THE

HALF BROTHERS

By ALEXANDRE DUMAS

AUTHOR OF "MONTE CRISTO"

Fredonia Books
Amsterdam, The Netherlands

The Half Brothers

by
Alexandre Dumas

ISBN: 1-58963-358-X

Reprinted from the original edition

Fredonia Books
Amsterdam, The Netherlands
http://www.fredoniabooks.com

In order to make original editions of historical works
available to scholars at an economical price, this
facsimile of the original edition is reproduced from
the best available copy and has been digitally
enhanced to improve legibility, but the text remains
unaltered to retain historical authenticity.

CONTENTS.

CONTENTS.

THE HALF BROTHERS.

CHAPTER I.

THE RENCONTRE.

ONE fine morning in the month of June, 1361, any one bold enough to expose himself in the open country to a heat of ninety degrees, might have seen advancing along the road from Pinchel to Coimbra, in Portugal, a figure which the present generation of men will thank us for describing. This strange apparition, however, could scarcely be termed a man; it was rather a complete suit of armour, consisting of a casque shaded by a red plume, above which glittered the point of the upright lance—a cuirass, " brassarts," and " cuissards," and a small buckler hung round the neck. This suit of armour was placed perpendicularly on the back of a charger of which nothing could be seen but his black legs and fiery eye, since, like his master, he was buried beneath his war harness, which was in turn covered with a white housing fringed with scarlet. From time to time the noble animal tossed his head and snorted, more from anger than exhaustion; for it was when some oxfly crept beneath the folds of his heavy accoutrements and tormented him with its sharp sting.

As to the rider, sitting firm and upright in his stirrups as though he were riveted to the saddle, he seemed to feel a pride in braving the intense heat of this burning sun which made the air like a breath of fire, and withered every blade of grass. Many, without fear of being accused of want of hardihood, would have thrown open the barred visor which made the inside of the helmet like the interior of an oven; but in the impassible countenance and perfect immobility of the chevalier might be seen that even in the desert he gloried in displaying the vigour of his constitution and his power of enduring the fatigues and hardships of a military life. We have said the desert—for in truth the region through which the chevalier was journeying merited no other name. It was a sort of ravine, just deep enough to concentrate within itself all the most ardent rays of the sun, and the heat was already such that for the last two hours it had been deserted by its usual occupants—the shepherds and their flocks, who came morning and evening to seek upon its slopes the few blades of dry and withered grass, having taken refuge behind hedges and bushes, where they lay sleeping in the shade. Far as the eye could reach, no other traveller was to be perceived bold, or rather fire-proof enough to tread a soil seemingly composed of the cinders of rocks calcined by the sun; the only token of animal life was a grasshopper—or rather myriads of them—which, entrenched between the pebbles, clinging to the blades of grass, or hanging on the branches of an olive-tree white with dust, kept up a ceaseless and monotonous chirp, their triumphal song announcing their conquest of the desert in which they reigned sole and undisputed sovereigns.

But we were wrong in saying that the eye might vainly seek another traveller besides the one we have endeavoured to describe; for at the distance of a hundred paces came a second figure scarcely less curious than the first, although of a type altogether different.

It was a man of about thirty years of age, crooked, bronzed, and dried up, squatted, rather than seated, on a horse as lean as himself, and sleeping in his saddle, without taking any of the precautions adopted by his waking companion—not even that of finding his way, a task he evidently left to those more interested than himself in his not losing it.

The chevalier, however, doubtless wearied at last with carrying both himself and his lance so upright, stopped for a moment to raise his visor and thus allow the hot vapour to escape, which began to mount from his iron casing to his brain; but before doing so he cast his eyes around him like a man who did not think courage the least in the world less estimable, when it was accompanied by a dose of prudence. It was during this rotatory movement he perceived his careless companion was asleep.

"Muscaron!" cried the iron-clad cavalier, after having raised the visor of his casque—"Muscaron! awake, sluggard, or by the precious blood of St. James, as the Spaniards say, you will never arrive safely at Coimbra with my baggage, for it will either be stolen from you or lost by the way. What! you still sleep!"

Indeed, the squire (for such was the rank of the person

t'was apostrophised) slumbered too profoundly for the simple sound of the human voice to awaken him. The chevalier, therefore, perceived that it was necessary to employ some more vehement measures—the more so as Muscaron's horse, seeing his leader pause, had thought proper to stop also, so that by this change from motion to immobility his master would only have the chance of enjoying a yet more profound repose. Detaching a small ivory horn, mounted in silver, from his belt, he applied it to his lips and blew a shrill blast, which made his own horse curvet and that of his companion neigh. This time Muscaron awoke with a start.

"Holà," cried he, drawing a sort of cutlass which hung at his belt, "what would you, robbers! what would you, Bohemians, grandsons of the devil!" and the brave squire began to thrust right and left, till finding he encountered nothing but air, he stopped and gazed in a bewildered manner at his master.

"Eh! what is the matter, Messire Agenor?" he asked, opening his eyes in astonishment. "Where are the villains who attacked us? Have they vanished into air, or did I annihilate them before I was fully awake?"

"The matter is this, sluggard," said the chevalier: "you have been dreaming, and whilst so doing have allowed my shield to trail at the end of its leather strap, thus dishonouring the arms of a brave chevalier. Come, arouse yourself, or I shall banish your slumbers by breaking my lance over your shoulders."

Muscaron impudently wagged his head.

"Ma foi! Sire Agenor, you will do well, for then at least *one* lance will be broken during our journey. Instead of opposing this project, I invite you with all my heart to put it into execution."

"What mean you by that, drone?" said the chevalier.

"I mean," said the squire, continuing carelessly to approach, "that during the sixteen days we have been journeying through Spain—the land you described as being so full of adventures—the only enemies we have encountered have been the sun and the flies, and all we have gained, dust and vermin. Mordieu, Sire Agenor, I am hungry, thirsty, and my purse is empty: I am thus a prey to the three greatest worldly calamities; and yet I see no signs of those grand conquests of infidel Moors which were to enrich our bodies and

save our souls, and about which I indulged in such delicious
dreams in my own fair province of Bigonia, even before I
became your squire, and how much more since!"

"Do you dare to murmur, when I do not complain?"

"I have good reason for it, Sire Agenor. I do not lack
boldness, but nearly our last franc went at Pinchel, to whet
your battle-axe, sharpen your sword, and furbish your armour;
so now all we want is an attack of brigands."

"Coward!"

"Hear me a moment, Sire Agenor; I did not say I was
afraid of it."

"What, then, do you say?"

"I say I hope for it."

"And why?"

"Because we will then plunder the robbers," said Muscaron, with the cunning look which was the chief expression
of his physiognomy.

The chevalier raised his lance with the very evident
intention of letting it fall on his squire's shoulders, he now
having approached near enough to permit this kind of cor-
rection being effectively used; but Muscaron, by a dodging
movement, in which he seemed well practised, avoided the
blow, whilst he held up the lance with one hand.

"Take care, Sire Agenor," said he; "don't indulge in such
jests, for I have hard bones and very little flesh to cover
them; an accident soon happens—one false stroke, and you
would break your lance, and then we should be obliged either
to manufacture a new shaft ourselves, or to appear before
Don Frederick with our armour incomplete, which would cast
a reflection on the honour of the Béarnaise cavalry."

"Peace, babbler! or if you must talk, mount yonder hillock
and tell me what you can see from its summit."

Muscaron made a circuit, so as to place himself beyond the
reach of his master's lance, and did as he was desired.

"Heavens!" he exclaimed, "what do I behold!" and he
crossed himself devoutly.

"What do you see?" demanded the chevalier.

"Paradise, or something little inferior to it," said Muscaron, still rapt in the most profound admiration.

"Describe to me your Paradise," said the chevalier, who
feared to be the dupe of some waggishness of his squire.

"Ah, Sire Agenor, what more would you have?" cried

Muscaron. "Here are orange-groves with golden fruit, a broad river with its silvery tide, and beyond that the sea itself glittering like a steel mirror."

"If you behold the sea," said the chevalier, who, still fearing this enticing picture would vanish like the mirage of the desert on his arriving at the summit of the hill, appeared in no haste to judge for himself—"If you behold the sea, you must also be able to discern Coimbra; and if you see Coimbra, we are at the end of our journey, for it is there my friend the grand master, Don Frederick, has appointed to meet me."

"Oh, yes!" cried Muscaron, "I can plainly see a large and handsome town, with a tall steeple!"

"Right," said the chevalier, beginning to believe that his squire was really speaking the truth; but at the same time resolving to inflict a heavy chastisement on him, should it after all prove to be only a jest. "Right, that is the town of Coimbra, and the spire of its cathedral."

"But," said Muscaron, "I see two towns and two steeples!"

"Two towns!" exclaimed the chevalier, in his turn arriving at the top of the hill. "Why, a moment ago none were to be seen, and now here are double the number we require."

"True enough," said Muscaron. "Look, Sire Agenor, cannot you see them, the one on the right and the other on the left of yonder clump of citron-trees, where the road branches off in two different directions? Now, which of these two roads must we follow? and which town is Coimbra?"

"In truth, this is a new and unforeseen difficulty," muttered the chevalier.

"And the worst of it is," said Muscaron, "that if we unfortunately take the road to the wrong town, we shall not be able to find at the bottom of our purse the wherewithal to pay for our lodging!"

The chevalier cast around him another sweeping glance, but it was this time in the hope of discerning some traveller from whom he might gain a little information.

"Accursed country!" cried he. "Or rather, accursed desert, for a country is supposed to be a place peopled with other inhabitants than grasshoppers and lizards!"

"Oh, for my fair France!" he continued, with one of those sighs which, at the thought of "fatherland," often escape from the lightest hearts; "France, where a kindly voice to cheer you on your way is never wanting!"

"And a good goat's-milk cheese to moisten your parched throat. See what comes of quitting one's own country! Ah, Sire Agenor, you have good reason to cry, France! France!"

"Silence, brute!" said the chevalier, who would not allow to Muscaron how well his words expressed his own thoughts.

"Silence!"—But our readers are sufficiently well acquainted with the worthy squire to be sure this was a command he did not blindly obey, and so he continued as though communing with himself. "And, besides, what is to become of us all alone in this cursed Portugal? Oh, how fine and imposing the 'Grand Companies' are; and, above all, how well you live in them! Oh, Sire Agenor, why are we not at this moment forming part of a grand company of horse on the route from Languedoc or Guienne!"

"You reason like a 'Jacques,'* Maitre Muscaron; do you know that?" said the chevalier.

"And so I am, or at least was, before I entered your service!"

"And do you boast of it, miserable fellow?"

"Don't speak against them, Sire Agenor, for the 'Jacques' have found means to eat as well as fight, in which they certainly have the advantage over us; for though it is true we fight but little, it is equally so that we eat still less."

"All this will not tell us which town is Coimbra," said the chevalier.

"No," replied Muscaron. "But here comes some one who perhaps may." And he pointed out to his master a cloud of dust raised by a little caravan, which, journeying at about half a league's distance behind them, was following the same road.

"Ah," cried the chevalier, "here is what we seek!"

"Yes," said Muscaron; "or who seek us!"

"Well, just now, you wished for brigands."

"But not for too many of them," said Muscaron. "In truth, Heaven seems inclined to overload us with favours. I asked for three or four brigands, and here is a whole troop of them! We wished for a city, and behold two! Come, then, chevalier," he continued, drawing nearer to his master; "let us consult together—two opinions are better than one, as you know, so give yours first."

"I propose," said the chevalier, "that we gain yonder

* Peasant.

grove of citron-trees through which the road passes; it will afford us at the same time shade and shelter, and we can there hold ourselves in readiness for either attack or defence."

"A most sensible opinion," said the squire, in a tone half-grumbling, half-convinced; "to which I unhesitatingly agree. Shade and security! that is all I ask for at the present moment. Shade—that is the half of water; and security—that is the three-quarters of courage. Let us, then, gain the grove of citrons, and that as speedily as possible."

But the two travellers had reckoned without their horses; the poor animals were so fatigued that, notwithstanding repeated spurrings, they could not be urged out of a walk. Fortunately this was attended with no other ill consequences than exposing their riders a little longer to the sun, as the troop against which all these precautions were taken was still at too great a distance to notice them. The grove once reached, they made up for lost time. The chevalier alighted, and throwing his bridle to his squire, seated himself at the foot of a solitary palm-tree which reared itself like the monarch of this odoriferous miniature forest. Muscaron secured the horse to a tree, and then went in search of such refreshment as the grove might afford. He returned in a few moments with a dozen sweet acorns, and two or three citrons, which he offered to his master, who shook his head.

"Ah!" said Muscaron, "I know well enough this is not very nourishing diet for men who have travelled four hundred leagues in sixteen days; but there is nothing for us but patience. We are about to present ourselves before the illustrious Don Frederick, Grand Master of St. James, and brother—or nearly so—to Don Pedro, King of Castile; and if he only fulfils the half of what his letter promises, in our next journey, we shall have fresh horses, mules with bells, and pages in rich habits, and shall see ourselves surrounded by girls from the posadas, muleteers and beggars—some presenting us with fruit, others wine, whilst the more generous will offer us their houses, entreating the honour of entertaining us; so that we shall want for nothing, precisely because we do not stand in need of their hospitality. Meanwhile we must scrunch acorns, and suck citrons."

"Well, well, Muscaron," said the chevalier, smiling, "this shall be your last fast, and in two days you shall have all you have described,"

"God grant it, monseigneur," replied Muscaron, casting up his eyes with a very doubtful look, as he raised his cap, ornamented with a long plume of the eagle of the Pyrenees. "I will endeavour to rise with the grandeur of my fortunes, and for that, use our past mishaps as stepping-stones."

"Bah!" cried the chevalier, "past miseries make future happiness!"

"Amen," responded Muscaron.

Notwithstanding this pious termination to his discourse, the worthy squire would, without doubt, have begun on some other topic, when all at once the measured trot of a dozen horses, or mules, the tinkling of bells, and the clang of steel, sounded in the distance.

"Be on your guard!" cried the chevalier. "Here comes the troop in question. Diable! judging from the haste they have made, the horses composing it must be less fatigued than ours."

Muscaron laid the remains of his acorns and citrons on a tuft of grass, and hastened to his master's stirrup, who in an instant was seated, lance in hand, in his saddle. At the same moment, they beheld from their leafy covert, a group of travellers, mounted on fine mules, and richly dressed—some in Spanish, some in Moorish costumes—appear on the brow of the hill. After this first troop rode a man who appeared to be their chief, and who, wrapped in a caftan of fine white wool, with silken fringes, allowed nothing to be seen of his countenance but a pair of sparkling eyes. There were in all twelve strong and well-armed men, without including their chief, and six led mules conducted by four servants. As we have before said, these twelve men rode in front, followed by the chief, and, behind him came the rear-guard, consisting of the four servants and their six mules; but in the midst of these was a painted and gilded litter, borne by two mules, which advanced at a foot pace, and so closely shut in with silken curtains, that the only way in which air could reach the interior, was through the holes in the carved frieze ornamenting it. This was the whole of the troop whose approach had thus been announced by the sound of bells, both great and small.

"Well," said Muscaron, not a little astonished, "this time, at least, we have real Moors to deal with, and I think I spoke too hastily! How black they are! one would take them to be the devil's body-guard. And how richly the miscreants are clothed! How unfortunate that they are so many, or that we are not a larger party, for it would doubt-less be very pleasing to Heaven for all these treasures to fall into the hands of good Christians like us. I say treasures; for no doubt this painted and gilded box, towards which the infidel every moment turns his head, contains his riches."

"Silence!" said the chevalier. "Do you not perceive they are consulting together, that two armed pages have advanced in front of the rest, and that they seem intending to attack us? Quick! give me my shield; hold yourself in readiness to assist me, if necessary, and they shall see of what stuff a chevalier of France is made!"

"Messire," said Muscaron, who appeared less eager than his master to assume a hostile attitude, "I think you are mistaken, these Moorish lords can never dream of attack-ing two inoffensive men; besides, one of the pages has been to consult his master, and he of the hidden face, instead of replying, has made signs for them to proceed; and, see! they continue their route without even unslinging their cross-bows, or having their arrows in readiness; so that instead of enemies, Heaven has sent us friends.

"Friends amongst the Moors! And what of our holy religion, Pagan?"

Muscaron felt that he deserved this rebuke, and respect-fully bent his head. "Pardon, messire," said he, "I should not have said friends. I know well enough no friendship can subsist between a Christian and a Moor. I should have said counsellors. And we are permitted to receive counsel from all the world, provided that counsel be good. I will go and interrogate these honest gentlemen, and they will point out our way."

"Well, be it so," said the chevalier. "But it strikes me they passed in rather too haughty a manner, and their chief did not respond to the courteous salutation I made him with my lance. However, go after them, and civilly inquire which of these two towns is Coimbra; add, that you come from Messire Agenor de Mauleon, and, in exchange for my name, demand that of the Moorish chieftain. Go!"

Muscaron, who was anxious to make the best possible appearance in the eyes of the strange troop, endeavoured to rouse his wearied horse; but the animal had been so long

deprived of shade and herbage, and, above all, found his present position so agreeable, that his master could not induce
him to quit it. The worthy squire was, therefore, obliged
to run after the troop, which, having continued to advance
during his struggle with his horse, had now disappeared
behind the olive-trees, on the brow of the declivity down
which the road wound.

Whilst Muscaron hastened to deliver his message, Agenor
de Mauleon, sitting as upright and as motionless as an equestrian statue, did not lose sight of the Moor and his companions. He perceived him stop at the sound of the squire's
voice, and his escort immediately halt also, as if those composing it were a part of their chief, and aware, by some
instinctive feeling, of his wishes, did not require even a sign
to express them.

So profound a silence reigned in this spot where all nature
seemed sleeping beneath the heat of the burning sky, the
air was so clear and the sea breeze so soft, that it bore,
without difficulty, Muscaron's words to his master's ear.
And Muscaron was acquitting himself, like not only a faithful, but a skilful ambassador.

"I salute your lordship," said he, "first, on the part of my
master, the honourable and valiant chevalier Agenor de
Mauleon, who awaits, at a little distance, your lordship's reply; and then, on that of his unworthy squire, who congra-
tulates himself on the happy chance which gives him the
honour of thus addressing you."

The Moor gravely inclined his head, and awaited in silence
the end of his speech.

"May it please your lordship to inform us which of these
two steeples we see below is that of Coimbra, and, also,
which of these fine palaces is that of Don Frederick, the
illustrious Grand Master of St. James, and the friend of the
noble chevalier who has the honour, through me, to request
this double information."

Muscaron, in order to enhance the consequence of both his
master and himself, had laid great stress on the words relative to Don Frederick, and as though to reward his tact,
the Moor listened attentively to this second part of his
speech, whilst his eyes gleamed with the fire peculiar to his
race; but he only replied by again bowing his head, then
pronouncing in an imperious and guttural tone a single Arab

word, the vanguard of his little troop resumed their march, the Moorish cavalier urged on his mule, and the rear-guard, bearing in their midst the closed litter, in their turn followed him.

Muscaron remained for a moment stupified and humiliated. As for the chevalier he did not precisely know whether the Arab word, which he understood as little as Muscaron, was uttered by the Moor in reply to the squire, or as a direction to his own troop.

"Ah!" suddenly exclaimed Muscaron, who would not acknowledge that he had received an insult, "no doubt he did not understand French; that was the cause of his silence; I ought to have spoken to him in Castilian."

But as the Moor was now too far distant for Muscaron, on foot as he was, to overtake him, and the prudent squire besides preferring a consoling doubt to a humiliating certainty, he returned to his master.

CHAPTER II.

COIMBRA.

AGENOR, furious at his squire's relation, which was confirmed by what he had himself overheard, for a moment entertained the idea of obtaining from the Moor by force what he had refused to courtesy; but when he endeavoured to urge his horse forward in pursuit of the impertinent Saracen, the poor animal manifested so little disposition to second his master's wishes, that the chevalier was obliged to pause on the steep and stony declivity we have before mentioned. The Moorish rear-guard observing the movements of the two Franks, turned from time to time, so as to avoid being surprised by them.

"Messire Agenor," said Muscaron, alarmed at these hostile demonstrations, which, however, the weariness of their horses deprived of all chance of proving dangerous—"Messire Agenor, have I not already told you that the Moor did not understand French; and moreover, did I not confess that, like you, indignant at his silence, the idea of interrogating him in Spanish did not occur to me until he was too distant to allow my putting it into execution? The blame, therefore, does not rest with him, but with me for not having sooner thought of this happy expedient. Besides," added he, perceiving that the chevalier was obliged to halt, "we are alone, and you see how worn-out your horse is."

Mauleon shook his head.

"That is all well and good," said he, " but the Moor did not behave naturally. He might not understand French, but the language of signs is known in every country of the globe. In pronouncing the word ' Coimbra,' you pointed alternately to the two cities ; so that he must necessarily have concluded that you were inquiring the way. I cannot at this moment overtake this insolent Moor, but by the blood of our Lord, which cries out for vengeance against these infidels, he had better not cross my path !"

"On the contrary, messire," said Muscaron, who, though prudent, was not wanting in either courage or rancour, "endeavour to meet with him, but not as he is now. For instance, meet him man to man, with the valets who guard this litter; you will charge the master, I the attendants, and we shall soon see what he keeps in this box of gilded wood."

"Doubtless some idol," said the chevalier.

"Or perhaps his treasures," said Muscaron. "Fancy plunging your hands into a great coffer full of diamonds, pearls, and rubies, for these accursed infidels make use of incantations, by the aid of which they discover buried riches. Oh, had we been only six, or even four in number, we would have had a sight of them ! Oh, France, France ! where are your valiant men-at-arms and gallant adventurers ?"

"Stay !" said the chevalier, who during this rhapsody had been buried in thought ; " I have just recollected something."

"What?" asked Muscaron.

"Don Frederick's letter."

"Well, messire?"

"Well, and this letter may, perhaps, give us some directions which I have forgotten relative to our route to Coimbra."

"Ah, ma foi ! that is thinking and speaking to the purpose. The letter, Messire Agenor, the letter ! if it be only to restore our spirits by the fine promises it contains."

The chevalier unfastened from his saddle-bow a small roll of perfumed leather, from whence he drew a parchment—it was Don Frederick's letter, which he preserved not only as a passport, but also as a talisman. It was as follows :—

"Noble and generous chevalier, Don Agenor de Mauleon, do you remember the lance you broke at Narbonne with

Don Frederick, Grand Master of St. James, when the Castilians visited France to fetch Donna Bianca de Bourbon?"

"He means Madame Blanche of Bourbon," said Muscaron, nodding his head with the air of a man professing to
understand Spanish, and who is unwilling to lose an opportunity of displaying his knowledge.

The chevalier glanced at Muscaron in the manner in
which he was accustomed to notice his squire's fanfaronnades,
and continued the perusal of his letter.

"I promised not to forget you, for you acted both nobly
and courteously towards me—"

"The fact is," a second time interrupted Muscaron, "that
your lordship could have introduced your dagger into his
throat, as easily and delicately as you did to Monsieur de
Lourdes, in the combat of the Pas de Larre ; for in this
famous tourney where you unhorsed him, and he, furious at
losing his seat, insisted of continuing the combat, *aux armes
emoulues,* instead of the courteous weapons of which you
had hitherto made use ; you had him' under your knee, and
instead of taking advantage of your victory, you generously
said to him—I think I hear the words—' Rise, Grand Master,
and be the honour of the Castilian cavalry!'" and Muscaron
accompanied these last words by a gesture full of majesty,
in which, without intending it, he parodied that of his
master on this memorable occasion.

"If he were thrown from his saddle," said Mauleon, "it
was from his horse being unable to bear the shock ; for these
half-Arab, half-Castilian coursers are worth more than ours
for the road, but less for the combat ; and he only fell under
me through catching his spur on the root of a tree at the
moment of receiving a heavy blow from my battle-axe, for
he is both an intrepid and a skilful chevalier. Nevertheless,"
continued Agenor, with a feeling of pride, which the modesty
he had just exhibited did not allow him to altogether repress, "the day on which this memorable passage of arms
at Narbonne took place was a bright one for me !"

"Without counting how you received the prize from the
hand of Madame Blanche of Bourbon, who, sweet princess,
became all pale and trembling at seeing the tourney at which
she expected to preside, changed into a veritable combat.
Yes, my lord," continued Muscaron, his heart palpitating at
the thoughts of the honours awaiting both his master and

B

himself at Coimbra, "you are right in calling it a bright day, for it will make your fortune."

"I hope so," said Agenor, modestly. "But let us continue;" and he resumed the perusal of his letter.

"To-day, I would recall to your remembrance the promise you made to grant to me alone, fraternity in arms. We are both Christians; join me then at Coimbra in Portugal, which I have just taken from the infidels, and I will give you an opportunity of distinguishing yourself against the enemies of our holy religion. You shall dwell in my own palace, and be treated as a brother at my court. Come, then, Agenor, for I have need of a companion who loves me—I who behold myself surrounded by artful and dangerous enemies.

"Coimbra is a town the name of which ought to be familiar to you, situated, as I have before said, on the River Mondego, in Portugal, at the distance of two leagues from the sea. You will only have to traverse friendly provinces. First, Arragon, which is the primitive domain left by Don Sancho the Great to Ramirio; then New Castile, the re-conquest of which from the Moors was begun by King Alphonso the Sixth, and completed by his successors. Then Léon, the theatre of the celebrated feats of arms of the illustrious Pelagio, whose history I related to you. Lastly, you must pass through Acqueda, and will then find yourself in Portugal, where I shall await you. Beware, unless you have a considerable retinue, of approaching too closely the mountains on your left, and put no trust in any Jews or Moors you may chance to encounter on your road.

"Adieu! Do you remember how for one whole day I styled myself 'Agenor' in your honour, and you called yourself 'Frederigo' in mine? How, too, on the same day, we bore each other's colours, and thus journeyed side by side, you wearing my scarf and I yours, until we reached Urgel, to which we were escorting our beloved queen, Donna Bianca of Bourbon? Come, then, Don Agenor, I need a brother and a friend—come!"

"Well," said Muscaron, "there is nothing in this letter to direct us."

"On the contrary, there is everything," said Agenor. "Did you not hear what I read? It is quite true that for one whole day I wore his scarf."

"And what then, messire?"

"Its colours were red and yellow; look well then, Muscaron, and try whether your piercing sight cannot discern in either of these two cities an edifice from the top of which waves a banner as yellow as gold and as red as blood, for this will be the palace of my friend Don Frederick, and the town in which it stands Coimbra."

Muscaron shaded his eyes with his hand to protect them from the bright sunshine which confounded all surrounding objects in a flood of golden light like a molten sea, and after allowing his gaze to wander from right to left and from left to right, he at last fixed it on the town situated on the right of the river, in one of the sinuosities that marked its course.

"In that case, Sire Agenor," said he, "Coimbra lies at the foot of yonder hillock, behind that wall of plantains and aloes, since from its principal edifice floats the banner you described, only it is surmounted by a red cross."

"The cross of St. James!" exclaimed the chevalier. "It would be so; but you are sure, Muscaron, that you are not mistaken?"

"See for yourself, messire."

"The rays of the sun are still so ardent that I cannot well distinguish distant objects; you must guide my eye a little."

"This way, messire, look this way—follow the course of the road till it branches off in two directions—you see it?"

"Yes."

"Follow the road to the right, which winds along the banks of the river. Look! look! the Moor's troop is entering one of the gates!"

The sun, which had hitherto been only a hindrance to the two travellers, at this moment came to their aid, by causing the suits of Moorish armour all damascened with gold to sparkle beneath his fiery rays.

"So," said the chevalier, "this Moor was himself going to Coimbra, and yet could not understand the name of his destination. Very well; the first favour granted me by Don Frederick shall be an opportunity of learning the reason of this insolence. But how happens it," continued the chevalier, still speaking to himself, "that so pious a prince as Don Frederick, whose name ranks among the ablest defenders of our holy religion, suffers the presence of Moors in his newly conquered city—the very city, too, from whence he has driven them?"

"What would you have, messire?" said Muscaron, without waiting to be interrogated. "Is not Don Frederick half-brother of Don Pedro, King of Castile."

"And what of that?" said Agenor.

"Is it possible that you are ignorant of the rumour which has even reached France, that the love of everything Moorish is innate in that family? They declare that they cannot exist without them; that he has them for counsellors, guards, and physicians—nay, has even Moorish mistresses."

"Be silent, Maitre Muscaron," said the chevalier, "and do not meddle with the affairs of his Majesty Don Pedro, who is a great prince, and the brother of my illustrious friend."

"Brother, indeed!" muttered Muscaron; "I have also heard it whispered that it was one of those Moorish relationships which will one day or other be terminated by either the bowstring or the scimitar! For my part, I would much rather have poor Guillonnes, who tends goats in the Vale of Andorra, for my brother, than Don Pedro, King of Castile."

"Whatever may be your own opinion," said the chevalier, "I forbid you to say another word on the subject. When we are about to receive hospitality from persons, the least we can do is not to speak ill of them."

"But we are not seeking it from Don Pedro of Castile," persisted the intractable Muscaron, "but from his brother, Don Frederick, Lord of Coimbra in Portugal."

"No matter; I order you to be silent," said the chevalier, sternly.

Muscaron raised his white cap, ornamented with a red tassel, and made a low bow, whilst a mocking smile, concealed by the masses of ebon hair which fell over his thin and bronzed cheeks, played on his lips.

"When your lordship is ready to continue your journey," said he, after a moment's silence, "your very humble servant is at your command."

"You must first consult your horse," replied Mauleon. "At all events, if he is unable to proceed, we can leave him where he is; and at nightfall, when he hears the howling of the wolves, he will gain the city of his own accord."

But the animal, on whom the squire had bestowed the name of the valley in which he was born, as though understanding the fate with which he was menaced, got up with more alacrity than could have been believed possible.

"Let us proceed," said Agenor; and he rode forward, again raising the visor of his casque, which he had lowered whilst awaiting the Moorish troop; and thus disclosing to view a noble countenance, heated and dusty, but full of character; a bold eye, fine and chiseled lips, teeth white as ivory, and a chin which, though beardless, bore on it the deep dimple which denotes indomitable will. In fact, Messire Agenor de Mauleon, as he confessed to himself on beholding his image mirrored in the bright shield which he now took from Muscaron's hands, was both a young and handsome chevalier."

This brief halt had refreshed the horses, and they proceeded at a tolerably rapid pace along the road, now infallibly indicated by the colours of the Grand Master of St. James, waving from his palace. As they approached the city, they perceived that, notwithstanding the intense heat of the day, the streets were full of people, and could distinguish the sound of trumpets and the chiming of bells filling the air with their joyous and ringing notes.

"If I had sent Muscaron on before me," said Agenor, "I should really believe that all these rejoicings were in my honour; but however flattering such a reception might be, I must nevertheless ascribe this tumult to some other cause."

As to Muscaron, who beheld in all this gaiety a promise of future festivities, he held up his head proudly, much preferring to be received by joyous people than sad ones.

The travellers were not mistaken; some great agitation reigned in the city, and if the faces of the inhabitants did not precisely wear the smiling mask of joy which this ringing of bells and flourish of trumpets seemed to demand, they still appeared like people whom some great and unexpected event had befallen. As to asking their way, that was quite unnecessary, they had only to follow the crowd which was hastening towards the principal square of the city. As they were endeavouring to force their way through the throng, and Muscaron, in order to open a passage for his noble master, was dealing blows right and left with the handle of his riding-whip, they suddenly beheld before them, shaded by lofty palm-trees and tufted sycamores, the magnificent Moorish Alcazar, erected by King Mohamed, and now occupied by the youthful conqueror, Don Frederick.

Notwithstanding their haste, Agenor and his companion paused to admire this vast and fantastic edifice, covered with exquisite stone fretwork, in imitation of the finest lace, and studded with marble mosaics, which appeared like large plates of topaz, sapphire and lapis-lazuli set by some architect of Bagdad for a palace destined for fairies or houries. In the western, or speaking relatively to Spain, the southern parts of France, there were few specimens of architecture besides the cathedrals of St. Trophime, and one or two ancient bridges ; the Franks had then no idea of the ogives and trefoils, which a hundred years later they borrowed from the East, to decorate their churches and the summits of their towers. The Alcazar of Coimbra was, therefore, a magnificent sight, even for our ignorant and barbarous ancestors, who at that epoch despised the Moorish and Italian civilization from which they afterwards so largely profited.

As Agenor and Muscaron stood silently gazing at it, they beheld a troop of guards, accompanied by pages, leading horses and mules, emerge from each of the two lateral gates of the palace. These two troops advanced towards each other, describing a quarter of a circle, and clearing a large space of ground in the form of a bow, in front of the principal entrance, to which was an ascent of ten steps. The mixture of the dazzling luxury of Africa with the more severe elegance of western costume, gave an irresistible fascination to this spectacle, of which both Agenor and his squire felt the influence ; as they beheld, on the one side, the purple and golden trappings of the Arab horses, and the gorgeous habits of their Moorish riders, and on the other, silks and chasings, rendered conspicuous by the haughty and commanding mien of their Frankish wearers, whose pride seemed shared by their very beasts of burden. Suddenly, the banner of the Grand Master appeared beneath the lofty arch carved in trefoils, which formed the central entrance to the Alcazar ; it was accompanied by six guards, and borne by a powerful man-at-arms, who placed himself in the centre of the vacant space.

Agenor immediately perceived that Don Frederick was either about to set out on a journey from one town to another, or to proceed in procession through the streets ; and was tempted, in spite of the poverty of his purse, to go in search of some hostelry where he might await his return, since he was unwilling to intrude his presence at this inopportune moment. But, at the same instant, he beheld emerge from one of the lateral arches of the Alcazar the vanguard of the Moorish chief, followed by the famous litter of gilded wood, borne between two white mules, which had been so strong and pious a temptation to Muscaron.

At last a burst of trumpets and cymbals announced the coming of the Grand Master, and four-and-twenty musicians, eight in a row, emerged from the central arch and descended the steps, still sounding their instruments. One of the powerful, but elegant dogs of La Sierra, with the pointed head of the bear, the glittering eye of the lynx, and the slender legs of the deer, bounded after them. His body was covered with long silken hair, which shone like silver, and round his neck was a heavy golden collar, studded with rubies, to which was attached a small bell of the same metal. His joy displayed itself by a thousand gambols : now he darted under the arch as though chiding the tardy footsteps of his master, and now returned to the side of a magnificently caparisoned snow-white charger, which acknowledged his caresses by a joyous neigh.

At last the Grand Master himself appeared, and a single cry, repeated by a thousand voices, rent the air, " Viva Don Frederick !"

Don Frederick advanced, conversing with the Arab chief who walked on his right, whilst on his left was a young page, whose black eyebrows and slightly compressed lips gave an expression of firmness to his handsome features, bearing an open purse full of gold pieces, in which Don Frederick, on arriving at the first step, plunged his white and delicate hand, and scattered a golden shower over the heads of the multitude, who redoubled their cries at a generosity to which they had been so little accustomed under the dominion of their former rulers. Their new master was of a majestic figure, which, even on horseback, lost none of its stateliness. The mixture of French and Spanish blood in his veins had given him long black hair, blue eyes, and a fair complexion ; and these blue eyes beamed with so sweet and benevolent an expression that the air resounded with blessings, and many, in their anxiety not to lose sight of him for a single instant, forgot to gather up the gold sequins. But suddenly, in the midst of these general acclamations, the trumpets and

cymbals, which had ceased for a moment, again sounded; but
whether by chance or whether influenced by the fear of
losing so good a master, instead of their former gay and
festive strains, they breathed only a sad and melancholy air,
whilst the bells, that newly invented link between heaven
and earth, instead of their joyous peals, only gave forth a
gloomy and discordant jangling, which sounded like a tocsin.
At the same time the dog rose upon his hind legs and placing
his paws on his master's breast, uttered so prolonged and
dismal a howl that every one shuddered.

There was a general silence, in the midst of which a
solitary voice from the crowd exclaimed—

"Do not go, Grand Master! Remain with us, Don Frederick!" But no one knew from whom this counsel proceeded.

At this cry, the Moor started, and his visage became of
that ghastly hue which is the pallor of these children of the
sun, whilst his anxious glance rested on Don Frederick, as
though he sought to read in his countenance his reply to this
isolated voice and general stupefaction. But Don Frederick
patted his howling dog, and turning with a sad smile to the
multitude, who gazed upon him with suppliant eyes and
clasped hands—

"My good friends," said he, "the King, my brother, summons me to Seville, where fêtes and tourneys await my
coming to celebrate our reconciliation; therefore, instead of
wishing to hinder my departure, rejoice at the amity subsisting between us."

But instead of manifesting any joy at this intelligence, the
crowd received it in gloomy silence. The page murmured a
few words to his master and the dog continued to howl.
Meanwhile, the Moor anxiously watched the people, the
page, the dog, and Don Frederick himself.

But the Grand Master's brow darkened—the Moor fancied
he hesitated, and hastened to address him.

"My lord," said he, "you know there are two books, one
of gold and one of brass, in which every man's destiny is
written beforehand. Yours is inscribed in golden letters,
therefore press boldly forward and accomplish it."

Don Frederick raised his eyes, which were fixed on the
ground, and cast them over the vast multitude, as if seeking
for one friendly visage, one encouraging glance. At the
same moment, Agenor, in his anxiety not to lose the smallest

detail of the scene passing before him, raised himself in his stirrups, and as if he instinctively comprehended what the Grand Master sought, waved his lance with one hand, and with the other lifted the visor of his casque.

Don Frederick uttered a cry of joy, his eyes sparkled, and a gay smile rested on his lips and lighted up his whole countenance.

"Don Agenor!" he exclaimed, pointing to the chevalier. The page, as though reading his master's wishes, waited to hear no more, but hastily quitting his side, forced his way towards Agenor, exclaiming,

"Come, Don Agenor! come!"

The crowd parted in a moment, and all eyes were fixed on the chevalier whom the Grand Master seemed to welcome with as much joy as Tobit of old did the divine companion sent him from heaven. Agenor dismounted, and throwing his bridle to Muscaron, to whom he also gave his lance, he hung his shield on the bow of his saddle and followed his young conductor through the crowd.

The Moor again started, for he recognised in his turn the Frank chevalier he had encountered on the route to Coimbra, and the squire to whom he had given no reply. Don Frederick held out his arms to Agenor, and the two young men embraced with all the ardour of their age.

"Will you accompany me?" asked the Grand Master.

"To the ends of the earth!" replied Agenor.

"My friends," said Don Frederick, in that sonorous and ringing voice which was the admiration of the multitude, "you may now see me depart without uneasiness, for my friend and brother, Don Agenor de Mauleon, the flower of French chivalry, goes with me." And on a sign from the Grand Master, amid the flourish of trumpets and beating of drums, his squire led forward his snow-white charger, whilst the people cried with one voice, "Long live Don Frederick, Grand Master of St. James!—long live Don Agenor de Mauleon, the Frank chevalier!"

The beautiful dog also approached the group and gazed intently at the two strangers; at sight of the Moor, he showed his white teeth with a low and menacing growl, but on the chevalier he lavished a thousand caresses. The page laid his hand on the dog's neck with a melancholy smile.

"My lord," said Agenor, "when you asked me to follow

you, and I gladly agreed to do so, I only consulted my zeal in your service; I did not reflect that having journeyed from Tarbes in sixteen days, my horses are nearly dead with fatigue and would be unable to proceed much further."

"What!" exclaimed Don Frederick, "did I not tell you that my palace—my horses—my arms—in short, everything that Coimbra can furnish, is at your disposal? Hasten to my stables, and there choose horses for yourself and squire—or rather do not leave me even for an instant; Fernand will procure for you everything you require. Let my war-horse Antrim be immediately saddled, and inquire whether Don Agenor's squire prefers a horse or a mule. As to the tired steeds, they shall follow in the rear-guard, where they will be properly cared for."

Meanwhile, the Moor, fancying the cavalcade was about to start, had descended to take a survey of his litter and to give sundry directions to those who guarded it; but finding the departure was delayed, and that the two friends remained in earnest conversation, he hastily returned to his former station beside the Grand Master, who immediately addressed him.

"My Lord Mothril," said he, "this chevalier is one of my friends, or rather more than a friend; for he is my brother-in-arms, and is about to accompany me to Seville, where I wish to offer his services to Don Pedro as captain of his guards, and if after that my kingly brother will resign him to me, I shall indeed be grateful, for his blade is invincible and his heart even truer than his sword."

The Moor replied in excellent Spanish, although his pronunciation somewhat partook of the guttural accent which Agenor had remarked on the road to Coimbra, when, on his uttering a single Arab word, his troop put themselves in motion.

"I thank your lordship for thus making known to me the rank and title of your friend, but chance has already caused me to be acquainted with the noble Frank. Unhappily, a traveller in a strange land, especially when, like myself, he belongs to a hostile nation, is obliged to distrust chance; therefore, when I met Don Agenor on the mountain I did not greet him with the courtesy he merited."

"What, then," said Frederick, "you have already met?"

"Yes, my lord," replied Agenor in French; "and I confess the tacit refusal of this Moorish lord to answer a simple inquiry as to our route, which I put to him through my squire,

somewhat annoyed me. We show more civility to strange
guests on the other side of the Pyrenees."

"Messire," said Mothril, still in Spanish, "you are mistaken on that point. The Moors still dwell in Spain, but it
is not their own land, and, except at Granada, they are themselves the guests of the Spaniards."

"So!" muttered Muscaron, who had insensibly approached
them, "he understands French well enough now."

"Let this slight difference between you be forgotten," said
Don Frederick; "for I am sure Mothril, the friend and
minister of his Majesty Don Pedro, will look with favour on
his brother's friend, the Chevalier de Mauleon."

The Moor silently bowed his head; and as Muscaron, in
his anxiety to discover what the litter contained, had approached it more nearly than he approved, he again descended the steps, and under pretence of giving some forgotten direction, hastened to place himself between his
treasure and the inquisitive squire.

Don Frederick took advantage of his absence to whisper
to Agenor, "In this Moor, you behold my brother's ruler,
and consequently mine!"

"Nay," said Agenor. "Why this bitter speech? Surely,
my lord, a chevalier of your princely blood and far-famed
valour need acknowledge no other ruler than God."

"And yet I am going to Seville," replied the Grand
Master, with a sigh.

"But why go there, my lord?"

"Because, my friend, his Majesty Don Pedro requests my
presence, and his requests are commands."

The Moor seemed divided between his unwillingness to
quit his litter, and his fear of allowing Don Frederick to
say too much to the Frank chevalier; but the latter feeling
prevailed, and he returned to his former station beside the
two friends.

"My lord," said he, addressing the young prince, "I regret
having to announce to you a piece of news which I fear will
disarrange all your plans. My secretary has just confirmed a
fact of which I was before almost certain—namely, that his
Majesty Don Pedro has already, as captain of his guards, a
brave man of Tarifa, in whom he places the greatest confidence, although he, or rather his ancestors, were born on the
other side of the Straits. I should therefore advise your

friend to remain at Coimbra, since he will be only giving himself useless trouble in visiting the court, the more so as it is well known that Donna Padilla dislikes the French nation."

"Well, so much the better," said Don Frederick; "I shall now be able to keep my friend with me."

"I have not come to Spain to serve under Don Pedro," said Agenor, proudly, "but to Portugal, to join Don Frederick, and I will not accept any service but his. Here is my master!" and he courteously saluted his friend.

The Moor smiled till his white teeth gleamed beneath his black beard.

"Heavens! what fine teeth he has!" said Muscaron. "He ought to be able to bite well."

At this moment the page appeared, leading the Grand Master's war-horse Antrim, and a mule for Muscaron; the exchange was soon made, Agenor de Mauleon mounted the fresh steed, Muscaron scrambled on his mule, and their wearied animals were consigned to the proper attendants.

At the Moor's invitation, Don Frederick descended the steps with the intention of, in his turn, mounting his charger. But again the beautiful dog, by leaping on his master and howling dismally, endeavoured to prevent his putting this design into execution; but Don Frederick pushed him aside with his foot, and springing into his saddle, gave the word to depart. Then, as if driven to desperation, the dog started up, and fixed his fangs deeply in the throat of the horse, which snorted with pain, and plunged with a violence that would have unseated any less practised cavalier than his rider.

"Why, Allan!" he exclaimed, addressing the dog by the title usually employed to designate his race. "Are you going mad!" And with the heavy thong of his riding-whip he inflicted so severe a blow on the infuriated animal, that he rolled to some paces distance.

"That dog ought to be destroyed," said Mothril.

Fernand cast a keen glance at the Moor. Allan retreated to the steps of the Alcazar, where he seated himself, and howled more dismally than ever. Then the people, who had remained silent spectators of this scene, raised their voices, and the cry which had before issued from a single mouth, was now echoed by a thousand more.

"Do not go, Don Frederick! Stay with us, Grand Master!

What need have you of a brother, when you have a faithful people? What can Seville offer more than Coimbra?"

"My lord," said Mothril, "must I return to my royal master with the intelligence that your dog, your page, and your people will not allow you to obey his summons?"

"No, Mothril," replied the young prince, "I am ready to depart; forward, my friends!" and waving his hand to the people, he placed himself at the head of the cavalcade—the crowd silently parting before it.

They now proceeded to close the gilded gates of the Alcazar, which grated on their hinges like the rusted portal of some empty sepulchre. As long as his master remained in sight, the dog, as though hoping he would change his resolution, and return, kept his position on the steps; but when a turn of the road hid him from view, he started off in pursuit, and in a few moments overtook him, as if, since he could not prevent his rushing into danger, he was at least resolved to share it with him. Ten minutes afterwards they left Coimbra, and took the same route travelled that same morning by both Mothril the Moor and Agenor de Mauleon.

CHAPTER III.
MUSCARON'S DISCOVERY.

THE Grand Master's troop, including the Frank chevalier and his squire, but not counting the Moor and his dozen guards, pages, and valets, consisted of in all thirty-eight men. The rich baggage was carried by sumpter mules, for eight days previous to the arrival of Mothril, Don Frederick had been apprised that his brother awaited him at Seville. He was, therefore, prepared for immediate departure, hoping that the Moor would be too fatigued to accompany him, and would remain behind; but in this he was disappointed, for weariness seemed alike unknown both to these sons of the desert and their fleet steeds.

On the first day, they journeyed ten leagues, and night having come, pitched their tents on the slope of the mountain, on the summit of which stands Pombal. During this stage, the Moor had exercised the most rigid surveillance over the two friends. Under pretence of making his excuses to the Frank chevalier, and redeeming his past rudeness by his present courtesy, he had never quitted Agenor's side,

except for the brief period necessary to exchange a few words
with the guardians of his litter.   But during this momentary
absence, which appeared to be occasioned by some sentiment
more powerful than any other, Agenor found time to say to
his friend—

"Deign to inform me, Don Frederick, from whence proceeds this persistence on the part of this Moorish lord to
share both our company and our conversation.   It can only
be his attachment to you ; for I fancy I received his somewhat tardy advances in a manner that would not inspire him
with any great liking for me."

"I know nothing about Mothril's attachment to me," replied Don Frederick ; " but I am well aware of his hatred
to Donna Padilla, the King's favourite mistress."

Agenor regarded him with the air of a man who hears
without understanding; but the watchful Moor was again
beside them, and Don Frederick had only time to whisper,
" Speak on some other subject."

Agenor hastened to obey, and gave utterance to the first
thought that presented itself to his mind.

" By-the-bye, Don Frederick," said he, " can you tell me
how our honoured lady, Blanche of Bourbon, Queen of Castile,
accommodates herself to Spain?   There has been much
anxiety in France about that fair princess, whose departure
was attended by so many good wishes, when you were sent
by her royal husband to escort her from Narbonne."

The words were still on his lips, when Agenor felt a sharp
blow on his left knee, and the young page, as though by the
wilfulness of his horse, passed between Don Frederick and
his friend; he gracefully apologized to the latter for both
himself and his horse, but at the same moment, gave him
a look which would have silenced even the most heedless
speaker.

Don Frederick felt that he must make some reply, since
in the situation in which he was placed, silence would bear a
worse interpretation than words.

" But," interrupted Mothril, who seemed to have as great
an interest in keeping up the conversation as Don Frederick
had in letting it drop, " has not the noble chevalier received
any news of Donna Bianca since her arrival in Spain?"

" Senor," said Agenor, with surprise, " during the last two
or three years I have been engaged with the grand companies

in making war against the English, the enemies of our King John, now a prisoner in London, and his Regent, Prince Charles, who will one day be called Charles the Wise, so famed is he already for his early prudence and virtue."

"I should have thought," said Mothril, "that the affair of Toledo made noise enough to reach your ears wherever you might have been!"

Don Frederick turned slightly pale, and the page laid his finger on his lips as a sign to Agenor to be silent. Agenor understood him, and contented himself with murmuring, "Spain, Spain! land of mystery!"

But this did not satisfy Mothril.

"Since you are no better informed of the fate of your regent's sister-in-law," said he, "I will myself relate what has happened to her."

"Nay, nay, my lord," interrupted Don Frederick. "The question asked by my friend was one of those idle ones which only require yes or no as an answer; not one of those long recitals, which to a stranger to Spain would be totally devoid of all interest."

"But," persisted Mothril, "if Don Agenor be a stranger to Spain, he is at least well acquainted with France, and Donna Bianca is his countrywoman; besides, the tale will not be long, and in visiting the Court of Castile, it is necessary for him to know what subjects of conversation are interdicted and what permitted."

Don Frederick sighed, and drew the hood of his large white mantle over his face, as though to shade his eyes from the last rays of the setting sun.

"It is said that you accompanied Donna Bianca from Narbonne to Urgel," continued Mothril. "Is my information correct, or have I been deceived?"

"It was the truth," replied the chevalier, who though rendered circumspect by the gloomy expression of his friend's countenance, and the warning looks of the young page, was incapable of dissimulation.

"Well, then, she continued her journey towards Madrid, traversing Arragon and part of New Castile under the guardianship of Don Frederick, who conducted her to Alcala, where the royal nuptials were celebrated with a magnificence worthy of so illustrious a pair. But, strange to say," continued Mothril, darting at Don Frederick one of the piercing glances habitual to him, " the King, whose motives still remain a mystery, next day returned to Madrid, leaving his young bride a prisoner, rather than a queen, in the castle of Alcala."

Mothril paused for a moment to see whether either of the two friends would say anything in Donna Bianca's defence ; but finding they both remained silent he resumed—

"From that time there was a complete separation between the royal pair, and more, a council of bishops pronounced a sentence of divorce. Thus," and he laughed ironically, " you may be sure, noble Frank, some grave cause of complaint existed against this strange princess for so respectable and holy an assembly to sever a link forged alike by policy and religion."

" Or rather," exclaimed Frederick, unable any longer to restrain his feelings, " the council was devoted to Don Pedro !"

" Nay," said Mothril, with that pretended simplicity which gives a sharper and more bitter signification to some seeming jest, " how is it possible to suppose that these thirty-two holy personages, whose mission is to direct the consciences of others, would do violence to their own? It is impossible ; for what would be thought of a religion represented by such ministers?"

The two friends still remained silent, and Mothril continued—

"About this time the King fell ill, and fears were entertained for his life.   Then, hitherto secret ambitions began to show themselves.   Don Henry de Transtamare—"

" My lord," said Don Frederick, eagerly embracing this opportunity of interrupting the Moor, " you forget that Don Henry de Transtamare is my twin brother, and that I will not allow you to speak ill of him in my presence, any more than of Don Pedro, King of Castile !"

" Forgive me, illustrious Grand Master," said Mothril. " In seeing Don Henry so rebellious, and you so well disposed towards my royal master, I forgot the relationship between you.   Henceforth I will only speak of Donna Bianca."

" Accursed Moor !" muttered Don Frederick between his teeth.

Agenor darted at the Grand Master a look which seemed to say, " Shall I rid you of this infidel, my lord?   It is soon done ;" but the Moor appeared unconscious of either the words or the glance, and went on with his tale.

"I was saying that ambitious projects began to be formed, many relaxed in their allegiance ; and at the very time Don Pedro hovered on the brink of eternity, the gates of the castle of Ancala one night opened of themselves, and Donna Bianca issued from them attended by an unknown knight, who escorted her to Toledo, where she remained concealed. But it was the will of Allah that the prayers of all his subjects, and doubtless of his own family, should be heard, and our beloved King, Don Pedro, restored to health and strength. On learning Donna Bianca's flight, assisted by this unknown knight, he resolved, as some say, to send her back to France, or, as others declare, to confine her in a still stricter prison than her former one. But whatever might have been the intentions of her royal spouse, Donna Bianca, forewarned of the orders he had issued for her arrest, one Sunday in the midst of divine service took refuge in the cathedral of Toledo, declaring to the people assembled there that she placed herself under the protection of the God of the Christians, and claimed the rights of sanctuary. It appears," continued the Moor, glancing alternately at Don Frederick and his friend, "that Donna Bianca is very beautiful ; as for myself, I have never seen her. Well, this beauty—the mystery attached to her misfortunes, and who knows, perhaps, some secret influence that had been long at work—moved all hearts in her favour. The bishop, one of those who had declared her marriage null and void, was driven ignominiously from the church, which now assumed the appearance of a fortress prepared to defend the fugitive princess against the royal guards, who were now seen approaching."

"What !" exclaimed Agenor, in a tone of horror, " attempt to seize Donna Bianca in a church ? Christians consent to violate the rights of sanctuary !"

"Oh, yes !" answered Mothril, " Don Pedro first addressed himself to his Moorish archers, but they entreated him to consider that the sacrilege about to be committed would be rendered even more heinous by employing infidels in its performance, and his Majesty respected their scruples. He then applied to the Christians, who immediately assented to his wishes. What would you have, noble Frank ? All religions are full of similar contradictions, therefore that one must be the best in which the fewest exist."

"Do you mean to assert, infidel that you are, that the

c

religion of the Prophet is better than the Christian faith ?"
exclaimed Don Frederick, angrily.

"No, illustrious Grand Master; I mean to say nothing of
the sort, and Allah preserve a poor insignificant atom of dust
like me from expressing any opinion on such a subject. No;
at the present moment I am a simple narrator of the adventures of Madame Blanche of Bourbon, as the French call
her, or as we say in Spain, Donna Bianca."

"Invulnerable !" murmured Don Frederick.

"Thus," resumed Mothril, " the royal troops committed
the frightful sacrilege of forcing their way into the cathedral,
from whence they would have torn Donna Bianca, when
all at once a knight in iron armour, with his visor down—
doubtless the same one who assisted the princess in her
flight—rode furiously into the sacred edifice."

"Rode !" exclaimed Agenor, involuntarily.

"Yes," said Mothril, "it was doubtless a profanation,
unless his name, his rank, or some military order gave him
the right of doing so. Many privileges of this description
exist in Spain. The Grand Master of St. James, for instance, has the right of entering any church in Christendom
without removing either his helmet or his spurs. Is it not
so, Don Frederick?"

The young prince gloomily replied in the affirmative.
"Well," continued the Moor, "this knight entered the
cathedral, repulsed the guards, and summoned all the people
to arms ; a revolt took place, the King's troops were driven
from the town, and the gates closed against them."

"But my royal brother has since then amply revenged
himself," said Don Frederick. "And the two-and-twenty
heads he caused to fall in the public square of Toledo have
rightly earned for him the surname of 'the Judge.'"

"Yes, but among these two-and-twenty heads, there was
not that of the rebel knight, for no one knew who he was."

"And what was the fate of Donna Bianca ?" asked Agenor.

"She was conveyed to the castle of Xeres, where she still
remains prisoner, although her crime perhaps merited a more
severe punishment."

"My lord," said Don Frederick, "it is not for us to decide
on the punishment or reward merited by those whom God
has elected to reign over us. They are second only to him,
and it is for him to judge their actions."

"My lord speaks truly," answered Mothril, crossing his hands meekly on his breast, and bowing to his horse's neck, "and his slave was wrong in speaking as he has done!"

They had now arrived at the spot agreed upon for their evening halt, and the attendants commenced preparing the tents. No sooner had the Moor quitted them to superintend the arrangement of his litter, than Don Frederick approached Agenor, and said hastily—

"Never again speak to me of anything concerning the King or Donna Bianca—nay, even of myself before that accursed Moor, who every moment tempts me to set my dog at his throat. Let us refrain from conversing together until our evening repast, when we shall be alone, and at liberty to say what we please. Then, at least, Mothril the Moor is obliged to release us from his presence, for he does not eat with Christians, besides, he has his litter to watch over."

"Then this mysterious litter contains some treasure?"

"Yes," said Don Frederick, smiling.

Agenor had already during this day's journey been guilty of so many indiscretions, that, dreading to commit some fresh one, he asked no further questions, but his curiosity was not the less lively from being thus repressed.

Fernand now approached to receive his master's orders, for his tent had just been pitched in the centre of the camp.

"Let our supper be served, good Fernand," said the prince; "for Don Agenor must be both hungry and thirsty."

"And then I may return to you?" said Fernand. "You know, my lord, to whom I gave a promise never to quit your side."

A slight flush mounted to the Grand Master's cheek.

"Yes, remain with us, boy," said he; "I have no secrets from you."

The evening repast was served in Don Frederick's tent, and, as he expected, Mothril did not make his appearance.

"Now we are alone," said Agenor; "since, as you say, you have no secrets from this young man, I do not count his presence—tell me, my dear lord, all that has taken place, so that in future I may avoid the errors into which I have fallen to-day."

Don Frederick cast an uneasy glance around him. "This tent," said he, "is but a slight protection against prying eyes and ears."

"Then," said Agenor, "let us talk of other things. Notwithstanding my very natural curiosity, I can wait for a more convenient opportunity. Besides, it will be strange if, in spite of Satan himself, we do not find means of exchanging a few words between this and Seville."

"If you were not so fatigued," said Don Frederick, ",I should propose our quitting the tent accompanied by Fernand, and wrapped in our mantles, and armed with our swords, proceeding to some sufficiently exposed spot on the surrounding plain to render it impossible for the Moor, even if he returned to his original form of a serpent, to approach within fifty paces of us to overhear our conversation."

"My lord," replied Agenor, with a smiling consciousness of his youthful vigour, "I am never fatigued. Frequently, on my return home after a day spent in chasing the izard on the loftiest peaks of our mountains, my noble tutor, Ernanton de St. Colombe, has said to me, 'Agenor, they have discovered traces of a bear, I know his haunts—will you accompany me in pursuit of him?' And I have only paused to disencumber myself of the game I carried before setting out after this new quarry."

"Come, then," said Frederick.

They unfastened their helmets and cuirasses, and wrapping themselves in their cloaks—less to shield themselves from the night air, which is always cold among the mountains, than from the concealment they afforded—quitted the tent and proceeded in the direction that would soonest take them beyond the limits of the camp. The dog wished to follow them, but on receiving a sign from his master, he again laid down in front of the tent; for the beautiful creature was so well known, that he would have immediately betrayed the incognito of the two friends. But they were almost immediately stopped by a sentinel.

"Who is this soldier," demanded Don Frederick, stepping back.

"Ramon, the cross-bowman, my lord," replied Fernand. "I was resolved that good watch should be kept over your slumbers, and, therefore, myself placed a line of sentinels. You know to whom I have sworn to guard you even with my life."

"Well, then," said the Grand Master, "to him at least there will be no danger in revealing our names, so tell him who we are."

Fernand approached the sentinel and spoke to him for a moment in a low voice; the man immediately lowered his cross-brow, and with a respectful salutation drew back to let them pass. They had, however, scarcely proceeded fifty paces further, when a white and motionless form appeared through the gathering obscurity. Surprised at such an appearance, they walked up to the seeming phantom, and discovered it to be a second sentinel enveloped in his caftan, who lowered his lance, exclaiming in guttural Spanish, "No one passes here!"

"And who is this," again asked Don Frederick.

"I do not know him," said Fernand.

"What, then! he has not been placed here by you?"

"No, my lord, you see he is a Moor."

"Let us pass," said the prince, in Arabic.

But the Moor shook his head, and continued to present the barbed head of his lance at the Grand Master's breast.

"What is the meaning of this?" exclaimed Don Frederick, angrily. "Am I, the Grand Master of St. James, the brother of the King, a prisoner in my own camp. Holà, my guards, holà!"

At the same moment, Fernand drew a small golden whistle from his belt, and blew a shrill call. But before the guards, or even the Spanish sentinel, who was but at fifty paces distance, could obey the summons, the dog, hearing his master's voice calling for help, came rushing up to him, his coat bristling with rage. With a bound like that of a tiger, he sprung on the Moor, and, in spite of the protecting folds of his mantle, seized him so rudely by the throat that the man fell to the ground uttering cries of pain and terror, which brought both Moors and Spaniards to the spot—the former gliding about in the darkness like white-winged birds—the latter each bearing a torch in one hand and a sword in the other.

"Here, Allan!" cried Don Frederick, and at his summons the faithful dog slowly and unwillingly released his hold, and returned to his master's side, where he stood ready at the slightest signal to resume the attack.

At the same moment, Mothril appeared. The Grand Master turned to him with all the double majesty of his princely birth and princely nature.

"Speak, Mothril," said he. "Who has presumed to place

sentinels in my camp? This man is one of your retinue—
by whom has he been stationed here?"

"Place sentinels in your camp, my lord?" replied Mothril,
with the most profound humility. "Believe me, your slave
could never have been guilty of such presumption! I stationed my trustworthy follower"—and he pointed to the
Moor, who had now risen on his knees, and was clasping his
wounded throat with both hands—"to keep watch for fear
of nocturnal surprises, and he has either exceeded my orders,
or else he did not recognise your highness. In any case,
since he has thus offended the brother of my King, and he
judges him deserving of death, he shall die!"

"Not so," said Don Frederick: "it is the evil intention
that makes the crime; and since you assure me that yours
was good, it is for me to make your follower some recompence for the rough treatment he has received from my dog.
Fernand, give this man your purse."

Fernand approached with visible repugnance, and flung
his purse to the wounded Moor, who eagerly picked it up.

"Now, my lord," said Don Frederick, with the air of a
man who brooks no contradiction, "thanks for your solici-
tude for my safety, but it is quite unnecessary; my guards,
and my own good sword, are sufficient for my defence, therefore employ yours in guarding yourself and your litter; and
since you now know that I have need of neither you nor
yours, return to your tent and sleep in peace!"

The Moor silently bowed his head, and the prince passed
on. Mothril watched him out of sight, and when the three
forms of the prince, the chevalier, and the page were lost in
the obscurity, he approached the sentinel.

"Are you hurt?" he inquired.

"Yes, my lord," was the sullen reply.

"Severely?"

"The accursed animal's teeth met in my throat."

"Are you in too much pain to think of revenge?"

"Ah, no! my lord; the sweet taste of revenge takes away
the sting of the pain—only tell me what to do!"

"You shall know when the proper time arrives. Now
come with me," and they both returned to the camp.

Meanwhile, Don Frederick, accompanied by Agenor and
Fernand, pursued their way across the wild and gloomy
expanse of country to which the Sierra d'Estrella forms the

horizon. The dog ran, now before, now behind them; and had they been followed, his unerring scent would have immediately warned them of the presence of a spy. When he judged that they had proceeded far enough to prevent the sound of their voices reaching the camp, Don Frederick paused, and laid his hand on his friend's shoulder.

"Listen, Agenor," said he, in those deep accents which seem to proceed from the heart, "never again speak to me of Donna Bianca! Her name pronounced in the presence of strangers would make my cheek flush and my hand tremble; but to mention it when we were alone would make my very soul die within me! This is all I may now tell you. The unhappy lady has been unable to win the affections of her royal spouse. He prefers Maria Padilla, the haughty and ardent Spaniard, to this pure and amiable princess. One day, perhaps, I may tell you more, but from henceforth, Agenor, name her not. Alas! she is too constantly in my thoughts to need her being recalled to my remembrance!" And as he said this, he drew his mantle closer around him, as though to isolate himself with his great sorrow.

Agenor stood deep in thought beside his friend. He endeavoured, by recalling past events, to penetrate so far into Don Frederick's secret as to discover how he could be of service to him; for he rightly conjectured that the summons he had received bore some reference to this mysterious subject. The prince understood what was passing in his mind, and continued—

"But this is what I wished to say to you. We shall one day be as formerly, always together; and then, as I have no need of precaution with my brother, you will at last, without the subject being mentioned between us, be able to sound the frightful abyss at which I myself shudder. But for the present we must go to Seville, where fêtes and tournaments await me. The King says he wishes to do me honour, and as a proof of it has sent me, as you see, his friend and counsellor, Don Mothril."

Fernand shrugged his shoulders, in token of his hatred and contempt for the Moor.

"I obey the summons," continued Don Frederick, as if pursuing a train of thought. "But even on quitting Coimbra my suspicions were aroused, and have since been confirmed by the surveillance exercised over me. I am therefore resolved to watch, not only with my own eyes, but with those of my faithful Fernand; and even if he is forced to quit my side on some secret and indispensable mission, you, Agenor, will remain with me, for I love you both equally." And he extended to each of the young men a hand, which Agenor respectfully pressed, and Fernand covered with kisses. They then returned to the camp, but had scarcely passed the first tent, when they again encountered Mothril, at the sight of whom Don Frederick could not conceal the annoyance caused him by this continued intrusion.

"My lord," said the Moor, "on perceiving that no one in the camp slept, an idea occurred to me. Since the days are so sultry, would it not be more agreeable to your highness to travel by night? The moon is rising, and by at once continuing our journey, your royal brother would be spared at least a few hours of impatience."

"But you and your litter?" said Don Frederick.

"Oh, my lord," replied Mothril, "I and mine are always at your command!"

"Well, then," said the Grand Master, "I am willing to do as you propose; give orders for our departure."

Whilst they were striking the tents and saddling the horses and mules, Mothril approached the wounded sentinel.

"If we travel ten leagues to-night," said he, "shall we cross the first chain of mountains?"

"Yes!" replied the soldier.

"And if we set out to-morrow, towards seven o'clock in the evening, by what time shall we arrive at the ford of La Zezera?"

"By eleven o'clock."

As the Moor predicted, this mode of travelling proved agreeable to every one, more especially to himself, as it enabled him to more effectually guard his litter from the prying gaze of Muscaron; for the worthy squire was tormented by a ceaseless anxiety to discover what species of treasure was enclosed in this golden casket, over which the Moor kept such careful watch. Thus, like a true son of France, he took no account of the exigencies of the new climate in which he found himself, but at the next halt, and during the most intense heat of the day, commenced his researches. The burning rays of the sun fell almost perpendicularly; the whole camp appeared deserted. Don Frederick, the better to indulge in his gloomy reflections, had retired to his own tent, and Agenor and Fernand were conversing in theirs, when Muscaron suddenly appeared on the threshold, with the smiling look of a man who has at last achieved some long-wished-for project.

"Messire Agenor," exclaimed he, "I have made such a discovery!"

"What is it?" said the chevalier, who was accustomed to his squire's facetiousness.

"Why, that Don Mothril speaks to his litter, and his litter answers him!"

"And what do they say to each other?" asked his master.

"I heard their conversation plainly enough," replied Muscaron; "but I could not understand what they were talking about, because both the Moor and his litter spoke Arabic."

Agenor shrugged his shoulders.

"What do you say to this, Fernand?" said he. "According to Muscaron, Don Mothril's treasure can speak!"

"There is nothing astonishing in that," said the page, "supposing the treasure to be a woman!"

"Ah!" exclaimed Muscaron, thoroughly crest-fallen; "I never thought of that!"

"Is she young?" demanded Agenor, eagerly.

"Probably so."

"Beautiful?"

"Ah, now, Don Agenor, you ask me a question which, I fancy, few persons even composing Don Mothril's suite itself would be able to answer."

"Well, then, I will find out for myself!" said Agenor.

"But how?"

"Since Muscaron has managed to approach the tent near enough to overhear their conversation, I shall surely be able to do the same. We hunters are accustomed to glide from rock to rock to surprise the izard on our mountain peaks, and this Mothril cannot be more wary or easily scared than one of those timid animals."

"Be it so!" said Fernand, carried away by an impulse of giddy and adventurous youth. "But on condition that I accompany you."

"Come, then; meanwhile Muscaron will keep watch."

Agenor had not deceived himself, nor was any excessive caution necessary. The noonday sun poured down its most burning rays, the whole camp appeared abandoned, for the

Spanish and Moorish sentinels had sought the shade of some projecting rock or solitary tree; so that, with the exception of the tents, which gave the country a momentary appearance of being inhabited, you might have fancied yourself in a desert.

Mothril's tent was on the extreme verge of the camp, and whether to afford it a little shade, or to render it yet more isolated, was pitched in the centre of a clump of trees. Under this the litter had been carefully placed, whilst a large piece of Turkish stuff hung before the door effectually prevented any eye from penetrating the interior.

After receiving the necessary directions from Muscaron, whom they left to watch all that took place within the camp. the two young men made a detour, and without difficulty gained the outskirts of the little wood, where carefully parting the branches, the rustling of which would have betrayed their presence, they advanced with stealthy footsteps and almost suspended breath until they safely reached the circular curtain dividing them from the Moor and his litter, of whom, though concealed from their sight, they could distinctly hear the conversation.

"Oh!" said Agenor, "we shall not learn much, for they are speaking Arabic!"

Fernand laid his finger on his lips.

"I understand Arabic," said he, "let me listen. Strange!" he exclaimed, after a moment's silent attention. "They are talking of you!"

"Of me?" said Agenor. "Impossible!"

"I am not mistaken, it is the fact."

"And what are they saying?"

Don Mothril has hitherto been the only speaker; he has just asked: "Is it the chevalier with the red plume?"

At the same moment, a clear and melodious voice—one of those which wake an echo in the heart—replied, "Yes, it is the knight with the red plume, he is both young and handsome!"

"Young, certainly," said Mothril, "for he has scarcely seen twenty summers; but I deny his being handsome."

"He carries his armour well, and appears so brave!"

"Brave! he, a mere plunderer—a vulture of the Pyrenees, come to batten on the corpse of our unhappy Spain!"

"What is he saying?" inquired Agenor.

The page laughingly repeated Mothril's speech, word for word. The angry blood mounted to the chevalier's brow;

he grasped the hilt of his word, and half drew it from its scabbard, but Fernand checked him.

"My lord," said he, "this is the reward of listeners; doubtless my turn will come next."

But the sweet voice continued, still in Arabic: "He is the first French knight I ever beheld, therefore pardon me a little curiosity. They say that the knights of France are all famed for their gallantry. Is this one in the service of Don Pedro?"

"Aïssa," said the Moor, in a tone of concentrated rage, "speak to me no more of this young man!"

"Nay," replied the voice, "were not you the first to speak of him when we met him on the mountains? and when, after having promised to halt beneath the clump of trees at which he had arrived before us, you obliged me, weary as I was, to continue my journey, in order to reach Coimbra before the French knight had been able to obtain speech with Don Frederick."

Fernand laid his hand on the chevalier's arm—it seemed as though at that moment the veil was about to be dropped, and the secret intentions of the Moor revealed.

"What, then, is he saying?" anxiously inquired Agenor; and Fernand repeated what he had just heard.

Then the female voice resumed, in accents which went to the chevalier's heart, although he did not understand their signification—

"But since he is not brave, why do you dread him thus?"

"I distrust all the world, but dread no man," replied Mothril. "But I think it needless for you to concern yourself about a man whom you will soon lose sight of for ever."

Mothril pronounced these last words in a tone that left little doubt of their signification. Besides, Fernand's sudden start at once told Agenor that he had heard something of importance.

"Be on your guard, Sir Chevalier!" said he. "Either from political causes or some private jealousy, you have an enemy in Don Mothril."

Agenor smiled disdainfully.

They again listened, but the conversation had ceased, and a few seconds afterwards they perceived through the trees that Mothril had quitted the tent, and was wending his way towards the camp.

"Now is the moment to see and speak to that fair Aïssa, who expresses such sympathy with the chevaliers of France," said Agenor.

"To see her, if you will," said Fernand; "but not to speak to her; for depend upon it, Mothril has not left her unguarded."

With the point of his dagger, he then made a slit in the seam of the tent, which, narrow as it was, revealed a glimpse of the interior.

Aïssa was reclining on a sort of couch of purple stuff, broidered with gold, plunged in one of those mute and smiling reveries peculiar to Eastern women, whose lives are entirely composed of physical enjoyments. In one hand, she held a musical instrument called a guzla, the other was buried among her black and pearl-braided tresses, which formed a charming contrast to her small and taper fingers, with their henna-stained nails. Her fawnlike eyes beamed with a soft and dreamy expression beneath their heavily fringed eyelids; their gaze seemed endeavouring to fix itself on the object then occupying her thoughts. "How lovely she is!" murmured Agenor.

"My lord," said Fernand, "remember she is a Mooress, and consequently an enemy of our holy religion."

"Bah!" said Agenor, "I will convert her."

At this moment, Muscaron coughed—the concerted signal in case any one approached the wood; and the two young men left their post of observation, and cautiously returned the way they came.

On entering the camp, they perceived a small troop, composed of about a dozen Arab and Castilian horsemen, advancing towards them, on the route from Seville. The Moor, who was on his way to the Grand Master's tent, paused to receive them; for these horsemen were the bearers of a despatch from Don Pedro to his brother Don Frederick, accompanied by a letter to himself, which having read, he invited the new comers to await his return, in case it was the Grand Master's pleasure to require any explanations, and proceeded on his mission.

"Again!" exclaimed the young prince, as he crossed the threshold.

"My lord," said Mothril, "my excuse for thus intruding on your privacy must be this packet, addressed to you by your royal brother, which I have hastened to bring to you."

And he offered the letter to Don Frederick, who took it with a certain hesitation; but on reading the first few lines his countenance brightened. It was as follows:—"Hasten, my well-beloved brother, for Seville is in joyful expectation of the arrival of the Grand Master of St. James, and already knights of every nation have flocked to my court. All who accompany you will be welcome; but do not encumber yourself with a large retinue, for my glory will be to behold you—my happiness in beholding you soon!"

At this moment, Agenor and Fernand, to whom the sight of this troop of strange horsemen had caused some disquietude, in their turn entered the tent.

"Here," said the young prince, giving Agenor the King's letter, "read this, and see what a reception awaits us."

"Will not your highness address a few words of welcome to the bearers of this despatch?" asked Mothril.

Don Frederick made a sign in the affirmative, and left the tent; then, when he had thanked the messengers for their speed (for he learned they had been only five days in journeying from Seville), Mothril said to their chief, "I will retain your men, to do honour to the Grand Master; but for yourself, return to Don Pedro with the swiftness of the swallow, and announce to him that the prince is on his road to Seville." Then he added, in a lower tone, "Hasten to the King, and tell him I will not return without the proof I promised him."

The Moorish cavalier inclined his head, and without uttering a single word, or pausing to refresh either himself or his horse, departed with the speed of an arrow.

This secret communication had not escaped the notice of Fernand, who, though unable to overhear the nature of it, thought it his duty to say to his master that this sudden departure of the chief of the newly arrived troop was the more suspicious from the fact of his being a Moor, and not a Castilian.

"Listen," said Don Frederick, when they were once more alone. "This danger, whatever it may be, menaces neither you, Agenor, nor myself; we are strong men, and need fear nothing; but in the castle of Medina Sidonia, there is a feeble and defenceless being—a woman who has already

suffered too much on my account.   You must therefore at
once set out, and by some means or other, which I leave to
your ingenuity, contrive to warn her to be upon her guard.
What I could not venture to say in a letter, you can tell her
by word of mouth."

"I am ready to set out as soon as you please," replied
Fernand.   "You know I am always at your command."

Frederick seated himself at the table, and wrote a few
lines on a slip of parchment, which he sealed with his own
seal.   As he finished his task, Mothril again entered the
tent.

"You see," said Don Frederick, "that I am, on my part,
writing to his Majesty Don Pedro; for it seems to me, that
allowing his messenger to depart charged with only a verbal
response, has the appearance of receiving his letter very
coldly.   Fernand shall therefore set out to-morrow morning."

The Moor only replied by a silent inclination of the head,
and in his presence the Grand Master enclosed the parchment in a small bag, broidered with fine pearls, and gave it
to the page.

"You know all you have to do?" said he.

"Yes, my lord, all."

"But," said Mothril, "since your highness wishes to benefit
this Frank chevalier, why not despatch him on this mission
instead of this page, whose attendance is so necessary to
your comfort?   He shall be escorted by four of my people,
and by thus bearing to the King his brother's letter, will at
once win the favour you are so anxious to obtain for him."

This crafty proposal at first embarrassed Don Frederick;
but Fernand came to his assistance.

"Pardon me, my lord," said he, "but it appears to me,
that no one but a Spaniard should be sent as messenger to
the King of Castile.   Besides, your choice first fell upon me,
and, except at your express desire, I decline to relinquish
the honour of this mission."

"Good," said Don Frederick, "then we will make no
change in our arrangements."

"Your highness is master," said Mothril, "and it is the
duty of your slaves to execute your wishes.   I therefore
come to learn them."

"Concerning what?"

"Our departure; for I fancy we agreed to journey by

night, as we did yesterday, unless your highness found our nocturnal march disagreeable."

"No; quite the contrary."

"Then, since we have only an hour or two more of daylight remaining, it is time to set out," said Mothril.

"I shall be ready by the time you have given the necessary orders."

The Moor retired.

"Listen," said Don Frederick to Fernand. "We shall have to cross the river, which rising in the Sierra, falls into the Tagus; there is sure to be some confusion in effecting the passage, therefore the moment you reach the opposite side, take advantage of it, and steal away, for I fancy you are not more anxious than myself for the Moor's proffered escort. Only be very prudent during your journey, and doubly so when you arrive at your destination, for you know how rigorously *she* is guarded."

Not a moment was lost in preparing for departure, and the cavalcade again set out in its usual order of march, that is to say, a party of Moorish horsemen led the way, then came Don Frederick, closely attended by Mothril, and the litter and its guard brought up the rear.

By ten o'clock, they had crossed La Sierra, and, descending into the valley an hour afterwards, what seemed to be a long undulating silver ribbon, gleaming in the moonlight, appeared through the trees growing on the mountain slope.

"Here is La Zezera," said Mothril. "With his highness's permission, I will cause the depth of the ford to be sounded."

As this would give Don Frederick an opportunity of remaining alone for a moment with Agenor and Fernand, he hastily assented to the Moor's proposal. Mothril, as we are already aware, never moved without his litter, therefore before proceeding to the ford, he caused the rear-guard to advance with the precious burden, which, until he had discovered its real nature, gave so much anxiety to Muscaron.

"Now," said Agenor, "it is my turn to ask a favour of your highness. We Franks are accustomed to cross rivers at any convenient spot that may present itself, and I am extremely desirous of reaching the opposite side of this one at the same moment as the Moor."

This gave Don Frederick an opportunity of giving his last instructions to Fernand without any one overhearing them.

"As you will," said he to Agenor. "But do not expose yourself to any needless danger; remember, I have need of you."

"My lord,' said the chevalier, "we shall meet on the opposite side.' And making a circuit in the opposite direction to that taken by the Moor and his litter, he disappeared with his squire among the sinuosities of the mountain.

CHAPTER IV.

THE PASSAGE OF THE RIVER.

THE Moor, having been the first to set out, was the first to arrive at the ford, with the depth of which he was seemingly well acquainted, since he unhesitatingly descended to the water's brink, buried to the waist in the rose-laurels which in the southern parts of Spain and Portugal are generally to be found in profusion on the river banks. At a sign from him, the conductors of the litter, after receiving the requisite directions as to the course they were to take, which was besides indicated by a little wood of orange-trees, took the mules by their bridles, and led them into the stream, which they crossed without the water rising higher than the stomachs of the animals. Notwithstanding the Moor's certainty of the safety of the ford, he watched the transit with anxious eyes, until he saw the precious litter deposited on the opposite bank. Then alone he cast a hasty glance around him, and stooping to a level with the laurels, said in a low tone,—" Are you there?"

" Yes," replied a voice.

" You will be able to recognise this page?"

" It is the one who whistled to the dog."

" The letter is in a pearl-embroidered bag, which he carries in a little pouch at his side—and it is this pouch I require."

" You shall have it," replied the voice.

"Then I may call him; you are at your post?"

" I shall be at the proper time."

Mothril retraced his steps, and rejoined Don Frederick and Fernand. Meanwhile, Agenor and Muscaron, in their turn, reached the sloping bank of the river. As he had said, the chevalier, regardless of the depth of the water, urged his horse into the current, which was at first shallow enough, but after he had accomplished about three-quarters of the distance, began gradually to deepen. The brave horse lost his footing, but encouraged by the hand and caresses of his master, swam boldly forward, and safely gained the opposite side. Muscaron followed his master like his shadow, and after having executed, as far as possible, exactly the same manœuvres, was, according to his usual custom, about to felicitate himself on his prowess; but Agenor, laying his finger on his lips, warned him to be silent. They ascended the bank without any sound, besides the light rippling of the water, being heard to betray their passage.

Agenor checked his horse, and springing to the ground, flung his bridle to Muscaron; then making a circuit, he gained the further extremity of the orange-grove, in front of which he perceived the gilded frieze of the litter glittering in the moonlight. But he would have easily discovered it, even without this to guide him, for the sweet notes of the guzla, ringing on the night air, showed that Aïssa was thus beguiling the time until her guardian should rejoin her. At first she struck only a few vague and uncertain chords, as though her fingers were straying unconsciously over the strings; but at last her rich voice broke out in words, which, though originally Arabic, were now translated into the purest Castilian. Thus it was evident that the fair Aïssa understood Spanish, and the chevalier would consequently be able to converse with her. He continued to approach, guided by the music.

Aïssa had drawn aside the curtains of her litter, on the side furthest from the river; and her attendants, doubtless in obedience to their master's commands, had retired to some twenty paces' distance. The Moorish girl reclined on her cushions, watching the pure, pale moon as she pursued her course through the cloudless sky; her attitude, like that of all Eastern women, was full of natural and voluptuous grace. She seemed to inhale at every pore the perfume borne by the warm southern breeze from the fragrant groves of Cintra. Her song, one of those Eastern compositions, was as follows:—

"It is the hour, the evening hour,
   When resting from his weary flight
In some lone vale, the nightingale
   Pours forth his song upon the night.
It is the hour, the tranquil hour,
   When earth is hushed in peaceful rest;
And sweeter still, the scents that fill
   The dewy rose's fragrant breast.

D

It is the hour, the silent hour,
    The murmuring rill forgets to play—
No sound is heard, save that lone bird,
    Pouring to Heaven his plaintive lay.
' Oh ! thou, the maiden's cherished flower,
    Why dost thou only thus unclose
To the dark night thy beauty bright ?'
    Thus sung the sweet bird to the rose.
The flower replied, ' Ah, wondrous bird,
    Why only when all sounds are still
In vale and grove, thy lays of love
    With melody all bosoms thrill ?'
' My song is to the modest flower,
    That shuns the burning eye of day.'
' My perfume sweet ascends to greet
    The bird that loves the moon's pale ray !' "

As she concluded, and the last chords vibrated on the still air, Agenor, unable any longer to restrain his impatience, appeared in the moonlit space between the little wood and the litter. At so sudden an apparition, most women would have cried out; the Moorish maiden, on the contrary, started from her recumbent position, and drew a small poniard from her girdle; but almost immediately recognising the intruder, she sank back again, and resting her head on one of her softly moulded hands, laid a finger of the other on her lips, to warn him to approach without noise.

Agenor obeyed. The long curtains of the litter and heavy trappings of the mules formed a sort of screen, and effectually concealed him from the eyes of the two attendants, who were besides engaged in watching the preparations making on the other side of the river for the crossing of Don Frederick and Fernand. He therefore boldly approached, and taking her hand, pressed it to his lips.

" Aïssa loves me, and I love Aïssa !" he whispered.

" Then are men of your nation necromancers," said she, "to read in women's hearts the secret they only confess to solitude and night ?"

" No," said the chevalier; "but we know that love awakens love. Do not tell me I am so unhappy as to be mistaken !"

" No," replied the young girl. " Since Don Mothril has carried me about with him, watching over me as if I were his wife instead of his daughter, I have passed many handsome Moorish and Castilian knights without my thoughts being diverted from my prayers, or my eyes wandering from the pearls of my bracelet; but with you it was different. From the moment I met you on the mountain, I longed to quit my litter and fly to you! You are astonished at my frankness, but I have not been brought up in cities. I am a flower of the desert; and as that flower yields up its perfume to the hand that gathers it, and then fades away, so I offer you my love, and shall die if you reject it!"

If Agenor were the first man that had attracted the notice of the fair Aïssa, she was no less the only woman who, by the melody of her voice and charms of her look and gestures, had been able to make any impression on his hitherto insensible heart. He was, therefore, about to make a fitting reply to this strange avowal of a passion almost surpassing his own, when suddenly a loud cry of terror and despair rang through the air, making them both start, and Don Frederick's voice was heard shouting from the opposite bank,

"Help, help, Agenor! Fernand is drowning!"

The Moorish maiden leant hastily out of her litter, and touching his brow with her lips, said, simply, " But I shall see you again?"

"On my soul, yes!" replied Agenor.

"Then hasten to the page's rescue!" said she, pushing him away with one hand, and with the other drawing around her the curtains of her litter.

By making a slight detour, a few steps brought the chevalier to the brink of the river. In a moment he divested himself of his sword and spurs, and as he was fortunately without armour, plunged into the stream, and swam rapidly towards the place where the agitation of the water marked the spot where Fernand had disappeared. This is what had taken place.

As we have before related, Mothril, after witnessing the safe arrival of his litter, and communicating his instructions to the concealed Moor, had returned to Don Frederick, whom, with Fernand and the rest of his retinue, he found awaiting him at a little distance.

"My lord," said he, " the ford is found, and as you may perceive, my litter has already crossed without difficulty. Nevertheless, in order to take every precaution, I will myself act as guide, first to your page and then yourself ; the rest of the party can follow."

This arrangement corresponded so well with Don Frederick's wishes that he did not dream of making any objection to it ; in fact, nothing could have better facilitated the execution of the project concerted between himself and Fernand.

D 2

"Good," said he to Mothril, "Fernand shall cross first; and, as he ought to precede us on the route to Seville, can at once proceed on his journey, whilst we complete the passage of the river."

Mothril inclined his head, as though he saw nothing to object to in this plan.

"Do you wish to send any message to my brother, Don Pedro?" asked the prince.

"No, my lord," replied the Moor, "my own messenger has already set out, and will arrive before yours."

The Grand Master devoted the short space of time before they reached the ford to giving a tender exhortation to Fernand. He dearly loved this young page, who had been in his service from a child, and to whom, boy as he was, he did not hesitate to confide his most cherished secrets; and on his side Fernand was devotedly attached to his noble master.

Mothril awaited them at the ford. Everything around was calm and tranquil. The landscape, illumined by the gleaming river, and the bright moonlight, here and there broken by the heavy mountain shadows, seemed like one of the fairy scenes we behold in our dreams. It would have been impossible for even the most fearful person to imagine that in this glorious repose of nature lurked even the semblance of a danger. Thus Fernand, who, like most youths of his age, was naturally brave and adventurous, fearlessly urged his horse into the stream after Mothril's mule. For about fifteen paces neither of the two animals got out of their depth, but then the Moor insensibly bore to the right.

"You are straying from the path, Mothril," cried Don Frederick from the bank. "Take care, Fernand! take care!"

"Do not be uneasy, my lord," replied Mothril; "I am leading the way, therefore if any danger exist I shall be the first to encounter it."

This reply was so plausible, that although the Moor diverged more and more from the straight line, Fernand only imagined he did so in order to more easily stem the force of the current.

Mothril's mule now lost its footing, and Fernand's horse also began to swim, but this mattered little to the young page, who, had it been necessary, would have found no difficulty in himself swimming across the stream. The Grand

Master continued to watch their progress with growing uneasiness.

"You are going wrong, Mothril!" cried he; "keep more to the left, Fernand."

But Fernand finding that his horse was swimming vigorously, and that the Moor still preceded him, far from feeling alarm at what he regarded as a mere trifle, turned gaily to his master, saying, "Do not be afraid, my lord; I am following Don Mothril, therefore I must be in the right path."

But as he did so, a singular vision presented itself in the sort of wake left by his steed, namely, the head of a man, which, though it immediately sank beneath the water, did not disappear so quickly, but that he distinctly caught sight of it.

"Don Mothril," said he, "I fear we have really mistaken the ford; your litter did not cross here; nay, I fancy I can see it glittering in the moonlight near yonder grove of orange-trees, quite at our left."

"We have almost passed the deep water," replied Mothril; "in an instant more we shall feel the bottom."

"You are going wrong!" again exclaimed Don Frederick, but they were now so far distant that his voice was scarcely audible.

"It is a fact," said Fernand, who began to be slightly uneasy on witnessing the vain struggles of his horse against the force of the current by which he seemed to be irresistibly carried away, whilst Mothril having ·his mule under full command, remained at some distance on his left.

"Don Mothril!" cried the page, "there is some treachery in this!"

He had scarcely uttered these words when his horse gave a sudden snort, and plunging on one side beat the water violently, but without, as before, swimming with his right hind leg. Almost immediately afterwards he again gave a dismal neigh, and ceased to use the left limb also; then having no other support than his two forelegs, his hind-quarters insensibly sank beneath the water. Fernand saw that the moment was now come to throw himself into the river, but he vainly attempted to release his feet from the stirrups, and to his horror discovered that he was fastened to his sinking steed.

"Help! help!" he exclaimed, and it was this cry of despair

that, reaching Agenor, awoke him from the ecstasy in which
he was plunged by the voice and aspect of the Moorish maiden.

The poor horse sank deeper and deeper, till only his
nostrils, through which the breath came with a roaring
noise, appeared above the surface, whilst his fore feet wildly
beat the water, and dashed it in showers around him.

Fernand endeavoured to utter a second cry for help, but
dragged down by the secret power against which he had
before vainly attempted to struggle, he also disappeared in
the abyss. His hand, raised to Heaven as though demanding vengeance or succour, appeared for a moment, and then,
like the rest of his body, vanished beneath the stream. All
that remained was a sort of eddy, to the surface of which
rose numerous blood-stained bubbles.

Two friends had hastened to Fernand's rescue; on the one
side, Agenor, and on the other, the faithful dog, which was
accustomed to obey the page's voice almost as implicitly as
his master's. But their search was vain, although Agenor
remarked that the dog thrice dived at one particular spot,
and returned the third time with a fragment of stuff in his
mouth. Then, as if he had done all in his power for his
unfortunate friend, he swam slowly towards the shore; and
crouching at his master's feet gave one of those piercing and
despairing howls which make even the firmest nerves thrill.
The night was consumed in fruitless researches, for Don
Frederick, who in his turn had safely crossed the river,
could not tear himself away from the watery grave from
which he every moment vainly hoped to see his friend emerge.
Allan lay howling at his feet, while Agenor gloomily and
thoughtfully held in his hand the morsel of cloth brought him
by the dog, and impatiently awaited the daylight.

Mothril, who for some time had been groping amongst
the rose laurels, as if searching for the lost youth, now presented himself in feigned despair, repeating, Allah! Allah!
and pretending to console the Grand Master by those idle
phrases, which only add poignancy to suffering.

Day at last broke; its first rays found Agenor sitting
beside the Grand Master. He had evidently awaited this
moment with the utmost impatience; for scarcely had the
first glimmer of light appeared than he approached the door
of the tent, and carefully examined the fragment torn from
the pourpoint of the unfortunate page. But this examina-

tion seemed only to confirm his previous suspicions, for he sadly shook his head.

"My lord," said he, "this is not only a very lamentable, but also a very strange occurrence!"

"It is indeed," replied Frederick. "Ah! why has Providence inflicted this fresh sorrow upon me?"

"My lord," said Agenor, "I fear this blow has come from some other hand than that of Providence. Look carefully at this last relic of the friend you mourn. Do you observe nothing?"

"What do you mean?"

"The pourpoint of our unhappy Fernand was as white as an angel's robe, and the river is as limpid and clear as crystal; and yet look, my lord! this morsel of stuff is tinged with red; there has been blood upon it!"

"Blood!"—"Yes, my lord."

"Allan must have wounded himself in his attempts to seize the body of his friend, for, as you see, his head is also tinged with the same reddish hue."

"I at first thought the same, but after the most careful scrutiny can find no trace of a wound; that blood did not come from Allan."

"But might not Fernand have himself struck against some rock?"

"My lord, I have dived at the spot where he disappeared, and the water is nowhere more than twenty feet in depth. But here is something that will perhaps guide us. Do you perceive this rent in the stuff?"

"It has been torn by the dog."

"Not so; for here are the distinct marks of the animal's teeth; this cut has been made by some sharp instrument— by the blade of a poniard."

"Horrible!" exclaimed Don Frederick, starting up, pale with rage and terror. "But you are right! Fernand was an excellent swimmer, and his horse, bred in my stables, has a hundred times before crossed far more rapid streams than this. There has been treachery, Agenor! there has been crime!"

"I do not doubt it, my lord; but what cause could there be for it?"

"Ah, true! you did not know that, on reaching the shore, Fernand was to quit me; not to join Don Pedro, as I told the Moor (who cannot have believed me), but to fulfil a

secret mission with which I had charged him. My poor
friend—my firm and faithful confidant, whose heart beat only
for me! Alas! it is for me, and through me, he has died!"

"That may be, my lord; but it is the duty of us all to
die for your highness."

"Alas! who can foresee the consequences that may result
from this death?"

"Although I do not enjoy your friendship in the same
degree as Fernand," said Agenor, sadly, "I will serve you as
faithfully as he has done."

"You are right, Agenor," said the prince, holding out
his hand, and regarding him with the infinite sweetness that
was one of his most astonishing characteristics. "I had
divided my heart between you and Fernand; but he is
gone, and you are now my sole remaining friend. I will
prove it by telling you the mission on which he was despatched. It was to bear a letter to your countrywoman,
the Queen, Donna Bianca."

"Ah! here is the cause, then," said Agenor, "and where
was this letter?"

"In the little pouch which hung at his belt. If Fernand
has been really assassinated (and, like you, I now believe such
to be the case), if the murderers have dragged the corpse,
which we have vainly endeavoured to discover, to some distant and lonely spot on the river banks, my secret is discovered, and we are lost!"

"Then, my lord," said Agenor, "why proceed to Seville?
You are still near enough to Portugal to return to your good
town of Coimbra, and place yourself in safety behind its
ramparts".

"Not to go to Seville, would be to abandon her—and to
fly, would give rise to suspicions, which will never exist, if
this death of Fernand's be, after all, the result of accident.
Besides, Don Pedro has Donna Bianca in his power, and
through her, attracts me towards him. I will go to Seville."

"But how can I serve you?" said the chevalier. "Cannot
I replace Fernand? Cannot you give me a duplicate of
the letter entrusted to him, and some token by which
I may be recognised as your messenger. I am no boy
of sixteen; nor do I wear a silken doublet, but a stout
cuirass which has turned aside far more dangerous weapons
than your Moorish canjiards and yataghans. Give it me; and

since to reach her is an eight days' journey, I promise she shall safely receive your billet in four!"

"Thanks, my brave Frank; but if the King is already forewarned, the danger would be doubled. The means I employed were not good, therefore God would not allow them to succeed. Now we must shape our course according to circumstances. We will continue our route as though nothing had happened; but when we are within two days' journey of Seville, watch an opportunity of leaving me, unobserved, make a detour, and whilst I go in at one gate, you, in your turn, enter the city by the other. Then, at night, steal into the King's Alcazar, and conceal yourself in the first court—the one overshadowed by magnificent plane-trees, and in the midst of which is a marble basin, ornamented with lions' heads. You will observe three windows hung with purple—these mark the apartments I usually occupy when on a visit to my brother. Come under those windows at midnight. I shall then know from Don Pedro's reception what we have to hope and what to fear. I will then speak with you; or, if unable to do that, will throw you a letter, containing instructions how to act. Only swear, that whether they be written or spoken, you will put them into instant execution."

"My lord," said Agenor, "I swear to you to fulfil your wishes on every point."

"Good," said Don Frederick. "Now I shall feel rather more tranquil; poor Fernand!"

"My lord," said Mothril, appearing on the threshold of the tent, "will your highness deign to remember that during last night we only performed half our allotted distance; therefore, if it please you to continue our journey, we shall arrive in three or four hours' time on the borders of a lofty forest, which I know from having halted there on a previous occasion, where we can repose during the heat of the day."

"Yes; let us set out," said Don Frederick. "Since I have lost all hope of again beholding Fernand, I have nothing to detain me here."

The cavalcade accordingly resumed its march; but not without the two friends many times turning their heads towards the river, and repeating, with a sigh, "Poor Fernand!" Thus Don Frederick continued his journey towards Seville.

CHAPTER V.

MARIA PADILLA.

THERE are some cities which by the advantages bestowed on
them by nature, no less than by the treasures of beauty
with which they are enriched by man, assume, as if by right,
a position as sovereigns of the surrounding countries.   Such
a one is Seville, that queen of beautiful Andalusia, who is
herself one of the fairest provinces of Spain.   The Moors, by
whom she was conquered with joy, preserved with affection,
and quitted with regret, left on her brow the Eastern diadem
which for three ages had rested there.   One of the palaces,
with which during their sojourn there they had endowed
their favourite sultana, was now inhabited by Don Pedro,
and thither we are about to transport our readers.

Upon a marble terrace, where fragrant orange and citron-
trees, mingled with myrtles and pomegranates, cast so thick
a shade that it was almost impervious to the sun, Moorish
slaves were waiting until the fiery beams of day were
quenched in the bosom of ocean.   As soon as the evening
breeze rose they hastened to sprinkle the marble pavement
with attar of roses and benzoin, so that the passing air bore
with it the mingled perfumes of nature and art, like beauty
heightened by a tasteful toilet.   They then spread beneath
these hanging gardens of this modern Babylon silken couches
and downy cushions, since with the coming of night Spain
appeared to return to life, and with the freshness of evening
the streets, the promenades, and the terraces again began to
show signs of being inhabited.   Presently the tapestry
dividing the terrace from a vast apartment was drawn aside,
and a man appeared, on whose arm leant a beautiful woman,
of between four and five and twenty years of age, with
black silky hair, dark soft eyes, and that clear brown complexion which in Eastern women compensates for the absence
of colour.   The man, on the contrary, who was perhaps
eight and twenty, was tall, fair haired, and bore in his blue
eyes and pale complexion, which not even a Spanish sun
could tinge of a darker hue, all the peculiar characteristics
of the northern races of Europe.   The woman was Donna
Maria Padilla ; the man, his Majesty Don Pedro.   They
silently advanced beneath the overhanging canopy of verdure,
but it was easy to perceive that this silence did not proceed

from lack of subjects of conversation, but from the too great preoccupation of their thoughts. The fair Spaniard did not notice even by a glance the Moorish slaves who stood awaiting her orders, or the riches by which she was surrounded. Although born in mean circumstances, almost poverty, she had become familiarized with all that the most dazzling luxury could furnish during the time she had sported with the sceptre of Don Pedro, as a child does with a rattle.

"Pedro," said she, at last interrupting a silence which they had hitherto both seemed unwilling to break, "you are mistaken in declaring that I am your loved and honoured mistress. I am a humiliated slave; that is all, my lord!"

Don Pedro smiled, and almost imperceptibly shrugged his shoulders.

"Yes," said Maria, "a humiliated slave! I have said it, and I repeat it!"

"How is that?" said the King. "Explain yourself."

"Oh, that is easily done, my lord! Here is the Grand Master of St. James, they say, about to visit Seville to attend the tourney for which you are making preparations. His apartments, enriched at my expense, are ornamented with the rarest hangings and most costly articles of furniture, which you have caused to be transported from your own palace."

"He is my brother," replied Don Pedro. Then he added, with an expression, the meaning of which was only known to himself, "My well-beloved brother!"

"Your brother!" returned Maria Padilla. "For my part, I thought he was the brother of Henry de Transtamare."

"Yes, senora; but they are both the sons of my late father King Alphonso."

"And you treat him like a king; but I comprehend, he has almost a right to these honours, since he is beloved by a queen."

"I do not understand you," said Don Pedro, turning pale, but allowing no other sign to escape him of the blow which had struck him to the heart."

"Ah, Don Pedro! Don Pedro!" said Maria, "you are either very blind, or very philosophical!"

The King made no reply, except by turning abruptly towards the east.

"Well, at what are you gazing?" cried the impatient Spaniard. "Do you wish to see whether your well-beloved brother has arrived?"

"I was observing whether the towers of Medina Sidonia were visible from this royal terrace."

"Yes," said Maria Padilla; "I know that you are about to reply as usual that the Queen is confined there; but how happens it that you, whom men surname 'the Judge,' punish one and not the other?—that the Queen is a prisoner, and her accomplice loaded with honours?"

"How has my brother, Don Frederick, offended you, senora?" asked the King.

"If you loved me, you would not have occasion to ask such a question, for you would have already avenged me! How has he offended me? He has pursued me, not with his hatred—that would be nothing, for it is sometimes an honour to be hated—but with his contempt."

The King made no reply. His was one of those impenetrable hearts in which it was impossible to read his real feelings beneath the iron mask by which they were concealed.

"Oh, how easy it is," continued Maria, disdainfully, "to assume the semblance of virtues not one's own! How easy for an artful woman to veil her unworthy passions by a timid look, and shelter herself beneath the prejudice that the maidens of France are cold and insensible compared with the daughters of Spain!"

Don Pedro still remained silent.

"Pedro! Pedro!" exclaimed Maria, doubly irritated at finding her sarcasms had no effect on the invulnerable prince, "you would do well to listen to the voice of your people. Hear how they cry, 'Maria Padilla, the royal courtesan—the shame of her kingdom. Look at her!—guilty and criminal as she is, she has dared to love her sovereign, not for his rank, but for himself! Let us curse her, as we have already done La Cava, for such women are the destruction of both the King and the people!' Such is the voice of Spain. Listen to it, Don Pedro! But if I were queen, they would say, 'Ah, poor Maria Padilla! you were very happy when you were a young maiden, and sported with your companions on the banks of the Guadalquiver; poor Maria Padilla, you were very happy when the King won your girlish heart by a semblance of affection. Your family was so illustrious, that the first lords of

Castile wooed you as their bride, but you committed the crime of preferring your sovereign. Poor inexperienced young girl! You did not then know that kings are, after all, only men; that he whom you have never wronged, even in thought, even in a dream, nevertheless deceives you, and forgetting your fidelity and devotion, gives his heart to others. If I were queen, all this would be said of me, and I should be regarded as a saint!—yes, as a saint, for is not that the title bestowed on a woman I know, who has betrayed her husband for love of his brother!"

Don Pedro, whose brow insensibly darkened, passed his hand over his eyes, and his countenance immediately became calm, almost smiling.

"In short, senora," said he, "you wish to be queen, although you know that to be impossible, since I am already married twice over. Ask anything in reason, and I will grant it you."

"I fancied I might at least demand as much as Juana da Castro."

"Juana da Castro asked nothing, senora; it was demanded by necessity, that inexorable ruler even of Kings. She belonged to a powerful family, and I was obliged to secure allies at home, whilst by repudiating Blanche I was making enemies abroad. Now, at the very moment when war menaces me on every side, when my other brother, Henry de Transtamare, has caused Arragon to revolt against me, has taken Toledo, and is besieging Toro, so that I have more difficulty in reconquering my own near possessions than I should have in driving the Moors from Granada, you would have me seize on the person of Don Frederick and consign him to a prison. Can you for an instant forget that I have myself been a captive, obliged to dissimulate, to bow the head, and smile at those whom I would fain have bitten, and to chafe like a child beneath my mother's ambitious will? That it cost me six months of dissimulation to enable me to find the door of my own palace open for a single instant? That I was obliged to fly to Seville, and then tear piece by piece from the hands of those who had seized upon them the possessions left me by my father, King Alphonso; to cause Garcilaso to be poniarded at Burgos—Albuquerque poisoned at Toro—four-and-twenty heads to fall at Toledo, thus causing my surname of the Judge to be changed into that of 'the Cruel,' without knowing which title **will** be handed down to posterity; and to crown all, that for a supposed crime, I have consigned a French princess to the prison of Medina Sidonia, where she remains in solitude and almost misery, merely because it is your pleasure to behold her thus ?"

"Ah, not because it pleases me !" exclaimed Maria Padilla, with flashing eyes, "but because she has dishonoured you."

"Not so, senora," said Don Pedro, "for I am not one of those who rest the honour or dishonour of kings on so frail a thing as a woman's virtue. What to other men is an occasion of joy or grief, is to us sovereigns merely a political means of arriving at some desired end. No, I have not been dishonoured by Queen Blanche, but I was forced to espouse her against my inclination, and therefore I seized on the opportunity, which she and my brother were imprudent enough to afford me, and under pretence of having conceived terrible suspicions against them, I have degraded and humiliated the daughter of the first house in Christendom. Thus, if you love me as you say, you should pray Heaven to guard me from misfortune ; for the Regent, or rather, the King of France is her brother-in-law, and he is a great prince, with powerful armies, commanded by the first general of the age, Bertrand Duguesclin."

"Ah, King, you are afraid !" said Maria Padilla, preferring Don Pedro's anger to this cold imperturbability, which by always giving him the mastery over himself, rendered him the most subtle and dangerous prince in the world.

"Yes, senora," returned the King, "I am afraid of you ; for hitherto you alone have had the power to make me commit the faults of which I have been guilty."

"Nay, it appears to me that a monarch who selects both his counsellors and attendants from among Moors and Jews, should ascribe his faults to them, not to the woman he ought to love."

"Ah, you also have fallen into the common error," said Don Pedro, shrugging his shoulders. "My Moorish counsellors, my Jewish agents ! Ah, senora, I receive counsel from where there is intelligence, and draw my resources from where there is wealth. If you and the rest of my accusers will take the trouble to cast your eyes over Europe, you will find that civilization belongs to the Moors, and riches

to the Jews. By whom were the Mosque of Cordova, the
Alhambra of Granada, the Alcazars that ornament our cities—
nay, even the very palace in which we now are, built except
by the Moors? In whose hands lies commerce? In the
hands of those who know how to gather up the gold, scattered by careless nations—the Jews. You see, then, that
these despised races are the fitting ministers and agents of a
King who wishes to live free and independent of his neighbours. Well, this, which during the last six years I have
endeavoured to accomplish, has given rise to all these calumnies and bitter emnities against me. Those who wished
to occupy confidential posts about me, have become my most
implacable enemies; and the cause is simple enough, I have
done nothing for and required nothing of them. I keep them
at a distance from me; but you, Maria, on the contrary, I
have raised from your former position, and placed as near my
throne as possible. I have given you as much of my heart
as a King may bestow; in short I, whom you accuse of loving
nothing, have loved you."

"Ah, if you had loved me," said Maria, replying woman-
like, rather to her own thoughts, than to Don Pedro's refu-
tation of her accusations, "I should not be thus condemned
to tears and shame for having been devoted to my King, for
I should ere this have been avenged.'

"Good heavens! wait," said Don Pedro, "and you shall
have your revenge! Do you think that I bear Don Frederick any real affection, or that I should not be glad of
an opportunity to rid myself of all this race of bastards?
Well, if Don Frederick has really outraged you, which I
doubt——"

"Is it not outraging me," interrupted Maria, pale with
anger, "to counsel you, as he has done, to discard me, and
again receive Queen Blanche as your wife?"

"And you are sure he has done this, Maria?"

"Oh, yes!" said the Spaniard, with a menacing gesture;
"I am as certain of it as I am of my existence."

"Then if he advises me thus, you have erred in accusing
him of being the Queen's lover; for jealous as you are, you
can surely comprehend that they would have otherwise both
rejoiced in the liberty of action afforded a despised woman."

"You are too subtle a reasoner for me, sire," said Maria,
rising, unable any longer to contain her fury; "I therefore

salute your Majesty, and will endeavour to avenge myself
without your aid."

Don Pedro gazed at her in silence, and suffered her to
depart without attempting to recall her by even a gesture;
and yet this was the only woman who had been able to
inspire him with anything approaching real affection; but,
on that very account, he feared her almost as he would have
done an enemy. Repressing, therefore, his first faint feeling
of pity, he remained extended idly on the cushions she had
just quitted, with his eyes fixed on the route from Portugal,
of which this lofty balcony commanded a view.

"Horrible lot of kings!" he murmured. "I love this
woman, and yet dare not allow either herself or others to
perceive it, lest she should abuse it; for no one must imagine
themselves possessed of sufficient power over the King to
demand satisfaction for injuries, or to influence in any way
his actions. No one must be able to say the Queen has outraged her husband, who knows it, and yet has not sought
his revenge. Oh!" he continued, after a moment's pause,
during which his usually impassible countenance betrayed all
that was passing in his mind—"God knows, I do not lack
the inclination to avenge myself, but if I take too violent
measures, my kingdom will perhaps be the price of this imprudent justice. As to Don Frederick, the King of France
has nothing to do with either his living or dying—that concerns only me. But will he come to Seville, or if he comes,
will he not have had time to warn his accomplice?"

As Don Pedro said these words, he observed in the direction of the Sierra d'Aracena something like a cloud of dust.
This increased in size till it gradually became more transparent, and he discerned first the white-robed Moorish horsemen, and then the tall form of Mothril riding beside his
gilded litter."

"Alone!" murmured Don Pedro, when he had carefully
scanned the whole group. "Where, then, is the Grand
Master? Can he have refused to come to Seville, and shall I
be obliged to seek him at Coimbra?"

The troop continued to advance, and in a few moments
disappeared beneath the gateway leading into the city. The
King followed it with his eyes as it wound through the tortuous streets of the city until it reached the Alcazar, where
it evidently intended to halt.

As the Moor possessed the right of free entry to the King, he presented himself in a few moments on the terrace, where he found his royal master standing with his eyes fixed on the route by which he had just arrived. His countenance was gloomy, and he made no attempt to conceal his disquietude. Mothril crossed his hands on his breast and bowed almost to the earth, but Don Pedro only replied to his salutation by an impatient gesture.

"The Grand Master?" demanded he.

"Sire," said Mothril, "I have hastened back, for the important intelligence I have to communicate makes me hope you will deign to listen to the voice of your faithful servant."

Don Pedro, accustomed as he was to read the hearts of those about him, was at this moment too much occupied by the passions agitating his own, to observe all the crafty precaution implied both in the words of Mothril and his feigned embarrassment.

"The Grand Master?" he repeated, stamping his foot.

"My lord," said the Moor, "he will cóme."

"Why have you quitted him? Why, if he be innocent, has he not willingly obeyed my summons? and why, if he be guilty, have you not brought him by force?"

"My lord, the Grand Master is not innocent, and yet rest assured he will wait upon you. He might, it is true, have attempted to fly, had he not been so closely watched by my people, who lead rather than escort him. My reason for preceding him was to speak with your Majesty on what still remains to be done, not of things that are already accomplished."

"Then you are certain he will come?"

"Sire, by to-morrow night he will be at the gates of Seville. You see I have been diligent."

"And no one knows of this journey?"

"No, sire."

"You understand the importance of my question, and the gravity of your reply?"

"Perfectly, sire."

"Well, what are these important news?" said Don Pedro, whose countenance having had time to regain its usual indifferent expression, did not betray the horrible oppression at his heart.

"The King knows how jealous I am of his honour."

"Yes, Mothril," interrupted Don Pedro, frowning; "and

E

you also know that these insinuations, though pardonable
from Maria Padilla—that is to say, from a jealous woman to
a perhaps too patient lover—are not so from a minister to
his sovereign.   All comments on the irreproachable conduct
of Queen Blanche are forbidden, and this, if you have forgotten, I again repeat to you."

"Don Pedro," said the Moor, "I can understand that a
monarch powerful, happy, loving, and beloved, as yourself, has
no room in his breast for either envy or jealousy; but yet,
great as your felicity may be, it must not render you blind."

"This time you have learned something," said the King,
fixing his keen glance on the Moor.

"My lord," he replied coldly, "your Majesty has more than
once thought on the dangers by which you are surrounded,
and reflected in your wisdom what would become of the kingdom of Castile in case of anything happening to you, since
you have no heirs."

"No heirs!"

"At least legitimate ones," continued the Moor. "So that
the kingdom would fall into the hands of either Henry, Don
Frederick, or Telo, whichever of the three was the boldest or
most successful."

"What is the meaning of all this, Mothril?" said Don
Pedro.   "Would you counsel me to contract a third marriage? But I warn you; the two first have not been so
happy as to tempt me to follow your advice."

These words, extorted from the King by some violent feeling of chagrin, made the Moor's eyes sparkle, for it revealed
the secret torments he had so long endured.   Mothril had
now learnt nearly all he wished—one word more would disclose the whole.

"Sire," said he, "why should not this third wife be a
woman with whose character you are already well acquainted.
For instance, marry Donna Maria Padilla, since you love,
and cannot separate from her, and she is of sufficiently high
birth to be raised to the throne.   By this means your sons
would be the rightful heirs to the crown, and none could
dispute it with them."

Mothril had not hazarded this last attack without due
consideration, but with a rapture known only to those whose
stake is a kingdom, he saw a dark cloud of vexation gather
on his sovereign's brow.

"I have already uselessly severed the tie between myself and the King of France," said he; "I cannot now break that binding me to the house of De Castro."

"Good!" murmured Mothril. "The less real love remaining in his heart, the less reason to fear her influence."

"Come," said Don Pedro, "continue your recital. You say you have something important to communicate."

"I have only to tell you a piece of news, which will entirely dissolve your relations with the King of France."

"And this news?—quick!"

"Sire," said Mothril, "first permit me to leave you for a moment, to give some directions to the guardians of the litter you see below. I am uneasy at having thus left alone a person who is very dear to me."

Don Pedro looked at him in astonishment.

"Go," said he; "but return speedily."

The Moor descended to the court, into which he caused his litter to be conveyed; whilst Don Pedro, leaning over his balcony, carelessly watched his minister's movements. In a few seconds Mothril re-appeared.

"Sire," said he, "will your Majesty deign to allot me my usual apartments in the Alcazar?"

"Yes, certainly."

"Then permit me to have the occupant of the litter conveyed within the palace."

"A woman?" inquired Don Pedro.

"Yes, sire."

"A favourite slave?"

"My daughter, sire."

"I did not know you had a daughter, Mothril."

The Moor made no reply; he had inspired the King with both doubt and curiosity, and he asked no more.

"Now," said Don Pedro, recollecting the importance of what he wished to hear, "tell me what you know about Queen Blanche."

CHAPTER VI.

THE MOOR'S MISSION.

MOTHRIL approached the King, and assuming an expression of the most profound compassion, the sentiment of all others which—coming from an inferior—was the most likely to wound Don Pedro, "Sire," said he, "before commencing my

E 2

recital, I beseech you to recal, word for word, the instructions you gave me."

"Proceed," said the King; "I never forget what I have once said."

"Your Majesty ordered me to repair to Coimbra, and inform the Grand Master that you awaited him at Seville. I did so. You charged me to hasten his departure, and after one hour's rest, I set out on my return."

"Good," said Don Pedro; "I know you are a faithful servant, Mothril."

"Your Majesty added: 'You will watch during this journey that the Grand Master warns no one of his movements.' Well, the day following our departure, Don Frederick—but, in truth, notwithstanding your Majesty's commands, I scarcely know whether I ought to tell you what took place."

"Speak! 'The day following your departure?'"

"The Grand Master wrote a letter."

"To whom?"

"To the very person your Majesty apprehended he would."

"To Queen Blanche!" exclaimed Don Pedro, turning pale.

"To Queen Blanche, sire."

"Moor," said Don Pedro, "have you reflected on the gravity of such an accusation?"

"I have only thought of serving my King."

"You may yet discover you were mistaken."

"Sire, I was not mistaken," said Mothril, shaking his head.

"Take care! I must have this letter," said Don Pedro, menacingly.

"It is here," replied the Moor, coldly.

Don Pedro, who had advanced a step towards him, suddenly recoiled.

"Ah, you have it!" he exclaimed.

"Yes, sire."

"This letter, written by Don Frederick to Blanche of Bourbon!"

"Yes, sire; and I will give it your Majesty when you are less enraged than at the present moment."

"I enraged!" said Don Pedro, with a forced smile. "I was never calmer."

"No, sire, you are not calm; your eye blazes with indignation—your lips are white—your hand trembles, and seeks the hilt of your dagger. Why need you conceal it? It is very natural, and in such a case vengeance is allowable. That is why, guessing your Majesty's wrath would be terrible, I endeavoured to soften it beforehand."

"Give me the letter, Mothril!" exclaimed the King.

"But, sire?"

"Give it me, I say, without any more delay. I *will* have it."

The Moor slowly drew from beneath his robe the pouch of the unfortunate Fernand.

"My first duty," said he, "is obedience to my sovereign, whatever may be the result of it."

The King carefully examined the pouch, from which he drew the pearl-embroidered bag, and eagerly seized on the letter it contained. His brow again contracted, for the seal had evidently been broken, but without making any remark, he read as follows:

"My Queen, the King summons me to Seville. I promised to inform you of any great event in my life, and this appears to me to be something decisive. But whatever may be the reason of it, I should care little for the vengeance of Donna Padilla—for it is doubtless at her instigation—if I were only sure that you, illustrious lady and beloved sister, were safe from her attacks. I am ignorant of what awaits me—it may be imprisonment, it may be death. If imprisonment, I shall no longer be able to defend you; and if I am to die, I profit by these brief moments of remaining freedom, to tell you that my arm and heart are alike yours until chains bind one and death stills the other. Fernand will convey you this intelligence—perhaps, this adieu. Farewell, my sweet friend and Queen, we shall meet again, if not in this world, at least in heaven.   DON FREDERICK."

"Where is this Fernand?—where is he?" cried Don Pedro, whose livid pallor was frightful to behold.

"Sire," answered Mothril, in a perfectly natural tone, "this Fernand was the Grand Master's page. He set out with us, and on the evening of the following day was charged with this message; the same night he chanced to be drowned in crossing the Zezera, and I found this packet on the body."

Don Pedro needed no further explanations to enable him to understand what had happened.

"Ah!" said he. "Then *you* found the corpse?"

"Yes, sire."

" Before any one else !"

" Yes, sire."

" Then no one is aware of the contents of this letter ?"

" Sire," said Mothril, " pardon my audacity—my anxiety for my King's interests perhaps carried me beyond the bounds of discretion—but I opened the pouch, and read the letter."

" But you alone? for in that case it is the same as though it had been unread."

" Without doubt, sire, since it has been in my possession."

" But before that ?"

" Ah, sire, I can answer for nothing that may have taken place beforehand ; the more so as the page was not alone with his master; there was an accursed Giaour—a dog—a Christian ! Pardon, sire !"

" And who was this Christian ?"

" A French knight, whom he called ' his brother.' "

" I should have thought," said Don Pedro, smiling, " that he would have conferred some other title on his friends."

" Well, he had no secrets from this Christian, therefore it would not be astonishing if he shared his confidence with the page. In that case, the crime would be made public."

" Don Frederick is approaching?" said Don Pedro.

" He is following me, sire."

Don Pedro paced to and fro for some moments, with his arms folded, his head drooping on his breast, and a heavy frown on his brow; it was easy to perceive that a terrible storm was raging within him.

" I must begin with him," he at last said, gloomily.

" Besides, it is my only means of excusing myself in the eyes of France. When King Charles sees that I have not spared my own brother, he will no longer doubt his criminality, and will pardon my treatment of his sister-in-law."

" But are you not apprehensive, sire, of the world mistaking your motives, and believing that in the person of the Grand Master you strike not the lover of Queen Blanche, but the brother of Henry de Transtamare—your competitor for the throne ?"

" I will make the letter public," said the King. " His blood shall wash out the stain. Go; you have served me faithfully."

" But, now, what are your Majesty's orders ?"

" Let them prepare the Grand Master's apartments."

Mothril left the terrace. Don Pedro was alone, and his

thoughts assumed, if possible, a yet more gloomy cast. The proud and jealous nature of the man began to re-awaken in the impassible *king*. He beheld mockery attached to his name, and fancied he could already hear the tale of the amours of Queen Blanche and Don Frederick echoed from mouth to mouth, with all the exaggerations attached to the faults of kings. Then, as he fixed his eyes on the windows of Donna Padilla's apartments, he fancied he could discern her standing behind its hanging draperies, with a smile of triumphant malice on her lips.

"She will believe, and so will others, that she has instigated me to what I am about to do ; and yet it is not so," said he, impatiently turning away his head, and gazing vacantly around him.

At this moment two Moorish slaves passed along the lower terrace of the Alcazar, each bearing a sort of censer, whence arose a bluish vapour, the ravishing perfume of which was borne to the King by the mountain breeze. Behind them came a female figure, whose tall and graceful form was concealed beneath a large Arab veil, which only allowed her eyes to be visible. Mothril respectfully attended her, and when they reached the entrance of the apartment she was to occupy, almost prostrated himself before her. The intoxicating perfume—the dark eyes gleaming through the thick veil—the Moor's respectful demeanour—all formed so strong a contrast to the passions agitating his breast, that Don Pedro felt himself insensibly refreshed and restored to equanimity— as though this apparition had at once recalled him to youth and pleasure. He waited impatiently for nightfall, and then, under cover of the darkness, descended from the apartment and stole towards the kiosk occupied by Mothril. By cautiously raising the heavy wreaths of ivy, and the branches of an immense rose-laurel, which shielded the interior of the apartment from indiscreet eyes better than any tapestry, he was enabled to discern the fair Aïssa, seated on a pile of silken cushions worked with silver. She was attired in a dress of transparent gauze ; her naked feet decorated according to the Eastern fashion with costly rings and anklets. Her brow was calm and thoughtful, her eyes cast down in a dreamy reverie, and her lips parted in a smile that displayed her fine teeth, as white and regular as two rows of pearls. Mothril had reckoned on the King's curiosity being excited. He watched and listened, and at last distinguished the rustling of the branches and the King's quick breathing. He however appeared to be quite unconscious of the royal presence; only when the young girl allowed her coral pounce-box to escape from her careless fingers, he hastened to pick it up, and presented it to her almost on his knees. Aïssa smiled.

"Why, during the last few days, have you shown me all this deference?" said she; "a father owes only tenderness to his child—it is the child who should show deference to the father."

"Whatever Mothril does, it is his duty to do," replied the Moor.

"But, my father, why show me more homage than you exact for yourself?"

"Because more is due to you," said he. "The day will come when all will be revealed to you, and then, Donna Aïssa, you may perhaps no longer deign to call me your father."

These mysterious words made an indefinable impression on not only the King, but Aïssa herself; but notwithstanding her entreaties, Mothril refused to explain them, and soon after retired. Aïssa's attendants now entered, bearing in their hands large fans of ostrich feathers, with which they proceeded to fan their fair mistress, while the softest music vibrated on the air, without either the musician or the instrument being visible. Aïssa closed her large eyes, heavy with happy thoughts.

"Of what is she thinking?" murmured the King, observing a light shadow pass across her face.

She was dreaming of the handsome French knight. The attendants approached to close the *jalousies*.

"Strange!" said the King, thus obliged to quit this dangerous contemplation. "One would almost fancy she pronounced some name." Nor was he mistaken; she had murmured the name of Agenor.

But although the *jalousies* were closed, Don Pedro was not in a fit state of mind to return to his apartments, for at this moment his heart was a prey to such conflicting emotions as to banish all hopes of either slumber or repose. Only wishing for the freshness of the night air and its silent calm, he continued to wander about the gardens, always returning, as by some irresistible attraction, to the kiosk, where slumbered the Moorish maiden. Occasionally, he passed by the windows of Maria Padilla's apartments, and gazed up at the gloomy casements—then, fancying the haughty Spaniard had retired to her couch, he continued his way, which, by a detour more or less long, invariably conducted him towards the kiosk. Don Pedro was mistaken; Maria Padilla was not sleeping, but enveloped in a sombre-coloured mantle, was seated in the darkness beside her window, from whence, with a heart throbbing with scarcely less violent emotions than those agitating the King, she watched his every movement, and we might almost say, read his every thought. But there were other eyes no less busily employed in reading the King's heart. The Moor still remained anxiously observing the success of his intrigue. When the King approached the kiosk, he trembled with joy; but when he raised his eyes towards the casement of the favourite, as though hesitating whether to join her, he muttered under his breath menaces which his hand, instinctively grasping his poniard, seemed ready to execute. It was under the influence of these two regards, alike piercing and venomous, that Don Pedro passed the night; till overcome by fatigue, he an hour before daybreak flung himself on a bench, and slept that agitated and fevered slumber which is only additional suffering.

"You are not yet as I wish you to be," said Mothril, on seeing the King thus succumb beneath his fatigue. "I must rid you of this Donna Padilla, whom you pretend you no longer love, and yet cannot tear yourself away from." And he let fall the corner of the curtain he had raised whilst he gazed into the garden.

"Now," said Maria Padilla to herself, "for one last trial of strength; but it must be prompt and decisive, and before this woman—for it was doubtless a woman at whom he was gazing through the *jalousies*—has acquired any influence over him." And she gave orders to her people, which by daybreak caused a great stir in the palace.

When Don Pedro awoke and returned to his apartments, he heard the tramping of horses and mules in the court, and the hurried footsteps of women and pages in the corridors. He was about to inquire the cause of this unusual bustle, when his door opened, and Maria Padilla appeared on the threshold.

"For whom are these horses waiting, senora," said the King. "And what are all these busy servants about?"

"They are preparing for my departure, sire, which I have hastened as much as possible, in order to relieve your Majesty of the presence of a woman who can no longer contribute to your happiness. Besides, my enemy arrives to-day, and as you doubtless intend, in your overflow of fraternal tenderness, to sacrifice me to him, I spare you the trouble by yielding him my place."

Maria Padilla was considered the handsomest woman in Spain. So great was her influence over Don Pedro, that contemporary writers, convinced that her beauty alone could never have enabled her to attain to such power, preferred attributing to magic what was in fact only the effect of the natural charms of the supposed sorceress. Thus, as she now stood in all the lustre of her five-and-twenty summers, with her long black hair falling negligently over her simple woollen robe, which, according to the fashion of the fourteenth century, fitted closely to her rounded arms and fine form, she again realized for Don Pedro, perhaps not all he had dreamed of, but all he had ever known of real affection and gentle emotions. She was his household fairy, the flower of his life, the casket in which was enshrined all his happy memories. He gazed sadly upon her.

"I am only astonished that you have not quitted me before this, Maria," said he; "but you have now chosen a fitting moment, when my brother Henry revolts against me, Don Frederick betrays me, and the King of France threatens me with war. It is true, that women soon cease to love the unhappy!"

"Are you unhappy?" exclaimed Maria Padilla, advancing with outstretched hands. "That is enough for me; I will remain. At another time I should have asked, 'Pedro, will my remaining add to your happiness?'"

The King on his side leaned forward, and catching one of her fair hands in his own, pressed it to his lips. "You are wrong, Maria," said he; "I love you; but to obtain a corresponding affection to your own, you should not have bestowed it on a king."

"Then you do not wish me to go?" said Maria, with one of those adorable smiles which rendered Don Pedro oblivious of all the world beside

"No," he replied; "if once for all you consent to share with me my future fate, as you have already done my past."

Maria approached the open window near which she was standing, and by a gesture as queenly as though she had been born to grace a throne, signed to the crowd of waiting attendants to re-enter the palace. At the same moment, Mothril made his appearance; for this prolonged conference between the King and Donna Padilla had begun to render him uneasy.

"What is it?" inquired Don Pedro, impatiently.

"Your brother, Don Frederick, is drawing near the city, sire," replied the Moor. "I can discern his escort on the route from Portugal."

At these tidings, the King's eyes gleamed with an expression of such intense hatred that Maria Padilla plainly saw she had nothing to fear in this direction; and having presented her cheek to Don Pedro, who touched it with his pale lips, she smilingly returned to her apartments.

CHAPTER VII.

THE ALCAZAR.

IN fact, as Mothril said, the Grand Master was rapidly drawing near Seville, which he reached about noon—that is to say, during the hottest part of the day. The Moorish and Christian horsemen forming his escort were covered with dust, and their beasts were bathed in sweat. Don Frederick glanced at the walls of the city, expecting to behold them crowded with soldiers and people, as is usual on *fête* days, but no one was to be seen except the ordinary sentinels.

"Should not the King be apprised of your highness's approach?" asked one of his officers, preparing, if the answer were in the affirmative, to start for that purpose.

"Do not trouble yourself," said Don Frederick, with a melancholy smile. "The Moor started in advance of us, and my brother is already apprised of it. Besides," he added in a bitter tone, "do you not know that my arrival is to be celebrated by *fêtes* and *tourneys?*"

The Spaniards gazed in astonishment around them, for nothing indicated these promised festivities—everything, on the contrary, wore a dull and gloomy aspect. They questioned the Moors, but they made them no reply. They entered the city; the streets were deserted, the doors and windows of the houses closed, as is customary in Spain during the heat of the day ; the only sound to be heard was that of one or two doors opening to allow egress to some few awakened sleepers, curious to know, before resuming their slumbers, to whom this troop of horsemen, entering the city at an hour when the Moors themselves, those children of the sun, sought the shade of the woods or freshness of the river, could possibly belong. The Christians rode first, the Moors, double their number, formed the rear-guard. Don Frederick silently observed this manœuvre ; the aspect of the town which, instead of finding, as he expected, full of life and gaiety, was as silent and gloomy as a tomb, had already awakened terrible suspicions in his breast. An officer approached him, and said in a low voice, " Have you remarked, my lord, that they have closed the gate by which we entered ? "

The Grand Master made no reply. They continued to advance, and soon discovered the Alcazar, where Mothril, attended by several of Don Pedro's officers, waited to receive them. The anxiously expected little troop entered the court, the gates of which, like those of the city, were immediately closed behind them. Mothril followed the prince with every mark of the most profound respect ; but as he alighted from his horse he approached him, saying, " You are aware, my lord, that it is not customary to enter the palace armed with any weapon ; shall I, therefore, cause your sword to be conveyed to your apartment?"

Don Frederick's long-repressed wrath only needed this occasion to burst forth. " Slave ! " he exclaimed, " has servitude so brutalized you that you can neither recognise your princes nor respect your masters? Since when has the Grand Master of St. James of Calatrava, who has the right of entering every church in Christendom helmed and spurred, and thus addressing God, been forbidden to enter the palace of his brother, and speak to him with his sheathed sword by his side ?"

Mothril listened respectfully, and humbly bowed his head. " Your highness has spoken truly," said he ; "and your slave forgot, not that you were a prince, but that you were the Grand Master of St. James of Calatrava. All these privileges are Christian customs, and it is therefore not astonishing when a poor infidel like myself is either ignorant of, or forgets them." At this moment another officer approached Don Frederick.

" My lord," said he, "is it true that you wish us to quit you ?"

" Who has said so ?" asked Don Frederick.

"One of the guards at the gate, my lord."

"And what was your reply?"

"That we only received orders from our lord, Don Frederick."

The prince hesitated for a moment; he was young, vigorous, and brave, and surrounded by a sufficient body of men to make a long defence.

"My lord," continued the soldier, seeing that his master was considering, "only say the word, and we will free you from the snare into which you have fallen. We are thirty good men, armed with lance, poniard, and sword."

Don Frederick glanced at Mothril, and surprising a smile upon his lips, followed the direction of his gaze. The terraces surrounding the court were crowded with archers and cross-bowmen, with their weapons unslung, and prepared for action.

"I should only cause the slaughter of these brave men," said Don Frederick to himself. "No, since I am all they want, I will enter alone." He turned calmly to his companions. "Retire, my friends," said he; "I am in the palace of my brother and my King—treachery does not dwell in such habitations. But if I should be mistaken, remember that I have been warned that treason was at work, and would not believe it." The soldiers bowed, and one by one departed. Don Frederick remained alone with the Moors and Don Pedro's guards. "Now," said he, turning to Mothril, "I wish to see my brother."

"Your highness's desire shall be at once gratified," replied the Moor; "for the King impatiently awaits you." He drew back to allow the prince to ascend the steps of the Alcazar.

"Where is my brother?" asked the Grand Master.

"In the terrace apartment, my lord."

This was next the one usually occupied by Don Frederick himself during his visits to the King; he therefore paused at the door, saying, "Cannot I enter my own chamber, and rest for a few moments before presenting myself to the King?"

"My lord," said Mothril, "when you have once seen his Majesty, you will be able to rest as long as you please."

There was a sudden movement among the Moorish attendants; Don Frederick turned round. "The dog!" they exclaimed; and in fact the faithful animal, instead of accompanying the horse to the stables, had followed his master, as though guessing the dangers menacing him.

"The dog is mine," said the prince.

The Moors drew back, less from respect than fear, and the dog joyfully leaped up and laid his paws upon his master's breast.

"Yes," said he, 'I understand you, and you are right; Fernand is dead, Agenor is far away, and you are my sole remaining friend."

"My lord," said Mothril, with an ironical smile, "is it also one of the privileges of the Grand Master of St. James to enter the King's presence followed by his dog?"

A dark cloud gathered on Don Frederick's brow. His hand involuntarily sought his poniard. The Moor was close beside him—one prompt and decisive movement and he was revenged on this insolent and mocking slave.

"No," said he to himself; "the King's majesty overshadows all those who surround him, therefore I will do nothing to outrage it." He coolly opened the door of his apartment and signed to his dog to enter it, which he did. "Wait for me here, Allan," said he. The animal stretched himself on a lion's skin, and his master closed the door. At the same moment a voice was heard exclaiming, "My brother! where is my brother?"

Don Frederick recognised the King's voice and advanced towards the spot from whence it proceeded. Don Pedro, looking pale after his sleepless night, and sullen and morose with secret rage, had just left his bath. He cast a severe glance at Don Frederick, who prostrated himself before him.

"I am here, my King and brother," said he. "You summoned me, and behold me at your feet; I have come with all speed to see and wish you prosperity."

"But how is it, Grand Master, that your words agree so little with your actions?" said the King. "You say you come to wish me prosperity, and yet all the while you are conspiring with my enemies against me."

"My lord, I do not understand you," said Don Frederick, rising; for after this accusation he would not remain kneeling another moment. "Is it really to *me* you address such words?"

"Yes, to you, Don Frederick, the Grand Master of St. James."

"Then, sire, you call me a traitor!"

"Yes, for a traitor you are!" replied Don Pedro.

The young prince turned pale, but still restrained himself.

"But why so, my King?" he asked in a tone of infinite sweetness. I have never offended you, at least knowingly;

on the contrary, in many encounters, particularly with the Moors, now your friends, I wielded a sword full heavy for my youthful arm."

"Yes; the Moors are my friends," exclaimed Don Pedro; "and it is well I have found them such, since in my own family I have nothing but enemies."

The more unjust and outrageous the King's reproaches became, the more proudly and intrepidly Don Frederick bore himself.

"If you allude to my brother Henry," said he, "I have nothing to say, for the matter does not concern me. He has done wrong in rebelling against you, for you are our rightful lord both by age and birth; but he wishes to be King of Castile, and they say ambition renders us oblivious of everything. For myself, I am not ambitious, and pretend to nothing. I am Grand Master of St. James; but if you know a worthier one, I am ready to resign my post into your hands."

Don Pedro made no reply.

"I have taken Coimbra from the Moors, and settled there as in my own dominions. No one has any claim to my city; but will you have Coimbra, brother? It is a fine sea-port."

Don Pedro still remained silent.

"I have a small army," continued Don Frederick, "but I only retain it at your good pleasure. Will you have my little troop, brother, to assist you against your enemies?"

Don Pedro made no reply.

"I have no wealth, except the fortune of my mother, Donna Eleonora de Guzman, and what I have won from the Moors. Will you have my money, brother?"

"I want neither your post, your city, your soldiers, nor your treasures, but only your head!" exclaimed Don Pedro, no longer able to restrain his fury at the self-possession of the young prince.

"My life, my King, is yours, like everything else; only why require the head, when the heart is innocent?"

"Innocent!" repeated Don Pedro; "do you know a Frenchwoman named Blanche of Bourbon?"

"I know a French princess of that name, whom I regard equally as a Queen and a sister."

"Well, then, that is what I mean to say," said Don Pedro; "you regard as a Queen and a sister the enemy of your brother and your King."

"Sire," said the Grand Master, "if you regard those you have injured, and who cherish the remembrance of their wrongs, as your enemies, the lady of whom you speak may perhaps be one of them; but on my soul, you might as well consider the flying gazelle wounded by your arrow as your foe."

"I regard as my enemy any one who causes my cities to rise in revolt against me, as she has caused Toledo,—any one who arms my brothers against me, as she has armed, not my ambitious brother Henry, as you just now termed him, but my hypocritical one, Don Frederick."

"Brother, I swear to you."

"Do not swear; you will only perjure yourself."

"Brother !"

"Do you recognise that?" said the King, drawing the Grand Master's letter from the pouch.

On beholding this proof of his love in the hands of the King—a sure token of Fernand having been assassinated—Don Frederick felt his firmness give way. Overcome by this crushing weight of misfortune, and the terrible consequences he at once foresaw, he sank on his knee at his brother's feet, and bowed his head on his breast. A murmur of astonishment broke from the group of courtiers assembled together at the lower end of the gallery. The sight of Don Frederick thus kneeling before his brother in evident supplication, only impressed them with an idea of his guilt; they did not imagine that his prayers were for another.

"Sire," said Don Frederick, "I take God to witness that I am innocent of the crime with which you reproach me."

"It is to God, then, you can declare so; for my part, I do not believe you."

"How can my death wash away a stain, when I am guiltless?"

"Guiltless!" exclaimed the King. "What, then, do you term this?" And carried away by his rage, he struck his brother on the face with the letter he had written to Blanche of Bourbon.

"Nay, sire," said Don Frederick, recoiling, "kill me if you will, but do not insult me. I have long known that by dwelling among courtiers and slaves, men become cowards; and you, King, are a coward, for you have outraged a prisoner."

"Ho, guards!" cried Don Pedro, "lead him to immediate execution !"

"One moment," interrupted Don Frederick, extending his hand majestically towards his brother; "furious as you are, you must pause, and listen to what I have to say. You have wronged, and suspected an innocent woman, and by so doing have outraged the King of France; but you dare not at your pleasure thus outrage God. I demand an hour before I am murdered to offer up my prayers to my Supreme Master, for I am not a Moor."

Don Pedro was almost mad with rage; but there were bystanders, and he restrained himself.

"Be it so," said he; "you shall have an hour—go!" All the witnesses of this terrible scene were chilled with affright.

"Be ready in an hour," exclaimed the King, with flashing eyes.

"Fear not," replied the young prince; "I shall die only too soon for you, for I am innocent."

For the space of an hour, the Grand Master remained alone in his chamber, commending his soul to his Maker; at the end of that time, finding his executioners did not make their appearance, he went into the gallery, exclaiming, "You keep me waiting, Don Pedro, the hour is past!"

The executioners appeared.

"By what death am I to die?" inquired Don Frederick. One of them drew his sword; the prince examined it and passed his finger along its edge. "Take mine," said he, drawing it from his sheath, "it is sharper."

The soldier took the weapon. "When you are ready, Grand Master," said he.

Don Frederick signed to them to wait a moment; then approaching the table, he wrote a few lines on a strip of parchment, which he rolled up and placed between his teeth.

"What is that for?" inquired the soldier.

"It is a talisman which renders me invulnerable. Now strike—I defy you!"

"Do you think there is any virtue in it?" said one soldier to the other.

"We shall soon see," was the reply.

The young prince bared his neck, and twisted up his long hair; then kneeling down with clasped hands and smiling lips, he said, "Strike."

The sword gleamed in the executioner's uplifted hands, it descended like a flash of lightning, and the Grand Master's

F

head, severed at one stroke from the body, rolled on the
ground. At the same moment a frightful howl resounded
through the palace. The King, who was listening at the door
of his apartment, retreated in dismay; the soldiers rushed
from the chamber, and nothing remained but a pool of blood,
a head severed from the body, and a dog, which, bursting
through a door, came and crouched beside the mangled
remains of his master.

CHAPTER VIII.

THE BILLET.

THE first grey shadows of evening fell mournfully around the
desolate palace. Don Pedro was seated, gloomy and uneasy,
in one of the lower apartments, in which he had taken refuge,
not daring to remain in his own, which was contiguous to
the one where lay the corpse of his murdered brother. Near
him sat Maria Padilla, weeping bitterly.

"Why these tears, senora?" said the King, with sudden
sharpness. "Have you not now obtained what you so long
and earnestly desired? You demanded the life of your enemy.
Well, you ought to be satisfied, for he no longer exists."

"Sire," said Maria, "I have, perhaps, in a momentary fit
of foolish pride—a burst of senseless anger—desired his death.
God pardon me for ever having allowed such a wish to enter
my heart; but I think I may reply, that I never demanded it."

"Ah, thus it is with women!" said the King. "Ardent
in their desires, but timid in their resolutions, they are
always wishing, and when those wishes are gratified, deny that
they ever formed them."

"Sire," said Maria, "in Heaven's name, never tell me that
you sacrificed the Grand Master to please me; for such a
belief would be my torment in this life, and an eternal remorse in the life to come. No, say what is really the truth,
that you sacrificed him to your honour. Nay, I will not
allow you to quit me without the assurance that it was not
I who instigated you to this murder."

"I will say anything you please, Maria," said the King,
coldly, as he rose and advanced to meet Mothril, who had
just entered the room with all the rights of a minister and
the privileges of a favourite.

Maria at first turned away her head to avoid the sight of

this man, for whom Don Frederick's death, although serving her interests, had redoubled her hatred. She retreated into the embrasure of a window, and from thence, whilst the king was conversing with the Moor, she amused herself by watching the movements of a knight clad in complete armour, who, profiting by the confusion which the sudden execution of the young prince had caused to reign throughout the palace, had entered the court without either guards or sentinels troubling themselves to inquire whither he was going. This knight was Agenor, on his way to keep his appointment with his friend, and pursuing his search for the purple curtains indicated by Don Frederick as belonging to his apartment. Mariá Padilla, without knowing who he was, mechanically followed him with her eyes until he was out of sight, and then turned her gaze upon the King and his minister. Don Pedro was speaking rapidly, and by his gestures was evidently giving some terrible orders. A sudden light broke on Donna Padilla's mind, and with the rapid intuition of her sex she at once guessed their object. She approached Don Pedro at the moment he signed to Mothril to retire.

"Sire," said she, "you will not give two similar orders in one day."

"You have overheard it, then?" said the King, turning pale

"No, but I guessed it. Oh, sire, sire!" she continued, falling on her knees before him, "I have often complained of—often excited you against her, but do not kill her, or you will say as you did about Don Frederick, that it was because I demanded it."

"Rise, Maria," said the King, gloomily, "and cease these useless supplications. Everything was arranged beforehand. I must complete my task now it is once begun. The death of one involves the death of the other. If Don Frederick were the only victim, the world would say that I sacrificed him to my private vengeance, and not that he suffered to expiate his crime."

Donna Maria regarded him with horror, like a traveller who starts back terrified from the brink of an abyss.

"Oh, all this will recoil upon me!" she exclaimed. "They will say that this double murder has been committed at my instigation; and yet, my God, you see I vainly pray, I supplicate, I entreat him to spare me being haunted by this woman's spectre!"

"No; for I will publicly proclaim my shame and their crime," said the King. "I will publish Don Frederick's letter to his sister-in-law."

"But," cried Donna Maria, "you will not find a Spaniard who will consent to lay violent hands on his Queen!"

"Therefore I have chosen a Moor," replied the King. "Of what use would Moors be if they did not do what Spaniards refuse?"

"Oh, I wished to leave this morning," cried Maria. "Why did I remain? But the evening is not too far advanced; there is yet time! Suffer me, therefore, to quit this palace; my house is always open to you, and you can visit me there."

"Do as you please, senora," replied the King, to whom by a strange revival of recollection, at that moment appeared the image of the Moorish maiden of the kiosk, lying buried in soft slumber, guarded by her women with their large fans— "Do as you please, for I am weary of continually hearing you threaten to take your departure without ever really doing so."

"O God!" cried Donna Maria, "you are witness that I leave him, because, after being accused of being the cause of Don Frederick's murder, I vainly entreat that the life of Queen Blanche may be spared!" and before Don Pedro could prevent her, she opened the door and was about to hasten from the apartment, when suddenly a loud noise resounded through the palace; persons were seen running to and fro a prey to the wildest terror, and cries were heard of which none seemed to know the cause. It seemed as if a sudden frenzy had spread through the palace.

"Listen!" said Maria, "listen!"

"What is the meaning of this tumult," asked Don Pedro, also approaching the door. "Speak, Mothril," he continued, addressing the Moor, who stood motionless on the other side of the vestibule, with his eyes fixed on some object invisible to Don Pedro. One hand grasped his poniard, and with the other he wiped away the sweat that hung in heavy drops upon his brow.

"Horrible! horrible!" repeated a number of voices.

Don Pedro impatiently stepped forward, and was in his turn greeted by a frightful spectacle. At the top of the wide marble staircase appeared Don Frederick's dog, bloody and terrible, with his hair bristling like a lion's mane. He held in his mouth his master's head, and drew it gently along the pavement by its flowing hair. Before him fled the palace guards and attendants, uttering the cries which had reached Don Pedro's ears. Brave, rash, insensible as he was, the King endeavoured to escape from this horrible scene, but like the Moor his feet seemed rooted to the ground. Meanwhile the dog descended the stairs, leaving behind him a broad red stain. When he drew near the King and Mothril, as if recognising in them the two murderers of his beloved master, he laid the head gently on the ground, and gave so piteous a howl that Maria fainted, and the King trembled as though the angel of death had touched him with his wing; then he took up his precious burden, and disappeared in the court.

The tumult had also been heard by the armed knight whom Maria Padilla had remarked entering the Alcazar, and like a good Christian, he crossed himself, and uttered a prayer to be preserved from evil. The sight of this crowd of flying domestics running against and falling over one another, struck him with a sudden stupor almost resembling terror. He leant against a plane-tree, and watched, with his hand on his poniard, this rapid procession of pale shadowy figures. At last the dog appeared, and on perceiving him, guided by that subtle instinct which made him recognise in the knight his master's friend, came straight to him. Agenor was speechless with horror. This fierce dog, bearing this gory head, like a wolf carrying away its prey—this crowd of affrighted domestics, flying with pale looks and cries of terror, seemed to him like one of those frightful dreams haunting the couch of the fevered patient. The dog continued to approach him, giving signs of joyful recognition, and at last laid the dust-stained head at his feet, whilst he again made the place re-echo with his piteous howls.

Agenor remained for a moment silent and motionless with horror; then, partly guessing what had occurred, he stooped down, and parting the beautiful hair, recognised—dimmed by the shadows of death—the soft blue eyes of his friend. The expression of the mouth was as calm and composed as when living, and it almost seemed as though his habitual smile lingered on the violet lips. Agenor fell on his knees, and large tears rolled silently down his bronzed cheeks. He raised the head reverently from the ground, intending to convey it where the last sad rites might be paid it, and then, alone, he remarked a small roll of parchment held tightly between the teeth of the unfortunate prince. He separated them with the point of his dagger, and eagerly unfolding the little roll, read as follows:—" My friend, our gloomy presentiments have not deceived us. I am doomed to death by my brother. Warn Queen Blanche, for she also is menaced with danger. You possess my secret—guard my remembrance."

"Yes, my prince," said the chevalier, mournfully; " I will religiously execute your last wishes. But how shall I escape from this place? I no longer know where I entered it. My brain reels, my memory fails me, and my poniard falls from my trembling hand when I attempt to restore it to its sheath." In fact, the chevalier rose from his knees, pale, bewildered, almost mad, walking blindly along, striking himself against the marble columns, and stretching out his hands like a drunken man fearing to injure himself. At last he found himself in a magnificent garden, planted with orange-trees, pomegranates, and rose-laurels, and small cascades of water, falling like jets of silver into their porphyry basins. He hastened to one of these basins, drank greedily, and bathed his burning brow in the icy water. A feeble light glimmering among the trees attracted his attention, and served him as a guide. He proceeded towards it; a white figure leaning over a trellised balcony recognised him, and with a sigh murmured his name. Agenor raised his head and beheld a female form leaning towards him with extended arms.

"Aïssa! Aïssa!" he exclaimed, and in a moment was beside her. The young girl flung herself into his arms, but suddenly recoiling, exclaimed, in a tone of terror,—" Oh, heavens! Frank, you are wounded?"

Agenor's hands were indeed stained with blood; but, instead of replying, he grasped her arm and pointed to the dog, which still followed him with his ghastly burden. At this terrible sight, Aïssa uttered a cry of terror which reached the ears of Mothril, who was just entering his apartments. His voice was heard calling for torches, followed by the approaching footsteps of himself and his attendants.

"Fly!" exclaimed the young girl, "fly! He will kill you, and then I shall die too—for I love you!"

"And I love you, Aïssa," said the chevalier, hurriedly; "be faithful to me, and you will see me again." Then pressing her to his heart, and imprinting a kiss upon her lips, he lowered the visor of his casque, drew his long sword, and leaping from the low balcony hastened away, breaking through the thickets of shrubs and trampling down the flowers. He soon forced his way out of the garden, crossed the court, rushed through the gate, and, somewhat surprised at no attempt being made to detain him, rejoined Muscaron, whom he found at a little distance, sitting firmly in his saddle, and holding by the bridle the black charger, Don Frederick's gift. He heard behind him a low fierce growl, and turning his head, at once perceived the reason of the little eagerness shown by the guards to bar his progress. The dog, unwilling to lose sight of his only friend, still followed him.

Meanwhile, Mothril, alarmed by the cries he had heard, hurried to Aïssa, whom he found standing, pale and agitated, beside the casement. He began to question her, but she preserved a gloomy silence, and he then began to suspect what had really taken place.

"Speak, Aïssa!" said he, "some one has been here!"

"Yes," replied Aïssa; "the head of the King's brother!"

Mothril regarded her more attentively. On her white robe remained the impress of a bloody hand.

"The Frank has been with you!" he exclaimed furiously.

But this time Aïssa's proud eye silently confronted him, but she made no reply.

CHAPTER IX.
MEDINA SIDONIA, OR QUEEN BLANCHE.

ON the day following this terrible one, and as the first rays of the sun were gilding the summit of the Sierra d'Aracena, Mothril, muffled in a large white mantle, took leave of his master on the lowest step of the Alcazar.

"I will answer for my slave, sire," said he. "He is the man you need for your task of vengeance; his arm is swift and sure; besides, I shall keep a watch over him. Meanwhile, let this French knight, the accomplice of Don Frederick, be diligently sought for, and if he falls into your hands, above all, show him no mercy."

"Good," said Don Pedro. "Go, and return speedily."

"In order to use greater expedition, sire," continued the Moor, "my daughter will accompany me on horseback, instead of in her litter."

"But why not leave her at Seville?" said the King. "Has she not her own house, her duennas, and female attendants?"

"Sire, I cannot leave her behind me. Wherever I go, she must accompany me. She is my most precious treasure, and as such I watch over her."

"Ah, Moor! you are thinking of the tale of Count Julian and the fair Florinda."

"I have reason to recollect it, sire, since to her the Moors owe their entrance into Spain, and, consequently, I the honour of being your Majesty's minister."

"But," said Don Pedro, "you never before told me that you possessed so fair a daughter."

"She is very beautiful, it is true," said the Moor.

"So beautiful that you worship her on your knees—is it not so?" interrupted the King.

Mothril feigned to be greatly disconcerted by these words. "I, sire?" he exclaimed. "Who can have told your Majesty such a thing?"

"No one told me; I saw it myself," said the King. "She is not your daughter."

"Ah, my lord," said Mothril, "do not imagine that she is either my wife or my slave."

"But what is she, then?"

"One day your Majesty will know all, meanwhile I hasten to execute your commands." And taking a respectful farewell of Don Pedro, he set out.

"The Moorish maiden, muffled in a long white mantle which only allowed her dark eyes and arched brows to be visible, formed, as Mothril had said, one of his suit; but he spoke falsely in declaring that she was to accompany him on the whole of the journey. At two leagues' distance from Seville, he left the direct route, in order to place her with a rich Moorish lady, in whose care he left her, and rapidly pursued his journey without further interruption. He soon crossed the Guadalquiver, at the very spot where Don Roderick disappeared after the famous battle which lasted seven days, and between Cadiz and Tariffa beheld the fortress of Medina Sidonia rearing itself in the air, and laden with all the gloom hanging over the dwelling of captives. It was here that a pale, fair girl had long dwelt with one solitary companion of her own sex. Her guards were as numerous as though she had been the most dangerous prisoner, and their pitiless eyes unceasingly watched her, whether she wandered with bowed-down head and arms hanging listlessly by her side through the scorched-up and desert gardens, or pensively reclined beside her iron-stanchioned casement, sadly gazing on the changing waves of the vast ocean, envying them their liberty. This was Blanche of Bourbon, the neglected and repudiated wife of Don Pedro. She passed her days in bitter tears and vain regrets for having sacrificed for this vain phantom of a crown the happy future she had once read in the blue eyes of Don Frederick.

When the unhappy princess beheld the blithe grape-gatherers returning homeward with their lovers from their daily labour, and listened to their merry songs, her heart swelled, and tears burst from her eyes as she thought that had her birth been humble, she might have been as free and as happy as they were. Then she invoked a cherished image, and murmured an oft-repeated name.

Medina Sidonia, since Blanche of Bourbon had been imprisoned there, had become like some spot on which rested a curse. Every passing traveller was suspected of being a friend or an accomplice, and was obliged by the guards to avoid a near approach to the fortress. During the whole of the weary day the Queen had but one brief interval of liberty, or at least solitude; and this was when the sentinels, themselves ashamed of all these precautions taken to guard a feeble woman, leant on their lances, and took their siesta either beneath some green plane-tree or under the shadow of the wall. Then the Queen sought the terrace overlooking the moat, and if she caught a chance sight of any distant traveller, she would hold out her supplicating hands, hoping to find in him a friend who could give her some tidings of her brother, King Charles. But no one had yet replied to the prisoner's mute appeal. One day, however, she perceived on the road from Arcos two horsemen, one of whom, notwithstanding the intense heat of the sun, which was reflected like a globe of fire in his helmet, appeared perfectly at his ease in his full suit of armour. He bore his lance so proudly, that she at once saw he was a valiant chevalier, and some irresistible attraction prevented her withdrawing her gaze from him. He advanced at his vigorous black horse's fullest speed, and although he evidently came from Seville, and was directing his course towards Medina Sidonia, Blanche experienced

rather a feeling of joy than sorrow at his approach, although
all former messengers from thence had only been the heralds
of fresh misfortunes. The chevalier in his turn perceiving
her, checked his horse.

The prisoner's heart throbbed with a vague feeling of hope ;
she leant over the ramparts, made the sign of the cross, and,
as usual, held out her clasped hands. The unknown knight
immediately set spurs to his horse, and came at full gallop in
the direction of the terrace where she stood. The Queen's
terrified gestures warned him of the near vicinity of the sentinel, who leaned sleeping against a sycamore tree.

The knight dismounted, and beckoning to his squire, conversed with him for some minutes in an undertone. The
squire led the two horses behind a rock, which concealed
them from sight ; he then rejoined his master, and they both
took shelter in an enormous clump of myrtle and mastic
trees, which stood within earshot of the terrace. Our worthy
chevalier—who, like Charlemagne, could not for his life have
traced with his pen anything but rude figures, bearing some
resemblance to a sword or a poniard—ordered his less illi-
terate squire to write a few words on the broad white surface
of a pebble with the pencil he always carried about him.
Then making signs to the Queen to draw a little on one side,
he sent it, by the vigorous exertion of his strong arm, whirling through the air, till it fell on the pavement at a few paces,
distance from the captive. The noise of its fall partly aroused
the drowsy sentinel, but on opening his eyes, and perceiving
nothing but what he saw every day—viz., the desolate Queen
standing sadly at her accustomed post, he again closed them,
and soon slept profoundly. The Queen hastily picked up the
pebble, and read these words inscribed on its smooth surface :—" Are you the unfortunate Queen Blanche, my King's
sister ?"

The Queen's reply was sublime in its sad and simple majesty ; she crossed her arms over her breast, and bowed her
head—a movement that caused two large tears to roll down
her pale cheeks. The chevalier bowed respectfully, and again
applied to his squire, who had already furnished himself with
another pebble.

" Write as follows," said he : " Madame, can you be on the
terrace to-night, at eight o'clock, for I have a letter from
Don Frederick to place in your hands ?"

The squire obeyed, and the second missive arrived as happily as the first. Blanche made a joyful gesture, but after long consideration, replied in the negative.

"Is there any means of reaching you?" asked Agenor, who was forced to trust to either the language of pantomime or to his pebbles, which his wearied arm could now scarcely launch across the moat, for fear the sound of his voice should awaken the slumbering sentinel.

The Queen pointed to a sycamore-tree, by means of which he could mount the wall, and reach a little door leading to the tower in which she was confined. The chevalier bowed— he understood her. At this moment the sentinel awoke, and resumed his rounds. The chevalier remained in his place of concealment, until his attention was attracted by something passing elsewhere, then he glided with his squire behind the rock where his horses were secured.

"Master," said Muscaron, "we have undertaken a difficult task. Why did you not at once deliver the Grand Master's letter to the Queen? For my part, I should have done so."

"Because it might have chanced to become unfastened by the way, and if the letter were lost, the Queen would not put faith in me. This evening, then, we must find some means of gaining the terrace unobserved by the sentinel."

Night came on, it was past seven o'clock, and yet Agenor had not discovered any method by which his object might be attained; for he wished, if possible, to avoid violence, and to effect an entrance rather by stratagem than force. But, as usual, Muscaron was of a totally different opinion to his master.

"Take it which way you will, Sire Agenor, we shall be forced to attack some one, and therefore your scruples appear to me rather out of place. Murder is as great a sin at eight o'clock as at half-past seven—to kill is always to kill. I therefore maintain that, of all the plans you propose, mine is the only practicable one."

What is it?"

"You shall soon see. Yonder sentinel is a villanous Moor, a frightful miscreant who stands rolling his white eye-balls as if he already felt the flames that will one day be his portion. Therefore, my lord deign to repeat an ' In manus,' and thus mentally baptize, this infidel."

"And what good will result form that?" asked Agenor.

"The only thing which under these circumstances should give us the least concern. We shall kill his body and save his soul!"

The chevalier did not yet understand what means Muscaron intended to employ. However, as he had great confidence in his squire's inventive powers, which he had had reason on more than one occasion to admire, he repeated the stated prayer.

Meanwhile, Muscaron, with as much coolness as though he were only preparing to win a silver cup at some village fête, unslung his cross-bow, fitted an arrow in it, and took aim at the Moor. A sharp whistling sound was almost immediately heard, and Agenor, who had not taken his eyes from off the sentinel, beheld him suddenly stagger and stretch out his arms. He endeavoured to cry out, but choked with blood, sank on the wall over which he leaned; and thus supported remained almost upright, but perfectly motionless.

The chevalier turned to Muscaron, who with a smile upon his lips was returning the cross-bow, from which he had just directed the arrow now planted in the Moor's heart, to its place at his side.

"Do you see, Sire Agenor," said he, "there is a double advantage in what I have just done. Firstly, in sending this infidel to Paradise in spite of himself; and secondly, in killing him before he had time to cry out 'Who goes there?' Now forward! for there is nothing more to hinder us; the terrace is deserted, and the way open."

They plunged into the moat, and swam across it. The water glistened on the chevalier's armour as if it had been the scales of a fish; but Muscaron with his usual care for himself, had divested himself of his clothes, which he carried over in a packet on his head. When they reached the foot of the sycamore he hastily attired himself; and whilst his master was freeing himself from the water which poured in streams from every joint of his armour, he grasped the branches of the tree, and was the first to gain its summit, which was on a level with the ramparts.

"Well," asked Mauleon, "what do you see?"

"Nothing, except the door which you will be able to force open with two blows of your battle-axe," replied the squire.

Mauleon, who had by this time mounted beside his squire, was able to convince himself of the truth of what he said.

The coast was clear, and nothing but this slight door separated them from the stairs communicating with the apartments of the captive Queen. As Muscaron had said, Agenor,
by introducing the point of his battle-axe between the stones,
found no difficulty in forcing back first the lock, and then
the two bolts. The door opened, and revealed a winding
flight of steps, serving as a back staircase to the Queen's
apartments, the principal entrance to which was in the
inner court. At the top of the first flight they found a
door at which the chevalier knocked three times without
receiving any reply.

" Do not be alarmed, madame, it is I !" said Agenor, fancying the Queen was afraid of some surprise.

" I heard your approach," answered the Queen from within.
" But are you not deceiving me ?"

" I am so far from doing so, madame," replied Agenor,
" that I am opening a door for your escape. I have slain
the sentinel ; the moat can be crossed in a few minutes, and
in a quarter of an hour we shall be in the open country."

" But have you the key of this door ?" asked the Queen,
" for I am locked in."

Agenor replied by executing the same manœuvre that had
already proved so successful with the lower door, and in an
instant it gave way like the former one.

" Thank God !" ejaculated the Queen on beholding her
liberators. Then she added, in a trembling and almost
inaudible voice, " But Don Frederick ?"

" Alas ! madame," said Agenor, sadly, as falling on one knee
he presented the parchment to the Queen, " here is his letter !"

By the light of the lamp Blanche read the billet. " But
he is lost !" she exclaimed. " This is the last adieu of a man
on the point of death." Agenor was silent. In Heaven's
name !" exclaimed the Queen, " by your friendship for the
Grand Master, I conjure you to tell me whether he be dead
or living ?"

" In either case, madame, you see Don Frederick entreats
you to fly."

" But if he be no more !" exclaimed the Queen, " why
should I fly—why wish to live ?"

" To obey his last wishes, madame; and demand vengeance
in your name and his, from the King of France."

At this moment the inner door of the apartment opened,

and Blanche's nurse—who had followed her from France—
appeared on the threshold, with pale and terrified looks.
"Oh, madame?" said she, "the castle is full of armed men,
just arrived from Seville, and they say that an er.voy from
the King desires an interview with you."

"Come, madame," said Agenor, "we have no time to lose."

"On the contrary,' said the Queen, "if they missed me
at this moment, they would pursue, and infallibly overtake us.
It will be better for me to receive this envoy, and when all
suspicions are lulled by my presence and conversation, we
will fly."

"But, madame," returned the chevalier, "suppose this
envoy harbours evil intentions towards you, or has received
orders to injure you?"

"I shall learn from him whether Don Frederick is dead or
living," replied the queen.

"Well, madame," said Agenor, "if that be your only motive
for receiving this messenger, I will myself tell you the mournful truth. He is dead!"

"Then," said Queen Blanche, "what matters this man's
business with me? Think only of your own safety, Sire
Mauleon. Go and announce to this envoy that I will wait
on him," she added, addressing her nurse. Then when the
chevalier still attempted to detain her, she enforced obedience
on him by a queenly gesture, and left the apartment.

"My lord," said Muscaron, "if you will be advised by me,
you will let the Queen manage her own affairs as she chooses,
and bethink yourself of retracing your steps; if not, we
shall perish here miserably—something tells me so. Let us
delay the Queen's flight until to-morrow, and forthwith. . . ."

"Silence!" interrupted the chevalier. "If I am alive,
the Queen shall be free to-night!"

"Then, at least, my lord," said the prudent Muscaron,
"let us replace the doors, so that if they visit the terrace,
they will perceive nothing of what has passed.—But they
will find the Moor's body."

"Throw it into the moat," said the chevalier.

"That is a good idea; but will only serve us for an hour,
at the most. The obstinate fool will return to the surface of
the water," replied Muscaron.

"An hour in some cases, is worth a lifetime," said the
chevalier.

"I would willingly be in two places at once," said Muscaron. "If I do not leave you, they will discover the dead Moor, and yet I dread lest some evil should happen to you during my absence."

"And what could happen to me whilst I have my sword and poniard?"

"Hum!" said Muscaron.

"Go, then; you are losing time."

Muscaron advanced three steps towards the door, and then suddenly stopped. "Ah, my lord," said he, "do you hear that voice?" In fact, a few words spoken in a loud tone, now reached them, and the chevalier listened attentively.

"If it were not impossible!" he exclaimed, "I should declare that was Mothril's voice."

"Nothing is impossible to Moors, hell, and magic," said Muscaron, hastening towards the door with a rapidity that showed his anxiety to find himself in the open air.

"If it be Mothril, the greater reason for not leaving the Queen!" exclaimed the chevalier ; "for if it be Mothril, she is lost!" And he made a movement to follow his generous inspiration.

"My lord," remonstrated Muscaron, holding him back by his surcoat, "you know I am not cowardly, only prudent. I do not deny it, I rather boast of it. Well, then, at least wait a few moments ; after that, I will follow you, to hell itself!"

"You are, perhaps, right," said Agenor. "Let us wait, then."

They still continued to hear the same voice, which, little by little, became sterner and gloomier, whilst that of the Queen, which had hitherto been low, assumed a more energetic tone. To this strange kind of dialogue succeeded a short silence, broken by a horrible cry. Agenor, unable longer to restrain himself, rushed into the corridor.

CHAPTER X.

THE QUEEN'S RING.

THIS is what had taken, or rather, was taking place.

Blanche had scarcely traversed the corridor, and followed her nurse up the few stairs leading to her chamber, when the heavy tread of a troop of soldiers sounded on the grand staircase of the tower. The troop, however, paused at the top of the first flight of stairs, and only two men ascended higher, one of whom remained in the corridor, whilst the other continued his way towards the Queen's apartments. He knocked at the door.

"Who is there?" inquired the trembling nurse.

"A soldier, who brings a message from his Majesty Don Pedro to Donna Bianca," replied a voice.

"Admit him," said the Queen.

The trembling nurse opened the door, and recoiled at sight of a tall man, wearing a soldier's costume—that is to say, a coat of mail covering the whole body—and muffled in a large white mantle, the hood of which concealed his face, and its heavy folds his hands.

"Retire, good nurse," said he, with the slightly guttural accent which distinguished the Moors, no matter how well they were acquainted with the Castilian language. "Retire; I have to converse with your mistress on business of importance."

The nurse's first impulse was to remain, in spite of the Moor's injunction; but her mistress, whom she interrogated by a look, signed to her to retire, and she obeyed. But she quickly repented having done so, when on reaching the corridor, she beheld the second soldier standing mute and motionless against the wall, evidently holding himself in readiness to execute the orders of the one now closeted with the Queen. When she had passed this man, and found herself separated from her mistress by these two strange visitors, as by some impassable barrier, she at once understood that Blanche was lost. The young Queen advanced with her usual calm majestic mien towards the pretended soldier, who held down his head, as if unwilling to be recognised. "Now we are alone," said she; "speak."

"Senora," replied the unknown, "it has come to the King's knowledge, that you have been in correspondence with his enemies, which you know amounts to high treason."

"And has the King only discovered this to-day?" said the Queen, with the same quiet dignity. "Then it appears to me I have already been sufficiently punished for a crime of which he has hitherto been ignorant."

The soldier raised his head and replied, "Senora, this time the King does not allude to the enemies of his throne, but to those of his honour. The Queen of Castile ought to be above all suspicion, and yet she has given room for scandal."

"Perform your mission," said the Queen, "and then leave me."

The soldier paused a moment, as though hesitating how to proceed; at last he said, "Have you heard, senora, the tale about Don Guttière?"

"No," replied the Queen.

"Yet it is quite recent, and has caused a great sensation."

"I am ignorant of all recent events," said the Queen. "And it would be difficult for any sensation, however great, to penetrate these castle walls."

"Then I will relate it to you," said the messenger.

The Queen, thus forced to listen, remained standing, calm and dignified.

"Don Guttière," said the messenger, "had espoused a beautiful young lady of sixteen; precisely the age at which your Highness was united to Don Pedro." The queen took no notice of this allusion, marked as it was. "This lady," continued the Moor, "before becoming the Senora Guttière, was styled Donna Meucia, and under this, her maiden name, was beloved by a young nobleman, who was no other than the King's half-brother, Don Henry de Transtamare." The Queen started. "One evening, on returning home, Don Guttière found her all trembling and agitated; he questioned her, and she pretended that she had been alarmed by finding a man concealed in her chamber. Don Guttière took a taper, and commenced a search, but found nothing except a dagger of such rich workmanship, that he at once saw it could not have belonged to a simple gentleman. The name of the maker was on the hilt. He went in search of him, and demanded from him the name of the person to whom he had sold that poniard. 'The Infant Don Henry, brother to his Majesty Don Pedro,' replied the man. Don Guttière had learnt all he wished. He could not revenge himself on Don Henry, for he was an old Castilian, too full of respect and veneration for his rulers to steep his hands in royal blood, notwithstanding the injury he had received. But Donna Meucia was only the daughter of a simple gentleman, so he could revenge this injury on her, and he did so."

"But how?" asked the Queen, carried away by her interest in a recital of adventures so strongly resembling her own.

G

" Oh, in a very simple manner," replied the soldier. " He watched at the door of a poor surgeon, named Ludovico, and as he was entering his house, seized him, held a poniard to his throat, bandaged his eyes, and conveyed him to his own dwelling. On his arrival there, he removed the bandage from his prisoner's eyes. A woman lay bound upon a bed, with two lighted tapers placed, one at her head, and one at her feet, as though she were dead. Her left arm especially, was so firmly fastened down, that all efforts to release herself from her bonds would have been fruitless. The surgeon was speechless with astonishment—he did not know what to think of this strange scene. 'Bleed this woman,' said Don Guttière, 'and let the blood flow until she dies.' The surgeon would have resisted, but he felt the sharp point of Don Guttière's dagger passing through his clothes, and ready to pierce his breast, and he obeyed. That same night a man, pale and covered with blood, threw himself at Don Pedro's feet. 'Sire,' said he, 'I have been carried this very night with my eyes bandaged, and a poniard at my breast, to a house where I have been compelled by violence to bleed a woman to death."

" ' And by whom were you compelled to do this ?' asked the King. 'What is the name of the murderer ?'

" ' Of that I am ignorant,' replied Ludovico. ' But without any one seeing me, I dipped my hand in the basin, and pretending to stumble as I left the house, I laid my bloody hand upon the door; therefore, sire, if you cause a search to be made, the door bearing the mark of a bloody hand is that of the guilty person.'

" Don Pedro took with him the Alcalde of Seville, and they together commenced a search through the city, until they found the terrible sign spoken of by the surgeon. They knocked at the door, which was opened to them by Don Guttière himself, who from his window had recognised his illustrious guest.

" ' Don Guttière,' said the King, 'where is Donna Meucia ?'

" ' You shall see her, sire,' replied the Spaniard, and he conducted them to the chamber where stood the lighted tapers and the still reeking basin of blood.

" ' Here, sire, is the person you seek,' said he.

" ' What has this woman done ?' asked the King.

" ' Sire, she has betrayed me.'

" ' But why have you revenged yourself on her, and not on her accomplice ?'

" Because her accomplice is the Prince Don Henry de Transtamare, brother to his Majesty Don Pedro.'

"'Have you proof of what you assert ?' said the King.

" ' Here is the prince's own dagger, which he let fall, and I picked up.'

" ' Good,' said the King, ' let Donna Meucia be buried, and cleanse your door from the mark of a bloody hand, which at present stains it.'

" ' Not so, sire,' answered Don Guttière, 'every man, holding a public office, places over his door some sign indicating his trade or profession. I am the physician of my own nonour, and the bloody hand is my sign.'

" ' Be it so,' said Don Pedro ; ' let it remain there as a warning to your second wife, if you contract another marriage, and a lesson to her to preserve both her respect for and her fidelity to her husband.' "

" And was this all that was done to him ?" asked Blanche.

" Yes, senora," replied the messenger ; " and on his return to the palace Don Pedro banished the Infant Don Henry."

" Well, how does this history relate to me, and in what do I resemble Donna Meucia?" asked the Queen.

" In this, senora; like you, she betrayed her husband; and, like Don Guttière, whose conduct he approved and pardoned, Don Pedro has already punished your accomplice."

" My accomplice ! What mean you, soldier ?" murmured Blanche, to whom these words recalled the contents of Don Frederick's letter. and her late terror.

" I mean that the Grand Master is dead," replied the soldier, coldly. " Dead, for traitorously conspiring against his king's honour; and that you, guilty of the same crime, must, like him, prepare for death."

For a moment Blanche was speechless with horror—not at her own sentence, but at the tidings of her lover's death. " Dead!" she murmured. " Then it is really true—he is dead!" It is impossible to describe the grief and despair embodied in these few words.

" Yes, senora," said the soldier; " and I have brought with me thirty men to escort the Queen's body from Medina Sidonia to Seville, so as to accord her, in spite of her guilt, the honours due to her rank."

"Soldier," said the Queen, "I have already told you that his Majesty Don Pedro is my judge—you are only my executioner."

"It is so, senora," said he, drawing from his pocket a long flexible silken cord, at the end of which he made a running knot. This cold-blooded cruelty revolted the Queen.

"Is it possible," she exclaimed, "that Don Pedro has found in all his dominions a Spaniard so base as to undertake this infamous office?"

"I am not a Spaniard—I am a Moor," retorted the soldier, raising his head and flinging back the white hood that had hitherto concealed his face.

"Mothril!" exclaimed the Queen; "Mothril, the scourge of Spain!"

"A man of illustrious birth, senora, whose touch will not dishonour even a queen's head." And he advanced towards her with the fatal cord in his hand, whilst she, with the instinctive love of life, retreated from him step by step.

"Oh, you will not kill me thus in a state of sin!" she cried, imploringly; "without even a prayer!"

"Nay, senora," replied the ferocious messenger, "you cannot be in a state of sin if, as you say, you are innocent."

"Wretch! thus to insult your Queen before murdering her! Oh, coward! why have I not one of my brave countrymen here to defend me?"

"Yes," replied Mothril with a laugh; "but unfortunately your brave countrymen are on the other side of the Pyrenees, and unless God permits a miracle to take place——"

"Oh, God is great!" cried Blanche. "Help, chevalier! help!" and she rushed towards the door; but before she reached the threshold, Mothril flung the fatal cord over her head and drew it sharply towards him. It was at this moment that Blanche, feeling the cold silk encircling her throat, uttered that lamentable cry which caused Agenor, in spite of his squire's counsels, to rush to the spot from whence it proceeded.

"Help!" cried the Queen in a stifled voice, and struggling wildly on the ground.

"Call! call!" said the Moor, tightening the cord which his unhappy victim grasped with her two clenched hands. "Call, and we shall see whether either God or your lover comes to your aid."

Suddenly the sound of spurs rung on the pavement of the

corridor, and the chevalier striding across the threshold confronted the astonished Moor. The Queen gave a moan of mingled joy and suffering. Agenor raised his sword, but Mothril's strong arm forced his victim from her recumbent position, and held her half lifeless body like a shield before him. The groans of the unhappy princess had now subsided into a hollow, half suffocated murmur—her features were distorted by the violence of her agony, and her lips had turned blue.

"Kebir!" cried Mothril in Arabic; "Kebir, help!" And he shielded himself not only with the Queen's body, but with one of those redoubtable scimitars whose curved blades cut off a head as easily as an ear of corn.

"Ah, miscreant!" cried Agenor, "you would kill a daughter of France!" And he endeavoured to strike Mothril with his sword above the Queen's head. But at the same moment he found himself seized round the waist, and dragged back by Kebir, whose arms encircled him like an iron belt. He turned to free himself from this new adversary, but it was a precious moment lost. The Queen had again fallen on her knees; she no longer sighed or moaned, but was to all appearance dead.

Kebir was meanwhile seeking a place unprotected by armour where, by loosing his grasp for a moment, he could plunge into the chevalier's body the dagger he held between his teeth.

This scene had taken place in almost less time than it takes a flash of lightning to illumine the face of the heavens and then disappear. It only occupied the few seconds necessary for Muscaron to follow the footsteps of his master, and in his turn reach the Queen's chamber. The cry he uttered on beholding what was passing was Agenor's first intimation of his unexpected reinforcement.

"The Queen first!" he exclaimed, still struggling in the grasp of the robust Kebir.

There was a momentary silence, then something whistled past Agenor's ear, and the Moor relaxed his hold. An arrow from Muscaron's crossbow had pierced his throat.

"Quick to the door!" cried the chevalier; "cut off all communication; now I will slay this wretch!" And shaking off the still clinging body of Kebir, which fell heavily to the ground, he rushed upon Mothril, and before he had time to defend himself, dealt him so violent a blow, that his sword cut through the double coat of mail defending his head and entered his neck. A mist swam before the eyes of the Moor,

a torrent of thick blood inundated his beard, and he fell
forward upon Blanche, as though even in his last agonies he
sought to complete the suffocation of his victim.

Agenor kicked the body on one side, and bending over the
prostrate Queen, unfastened the fatal cord, now almost buried
in the delicate flesh. A long sigh was the only indication of
life—her whole person seemed paralysed.

"The victory is ours!" cried Muscaron. "My lord, raise
the lady's head, I will take her by the feet, and let us thus
carry her away."

The Queen, as though she had heard and understood these
words, and wished to aid her liberators, raised herself by a
convulsive movement, and the blood returned to her lips.

"Useless, useless," she murmured. "Leave me, for I am
already more than half in the grave. Only give me a cross,
that I may die pressing the symbol of our redemption to
my lips."

Agenor held the hilt of his sword, which was in the form
of a cross, to her lips.

"Alas, alas!" said the young Queen, faintly. "Life's journey
has ended for me almost as soon as begun. God will pardon
my sins, for I have truly loved, and deeply suffered."

"Come, come," said the chevalier; "there is yet time—
we may still save you."

"No, no!" gasped Blanche, clasping the chevalier's hand.
"All is finished for me; you have done all you could, therefore now fly; quit Spain—return to France—find my sister,
—relate to her what you have witnessed, and let her avenge
us. I go to tell Don Frederick how noble, how true a friend
you have proved yourself." Then drawing a ring from her
finger, she gave it to the chevalier, saying, "You will return
her this ring, which, at the moment of my departure, she gave
me from her husband, King Charles." And a second time
raising herself towards the cross of Agenor's sword, she expired at the moment she touched the sacred symbol.

"My lord," cried Muscaron, whose head had been turned
towards the corridor. "They are coming—and in a body!"

"They must not find the body of my Queen confounded
with those of her murderers. Assist me, Muscaron." So
saying, he raised the corpse, and seated it majestically in a
chair, of carved wood, with its foot resting on the gory head
of Mothril, as painters and sculptors represent the Virgin's

foot placed on the bruised head of the serpent. "Now let us go," said Agenor, "unless we are already surrounded."

Five minutes later, the two Franks found themselves once more beneath the blue vault of heaven; and retracing their steps by means of the sycamore, came in sight of the dead sentinel, who, still supported by the wall against which he leaned, seemed staring at them with the lustreless eyes that death had forgotten to close. They had already reached the opposite side of the moat, when lights moving to and fro, and the sound of loud cries, showed them that the secret of the tower was discovered.

——————

CHAPTER XI.
CAVERLEY.

AGENOR on his way back to France pursued as far as possible the same route he had taken to enter Spain, hoping that by thus travelling humbly and alone, and consequently inspiring neither fear nor envy, he should be enabled to honourably acquit himself of the mission with which the dying queen had charged him. Nevertheless, it was necessary for him to be on his guard against, firstly, the Lepers, who report said poisoned all the fountains with a mixture of human hair, adders' heads, and frogs' feet. Secondly, the Jews, the allies of the Lepers, and of all men and things generally that could injure the Christians. Thirdly, the King of Navarre, the enemy of the King of France, and consequently his subjects. Fourthly, the "Jacques" or peasantry, who after having long excited the people against the nobles, had at last arrived at the pitch of raising the flail and the pitchfork against the sword and the battle-axe. Fifthly, the English, treacherously posted in all parts of the fair kingdom of France; in Bayonne, at Bordeaux, in Dauphiny, in Normandy, in Picardy, even in the faubourgs of Paris. And sixthly and lastly, the Free Companies, those heterogeneous assemblies, forming for the traveller, the landowners, the inhabitants, for beauty, riches or power, a foe uniting the qualities of the Jew, the Navarrais, the English, and the Jacques, without counting the other countries of Europe, which seemed to have each furnished a sample of the worst part of their population to swell the ranks of each of the bands now desolating France. There were even Arabs in this rich medley of nations styled the Free Companies : only by the spirit of contradiction they had become Christians—a charge that was quite allowable, since, on their side, the Christians had become infidels. Apart from these inconveniences, of which we have only given a brief programme, Agenor travelled in the most peaceable manner possible.

In these times it was necessary for the traveller to follow the example, and imitate the manœuvres of the thievish sparrow, which at every hop, every flight, turns its head towards the four cardinal points, expecting to see either a gun, a net, a dog, a rat, or a child.

Muscaron was this restless and thievish bird ; for, having been appointed by Agenor pursebearer, he was anxious that its scanty store of golden pieces should not become absolutely exhausted. Thus, he descried the Lepers afar off ; recognised the Jews at five hundred paces' distance ; saw the English forces in every clump of trees ; politely saluted the Navarrais, and displayed his short knife and crossbow to the Jacques. As to the Free Companies, he did not fear them as much as his master did, or rather he did not fear them at all ; for, as he remarked, " If, my lord, they take us prisoners, we must enter their ranks and purchase our freedom by the liberty of which we deprive others."

" That will be all well and good," said Agenor, " when I have fulfilled my mission. Then I care not what happens ; but meanwhile I trust nothing of the kind will befall us."

They passed without any difficulty through Roussillon, Languedoc, Dauphiny, Lyonnais, until they arrived at Chalons-sur-Saône ; and here they suffered for their feeling of undue security ; for, convinced that, near as they were to the end of their journey, no misfortune would now happen to them, they ventured to travel by night, and at daybreak on the following morning fell into so numerous and well laid an ambuscade that it was impossible for them to make any resistance. Besides, the prudent Muscaron laid his hand upon his master's arm, as he was inconsiderately going to draw his sword, and he was thus taken without having struck a single blow.

What they, or rather the chevalier, had most dreaded had now come to pass ; they were both in the power of the captain of one of the companies named Hugh Caverley, a man who was at once English by birth, a Jew in mind, an

Arab in character, a Jacques in tastes, a Navarrais in cunning, and, besides this, almost a Leper; for, as he said, he had made war in hot countries until he had become so accustomed to the heat that he could not now divest himself of either his suit of armour or his iron gauntlets. As to his detractors, and, like all persons of transcendent merit, the captain was not without them, they simply asserted that the reason why he never laid them aside was to avoid communicating to his numerous friends the unfortunate disease he had contracted in Italy.

Agenor and Muscaron were immediately conducted before this chief, who insisted on all occasions on seeing and hearing for himself; as he always pretended being afraid lest his men should allow some prince, disguised as a peasant, to escape them, and thus lose an opportunity of making their fortunes. In the course of a few moments he made himself acquainted with all of Agenor's affairs that he felt himself at liberty to disclose; as to the Queen's mission, that had nothing to do with their present subject of conversation, which was only relative to ransom.

"Excuse me," said Caverley, "I was lying in ambush on the road, like a spider under a beam, waiting for somebody or something. You came and I took you prisoner, but without harbouring any evil intentions towards you. Alas! since King Charles has been regent—that is to say, since the end of the war, we have been scarcely able to gain our daily bread. You are a charming chevalier, and were we living in ordinary times I would courteously allow you to depart; but when there is a famine in the land, you see we must pick up the crumbs!"

"Here are mine," said Mauleon, showing his poorly-filled purse to the rough soldier, "and I swear to you by all I hold sacred that I possess nothing else, either in money or land! Thus of what service can I be to you? Let me go!"

"First, my young friend," said the captain, examining with a critical eye the vigorous frame and martial air of the chevalier—"First, you will produce a superb effect in the front rank of my company. Then you have your horse and your squire, though it is not on that account you will prove a precious hostage for me."

"A hostage!"

"Undoubtedly; so that in case King Charles takes one of

my men prisoner, and threatens to hang him on a tree, I
shall be able to menace him with treating you in the same
manner; and if he really puts his threat into execution, I
shall do the same. It would vex him to have one of his
gentlemen hanged! But, pardon me!" continued Caverley,
" I remark on your hand a jewel which has hitherto escaped
my notice,—something in the shape of a ring. Come, let
me look at it, chevalier; I am rather a connoisseur in
trinkets, especially when the value of the material enhances
that of the workmanship."

Mauleon at once understood the sort of man with whom
he had to deal. Caverley was one of the leaders of the
band; he had become the chief of a horde of robbers, because,
as he himself said, he no longer found anything to do in pursuing his honest trade of a soldier.

"Captain," said Agenor, drawing back his hand, "do you
respect anything in the world?"

"Everything that inspires me with fear," replied Caverley.
"It is true I fear nothing,"

"That is unfortunate," said Agenor, coldly; "as without,
what this ring is worth—"

"Three hundred livres Tournois," interrupted Caverley,
glancing at it. "Counting only the value of the gold, and
not the workmanship."

"Well, this ring which you acknowledge to be worth
three hundred livres Tournois, would have brought you in a
thousand, if you had feared anything."

"But pray inform me how, my young friend? We are
never too old to learn, and for myself, I am always glad to
acquire information."

"Have you at least a word of honour, captain?"

"I believe I had one formerly, but from having given it
so frequently, nothing now remains of it."

"But, at least, you will put faith in a word of honour that
has never been lightly given, and is therefore not worn out?"

"I would put faith in the word of only one man living,
chevalier, and you are not he."

"But who is he?"

"Bertrand Duguesclin!—would he be answerable for you?"

"I do not know him; at least, personally," said Agenor;
"but, stranger as he is to me, if you let me go where I wish—
if you let me return this ring to its destined owner, I pro-

mise you, in the name of Messire Duguesclin, not a thousand livres, but a thousand gold crowns."

"I prefer the three hundred livres the ring is worth, down on the nail," said Caverley, laughing, and extending his hand towards Agenor.

The chevalier drew back hastily; and approaching a window overhanging the river, "This ring," said he, snatching it from his finger, and holding it over the Saône, "belonged to Blanche, Queen of Castile; I am bearing it from her to the King of France. If you will give me your word that you will allow me to depart, I will trust in it, and on my side promise you a thousand gold crowns. If, on the contrary, you refuse, I will fling the ring into the river, and you will lose both gain and ransom."

"Yes; but *you* will still be in my power, and I shall hang you."

"That would be a very poor recompence to so shrewd a calculator as yourself; and as a proof that you do not think my death worth a thousand crowns, you do not say no to my proposition."

"I do not say no, because——"

"Because you are afraid to do so, captain; say so, and the ring is lost—after that, hang me if you please. Well, do you say yes or no?"

"Faith!" exclaimed Caverley, struck with admiration, "you are what I call a fine fellow—even your squire has not flinched. Devil take me, I like you, chevalier!"

"Very well, I feel properly grateful; but answer! Yes, or no—that is soon said, and I require nothing more."

"Well, then, yes."

"So much the better," said the chevalier, returning the ring to his finger.

"But on one condition, however," said the captain.

"What is that?"

Caverley was about to reply, when a violent tumult at the other end of the village—or rather in the camp, which was situated on the banks of the river, and half buried in the woods—attracted his attention. Several soldiers made their appearance at the door of the tent, crying, "Captain! captain!"

"Well, well," said Caverley, who was accustomed to this kind of hasty summons; "I am coming." Then turning towards the chevalier. "Remain here," said he: "twelve men shall guard you—I hope I show you enough respect then !"

"Be it so," said the chevalier; "but warn them not to approach me, for at the first step they make towards me, I will fling the ring into the Saône."

"Do not go near him, but nevertheless keep him in your sight," said Caverley to his bandits; and saluting the chevalier, without having even for an instant raised the visor of his helmet, he proceeded, at his usual careless pace, towards that part of the camp where the noise was loudest.

During his absence, Manleon and his squire stood together near the casement; their guards were ranged on the opposite side of the apartment, and remained stationary before the door. The tumult continued, but gradually grew fainter until it at last altogether died away; and half an hour after his quitting them, Hugh Caverley returned to his prisoners, accompanied by a fresh captive, who had fallen into the hands of his bandits, who were spread over the face of the country like a net to catch larks. The new comer appeared to be a country gentleman; tall, and of commanding mien, but accoutred in a rusty helmet, and a cuirass which looked as as though it had been picked up by one of his ancestors on the battle-field of Roncevaux. The first feeling excited by his appearance was that of laughter, but there was a certain pride in his bearing and boldness in his countenance, to which he nevertheless endeavoured to give an expression of humility, that commanded, if not the respect, at least the circumspection of the jesters.

"Have you searched him thoroughly ?" asked Caverley.

"Yes, captain," replied a German lieutenant, to whom Caverley owed the happy choice of the position he now occupied—a choice which had not been influenced by the superiority of the position itself, but by the excellence of the wines which at that epoch were to be found on the banks of the Saône.

"When I say him," added Caverley, "I mean him and his men."

"Be easy, captain; the operation has been rigorously performed," said the German lieutenant.

"And how much have you found upon them ?"

"A gold mark, and two silver ones."

"Bravo !" exclaimed Caverley; "this seems to be a lucky

day." Then turning to his new captive, "Now," said he, "let us have a few words together, my Paladin; although you bear a strong resemblance to the nephew of the Emperor Charlemagne, I shall be glad to hear from your own lips who you are. Come, tell me frankly, without restriction, without reserve."

"I am, as you may tell from my accent," said the unknown, "a poor gentleman of Arragon, come on a visit to France."

"You are in the right," said Caverley. "France is a fine country."

"Yes," added the lieutenant, "only you have chosen a bad time for your visit."

Mauleon could not repress a smile; for he, better than any one, appreciated the justice of the remark. As to the stranger, he remained unmoved.

"Let us see," said Caverley, "you have as yet only informed us of your country; just half of what we wish to know. Now, what is your name?"

"You will not recognise it, if I tell you," replied the unknown.

"Unless you are either Jew, Turk, or Moor, you have at least a Christian name," said the captain.

"I am called Henry."

"Good. Now raise your visor a little, and let us see your face." The unknown hesitated, and glanced around him, as though to assure himself that there was no one present to whom he was known.

Caverley, irritated at this delay, made a sign to one of his men, who drew near the prisoner, and striking the spring of his helmet with the hilt of his sword, raised the visor covering the face of the stranger. Mauleon gave a cry, for the face thus disclosed was the living portrait of the unfortunate Don Frederick, of whose death there could not be the least doubt, for he had held his head in his hands. Muscaron turned pale with affright, and hastily crossed himself.

"Ah! ah! you are acquainted with each other," said Caverley, looking alternately at Mauleon and the knight in the rusty helmet.

At these words, the unknown looked uneasily at Mauleon; but as his first glance convinced him that he beheld the chevalier for the first time, his countenance resumed its serenity.

"Well?" said Caverley.

"You are mistaken," said the new comer, "I am not acquainted with this gentleman."

"And you?"—"Neither am I with this chevalier."

"Why, then, did you cry out just now?" inquired the captain, who, notwithstanding the double denial of his two prisoners, was still incredulous.

"Because I thought that in striking up his visor, your soldier would have split open his head."

Caverley laughed. "We bear, then, a sad reputation," said he. "But tell me frankly, chevalier, do you, or do you not, know this Spaniard?"

"Upon my knightly word," said Agenor, "I behold him to-day for the first time." But whilst taking this oath, which was the exact truth, Mauleon's heart throbbed wildly at this strange resemblance.

Caverley looked from one to the other; but the unknown had resumed his impassible demeanour, and appeared like a marble statue. "Come," said Caverley, impatient to solve this mystery, "you are the first comer, Chevalier de . . . . I forgot to ask your name."

"I am called Agenor de Mauleon," replied the chevalier.

Caverley cast a rapid glance at the unknown, to see if the name first pronounced by the chevalier made any impression on him; but not a muscle of his face moved.

"Come, then, Chevalier de Mauleon," said Caverley, "since you are the first comer, let us conclude your affair first, then we will pass to the Chevalier Henry's. Thus we were saying: the ring for two thousand crowns."

"A thousand crowns," said Agenor.

"You think so?"—"I am certain of it."

"It may be so. Well, then, the ring for a thousand crowns; but you must certify to me, that it is really the ring of Blanche of Bourbon." The unknown, in his turn, made a movement of surprise, which did not escape Mauleon.

"Queen of Castile," continued Caverley.

"Queen of Castile," replied Mauleon.

The unknown redoubled his attention.

"Sister-in-law to his Majesty Charles V.?"

"Yes, sister-in-law to his Majesty."

The unknown was eagerly listening.

"The same," continued Caverley, "who is now prisoner in the castle of Medina Sidonia by order of her husband. Don Pedro?"

"The same who has just been murdered by her husband Don Pedro's orders," said the unknown, in a cold but impressive voice.

Mauleon regarded him with astonishment.

"Ah, ah!" said Caverley, "the matter now becomes complicated."

"How did you learn this?" asked Agenor. "I thought I was the first to bring these tidings to France."

"Did I not tell you," replied the unknown, "that I was a Spaniard, and just arrived from Arragon? I heard of this catastrophe, which at the time of my departure was making a great noise in Spain."

"But if Queen Blanche of Bourbon is dead," said Caverley, "how did you become possessed of her ring?"

"Because she gave it to me just before her death, charging me to convey it to her sister, the Queen of France ; and at the same time to tell her, how, and by whose hand, she died."

"Then you were present at her last moments?" inquired the unknown knight, abruptly.

"Yes," said Agenor, "and it was I who killed the assassin."

"A Moor?"—"Mothril himself," replied Agenor.

"Good ; but you did not kill him."

"How?"—"You only wounded him."

"Morbleu!" exclaimed Muscaron. "If I had only known that!—and I had still eleven shafts in my quiver."

"Come," interrupted Caverley. "This may be very interesting to you two, but it does not concern me the least in the world, since I am neither Frenchman nor Spaniard."

"You are right," said Agenor. "It is then an understood thing, that you keep all you found on us ; but restore myself and squire to liberty."

"There was nothing said about the squire," said Caverley.

"Because there was no occasion for it," said Agenor. "It was a matter of course. You leave me, then, this ring, and in exchange I am to give you a thousand crowns."

"All right," said the captain. "But there is still a little condition."—"A condition!"

"Which I was about to name to you at the moment we were interrupted."

"True," said Agenor, "I remember; and what is this condition?"

"That besides these golden crowns at which I value your

release, you shall engage to serve under me during the first campaign on which it shall please King Charles to employ us, or that I shall undertake on my own account." Agenor gave a start of surprise. "Yes," continued Caverley, "these are my conditions—it must be thus or not at all. You must enrol yourself in the company, and then you are free—at least for the present."

"But suppose I do not return?" said Mauleon.

"Oh, you will come back," said Caverley, "since you have given your word."

"Well, be it so; I accept your terms, but with a single reservation."—"What is that?"

"That under no pretext whatever you require me to draw my sword against the King of France."

"You are right," said Caverley, "I did not think of it—I who own no sovereign but the King of England, and yet— Then we will write an agreement which you must sign."

"I cannot write," said Agenor, who shared without shame in the general ignorance of the nobles of that period, "but my squire can."

"Then you can make a cross," said Caverley.—"I will do so."

He took up a scrap of parchment and a pen and gave them to Muscaron, who wrote after his dictation:—"I, Agenor, Chevalier de Manleon, engage to return to Messire Hugh de Caverley, wherever he may be, immediately my mission to King Charles V. is fulfilled, and to serve under him, both me and my squire, during his campaign, provided this said campaign be not directed against the King of France or Monseigneur le Comte de Foix, my feudal lord.'

"And the thousand crowns?" suggested Caverley.

"You are right," said Agenor. "I forgot them."

"So it seems, but I have a good memory."

Agenor continued to dictate to Muscaron :—"I also engage to remit to the said Sir Hugh Caverley the sum of one thousand crowns, which I owe him in exchange for the present liberty he has granted me." The squire added the date of the day and year. The chevalier then seized the pen almost as he would a poinard, and boldly made a mark in the form of a rude cross.

Caverley took the parchment, perused it with the most scrupulous attention, scattered some sand over the still wet writing, and then carefully folding it, placed it in his sword belt.

" There," said he, " now that is done'; now you may depart
—you are free."

" Listen," said the stranger. " Since I am summoned to
Paris on affairs of moment, and have no time to lose, I offer
to ransom myself on the same terms as this chevalier. Will
that suit you? Answer, and that quickly."

Caverley burst into a laugh—"I do not know you," said he.

" Then what more do you know about Agenor de Mauleon,
who, from what I can gather, has only been an hour in your
hands?"

" To close observers like ourselves," said Caverley, " an hour
is more than sufficient to make us acquainted with a man's
character ; and during the hour the chevalier has passed with
me he has done something which has made me know him
thoroughly." The Spanish knight smiled strangely.

" Then you refuse me?" said he.—" Decidedly."

" You will repent it."—" Bah !"

" Listen : you have taken all I possess; at the present
moment I have nothing more to offer you. Keep my equipages, detain my attendants as hostages, and let me depart
alone with my horse."

" Faith! you would do me a great favour, truly! Your
equipages and attendants already belong to me."

" Then at least let me say two words to this young noble,
since he is free."

" Two words àpropos of ransom?"

" Certainly. At how much do you estimate it ?"

" At the sum we found upon you and your people—a gold
mark and two silver ones."

" Be it so," said the stranger.

" Well, then," said Caverley, " you may say what you please
to him."

" Listen to me for a moment, chevalier," said the stranger,
and they both drew aside in order to converse more at their ease.

CHAPTER XII.

THE TWO RANSOMS.

CAPTAIN CAVERLEY anxiously watched the progress of the
conversation between the two young men; but the Spaniard
had drawn Agenor out of earshot of the adventurer.

" Sir Chevalier," said he, " we are out of hearing, it is true,

H

but not out of sight; therefore, lower the visor of your helmet so as to render yourself unintelligible to those surrounding us."

"And before you lower yours, senor," said Agenor, "permit me to gaze for a few moments upon your face. Believe me, I experience at the sight of your features a melancholy pleasure which you cannot comprehend."

The unknown smiled sadly. "Sir Chevalier," said he, "contemplate me at your leisure, for I shall not lower the visor of my helmet. Although scarcely five or six years older than yourself, I have already suffered enough to be sure of keeping a command over my countenance. It is an obedient servant, and never betrays more than I choose, and if it recalls to you the features of some beloved friend, so much the better, it will encourage me to ask you to render me a service."

"Speak," said Agenor.

"You seem to hold a high place in the esteem of the bandit who has made us prisoners; but it is not so with me, for whilst he detains me captive, he suffers you to continue your journey."

"Yes, senor," said Agenor, astonished to find that since they had conversed apart, the Spaniard, although still retaining a slight accent, expressed himself in the purest French.

"Well," continued the unknown, "however great may be your need of pursuing your journey, mine is not less urgent; and at whatever price, I must be delivered out of the hands of this man."

"Senor," said Agenor, "if you swear you are a true knight, and give me your knightly word, I will on my part pledge my honour to Caverley, and induce him to allow you to depart with me."

"And this," exclaimed the stranger, joyfully, "was the very service I was about to ask you to render me. You are as intelligent, as courteous, chevalier."

Agenor bowed. "Then you are noble?" said he.

"Yes; and I might even add, that few gentlemen could boast of having more noble blood in their veins than myself."

"Then," said the chevalier, "you have another name?"

"Undoubtedly," replied the Spanish knight; "and in this very thing will the greatness of your courtesy display itself; for you must be satisfied with my word of honour, without knowing my name, for this I cannot disclose."

"Not even to the man whose honour you implicate—the

man whom you request to be answerable for you?" asked Agenor, in surprise.

"Sir Chevalier," replied the unknown, "I reproach myself for a concealment unworthy of us both; but grave interests, not altogether my own, render it necessary. Obtain my liberty at what price you will, and on my knightly word, I will pay it. Then, if you will let me add a word, it will be to assure you, that you will never repent having assisted me on this occasion."

"Enough!—enough!" said Mauleon. "Ask a service of me if you will, my lord; but do not try to bribe me to do it."

"Some day, Sire Agenor, you will appreciate my motives for acting thus. I might have deceived you for the moment, by giving you a false name, with which, as you did not know otherwise, you would have been obliged to be content."

"I was just thinking the same thing," said Mauleon. "If Captain Hugh Caverley still continues to hold me in his good graces, you shall be free at the same time as myself, my lord."

Agenor left the stranger where he was, and returned to Caverley, who was impatiently awaiting the close of the conference.

"Well, my good friend," said he, "have you made any greater progress than myself towards finding out who this Spaniard really is?"

"A rich merchant from Toledo, come to trade in France, and who pretends that his detention will do him great injury. He asks me to be security for him. Will you accept me?"

"Are you willing to become so?"

"Yes. Having for a short time shared his situation, I naturally commiserate him. Come, captain, be merciful to him."

Caverley considered for a moment. "A rich merchant," said he, "who has need of his liberty to pursue his business."

"Master," whispered Muscaron, "I think that was a rather imprudent speech of yours."

"I know what I am about," replied Agenor. Muscaron bowed in acknowledgment of his master's superior prudence.

"A rich merchant!" again repeated Caverley. "The devil! You understand it will cost him more than if he were merely a simple gentleman. And our first price of one gold mark and two silver ones does not stand good."

"That is why I told you frankly, captain, what he really was; for I did not wish to hinder you demanding from him a ransom equivalent to his position."

"Decidedly, chevalier, you are, as I said before, a good fellow. And how much does he offer? Has he not hinted at that during this long conversation?"

"Why," said Agenor, "he told me to go as far as five hundred gold or silver crowns."

Caverley did not immediately reply, he was still calculating.

"Five hundred gold crowns would do for a simple merchant; but you said a *rich* one, do you remember that?"

"Yes," said the chevalier; "and I also see, captain, that I ought not to have told you that. But since one must pay the penalty of one's faults, fix his ransom at a thousand crowns, and if I am obliged to pay five hundred for my indiscretion, why I must."

"That is not enough for a rich merchant," said Caverley; "at the most, it is only a chevalier's ransom."

Agenor glanced at the person for whom he was acting, to see whether he might increase the offer. The Spaniard made a sign in the affirmative. "Then," said the chevalier, "let us double the sum, and say no more about it."

"Two thousand gold crowns!" said the robber captain, beginning to be himself astonished at the price placed upon his person, by the unknown. "Two thousand crowns! Then he must be the wealthiest merchant in Toledo. No, faith! I fancy I have made a good stroke, and I mean to profit by it. Let him double the sum, and then we shall see."

Agenor looked at his client, who repeated his former sign. "Well," said the chevalier, "since you are so exorbitant, we will go as far as four thousand gold crowns."

"*Four thousand!*" exclaimed Caverley, at once stupefied and delighted. "Then he must be a Jew, and I am too good a Christian to release a Jew for less than——"

"For less than how much?" repeated Agenor.

"For less than——." The captain himself hesitated to utter the enormous sum upon his lips; "for less than ten thousand crowns! Faith! then, I have said it, and on my word it is a mere nothing."

The unknown made another almost imperceptible sign of assent.

"Your hand upon it," said the chevalier, holding out his own. "We agree to give this sum, so it is a bargain."

"Stop a moment," exclaimed Caverley; "for by the Pope I will not accept any chevalier's security for ten thousand crowns. A prince alone could offer a guarantee for such a sum; and even then, I question whether I would accept it."

"Traitor!" exclaimed Mauleon, striding up to Caverley, and laying his hand upon his sword. "Then you doubt my honour?"

"Nay, nay, boy," said Caverley; "it is not you I doubt, but him. Fancy him, when once out of my claws, paying me ten thousand crowns. No, at the first cross-road you come to, he would turn to the left, and you would never again catch sight of him. He would never have been so munificent in words, or at least in gestures, if he had had any intention of paying what he promised."

Notwithstanding the impassibility of which the stranger had boasted, Agenor observed the angry colour rise in his cheek; but he almost immediately recovered himself, and beckoned to Agenor to draw near him.

"Do not go near him," said Caverley, "it is only to seduce you by fine words, and to leave the weight of the ten thousand crowns on your shoulders." But the chevalier instinctively felt that the Spaniard was more than he seemed. He therefore approached him with entire confidence, not unmingled with respect.

"Thanks, loyal gentleman," said the stranger, in a low voice. "You have done well in thus engaging yourself for me on my bare word. You have nothing to fear, for were it my pleasure to do so, I could pay Caverley this very moment. I have in my horse's saddle gold and jewels to the amount of more than three hundred thousand crowns. But this wretch would take my ransom, and then refuse to restore me to liberty. You must therefore change horses with me, and set out, leaving me here. At the next town rip open the saddle, and you will find a leathern bag. From this take diamonds sufficient to produce ten thousand crowns; provide yourself with a suitable escort, and return hither to me."

"But, my lord," said Agenor, in astonishment, "who are you to be possessed of such resources?"

"Nay, I think I have shown you enough confidence by thus putting in your hands all I possess, without telling you who I am."

"My lord," replied Mauleon, "now I begin in truth to tremble. This strange resemblance—these riches—the mystery enshrouding you. My lord, I have interests—sacred interests—to defend in France, and these are perhaps opposed to yours."

"Answer me," said the unknown, in the tone of one accustomed to command. "You are going to Paris, are you not?"

"Yes," replied the chevalier.

"In order to deliver to King Charles V. the Queen of Castile's ring?"—"Yes."

"You are going in her name to demand vengeance on his Majesty Don Pedro?"—"Yes."

"Then be under no uneasiness," said the unknown, "my interests are the same as your own. Don Pedro has murdered my Queen, and I also am sworn to avenge Donna Bianca."

"Is what you say really true?" exclaimed Agenor

"Sir Chevalier," replied the unknown in a firm and majestic tone, "look at me well. You pretend I resemble some one of your acquaintance—who is that some one? Tell me."

"Oh, my unhappy friend!" exclaimed the chevalier. "Oh, my noble Grand Master! My lord, you might, from your great resemblance to him be taken for his Highness Don Frederick."

"Yes," said the unknown, smiling, "is it not a strange resemblance—the resemblance of a brother?"

"Impossible!" exclaimed Agenor, regarding the Spaniard with almost terror.

"Proceed to the next town, Sir Chevalier, sell the diamonds to a Jew, and tell the captain of the Spanish troop there that Don Henry de Transtamare is the prisoner of Captain Caverley. Calm yourself, for I see you tremble in your armour—remember we have eyes upon us."

Agenor, in fact, shook with surprise. He saluted the prince with more respect than was perhaps needed, and hastened to Caverley, who advanced to meet him half way.

"Well," said the captain, laying his hand upon his shoulder, "he deals in fine words and golden promises; and you, boy, are their dupe. Is it not so?"

"Captain," replied Agenor, "this merchant's words are indeed golden; for he has pointed out the means of paying you his ransom before nightfall."

"The ten thousand gold crowns?"—"Yes."

"Nothing can be easier," said the unknown, coming forward. "The chevalier has only to proceed on his journey until he arrives at a certain spot of which he knows, where I have placed a sum of money. This he will bring back to you in ten bags, each containing a thousand crowns; and when you have convinced yourself by sight and touch of their being genuine, and have safely deposited them in your coffers, you will let me depart. Is that too much to ask, or is it agreed upon?"

"Agreed! Yes, faith, if you perform all you promise," said Caverley, fancying himself in a dream. Then turning to his lieutenant, "Here," said he, "is a man who holds himself in high estimation; we shall see whether he will pay the price at which he values himself."

Agenor glanced at the prince.

"Sire de Mauleon," said he, "in remembrance of your good offices and the debt of gratitude I owe you—according to the fraternal custom of chevaliers, exchange sword and steed with me. You will, perhaps, suffer by the exchange; but I will repay you at some future time." Agenor thanked him.

Caverley, who overheard them, began to laugh. "He is still robbing you," said he, in an undertone, to the young man. "I have seen his horse. and it is not equal to yours. Decidedly, he is neither knight, merchant, nor Jew—he is an Arab."

The prince quietly seated himself at the table, and signed to Muscaron to prepare a second engagement, similar to the former one. When he had done so, Agenor, as security for the prince, affixed his cross to it, as he had done to his own; then, after Captain Caverley had examined it with his usual care, the chevalier set out for Châlon, which could be seen on the other side of the Saône. Here everything took place as the prince had directed. Agenor found in the saddle the little bag of diamonds, some of which he sold for twelve thousand crowns; for the prince having been entirely despoiled by Caverley, his purse needed replenishing. Then proceeding to the camp, he found the Spanish captain mentioned by Don Henry de Transtamare—recognised him—recounted the mishap that had befallen the prince—and caused him and his men to accompany him as far as a little wood, at about a quarter of a league's distance. Here the Spaniards stopped, and Agenor continued his way alone.

The affair was concluded more peaceably than Agenor had dared to hope. Caverley counted and re-counted his gold crowns, heaving deep sighs; for the idea had only just occurred to him, that from a man who paid so promptly, it would only have been necessary to ask double the sum he had demanded, to obtain it. Nevertheless, he was obliged to come to a speedy decision, and, since the chevalier had strictly kept his promise, fulfil his own. He therefore allowed the two young men to depart, but not without re-minding Agenor that he was not yet out of his debt, and that he owed him, not only a thousand crowns, but also his services during the next campaign.

"I trust you will never return to these bandits," said the prince, when they were out of hearing.

"Alas!" said Agenor, "I must. Nevertheless . . . . "

"I will pay the sum for your ransom."

"But you cannot ransom my word, my prince," said Age-nor. "And that has been given."

"Mordieu!" said the prince. "I did not give mine, and as sure as we both exist, I will hang Caverley, by which means I shall not have to regret his profiting by my crowns."

They soon reached the little wood, where the Spanish captain and his twenty lances lay concealed, and Don Henry, overjoyed at having got off so easily, at last found himself with his friends. Such was the issue of the dilemma in which the prince found himself, and from which, thanks to the word of a chevalier, he was at last extricated.

Agenor, on his side, who had set out without either money or friends, now found himself with a treasure almost at his disposal, and a prince for his protector. Upon that, Mus-caron made a thousand dissertations, each more ingenious than the former, and terminated them by too important a question for us to pass over.

"My lord," said he, "I cannot understand how, having twenty lances at your disposal, you have journeyed with only one squire, and two or three attendants?"

"My good friend," replied the prince, laughing, "it was because my brother, Don Pedro, has placed spies and assas-sins on all the route leading from Spain to France. A bril-liant train would have caused me to be recognised, and I wish to preserve my incognito. At present, obscurity suits me better than broad daylight; besides, I wish it to be said,

Don Henry left Spain with only a handful of attendants, and re-entered it with a large army. Don Pedro, on the contrary, was surrounded by his army, and he had fled from Spain alone."

"Brothers!" murmured Agenor, "Brothers!"

"My brother killed my brother," said Don Henry, "and it is his death I shall avenge."

"Master," said Muscaron, taking advantage of the moment when the prince turned aside to speak to his lieutenant, "Don Henry would not be deprived of this pretext for ten thousand more crowns."

"How he resembles the noble Grand Master! Have you remarked it, Muscaron?"

"Master," said Muscaron, "Don Frederick was fair haired, this one is red. The Grand Master's eyes were blue—Don Henry's are grey. One had a nose like the eagle's bill—this one has the beak of the vulture. The first was slender—the second is lean. Don Frederick had fire on his cheeks—this one has blood; therefore it is not Don Frederick he resembles, but Don Pedro. Two vultures, Messire Agenor!—two vultures!"

"It is true," thought Mauleon, "and they will rend one another over the body of the dove."

CHAPTER XIII.

THE FULFILMENT OF THE MISSION.

IN the garden adjoining a handsome hotel, in the Rue St. Paul which in many parts was but half complete, was walking a young man, between five and six and twenty years of age, attired in a long sad-coloured robe, turned up with black velvet, and confined round his waist by a cordeliere, the tassels of which fell to his feet. Contrary to the custom of the times, he wore neither sword, dagger, nor ineed any distinctive mark of nobility. His only decoration was a sort of small coronet of golden *fleurs-de-lys* encircling one of the small black velvet caps which preceded the fashion of hoods. This man possessed all the characteristics of the pure French race. He had fair hair, cut squarely over his forehead, in token of high birth; blue eyes, and chestnut beard. His face, although denoting the age we have before said, did not bear the impress of a single passion, and its grave and thoughtful expression indicated the man of deep thought and long meditations. From time to time he paused, and let his head drop on his breast, and his hand fall listlessly at his side, when it was fondly licked by two large dogs, which kept close to his side, stopping when he stopped, and going on when he resumed his walk. At a little distance, a careless young page stood leaning against a tree, toying with a beautiful falcon he bore upon his wrist, and whose golden bells showed it was a favourite. Still further off, and in the more retired spots of the garden, could be heard the joyous songs of the birds, which had already taken up their abode in the shady alleys of the new royal domicile; for this pensive man was no other than King Charles V., who governed the kingdom of France, while his father, King John, the slave of his given word, remained prisoner in England, and who had just built this handsome new hotel to take the place of the palace of the Louvre and the palace of La Cité, in which the studious monarch—the only one on whom posterity has conferred the title of the Wise—did not find enough solitude and tranquillity. The numerous domestics belonging to this sumptuous dwelling, were to be seen passing to and fro through the green alleys; and rising above the sounds of their voices, the impatient cries of the falcon, and the distant warbling of the birds, was occasionally heard, like approaching thunder, the roar of the enormous lions procured from Africa by King John, and now kept in deep pits.

King Charles V. was thus pacing one of these garden paths, turning back when he had reached a certain spot, so as not to lose sight of the door of the hotel, from which six steps descended to a terrace communicating with this path. He paused from time to time, and fixed his eyes upon this door, seeming to expect some one, and then, although he was evidently anxious for the appearance of this person, resumed his walk at the same pace, and with the same melancholy serenity, without his countenance displaying the slightest impatience at his disappointment. At last, a man attired in black, and holding in his hand an ebony writing-case and a roll of parchment, appeared at the top of the flight of steps. He cast a hasty glance over the garden into which he prepared to descend, and perceiving the King hastened to him,

"Ah! is it you, doctor?" said Charles, advancing a few

sters to meet him, "I was waiting for you. Do you come from the Louvre?"

"Yes, sire."

"Has a messenger arrived from any of my ambassadors?"

"No, sire : there are only two chevaliers, who have just arrived—seemingly from a long journey, and who desire to be instantly presented to your Majesty, to whom they say they have to communicate matters of the utmost importance."

"What have you done?"

"I have brought them with me, and they await you Majesty's pleasure in one of the saloons of the hotel."

"And no tidings of his Holiness Pope Urban V. ?"

"No, sire."

"Nor of Duguesclin, whom I sent to him?"

"Not yet, but it cannot be long before we receive them, for it is ten days ago since he wrote to your Majesty that he should next day leave Avignon."

The King remained for a moment buried in profound, almost anxious thought ; then, as if taking a sudden resolution, "Now, doctor," said he, "let us see the dispatches." And, trembling, as if each fresh letter must necessarily apprise him of some new misfortune, the King seated himself in an arbour of honeysuckle, through the green leaves of which fell the warm rays of the August sun.

The person designated by the King as doctor opened the portfolio he carried under his arm, and drew from it several large letters ; one of these he opened at hazard.

"Well?" inquired the King.

"Advices from Normandy," replied the doctor. "The English have burned a town and two villages."

"In spite of the peace !" murmured the King. "In spite of the treaty of Bretigny, which has cost us so dear !"

"What will you do, sire?"

"I will send money," said the King.

"Advices from Forez."—"Go on," said the king.

"The Free Companies have assembled on the banks of the Saône. Three towns have been sacked—the crops destroyed—the vines torn up—the cattle slaughtered. A hundred women have also been carried away."

The King buried his face in his hands.

"But is not John of Bourbon there?" said he. "He promised to rid me of these brigands."

"Listen, sire," said the doctor, opening a third despatch; "here is a letter in reference to him. He met the Free Companies at Brignais; he gave them battle, but—" the doctor paused and hesitated.

"But—" repeated the King, taking the letter from his hands. "Let me see what is the matter."

"Read it yourself, sire."

"Defeated and slain!" murmured the King. "A prince of the House of France slaughtered by bandits, and yet our Holy Father gives me no reply, although the distance to Avignon is not great."

"What are your commands, sire?"

"Nothing; what would you have me order in Duguesclin's absence? And in the midst of all this, has not a despatch arrived from the brother of the King of Hungary?"

"No, sire," replied the doctor, who beheld the weight of calamity thus falling on the poor King every moment grow heavier.

"And Brittany?"—"Still continues in open war; the Earl of Montfort has been hitherto successful."

Charles V. raised his eyes to heaven with a look more dreamy than despairing. "Great God!" he murmured, "have you, then, abandoned the kingdom of France? My father was a good king, but too warlike; for myself, I have piously received the trials thou, my God, hast sent me. I have always endeavoured to spare the blood of thy creatures, regarding those thou hast placed me to reign over as men of whom I shall have to render thee an account, and not as slaves whose blood I may shed at pleasure. Nevertheless, no one is pleased with my humanity—not even thou, my God. I wish to stem this tide of barbarity which is hurrying the world towards chaos. I am sure of the goodness of my intention, and yet no one assists—no one comprehends me." And the King let his head droop moodily on his hand.

At this moment a flourish of trumpets, accompanied by loud acclamations, echoed through the streets, reaching even the King's ears. The page ceased toying with his falcon, and exchanged an interrogative glance with the doctor.

"Go, and see what it is," said the doctor. "Sire," he continued, turning to the King, "do you hear those trumpets?"

"I prayed to heaven for peace and philosophy," said the

King, "and it has replied to my prayers by the sounds of war and violence."

"Sire," said the page, running towards them, "it is Messire Bertrand Duguesclin, who has just returned from Avignon, and is this instant entering the city."

"He is welcome," said the King, as if speaking to himself; "although he comes attended by more noise than I could wish." And he rose hastily from his seat, and advanced towards the hotel to receive him. But before he had reached even the end of the alley, a great crowd of people, guards, and knights, half wild with delight, appeared beneath the arch leading into the garden. In the midst of them was a man of middle height, with a large head, broad shoulders, and legs bowed from constantly being on horseback. This man was Messire Bertrand Duguesclin, who, with his vulgar but pleasant face and intelligent eyes, smiled upon and thanked the populace, the guards, and the knights, who loaded him with blessings.

As the King appeared, they all bent before him, and Bertrand Duguesclin hastily descended the steps to offer his homage to his sovereign.

"They prostrate themselves before me," muttered Charles, "but they smile upon Duguesclin—they respect me, but they love him. It is because he is the emblem of the false glory that exercises so powerful an influence over vulgar minds, and that I represent Peace—that is to say, in their short-sighted estimation, shame and submission. These people belong to the age in which they live—it is I who do not belong to mine; and they would rather die than have a change, alike foreign to their tastes and habits, imposed upon them. Nevertheless, whilst God grants me strength I will persevere." Then turning his calm and benignant gaze on the knight kneeling before him, he extended his hand with the grace peculiar to him, saying, "You are welcome."

Duguesclin touched the august hand with his lips. "Good King," said he, rising, "I am here. I have used despatch, as you see; and I bring you news."

"Good ones?" asked the King.

"Yes, sire, very good. I have raised three thousand men."

The populace uttered shouts of joy at hearing of the arrival of this reinforcement, conducted by so brave a general.

"Then all goes well," said Charles, unwilling to damp the
joy Duguesclin's words had caused the whole of the admiring
assembly. Then he added, in an undertone, "Alas, messire!
there was rather occasion to suppress six thousand lances than
to raise three thousand more. We shall always be able to
find soldiers enough when we know how to employ them."

And taking the arm of the worthy chevalier, who was lost
in astonishment at the honour done him, he ascended the
steps and passed through the crowd of people, courtiers, guards,
chevaliers, and women, who seeing the good understanding
existing between the King and the general on whom all their
hopes were fixed, rent the air with their cries of "Nöel."

Charles V. returned their salutations by smiles and gestures,
and conducted the Breton knight through a large gallery,
destined, at a future period for an audience chamber, and leading to his apartment. The shouts of the crowd followed them,
and were heard even after the great doors were closed behind
them.

"Sire," said Bertrand, joyfully, "by the aid of Heaven and
our brave people's love, you will recover your entire heritage,
and I am very certain that by two years of well-directed war—"

"But to make war, Bertrand, requires money—much
money—and our coffers are empty."

"Bah, sire!" said Bertrand; "a little tax upon the agricultural districts—"

"There are no longer any agricultural districts, my friend—
the English have ravaged everything, and our worthy allies,
the Free Companies, have finished devouring what the
English spared."

"Then, sire, you can levy a tax of a franc a head on all
members of the clergy, and take a tithe of their possessions—
they have taken one of ours long enough."

"It was for that I sent you to our Holy Father, Pope
Urban," said the King. "Does he grant us authority to
levy this tax?"

"No! quite the contrary, sire; he complains of the poverty
of the clergy, and asks for money."

"Then you see plainly, my friend," said the King, with a
faint smile, "that there is nothing to be done in this direction."

"Yes, sire; but he bestows a great favour on you."

"Any favour that costs much, Bertrand, is no longer one
for a king whose coffers are empty."

"Sire, he bestows it on you gratuitously."

"Then tell me quickly, Bertrand, what this favour is."

"Sire, at this moment the Free Companies are the scourge of France; is it not so?"

"Yes, certes, but has his Holiness discovered any means of getting rid of them?"

"No, sire, that is beyond his power, but he has excommunicated them."

"Ah, we only needed this to complete our destruction!" exclaimed the King, in despair; whilst Bertrand, who had triumphantly announced this piece of news, remained ignorant of the cause of his annoyance.

"From robbers they will become assassins—from wolves, tigers—for there were, perhaps, some few among them who still feared God, and they restrained the rest. Now they will have nothing either to fear or to restrain them—we are lost, my poor Bertrand!"

The worthy chevalier knew the fine mind and profound wisdom of the King. He possessed this quality, so precious in a man of inferior capacity, deference for a judgment superior to his own. Thus, he immediately began to reflect, and his natural good sense soon proved to him that the King was right.

"It is true," said he. "They will laugh finely when they learn that our Holy Father has treated them like Christians; and in return they will treat us like Jews and Mahometans."

"You see plainly, my dear Bertrand," said the King, "in what a position we stand."

"Ma foi! I never dreamt of it," said the chevalier. "I thought I was bringing you good news. Let me return to the Pope, and tell him there is no need for haste in the matter."

"Thanks, Bertrand," replied the King.

"Excuse me, sire, I am a bad ambassador—my business is to mount my horse and charge when you cry out, 'To horse, Duguesclin!' But in all matters discussed by pen instead of sword strokes, I confess, sire, I am but a poor politician."

"Nevertheless, my dear Bertrand," said the King, "if you will assist me, all may yet be saved."

"How—if I will aid you, sire? That I will, right willingly—my arm, my sword, my body, are all at your disposal."

"Ah, you do not understand me!" said the King, with a sigh.

" Ah, sire, that is very possible, for my head is rather thick, which is on the whole a happy thing for me; for I have received so many knocks upon it, that if nature had not made it of this consistency, it would have been by this time seriously damaged!"

" I was wrong in saying you could not understand me, my dear Bertrand ; I should have said you would not."

" That I would not !" repeated Bertrand in astonishment.

" Yes, my dear Bertrand," said the King, " because we are not in general willing to understand things foreign to our natures, our habits, and our inclinations ; and what I am about to ask you will at first appear both strange and singular."

" Go on, sire," said Duguesclin.

" Bertrand," continued the King, " you are acquainted with the history of France—are you not?"

" Not very well, sire. I know a little about Brittany, because that is my own province."

" But at least you have heard of all the great defeats, which at various times have reduced the kingdom down to the brink of ruin?"

" Oh, as to that, yes, sire! Your Majesty, doubtless, refers to the battle of Coutray, for instance, where the Comte d'Artois was slain ; or the battle of Creçy, where Philip of Valois was obliged to fly ; or lastly, to the battle of Poitiers, where King John was made prisoner."

" Well, Bertrand," continued the King, " have you ever reflected on the cause of these defeats?"

" No, sire, I reflect as little as possible ; it fatigues me."

" Yes, I understand that ; but I have myself reflected on this subject, and discovered the cause."

" Really, sire !"—" Yes, and I will tell it you."

" I am all attention, sire."

" Have you ever remarked that immediately the French assemble on the field of battle, instead of entrenching themselves, like the Flemings, behind their pikes, or, like the English, behind their lances, or taking advantage of a propitious moment to make the attack, they charge pell-mell, regardless of their position, each man having but one thought, that of being foremost, and dealing the most blows? It is this absence of unity—for each one consults only his own will, and obeys but one law, that of his own caprice—that enables the Flemings and the English, who are steady and disciplined troops, obeying the voice of a single leader, and striking together—to almost always defeat us."

"It is true," said Duguesclin, "all takes place much as you say; but how is it possible to prevent the French charging when the enemy is before them?"

"Yet it must come to that, my good Duguesclin," said Charles.

"That might be possible if the King himself were at our head; his voice might perhaps be heard."

"You are mistaken in that, my dear Duguesclin," said the King. "My nature is known to be pacific, altogether different from that of my father, King John, and my brother, Philip. It is believed that fear alone hinders me from marching against the enemy, since it is the custom of the Kings of France to lead their armies wherever an enemy presents itself; therefore it is only by a well-known courage, an established renown, a spotless reputation, that such a miracle could be accomplished. It is by Bertrand Duguesclin, if he chooses!"

"By me, sire!" exclaimed the chevalier, with eyes opened to their widest extent.

"Yes, by you, and you alone, since, thank God, it is well known that you love danger; and that, when you avoid it, no one can suspect that your caution proceeds from fear."

"Sire, you are very good to say so; but all these knights and gentlemen, whom will they obey?"—"You, Bertrand."

"Me, sire!" repeated the chevalier, shaking his head. "A poor countryman like me give orders to your nobles, one half of whom are of far higher rank than myself!"

"Bertrand, if you will assist—if you will serve—if you will understand me, with one word I will make you greater than them all."

"You, sire?"—"Yes, I," replied Charles V.

"And how will you do it, sire?"

"I will make you Lord High Constable."

Bertrand burst out laughing. "Your Majesty is pleased to jest with me," said he at last.

"Not so, Bertrand," said the King. "On the contrary, I am speaking seriously."

"But, sire, that sword with its blade decorated with *fleurs-de-lys* is accustomed to glitter only in almost royal hands."

"And that is precisely the misfortune of nations," said

I

the King ; " for the princes on whom this sword is conferred
regard it rather as an appendage of their rank than a reward
for their services.   Receiving it in virtue of their birth, as it
were, and not from the hands of the King, they forget the
duties imposed by it ; whilst you, Duguesclin, each time you draw
it from its scabbard, will think of the King who gave it you,
and the recommendations by which it was accompanied."

" The fact is, sire," said Duguesclin, " that if I were ever
to have such an honour conferred on me—but, no ; it is impossible !"

" How impossible ?"

" Yes, yes, it would only be wronging your Majesty ; besides they would not consider my rank high enough to yield
me obedience."

" Only obey me," said Charles, his face assuming a determined expression, " and I will see that you are obeyed by
others."   Duguesclin shook his head doubtfully.   " Listen,
Duguesclin," continued the King, " do you believe our too
great bravery to be the sole cause of our being beaten ?"

" Ma foi !" said Duguesclin, " I confess I never thought
that ; but on reflection, I am of your Majesty's opinion."

" Very well, then, my good Bertrand, all will go well.   We
must not attempt to fight the English, but to drive them
from the country ; and for this, no battles, Duguesclin, no
battles ! only skirmishes, encounters, and ambuscadoes.   We
must destroy our enemies in detail, one by one, on the borders
of woods, the fording of rivers, in the villages where they
are lingering.   The means will be longer, I well see, but they
will be more sure."

" Good heavens ! yes, sire ; I know it well, but your nobles
will never consent to wage such a war !"

" But by the Holy Trinity they must consent to wage it,
when there are two men resolved upon it, and these two
King Charles V. and Bertrand Duguesclin."

" But for that it is requisite for the constable to possess
the same power as King Charles."

" You shall possess the same, Bertrand ; I will cede to you
my right of life and death."

" Over the peasantry, yes, sire ; but over the gentlemen ?"

" Equally so over the gentlemen."

" Reflect, sire ; you have princes in your army,"

" You shall have power over them all, the princes as well

as the gentlemen. Listen, Duguesclin, I have three brothers, the Dukes d'Anjou, Burgundy, and De Berry. Well, these shall be, not your lieutenants, but your men ; they will teach obedience to the other nobles, and if one of them fails in obedience to you, you shall summon the headsman, and he shall lose his head on the spot as a traitor."

Duguesclin regarded the King with astonishment, for he had never before heard him, generally so mild and merciful, speak with a similar determination.

The King's look confirmed what his lips had just uttered.

"Well, sire," said Duguesclin, "since you place these means at my disposal, I will obey your Majesty—I will try."

"Yes, my good Duguesclin," interrupted the King, laying both his hands on the chevalier's shoulders, "you will not only try, but you will succeed. Meanwhile, I will occupy myself with finance. I will replenish my treasury coffers. I will finish building my fortress of the Bastile, repair the walls of Paris, or rather re-enclose it. I will found a library ; for it is not enough to merely nourish men's bodies, their minds also have need of food. We are at present mere barbarians. Duguesclin : thinking more about removing the rust from our cuirasses than from our intellects. The Moors, whom we despise, are our superiors ; they have poets, historians, and legislators, whilst we have nothing of the kind."

"True, sire," said Duguesclin ; "yet we appear to do very well without them."

"As England does without the sun, because she cannot do otherwise ; but if the good God preserves my life and your courage, Duguesclin, we two will bestow on France all that is now wanting in her, and in order to do this, the first thing to give her is peace."

"And above all," said Duguesclin, "to find means of ridding her of those Free Companies, although that could only be accomplished by a miracle."

"Well, then, God will perform this miracle ; we are both too pious Christians, and our intentions are too good for Him not to come to our aid."

At this moment the doctor ventured to open the door.

"Sire," said he, "your Majesty forgets the two chevaliers."

"Ah, true !" exclaimed the King. "But it was because Duguesclin and I were just finding out how to make France the first country in the world. Now let them enter."

The two chevaliers were immediately introduced. The King advanced towards them. Only one of them had his visor raised. He was unknown to the King, but the smile with which he greeted him was not the less benevolent on that account.

"You demanded an interview with me, chevalier, and they tell me on important business?" said the King.

"It is true, sire," replied the chevalier.

"You are welcome, then," said Charles.

"Do not welcome me too hastily, my King," said the young man, "for I am the bearer of sad tidings."

A melancholy smile hovered for an instant on the King's lips. "Sad tidings!" he repeated, "it is long since I received any other. But we are not one of those who confound the messenger with the tidings he brings. Speak, then, chevalier.'

"Alas, sire!"

"From what country do you come?"—"From Spain, sire."

"It is long since we heard anything good in that direction, therefore whatever you may have to tell will not surprise me."

"Sire, the King of Castile has put to death the sister of our Queen." Charles made a gesture of horror; the chevalier continued :—"He first dishonoured her by calumny, and then caused her to be assassinated."

"Assassinated! my sister assassinated!" exclaimed the King, turning pale; "impossible!"

The chevalier, who was kneeling at his feet, rose abruptly. "Sire," said he, in an agitated voice, "it is unjust for a monarch thus to insult a loyal subject, who has already suffered so deeply in the service of his prince. Since you will not believe my statement, here is the Queen's ring—you will perhaps credit that more than me."

Charles V. took the ring and carefully examined it; then by degrees his breast swelled and his eyes filled with tears. "Alas! alas!" said he; "it is really hers—I recognise it, for it was my gift to her. Do you hear, Bertrand?—another blow," he continued, turning to Duguesclin.

"Sire," said the worthy chevalier, "you owe this young man an apology for your hasty speech to him."

"Yes," said Charles, "yes; but he will pardon me, for I am overcome with grief. At first I would not believe it, and even now I cannot."

The second chevalier approached and raising the visor of his casque—"Will you believe me, sire," said he, "if I confirm what he has just said? Will you believe me, a child of France, who studied chivalry by your side, and whom you so fondly loved?"

"My boy! my son, Henry de Transtamare!" cried Charles. "Oh, thanks! in the midst of all these miseries you have returned to me!"

"I am come, sire, to deplore with you the cruel death of the Queen of Castile, and to seek safety by placing myself under your protection; for if Don Pedro has murdered your sister, Donna Bianca, he has done the same to my brother, Don Frederick."

Bertrand Duguesclin became crimson with anger, his eyes blazed with indignation and the desire of vengeance. "He is a wicked prince," cried he; "and if I were only King of France—"

"Well, what would you do?" interrupted Charles, turning quickly towards him.

"Sire," continued Henry, still kneeling, "save and protect me!"

"I will endeavour to do so," said the King. "But how was it that you, a Spaniard, coming direct from Spain, and deeply interested in this affair, remained in the background, while this chevalier recounted it to me?"

"Because, sire," replied Henry, "this chevalier, whom I recommend to you as one of the noblest and most loyal I know, has rendered me a signal service; and I therefore simply accorded him the honour he merited in letting him speak to you first. He has not only rescued me from the hands of the captain of one of the Free Companies, and since been my loyal companion, but no one is better fitted to speak to your Majesty on this subject than himself, for he was a witness to the dying agonies of the Queen of Castile, and held in his hand the gory head of my unfortunate brother."

At these words, broken by sobs and tears, Charles appeared to be almost distracted with grief, and Bertrand Duguesclin stamped his foot violently on the ground.

Henry watched between the fingers of the gauntleted hand with which he had covered his eyes the effect produced by what he had said, and this surpassed his hopes.

"Well," exclaimed the enraged King, "these tidings shall be made known to my people, and may God punish me if in my turn I do not unchain the demon of war which I have so long

kept fettered in his den. Yes, though I die in the struggle!
—though I fall on the body of my last man!—though France
herself be swallowed up, my sister shall be avenged!" But
as Charles grew animated, Bertrand became thoughtful.

"Such a king as Don Pedro dishonours the throne of
Castile!" cried Henry.

"Marshal," said Charles, addressing himself to Bertrand,
"your three thousand lances will now be useful to us."

"I raised them for France, and not to pass beyond the
mountains—that will make us too many wars at one time.
What your Majesty has just said makes me reflect that whilst
we are making war on Spain, the English will re-enter France,
and unite their forces with the Free Companies, and then we
should succumb to them."

"It is, doubtless, God's will to thus order the destinies of
the kingdom," said Charles; "but it will be known why the
King of France thus sacrifices his fortunes. The nation may
perish, but at least in a more just and important cause than
the possession of a tract of land or an ambassador's quarrel."

"Ah, sire!" said Bertrand, "if you only had money!"

"I have money," replied the King in a low tone, as though
fearing lest his words should be heard beyond the apartment;
"but that will not restore either my sister or his brother to life."

"True, sire," said Duguesclin; "but it will enable us to
avenge them, and that without impoverishing France."

"Explain yourself," said Charles.

"With money, sire," answered Bertrand, "we could enrol
under our banner some of the captains of these companies.
They are devils, to whom it matters little for whom they fight,
so long as they fight for money."

"And I," said Mauleon, timidly, "if your Majesty will
permit me to say a single word—"

"Listen to him, sire," said Henry; "for, notwithstanding
his youth, he is as wise as he is brave and loyal."

"Speak," said Charles.

"I believe, sire, I understood you to say that these Free
Companies were a great expense to you?"

"They devastate my kingdom, chevalier, and ruin my
subjects."

"Well, sire," said Mauleon, "there are, perhaps, means of
delivering you from them."

"Oh, speak! speak!" exclaimed the King.

"Sire, at this moment all these bands are assembled together on the banks of the Saône. No longer finding prey in the States ruined by war, they will turn like famished ravens towards the first repast that offers. Therefore, let Messire Duguesclin (who is known and respected to the last man among them) go to them, place himself at their head, and offer to lead them to Castile, where there is so much to pillage and to burn, and you will see them, in their trust in this great captain, with one accord march beneath his banner on this novel crusade."

"But if I were to go to them," said Bertrand, "should I not run some risk of being detained by them and forced to pay ransom? I am only a poor Breton knight."

"Yes," said Charles; "but you have kings for your friends."

"And I," said Mauleon, "humbly offer myself to introduce you to the most redoubtable amongst them, Sir Hugh Caverley."

"Who are you, then?" demanded Bertrand.

"No one, messire—or at least a person of very little consequence, but I fell into the hands of these bandits, and taught them to respect my word, since it was on that they released me. And when I quit your Majesty's presence it will be to carry back to them the thousand crowns I owe them, with which Don Henry has kindly presented me, and to enrol myself for one year in their company."

"You among these bandits!" said Duguesclin.

"Messire," said Mauleon, "I pledged my word, and it was only on this condition they let me out of their hands; besides, when you command them, they will no longer be bandits, but soldiers."

"And you think they will go?" said the King, animated by hope. "You think they will quit France—consent to abandon the kingdom?"

"Sire, I am sure of what I say," said Mauleon; "and here are at once twenty-five thousand soldiers for you."

"And·I will lead them so far," said Bertrand, "that not a soul among them shall ever return to France. I swear it to you, my good King! They wish for war—by Heaven, they shall have it!"

"That is what I was about to observe," said Mauleon, "and Messire Duguesclin has completed my thought."

"But who, then, are you?" demanded the King, eyeing him with astonishment.

"Sire," replied Agenor, "I am a simple chevalier of Bigorre, serving, as I before told your Majesty, in one of the Free Companies."

"Since when?" asked the King.—"Four days ago, sire."

"And what was the cause of your joining them?"

"Relate the circumstances, chevalier," said Don Henry; "for the recital only reflects credit upon you."

And Mauleon related to King Charles V. and Duguesclin the history of his engagement with Caverley in a manner that charmed the King, who understood and appreciated wisdom as much as the marshal did valour.

CHAPTER XIV.

THE AMBASSADOR.

CHARLES V. was too wise a prince, and had too deeply studied the affairs of his kingdom, not to perceive at the first glance the advantages that would result from a disposition of events such as Mauleon suggested, and offered to prepare the way for. The English, deprived of the aid of the Free Companies— those scourges of the country—would necessarily find themselves obliged to hire troops to replace those which paid themselves by making on their own account a lucrative war that ruined the kingdom. The result of this must be a truce with France, during which, new institutes would give the inhabitants a little repose, and permit the King to finish the great works he had commenced for the embellishment of Paris, and the amelioration of financial affairs. As to the war with Spain—Duguesclin saw nothing to prevent it—the French cavalry was superior in strength and tactics to any other in the world, therefore the Castilians ought to be beaten. Besides Bertrand reckoned on getting cheaply rid of his companies; knowing that the dearer the victory cost him, the better it would be for France ; and that the more corpses strewed the Spanish battle-field, the fewer robbers there would be for him to lead back.

The politics of this period were utterly selfish, or at least purely personal. The world had not yet conceived the idea of putting into circulation those principles of international rights which have since then so simplified questions of war between hostile sovereigns. Each monarch made war on his own account, and with his own resources, and by this means acquired—either by persuasion, strength, or money—power of which many of them were not slow to avail themselves.

"Don Pedro has put his brother to death and murdered my sister," said King Charles to himself. "But he will make it appear that he was in the right, unless I manage my affairs so as to prove him in the wrong."

Don Henry de Transtamare said, "I am the eldest son, for I was born in 1333, and my brother Don Pedro in 1336. My father, King Alphonso, was affianced to my mother Eleonora de Guzman, therefore, although he did not actually espouse her, she was in reality his lawful wife. Chance alone has made me what the world calls illegitimate. But if this excellent reason were not sufficient, Heaven itself sends me both private injuries and political crimes to revenge. Don Pedro has attempted to dishonour my wife—he is the assassin of my brother Don Frederick—and to crown all, he has put the sister of the King of France to death. Thus I have good reasons for wishing to dethrone him, more especially as, if I succeed, I shall in all probability ascend the throne in his stead."

Don Pedro said to himself, "Legitimate son and rightful King, I espoused—in virtue of a treaty which gave me France as an ally—a young princess of the blood royal, named Blanche of Bourbon. Instead of loving me, as was her duty to do, she had bestowed her affections on my brother, Don Frederick; and as if this was not enough for me, after having been constrained to contract a political alliance, my wife took part with my brothers, Henry and Tello, who were making war against me; thus committing the crime of high treason. More, she caused her name to be coupled with Don Frederick's;—this was a capital crime, therefore I had a right to put them both to death."

But when he cast his eyes around him to convince himself that this right was well founded, he only beheld his Castilians, his Moors, and his Jews, whilst Don Henry had on his side Arragon, France, and the Pope. The game was not equal, therefore Don Pedro—one of the cleverest princes of the period—secretly confessed to himself that, although he began by thinking himself in the right, it was not improbable that he might end by finding himself in the wrong.

Preparations were quickly commenced at the court of France. King Charles lost no unnecessary time in placing

the sword of high constable in the hands of Bertrand Duguesclin, and in ·delivering an harangue to the princes and
nobles of his army, in which—after informing them of the
honour he had conferred on a Breton gentleman—he invited
them to obey the new constable, as they would himself. Then,
as it was above all things necessary to secure the co-operation
of the Free Companies in the projected expedition, before
any rumour of it should be bruited abroad, for fear of Don
Pedro bribing them—not to join him in Spain—but to remain in France, which would effectually hinder the King
from leading his forces elsewhere, the King took leave of the
constable and the chevalier who was to introduce him.

Prince Henry de Transtamare, assured of the King's aid
and protection, accompanied them as a simple knight. The
journey was accomplished without any adventure. The ambassadors were only attended by their squires, their personal
attendants, and a dozen men-at-arms. They speedily arrived
in sight of the Saône and the innumerable tents of the Free
Companies, who deserting the already ravaged borders of
France, were little by little approaching its centre, like hunters
driving the game before them, and like another horde of barbarians awaiting the coming of a second Aétius, had united
their banners on its fertile plains.

Agenor left the constable in safety at the stronghold of
La Rochfort, which still belonged to King Charles; and after
taking this precaution, set out alone, and without hesitation
again cast himself into the nets of the robbers. The captain
on that day commanding the outposts, and before whom
Agenor was brought, was one almost as well known as Sir
Hugh Caverley himself, and styled "The Green Knight."
The chevalier, however, not being disposed to pay two ransoms, demanded Sir Hugh Caverley, and was accompanied to
his tent by the Green Knight himself. The redoubtable
chief of the adventurers uttered an exclamation of satisfaction on perceiving his ancient prisoner, or rather his future
associate. Before entering into any explanation, Agenor beckoned Muscaron forward, who drew from a leathern bag—tolerably well filled through the munificence of King Charles
and Prince Henry de Transtamare—a thousand crowns, which
he arranged upon the table.

" Ah ! this is a good sign, comrade," said Sir Hugh, when
the last pile of money had been built beside the nine former

ones. "I confess I did not expect to see you so soon again. Then you are already reconciled to the idea of living amongst us, which at first caused you such consternation ?"

" Yes, captain, since a true soldier can live anywhere and everywhere. And then, besides that, I thought good news could never arrive too soon ; and I have brought you some of a nature that I am very sure you are far from expecting."

" Bah !" said Caverley, who began to suspect from this commencement, that Mauleon was laying a trap for him, so as to free himself from his plighted word. " Bah ! extraordinary tidings, you say ?"

" Sir Captain," replied Mauleon, " I spoke about you the other day to the King of France—to whom, as you know, I was sent by his dying sister—and related to him the courteous treatment I had experienced at your hands."

" Ha ! ha !" said Caverley, highly flattered ; "then the King of France knows me ?"

" Certes, captain, the ravages you have committed on his kingdom are enough to make him know you ; the cries of roasted monks, the lamentations of ravished women, the complaints of citizens forced to pay heavy ransoms, have made your name ring in his ears."

Caverley fairly quivered with pride and pleasure beneath his black armour ; there was something terrible in the joy of this iron statue. " Then it is thus," said he, "that the King knows me, that Charles V. knows the name of Hugh Caverley !"

" He knows, and I will answer for it, will not forget it !" replied Mauleon.

" And what did he say to you about me ?"

" The King said to me, ' Chevalier, go and find this good Sir Hugh, or rather,' he added"——the captain seemed to hang with suspended breath on the words falling from Mauleon's lips—" ' or rather,' " continued Agenor, " ' I will send him one of my best servants.' "

" One of his best servants !"—" Yes."

"But a gentleman, I hope ?"—" Parbleu !"

" Of high rank ? "—" Very."

" His Majesty does me much honour," replied Caverley, re-assuming his grumbling tone ; "but this good King Charles V. must require something of me, then ?"

" He wishes to enrich you, captain."

"Young man—young man," said the adventurer, with sudden coldness, "do not jest with me, for it is a game for which those who play at it, pay dearly. The King of France may possibly require something of me—my head, for instance —for I well know he would not be sorry to have it; but however cleverly he may set about it, I regret to tell you, chevalier, that he will not obtain it through your interposition."

"This is the result of always having done evil!" said Mauleon, gravely; his noble countenance inspiring the robber with a feeling of almost respect. "You mistrust and accuse every one, and even calumniate the King, who deserves the love of the most honest man in his kingdom! I begin to think, captain," continued he, shaking his head, "that the King has been wrong in sending his deputy to you—an honour mutually rendered between princes—for you are now speaking like a robber captain instead of a prince."

"But," said Caverley, somewhat nettled at this bold speech, "it is wise to be cautious, my dear friend; and frankly, how could the King regard me with favour after the cries of those roasted monks, ravished women, and plundered citizens, ringing in his ears, as you just now so eloquently described?"

"Very well," said Mauleon: "then I see what course remains for me to pursue."

"And what is that?" asked Sir Hugh.

"To send and inform his Majesty's ambassador that his mission is at an end—inasmuch as the captain of a band of adventurers doubts the word of his Majesty King Charles V.!" and Mauleon strode towards the door of the tent to put his threat into execution.

"Stay! stay!" exclaimed Caverley; "I have not uttered a syllable of what you think, or thought a word of what you say. Besides, there will be plenty of time to send back this ambassador. Now, on the contrary, let him come hither, and he shall be made welcome."

Mauleon shook his head. "The King of France distrusts you," said he, coldly. "And he will not allow one of his principal servants to enter your camp, without your giving him a sufficient guarantee for his safety."

"By the Pope!" roared Caverley, "you insult me, comrade."

"Not so, my good captain," retorted Agenor; "for you set us the example of distrust."

"But, mordieu ! does not every one know that the envoy of a king is sacred, even to us who hold few things so? Is this one, then, anything particular?"

"Perhaps so."—"Then I will see him, if only out of curiosity?"

"In that case, sign a regular safe-conduct."—"That is easily done."

"Yes ; but you are not alone here, captain, and I came to you in particular, because you are the first leader amongst them ; and I had, besides, the advantage of being connected with you, and not with the others."

"Then the message is not to me alone?"

"It is to all the leaders of the Free Companies."

"Then is it not only me the good King Charles wishes to enrich?" said Caverley, in a discontented tone.

"His Majesty King Charles is powerful enough to enrich, if he chooses, all the thieves in the kingdom !" replied Mauleon, with a laugh far surpassing Caverley's in irony.

It appeared as if this rough mode of speech was the only one in which to address the robber captain, for this sally put all his ill-humour to flight. "Fetch hither my clerk," said he, "and let him write a regular safe-conduct."

A tall, lean, trembling man, clad all in black, came forward ; he was the schoolmaster of the neighbouring village, whom Captain Hugh Caverley had in the interim elevated to the dignity of his secretary. He wrote under Muscaron's inspection the most precise and complete safe-conduct that had ever issued from a doctor's pen. Then, the captain, causing a page to summon his fellow-leaders, commenced —either because he could not write, or had some reason best known to himself for declining to remove his iron gauntlets —by himself placing the impression of his dagger's hilt beneath the writing, whilst the other chiefs, in turn, affixed beneath this monogram, some their crosses, some their seals, and some even a flourishing signature ; and all, while executing this manœuvre, laughed heartily among themselves, esteeming themselves far superior to any princes on earth— they who granted safe-conducts to the ambassador of the King of France. When all the seals and signatures had been affixed to the parchment, Caverley turned towards Mauleon. "And the name of this messenger," said he. "You will learn it when he comes," said Agenor. "That is to say, if he deigns to acquaint you with it."—"It is some baron," said the Green Knight, laughing, "whose chateau we have burned, and wife carried away, and who is coming to see if there is no means of bartering his horse or his ger-falcon for his loving spouse!"

"Don your best armour," said Mauleon, proudly, "and let your pages, if you have any, be arrayed in their richest attire; bid them, also, if you would avoid committing a great error unworthy of men learned in the science of arms, keep silence, when the person I shall announce, enters." And Mauleon quitted the camp with the air of a man who felt the responsibility of what he has undertaken.

A murmur of surprise and doubt ran through the group. "He is mad!" exclaimed several voices.

"Oh, you do not know him," said Caverley. "No, no; he is not mad, and we may expect something new."

Half the day had passed away. The camp had resumed its usual aspect. Some of the men were bathing in the river —some sat drinking and carousing beneath the trees, and others were wrestling on the grass. Bands of plunderers were seen returning homewards, their coming heralded by mingled cries of joy and distress, followed by the spectacle of dishevelled women, and slaughtered men dragged along at the tails of their horses. Cattle, terrified at their new mas-ters, were being driven, bellowing, towards the tents where they were immediately slaughtered and prepared for the evening repast, whilst the chiefs proceeded to inspect the results of the expedition, and to choose their share of the booty, the division of which did not take place without sun-dry grave conflicts between drunken or greedy soldiers. At a little distance the fresh recruits were being drilled; pea-sants who, torn from their huts, and forced to take up arms with them, would at the end of three or four years, forsake everything to become, like their new companions, men of blood and rapine. Troops of valets and crowds of soldiers' boys were straying about, or preparing their masters' re-pasts. Barrels, with the heads staved in, broken furniture and rags of all description, strewed the ground, whilst herds of enormous dogs, without masters, prowled around these various groups in quest of food, pilfering the robbers, and terrifying the children.

All at once, at the entrance of this camp, which we have

attempted to describe, but of which, the sight alone could give any just idea, resounded the loud burst of four trum pets, and four trumpeters appeared, preceded by a white banner, covered with numberless *fleurs-de-lys*, which at this period formed the arms of France. This immediately gave rise to great confusion in the camp of the adventurers. The drums beat, the under officers hastened to re-assemble the stragglers and guard the principal posts. Soon, amidst a throng of curious and astonished faces, appeared a solemn *cortége*. First came the four trumpeters, whose flourishes had aroused the camp ; then a herald man-at-arms, bearing aloft the naked sword of the constable, with its golden hilt, and blade ornamented with *fleurs-de-lys ;* and lastly, preceded by a dozen men-at-arms, or rather a dozen iron statues, came a knight of proud bearing, with his visor closed. His powerful horse champed a golden bit, and a long sword, the hilt polished by constant use, glittered at his side. Near this knight, but a little behind him, came Mauleon. He conducted the whole troop to the general tent where the chiefs were assembled in council. The deep silence of astonishment and expectation now reigned in the camp, which a few moments before rang with noisy clamour. The knight who appeared to be the leader of the little troop, dis-mounted, and waving the banner of France to the sound of the trumpets, entered the tent. The chiefs did not rise from their seats, but glanced meaningly at each other.

"This is the banner of his Majesty the King of France," said the knight, in a clear and distinct voice, bowing before it as he spoke.

"We recognise it perfectly," said Sir Hugh Caverley, rising to reply to the stranger; "and we wait for the envoy of his Majesty to declare his name, to enable us to bow before him, as he has himself just done before the royal standard of his master."

"I am Bertrand Duguesclin," said the knight, calmly, and at the same time raising the visor of his casque, "Constable of France, and deputed by his Majesty King Charles V. to treat with the leaders of the Free Companies, to whom God grant all joy and prosperity."

He had scarcely concluded his speech before all heads were uncovered and all swords drawn from their scabbards and brandished in the air with the wildest enthusiasm. He was

greeted on all sides by welcoming shouts, and this electric fire
spreading like a train of gunpowder throughout the camp,
the whole army assembled about the door of the tent, clashing
their swords and pikes, and crying out, "Noël! Noël! good
luck to the brave constable!"

Bertrand bowed with his usual humility, and saluted them,
amidst thunders of applause.

CHAPTER XV.
THE FREE COMPANIES.

THIS first moment of enthusiasm soon gave place to such deep
attention that the constable's words, clearly and distinctly
pronounced as they were, pierced the ranks of the crowd and
were plainly heard at the other end of the camp, where, to
the last man amongst them, they were eagerly listened to.

"Sir Captain," commenced Bertrand, with that almost ob-
sequious politeness which gained him the hearts of all those
with whom he had dealings, "the King of France sends me
to you, that by your aid I may accomplish, perhaps, the only
object worthy of brave warriors like yourselves." This was a
flattering exordium, but the general character of mind among
the captains of the Free Companies being distrust, their ignorance of the constable's ultimate designs somewhat damped
their enthusiasm; seeing, therefore, that he must proceed to
particulars, and profiting by the impression he had just made,
he continued:—" You have each of you won enough glory to
be indifferent about winning more, but not one among you is
possessed of sufficient wealth to say, 'I am rich enough.'
Besides, you ought by this time to have arrived at that point
where men wish to unite the honour of their profession with
the profit that should accrue from it. Thus, worthy captains,
figure to yourselves what an expedition would be directed by
you against a rich and powerful prince, whose spoils, falling
into your hands by the rights of legitimate war, would furnish
you with trophies as glorious as productive. I am myself an
adventurer like yourselves—like you, a soldier of fortune.
Are you not, then, like me, weary of the oppression we
have exercised over enemies weaker than ourselves? Would
you not rather hear, instead of the sobs of children and the
cries of women, which fell on my ears as I passed through
the camp, the flourish of trumpets announcing a real engage-

ment, and the tramp of an enemy whom we must fight to conquer? In short, brave knights of all nations, who have, consequently, all of you your national honour to sustain, would you not be glad, setting aside the riches and glory I have promised you, to unite together in a cause glorious to humanity? For, after all, what a life we lead! No God-elected prince authorizes our rapine and our exactions. The blood we shed too often cries aloud for vengeance, and its voice not only mounts up to Heaven, but sometimes, in spite of ourselves, shakes our souls, hardened by the horrors of war."

This time a long murmur of approbation ran through the ranks of captains; for the voice of this rude breaker of lances, the most famous skirmisher of the period, had a great effect upon them. All had witnessed Bertrand's prowess in the hour of battle—many had felt the keen edge of his sword, or the force of his stalwart arm; and they seemed with one accord inclined to follow the opinion of such a soldier.

"My friends," continued Bertrand, overjoyed at perceiving the effects of the first part of his discourse, "this is the plan his Majesty Charles V. has confided to me to execute. In Spain, the Moors and Saracens have become more insolent and more cruel than ever; but in Castile reigns a prince worse than either Moors or Saracens, for he has murdered his brother, a belted knight, wearing both chain and golden spurs, and assassinated his wife, the sister of our King Charles —by this means setting the chivalry of the whole world at defiance; for whilst there is a chevalier remaining in Christendom such a crime could not be allowed to go unpunished." This second part of his speech made but a slight impression on the adventurers. Although killing his brother and assassinating his wife might be somewhat irregular acts, they did not appear to them crimes of sufficient magnitude to render it necessary to embroil twenty-five thousand honest fellows to avenge them. Duguesclin perceived that his cause was weakened; but, without being discouraged, he resumed :—"See, comrades, if a more glorious, and above all more useful, crusade was ever contemplated. You know Spain—some of you have passed through it, and all have heard speak of it;—Spain, the land of silver mines—Spain, with its palaces paved with Moorish treasures, and where Moors and Saracens are rolling in wealth the spoils of half the world—Spain, where the women are so fair that for the love of one of them King Roderigo lost his

K

kingdom. Well, it is thither I will lead you, if you are willing to follow me; it is thither I go, accompanied by a few brave hearts, chosen among the best lances of France, to learn whether the Spanish knights are as cowardly as their master, and to prove whether the temper of their blades equals that of our battle-axes. Say, captains, will you join me?"

The constable terminated his discourse. Hugh Caverley, who during this harangue had appeared as excited as if the demon of war was already urging his war-horse on to battle, hastily went round the circle of chiefs, asking each one's opinion, after which he returned to Bertrand Duguesclin, who stood leaning on his long sword, and conversing quietly with Agenor and Henry de Transtamare, whose heart was beating violently, since for him, unknown and unnoticed as he was among the crowd, the result of this scene was either a throne or obscurity—life or death. Men of this stamp, in place of a heart, possess only ambition, and to this every wound is a fatal one. The chiefs deliberated for a few moments, then Hugh Caverley approached the constable, and, in the midst of a profound silence, said to him:—

"Honoured Bertrand Duguesclin, beau sire, brother and companion, you, who are the very mirror of chivalry, know that, for your valour and loyalty, we are ready to serve you. You shall be our chief and not our associate—our captain and not our equal; we belong to you, and will follow you to the ends of the earth. Give the word of command, and whether they be Moors, Saracens, or Spaniards, we will march against them. Only there are many English knights among us who love King Edward and his son, the Prince of Wales; with these exceptions, they will war against all who come in their way. Do you agree to that, beau sire?"

The constable bowed to the assembly with every sign of profound gratitude, and added a few words expressive of his sense of the honour done him by such warriors; and in that Bertrand spoke only the truth, for such homage rendered to his superiority was most flattering to a man of the fourteenth century, whose whole life was that of a soldier.

The news of this determination excited in the camp an enthusiasm difficult to describe. The prospect of exchanging the hard and uncertain life of adventurers for a sojourn beneath the bright sky of a new and almost virgin land, rich in wine and beauty—of re-conquering the spoils of the Moors,

Saracens, and Spaniards—all these were dreams that har-
monized well with the reality of having for their leader the
mirror of European chivalry, as the constable was styled by
Sir Hugh Caverley. Thus the constable was received with
frantic delight, and reached the tent prepared for him in the
highest part of the camp, beneath an archway of lances crossed
above his head by the wild soldiery, who bowed not before
the banner of France, but him who bore it.

"My lord," said Bertrand to Henry de Transtamare when
they were alone, and whilst Hugh Caverley and the Green
Knight were engaged in congratulating Agenor on his return,
and particularly on the circumstances attending it—"My lord,
you ought to be well satisfied, for the rudest part of our task
is accomplished. We are all content. These rascals will
fasten like greedy blood-suckers on these Moors, Saracens, and
Spaniards, and sting them outrageously. They will at the
same time benefit us and themselves—while enriching themselves, they will gain you a throne. I reckon on the fevers
of Andalusia, mountain ambushes, the passage of the rivers,
whose rapid current carries away here both men and horses;
the enervating influence of wine and voluptuousness, laying
low half these bandits. The others will perish, I trust, beneath
the swords of the Saracens, Moors, and Spaniards. We shall
then indeed be victors. I will place you on the throne of
Castile, and then, to the great satisfaction of King Charles,
return to France with my soldiers, whom, by the sacrifice of
these scoundrels, I shall avoid losing."

"Yes, messire," replied Henry de Transtamare; "but do
you not fear some unexpected movement on the part of Don
Pedro? He is an able general, and full of resources."

"I do not look so far ahead, prince," replied Duguesclin.
"The more trouble we have, the more glory we shall obtain,
and the more Green Knights and Hugh Caverleys we shall
leave on the good soil of Castile. How to effect our entrance
into Spain is the only thing that troubles me, since it is all
very well to make war on Don Pedro and his Moors and
Saracens, but not on entire Spain; for that, five hundred
companies would not suffice, and it is a very different matter
to support an army in Spain and in France."

"I have arranged," replied Henry, "to precede you, and
announce your coming to the King of Arragon, one of my
friends, who, for love of me and hatred of my brother Don

Pedro, will grant you free passage through his dominions, as well as assist you with men and money ; so that, if by chance we are defeated in Castile, we shall have some place to fall back upon."

"It is easily seen, my lord, that you were brought up by the good King Charles, who sheds his wisdom on all around him. Your counsel is full of prudence. Go, then, but beware lest you are taken prisoner, for then the war would at once be ended ; for, if I mistake not, our only object is the making and unmaking of a king."

"Ah, messire," said Henry, annoyed at the shrewdness of the man he had hitherto regarded as merely a rough soldier, "were Don Pedro once dethroned, would not you be glad to replace him by a faithful friend to France ?"

"Believe me, prince," replied Duguesclin, "Don Pedro would be a faithful enough friend to France, if France would only reciprocate the friendship. But that is not the point under discussion, and the question is decided in your favour. This miscreant, assassin—this Christian king, who disgraces Christianity, ought to be punished, and you will serve as well as any other for the instrument of God's justice. Therefore, my lord, since all is understood and arranged between us, set out at once ; for I am anxious to reach Spain before Don Pedro has time to unloose his purse-strings, and play us, as you say, some trick."

Henry made no reply ; he felt humiliated to the bottom of his heart at the protection of a simple gentleman to which he was forced to submit, under penalty of failing in his enterprise. But his ambition, and the crown he beheld glitter in his dreams of the future, consoled him under this passing humiliation. Thus, whilst Bertrand led the principal leaders of the Free Companies to Paris, in order to present them to King Charles, who by loading them with honours and largesses, disposed them to die merrily in his service, Henry, followed by Agenor, attended by his faithful Muscaron, re- turned to Spain by a different route from the one they had before pursued, for fear of meeting with those who, notwith- standing their being furnished with safe-conducts by not only Captain Caverley but also Bertrand Duguesclin, might still cause them no little uneasiness.

Don Henry, almost certain of not being recognised beneath he costume and under the name of a simple knight, wished to assure himself of the feeling of the English towards him, and to try whether it were possible to win over the Prince of Wales to his side; a result which did not seem impossible, after the eagerness displayed by the captains to follow Bertrand Duguesclin, a proceeding that plainly showed no cause had as yet been espoused by the Black Prince. To have as ally the son of Edward III., the youth who won his spurs at Crecy—the young man who defeated King John at Poitiers, was not only to double the moral force of his cause, but to pour into Castile five or six thousand more lances—that being the amount of troops of which the prince was able to dispose, without weakening his garrison of Guyenne.

The Black Prince held his court at Bordeaux, between which and France, if not peace, at least a truce subsisting—the two chevaliers entered without difficulty; it is true that it being the evening of a fête-day they were unnoticed amid the tumult. Agenor had at first proposed to Prince Henry to accompany him to the residence of his guardian, Messire Ernauton de St. Colombe, who had a house in the town, but the fear of his companion not being able to entirely conceal his secret made him refuse this offer. However, having learnt by his unsuccessful applications at all the auberges of the impossibility of his obtaining lodgings, owing to the great number of people assembled there, he was at last obliged to avail himself of Agenor's invitation. They therefore wended their way towards the dwelling of Messire Ernauton, which was situated in one of the environs of the city, after it having been fully understood between them that the title of prince was not to be pronounced, and that he was to pass as a simple chevalier, friend and brother-in-arms to Agenor. Chance befriended the travellers, for Messire Ernauton was at that moment absent on a visit to Mauleon, where he possessed a small property. Two or three servants alone remained at Bordeaux, and welcomed the young man as if he had been the son instead of the ward of the old chevalier. During the four years that had elapsed since Agenor last visited Bordeaux, a great change had taken place in the house. The immense gardens, forming a retreat alike inaccessible to the gaze of men and the rays of the sun, were now separated from the dwelling by a high wall, and seemed to form a separate residence. On questioning the old servants he learnt that the gardens, beneath whose sycamores and plane-trees his careless youth had been passed, had been sold by his guardian to the Prince of Wales, who had erected in them a magnificent mansion, where he entertained those guests whom he either could not or would not openly receive in his palace.

Don Henry made Agenor repeat this explanation in all its details, since, if our readers remember, he had come to Bordeaux for the express purpose of seeing the Black Prince, in the hope of gaining him as a friend. But it was now late, and the two travellers were both fatigued by their long journey; the prince therefore gave orders to the attendants to prepare his chamber, and retired immediately after supper. Agenor followed his example and sought his own room, which being situated on the first floor of the house, over-looked the beautiful gardens before mentioned. Instead of, like the prince, seeking his couch, he seated himself at the window, and fixing his eyes on the fine trees through whose foliage glimmered the moonlight, he occupied himself in re-tracing, with all the poetry of his twenty years, his progress down the tide of life from the flower-strewn course of in-fancy. The sky was cloudless, the air calm and sweet, the river glittered in the distance like the silver scales of an immense serpent ; but by a freak of imagination, whether from the similarity of the landscape at the same hour, or that the recollection of the orange-trees of Portugal was recalled by the sweet perfume of those of Guyenne, his thoughts tra-versed with fiery wings the distant mountains, and rested at the foot of the Sierra d'Estrella on the borders of that little river falling into the Tagus, on the opposite bank of which, attracted by the sound of her guzla, he had for the first time spoken of love to the beautiful Moorish maiden.

All at once, in the midst of these intoxicating reveries, a light proceeding from the mysterious palace twinkled like a star through the foliage, and a moment afterwards, by some strange miracle which Agenor took for a deception of the senses, he heard the sounds of a guzla. He tremblingly listened to the preluding chords, followed by a rich melodious voice, which it was impossible not to recognise after having once heard it, chanting in Castilian the following old Spanish romance :—

" Slow riding o'er the flowery mead
  There came a knight of Spanish race,
His lagging dogs of matchless breed,
His tired hawk, and weary steed,
  Proclaim'd him wending from the
    chase.

Beneath an oak tree's pleasant shade,
  He laid him down at close of day ;
The wind like distant clarions played,
The whispering leaves low music made,
  As tender as a lover's lay.

When 'midst the overhanging green,
  Sudden appeared a witching face,
The glorious eyes of azure sheen,
Gleaming the golden locks between
  With wild, almost unearthly grace.

And sounded on his startled ear,
  A gentle voice in accents mild ;—
' Oh fear not, gallant cavalier,
A magic spell detains me here,
  A royal father's only child !

  ' Condemn'd within this oak to dwell
  Until my fifteenth year be past ;
  To-morrow will unloose the spell,
  Oh, take me from my woodland cell,
  And let my lot with thee be cast !' "

Agenor stayed to hear no more ; he bounded from his seat, as though to shake off the illusion, and gazing eagerly on the plane-trees in the garden, he murmured with a feeling of feverish hope, " Aïssa ! Aïssa !"

CHAPTER XVI.

THE UNEXPECTED MEETING.

AGENOR once certain that it was Aïssa's voice he had heard, and yielding to an impulse very natural with a young man of twenty years of age, seized his sword, wrapped himself in his mantle, and prepared to make his way into the garden. But as he was about to spring from the window he felt a hand laid upon his shoulder ; he turned and beheld his squire.

"Master," said he, " I have always remarked, that although some few of the follies we commit are caused by passing through doors, the remainder—that is to say, the greater part—are committed by passing through windows."

Agenor was about to continue his descent, but Muscaron restrained him with respectful violence.

"Release me !" said the young man.

" Messire," said Muscaron, " I only ask you to grant me five minutes' attention, then you shall be at liberty to commit as many follies as you please."

"Do you know where I am going?"—"I fancy so."

"Do you know who is in the garden?"—"The Moorish girl."

"You have said it, Aïssa herself ! Now do you expect to keep me here ?"

"That depends, master, whether you are reasonable or mad."

"What do you mean?"

"That the Moorish girl is not alone."

"No; she is doubtless with her father, who never leaves her."

"And her father is himself always guarded by a dozen Moors."

"Well?"

"Well, they are all there wandering about beneath the trees. You might strike one of them and kill him, but a second would come at his cries. You might kill him also, but a third, a fourth, a fifth, would run to the rescue; there would be a struggle, a combat, a clashing of swords; you would be recognised, taken prisoner, perhaps killed."

"Be it so! I will see her, notwithstanding."

"Fie, master! A Moorish girl!"

"I am resolved to see her."

"I do not wish to hinder you, only do it without risk."

"Do you know any means of doing so?"

"Not of myself, but the prince will furnish you with means."

"How! the prince?"

"Undoubtedly; do you think Mothril's presence at Bordeaux will be less interesting to him than to yourself, or that when he hears of it, he will not be as anxious about what brings the father here as you are about the daughter?"

"You are right," said Agenor.

"Ah! you see it," said Muscaron, complacently.

"Well, go and inform the prince. I shall remain here so as not to lose sight of this little light."

"And you will have patience to await our coming?"

"I will listen," said his master.

Meanwhile, the sweet voice continued to sound upon the night air to the guzla's tinkling accompaniment.

Agenor no longer beheld before him the garden at Bordeaux. It was the garden of the Alcazar, with its Moorish kiosk and overhanging verdure. Each succeeding note of the guzla sank more deeply into his heart, filling it with delicious intoxication. He had scarcely fancied himself a moment alone, when he heard the door open, and Muscaron entered, followed by the prince, muffled like himself in his mantle, and bearing his sword in his hand. A few words were sufficient to make the prince acquainted with the state of affairs, for Mauleon had already related to him without reservation his former relations with the Moorish maiden, as well as Mothril's furious jealousy.

"Then," said the prince, "you should endeavour to obtain speech with this maiden. We should learn more from her than from all the spies in the world. A woman held in slavery often governs her tyrant."

"Yes, yes," cried Mauleon, burning with impatience to join Aïssa; "I am ready to obey your highness's commands."

"You are sure it was her voice you heard?"

"I heard it as distinctly as I now hear yours, monseigneur. Her voice came from yonder—it still vibrates on my ear, and would guide me through the darkness of hell itself."

"Our greatest difficulty will be to gain an entrance into the house, without falling in with some armed troops."

"You say *our*, monseigneur."

"Undoubtedly, I accompany you; but be it well understood, I shall keep on one side, and leave you at liberty to converse with your mistress."

"Then, monseigneur, there is nothing more to fear. Two chevaliers like ourselves are worth ten Christians and twenty Moors."

"True, chevalier; still be on your guard. See your mistress, but take all needful precautions."

"Yes; prudence, prudence!" muttered Muscaron.

"Yes; but by too much prudence I may lose her altogether," said Agenor.

"Rest easy," said Don Henry. "On my princely word, if ever I mount the throne of Castile, she shall be my first confiscation from the Moors. Meanwhile, let us try and win this throne."

"I await your highness's commands," replied Mauleon, with difficulty curbing his impatience.

"Good," replied Don Henry; "I know you are a well-disciplined soldier, and yet you will be none the worse for obeying me. We are captains, and therefore ought to know how to discover the weak side of a place. Let us descend into the gardens, examine the wall, and when we find a favourable spot, scale it."

"Ah! my lord," exclaimed Muscaron, "that would not be a difficult task, for I have seen a ladder in the courtyard. All parts of the wall would be equally favourable; but on the other side are Moors armed with scimitars, and forests of pikes. My master knows I am brave enough, but when

the lives of so illustrious a prince and so worthy a chevalier
are in question——"

"Speak only for the prince!"

"This good squire pleases me," said Henry; "he is prudent, and will make an invaluable vanguard." Then raising
his voice, "Perago!" said he, addressing a squire, who stood
at the door of the apartment, "are you armed?"

"Yes, monseigneur," said the person addressed.

"Then follow us."

Muscaron saw there was nothing more to be said; all he
had gained by his remonstrances was, that they made their
descent by the door instead of the window. There was, as
he said, a ladder in the courtyard; this he placed against the
wall. The prince mounted first, then Agenor, Perago, and
lastly Muscaron himself, who drew up the ladder after him,
and placed it on the other side.

"Stay and guard this ladder," said the prince; "for the
manner in which you spoke has given me full confidence in you."

Muscaron seated himself on the lowest rung of the ladder;
Perago was placed in ambush behind a fig-tree at twenty
paces' distance, whilst Henry and Agenor continued their
way, carefully keeping in the heavy shadow of the trees,
which naturally hid them from the observation of those in
the light. They were soon so near the dwelling, that although
the sound of the guzla had ceased, they could distinctly hear
the sighs of the musician.

"Prince," said Agenor, who could no longer restrain his
impatience, "wait for me in this bower of honeysuckle.
Before ten minutes have elapsed, I shall have spoken to the
Moorish maiden, and learnt from her the reason of her
father's visit to Bordeaux. If I am attacked, do not risk
your valuable life, but gain the ladder. I will warn you by
a single cry of 'To the wall!'"

"If you are attacked," replied Henry, "remember that
with the exception of Don Pedro my brother, and Bertrand
Duguesclin my master, perhaps no one can equal me in the
use of the long rapier. Then you shall see, chevalier, that I
do not boast without reason."

Agenor thanked the prince, who drew back into the dark
shadow of the trees, and continued his way towards the house,
between which and the grove lay a space brilliantly lighted
by the rays of the moon. For a moment he stood hesitating

whether to expose himself to this glare of light, when suddenly a side door of the house opened, creaking on its hinges, and gave egress to three men conversing together in an undertone. The one nearest to Agenor—who remained mute and motionless beneath the shadow of a plane-tree—was easily recognised by his white burnous as Mothril. The centre one was a knight in black armour, and the third attired in a magnificent Castilian costume and purple mantle.

"My lord," said this last one gaily, addressing the knight in black armour, "you must not bear Mothril malice for having refused to show you his daughter this evening, when he scarcely consented to allow me, who journeyed in his company night and day for six weeks, so much as a glimpse of her." The black knight made some reply, but Agenor did not wait to catch what he said. He had now heard all he cared to hear, that Aïssa was alone. At the sound of her father's voice, she had even risen, and, curious as a Christian, approached the window to watch the three mysterious promenaders. The chevalier rushed from the thicket, and in two bounds stood beneath the window, which was about twenty feet from the ground.

"Aïssa," said he, "do you know me?"

Mistress of herself as she was, the young girl started back with an involuntary cry; but almost immediately recognising him who occupied her whole thoughts, she held out her arms to him, saying in her turn, "Is it you, Agenor?"

"Yes, my love, it is I; but now, after so miraculously finding you again, how shall I reach you? Have you a silken ladder?"

"No," said Aïssa; "but I will have by to-morrow. My father passes the night at the prince's palace, so come to-morrow; but be careful to-night, for they are near at hand."

"Who are near at hand?" asked Agenor.

"My father, the Black Prince, and the King."

"What King?"—"Don Pedro."

Agenor thought of Henry, who was perhaps on the point of finding himself face to face with his brother.

"To-morrow, then," said he, hastily regaining the grove, and disappearing beneath its covert.

Agenor was only partially mistaken. The three promenaders had proceeded towards the spot where Henry was concealed. Mothril was the first the prince recognised.

"My lord," he was saying, as they came within ear-shot, "your highness is wrong in thus continually dwelling on Aïssa. The son of the King of England, the glorious Prince of Wales, is not come here to see a poor African girl, but to decide with you on the destinies of a great kingdom."

Henry, who had leaned forward, in order to hear better, here drew hastily back. "The Prince of Wales!" he muttered, with inexpressible surprise, and gazing curiously on his black armour, so celebrated throughout Europe, since the bloody battles of Crecy and Poitiers.

"To-morrow," said the prince, "I will give you an audience; and before we separate, I trust that all will be arranged. The affair can then be made public. To-day, I must conform to the wishes of my royal guest, and avoid awakening the curiosity of the courtiers. Nevertheless, before concluding anything, I ought to know the precise intentions of his Majesty Don Pedro, King of Castile." And so saying, the Black Prince bowed courteously to the noble in the purple mantle.

The cold sweat broke out on Henry's brow; but he felt very differently when a well-known voice replied, "I am not the King of Castile, monseigneur, but a suppliant forced to seek for help far from my kingdom; for my most cruel foes are those of my own family. Of my three brothers, one aimed at my honour, the other two at my life. The first one I killed, but Henry and Tello still remain. Tello is in Arragon, endeavouring to raise an army against me; Henry is in France with King Charles, flattering him with the prospect of conquering my kingdom; so that France, weakened by your victories, might gain in Castile fresh strength to resist you. I have therefore thought, monseigneur, that it would be politic for you to espouse the cause of a legitimate monarch, to continue—with the resources of men and money he offers you—the war with France, which this rupture of the truce permits you to make. I await your highness's reply, to know whether or not I must despair of my cause?"

"Certes, no; you must not despair, Don Pedro, for, as you say, your cause is a just one. But although Viceroy of Guyenne, I was unwilling to support alone the weight of my vice-royalty. At my request, my father granted me the aid of a council of wise men. These I must consult, but rest assured that if the opinions of the majority coincide with my own, and yield to my wish to serve you, never will a more faithful, or I may say more energetic ally have fought under your banner. To-morrow, sire, when you come to the palace my answer will be more explicit. Meanwhile, do not show yourself; secrecy is above all things necessary for our success."

" Oh, rest easy ! no one knows us here."

" And this house is safe," said the prince, laughing. " Even safe enough to set Senor Mothril's mind at rest on the subject of his daughter."

The Moor stammered a few words which Henry could not catch, for the three promenaders were already at some distance from him. Besides one wild, burning, almost irrepressible desire had taken possession of him since hearing the sound of this accursed voice. There at a few feet from him stood his mortal enemy, rising like a spectre between him and his desired end ; there within reach of his sword was the man thirsting for his blood, and for whose blood he also thirsted. A single blow, dealt by a hand guided by hate, would terminate the war, decide the question for ever. This thought made the prince's heart bound, his hand moved towards his sword. But Henry was not a man to yield to a first impulse, even though prompted by mortal hatred. " No," said he, " I could slay him, and that is all. His death is not enough ; I must succeed him on the throne. I could slay him, but the Prince of Wales would avenge his assassinated guest by either causing me to perish miserably or dooming me to eternal imprisonment. Yes," he continued, after a moment's pause, " and if I were even able to save myself, I should find on my return Tello upon the throne, and then the struggle would recommence."

This consideration stayed his arm, and returned his half-drawn sword to its sheath. Certes, the spirits of darkness must have laughed to see their sister Ambition for the first time snatch a poniard from the hand of one of her children.

Agenor now rejoined him, radiant with happiness, and forgetting war, intrigues, and princes, whilst he crushed his iron gauntlets together, fancying he was already crushing his enemies, and clinging to the steps of the throne of Castile.

CHAPTER XVII.

THE BLOOD-HOUND.

THE secret of Mothril's journey to Bordeaux was now ex-plained, and Aïssa had no information to give the chevalier on this subject. But for them remained a thousand subjects of far more importance—the never-ending confidences of love, which sweet as they are to all lovers, were doubly so to Agenor and Aïssa, who had never before experienced their happiness. Prince Henry de Transtamare, on the other hand, understood his brother's plan as well as if he had himself been informed of all particulars, and knew beforehand what would be the Prince of Wales' reply, as well as if he had already assisted at the morrow's council. Nothing, therefore, remained for him to do, convinced as he was that Don Pedro would obtain the help of the English, but to quit Bordeaux before the alliance was sworn between them; since if he were recognised he would become a prisoner of war, and Don Pedro, to finish the quarrel at one blow, would be very likely to have recourse to those expeditious means, which ambition alone had prevented Henry making use of against his brother.

After some conversation between the prince and Agenor, in which it was agreed that the prince should at once set out for Arragon, so as to be in readiness to receive the first com-panies despatched by the constable, Henry in his turn began to think of his companion's private affairs.

" And your love ?" said he.

" My lord," replied Agenor, " I will not conceal from you that the thought of it makes me very sad. It was so sweet to find at a few paces' distance the happiness of which I had so long dreamt, and which, I feared, I should all my life pursue without attaining it."

" Well," said the prince, " and what change has taken place ? What hinders you, who have neither a brother to fight, nor a throne to win, from enjoying this passing happiness ?"

" My prince, are you not about to depart ?" said Agenor.

" Undoubtedly," replied the prince ; " for notwithstanding the tender friendship I feel for you, dear Agenor, you can well understand I must not let it weigh against the interests of a kingdom and the happiness of a nation. If it concerned your life, that would be another thing ; for to your safety I would sacrifice even my fortune and my ambition." And the subtle eyes of the prince sought to meet the open glance of Agenor, to read in it his gratitude.

"But," he continued, "I will not sacrifice my crown to the—forgive me if I say—mad passion you have conceived for this daughter of the traitor Mothril."

"I know it, monseigneur, and I should have been a fool to have even formed such a hope. Therefore, poor Aïssa, adieu !" And he gazed so sorrowfully at the pavilion among the sycamores, that the prince began to smile.

"Happy lover," he muttered, while his brow became overcast, "I also have experienced this charming torture which makes the young heart thrill with all generous emotion."

"You call me happy, monseigneur !" exclaimed Agenor. "If all the hopes of a youthful heart destroyed at the very moment of their being accomplished constitutes misfortune, I am the most unfortunate of men."

"You are right, Agenor," said the prince; "think then only of the present moment ; you neither desire riches, nor strive for a crown ; you ask but a sweet word, or claim a first kiss ; your treasure is a woman, your throne the flowery bank on which she was to have been to-morrow seated beside you. Then do not lose this meeting, it will perhaps prove one of the fairest pearls locked up in the casket of memory !"

"Then, monseigneur," said Agenor, "you intend setting out alone?"

"This very night. I wish to quit the English territories, for by daybreak, as you are well aware, I must be upon neutral ground. I shall remain for three or four days at Navarre and Pampeluna ; hasten to join me there, for I cannot wait longer for you."

"But, my prince," said Agenor, "in spite of all the happiness promised me in beholding her I love, I cannot consent to leave you thus when danger menaces you."

"Do not exaggerate circumstances, Agenor. No danger menaces me in departing this evening. Besides, Perago will accompany me, and you know he is a good swordsman. Only rejoin us as soon as possible."

"But, monseigneur !"

"Listen. If you love this Moorish girl as you say——"

"Ah, monseigneur ! you cannot tell how I love her, although I have scarcely exchanged two words with her."

"Two words of our brave Castilian tongue are enough, provided they are well chosen. I was saying, that if you really love this Moorish girl, it will be a double triumph for you, for you will rob Mothril of a daughter and hell of a soul!"

These words were those of both a King and a friend. Agenor understood that Henry de Transtamare had already begun to assume both characters; and in order rightly to fill his own, bent his knee to the prince, to whom his interests were in reality so indifferent, that his thoughts were already straying across the Pyrenees. It was then agreed that the prince, after taking a few hours' repose, should set out for the frontier. As to Mauleon, feeling himself free, and his golden fetters loosed for a moment, he was no longer on earth but in heaven itself.

Lovers' slumbers, if not deep, are at least prolonged; they are so full of dreams of happiness, that it is very difficult to awake from them. Thus when Agenor opened his eyes the sun was already high in the heavens. He called Muscaron, and learnt from him that the prince had mounted his horse at four o'clock that morning, and hurried from Bordeaux, like a man conscious of the danger and difficulty of his position.

"Good," said he, after listening to the squire's recital and the comments he thought fit to make upon it: "we shall remain here to-night and perhaps to-morrow; but during the time it is agreed that we neither go out nor let any one see us. We shall therefore be refreshed and ready for our departure, which may take place at any moment. As to you, my friend, tend the horses carefully, so that we may be able to overtake the prince, even if double strength and courage be necessary to do so."

"Ho! ho!" said Muscaron, who, our readers will remember, was quite at his ease with his young master, particularly when he was in a good humour; "then we are now engaged in something besides politics. If I knew what it was, I might perhaps assist you."

"You will see at midnight; meanwhile, remain quiet, and do as I tell you."

Muscarón, who was always on the best terms with himself, from the immense confidence he possessed in his own resources, rubbed down his horses, gave them a double allowance of provender, and waited patiently till midnight, without putting so much as his nose out of a single window. It was not so with Agenor, whose eyes, through the crevices of the jalousies, were fixed on the neighbouring dwelling. But Muscaron and his master having both risen late, had neither of them observed, at daybreak, in Don Pedro's garden, a man stooping down, and examining with visible anxiety the traces of footsteps left on the fresh soil, and the crushed and broken branches of the shrubs surrounding Aïssa's pavilion. Mothril, for it was he, examined, with the sagacity peculiar to his race, the different footprints, following them as a blood-hound does the scent.

"Yes," he muttered at last, with flashing eyes and dilated nostrils; "yes, these are really my footsteps in this path; I recognise them by the form of my slippers. Beside them are the deeper ones of the Prince of Wales, made by his iron heels; and these faint traces are Don Pedro's, for he walks as lightly as a gazelle. The traces of our three footsteps continually follow one another; but these—these—I do not know them!" And he drew near the thicket of honeysuckle where Mauleon had remained so long concealed. "Here," muttered he, "they are deep, impatient, and unequal. Whence do they come, and whither were they proceeding?—towards the house? Yes, they are here, at the foot of the wall, and even more deeply indented in the earth. The person has here stood on tip-toe, doubtless endeavouring to reach the balcony. There is no doubt Aïssa was his object; but now to discover whether Aïssa was in league with him." And the Moor bent over the footsteps, and examined them with serious uneasiness. After a moment's silence, he resumed, "This is the footstep of a man booted like the French cavaliers; here is the trace of his spur. Let me see whence it comes." And Mothril followed the track leading back to the bower of honeysuckle, where his investigation recommenced.

"Another person has been stationed here," said he; "for the footprints are not alike. He was doubtless on the look-out for us, while the other went on to Aïssa. We must have brushed against this one. What were we speaking of when we passed by here, for he must have overheard it?" And Mothril endeavoured to recollect the words that had fallen from his own and his companions' lips as they drew near the spot. But the Moor's chief anxiety was not about politics; he therefore quickly resumed his examination of the footsteps. He thus tracked them to the wall, and then discovered that

L

three men had descended. One had proceeded as far as the fig-tree, in which he had concealed himself, for the lower branches of the tree were broken. This he concluded was only a sentinel; the second had advanced as far as the bower of honeysuckle, and was doubtless a spy; the third had reached the thicket, had remained stationary an instant, and from thence had gained Aïssa's pavilion. This was certainly a lover.

Mothril followed the traces until he found himself at the foot of the wall separating Ernauton de St. Colombe's house from the garden sold to the Prince of Wales; and here everything became as clear to him as though it were written in a book. The foot of the ladder had made two holes in the ground, and the top of it had grazed the coping of the wall.

"They all three came from there," exclaimed the Moor. He raised himself above the coping of the wall, and suffered his eager gaze to stray over Ernauton's garden; but it was still early, and, as we before said, Agenor and Muscaron slept late. Mothril therefore beheld nothing but the trace of footsteps approaching the house. "I will watch," said he.

During the day the Moor caused inquiries to be made in the neighbourhood; but Ernauton's servants were discreet; besides, they did not know Henry de Transtamare, and by most of them Agenor himself was beheld for the first time. Their information, that their guest was the godson of Messire Ernauton de St. Colombe, conveyed so little to either Mothril or his Moorish spies, that he resolved to trust only to himself.

Night arrived. His Majesty Don Pedro was expected, with his faithful ambassador, at the Prince of Wales' palace. Mothril was ready at the appointed hour to accompany the prince, and entered the council chamber with the air of a man who would not allow his secret anxieties to interfere with the performance of his duty. Meanwhile Mauleon, after witnessing the Moor's departure, and knowing that Aïssa was now alone, took his sword, as he had done on the preceding evening, and bidding his squire have the horses all ready saddled in the court-yard, reared the ladder against the wall in the same spot as before, and descended without accident into the Prince of Wales' garden.

Aïssa knelt beside her open window, inhaling the cool evening air and the perfume of the surrounding flowers.

Suddenly she heard a rustling of leaves; she leaned forward, blushing with pleasure, from among the wreathing blossoms with which the balcony was overhung. A light footstep was then heard, and Mauleon appeared in the wide moonlit space between the thicket and the house. The Moorish girl had only waited for this; she sprang up lightly as a swallow, and clinging to a long silken cord attached to the balcony, safely reached the ground, and flung herself into Agenor's arms.

CHAPTER XVIII.

LOVE.

AGENOR silently drew the Moorish maiden into the honey-suckle bower, in which, on the preceding evening, Don Henry had found shelter, and there, seating her on a mossy bank, flung himself at her feet.

"You expected me, then?" said he.

"Yes," replied Aïssa; "not only since yesterday, but from the first day I beheld you, I knew we should meet again."

"You love me, then!" said Agenor, overjoyed.

"Yes," replied Aïssa; "I love you because you are brave. Why do you love me?"

"Because you are beautiful," said the young man.

"True; all you know of me is my face, whilst I have heard of your exploits."

"Then you know I am your father's enemy?"—"Yes."

"And that it is war to the death between us?"

"I know it."

"And you do not hate me for it?"—"I love you."

"You are right. I hate this man because he drew my brother-in-arms, Don Frederick, on to his death. I hate him because he murdered the unhappy Blanche of Bourbon; and lastly, because he guards you as if you were his slave, instead of his daughter. Are you really his daughter, Aïssa?"

"I know not. It seems as if one day in my early child-hood I awoke from a deep sleep, and on opening my eyes this man's face was the first that presented itself. He called me his daughter, and I called him father. But I do not love him—he terrifies me."

"Is he, then, cruel or severe to you?"

"On the contrary; no queen is treated with more defe-rence. My slightest wish is a command; I have only to

L 2

make a sign, and I am obeyed. I seem to occupy all his thoughts. I know not what projects he has formed concerning me, but sometimes his gloomy and jealous tenderness frightens me."

"Then you do not love him as a child should her father?"

"I fear him, Agenor. Listen: sometimes, during the night, he glides like a spirit into my chamber, and makes me shudder; he approaches my bed with footsteps so noiseless that he does not even awaken the women sleeping on their mats around me; he passes through the midst of them as though his footsteps did not touch the earth. But I cannot sleep: beneath my eyelids, quivering with fear, I behold his terrible smile. He draws near me, and bends over my couch; his breath scorches my face, and the kiss by which he fancies he protects my slumbers, burns on my brow or my lip like the touch of red-hot iron. Such is the feeling of terror with which each night I fall asleep, such are the visions that haunt me—visions full of reality! And yet something tells me that I am wrong to tremble, since, as I told you, I exercise a strange dominion over him, either sleeping or waking. I have often seen him quake at a frown, and never can his proud and piercing eye sustain the gaze of mine. But why talk of Mothril, my brave knight? You are not afraid of him—you, who fear nothing?"

"Assuredly not; I only fear for you!"

"Ah! that proves you love me," said Aïssa, with a bewildering smile.

"Aïssa, I have often wondered at the indifference with which I regarded my fair countrywomen; but I now know the reason of it. It was that my heart might belong entirely to you. But listen, Aïssa; in my country, the women that we love become friends beside whom we live and die, and when they have received our plighted troth are sure of never being consigned to the depths of some harem, where they are obliged to serve the newer and more favoured mistresses of those they have loved. Therefore, become a Christian, Aïssa, and my wife."

"I was going to ask you to teach me how to become one," replied the Moorish girl.

"Fly with me, then!" said Agenor, and springing to his feet he took his mistress in his strong arms, and bore her swiftly towards the part of the wall where he had placed the ladder, scarcely feeling the weight of his fair burden, as he passed with the speed of an arrow through the clumps of trees and alleys of verdure. He was already within sight of the wall, rendered all the darker by the neighbouring trees, when Aïssa glided with the agility of an adder from his arms. Agenor stopped suddenly. The Moorish girl was crouching at his feet, with her outstretched hand pointing towards the wall.

"Look!" whispered she, and Mauleon, following the direction of her finger, perceived a white figure bending down behind the ladder.

"Can this be Muscaron?" said he to himself, "who, alarmed for my safety, is thus on the look-out for me? But, no!" he continued, shaking his head, "Muscaron is too prudent to expose himself to the chance of receiving a sword-cut by mistake." The shadowy figure sprang up, and a bluish ray flashed from its belt.

"Mothril!" exclaimed Aïssa.

Aroused by this terrible word, Mothril drew his sword. The Moor had evidently not observed the young girl, or in the strange group formed by a Christian warrior carrying off a Moorish maiden had not recognised her; but the moment he heard her exclamation, and beheld her tall and graceful form emerge from the shade, he uttered a terrible cry, and rushed blindly on Agenor. But love was even swifter than hate; by a movement rapid as thought, Aïssa drew down the visor of the chevalier's helmet, and the Moor found himself facing a statue of iron, encircled by the arms of his daughter.

Mothril paused suddenly. "Aïssa!" he murmured, despairingly, and his arm fell at his side.

"Yes, Aissa!" she replied, with a wild energy that redoubled Mauleon's love, and made a cold shudder run through the Moor's veins. "If you wish to kill me, strike! As to *him*, you well know he does not fear you." And she designated Agenor by a gesture.

Mothril stretched out his hand to seize her; but she retreated, and left him confronted with the motionless form of Agenor, standing sword in hand. His eye gleamed with such deadly hate, that the chevalier raised his weapon, but his arm was arrested by Aïssa.

"No," said she; "do not strike him in my presence! you are strong, well armed, and invulnerable, therefore pass by him, and depart."

"Ah !" exclaimed Mothril, overturning the ladder with a blow of his foot. "You are strong, well-armed, and invulnerable—we will prove that." At the same moment he gave a shrill whistle, and a dozen Moors, armed with scimitars and battle-axes, appeared.

"Ah, dogs of infidels !" cried Agenor, "come on, and we will see."

"Death to the Christian !" cried Mothril—"Death !"

"Fear nothing," said Aïssa, and she advanced with a calm and firm step between the chevalier and his adversaries.

"Mothril," said she, "it is my will that this young man quit this spot safe and sound,—do you hear ? Woe to you, if so much as a hair of his head be harmed !"

"Then you love this miscreant !" exclaimed Mothril.

"I do," replied Aïssa.

"Then the greater reason he should die. Strike !" cried Mothril, himself lifting his poniard.

"Mothril," repeated the young girl, knitting her brows, and darting upon him her lightning glance, "did you not understand what I said, or must I a second time tell you it is my will that this young man depart this very moment?"

"Strike !" vociferated Mothril, furiously.

Agenor made a movement to defend himself.

"Wait," said Aïssa, "and you shall see the tiger become a lamb." She drew from her girdle a sharp, finely-tempered poniard, and uncovering her beautiful bosom pressed the dagger point on the fair flesh till it began to yield to the dangerous pressure. The Moor uttered an agonized cry. "Listen !" said she; " I swear, by the god of the Arabs, whom I now renounce, and the God of the Christians, whom I will henceforth worship, that if any evil happens to this young knight, I will plunge this dagger into my heart."

"Aïssa !" cried the Moor, "in mercy refrain ! You will drive me mad !"

"Throw aside your cangiar, then," said the Moorish girl. Mothril obeyed.

"Command your slaves to retire."

The Moor made a sign, and they disappeared. Aïssa cast a long glance around her—like a queen, assuring herself that she is obeyed; then turning to the chevalier she said, in a low voice, "Come hither, Agenor, and let me bid you adieu."

" " Cannot you fly with me ? " he asked in the same tone.

" No ; for he would rather kill than lose me. I remain to save us both."

" But you will still love me?" said the young man.

" Look at yonder star," said Aïssa, pointing to one of the most brilliant constellations then glittering in the heavens, " and believe that it will be extinguished before love expires in my heart!" and lifting the visor of his helmet, she pressed a long kiss upon his lips, whilst the Moor ground his teeth with fruitless rage.

" Now go," said Aïssa, " but hold yourself prepared for everything." And placing herself at the foot of the ladder, which Agenor had again reared against the wall, she smilingly regarded her lover ; meanwhile extending her hand towards the baffled Moor, like the wild-beast tamer, who by a gesture subdues the animal apparently ready to devour him.

" Adieu !" said Agenor once more. " Remember your promise."

" Adieu !" responded Aïssa. " I will keep it." Agenor waved her a last farewell, and sprang lightly over the wall, followed by a cry of rage from the Moor at seeing his prey thus escape him. " Now," said Aïssa, addressing Mothril, " do not let me see that you watch me too closely, or make me suspect that you treat me as a slave, for you see I have the means of freeing myself. It is growing late ; let us return to the house, my father."

Mothril allowed her to indolently and dreamily retrace her steps to the pavilion. He picked up his long poniard, and passed his hand across his brow. " Girl !" he muttered, "in a few months, perhaps a few days, you shall not thus daunt Mothril."

As the young girl reached the threshold of the pavilion, the Moor overheard the sound of footsteps behind him.

"Enter quickly, Aïssa!" he exclaimed. "Here is the King."

The young girl passed through the door, and closed it behind her as leisurely as though she had not heard him. The Moor watched her disappear. An instant afterwards, the King was at his side.

" Well," said the King, " victory, friend Mothril ! we have carried the day ; but why did you leave the council just as they were entering into consultation ? "

" Because, my lord," said Mothril, " I did not think the

presence of all these powerful princes the fit place for a poor Moorish slave."

" You lie, Mothril ; you were uneasy about your daughter, and returned home to watch over her."

" Ah, my lord !" said Mothril, smiling at the pre-occupation of Don Pedro, " one would imagine, on my honour, that you thought of her even more than I do."

They both re-entered the house ; but not without Don Pedro casting an anxious glance towards the pavilion, at the window of which appeared the shadowy form of a woman.

CHAPTER XIX.

BERTRAND DUGUESCLIN'S ARITHMETIC.

WHILST Prince Henry de Transtamare and his companion Agenor wended their way towards Bordeaux, where the events we have just related awaited them, Duguesclin, furnished with full power, had assembled the principal leaders of the Free Companies, and explained to them his plan of the campaign. But these robbers possessed more military tactics than one would have imagined, and against all his warlike projects they brought one unanswerable argument—the want of money.

" True," said Duguesclin, " I have already been thinking about that ; but," he added, " you will have plenty after the first battle."

" But in the meantime," said the Green Knight, " how are we to live and pay our men ?"

" Unless," added Caverley, " we continue to prey upon the French peasantry ; but their cries and complaints—and the poor devils are always crying out—would wound the ears of our illustrious constable. Besides, what is the good of becoming honest captains if we are obliged to plunder the same as when we were adventurers ?"

" Your argument is very just," said Duguesclin.

" I would add," remarked Claude l'Ecorcheur, another worthy member of this band of wolves, who passed for less ferocious than Hugh Caverley, but a thousand times more treacherous and greedy, " that we are now the allies of his Majesty the King of France, seeing that we are about to avenge the death of his sister-in-law ; and that we should be unworthy of this honour—an unspeakable one for simple adventurers like ourselves—if we did not, for the present at least, cease destroying the country of our royal ally."

"Your remarks are both judicious and profound," said Duguesclin; "but can you point out to me any means of obtaining money?"

"It is our business to receive, not to obtain it," retorted Caverley.

"That fact is indisputable," replied Duguesclin, "and the doctor himself is not a better logician; but, come—how much do you ask?"

The chiefs looked at one another, and Caverley, as if the care of the general interests had been left to him, replied, "On my word, as a captain, Messire Bertrand, we will be reasonable."

At this promise Duguesclin felt a cold shudder run through his veins. "I await your reply," said he; "speak."

"Well, then," resumed Caverley, "until we arrive in an enemy's country, let his Majesty Charles V. pay us only a gold crown per man. It is not much, certainly, but we take into consideration the honour of being his allies, and will be moderate in our demands. We have, as one may say, fifty thousand men."

"Almost," said Duguesclin. "More or less. A few less, I fancy."

"Never mind," said Caverley, "we undertake to do as much with those we have as others would do with fifty thousand, therefore it is exactly the same as though we had them."

"Then that is fifty thousand gold crowns?" said Duguesclin.

"Yes!" answered Caverley; "for the men."

"Well?" asked Duguesclin.—"Then there are the officers."

"True, I forgot the officers. Well, how much must be given to the officers?"

"I think," interrupted the Green Knight, doubtless fearing lest Caverley should not estimate them highly enough—"I think that these honest fellows, who are for the most part brave and experienced men, are well worth five gold crowns a head; remember that nearly all of them have valets and grooms to keep, besides three horses."

"Peste!" cried Bertrand; "here are officers better served than those of the King, my master."

"We will hold to that," said Caverley.

"And you say five crowns for each man?"

"It is the lowest price that, in my opinion, could be demanded for them. I should have said six myself, but since the Green Knight has named a price, I will abide by what he has said."

"Accursed rogues!" thought Bertand, whilst his countenance assumed its most gracious expression, "how I would hang you all if I were only strong enough." Then he said aloud, "Gentlemen, you perceive by my momentary silence, that I have reflected on your demands, and the sum you name does not seem to me exorbitant. And how many officers have you?"

Caverley drew himself up, and after having mutely interrogated his friends, replied, "I have a thousand."

This was just double the real number.

"And I eight hundred," said the Green Knight. He followed the example of his colleague.

"I a thousand," said Claude l'Ecorcheur. He tripled the number.

The rest imitated this generous example, and the number of officers was announced to be four thousand.

"Then there is an officer to every eleven soldiers," exclaimed Duguesclin, in feigned admiration. "What a magnificent army it ought to be, and what discipline maintained in it."

"Yes," responded Caverley, modestly; "it is well enough managed."

"Then that amounts to twenty thousand crowns," said Bertrand.

"Gold ones," amended the Green Knight.

"Pardieu!" continued the constable; "twenty thousand gold crowns, which, added to those already accorded, make precisely seventy thousand.

"It is right to a carolus," said the Green Knight, who admired the constable's facility in addition.

"But," resumed Caverley—

Bertrand did not allow him to complete his sentence, "But," said he, "I understand—we are forgetting the leaders."

Caverley opened his eyes to their widest extent. Bertrand not only at once divined his objections, but even went beyond them. "You are forgetting yourselves," continued Bertrand. "What noble disinterestedness! But I do not forget you, therefore let us count. You are ten in number, are you not?"

The adventurers counted after Duguesclin; they would

willingly have made themselves out twenty, had that been possible.

"Ten leaders," they repeated.

"Which, at three thousand gold crowns each, makes thirty thousand crowns, does it not?" said Duguesclin.

At these words the chiefs, dazzled and bewildered by so much munificence, started from their seats, brandishing their heavy swords and waving their helmets in the air, as they thundered rather than shouted, "Noël! Noël! Success to our brave constable!"

"Ah, brigands!" muttered the object of their applause, hypocritically casting down his eyes, as though overpowered by their acclamations. "By the help of our Lord, and Our Lady of Mount Carmel, I will lead you to a place from whence not one of you will return." Then he added aloud, "In all, one hundred thousand gold crowns, which will settle all our accounts."

"Noël! Noël!" repeated his auditors, wound up to the highest pitch of enthusiasm.

"Now, gentlemen," said Duguesclin, "you have my knightly word that this sum shall be paid you before the commencement of the campaign. Only you understand I cannot give it you immediately, as I do not carry the royal treasury about with me."

"True," said the chiefs, too overjoyed to be more exacting than they had already been.

"Then, messires, it is understood that you give credit to the King of France on the word of his constable; and," he added, proudly raising his head, "that word is inviolate; but as loyal servants we ought to set out immediately, and if at the moment of entering Spain the money is not forthcoming, you will nevertheless have two guarantees for it—firstly, your liberty, which I will restore to you; and secondly, a prisoner, who will be well worth a hundred thousand crowns."

"What prisoner?" inquired Caverley.

"Myself," replied the constable; "for if the women in my province had to spin night and day to earn the sum for my ransom, it would be paid."

"It is a bargain!" exclaimed the adventurers with one voice, and they touched the constable's hand in token of alliance.

"When do we set out?" asked the Green Knight.

"Immediately, if you will, messieurs."

"Immediately!" repeated Caverley. "In fact, comrades,

since there is nothing more to be gained here, the sooner we change our quarters the better." Each leader then hastened to his post; the banners waved, the drums beat, and a general movement took place throughout the whole of the camp. Two hours later the tents were all struck, and the pack-horses bending beneath the weight of their burdens; horses were neighing, and groups of lances gleaming in the sun like flashes of lightning.

Towards noon the army commenced its march, descended the Saône, and formed itself into two columns, one on either bank. One would have fancied it was the migration of a horde of barbarians about to fulfil one of those terrible missions given them by Heaven, as they followed the footsteps of one of those scourges of God—Alaric, Genseric, or Attila. Nevertheless, these followed the good constable, Bertrand Duguesclin, who, seated on his powerful charger, with his head bowed on his broad breast, was muttering thoughtfully to himself—"This is all very well, provided it lasts. But where am I to get this money; and if I do not get it, how will the King be able to assemble an army numerous enough to bar the return of these brigands, who will pour down the Pyrenees more rapacious than ever?"

The good constable continued his journey buried in gloomy thought, turning from time to time to watch the noisy multitude surging around him, whilst his busy brain did more work than the brains of all the fifty thousand adventurers put together. All at once, just as the sun was sinking behind the purple and golden clouds veiling the horizon, the worthy constable, whose taciturnity had begun to surprise those around him, raised his head, shook himself like a conqueror in a fray, and called to his domestics, "Ho, Jacquelard! Ho, Berniquet! a cup of wine—and the best you have in your stores!" Then he murmured behind his visor, "By our Lady of Auray, I fancy I know where to lay my hand on these hundred thousand crowns, and that without in any way wronging our good King Charles." Then turning towards the leaders of the adventurers, who had begun to grow uneasy at seeing their chief so thoughtful, "Come, messieurs!" he cried, in his sonorous voice; "what say you to a cup of wine?"

This was an irresistible invitation; they gathered round him, and each quaffed a generous flagon of wine of Chalons to the health of the good King Charles.

CHAPTER XX.

URBAN V.

THE army continued their march until they reached Avignon. Here Pope Urban V. held his court; who, first Benedictine, then Abbé of St. Germain d'Auxerre, and Prior of St. Victor of Marseilles, had been elected Pope under the condition that he should not in any way disturb the terrestrial beatitude of the cardinals and the Roman princes; a condition which he took care from the moment of his election rigidly to keep, thanks to which he reckoned on living, as long as possible, and dying at last in the odour of sanctity.

Our readers may remember that the successor of St. Peter had been touched by the complaints of the King of France respecting the Free Companies, and that he had excommunicated them, a masterpiece of diplomacy of which King Charles, in his wise foresight, had so plainly shown the evil consequences to Duguesclin, as to leave in his mind a very strong desire to restore things to their normal condition. Thus, the brilliant idea that had occurred to Bertrand on the road from Chalons to Lyons was, to proceed with his fifty thousand adventurers, and pay a visit to Pope Urban V. Thus it fell out all for the best, that as the adventurers approached the States of this pontiff, to whom, inoffensive as the excommunication had proved, they all more or less bore malice, their warlike and ferocious instincts began to revive. They had, indeed, been too long peaceable.

When they were within two leagues of the town, Bertrand ordered a halt, assembled the leaders, and commanded them to widen their ranks, so as to present an imposing front to the town as they surrounded it, forming an immense bow, of which the river represented the string. He then mounted his horse, and attended by a dozen men-at-arms and the French cavaliers forming his suite, presented himself at the gate of Vaucluse, demanding to speak to the Sovereign Pontiff.

Urban, on beholding this horde of barbarians pour down upon him like an inundation, had assembled an army of two or three thousand men, and knowing the power of his supreme arm, was prepared to deal a signal blow with the keys of St. Peter on the heads of the adventurers. But it must be confessed that in the depth of his heart lurked the thought that the brigands, overwhelmed with their excommunication, were

come to ask his pardon, and to offer to redeem their sins by
some new crusade, trusting to this display of their strength
and number to give due value to the humility of their submission. He summoned the constable to his presence, with
a haste that greatly surprised him. His Holiness was dining
at the time on his terrace, shaded by orange-trees and rose-
laurels, in company with his brother, the Abbot Angelo
Grinvald, to whom was promised the bishopric of Avignon,
one of the principal seats of Chistianity.

"*You*, Messire Bertrand Duguesclin!" exclaimed the Pope.
"Are you, then, with this army, which has suddenly arrived
here, without our knowing for what purpose or whence it
comes?"

"Alas! Holy Father," said the chevalier, "I command it;"
and he knelt before him.

"Then I breathe again!" said the Pope.

"And I also!" said Angelo, drawing a deep breath.

"You breathe again, Holy Father?" said Bertrand; and,
in his turn, he heaved as deep a sigh as if he had inherited
the pontifical oppression.

"Yes, I breathe again, because I now know their intentions."

"I do not think so, Holy Father," said Bertrand.

"With such a leader as yourself, constable—a man who
respects the Church——"

"Yes, Holy Father, yes, I respect the Church!"

"Well, then, my son, you are welcome; but let me hear
what your army wants with me?"

"First," said Bertrand, evading the question, and delaying
the explanation as long as possible, "your Holiness will
doubtless learn with pleasure that there is every chance of a
war against the infidels."

Urban V. cast a glance at his brother, as much as to say,
"Well, was I mistaken?" Then, satisfied with this fresh proof
of his self-ascribed infallibility he turned to the constable.
"Against the infidels?" he repeated, with unction.

"Yes, Holy Father."

"And against what infidels, my son?"

"The Moors of Spain, Holy Father."

"It is a pious thought, constable, and worthy of a Christian hero—for I presume it originated in you."

"Yes, Holy Father, in me and good King Charles."

"You will share the glory, and God will bless alike the

head that conceived and the arm that executes. Thus, your aim——"

"Our aim is to exterminate them, Holy Father (and God grant we may be successful), and to consecrate the chief part of our spoils to the glorification of the Catholic religion."

"Embrace me, my son," said Urban, touched to the heart, and struck with admiration for the valiant sword thus drawn in the service of the Church.

Bertrand disclaimed so great an honour, and contented himself with kissing the hand of his Holiness. "But," resumed the constable, after a moment's pause, "you are aware, Holy Father, that the soldiers now about to make this heroic pilgrimage are the same your Holiness thought fit to excommunicate not long ago."

"I had good reasons for doing so, and I think you, my son, were then of the same opinion."

"Your Holiness is always in the right," said Bertrand, taking no notice of the allusion to himself; "but still they are excommunicated, and I will not conceal from you that it will have a detestable effect on men about to fight in defence of the Christian religion."

"My son," said Urban, emptying his glass filled with golden Monte Pulchiano; "my son, the Holy Church is neither intolerant nor implacable, but shows mercy to all sins, provided the sinner sincerely repents; and if you, one of the pillars of the faith, guarantee their return to orthodoxy——"

"Oh, certes, yes, Holy Father."

"Then I will revoke the anathema, and consent to let only a portion of my displeasure rest upon them. You see I am full of indulgence," added the Pope, smiling.

Bertrand bit his lips as he thought how much deeper in error his Holiness would get? Urban continued, in a voice full of gentleness, but yet not wanting in that firmness which sits so well on one who pardons without being ignorant of the gravity of the offence he wishes to forget, "You understand, my son, that these men have amassed unholy riches; therefore, as it is said in Ecclesiastes, 'Omne malum in pravo femore.'"

"I do not understand Hebrew, Holy Father," said Bertrand, humbly.

"Therefore I spoke in simple Latin, my son," said Urban, smiling; "but I forgot that warriors are not Benedictines.

This, then, is the meaning of what I said, and which you will perceive is marvellously applicable to the present case,—"The greatest of all evils is ill-acquired wealth."

"How good!" said Duguesclin, smiling beneath his thick moustache, as he thought of the manner in which this proverb would soon be turned against his Holiness.

"Therefore," continued Urban, "I have decided; and this I swear to you, my son, only out of regard to you, that these miscreants—for miscreants they are, notwithstanding their repentance of their misdeeds—shall forfeit a tenth of their ill-gotten possessions, and have the sentence of excommunication taken off them.   Therefore, my son, although I act spontaneously, and without being urged by you, impress on their minds the favour I confer on them, for it is immense!"

"It is immense," replied Bertrand; "but I doubt whether they will receive it with the gratitude it deserves."

"Is it not, my son?" said Urban.   "Then let us consult together at what sum we ought to fix this removal of excommunication."   And he turned towards his brother, as though to ask his opinion on this delicate question.

"Holy Father!" said Angelo, throwing himself back in his chair, and shaking his head, "it will require a great deal of gold to compensate for the withdrawal of your spiritual displeasure!"

"Without doubt, without doubt!" resumed Urban; "but we are clement; indeed everything disposes us to clemency. The skies are so bright at Avignon, and when the 'mistral' allows us to forget that it is slumbering in the caverns of Mount Ventoux, the air so pure that these blessing from the hand of the Lord speak to men of mercy and fraternity. Yes," continued the Pope, holding out his golden cup to a young page clad in white, who immediately replenished it, "yes, decidedly all men are brothers."

"Then," said Bertrand, "permit me to inform your Holiness in what capacity I am come hither.   I come as the ambassador of the brave fellows of whom we speak."

"And as such crave our indulgence for them; is it not so?"

"Yes, Holy Father; for, in the first place, your blessing is an excellent thing for us poor soldiers, whose lives are not safe one moment after another."

"Oh, it is yours, my son; but we will now speak of our mercy, or, if you like it better, our pardon!"

"We reckon upon that as well, Holy Father."

"Yes; but you know the only conditions on which we can accord it you?"

"Alas!" said Duguesclin, "a condition impossible to accept; "your Holiness forgets what we are about to do in Spain!"

"In Spain?"

"Yes, Holy Father, did you not say we were going to fight for the Christian Church?"—"Well?"

"Then in setting out on this expedition, the army have a right to claim not only your full pardon and indulgence, but also your aid."

"My aid, Messire Bertrand?" exclaimed the Pope, who began to grow uneasy. "What mean you by these words, my son?"

"I have always understood, Holy Father, that the apostolic seat was both rich and generous; that the propagation of the Christian faith was greatly to its advantage, and that it could pay for it."

"What are you saying, Messire Bertrand?" interrupted Urban, starting from his fauteuil in undisguised anger.

"I see that your Holiness perfectly understands me," said the constable, rising and brushing the dust from his knees.

"Not so," said the Pope, who would not understand; "not so; explain yourself."

"Thus, then, Holy Father, these gallant soldiers—somewhat miscreant, I own, but very repentant—whom you behold here assembled in number like the leaves of the forest or the sands of the sea; these soldiers, I say, under the command of Sir Hugh Caverley, Claude l'Ecorcheur, Le Bègue de Vilaine, the Green Knight, Oliver de Mauny, and other illustrious leaders, await a subsidy from your Holiness before commencing their campaign. The King of France has promised them one hundred thousand crowns; he is a pious prince, and deserves canonization neither more nor less than a Pope. Therefore your Holiness, who is the keystone of the arch of Christianity, may well give, for instance, two hundred thousand crowns."

Urban again started from his fauteuil; but this elasticity in the muscles of his Holiness—an elasticity that could only proceed from strong nervous excitement—did not in the least discompose Bertrand, who remained standing in the same firm but respectful attitude.

"Messire," said the Pope, "I perceive that the society of

M

brigands is not without its contaminating effects; and it appears to me that certain persons (who shall be nameless), who have hitherto enjoyed the favour of the Holy See, would have met with a better reward for their merit had they submitted to its rigour." To the Pope's astonishment these terrible words, from which he expected great results, found the constable quite unmoved.

"I," continued his Holiness, "have 6000 soldiers."

Bertrand remarked to himself that Urban V., like Sir Hugh Caverley or the Green Knight, doubled the number of his men, which struck him as being—notwithstanding the urgency of the case—somewhat hazardous for a Pope to do.

"I have 6000 soldiers in Avignon, and 20,000 inhabitants in a state to carry arms; the town is fortified, but had it neither ramparts, moats, nor men to defend it, I have the tiara of St. Peter on my brow, and by invoking God, would alone arrest the progress of these barbarians, less courageous than those of Attila, whom Pope Leon stayed before Rome."

"Ah, Holy Father, reflect! Arms, either spiritual or temporal, rarely succeed when taken up by the Vicars of Christ against the Kings of France, the eldest sons of the Church. Witness your predecessor, Boniface VIII., who received— God forbid that I should excuse such an outrage—who received, I say, a blow from Colonna, and who perished miserably in prison. You already see of what use the excommunication has been; since those you excommunicated, instead of dispersing and taking to flight, have on the contrary assembled sword in hand to demand your pardon. As to temporal arms, your 6000 soldiers and 20,000 unskilful inhabitants, would be of little service. Even reckoning each of these honest shopkeepers as a soldier, they number in all only 26,000 men against 50,000 tried warriors, fearing neither God nor the devil, and far better accustomed to Popes than the soldiers of Attila, who beheld one for the first time. It is above all, on this account, that I would entreat your Holiness to pause before engaging with these adventurers."

"What would they dare?" exclaimed Urban, his eyes sparkling with anger.

"Holy Father, I know not what they would dare, but they are bold fellows."

"What, the Lord's anointed!—the wretches!—what, Christians!"

"Pardon me, Holy Father; they are not Christians, but excommunicated men. What would you have restrain them? Ah, were it otherwise, they might have the dread of excommunication before their eyes, but as it is they fear nothing."

The more forcible the argument became, the more the Pope's anger increased. He rose from his seat, and advanced towards Bertrand. "And you who give me this strange advice," said he, "have you no fears for your own safety?"

"I am in far less danger than your Holiness yourself," retorted Bertrand with a coolness that would have disconcerted St. Peter himself. "Since admitting what I do not suppose possible, namely, that some disaster befel me, I can answer for it beforehand that there would not long remain one stone upon another of the good city of Avignon, or the magnificent palace, solid as it is, you have built there. Oh, these scoundrels are famous destroyers, and make a fortress crumble in as short a time as it would take a regular army to demolish a village. But they would not stop there; they would pass from the castle to the garrison, from the garrison to the inhabitants, till not a bone would remain of your thirty thousand men, which would cause many souls to be lost all through the fault of your Holiness. Thus, knowing your prudence, I feel more in safety here than in my own camp."

"Nevertheless," cried the enraged Pope, "I persist in what I said! I will wait!"

"In truth, Holy Father," replied Duguesclin, "I swear to you on my faith as a gentleman, that I do not recognise you in this refusal. I now see my mistake, but I was convinced that your Holiness would have anticipated this request; and following the example of our good King Charles, the two hundred thousand crowns would have been offered by the Holy See. Believe me, Holy Father," continued the constable, assuming the air of one deeply pained, "it is very sad for a good Christian like myself to behold the first Prince of the Church refuse his assistance to a pious enterprise such as we project. The worthy leaders will never credit it!" and saluting Urban, who remained stupified at the aspect of affairs, more humbly than ever, the constable quitted the terrace, descended the steps, and rejoining his suite, who began to be uneasy at his absence, at the gate of the palace, returned to the camp.

CHAPTER XXI.

THE LEGATE'S VISIT TO THE CAMP.

DUGUESCLIN, on his return to the camp, began to foresee that he should have great difficulty in putting his plans, which were intended to have three grand results—viz., to pay the adventurers, defray the expenses of the campaign, and assist the King in completing the Hotel St. Paul—into execution, in case the Pope remained in his present way of thinking. But Duguesclin was a Breton; that is to say, more obstinate than any pope, either past, present, or to come; and he was besides urged on by Necessity, that inflexible goddess, represented by the ancients as being armed with a rod of iron. He therefore armed his men, and ordered his Bretons who had arrived two days before under the conduct of Oliver de Mauny, and Le Bègue de Vilaine, to proceed towards Villeneuve; so that from the heights of the terrace, which he had not yet quitted, his Holiness beheld the long blue line of troops winding like an azure serpent, on whose coils the setting sun cast a glowing reflection, brighter than gold, and more terrible than the papal anathema.

Urban V. was almost as good a general as a monk. He had no need to summon his captain-general to understand that a few steps further, and this serpent would enclose Avignon in its deadly coils. Wishing, therefore, to convince himself whether the Free Companies were as enraged against him as Duguesclin had represented, he determined to send his legate to their commander-in-chief, merely to judge of the state of the general mind.

The legate had not been present at the conversation which had taken place between his Holiness and Duguesclin. He was, therefore, ignorant that Duguesclin demanded more than a renunciation of the excommunication launched against the Free Companies. He set out mounted on a mule, and attended by a sacristan, his acolyte.

We have already said that the legate was forewarned of nothing, it having been the Pope's opinion, that to confide his fears to his ambassador would be the means of weakening his confidence in his master's power. Thus the legate advanced towards the camp, enjoying in imagination the genuflexions and signs of the cross which were to greet his coming. Meanwhile Duguesclin had harangued his troops,

and stated his disagreement with his Holiness in such terms
as would best raise their anger to a prudent height. The
legate reached the outskirts of the camp, smiling blissfully.
The English rushed to the palisades to behold him, folding
their arms with insolent composure.

"Oh!" they exclaimed, "what does this mule want with
us?"

The sacristan turned pale with rage at this insult; but
assuming the paternal tone familiar to members of the church,
"This," said he, "is the Pope's legate."

"Then," cried the robbers, "where are the money bags?
Is your mule strong enough to carry them all? Come, show
us them!"

"Money! money!" cried the rest, with one voice.

The legate, stupified at this unexpected reception, looked
at the sacristan, who crossed himself in terror, and they pursued their way through ranks of soldiers, who unceasingly
repeated the cry, "Money! money!"

Not a leader was to be seen; for, warned by Duguesclin,
they had all retreated to their tents.

The legate and his companions had now passed through
the line of English, and reached the French camp; when the
men no sooner perceived them, than they prostrated themselves before them. The legate thought they intended to do
him honour, and began to hold up his head again; but instead of the humble salutations he expected, he heard on all
sides loud bursts of laughter.

"Ah, good-day, Monsieur Legate!" cried one. "Has his
Holiness sent you to us instead of a regiment of cavalry?"

"Does his Holiness think to put us to the edge of the
sword with the jaw-bone of his ambassador's ass?" said
another. And thus saying, they struck the mule on which
the legate was seated with their switches, laughing and
jeering in a manner that alarmed him more than the demands
of the English.

The legate passed as rapidly as possible through the
second line. It was now the turn of the Bretons, but they
were even less inclined to jest than the others. They surrounded him with flashing eyes and clenched fists, exclaiming,
in their formidable voices, "Absolution! absolution!" And
this went on, until at the end of a quarter of an hour, it was
impossible for the legate to distinguish anything amid this

frightful tumult, which resembled the roaring waves, the growling thunder, and the whistling wind, spending their fury on some rocky coast.

The sacristan began to lose his assurance and to tremble in every limb. The legate's teeth had long ago chattered, and the cold sweat stood upon his brow; but he now grew paler and paler, and finding that his mule—upon whose back more than one wag had sprung behind him—was beginning to falter, he demanded in a timid voice, "Your leaders, messieurs—who will have the goodness to conduct me to your leaders?" It was not until then that Duguesclin, overhearing this lamentable voice, thought proper to interfere. He forced his way through the crowd, and confronted the legate.

"What, is it you, Monsieur le Légat? An envoy from his Holiness! What an honour for excommunicated men! Back, soldiers, back! Ah, monsieur, deign to enter my tent! Messieurs," he continued, in a somewhat angry tone, "I request you to respect Monsieur le Légat, he doubtless brings us some welcome reply from his Holiness. Will you, monsieur, take my hand to assist you in alighting from your mule? So, you are safe on the ground! Now, come." The legate did not wait for a second invitation; but seizing the hand tendered him by the Breton chevalier, he hastily dismounted, and traversed the crowd of soldiery assembled to stare at him, amid shrugs, buffooneries, laughter, and remarks which made the sacristan's hair stand on end.

"What society!" muttered the church rat, "what society!"

Once in his tent, Bertrand Duguesclin, amid profound reverences to the legate, asked his pardon for the rude conduct of his soldiery, in terms which restored a little courage to the crest-fallen ambassador, who, beholding himself out of danger, and under the protection of the constable, endeavoured to summon up all his dignity and commenced an harangue, of which the sense was that the Pope was willing to grant absolution to the rebels, but money to no one.

"Then, Monsieur le Légat, I fear we shall never be able to make honest men of our soldiers!" And the constable rose from his seat, whilst the colour mounted into his bronzed cheek.

The legate understood that the audience was terminated. He remounted his mule, and was preparing to return to Avignon, but Duguesclin stopped him.

"Stay, monsieur," said he, "do not go alone, or you may

chance to get cut down by the way, and that would greatly
annoy me." And the constable walked beside the legate's
mule until they reached the limits of the camp, saying
nothing himself, but accompanied by such menacing clashing
of arms and furious imprecations, that his departure, even
thus protected by the constable, appeared to the Pope's
envoy, far more terrible than his arrival. Once out of the
camp, the legate struck his mule with his heel, and hurried
towards Avignon, as though he feared being recaptured.

CHAPTER XXII.

THE POPE'S DECISION.

THE unhappy fugitive had scarcely reached Avignon, before
Duguesclin, by advancing his troops, completed the terrible
circle which had so terrified Urban, when, from the heights
of his terrace, he had beheld its gradual formation. By this
movement Villeneuve, La Begude, and Gervasy, were taken
without the slightest resistance, although at the former there
was a garrison of five or six hundred men. The constable
had charged Hugh Caverley with the execution of this movement and the occupation of these towns. He knew his
mode of proceeding, and felt no doubt of the impression that
would be produced on the minds of the inhabitants of Avignon
by this commencement of the campaign. In fact, that same
evening they beheld around them great fires—which if some
time kindling, when once lighted, soon burned fiercely—
and recognising by degrees the precise spots from whence the
flames proceeded, found that their country houses were the
fuel, and their olive-groves the matches. By the light of
these fires encircling the town, and showing the band of
English adventurers engaged in their nocturnal preparations,
the Pope assembled his council. The cardinals were even
more divided than usual in their opinions. Many were in
favour of redoubled severity, which would strike not only the
adventurers, but all France, with salutary terror. But the
legate, whose ears still rang with the cries of the excommunicated army, did not conceal from either his Holiness or his
council the impression he had received, and finished by
saying that, unless by the express command of his Holiness,
nothing would induce him to again go among them without
carrying with him all they asked.

" Well, well," said the Pope, greatly agitated and not a little alarmed ; " we shall see."

" Unfortunately, your Holiness, we see already, and that very plainly," remarked one of the cardinals.

" You see what ?" asked Urban.

" A dozen country houses in flames, among which I can distinguish my own. There, look, Holy Father ! at this very moment the roof is falling in !"

" The fact is," said Urban, "the case appears to me urgent."

" I," said another, whose country seat the flames were now approaching, " I am of opinion that your Holiness should at once send an ambassador to the constable, bidding him, in the name of the Church, stop the ravages his soldiers are committing on our property."

" Will you undertake this mission, my son ?" asked the Pope.

" With the utmost pleasure, your Holiness, if I were not so poor an orator.   Then the constable does not know me ; and it would be better, I think, to send some one with whose face he is acquainted."

The Pope turned to the legate, who rose, and crossing himself, said, " I am ready, Holy Father, to proceed to martyrdom."

" I give you my blessing," said the Pope.

" But what am I to tell them, your Holiness ?"

" Tell them to extinguish their fires, and my wrath shall be forgotten ; to cease to burn, and I will cease to curse."

The legate shook his head with the air of a man who strongly doubted the success of his mission, but set out with his faithful sacristan, equipped as before.   This time, as he drew near the camp, the legate assumed a cheerful aspect ; he had gathered an immense olive-branch, which he bore in his hand as a symbol of peace, and, as soon as he caught sight of the English in the distance, began to cry out to them, " Good news ! good news !"

Thus by the English, who, although ignorant of the language, understood his gestures, he was not on the whole badly received, whilst the French waited to hear further particulars, and the Bretons bowed as he passed them.   But when he was obliged to announce to Duguesclin that he had returned without bringing anything with him but the pardon promised during his last visit, he acquitted himself of his mission with tears in his eyes ; the more so, as when he had finished, the constable regarded him with an air that plainly said, "And you have dared to return, and make me such a proposition?"

Without further hesitation, the legate exclaimed, "Save my life, Messire Constable, save my life; for when your soldiers find that I, who announced myself the bearer of good tidings, have returned with empty hands, they will kill me."

"Hum!" said Duguesclin, "I will not deny it."

"Alas! alas!" cried the legate; "I told his Holiness truly when I said I was going to martyrdom."

"I confess," said the constable, "that they are now more like wehr-wolves than men. This excommunication has had an effect on them that surprises even myself. I thought them more thick-skinned; and in truth, if by this time to-morrow they have not each of them two or three gold crowns to heal the wounds inflicted by the papal thunderbolts, I will no longer answer for the consequences. To-morrow they will be capable of burning Avignon and the cardinals in it—nay, I shudder to think of it—the Pope himself."

"But," said the legate, "in order to bear them this reply, and warn them of these impending dangers, you must let me depart in safety."

"We do not wish to force his Holiness to anything," said Bertrand: "we wish his decision to be voluntary—the result of his own free will. I will therefore conduct you to the outskirts of the camp, and, for greater safety, you shall depart by a secret outlet."

"Ah! Sire Constable," cried the legate, "you are a true Christian."

Duguesclin kept his word. The legate quitted the camp safe and sound, but behind him the devastation, stayed for a moment by his announcement of good news, recommenced with redoubled fury. The inhabitants of Avignon beheld from the top of the walls—for they none of them dared to move beyond the city—the ruin spreading around them. The cardinals bemoaned their losses. The Pope then proposed to grant one hundred thousand crowns.

"Bring them, and then we shall see," was Bertrand's response.

The Pope summoned his council, and, after grave deliberation, it was decided that the money should be raised by a tax on the citizens.

"And if they complain," said the Pope to his treasurer, "tell them what you have witnessed, and that neither my prayers nor my supplications have been able to save my beloved people from an exaction so grievous to my heart. Ah," he added, with tears in his eyes, "nothing is so sad for a prince as thus to dispose of his subjects' money!"

"Which, on some future occasion, would have been so useful to your Holiness," said the treasurer, with a low bow.

"Nevertheless, it is God's will," ejaculated the Pope.

The next morning, at daybreak, the legate, no longer mounted on his mule, but with ten richly-caparisoned horses, wended his way towards the excommunicated camp. The soldiers uttered loud cries of joy on perceiving them, but instead of finding their general charmed, as he had expected, by this palpable proof of the submission of the Holy See, he found him, to his surprise, gloomily turning over a recently unsealed slip of parchment.

"Oh," said the constable, shaking his head, "this is a fine sum of money you have brought me."

"Is it not?" said the legate.

"Yes," said Duguesclin; "but one scruple stops me. Whence comes this money?"

"From his Holiness, since he sends it to you."

"True; but who found it?"

"Dame! his Holiness, I presume."

"Pardon, Monsieur le Légat, a churchman ought not to tell lies."

"But," said the legate, "I am witness——"

"Read that," said Duguesclin, giving him the slip of parchment he had been rolling and unrolling between his fingers.

The legate took it and read:—"Is it the desire of the noble Chevalier Duguesclin that an innocent and already oppressed city of poor, half-ruined tradesmen and starving artisans should be deprived of their last morsel of bread to pay for a war of caprice? This question is asked in the name of humanity of the most loyal of all Christian chevaliers by the city of Avignon, from the sweat of whose brow has been wrung a hundred thousand gold crowns, whilst his Holiness has in the vaults of his palace two millions, without counting the treasures of Rome."

"Well?" said Bertrand, angrily, when the legate had perused this missive.

"Alas!" said the legate, "his Holiness must have been betrayed."

"Then what is said of these hidden treasures is true?"

"They pretend so."

"Then, Monsieur le Légat," said the constable, "take back this gold; for it is not the bread of the poor, but the super-fluities of the rich, that men about to defend the cause of Christianity require. Listen to what Bertrand Duguesclin, Constable of France, says to you: if the two hundred thousand crowns of the Pope and his cardinals are not here before nightfall, this night I will burn, not the environs, not the town, but the *palace*, and with it its inhabitants; so that by to-morrow's dawn not a vestige shall remain of either Pope, cardinals, or palace!"

These noble words were hailed with such applause by men, officers, and leaders, that no doubt remained of the perfect unanimity of opinion. The ambassador, therefore, silently returned with his laden horses to Avignon.

"My children," said Bertrand, to those of his men who, having been too far distant to overhear what had passed, were astonished at the acclamations of their comrades, "the poor people had only one hundred thousand crowns to give us; it was too little, therefore the Pope will give us two hundred thousand." And, in fact, three hours afterwards, twenty horses bending beneath their load entered the constable's camp, and the legate having piled up three heaps of gold, the one containing one hundred thousand crowns, and the other two each fifty thousand, added to them the pontifical benediction, to which the adventurers replied by wishing him all sorts of prosperity.

Duguesclin then assembled the different leaders, and paid them the sums before agreed upon for the men, the officers, and their captains. When this was done, there still remained one hundred thousand crowns, of which Caverley anxiously inquired the destination.

"You are too prudent, captains," said Bertrand, "not to be aware that to an army commencing a campaign, a certain amount of money is necessary; therefore, these fifty thousand crowns are for the public coffer."

"And the remainder for the private one," said Caverley to his companions. "What a cunning fellow! Peste! I understand."

"Come hither, Messire Chaplain," continued Bertrand, "and let us together compose a little letter to the King of France, for whom I design this remaining sum of money."

"Oh, this is really noble!" exclaimed Caverley. "For myself, I would not do as much even for the Prince of Wales."

CHAPTER XXIII.
THE CUP AND THE LIP.

OUR readers may remember that we left Aïssa returning to her father's dwelling, after the scene in the garden, and Agenor making his way over the wall. Muscaron understood that there was nothing more to detain his master at Bordeaux; therefore, when the young man awoke from his reverie, he found his horse saddled, and his squire ready to set out. Agenor sprang in his saddle with a single bound, and setting spurs to his horse, quitted the town at full gallop, followed by Muscaron, grumbling as usual. They followed the traces of Prince Henry through Guyenne and Bearn, without overtaking him; and it was not until after crossing the Pyrenees and entering Arragon, that they were able to rejoin him. Here they met and recognised each other by the light of the flames proceeding from a little town which Sir Hugh Caverley had caused to be set on fire. It was thus the Free Companies signalized their entrance into Spain. Sir Hugh Caverley had displayed his taste for the picturesque by selecting for a beacon a town situate on an eminence, so that the flames lighted up for ten miles round the unknown land with which he longed to become acquainted.

Henry did not trouble himself about this freak of the English captain's, excepting by begging Bertrand Duguesclin to interpose his authority over those under his command, so as to have as little mischief done as possible. "For," as he judiciously observed, "as this kingdom may one day be mine, I should like it to fall to me in good condition, instead of being in a state of ruin." After receiving his promise to that effect, Henry retired with Mauleon to his tent, and the constable returned to his own. But Sir Hugh Caverley, instead of following their example and retiring to rest, waited until all was silent, and then summoned his secretary.

This secretary was a very important personage in the worthy captain's establishment; since whether Caverley either did not know how to write, or did not choose to hold a pen, his scribe was charged with the regulation of all the transactions that took place between the chief of the adventurers and the prisoners on whom he placed a ransom; and few days passed without his having some task of this kind to occupy him. The scribe presented himself with a pen in one hand, an inkhorn in the other, and a roll of parchment under his arm.

"Come here, Maitre Robert," said the captain, "and write me out a quittance and a pass."

"A quittance for how much?" demanded the clerk.

"Leave a blank for the sum, but do not spare space, for it will be a round one."

"In whose name?" again asked the scribe.

"Leave a blank for the name as well as the sum."

"And the same space?"

"Yes, for the name will be followed by no mean show of titles."

"Good, good," said Maitre Robert, applying himself to his task; "but where is the prisoner?"

"Things are in train to make one."

The clerk knew his patron's habits; he, therefore, did not hesitate for a moment to prepare the schedule, since the captain had announced that affairs were in train to make a prisoner, a prisoner would be forthcoming. He had scarcely penned the last word, when a sound, which seemed drawing nearer, was heard in the direction of the mountains. Caverley seemed to have divined, rather than heard, this sound; for before it reached the watchful ear of the sentinel, he had raised the canvas of his tent. At the same moment, by the faint glimmer of the now dying fire, a band of twenty or thirty Free Companions were seen approaching, surrounding a little group of prisoners, consisting of a knight, apparently in the very prime and flower of his age, a Moor, who seemed unwilling to quit, even for a moment, a curtained litter, and two squires. Caverley had no sooner convinced himself that the little troop really consisted of the persons we have just described, than he dismissed from his tent all its occupants, with the exception of his secretary. These quitted him with a reluctance they did not attempt to conceal, reckoning as they went the value of the new prize that had thus fallen into the hand of the bird of prey they called their captain. Caverley bowed profoundly to the new comers, then addressing the knight, "Sire," said he, "if my men have by chance been wanting in courtesy to your Majesty, pardon them, for they did not know you."

"Sire!" repeated the prisoner, in accents to which he endeavoured to give the intonation of surprise; but his countenance at the same time assuming a pallor that betrayed his secret uneasiness; "are you addressing *me*, captain?"

"Yourself, sire—Don Pedro, the redoubted King of Castile and Murcia."

The knight from pale became livid, and a forced smile struggled on his lips. "In truth, captain," said he, "I am sorry for you, but you make a great mistake in taking me for him you name."

"Faith! monseigneur, I take you for what you are, and think in truth that I have captured a capital prize."

"Think what you please," said the knight, making a movement as though to seat himself; "I shall have very little difficulty in convincing you to the contrary."

"In that case, monseigneur, you must not be so imprudent as to walk."

The knight clenched his hands. "And why not?" said he.

"Because your joints crack at every step you take, which is most agreeable music to the ears of a poor leader of a Free Company, like myself, on whom Providence has bestowed such a windfall as a king."

"Then it is only Don Pedro, whose joints make this noise in walking; may not another man be troubled with the same infirmity?"

"The thing is possible," said Caverley, "but I have a certain means of knowing whether I am in error, as you say."

"What is that?" said the knight, frowning, and evidently weary of these interrogations.

"Prince Henry de Transtamare is not a hundred paces from here; I will send for him, and we shall soon see whether he recognises his beloved brother." The knight made an angry gesture, in spite of himself.

"Ah, you colour!" exclaimed Caverley. "Come, then, confess, and I swear to you, by my word as a captain, that it shall be confined to ourselves, and that your brother shall never know I have had the honour of a few moments' conversation with your Majesty."

"Well; let us see what you require."

"I require nothing, as you know, monseigneur, since I am not certain of the identity of the person who has fallen into my hands."

"Then suppose I am really the King, and speak."

"Peste! how you say that, sire!—speak! do you think, then, that I have so little to say to you, that it may be comprised in two words? No, monseigneur—the first thing is to provide a guard worthy of your Majesty."

"A guard! Then you reckon on detaining me prisoner?"

"Such at least is my intention."

"And, I tell you, that if it even cost me half my kingdom, I will not remain here one hour longer."

"Ah, it will cost you quite that, sire; nor is it too much, since if you remain in your present situation you are almost sure to lose the whole of it."

"Name your price, then!" exclaimed the prisoner.

"I am considering my price," replied Caverley, coolly.

Don Pedro controlled himself by a violent effort, and seated himself on the opposite side of the tent, turning his back on the captain, who appeared to be buried in profound thought. After a moment's silence, he said,

"You shall give me, sire, half a million of gold crowns."

"You are a fool!" replied the prince. "You would not find them in all Spain."

"Three hundred thousand, then. I hope I am now reasonable enough?"

"Not half of it!" said the King.

"Then, sire," said Caverley, "I must write a line to your brother, Henry de Transtamare; he knows better than me what a royal ransom should be, and shall name yours."

Don Pedro clenched his hands, and the sweat started out at the roots of his hair, and rolled in heavy drops down his face. Caverley turned to his secretary—"Maitre Robert," said he, "go and request the Prince Henry de Transtamare to join me in my tent."

The clerk moved towards the door of the tent; but as he was about to pass through it, Don Pedro rose from his seat.

"I will give you the three hundred thousand gold pieces," said he. Caverley started with joy. "But as after parting with you, I might fall into the hands of other robbers of your class, who would again demand ransom, give me a receipt, and a pass."

"And you will count me out three hundred thousand pieces of gold?"

"Not so; for you must be aware that I do not carry such a sum of money about me; but you surely have among your number some one learned in diamonds?"

"I am so myself, sire," said Caverley.

"Good. Come hither, Mothril," said the King, beckoning to the Moor to approach, "you have heard what has passed?"

"Yes, sire," said Mothril, pulling out a long purse, through whose meshes the sparkling contents betrayed themselves.

"Prepare the receipt," said Don Pedro.

"It is already prepared," said the captain. "It has only to be filled up."—"And the pass?"

"It is already signed. I am too much your Majesty's very humble servant to keep you waiting."

A convulsive smile distorted the King's lips, as he approached the table, and read—"I, the undersigned, Hugh Caverley, leader of the English adventurers." The King did not read another word; his eyes flashed lightning. "Your name is Hugh Caverley?" said he.

"Yes," replied the captain, astonished at this sudden joy, of which he could not divine the reason.

"And you are the leader of the English adventurers?" continued the King.

"Most assuredly."

"One moment, then," said the King; "Mothril, return the diamonds to your purse, and the purse to your pocket."

"What do you mean by that?"

"I mean, that it is for me to give orders here, instead of obeying them," said Don Pedro, drawing a parchment from his bosom.

"Orders?" repeated Caverley, haughtily. "Learn, Sir King, that there lives but one man in the world who has a right to give orders to Captain Hugh Caverley."

"And behold his signature at the foot of this parchment," said Don Pedro. "In the name of the Black Prince, I command you, Hugh Caverley, to obey me."

Caverley shook his head, and cast a glance through the bars of his visor at the unrolled parchment in the King's hand; but no sooner did he behold the signature, than he uttered a cry of rage which brought all his officers, who, out of respect, had remained outside the tent, again about him.

In fact, this parchment was the safe-conduct granted by the Black Prince to Don Pedro, and an order to his English subjects to yield him obedience in all things, until he himself came to take the command of the English army.

" You see, I shall decidedly come off more cheaply than either of us imagined," said the King. "But rest easy ; I will recompense you, my brave fellow."

" You are right, Sir King," replied Caverley, with an evil smile, which was hidden by his closed visor. " You are not only free, but I await your commands."

"Well, then," said Don Pedro, "do as you before intended. Send Maître Robert to seek my brother, Prince Henry de Transtamare, and bring him here."

The secretary glanced at the captain, and receiving a sign in the affirmative, left the tent.

CHAPTER XXIV.
THE SAME CONTINUED.

THESE are the events, at present unknown to our readers, which followed the departure or rather the flight of Agenor, after the scene in the garden at Bordeaux.

Don Pedro had obtained from the Prince of Wales the protection he required to enable him to return to Spain, and sure of a reinforcement of men and money, he had set out with Mothril, furnished with a safe-conduct from the prince which gave him power and security in the midst of the English bands. The little troop had wended their way towards the frontier, where, as we have before said, Hugh Caverley had spread a veritable trap for them. And yet, notwithstanding the vigilance of the robber chief and the address of his men, it is probable that, thanks to his knowledge of the locality, Don Pedro would have skirted Arragon, and gained New Castile without accident, had it not been for the following episode.

One evening, whilst the King and Mothril were occupied in tracing on a large map of Spain the route they intended to pursue, the curtains of the litter gently opened, and Aïssa's head peeped between them. By a single look she summoned to her side a slave who was lying on the ground at a little distance from her.

"Slave," said she, " from what land are you ?"

ꝗ

"I was born across the sea," replied the slave, "on the shores that gaze upon Granada without envying her."

"And you would fain return to your own land—is it not so?"

"Yes!" sighed the slave.

"To-morrow, if you will, you shall be free."

"Lake Laoudiah is far away from here, and the fugitive would perish with hunger before he reached it."

"Not so; for the fugitive shall bear with him a string of pearls, each one of which is of sufficient value to support him during the whole journey." And Aïssa unclasped a costly necklace from her throat, and slid it into the slave's hand.

"And what must I do to gain at the same time my liberty and this string of pearls?" asked the slave, trembling with joy.

"You see," said Aïssa, "yonder grey line cutting the horizon—it is the camp of the Christians. How long would it take you to reach it?"

"Before the nightingale has finished his song," replied the slave, "I will be there."

"Listen, then, to what I am about to say to you, and let my words be engraven on your memory." The slave listened in silent ecstacy. "Take this letter," continued Aïssa, "gain the camp, and there inquire for a noble Frank chevalier named the Comte de Mauleon. Ask to be conducted to his presence, and give him this little pouch, in return for which he will give you a hundred pieces of gold—go!"

The slave seized the pouch, and concealed it beneath his coarse habit; and taking advantage of the moment when one of the mules strayed towards the neighbouring wood, he pretended to go in quest of it, and disappeared among the trees with the swiftness of an arrow. No one remarked his movements except Aïssa, who followed him with her eyes, and scarcely dared to breathe until he was out of sight. All took place as the Moorish girl had directed. The slave had scarcely emerged from the brushwood, when he encountered a sentinel, who immediately raised his cross-bow. This was what he sought. He made signs that he wished to speak to him, and the sentinel approached, but without lowering his weapon. The slave then told him he was on his way to the Christian camp, and asked to be conducted to Mauleon. This name, of which Aïssa exaggerated the importance, nevertheless enjoyed a certain notoriety among the companies since the brave conduct of Agenor on his arrest by Caverley's band, and above all since they were aware that to him was owing the constable's co-operation. The soldier gave a signal, and taking the slave by the wrist led him to another sentinel, placed at a hundred paces' distance, who, in his turn, conducted him to the last line of videttes, where, like a spider in the centre of his web, Sir Hugh Caverley was reposing in his tent in the midst of his troops. Immediately understanding by the slight agitation around him that something fresh had occurred, he appeared on the threshold of the tent. The slave was conducted straight to him, murmuring all the while the name of Mauleon, which had hitherto served him as a pass-word.

"Who sent you hither?" inquired Caverley, anxious to avoid any explanation.

"Are you the Comte de Mauleon?" said the slave.

"I am one of his friends," replied Caverley, "and one of his dearest ones besides."

"That is not the same thing," replied the messenger, "and I am ordered to deliver the letter I bring into no hands but his own."

"Listen," said Caverley, "the Count de Mauleon is a brave Christian chevalier, who has many enemies among the Moors and Arabs, who have sworn to assassinate him; we have therefore on our part resolved to allow no one to enter his presence without our first being made acquainted with the message of which he is the bearer."

"Well, then," said the slave, perceiving that all resistance was useless, and the captain's intentions, besides, seeming good to him, "I am sent by Aïssa."

"And who is Aïssa?" inquired Caverley.—"Mothril's daughter."

"Ha! ha!" said the captain, "his Majesty Don Pedro's chief counsellor?"

"Exactly."

"You see the case assumes a still darker aspect; and this message, doubtless, contains some witchcraft."

"Aïssa is no sorceress!" said the slave, shaking his head.

"No matter. I choose to read this missive."

The slave cast a hasty glance around him, to see whether flight were possible; but a group of adventurers had already gathered round him. He drew from his bosom Aïssa's little pouch, and held it out to the captain. "Read it," said he, "you will find in it something concerning me."

Caverley's elastic conscience did not need this invitation; he opened the little amber and benzoin-perfumed envelope, and drew from it a square of white silk, on which Aïssa had written in Spanish, as follows :—

"My DEAR LORD.— I write according to promise; Don Pedro and my father are preparing to pass with me through the defile, and thus reach Arragon. You can, therefore, at one blow secure both happiness and glory. Make them prisoners; and me—your willing captive—with them. If you choose to demand a ransom, they are rich enough to satisfy your ambition; if you prefer glory to money, and restore them their liberty, they are proud enough to publish your generosity; but if you set them free, my noble lord, you can keep me, and I have a coffer filled with rubies and emeralds worthy of a place in a queen's crown. Listen then, and remember what I say. To-night we set out. Post your men in the defile, in such a manner that we cannot pass through it without being observed. Our escort is at this moment feeble, owing to the rapidity of Don Pedro's march, which has prevented the six hundred men-at-arms in attendance on him from yet rejoining him, but it may at any moment become stronger. Thus, my noble lord, Aïssa will be yours without any one being able to take her from you; for you will have made her your prisoner by the force of your victorious arms. One of our slaves will bear you this message. I have promised that you will give him his liberty, and with it a hundred pieces of gold. Fulfil the desire of
                                    " Your Aïssa."

"Oh, oh !" said Caverley to himself. "A King! What good deed have I done lately, that fortune should send me such a prize? A King! This must be seen to; but first to get rid of this fool. Then," said he, "the Comte de Mauleon is to give you your liberty?"

"Yes, captain, and a hundred pieces of gold."

Hugh Caverley did not think fit to notice this latter part of his speech, he only called his squire. "Here," said he, "take your horse, and conduct this man two good leagues from the camp, then leave him there. If he asks you for money, and you have too much, give him some; but I warn you it will be your own gift. Go, my friend," continued he, turning to the slave, "your commission is performed—I am the Comte de Mauleon."

The slave prostrated himself before him.

"And the hundred pieces of gold?" said he.

"Here is my treasurer whom I have ordered to give them to you," said Hugh Caverley, pointing to the squire.

The slave rose joyfully and followed his conductor. He was scarcely a hundred paces from the tent before Caverley despatched a detachment to the mountains, and himself placed the sentinels, so that no person could pass through the defile without being seen. Then, after having given orders that no violence was to be shown to the prisoners, he returned to his tent to await the event. Nor had he long to wait; for the King, impatient to continue his journey, set off without any further delay. They were soon buried in the ravine, to Aïssa's great joy, who impatiently awaited the attack led, as she supposed, by Mauleon. Meanwhile, measures had been so taken by Caverley, and the number of his archers was so great, that not one of Don Pedro's suite made even an attempt to resist. But Aïssa, who had expected to see Mauleon at the head of the troop, began to be uneasy at his absence. Nevertheless, seeing the enterprise succeed according to her wishes, she fancied he was acting so through prudence, and as yet suspected nothing. Thus there was nothing astonishing in the worthy captain so easily recognising Don Pedro. It is true he somewhat dreaded Mauleon's wrath at the discovery of his secret relative to Mothril and Aïssa; but he immediately reflected, that it would be easy to ascribe it all to the treachery of the slave; and that he could besides make of this abuse of confidence a claim on Mauleon's gratitude, since, while making Don Pedro and Mothril pay a heavy ransom, he had resolved on resigning Aïssa to her young lover—an act of generosity for which he highly commended himself.

We have seen how the safe-conduct of the Prince of Wales, exhibited by Don Pedro, changed the whole aspect of affairs, and overthrew the bold and cleverly concocted schemes of Caverley. Don Pedro, after Robert's departure, was engaged in relating to the chief of the adventurers the particulars of the treaty concluded at Bordeaux, when a great noise was heard—the trampling of horses, the clashing of armour, and

the clank of swords against the sides of armed men.   Then
the curtains of the tent were rudely pushed aside, and the
face of Henry de Transtamare appeared, lighted up with a
sinister joy.   Behind him came Mauleon, glancing inquir-
ingly around him ; he caught sight of the litter, which his
eyes did not again quit.   On Henry's arrival, Don Pedro
drew back, looking as pale as his brother, and his hand involuntarily seeking his absent sword ; nor did he appear at
ease until in his retreat he encountered one of the supports
of the tent, against which hung a complete suit of armour,
and again felt in his grasp the cold steel of a battle-axe.   The
two brothers stood for a moment silently regarding each
other, and exchanging lightning-like glances of menace and
hate.   Henry was the first to break silence.

"I fancy," said he, with a dark smile, "that here is the
war finished before it is even commenced."

"Ah, you think so !" said Don Pedro, tauntingly, yet
threateningly.

"I so firmly believe it," replied Henry, "that I shall first
of all ask this worthy captain what price he demands for a
capture of such importance as the one he has just made ;
since had he taken twenty cities, or gained a hundred battles
—exploits for which we pay well—he would not have had
such claims on our gratitude as he has at present through
this single achievement."

"It is flattering," replied Don Pedro, "to be estimated at so
high a value, therefore courtesy for courtesy.   Supposing
yourself to be in my situation, Don Henry, at what sum
would you estimate your person ?"

"I believe he still mocks me !" exclaimed Henry, furiously.

"Let us see how all this will end," muttered Caverley—
who began to enjoy this scene, rather as an amateur-artist
than a greedy speculator—seating himself so as not to lose
the smallest detail.   Henry glanced at him, and then prepared to reply to Don Pedro.

"Well, be it so," said he, casting a glance of the most
deadly hatred at his brother.   "Friend Caverley, I will give
you for this man—once a king, but on whose brow no
longer rests the golden reflection of a crown—either two
hundred thousand gold crowns, or two good cities, which
you please."

"Well," said Caverley, stroking his iron-covered chin, as

he glanced through the bars of his still closed visor at Don Pedro. "The offer would be acceptable enough, but——"

"Well," said Henry, "what were you going to say?"

Mauleon could no longer restrain his impatient curiosity.

"The captain was doubtless about to say," interrupted he, "that Don Pedro is not the only prisoner, and that he wishes a value to be placed on the others also."

"Faith! this is what may be called reading a man's thoughts, and you are a brave chevalier, Sire Agenor," exclaimed Caverley. "Yes, on my soul, I have made other prisoners and noble ones, too; but . . . . " and he again hesitated.

"You shall be paid for them, captain!" exclaimed Mauleon, boiling over with impatience. "Where are they? Doubtless in this litter." Henry laid his hand on the young man's arm, and gently restrained him.

"Do you accept my offer, Captain Caverley?" said he.

"The answer rests with me, prince," said Don Pedro.

"Oh, do not assume the master here, Don Pedro," said Don Henry, disdainfully; "for you are no longer king. Therefore reserve your reply until I address you."

Don Pedro smiled, and turning to Caverley, "Explain to him, captain," said he, "how it happens that you cannot accept his proposal."

Caverley drew Agenor aside, and passing his hand over his iron visor, as if it had been his brow—"My brave friend," said he, "between good comrades like ourselves, there should be no deception."—Agenor regarded him with astonishment. "Well, then," continued the captain, "if you put faith in me, leave this tent immediately; and if you have a good horse, mount him, and spur him forward as long as he will go."

"We are betrayed!" exclaimed Mauleon, a sudden light breaking on his mind. "To arms, prince! to arms!"

Henry looked at him with astonishment, and mechanically laid his hand on the pommel of his dagger.

"In the name of the Prince of Wales!" exclaimed Don Pedro, who found the comedy was drawing to a close—extending his hand with a commanding gesture, "I require you, Messire Hugh Caverley, to arrest the Prince Henry de Transtamare.

The words were scarcely uttered, before Henry's sword was in his hand; but Caverley, raising the visor of his helmet for a moment, placed a trumpet at his lips, and at the sound, twenty adventurers rushed upon the prince, and immediately disarmed him.

"It is done," said Caverley to Don Pedro. "Now if you will take my advice, Sir King, you will retire, for there will soon be a shower of hard knocks, I can answer for it."

"How so?" asked the King.

"The Frenchman who has just passed through yonder door, will not allow his prince to be captured without breaking a few heads in his honour."

Don Pedro leaned towards the opening, and perceived Agenor with his foot in the stirrup, evidently about to seek assistance. The King seized a cross-bow, and fitting an arrow, aimed it at Agenor.

"David slew Goliath with a sling," said he. "It will be strange if Goliath cannot slay David with a cross-bow."

"Stay a moment, Sir King!" exclaimed Caverley. "What the devil are you about? You are scarcely arrived here before you upset everything. What will the constable say if I allow his friend to be slain?" and he struck up the cross-bow, just as Don Pedro had his finger on the trigger. The bolt fell harmless.

"The constable!" exclaimed Don Pedro, stamping his foot. "It was well worth making me miss my aim from such a fear. Set your snare, hunter, and capture this great Wild Boar also; by this means the chase will be finished at once, and on this condition, I will pardon you."

"It is easy to talk of such a thing. Take the constable, good!—just come and take the constable! Good God!" he continued, shrugging his shoulders, "what boasters these Spaniards are!"

"Sir Hugh Caverley, by heaven! I mean what I say." "Take the Constable! I am not curious; but faith, I should dearly like to see *you* make such a capture!"

"Here is one, already," said Don Pedro, pointing to Agenor, who was being led back prisoner. As he was passing through the camp at full speed, one of the adventurers, with a pruning-hook, had ham-strung his horse, which fell to the ground, with its rider under it.

So long as she believed her lover out of this affray, and exempt from danger, Aïssa had neither moved nor spoken—it appeared as though the conflicting interests by which she was surrounded were totally indifferent to her; but at the

approach of Mauleon, disarmed and in the hands of his enemies, the curtains of the litter were thrown back, and the
young girl's face appeared looking paler even than her long
veil of fine white wool, the usual head covering of Eastern
women. Agenor uttered a cry. Aïssa sprang from her litter,
and rushed towards him.

"Allah!" exclaimed Mothril, knitting his brows.

"What is the meaning of this?" demanded the King.

"Now for an explanation!" thought Caverley.

Henry de Transtamare cast on Agenor a dark and defiant
look, which he perfectly understood.

"You can speak to me, lady," said he, addressing Aïssa.
"But do so quickly, and aloud, for from the moment of our
becoming your prisoners to that of our death, there will probably be little time to lose for even those most deeply
attached to each other."

"*Our* prisoners!" exclaimed Aïssa. "Oh, that is not what
I wished, my noble lord : I had hoped quite the contrary."

Caverley began to feel greatly embarrassed ; this man of
iron almost trembled at the thought of the accusation about
to be brought against him by these two young people, both
of whom were in his power.

"My letter!" continued Aïssa. "Have you not received
my letter?"

"What letter?" asked Agenor.

"Enough, enough!" interrupted Mothril, whose projects
this scene began to destroy. "Captain, it is the King's
orders that you conduct Prince Henry de Transtamare to
his quarters, and this young man to mine."

"Caverley, you are a coward!" vociferated Agenor,
furiously, endeavouring to free his wrists from the rude
gauntlets encircling them.

"Faith! it was your own fault," retorted the captain. "I
told you to save yourself, and you would not, or you did so
too late, which amounts to the same thing."

"Hasten, gentlemen," said Don Pedro, "and let a council
be assembled this very night to judge the bastard who
calls himself my brother—the rebel who pretends to be
my King! Caverley, he offered you two cities. I am more
generous than he is, I will give you a province. Mothril,
summon my attendants ; before another hour is past, we
must be lodged in some strong fortress."

Mothril inclined his head, and went out; but he had scarcely gone ten paces, when he started back precipitately, making signs for silence.

"What is it?" inquired Caverley, with ill-disguised uneasiness.

"Speak, good Mothril," said Don Pedro.

"Listen," replied the Moor. In fact, a sound was heard like the rolling of thunder or the progress of a body of horsemen.

"Our Lady of Guesclin!" suddenly exclaimed a loud and sonorous voice.

"The constable!" muttered Caverley, who recognised the war-cry of the rude Breton.

"The constable!" repeated Don Pedro, knitting his brows, for he was no stranger to this terrible cry, even without having heard it.

The prisoners exchanged looks, and a hopeful smile played upon their lips. Mothril drew nearer his daughter, and clasped her more closely in his arms.

"Sir King," observed Caverley, in the grumbling tone which he never dropped, even in moments of danger, "you were wishing to snare the Wild Boar: I fancy here he comes to spare you the trouble."

Don Pedro beckoned to his soldiers to range themselves behind him. Caverley, determined to preserve his neutrality between his new leader and his ancient comrade, withdrew on one side; a triple row of guards surrounded the prince and Mauleon.

"What are you doing, Caverley?" said Don Pedro.

"I yield you the first place, sire, both as my King and my leader," said the captain.

"Good," said Don Pedro. "Let every one obey me, then."

The troops stopped. A sound was then heard of a man leaping from his horse; the clank of steel rang upon their ears, and immediately afterwards Bertrand Duguesclin entered the tent.

CHAPTER XXV.

THE WILD BOAR TAKEN IN THE SNARE.

BERTRAND raised his visor, and cast a single glance around the assembly. He bowed slightly to Don Pedro, more respectfully to Henry de Transtamare, and shook Caverley by the hand.

"Good day, Sir Captain," said he, calmly; "you have taken a rich prize. Ah, Sire de Mauleon, pardon. I did not perceive you." These words, which seemed to indicate a positive ignorance of the real state of affairs, stupified all present with astonishment. But Bertrand, far from remarking this almost solemn silence, continued, "I trust, Captain Caverley, that you have shown the prisoner all the consideration due, not only to his rank, but his misfortunes."

Henry was about to reply, but Don Pedro interrupted him.

"Yes, my lord constable, rest assured we have shown the prisoner all the respect he merited."

"*You*," said Bertrand, with an expression of countenance that would have done credit to the most skilful actor, "*you* have shown the prisoner respect. And pray, what may your highness mean by that?"

"Yes, Sire Constable," said Don Pedro, smiling; "I repeat that *we* have shown the prisoner all the consideration he merited."

Bertrand looked at Caverley, who stood unmoved, his face hidden beneath his visor.

"I do not understand you," said he.

"Dear constable," said Henry, rising with difficulty from his seat, for he had been wounded and half stifled in the affray, "Don Frederick's assassin is right; he is our master, and we, through treachery, are his prisoners."

"Hum!" said Bertrand, turning round with so evil a look, that more than one face in the assembly became pale. "Treachery, do you say? And who, then, is the traitor?"

"My lord constable," said Caverley, stepping forward, "the word treachery is a wrong one; it should rather be 'fidelity.'"

"Fidelity!" repeated the constable, with apparently increasing astonishment.

"Undoubtedly," replied the captain; "for we are English, are we not, and consequently subjects of the Prince of Wales?"

"Well, and what has that to do with it?" asked Bertrand, throwing back his broad shoulders as though to breathe more freely, and letting his heavy gauntleted hand fall on the hilt of his sword, "Who said, my good Caverley, that you were not a subject of the Prince of Wales?"

"Then, my lord, you will agree with me—for no one knows the laws of discipline better than yourself—that I must obey the orders of my prince."

"And his orders are these," said Don Pedro, holding out the parchment to Bertrand.

"I cannot read," said the constable, abruptly.

Don Pedro drew back the offered document, and Caverley, brave as he was, began to tremble.

"Well," continued Bertrand, "I fancy I understand it all now. His Majesty Don Pedro was taken captive by Captain Caverley, but on displaying the safe-conduct received from the Prince of Wales, was immediately restored to liberty."

"Exactly so," exclaimed Caverley, who for a moment hoped that Duguesclin, in his loyalty, would approve of what he had done.

"So far nothing could be better," said the constable. Caverley breathed more freely. "But," continued Bertrand, "there is still one thing obscure to me."

"What is it?" demanded Don Pedro, haughtily. "Only make haste, Messire Bertrand, for all these interrogations become wearisome."

"I have just finished," resumed the constable, with his terrible impassibility. "But what need was there for Captain Caverley, in setting Don Pedro free, to make Don Henry prisoner?"

At these words, and the attitude Bertrand assumed in pronouncing them, Mothril judged that the moment had arrived for summoning a reinforcement of Moors and English to Don Pedro's aid. Bertrand did not seem even aware of this manœuvre; only his voice became, if possible, still colder and sterner.

"I await a reply," said he.

It was Don Pedro who made it. "I am astonished," said he, "that French chevaliers should be so ignorant as not to be aware that there is double benefit to be derived from making a friend at the same time you defeat an enemy."

"Are you of that opinion, Maître Caverley?" demanded Bertrand, fixing on the captain a glance, menacing from its very serenity.

"I have no choice, messire," replied the captain; "I only obey."

"And I, on the contrary, command," said Bertrand.

"Therefore I order you to immediately set his Highness Prince Henry de Transtamare—whom I see yonder, guarded by your soldiers—at liberty. And, as I am more courteous than you, I do not require you to arrest Don Pedro in his stea.; although I, whose money you have at this moment in your pocket—I, who am your master, since I have hired you, have justly the right to do so." Caverley made a movement as if to speak; Don Pedro stretched out his arm.

"Make no reply, captain," said he. "There is but one master here, and that is myself. You will therefore please to obey me, and that immediately. Don Henry, Messire Bertrand, and you, Comte de Mauleon, I declare you all three my prisoners."

At these terrible words a deep silence reigned through the tent, in the midst of which, at a sign from Don Pedro, six men-at-arms detached themselves from the group, and approached the constable, with the intention of securing his person as they had already done that of Don Henry; but the worthy chevalier with one blow of his fist felled the first that presented himself, and raising his powerful voice, till the war-cry of Duguesclin echoed over the plain, drew his sword. In a moment the tent presented a scene of the most terrible confusion. Agenor had by a single effort pushed aside the two soldiers carelessly guarding him, and joined the constable, whilst Henry had unfastened with his teeth the cord binding his wrists. Mothril, Don Pedro, and the Moors formed a threatening group.

Aïssa, unmindful of all save her lover, had passed her head between the curtains of her litter, and was crying out, "Courage, my noble lord, courage!"

Caverley had retreated, taking with him his band of English, so as to preserve his neutrality as long as possible, only to be prepared in every case, he caused the "Bouteselle" to be sounded. The combat raged. Arrows, bolts, and leaden balls propelled by slings, whistled through the air, and showered on the three chevaliers, when suddenly a tremendous clamour was heard, and a troop of armed horsemen dashed into the tent, dealing blows right and left, overturning and crushing everything in their way.

From their cries of " Guesclin! Guesclin!" they were easily recognised as the Bretons commanded by Le Bègue de Vilaine, Bertrand's inseparable friend, whom he had posted at the barriers of the camp with instructions not to charge until they heard the cry of " Our Lady of Guesclin !"   Then ensued a moment of strange confusion, during which friends and enemies were mingled, confounded, and blended together; then the dust cleared away, and the first rays of the sun rising behind the mountains of Castile beheld the Bretons masters of the field.

Don Pedro, Mothril, Aïssa, and the Moors, had disappeared like a vision.   All that remained to show that they had not been engaged with a phantom host was a few dark corpses, stretched here and there, swimming in their blood.

Agenor was the first to discover this disappearance ; he sprang upon the first horse that came to hand, and without observing it was wounded, spurred towards the nearest hillock, from whence he could obtain a view of the plain. From thence he beheld in the distance five Arab horses entering the wood, and athwart the blue haze of morning could distinguish the white robe and floating veil of Aïssa. Without pausing to see whether he was followed or not, he by an impulse of wild hope urged his horse in pursuit, but after proceeding a few paces, the wounded animal fell to rise no more.   He came up to the litter, but it was deserted ; and the only trace he found of its occupant was a bouquet of roses all bedewed with tears.   Meanwhile, the English cavalry awaited in good order the word of command from their captain.   Caverley had so skilfully disposed his men that they enclosed the Bretons in a circle.   Bertrand perceived at a glance that the aim of this manœuvre was to cut off his retreat.   Caverley came forward. "Messire Bertrand," said he, "to prove that we are still loyal comrades, we will open our ranks and allow you to regain your quarters.   That will show you that the English are true to their word, and respect the chivalry of France."

Meantime, Bertrand as calm and silent as though nothing extraordinary had taken place had remounted his horse, and received his lance from his squire's hands.   He looked round and perceived Agenor had done the same, and that all his Bretons were behind him in good array and ready to charge.

"Sir Englishman," said he, "you are a double-dealer, and if I were strong enough I would hang you on yonder chestnut tree."

"Take care, Messire Constable !" retorted Caverley, "or

you will force me to make you prisoner in the name of the Prince of Wales."

"Bah !" said Duguesclin.

Caverley understood the menace contained in the constable's mocking exclamation, and turning to his men, " Close your ranks !" cried he.   They obeyed him, and presented a solid iron wall to the Bretons.

"Come, my men," said Bertrand to his brave followers, "it is drawing near breakfast time, our tents are below, let us return to them."   And he spurred his horse forward so rudely that Caverley had barely time to start on one side, and avoid the whirlwind of men and horses that came sweeping on.

When Caverley looked round he beheld a bloody gap ; and at five hundred paces' distance, the Bretons galloping along in as good order as if they had only passed through a field of ripe wheat.

"And yet I had resolved to have nothing to do with these brutes !" muttered he, shaking his head.   " Devil take these bullies and their bragging !   I lose by this bout at least a dozen good horses and four men, without counting—unfortunate wretch that I am !—a King's ransom.   Come, comrades, let us decamp.   From this moment we are Castilians. Let us change our standard." And the adventurers broke up their camp that very day, and set out to join Don Pedro.

CHAPTER XXVI.

THE POLITICS OF MESSIRE BERTRAND DUGUESCLIN.

SOME hours had now elapsed since the scenes described in the preceding chapter, and the positions of the different personages of our tale presented a sufficiently varied spectacle. On one of the distant mountain summits, which they had attained with a rapidity scarcely to be surpassed by the eagle's flight, reappeared the little fugitive troop, three things among them being distinctly visible, viz., Mothril's scarlet robe, Aïssa's white veil, and the steel point of Don Pedro's casque, which glittered in the sun like a tiny spark.   Along the mountain road Caverley's troop—ranged in order for battle—were wending their way, the foremost horsemen beginning to be lost in the wood that spread at its foot.   In the foreground of the picture stood Henry de Transtamare leaning against a gigantic tuft of broom, and from time to time ruefully contemplating his wrists still reddened by the pressure of the cords. These vestiges of the frightful scene that had taken place in the English leader's camp were the only proofs remaining that a few short hours before Don Pedro was in his power—that fortune had smiled on him for an instant only to precipitate him from the height of premature prosperity to the darkest and deepest abyss of uncertainty and helplessness.

Near Henry, several Bretons, exhausted by fatigue, lay stretched upon the grass, with their mantles drawn over their faces, buried in sleep. Le Bègue de Vilaine and Oliver de Mauny were not sleeping, but watching with profound attention the movements of the English, whose vanguard, as we have already said, was beginning to be lost in the wood, whilst its rear-guard was occupied in striking the tents and loading the mules with them. In the midst of the workers Caverley could be distinguished moving like an armed phantom among his men, and superintending the execution of his orders. Thus all these men scattered over the vast landscape, and wending their way like fugitive ants towards the four points of the compass, were, nevertheless, all actuated by the same feeling—the desire of vengeance.

Bertrand Duguesclin at last arose from the little hillock on which he was seated, and approached Prince Henry; but although his heavy footsteps seemed to shake the earth, they did not arouse the young man from his reverie. Bertrand continued to approach until his shadow, interposing between the sun and the prince, caused him to raise his eyes and fix them on the good constable, who stood before him leaning on his sword, with his visor half raised, and an encouraging smile on his countenance.

"Ah, constable!" said Henry, sadly shaking his head, "what a day!"

"Bah! monseigneur," said Duguesclin, "I have seen worse. Ma foi! we must remember that we might have been prisoners, and here we are free."

"Ah, constable, do you not see that everything has escaped us!"

"What do you call everything?"

"The King of Castile, by St. James!" exclaimed Don Henry, with a gesture of rage and menace that made Agenor who attracted by the loud tones of the prince had drawn near them, shudder, for he could not forget that this abhorred enemy was a brother.

Bertrand had not sought the prince's presence without a motive; he had, in fact, detected, on all visages an expression of lassitude strongly resembling the commencement of discouragement.   He leaned his two hands on the pommel ·of his sword:—" Pardon, monseigneur," said he, " if I distract your thoughts from their present course, but I wish you to listen to me for a moment."

"What is it, my dear constable?" said Henry, whom this preamble made very uneasy, for he had trusted entirely to the loyalty of the Bretons to accomplish the gigantic scheme of his usurpation.

" You just now said, monseigneur, that the King of Castile had escaped."—" Undoubtedly I said so."

"Well, then, monseigneur, it was an equivoque, and I engage to dispel the state of doubt into which you have thrown your faithful servants.   Is there any other King of Castile besides yourself?"

Henry raised his head like a bull that feels the sharp prick of the picador's dart:—"Explain yourself, dear constable," said he.

" That is easily done.   If you and I do not understand each other on this subject, neither will my Bretons and your Castilians; and the rest of the Spanish people will never know whether they are to cry ' Viva Don Henry!' or ' Viva Don Pedro!' "

Henry listened without understanding what the constable was driving at.   Nevertheless, as the reasoning appeared extremely logical, he made an affirmative sign of the head.

" Well?" said he at last.

"Well," resumed Duguesclin, "since two kings would cause confusion, let us begin by unmaking one."

" But to accomplish that, Sir Constable, we shall be obliged to go to war."

" Very well; but we have not yet gained one of those signal battles which at once dethrone a king; and whilst waiting for the day which will decide both your own fate and that of Castile, you are not certain whether you are, or are not, its king."

" But, my dear constable! am I not in your eyes its true monarch?"

"That does not suffice; you must be so in the eyes of all the world."

"And that, messire, appears to me impossible, without either winning a battle, being proclaimed king by the army, or taking some great city."

"That is exactly my opinion, monseigneur."—"Yours!"

"Undoubtedly; do you fancy that because I strike I never think? Be undeceived; I do not always do the one, and I sometimes do the other. You say you must wait until you have either won a battle, been proclaimed by the army, or taken a great city?"

"Yes; at least one of these things, and they all appear to me very difficult, if not impossible."

"And why, sire?"—"Because I am afraid."

"Ah, if *you* are afraid, sire, *I* fear nothing," replied the constable, quickly. "If you will not do it, I will."

"We shall fall from so great a height, constable, that we shall never rise again."

"So long as you do not fall into the grave, monseigneur, you are sure to rise again, at least while you have your Breton chevaliers by your side, and your good Castilian blade in your hand. Come, monseigneur, display your resolution."

"Oh, rest assured I shall show enough when there is occasion for it," said Henry, his eyes sparkling at the nearer prospect of the realization of his dream; "but at present I see no signs of either battle or army."

"No; but you see the city." Henry gazed around him. "Where are the kings crowned in this country, monseigneur?" asked Duguesclin.

"At Burgos."

"Well, then, although my geographical knowledge is not very extensive, it seems to me that Burgos is in our neighbourhood."

"Without doubt; at most twenty or five-and-twenty leagues from here."

"Then let us take Burgos."—"Burgos!" repeated Henry.

"Yes, Burgos. If you have any wish to possess it, I will give it you, as sure as my name is Duguesclin."

"What, such a stronghold as that, constable," said Henry, shaking his head doubtfully; "a capital city, containing, besides the nobility, a powerful middle class of Christians, Jews, and Mahometans, who, though usually divided, will unite to

Defend their privileges. Burgos is, in one word, the key of Castile, and seems to have been selected as the most impregnable sanctuary by those who place there the crown and the royal insignia."

"Then it is thither, if it please you, monseigneur, that we will proceed," said Duguesclin, calmly.

"My friend," said the prince, "do not allow yourself to be carried away by feelings of affection—an exaggerated gratitude. Let us consider our strength."

"To horse, monseigneur!" cried Bertrand, seizing the bridle of the prince's steed, as it wandered among the tufts of broom; "to horse! and let us march straight to Burgos." And, on a sign from the constable, a Breton trumpet gave the signal.

The slumberers were the first in the saddle, and Bertrand, who regarded his men with the mingled attention of a leader and affection of a father, remarked that the greater part of them, instead of, as usual, surrounding the prince, ranged themselves behind himself, as if recognising in him alone their true leader.

"It was time!" he whispered in Agenor's ear.

"Time for what?" demanded the person he addressed, starting as if just awoke from a dream.

"Time to restore our soldiers' activity."

"It is not a bad thing to do so," replied the young man; "for it is hard for men to be journeying they know not whither, nor for why."

"But you do not speak for yourself," said Bertrand; "yet I have always observed you the first in marches and skirmishes for the honour of our country."

"Oh, I, messire, ask for nothing better than to fight, and, above all, be on the march; and never is a march too rapid for me." And, saying these words, Agenor rose in his stirrups as if to enable his gaze to reach the mountains that bordered the horizon. Bertrand made no reply; he contented himself with consulting a goatherd, who assured him that the shortest route to Burgos was through Calahorra, a little town at scarcely six leagues' distance.

"Forward, then, to Calahorra!" said the constable, and he spurred on his horse, whilst behind him swept a formidable iron-clad squadron bearing in their midst Henry de Trans tamare.

CHAPTER XXVII.

THE MESSENGER.

It was towards the close of the second day's march that the small town of Calahorra presented itself to the notice of the little army commanded by Henry de Transtamare and Bertrand Duguesclin. This army, which had now been reinforced by all the scattered bands, amounted to nearly ten thousand men. The attempt they were about to make on Calahorra, the advanced outpost of Burgos, would prove almost decisive, since on their success in this quarter, which served as a mouthpiece for the sentiments of all Old Castile, depended, in a great measure, that of the whole campaign. Checked before Calahorra, Don Henry's march would become war; but that city passed without obstacle, he would advance upon the road to triumph. The gates of the city were closed, the soldiers guarding them were at their posts; sentinels, with their cross-bows on their shoulders, paced backwards and forwards on the walls. Everything was in a state of, if not menace, at least of defence.

Duguesclin led his little army to within bowshot of the ramparts, then causing a trumpet to sound a rally round the standard, he pronounced a discourse framed with the mingled assurance of a Breton and the address of a man brought up at the court of Charles V., and concluded it by proclaiming Don Henry de Transtamare King of the Two Castiles, Seville and Leon, in the room of Don Pedro, "murderer and base knight." These words, which Bertrand pronounced with all the force of his strong lungs, caused ten thousand swords to flash from their scabbards, and beneath the brightest sky in the world, at the hour when the sun was slowly sinking behind the mountains of Navarre, Calahorra beheld from her ramparts the imposing spectacle of a falling throne and a tottering crown. Bertrand having thus spoken, and received the response of his army, turned towards the town, as though to demand its views on the subject. The inhabitants of Calahorra—well fortified and furnished with arms and provisions as it was—did not long remain in doubt. The constable's attitude was significant, and that of his men with their raised lances no less so. They probably reflected that the weight alone of this body of cavalry would be sufficient to burst through their walls, and that the most simple method of avoiding this misfortune would be to open their gates. They, therefore, responded to the shouts of the army by enthusiastic shouts of "Viva Don Henry de Transtamare, King of the Two Castiles, Seville and Leon!" These first acclamations, pronounced in the Castilian tongue, deeply moved Don Henry. He raised the visor of his helmet, and advancing alone towards the walls, "Say," said he, "Viva *good* Don Henry, for I will be so good to Calahorra, that she shall always remember having been the first to hail me King of Castile."

It was no longer enthusiasm that reigned, but frenzy. The gates flew open as if by the touch of a fairy's wand, and a compact mass of men, women, and children issued from the town, and mingled with the royal troops. In an hour one of those splendid *fêtes* was organized of which Nature alone is sufficient to furnish the material—the wine, the flowers, the honey of this fair land. Lutes and dulcimers, accompanied by women's voices; perfumed tapers, the ringing of bells, and the chanting of monks,—all shed their intoxicating influence over the new King and his companions during the whole of that night. Bertrand, however, assembled his council of Bretons, and said to them, "Here is Prince Henry de Transtamare now proclaimed, if not crowned, King; you are no longer supporting an adventurer, but a prince possessing lands, fiefs, and titles. I wager that Caverley will regret being with us no longer." Then, in the midst of the profound silence always accorded him, not only as a leader, but as a warrior, as brave as prudent, and as experienced as brave, he unfolded all his designs, or rather his hopes, which were soon shared by his adherents. He finished his discourse just as they came to inform him that the prince desired his presence as well as that of the Breton leaders, and that he awaited their coming at the Government House of Calahorra, which had been placed at his disposal by the government. Bertrand, in obedience to the invitation he had received, immediately proceeded thither. Henry was already seated on a throne, with a circlet of gold—the mark of royalty—encircling the crest of his helmet.

"Sir Constable," said the prince, holding out his hand to Duguesclin, "you made me a king. I will make you a count. You have given me an empire: I offer you a domain. I style myself—thanks to you—Henry de Transtamare, King of

Castile, Seville, and Leon; and you shall call yoursel
thanks to me—Constable of France and Comte de Soria."

The plaudits of both leaders and soldiers proved to the
King that he had just performed an act of not only gratitude, but justice.

"As to you, noble captains," he continued, "my presents
will not be as great as you merit, but your future conquests,
by increasing my dominions and augmenting my wealth, will
render you also more rich and more powerful." He then
caused his gold and silver plate, his horses, equipages, and
everything precious that the palace of Calahorra contained,
to be distributed amongst them, and named the governor of
the town governor of the province. Then, coming forward
on the balcony, he distributed his remaining eighty thousand
gold crowns to the soldiers, and showing them his empty
coffers, "I give them into your hands," said he, "for we will
refill them at Burgos."

"At Burgos!" exclaimed captains and soldiers.

"At Burgos!" repeated the inhabitants, for whom this
night, passed in feasting and jollity, was a sufficient pledge
of fraternity.

Meanwhile the day had dawned; the troops were ready to
set out; already the royal banner floated among the pennons
of the different Breton and Castilian regiments, when a loud
noise was heard at the principal gate of Calahorra, and the
shouts of the populace, as they hurried towards the centre of
the town, announced some important event. This was the
arrival of a messenger. Bertrand quitted the council hall.
Henry drew himself up proudly.

"Make way for him," said he.

The crowd parted, giving to view a dark-complexioned
man enveloped in a white burnous, and mounted on an Arab
horse with smoking nostrils, long wavy mane, and legs as
slender as rods of steel.

"The prince, Don Henry?" said he.

"You mean the King," said Duguesclin.

"I know no other king than Don Pedro," replied the Arab.

"Here is one at least who uses no disguise," muttered
Duguesclin.

"Good," said the prince; "let us waive this discussion.
"I am he whom you seek."

The messenger bowed his head, without alighting from his
horse.

"Whence do you come?" said Don Henry.—"From Burgos."

"And from whom?"—"From his Majesty Don Pedro."

"Don Pedro at Burgos!" exclaimed Don Henry.

"Yes, my lord," replied the man.

Henry and Bertrand exchanged glances.

"And what does Don Pedro desire?" demanded the prince.

"Peace," returned the Arab.

"Oh! oh!" said Bertrand, whose honesty of purpose displayed itself, regardless of private interests; "this is good news."

Don Henry knit his brows. Agenor trembled with joy. Peace was to him liberty to seek Aïssa, and attempt to win her.

"And this peace," said Don Henry, sharply. "On what conditions will it be accorded us?"

"Answer, monseigneur," returned the envoy, "that you are as anxious for it as ourselves, and the King, my master, will be indulgent regarding the conditions."

But Bertrand had now reflected on the mission he had received from King Charles—a mission of vengeance towards Don Pedro, and destruction to the Free Companies.

"You cannot accept peace," said he to Don Henry, "before having gained sufficient advantage on your side to render the conditions good."

"I was thinking the same thing, but I waited for your opinion," said Don Henry, eagerly, for he dreaded being obliged to share what he wished to possess entirely.

"What is my lord's reply?" demanded the envoy.

"Answer for me, Comte de Soria," said the King.

"Willingly, sire," said Bertrand, bowing. Then turning to the messenger, he said, "Sir herald, return to your master, and inform him that we will treat for peace on our arrival at Burgos."

"At Burgos!" exclaimed the envoy, in a tone denoting more fear than surprise.

"Yes, at Burgos."

"The great city occupied by Don Pedro and his army?"

"Precisely," said the constable.

"This, then, is your reply, my lord," said the herald, turning towards Henry de Transtamare.

The prince made a sign in the affirmative.

"Then God preserve you!" said the envoy, covering his head with his mantle, and, bowing to the prince as he had done on his arrival, he turned his horse's head, and rode leisurely through the crowd, which, disappointed in its hopes, remained mute and motionless during his passage.

"Go a little faster, sir messenger," exclaimed Bertrand, "unless you wish us to arrive there before you."

But the horseman, without turning his head, without even appearing conscious that these words were addressed to him, allowed his steed to gradually pass from a gentle amble to a rapid trot, and from that to so swift a pace, that before the vanguard of the army had passed through the gates of Calahorra, to march upon Burgos, he had become invisible even from the ramparts.

Some news traverse the air like the atoms borne hither and thither by the wind. Thus by the evening of the day on which Don Henry, side by side with the constable, entered Calahorra, the tidings of his proclamation as King of the Two Castiles, Seville, and Leon, had reached Burgos, where Don Pedro had himself arrived only a quarter of an hour before. What eagle, in passing through the air, had let it fall from his talons? None could say; but in a few moments every one was convinced of its truth. Don Pedro alone doubted it.

"Even supposing," said he, "that this bastard has entered Calahorra, it is not probable that he has been proclaimed King."

"If he were not so yesterday," replied Mothril, "he is certain to be so to-day."

"Then let us march upon him, and declare war," said Don Pedro.

"Not so. Let us remain where we are, and declare peace," said Mothril.

"Peace!"

"Yes; and even purchase it, if it be necessary; for what does a promise cost—especially to you, sire?"

"Ah! ah!" said Don Pedro, who began to understand.

"Don Henry desires a throne," continued Mothril. "Give him one after your own fashion, you can cast him from it afterwards. If you make him King, he can no longer doubt you, who have placed the crown upon his brow. Is it, I ask you, so advantageous to have a ceaseless rival hovering about you, who may at any moment fall upon you like a clap of thunder, you know not from whence? Assign a kingdom to Don Henry, imprison him in a space well known to your-self; treat him as they do the sturgeon, whom they apparently set at liberty in a fishpond furnished with a thousand retreats, but where they are sure of finding him when they want him; whilst in the open sea he might escape them altogether."

"True," said Don Pedro, listening more and more attentively.

"If he demands Leon," continued Mothril, "give him Leon; as soon as he has accepted it, he must come and offer you his thanks, you will have him by your side, at your board, within reach of your arm, for a day—an hour—ten minutes. They say he is at Calahorra—then give him all the territory between there and Burgos, you will only be nearer him."

Don Pedro perfectly understood Mothril.

"Yes," said he, thoughtfully, "it was thus I drew near Don Frederick."

"Ah!" said Mothril, "I thought your Majesty had forgotten it."

"It is well," said Don Pedro, letting his hand fall on Mothril's shoulder, "it is well." And thereupon the King dispatched to Don Henry one of those indefatigable Moors who measure their days by the thirty leagues accomplished by their horses.

Mothril did not for a moment doubt that Don Henry would embrace their proposals, were it only in the hope of depriving Don Pedro of the second part of the empire, after accepting from him the first. But he reckoned without the constable. Thus, when the reply arrived from Calahorra, Don Pedro and his counsellors were at first struck with consternation, and exaggerated the consequences of it. It is true Don Pedro had an army, but the force of an army is weakened by its being besieged; he had Burgos, but could he depend on its fidelity? Mothril did not attempt to conceal from the King that the inhabitants of Burgos passed for being great lovers of novelty.

"We will burn the town," said Don Pedro.

Mothril shook his head. "Burgos," said he, "is not a town to allow itself to be destroyed with impunity. It is, in the first place, inhabited by Christians, who detest the Moors, and the Moors are your friends—by Mussulmans, who detest the Jews—and the Jews are your treasurers; and by Jews, who hate the Christians, and you have a good number

of Christians in your army. These people will tea.· one
another to pieces, instead of resisting Don Henry's army;
or, better still, each party will betray the two others to the
invader. Take my advice, sire, and find some means of
quitting Burgos, and that before they learn the news of Don
Henry's election.

"If I quit Burgos, it will be a lost city to me," said Don
Pedro, hesitating.

"Not so. On returning to besiege Don Henry, you will
find him in the same position we ourselves occupy to-day,
and the advantage you acknowledge he now has over us, will
then be ours; therefore, my lord, endeavour to effect your
retreat."

"To fly !" said Don Pedro, furiously, raising his clenched
hand towards heaven.

"He does not fly who departs only to return, sire," returned Mothril.

Don Pedro still hesitated, but what he himself beheld,
soon effected what counsel had failed to do. He observed
groups of persons gathering together on the thresholds and
in the highways, and overheard one of them say, "The King,
Don Henry !"

"Mothril," said he, "you were right. I think, in my turn,
that it is time to retreat." A few moments afterwards,
Don Pedro quitted Burgos, just as Don Henry's banner appeared on the summit of the mountains of Asturias.

CHAPTER XXVIII.

THE CORONATION.

THE inhabitants of Burgos, who had trembled at the idea of
being placed between two opposing forces, were no sooner
aware of Don Pedro's retreat than they became Don Henry's
most ardent partisans; and it was amid shouts and exclamations that he was conducted by the Bishop of Burgos to
the palace so recently tenanted by Don Pedro. Duguesclin
installed his Bretons within the city, and placed the French
and Italian companies—which had remained faithful to him
after the desertion of the English band—around it. The
most rigid discipline was everywhere enforced. The slightest
theft was to be punished by death to a Breton, and flogging
to a stranger; for the constable at once comprehended that

this voluntary conquest required great management, and that it was important that a good feeling should exist between his soldiers and these new adherents to the cause of the usurper.

"Now, my prince," said he, "for your coronation, if you please. Send for your fair princess, that she may be crowned at the same time as yourself. Nothing is so effective as these sort of ceremonies—I have observed it in France—as women and cloth of gold. And then, many persons little disposed in your favour, and yet asking nothing better than to turn their backs upon your brother, will be inspired with an ardent zeal for the new Queen, who, report says, is one of the finest princesses in Christendom. Besides," he added, "that is a point Don Pedro cannot contest with you, since he has murdered his wife; and when the world sees you so good a spouse to Juana of Castile, it will begin to inquire what he has done to Blanche of Bourbon."

The King smiled at these words, the logic of which he acknowledged; and which, whilst they convinced his reason, at the same time flattered his pride and ostentation. The Queen was therefore summoned to Burgos.

When the signal was given of her approach, Duguesclin placed himself at the head of his Bretons, and went to receive her at about a league from the city. The Princess Juana of Castile was really a lovely princess, and her beauty was heightened by her splendid attire, and almost regal equipage. "She was seated in a car," says the Chronicle, "hung with cloth of gold, and enriched with precious stones. The King's three sisters accompanied her, and their ladies of honour followed in equipages almost equally magnificent, whilst a crowd of pages, glittering with silk, gold, and jewels, pranced around them on their superb Andalusian coursers." The Queen was no sooner aware of Duguesclin's approach—whom she easily recognised by his gilded armour, and the sword of constable borne before him on a blue velvet cushion, sown with fleurs-de-lys—than she checked the white mules drawing her car, and hastily descended from it, followed by the King's sisters and their attendants, who imitated her movements without being aware of her intentions. The Queen advanced with outstretched arms towards Duguesclin—who on perceiving her, sprang from his horse—and embraced him as she would have done a brother.

"It is to you, illustrious constable," she exclaimed with deep emotion, "that I owe my crown. Thanks, chevalier; may God worthily reward you for it; for myself, I can only endeavour to equal the service by my gratitude." At these words, and, above all, at the royal salute—so great a mark of honour for the good constable—a cry of assent, almost formidable for the number of voices taking it up, burst from both army and people.

"*Noël* to the good constable," cried they, "joy and prosperity to the Queen Juana of Castile!"

The Queen then mounted a white mule, covered with housings, broidered with gold and precious stones, and harness of jeweller's work, studded with gems, a present from the bourgeois of Burgos. She placed Duguesclin on her right hand, choosing Oliver de Mauny, Le Bègue de Vilaine, and fifty other cavaliers to escort the King's sisters, who continued their way on foot, surrounded by their ladies of honour. They thus arrived at the palace, where the King awaited them, seated beneath a canopy of cloth of gold, and having near him the Comte de la Marche, who had that morning arrived from France. On perceiving the Queen, he arose from his seat; she, on her part, alighted from her mule, and bent the knee before him. He raised her, and after embracing her, said aloud—"To the monastery De las Huelgas." This was where the coronation was to take place. The crowd followed the King and Queen, shouting "*Noël!*"

Meanwhile, Agenor, avoiding all these *fêtes* and rejoicings, had retired to an obscure and distant lodging, accompanied by his faithful Muscaron. This last, however, not being in love, but on the contrary, curious and ferreting, as a bachelor squire should be, finding his master shut up in his own apartment, profited by his pre-occupation to leave him, and pay a visit to the town, where he witnessed the ceremonies, and when he returned at night to Agenor, had seen and heard all that had taken place. He found Agenor strolling about the garden of his dwelling, and there, anxious to communicate the news he had collected, he informed his master that the constable was no longer only Comte de Soria; for that before seating herself at table, the Queen had demanded a favour of the King, and it being granted, had conferred on Duguesclin the Comté de Transtamare.

"He is fortunate," said Agenor, absently.

"That is not all, messire," continued Muscaron. "Before the constable had time to rise, the King said to him—'Messire, the Comté de Transtamare is the Queen's gift. In my turn, I give you mine. I bestow on you the Duchy of Molina.'"

"They load him with honour, and it is only just," said Agenor.

"But that is not yet all, master," continued Muscaron. "All the world has tasted the royal munificence."

Agenor smiled bitterly, as he thought how he, who in his secondary position had rendered no less services to Don Henry, had been forgotten. "All the world?" said he. "How was that?"

"Yes, my lord, from the leaders down to the men. Indeed I asked myself, without ceasing, two questions,—first, how Spain could be large enough to contain all the King has given away; and, secondly, how these persons could find strength enough to carry away all that has been given them?"

But Agenor had ceased to listen, and Muscaron vainly awaited a reply. Meanwhile night had fallen, and Agenor, leaning against one of the balconies, carved in trefoils and hung with the flowers and foliage of creeping plants, listened to the distant sounds of revelry as they died away. At the same time the evening breeze cooled his brow, throbbing with burning thoughts, and the sweet and penetrating odour of the myrtles and jasmins recalled to him regretfully the gardens of the Alcazar and of Ernanton de St. Colombe. It was these remembrances that had distracted his attention from Muscaron's recital. But Muscaron, who knew how to deal with his master's humour—a task always easy to those who love us and are acquainted with our secrets—Muscaron, in order to bring back his thoughts, chose a subject which he fancied would effectually rouse him from his reverie.

"Do you know, my Lord Agenor," said he, "that all these grand festivities are only the prelude of war, and that an expedition against Don Pedro is to follow the ceremony of today, and give the country to him who has already seized upon the crown?"

"Well," replied Agenor, "be it so. We shall join this expedition."

"It is a long way to go, messire."

"Well, we shall go this long way."

"It is there," and Muscaron pointed to the distant horizon,

"that Messire Bertrand wishes to leave the bones of the Free Companies to rot!"

"Well, and our bones may perhaps rot there in company, Muscaron."

"That would certainly be a great honour for me, my lord, but"—"But what?"

"But it is quite true what they say, that the master is master, and the servant, servant—that is to say, only a poor machine."

"What do you mean by that, Muscaron?" asked Agenor, at last struck by his squire's pretended tone of complaint.

"I mean that there is an essential difference between us: it appears that you, a noble chevalier, serve your masters for honour, whilst I—"

"Well, you?"

"Well, I serve you—in the first place, also, for honour; then for the pleasure of your society; and lastly, for my wages."

"But I also receive wages," returned Agenor, with some bitterness. "Did you not see Messire Bertrand Duguesclin bring me, the other day, a hundred gold crowns from the new-made King?"

"I know it, master."

"Well," added the young man, laughing, "and did not you share these hundred crowns?"

"Yes, for I had them all."

"Then, you see, I receive wages, since you have had the benefit of them?"

"Yes; but this is what I grumble at; you have not been paid according to your merits. A hundred gold crowns! why, I could name thirty officers who have received five hundred, and besides that, been created by the King barons, or even royal seneschals."

"Which proves that the King has forgotten me, is it not so?"

"Absolutely."

"So much the better, Muscaron; so much the better. I care little for the forgetfulness of kings—then at least they do me no injury."

"What!" said Muscaron, "would you have me believe that you are happy, strolling idly and pensively about this garden, whilst your comrades are below there, quaffing wine out of golden cups, and returning the soft glances of the ladies?"

"It is so, nevertheless, Master Muscaron," replied Agenor;

"and when I say so, I beg you to believe it. I find more amusement alone with my thoughts beneath these myrtles, than a hundred of the chevaliers below will find in intoxicating themselves with Xeres wine at the royal palace."

"But it is not natural."—"Yet it is so, for all that."

Muscaron shook his head. "I should have waited on you at table," said he; "and it would have been flattering to have been able to say, 'I served my master at the coronation feast of King Henry de Transtamare.'"

Agenor in his turn shook his head, with a sad smile. "You are the squire of a poor adventurer, Master Muscaron," said he; "be contented that you are still alive, and have not yet perished with hunger—a fate which might as well have befallen us as many others. Besides these hundred gold crowns—"

"Undoubtedly I have these hundred gold crowns," said Muscaron; "but if I spend them, what then shall we have to depend upon? with what pay the doctors and leeches when, through your fine zeal for Prince Henry, we get our heads cloven?"

"You are a good servant, Muscaron," returned Agenor, laughing, "and your health is valuable to me; therefore, since it is getting late, seek your couch, and leave me to amuse myself in my own fashion with my thoughts. Go; and to-morrow you will be in a better humour for resuming your harness."

Muscaron obeyed. He retired smiling slyly, for he fancied he had awakened a little ambition in his master's heart; and trusted that this ambition would produce its effect. But it was not so. Agenor, wrapped in his love dreams, in reality never wasted a thought on either duchies or treasures; he was suffering from that sad heart-sickness which makes us regret, like a second fatherland, the country where we have known happiness. He was thinking with regret of the gardens of the Alcazar and at Bordeaux. Nevertheless, as when the sun has set a faint reflection of his light yet lingers in the sky, Muscaron's words dwelt in his memory after that worthy had quitted him.

"And yet," he murmured, "why should I care, because in the distribution of royal favours I have been forgotten? Kings are all ungrateful. Why should I care, because the constable has neither invited me to join the revelry nor distinguished me among my fellow-captains. Men are always forgetful and unjust. At the worst, when I am weary of their neglect and injustice, I can ask my dismissal."

"Softly, young man!" exclaimed a voice near him, which made him start back in almost alarm. "Softly, young man! we have need of you!"

Agenor turned, and beheld two men, muffled in dark mantles, appear in the depths of a verdant alley which he had imagined solitary, his pre-occupation having prevented his hearing their footsteps on the gravel. The one who had spoken came up to Agenor, and laid his hand upon his arm.

"The constable!" exclaimed the young man.

"Who comes to prove to you by his presence that he has not forgotten you."

"But you are not the King," said Agenor.

"True, the constable is not the King," said the second personage; "but I am, comte; nor do I forget that I am in part indebted to you for my crown."

Agenor recognised Don Henry. "My lord," he murmured, in confusion, "pardon me, I entreat you!"

"You are already forgiven, comte; only as you did not share the recompence of the others, you shall have something better still."

"Nothing, sire, nothing!" exclaimed Mauleon; "the world would think I asked for it."

Don Henry smiled. "Calm yourself, chevalier," said he, "I will answer for it they will not say that, since few men would ask for what I offer you. The mission is dangerous, but at the same time so honourable, that the eyes of the whole Christian world will be directed towards you. Comte de Mauleon, I am a king, and you are about to be my ambassador."

"O monseigneur! I was far from expecting such an honour."

"Come, no modesty, young man," said Bertrand. "The King at first wished to send me, but he reflected that he might need me here to lead the companies—men difficult enough to manage, I swear to you. I was recommending you to his Majesty—at the very moment you were accusing us of forgetfulness—as being firm, eloquent, and possessing a thorough knowledge of the Spanish tongue. Being a Bearnais, you are, in fact, half Spanish. But, as the King has just said, the mis-on is a dangerous one—it is to find Don Pedro."

"Don Pedro!" exclaimed Agenor, in a transport of joy.

"Ah! I see that pleases you, chevalier." observed Henry.

Agenor felt that his joy had made him indiscreet, he there-fore restrained himself. "Yes, sire," said he, "that pleases me, for I see in it an opportunity of being useful to your Majesty."

"You will, in fact, render me a great service," replied Don Henry. "But I warn you, my noble messenger, it will be at the peril of your life."

"Your orders, sire!"

"You must traverse the whole of Segovia, where Don Pedro ought now to be. I will give you as credentials a ring, one belonging to our brother, which Don Pedro will certainly re-cognise; but before accepting this mission, reflect well on what I am about to say."

"Speak, sire."

"I enjoin you, if attacked by the way, made prisoner, or even menaced with death, not to disclose the object of your journey. You would discourage my partisans too much, if you let them know that, at the height of my prosperity, I was making overtures of reconciliation with my enemy."

"Of reconciliation!" echoed Agenor, in surprise.

"It is the constable's will," said the King.

"Sire," said the constable, "I have no will, I only entreat It is true I am departing from my instructions in thus in-clining you to peace; but King Charles himself will in his wisdom approve of it when I say to him, 'Sire, they were chil-dren of the same father, two brothers, who, having unsheathed their swords against each other, might some day meet, and shed each other's blood.' Don Pedro offered you peace. You re-fused it, because by accepting it then, the world might have accused you of cowardice. Now you are victor and crowned king, in your turn offer it him, and it will be said that you are a magnanimous prince, the friend of justice, instead of the slave of ambition; and the states you now lose, will soon be restored to you by the arbitrary will of your subjects. If he refuses, you will no longer have anything to reproach your-self with. And he will have, of himself, rushed upon his own destruction."

"Yes," said Henry, sighing; "but shall I again find an opportunity of destroying him?"

"My lord," said Bertrand, "I have spoken according to

P

my conscience. A man wishing to walk in the straight path
ought not to say to himself that perhaps the end would be
equally attained by making detours."

"Be it so, then," said the King, apparently taking a resolution.

"Then your Majesty gives your consent?"

"Yes, beyond return."—"And without regret?"

"Oh, there you demand too much, Sire Constable!" said
Henry. "I give you full power to make peace, therefore ask
nothing more."

"Then, sire," said Bertrand, "permit me to give the
chevalier his instructions; those which we interrupted ——"

"Do not give yourself that trouble," replied the King,
quickly; "I will explain all that to the comte; besides," he
added in a lower tone, "you know what I have to give him."

"Very good, sire," returned Bertrand, who suspected nothing from the King's eagerness to get rid of him, and he
turned to depart, but had scarcely reached the threshold
before he retraced his steps.

"Remember, sire," said he, "a true peace; half the kingdom if necessary. A really prudent—really Christian manifesto—without anything hurtful to pride."

"Yes, certes," replied the King, colouring in spite of himself; "yes, rest certain that my intentions, constable ——"

Bertrand did not consider he had any right to insist
further; his suspicions seemed to be roused for a moment,
but the King dismissed him with so amicable a smile that
they slumbered again. The King followed his retreating
form with his eyes, and when it was lost among the trees
he turned to Mauleon. "Chevalier," said he, "here are your
credentials to Don Pedro, the jewel I spoke of; but let the
words just uttered by the constable be effaced from your
memory, so as to allow mine to be the more deeply engraven
there. I offer Don Pedro peace, and promise to abandon to
him the half of Spain from Madrid to Cadiz, but on one
condition."

Agenor lifted his head in astonishment, more at the tones
than the words of the prince.

"Yes," continued Henry, "I repeat all the constable has
said, but on one condition. You seem surprised, Mauleon,
that I have concealed something from the good chevalier;
but, listen, the constable is a Breton, a man obstinate in his

probity, but little aware of the slight value of oaths in Spain, a country where passions burn up the soul even more fiercely than the sun does the soil. He, therefore, cannot conceive the depth of Don Pedro's hatred to me. The loyal Breton forgets that he has destroyed my brother Frederick by treachery, and strangled his master's sister without even the mockery of a trial. He fancies that here, as in France, war is made only on the battle-field. King Charles knows better; it is his genius that inspires the orders I now give you." Agenor bowed, although at the bottom of his heart alarmed at these royal confidences. "You will therefore seek Don Pedro," continued the King, "and promise him in my name what I have said, provided the Moor Mothril and the twelve nobles of his court, whose names you will find on this parchment, are sent to me, together with their families and possessions, as hostages."

Agenor started. The King had said twelve of the chief nobles and their families, therefore if Mothril came to Don Henry's court he must be accompanied by Aïssa.

"In which case," continued the King, "you will conduct them hither."

Agenor trembled with joy, which did not escape the observation of the King, only he mistook the cause of it.

"You are afraid," said he; "but the danger is not very great, at least in my opinion."

"Your Majesty is mistaken," said Agenor; "it was not with fear I trembled."

"With what, then?" said the King.

"With impatience to enter on this campaign in your service; I would already fain be gone."

"Good; you are a brave chevalier!" exclaimed Henry. "You possess a noble heart, and if you will attach yourself to my fortunes, I promise you shall rise high in the profession of arms."

"Ah, my lord," said Mauleon, "you have already recompensed me more highly than I deserve."

"Then you are ready to set out immediately?"

"Immediately, sire."

"Go, then. Here are the three diamonds they call 'the three Magi,' they are each worth a thousand gold crowns to the Jews, and there is no lack of Jews in Spain. Here are also a thousand florins, but only for your squire's pouch."

"My lord, you overwhelm me with kindness," said Agenor.

"I will give you on your return," continued the King, "a troop of a hundred lances, equipped at my cost."

"Oh, not a word more, I entreat you, my lord!"

"But promise me not to inform the constable of the conditions I impose on my brother."

"Oh, do not fear, sire, for he would be opposed to them, and I am as unwilling as yourself to encounter his opposition."

"Thanks, chevalier," said Henry; "you are more than brave, you are intelligent."

"I am a lover," murmured Agenor; "and it is said that love supplies all the qualities in which one is deficient!"

The King proceeded to rejoin Duguesclin. Agenor awoke his squire, and two hours afterwards master and squire were travelling along by the bright light of the moon towards Segovia.

CHAPTER XXIX.

CURIOSITY.

DON PEDRO had by this time reached Segovia, a prey to the most bitter mortification. This first attack upon his ten years' sovereignty affected him more sensibly than did afterwards the checks sustained in battle, and the treachery of his best friends. To him who was in the nightly practice of wandering through Seville with no other weapon than his sword, or disguise than his mantle, this being obliged to pass cautiously through Spain, appeared in the light of an ignominious flight. But beside him—like the genius of old breathing on the anger in the heart of Achilles—rode Mothril, that veritable genius of hate and fury, unceasingly pouring his evil counsels into his ear, and offering to his lips the sweet and bitter fruit of vengeance—Mothril, ever prolific in schemes to foresee evil and avoid danger, and whose irresistible eloquence held out to the fugitive King more power, more resources, and more riches than he had ever dreamt of even in his most prosperous days. Thanks to him, the way lost half its length, for he knew where to find even at noonday the icy spring bubbling up beneath the shade of oaks and plane-trees; and how, during their passage through the towns, to awaken for Don Pedro's ears a few cries of joy or demonstrations of fidelity, the last faint reflections of expiring monarchy.

"Then they still love me," remarked the King, "or sti_l fear me, which is perhaps, after all, the best."

"Once more become King, sire, and you will soon see whether they will not all either adore or tremble before you," returned Mothril, with unextinguishable irony.

However, in the midst of Don Pedro's hopes, fears, and interrogatories, Mothril had remarked one thing with joy, his complete silence on the subject of Maria Padilla. This enchantress, who whilst in his presence, had exercised so great an influence over him that her power was attributed to magic, appeared to be now not only exiled from his heart, but banished from his very remembrance. This was because Don Pedro—imaginative, capricious—a passionate man in every acceptation of the word, had been since the commencement of his journey with Mothril under the dominion of other thoughts. This litter, kept constantly closed from Bordeaux to Vittoria; this female accompanying Mothril in their flight across the mountains, and whose veil once or twice ruffled by the wind gave a glimpse of one of those adorable Eastern Peris, with soft black eyes, raven hair, and clear yet dark complexion; these sounds of a guzla, breaking on the silence of night, keeping its love watches, whilst Don Pedro was sleepless with anxiety—all this had little by little banished the remembrance of Maria Padilla from his heart.

The King had thus arrived at Segovia, without any serious obstacle having opposed itself to his march. There nothing was changed, all was as he left it. He found here a palace and a throne, a good city, and faithful subjects, and he breathed again. The day after his return was signalized by the arrival of Caverley and his companions, who faithful to the oaths made to their sovereign, had come, with that nationality which has always made the power of the English, to join the ally of the Black Prince, who was himself expected by Don Pedro. Soon afterwards arrived an emissary of the Prince of Wales, that eternal and indefatigable foe to France, announcing his near approach with an army he had assembled at Auch.

Don Pedro's seat on the throne, shaken for an instant by the proclamation of Don Henry at Burgos, was now growing firmer than ever, and in the same proportion his partisans gathered around him. The presence of the Moors—now even more powerful than before about the King—was the only thing that somewhat damped their zeal; for this warlike race of Saracens swarmed round Mothril like bees round the hive containing their queen. Don Pedro, finding there was gold in the treasury, at once surrounded himself with that illusory luxury which attracts the hearts of men through their eyes.

As the Prince of Wales was so soon to make his entrance into Segovia, it was decided by him and his minister that magnificent *fêtes*, beside the lustre of which the ephemeral glories of Don Henry's coronation would grow pale, should restore the people's confidence, and make them confess that their true and only King was the one who not only possessed but dispensed the most. Meanwhile, Mothril had not relinquished his long-conceived project of gaining as much ascendancy over the passions of Don Pedro as he already possessed over his mind. Every night, the sound of Aïssa's guzla was heard, and, like a true daughter of the East, her songs were all of love; the sweet notes were borne upon the breeze to the ears of the prince, and steeped his senses in that delicious dreaminess which is the passing slumber of southern natures. Mothril impatiently awaited the moment when Don Pedro should betray by words the secret passion which he felt was awakened in his heart; but he waited in vain. One day, however, Don Pedro said abruptly, as if by a violent effort he had broken the chain that had fettered his tongue,

"Well, Mothril, are there no news from Seville?"

These words revealed the cause of all Don Pedro's uneasiness, for by Seville was meant Maria Padilla.

Mothril started—that same morning he had caused a Nubian slave, bearing a letter from Maria Padilla to the King, to be seized on the route from Toledo to Segovia, and thrown into the Adaja.—"No, sire," replied he.

Don Pedro fell into a gloomy reverie, then replying aloud to the secret voice of his conscience,—"Thus, then," said he, "is effaced from a woman's mind the devouring passion to which I have sacrificed wife, brother, honour, and crown; for who tears the crown from my brow? it is not Don Henry alone, but also the constable." And Don Pedro made a menacing gesture which foretold no good to Duguesclin in the event of his having the bad fortune to fall into his hands.

Mothril did not pursue this subject: he had another object

in view. "Donna Maria," remarked he, "wished, above all things, to be queen; and since they must believe at Seville that your Majesty is no longer King——"

"You have said so before, and I would not listen to you."

"I repeat it, sire, and you begin to believe me. I said so even before I received your orders to proceed to Coimbra in quest of the unfortunate Don Frederick."

"Mothril!"

"You know with what slowness—I might almost say with what repugnance—I executed this command."

"Silence, Mothril, silence!" exclaimed Don Pedro.

"But your honour was greatly compromised, my King."

"Yes; but no one can attribute their crimes to Maria Padilla."

"Undoubtedly not; but except through Maria Padilla you would never have known them—for I was myself silent, though not from ignorance."

"Then, since she was jealous, she must have loved me."

"You were a king, and by the death of the unhappy Blanche, she might become queen. Besides, jealousy is not always inseparable from love. You were jealous of Donna Blanche. Did you love her, sire?" At this moment, as if the words pronounced by Mothril had been some given signal, the sounds of the guzla made themselves heard, and Aïssa's voice reached Don Pedro's ears in an harmonious murmur, although he was too far distant to catch the words of her song.

"Aïssa!" murmured the King. "Is not that Aïssa who is singing?"—"I believe so, my lord," said Mothril.

"Is she not either your daughter or your favourite slave?" said Don Pedro, carelessly.

Mothril smiled, and shook his head. "Oh, no, sire, we do not bend the knee to either a daughter or a slave purchased with gold."

"Then who is she?" demanded Don Pedro, whose whole thoughts were for a moment concentrated on this young and mysterious girl. "Do you dare to mock me, accursed Moor?" So abrupt and violent was this attack, that Mothril recoiled .n almost affright. "Answer!" continued the King, a prey to one of those frenzies which convert a king into a madman, a man into a wild beast.

"Sire, I dare not tell you."—"Then conduct her to my presence," said the King, "that I may learn it from herself."

"Oh, my lord!" exclaimed Mothril, as though terrified at such a command.—"Let her be here forthwith, or I will myself drag her from her apartment!"

"My lord," replied Mothril, drawing up his tall form with the calm and solemn gravity of the Orientals, "Aïssa is of too noble blood to be touched by profane hands. Do not insult Aïssa, Don Pedro."

"And in what can the Moorish girl be insulted by my love?" asked the King. "My wives were the daughters of princes, and in more than one instance my mistresses have been equally noble."

"Sire," returned Mothril, "were Aïssa my daughter, as you suppose, I should say to you, 'Spare my child, Don Pedro; do not dishonour your servant.' But Aïssa has nobler blood in her veins than either your wives or mistresses, for she is the daughter of King Mohammed, the descendant of the great Mahomet, the prophet, and I command you to respect her!"

Don Pedro paused, subjugated by the proud authority of the Moor. "Daughter of Mohammed, King of Granada!" murmured he.

"Yes, the daughter of Mohammed, King of Granada, whom you put to death. I was, as you know, in the service of this great prince, and whilst your soldiers were pillaging his palace, I rescued her from a slave who was carrying her away in his cloak to sell her. That is now nine years ago. Aïssa was then scarcely seven years old. You heard that I was a faithful counsellor, and summoned me to your court. It was the will of Allah that I should serve you. You are my master, and the greatest of the great, and I have obeyed you; but the daughter of my ancient monarch has accompanied me hither. Poor child! she believes me to be her father, for she was brought up in a harem, without having ever beheld the majestic countenance of the late sultan. Now, sire, you possess my secret: your violence has wrested it from me; but remember, Don Pedro, that although, as heretofore, the devoted slave to your lightest caprice, I shall turn, like a serpent, against you, in defence of the only being dearer than yourself."

"But I love Aïssa!" exclaimed Don Pedro, carried beyond himself.

"Love her, then, Don Pedro, for she is at least your equal

in birth; love her—I do not hinder you, but obtain her love in return. You are young, handsome, powerful—why should not you be able to win this virgin heart?" As he uttered these words, barbed like a Parthian dart, and which sank deeply into Don Pedro's heart, Mothril raised the tapestry as though about to quit the chamber.

"But she will hate me—she ought to hate me—when she knows that I was the cause of her father's death."

"I never speak ill of the master I serve, sire," returned Mothril, still holding the raised tapestry. "And Aïssa knows nothing of you except that you are a good king and a great sultan." So saying, he let the tapestry fall behind him, and Don Pedro could hear his footsteps echo on the pavement as he proceeded towards Aïssa's apartments.

CHAPTER XXX.
FATHER AND DAUGHTER.

As we have before said, Mothril, on quitting the King, directed his steps towards Aïssa's apartments, where the young girl, shut in by grated lattices, and rigorously watched by her father, was sighing for air in default of liberty. Aïssa possessed none of the resources of the women of the present day; her only amusement was dwelling on the thought that she had inspired an affection equal to her own, and that, if he were alive, Agenor, who had already found means of three times reaching her, would do so again; and in her youthful confidence in the future, it seemed impossible that he could die. Therefore nothing remained for Aïssa but to wait and hope. Mothril entered, and, according to custom, prostrated himself before her.

"Aïssa," said he, "may I hope that you will listen favourably to what I am about to say?"

"I owe everything to you, and I am attached to you," replied the young girl, gazing at the Moor, as though wishing him to read in her eyes the truth of her words.

"Does the life you at present lead please you?" asked he.

"How?" demanded Aïssa, evidently desiring to know the object of this question.

"I wish to know if this secluded life is pleasing to you?"

"Ah, no!" replied the young girl, quickly.

"Then you would willingly change it?"—"Most assuredly."

" And what would give you most pleasure?"

Aïssa was silent; she dared not tell what she alone desired.

" You do not reply," said Mothril.

" I do not know what answer to make to your question," said she.

" Would you not like, for instance," continued the Moor, " to ride upon a fine Spanish horse, followed by ladies, cavaliers, dogs, and music?"

" That is not what I most desire, though I should like it well enough, provided——" she paused.

" Provided?" repeated Mothril, with curiosity.

" Nothing," replied the proud young girl, " nothing."

But, notwithstanding this reserve, Mothril perfectly understood the meaning of this " provided."

" So long as you are with me, Aïssa," he continued, " and whilst passing for your father (although that honour is not really mine), I am responsible for your happiness and repose; the only thing you desire cannot come to pass."

" And when will there be a change in all this?" demanded the young girl, with lively impatience.

" When a husband claims you." She shook her head.

" No husband shall ever claim me!" said she.

" You interrupt me, senorita," said the Moor; " and yet I am telling you things for your good."

Aïssa gazed earnestly at him.

" I was saying that a husband alone could give you liberty."

" Liberty," repeated the Moorish girl.

" Perhaps you scarcely know what freedom is," continued the Moor; " I will tell you. It is the right to go out without having the face veiled or being shut up in a litter—the right of receiving visits like the Franks—of giving *fêtes* and hunting parties, and enjoying grand festivities in the company of knights and nobles." Whilst Mothril was speaking, a faint blush mounted to the olive cheek of his auditor.

" But I have heard, on the contrary," said she, hesitatingly, "that the husband takes away this freedom, instead of giving it."

" It is sometimes the case after marriage, but before it, especially if he occupies some distinguished position, he allows his betrothed to do as I have said. Do you remember Maria Padilla?"

The young girl listened attentively.—" Well," said she.

" Well, was not Maria Padilla always queen of the revels,

the all-powerful mistress of the Alcazar—Seville—Spain
itself? Do you not recollect seeing her through our grated
jalousies, exercising her beautiful Arabian steed in the courts
of the palace, and assembling about her her favourite cavaliers for whole days together; whilst you, secluded and concealed, could not cross the threshold of your chamber, saw
no one but your women, and could confide to no one either
your thoughts or feelings."

"But," said Aïssa, "Donna Maria Padilla loved Don Pedro,
and it appears that in this country she who loves is free, and
may publicly declare her affection. Here women are chosen,
not bought, as in Africa. I say Donna Maria loves Don
Pedro; but, for myself, I should never love the man who
sought me in marriage."

"How do you know that, senora?" said Mothril.

"Who is he?" asked the young girl hastily.

"You question me very eagerly," said Mothril.

"And you reply very slowly," retorted Aïssa.

"I was going to tell you, that Don Pedro no longer either
loves, or is loved by, Donna Maria, and that the crown promised to her will be placed on a younger and fairer brow."

Aïssa raised her head in surprise. "And she who is no
longer beloved—what will become of her?" said she, thoughtfully.

"Oh," said Mothril, with affected carelessness, "she has
found other happiness. Some say she feared the issue of the
wars in which the King is about to involve himself; but others
assert, what is more probable, that she is about to espouse
another."

"And who is this other?" inquired Aïssa.

"A knight from the west," replied Mothril.

Aïssa fell into a profound reverie; these artful words revealed, as by some magic power, all the sweet future of which
she had dreamed, and yet from which, either through ignorance or timidity, she had not dared to lift the veil.

"Ah, they say that!" said she at last.

"Yes, certes," returned Mothril; "and had she remained
shut up in a harem or a convent, she would never have
attained that happiness."—"True," said the young girl.

"Thus, Aïssa, if the King addresses you, you will listen to
him. Remember, he is sad and irritated by misfortune, and
you can speak soothing words if you will."

" I will listen to the King, if it be your wish, my lord," said she.

"Good," thought Mothril to himself. "I knew that the voice of ambition would speak, if that of love were silent. At present she loves her Frank chevalier sufficiently to embrace any means of seeing him again—at this moment she would sacrifice the monarch to the lover. A little later I may, perhaps, have to watch that she does not sacrifice the lover to the monarch."

"Then you consent to receive the King, Aïssa ?" said he, aloud.

"I shall be his Majesty's respectful servant," replied the young girl.

"Not so, Aïssa, you are his equal; remember that, only avoid undue pride as much as undue humility. Adieu, I go to inform the King that you consent to be present at the serenade they give him every evening. All the court will attend, as well as many noble strangers. Adieu, Donna Aïssa."

" Who knows," murmured the young girl, "but what among these noble strangers I may behold Agenor."

Don Pedro, a man of sudden and violent passions, coloured with pleasure like a young novice, when he that evening beheld the beautiful Moorish girl, whose soft black eyes and olive complexion outshone anything in the way of beauty that Segovia had hitherto been able to produce, advance upon the balcony, resplendent beneath her gold-embroidered veil. Aïssa seemed like a queen, accustomed to the homage of kings. Instead of casting down her eyes, her gaze wandered over the assembly, often resting upon Don Pedro ; and more than once in the course of the evening he quitted the wisest counsellors and fairest ladies of his court to breathe a few low-toned words to the young girl, who replied without trouble or embarrassment—only a little absently perhaps—for her thoughts were elsewhere. All that evening the courtiers whispered together on the subject of the new mistress the King seemed so ready to give them ; and on his retiring to rest, Don Pedro publicly announced that he had confided the management of the pay of his troops to his prime minister Mothril, chief of the Moorish tribes employed in his service.

CHAPTER XXXI.

THE GROTTO.

WE left Mauleon and his squire journeying beneath the bright moonlight, in compliance with the wishes of the new King of Castile. Avoiding the easier and more frequented route from Burgos to Segovia, Agenor, like a true Bearnais, sought the mountains, much to Muscaron's disappointment, who, whilst munching his goat's-milk cheese and barley bread, and washing it down with coarse common wine, sighed for the roasted kid, olla podrida, and wine grown old in its leathern bottles, which he would have found on the plain. Towards the evening of the second day, they reached a little village not far from Segovia ; and here Muscaron, during his search for provisions for himself and master, learnt an important piece of news—viz., that Don Pedro had quitted Segovia, and proceeded with all his court to Soria. Without there waiting to refresh himself, the disappointed che-valier remounted his horse, and resumed his journey. There still remained nearly an hour of daylight, and the rays of the setting sun gilded their way ; but when the last pale reflec-tion had faded away, night in its turn came on with a rapi-dity the more unfortunate, since the last hour had revealed to the two travellers the steepness and consequent danger of their road. After proceeding for a quarter of an hour in this darkness, Muscaron suddenly stopped.

"Sire Agenor," said he, "the road is becoming worse and worse, or rather there is no longer any road at all. If you insist on our going further, we shall certainly be killed."

"The devil !" said Agenor, "I am not particular, as you know ; but, nevertheless, such a resting-place as this appears to me rather too exposed. Let us see if we cannot push forward.

"Impossible ! we are on a kind of platform, surrounded on all sides by precipices. Let us stay where we are ; in fact, make a regular halt, and trust to my acquaintance with mountains to find you some spot in which to pass the night."

"Do you then smell some thick savoury smoke," said Agenor, smiling.—"No, but I scent a pretty grotto, curtained with ivy and carpeted with moss."

"From which we shall first have to chase a horde of owls, lizards, and serpents."

"*Ma foi!* what does that signify, messire ? In our present

situation I care for no flying or creeping thing, it is only
walking ones I dread. Besides, you are not superstitious
enough to be afraid of owls, and serpents and lizards could
not find much to bite in your iron-sheathed limbs."

"Be it so," said Agenor. "Let us halt then."

Muscaron dismounted, and passed the bridle of his horse
over a rock, whilst Agenor still remained seated on his steed,
like an equestrian statue of cool daring. Meanwhile, the
squire with that instinct whose power is tenfold increased
by determination, began to explore the neighbourhood.
Scarcely a quarter of an hour had elapsed before he returned,
holding his drawn sword in his hand, and with a triumphant
expression of countenance.

"This way, master," cried he, "come and see our Alcazar."

"What the devil ails you?" said the chevalier. "You
seem to be soaked to the skin?"

"I have been doing battle with a forest of lianas, which
sought to make me prisoner, but by dint of hacking and
hewing I opened a passage for myself; then all the leaves
dripping with dew showered down upon my head. At the
same time out flew a dozen bats, and behold the place was
taken. Fancy to yourself an admirable grotto, carpeted
with fine sand."

"Indeed!" said Agenor, following his squire, but somewhat
doubting his fine words. But he was wrong to doubt; for
scarcely had he proceeded a hundred paces down a somewhat
steep descent to a place where further progress seemed to be
stopped by a wall, before he trampled upon branches of fresh
foliage, and felt his cheek fanned by the wings of the large
bats which hovered around him, anxious to retake possession
of their abode.

"Why, this is surely the cavern of the enchanter Maugis,"
said Agenor.—"Discovered by me, messire, and by me alone;
for devil take me, if it has ever entered any man's brain to
set foot there. These lianas date from the commencement of
the world."

"Good," replied Agenor. "But supposing this cave to be
unknown to man, can you say as much for the wolves, or
those little red bears which are found in the Pyrenees?"

"The devil!"

"Or those wild cats which tear open the throats of sleeping travellers in order to suck their blood?"

"Then, messire, do you know what we must do ?   One of us must keep watch whilst the other sleeps."

"That will only be prudent."

"Now, messire, have you any other objection to advance against this cavern of Maugis ?"

"Absolutely nothing. I even think it extremely agreeable."

"Then let us enter it, messire," said Muscaron.

They both dismounted, and cautiously entered the cavern, feeling about as they went—the chevalier with the end of his lance, and Muscaron with his sword; and after having advanced some twenty steps, encountered a solid and impenetrable wall, apparently formed by the solid rock, and without any visible cavity or retreat for noisome animals.   The cavern was divided into two compartments, and had evidently been the retreat of one of those pious hermits who in the early times of Christianity chose solitude as the path leading to heaven.

"God be praised!" ejaculated Muscaron; "our bedchamber is secure."

"In that case, lead the horses into the stable, and spread our supper," said Agenor, "for I am hungry."   Muscaron obeyed by leading the two animals into the kind of porch forming the first division of the cave, and then busied himself in the more important preparations for supper.   "What are you saying?" said Agenor, overhearing him grumbling to himself, as he pursued his employment.

"I was saying, messire, that I was a great fool not to have thought of a taper to light us. Happily, we can make a fire."

"Make a fire, Muscaron!   Of what are you thinking?"

"That fire drives away ferocious beasts is an axiom of which I have more than once had occasion to acknowledge the truth."

"Yes, but it attracts men; and at this moment I confess to you I stand in more fear of being attacked by a band of English or Moorish desperadoes than of a whole pack of wolves."

"Mordieu!" said Muscaron.   "It is, nevertheless, hard to devour such good provender without seeing it."—"Bah!" said Agenor.   "A hungry stomach has no ears, it is true, but it has eyes."

Muscaron this time acknowledged the force of his master's reasoning, and hastened to spread their repast at the entrance of the second cavern, so that the faint light without might reach them. All at once he ceased eating.

"Well, what is the matter?" said his master.

"Master, I fancied I heard something," said Muscaron; "but no doubt it was only fancy. It is nothing." And he continued his meal. But he soon paused again, and, as his back was turned towards the entrance of the cavern, Agenor could perceive his movements.

"Again!" said Agenor. "Are you mad?"—"No, my lord; neither am I deaf; I hear something, I tell you."

"Bah! you are dreaming," said the young man. "It is some stray bat flapping his wings against the wall."

"Well," said Muscaron, lowering his voice till his master could scarcely distinguish what he said, "I not only hear, but see something!"—"You see something?"

"Yes, and if you will turn round your eyes, you will see for yourself."

The invitation was so peremptory, that Agenor turned hastily round, and beheld in the gloomy depths of the cavern the flickering of a luminous ray, evidently proceeding from some flame, the light of which penetrated to the cavern through some fissure in the rock. This phenomenon was startling enough.

"Well, they have a light, if we are without one," said Muscaron.

"They?"—"Dame! our neighbours."

"Then you believe your solitary grotto to be inhabited?"

"I answered for this one, not the neighbouring one."

"Come, explain yourself."

"Do not you understand it, messire? We are on the crest of a mountain, and every mountain has two sides."

"True."

"You agree with me. According to my calculation, this grotto has two entrances. Chance has produced the separation we see. We have entered by the west—they by the east."

"But who are they?"—"I know nothing about them, messire; but we will find out. You were right in not allowing me to make a fire. Your lordship is as prudent as brave, and that is not saying a little."

"Come, let us see," said Agenor. They both penetrated, though not without beating hearts, into the depths of this subterranean retreat. Muscaron was the first to apply his eye to the crevice in the rocky partition.

" Look, master," whispered he; " it is worth the trouble."

Agenor did so, and started.

" Hem!" said Muscaron.—" Hush!" returned Agenor.

CHAPTER XXXII.

THE BOHEMIANS.

THE scene that presented itself to the eyes of our two travellers fully deserved their notice. They beheld a cavern closely resembling the one they themselves occupied. In the centre of it two females were seated, or rather crouched, beside a small coffer placed upon a stone larger than itself, in a fissure of which one of the women was endeavouring to fix a lighted taper, from whence proceeded the light that had attracted the observation of our two travellers. Both figures were miserably clad, and muffled in the thick and parti-coloured veils worn by the Bohemians of former days. They were therefore recognised by Agenor as two women of this vagabond race, and, to judge from their gestures and appear-ance, they were old ones. At a little distance stood a third figure, but as the flickering light of the taper did not illumine its face, it was impossible to say to what sex it belonged. Meanwhile, the two females were arranging piles of their baggage to serve as seats. These packages were to all ap-pearance poor, miserable, and squalid; the only thing that did not accord with this seeming misery was the coffer, which was of ivory, incrusted with gold. Presently a fourth figure advanced from the further end of the cavern, and approaching one of the females, addressed a few words to her which neither Muscaron nor Agenor could catch. The Bohemian listened attentively, and then by a gesture dismissed the new comer. Agenor remarked that this gesture was at once dignified and imperious. The standing figure followed the one who had spoken, and both disappeared in the depths of the grotto. Then the woman of the imperious gesture arose from her seat, and placed her foot upon the stone. The movements of all these persons were distinctly visible to our two travellers, but their words only reached their ears in a confused murmur.

" I wager, messire," whispered Muscaron, " that these two

Q

old sorceresses have at least three hundred years between them. These Bohemians live to the age of rooks."

"Truly, they do not appear to be young," said Agenor. Meanwhile the second female, instead of rising as the first had done, knelt before her, and busied herself in unlacing the thin leather buskin which covered her leg to the middle of the calf. "Ma foi!" said Agenor, "look if you like, Muscaron, but as to me I shall retire. Nothing is so ugly as the foot of an old woman."

The chevalier stepped back, but Muscaron, more curious than his master, remained at his post of observation. "Ma foi, messire!" he exclaimed, "this one, I assure you, is less frightful than you fancy. On the contrary, it is charming! Look, master."

Agenor ventured to do so. "Strange!" muttered he, "the proportions are exquisite. Ah, the gipsies are a magnificent race of people!"

The female then dipped a fine napkin in the crystal water, which trickled in drops like liquid diamonds from a part of the rocky side of the cavern, and carefully washed the foot of her companion, afterwards—much to the astonishment of the two gazers—rubbing it with perfumes, which she took from the gold-incrusted coffer.

"Perfumes! balms! Do you see that, master?" cried Muscaron.

"What does all this mean?" said Agenor, on beholding the Bohemian uncover a second foot no less delicate than the first.

"Messire," said Muscaron, "it is the Queen of the Gipsies making her toilette, and see, they are going to disrobe her!"

In fact, the Bohemian having washed, dried, and perfumed the second foot as she had done the first, passed to the veil, which she lifted with infinite respect and every possible precaution. Instead of disclosing, as it fell, the wrinkles of a woman turned a hundred, as Muscaron had predicted, it gave to view a charming face, with brown eyes, and olive-tinted skin, in which the two travellers could recognise a woman of six or eight and twenty, in all the lustre of her resplendent beauty. Whilst the two spectators remained gazing in speechless ecstasy, the old Bohemian spread upon the ground a carpet made of camel's hair, which, although a dozen feet in length, would have passed through the ring of a young girl. It was composed of that peculiar tissue, of which at that epoch the Arabs alone possessed the secret, and was woven of the hair of a still-born camel's foal. On this magnificent carpet the first Bohemian placed her naked feet, whilst the old woman having, as we before said, removed the veil from her head, commenced unfastening her loose robe, when Muscaron, unable any longer to restrain his admiration, uttered an exclamation which, doubtless, reached the ears of the two women; for the light was suddenly extinguished, and the most profound silence and obscurity reigned in the cavern, swallowing up, like oblivion, the reality of this mysterious scene. Muscaron instinctively managed to avoid the violent kick dealt him by his master, accompanied by the energetic apostrophe of "Fool!" and hastened to roll himself in his cloak, and stretch himself on the bed of leaves he had so carefully prepared. At the end of a few minutes, when he was convinced that the light would not reappear, Agenor flung himself down near him. Muscaron judged that this was the proper moment to obtain by his perspicacity pardon for his fault.

"This is how it is," said he, replying aloud to what was doubtless his master's secret thought, "they were journeying on the other side of the mountain along a path parallel with ours, and found on the opposite slope an entrance to the cavern similar to this one; for it is evident that this grotto is divided into two parts by yonder rock, which either the caprice of nature, or the fancy of man, has placed there like a gigantic partition."

"Beast!" was his master's sole response; but as this was pronounced in a somewhat softened tone, the squire continued—

"But now who are these women? Doubtless Bohemians. That may be; but wherefore those balms and perfumes, those bare white feet, that handsome face, that beautiful neck, which we should have seen if—fool that I was!" And he gave himself a violent slap on his face. Agenor could not help laughing. Muscaron overheard him. "The Queen of the Gipsies!" he continued, more and more satisfied with himself, "it is hardly probable, and yet I can see no other explanation for the truly fairy vision which I made vanish by my stupidity. Oh, beast that I am!" And he dealt himself another slap on the opposite cheek.

Agenor perceived that Muscaron no less curious than him-

self, was struck with real repentance for his indiscretion, and
he recollected that the Scripture urges the conversion, but
not the death of the sinner.

"What is your own opinion of these women, master?" at
last hazarded Muscaron.

"I think," said Agenor, "that the sordid habits the
younger one was laying aside were little in accordance with
the brilliant beauty which unfortunately we have only half
seen." Muscaron gave a deep sigh. "And," continued his
master, "that the balms and perfumes agreed still worse with
their squalid attire, all which makes me suspect that they
are two travellers, one of them rich and noble, journeying to
some distant city, and assuming this disguise to avoid
exciting the avarice of either robbers or soldiers."

"Wait, master, wait!" interrupted Muscaron, resuming his
accustomed place in the conversation, or perhaps one of
those women whom the Bohemians sell, and whose beauty
they tend, as the jockeys do their valuable horses as they
convey them from town to town." On this occasion Muscaron decidedly had the best of the argument, and Agenor
acknowledged by his silence that he was beaten. The fact
was, that Agenor, attracted, as every young man of five-and-
twenty, even if he were a lover, would be by the charms of
a pretty foot and lovely face, kept his secret discontent to
himself; for Muscaron might, after all, be right, and his
mysterious fair one be only an adventuress scouring the
country with a troop of Bohemians, and employing those
adorably white and delicate little feet in dancing the egg
dance, or treading the tight rope. Only one thing combated
this probability: the respectful demeanour of both the two
men and the old woman towards the unknown; but Muscaron, whose logical arguments drove the chevalier to despair, recalled to his recollection examples of jugglers treating
with equal consideration the favourite ape of the troop, or
the principal actor on whom the chief gains of the company
depended. The chevalier wandered in a maze of uncertainty
until slumber, that sweet attendant on fatigue, deprived him
of the faculty of thought of which during the last two or
three hours he had been making such immoderate use.
Towards four o'clock in the morning the first rays of sunrise,
casting their purple light on the floor of the grotto, aroused
Muscaron, who awoke his master Agenor opened his eyes,

collected his thoughts, and hastened to the cleft in the rock. But Muscaron shook his head in token that he had already been there.

"There is no one there!" observed he. In fact, there was sufficient light in the neighbouring grotto, now exposed to the rays of the rising sun, to enable them to distinguish objects; the grotto was evidently deserted. The Bohemians, earlier risers than the chevalier, had already quited it; balms, perfumes, coffer, all had disappeared.

Muscaron, always occupied with material things, proposed breakfast, but before he had finished pointing out the advantages of following his suggestion, he had gained the crest of the mountain, from whence, as he sat perched on its height like a bird of prey, he could see the windings of the mountain path, and the blue depths of the valley. From this elevation his eagle eye discerned at a considerable distance an ass bearing a single rider, whilst three other persons followed it on foot. These could be none other than the four Bohemians, apparently pursuing the path pointed out to Muscaron as leading to Soria. He communicated this discovery to his master, who eagerly exclaimed, "Haste, Muscaron! Let us mount our horse, and spur after them. These are our night birds; let us see what their plumage is like by day."

Muscaron, who was conscious of having many faults to repair, led out his master's horse already saddled, mounted his own, and silently followed his master, who urged his steed forward at a gallop. In half an hour they were within three hundred paces of the Bohemians, whom a clump of trees concealed for a moment from their sight.

CHAPTER XXXIII.
THE QUEEN OF THE GIPSIES.

THE Bohemians had once or twice turned round—a proof that they were aware of the approach of our travellers—a fact which made Muscaron, with most unusual timidity, give it as his opinion, that the clump of trees once passed, they would no longer behold the little troop, but that it would have disappeared in a manner as mysterious as itself. But Muscaron was not in a happy vein for prophesy that morning, for they again came in sight of the Bohemians quietly pursuing their journey. Agenor, however, remarked one slight change in their order of march—the woman whom they had beheld from afar seated on the ass, and whom they concluded to be her of the white feet and charming face, was now on foot like her companions, without presenting anything different from them either in walk or general appearance.

"Hola," cried Agenor, "hola, good people!" The men turned round, and Agenor remarked that their hands sought their belts, from whence depended their long knives.

"My lord," said Muscaron, always prudent, "did you see?"

"Perfectly," was the reply; then turning to the Bohemians, he continued, "Fear nothing, my brave fellows, my intentions are quite friendly; and were they otherwise, your knives would be poor offensive weapons against my cuirass and shield, or defensive ones against my lance and sword. Now, that point is settled, where are you going, my masters?"

One of the men knit his brow, and was about to make some rough reply, but the other stopped him, and said civilly, "Do you wish to follow us, that we may show you the way, senor?"

"Assuredly," said Agenor; "without counting the desire we have to be honoured with your company."

Muscaron made a most significant grimace.

"Well, then, senor," replied the Bohemian, "we are going to Soria."

"Thanks; that is most fortunate; for we are ourselves bound for Soria."

"Unfortunately, senor," replied the Bohemian, "your progress will be too rapid for poor foot passengers."

"I have heard it said," observed Agenor, "that your race can vie in speed with even the swiftest horses."

"It is possible," said the gipsy, "but not when we have two old women with us."

Agenor and Muscaron exchanged glances, which on Muscaron's side was accompanied by a grimace.

"True," resumed Agenor; "how are the women journeying with you able to support such fatigue?"

"They have always been accustomed to it, senor. They are our mothers, and we gipsies are only born for toil and privations."

"Ah, your mothers!" said the chevalier. "Poor women!"

For a moment Agenor feared that the fair unknown had

taken another route, but he almost immediately recollected how one of the women was at first mounted on the ass, and how she had only dismounted from it on perceiving him. The palfrey was a humble one, but at least it served to save the little delicate and perfumed feet he had beheld on the preceding evening. He approached the women, but they redoubled their speed.

"Let one of your mothers mount the ass," said he, "and I will take the other behind me on my horse."

"The ass is laden with our baggage, and is sufficiently burdened as it is," replied the Bohemian. "As to your horse, senor, your excellency doubtless jests, for it is too noble and spirited a steed to carry a poor old gipsy."

Agenor was meanwhile carefully observing the two females, and on the feet of one of them detected the doeskin buskins he had remarked in the grotto. "'Tis she!" he murmured, this time certain of not being mistaken. "Come, come, good mother in the blue veil!" he continued; "accept the offer I make you. Seat yourself behind me, and if your ass is already sufficiently laden, your companion shall ride behind my squire."

"Thanks, senor," replied the person he addressed, in a voice whose harmony dispelled the last doubts remaining in the chevalier's mind.

"Truly," he observed, in a tone of irony which made the two females start, and the men again lay their hands upon their long knives, "truly, that is a very sweet voice to come from the lips of an old woman."

"Senor!" angrily exclaimed the Bohemian who had hitherto remained silent.

"Oh, do not be uneasy," retorted Agenor, coolly; "if I guess from her voice that your companion is young, I also conclude from the thickness of her veil that she is handsome— there is nothing in that to call forth your knives." The two men made a step in advance, as if to protect their companion.

"Stay!" cried the young woman, imperiously. The men paused. "You are right, senor," said she; "I am young, and perhaps even handsome; but I ask you, what does that concern you, or why should you molest me on my journey because I am twenty or five-and-twenty years younger than I seem?"

Agenor had remained speechless with surprise at the accents of this voice, which denoted the woman of superior rank accustomed to command. Both the education and position of the unknown were then in harmony with her beauty.

"Senora," faltered he, "you are quite right; I am a chevalier."

"A chevalier? Be it so; but as to me, I am not a senora, but a poor Bohemian, a little less ugly, perhaps, than most women of my condition." Agenor made a gesture of incredulity. "Have you ever beheld the wives of nobles journeying on foot?" asked the unknown.

"Oh, this is a poor reason," retorted Agenor; "for scarcely a moment ago you were mounted on yonder ass."

"Granted," said the young woman; "but at least you will allow that my clothes are not those of a lady of quality."

"Ladies of quality sometimes disguise themselves when they have reasons for wishing to be taken for women of the people."

"Do you think," said the Bohemian, "that a lady of quality, accustomed to velvet and silken attire, would consent to clothe her feet thus?" and she pointed to her doeskin buskin.

"But at night the delicate foot, wearied with the day's fatigue, may be released from its imprisonment, bathed, and perfumed."

If the veil of the unknown had been raised, Agenor would have seen the blood rush to her cheek, and her eyes flash fire. "Perfumed!" she murmured, uneasily regarding him; whilst Muscaron, who had not lost a single word of the dialogue, smiled slily. Agenor did not attempt to give her any further uneasiness.

"Senora," said he, "I only meant to say that a very sweet perfume exhales from your person."

"Thanks for the compliment, sir knight; but since that was all you wished to say, you ought now to be satisfied with having said it."—"Which signifies that you wish me to leave you; is it not so, senora?"

"It signifies that I recognise you as a Frank, senor, not only from your accent, but from your gallant speeches; and it is dangerous to travel with Franks when one is only a poor young gipsy, extremely susceptible to courtesy."

"Then you insist on my quitting you?"

"Yes, senor; to my great regret, I must insist on it."

The two attendants, on hearing this response of their mistress, appeared inclined to enforce it.

"I will obey you, senora," said Agenor. "But, believe me, not on account of the threatening gestures of your two companions, whom I should like to meet in other society than yours, in order to teach them not to lay their hands upon their knives so often; but on account of the mystery surrounding you, which doubtless conceals some project, with which I do not wish to interfere."

"I swear to you, you neither interfere with any project, nor risk discovering any secret," replied the unknown.

"Enough, senora," said Agenor. "Besides," he added, somewhat piqued at the little effect produced by his good looks—"Besides, the slowness of your pace would hinder my arriving as speedily as it is indispensable for me to do at Don Pedro's court."

"What, are you on your way to Don Pedro?" said the young woman, quickly.—"Immediately, senora, and I take leave of you, wishing you all sorts of prosperity."

The young woman, as if forming a sudden resolution, raised her veil, and its coarse folds formed a framework to her face that if possible heightened the beauty and elegance of her features—of her winning glance and smiling lips. Agenor checked his horse, which had already made a few steps forward.

"Come, senor," said she; "it is clear that you are a discreet and delicate-minded chevalier; for though you have, perhaps, guessed who I really am, you have not persecuted me, as another would have done in your place."

"I have not guessed who you are, senora—only what you are not."

"Well, then, sir knight, since you are so courteous," said the fair traveller, "I will tell you the whole truth." At these words the two attendants exchanged glances of astonishment, but the false Bohemian smilingly continued—"I am the wife of one of Don Pedro's officers, and having been separated from my husband, who followed that prince to France, for nearly a year, I am endeavouring to join him at Soria. The country being, as you know, occupied by the soldiers of the two parties, and, as I should be a captive of some value for the men of the pretender, I have, to escape them, assumed this disguise, until I can reach my husband."

"Very good," said Agenor, this time convinced of the veracity of his fair acquaintance. "Well, I would have offered

you my services had not the urgency of my mission obliged
me to use the greatest celerity."

"Listen, senor," said the lady. "Now you know who and
what I am, and have acquainted me with your own position,
I will proceed as rapidly as you please, if you will permit me
to place myself under your protection, and travel under your
escort."

"Ah, senora," said Agenor, "then you have changed your
mind."

"Yes, senor; I have reflected that I might meet with persons as clear-sighted, but less courteous than yourself."

"Then, senora, how shall we manage it—at least, if you
will not accept my former proposal?"—"Oh, do not judge
my ass by his appearance; humble as he seems, he is as
high bred as your horse—he comes from Don Pedro's stables,
and for speed will bear comparison with the fleetest courser."

"But your attendants, senora?"—"Cannot your squire
take my nurse behind him, and the two others can follow on foot."

"It would be better, senora, to leave the ass to the two servants, who can take it in turns to ride—for your nurse to
mount behind my squire, as you say, and for you to do the
same behind me, as I at first proposed; by this means, we
shall make a respectable troop."

"Well, it shall be as you wish," replied the lady, and with
the lightness of a bird, she seated herself on the crupper of
Agenor's horse, whilst the two men placed the nurse behind
Muscaron, who no longer laughed. One of the men then
mounted the ass, and the other ran beside it, and the whole
party set out at full trot.

CHAPTER XXXIV.

THE FELLOW-TRAVELLERS.

It is very difficult for two beings, young, handsome and intelligent, to thus journey together on the same steed without
a degree of intimacy springing up between them. The young
woman, in right of her sex, began by asking questions.

"Then, sir knight, I guessed rightly," said she. "And you
are a Frank?"

"Yes, senora."—"And are bound for Soria?"

"Oh, that you did not guess—I told you so."

"True. Doubtless, to offer your services to Don Pedro?"

Before replying categorically to this question, Agenor reflected that, as he was conducting this lady to Soria, and would see the King before she did, there was nothing to fear from any indiscretion; besides, he had many things to say before he came to the truth.

"Senora," said he, "this time you are mistaken—I do not intend offering my services to Don Pedro, because I already belong to Don Henry de Transtamare, or rather, to the constable, Bertrand Duguesclin, and I am bearing offers of peace to the vanquished King."

"To the vanquished King!" repeated the lady, in a haughty tone, which she immediately modified into one of surprise.— "Undoubtedly vanquished!" replied Agenor, "since his competitor is crowned King in his place."

"Ah, true," said the young woman, carelessly. "Then you are bearing offers of peace to the vanquished King?"

"Which he will do well to accept," resumed Agenor, "since his cause is lost."

"You think so?"—"I am sure of it."

"And why so?"

"Because, surrounded by evil, and, above all, badly counselled as he is, it is impossible for him to make any resistance."

"Surrounded by evil?"—"Undoubtedly; subjects, friends, mistress—all plunder him and incite him to do wrong."

"Then, his subjects?"—"Abandon him."

"His friends?"—"Plunder him."

"And his mistress?" said the young woman, hesitatingly.

"His mistress incites him to do wrong." The stranger frowned, and something like a cloud passed across her brow.

"You doubtless allude to the Moorish girl," said she.

"What Moorish girl?"—"The King's new passion."

"What!" ejaculated Agenor, with flashing eyes.

"Then have you not heard the report, that the King is madly enamoured of the daughter of Moor Mothril?"

"Of Aïssa!" exclaimed the chevalier.

"You know her?" said the young woman.—"Undoubtedly."

"Then how is it you are ignorant that this infamous miscreant has made, or is about to make, her the King's declared mistress."—"Stay! exclaimed Agenor, becoming deadly pale. "Do not speak thus of Aïssa, unless you wish our friendship to be at an end."

"But how can I speak otherwise, senor, since I say nothing

but the truth. The King accompanies her everywhere—walks beside her litter, gives concerts and *fêtes* in her honour, and brings the court to her dwelling."

"You know this to be the case?" said Agenor, trembling.

"I know many things, sir knight," said the stranger; "for we members of the household soon learn the n·ws."

"Oh, senora, you cut me to the heart!" said Agenor, sadly.

"I cut you to the heart!" said the lady, in surprise. "Are you then acquainted with this girl?"

"Alas! I love her to distraction" said the chevalier, in despair.

The young woman made a gesture of compassion.

"But she does not love you, then?" said she.

"She told me she loved me. Oh, this traitor Mothril must have used towards her either force or magic!"

"He is a wretch," said the young woman, coldly, "and has already done the King much harm. But what do you think is his aim in acting thus?"

"That is very simple—he wishes to supplant Donna Maria Padilla."

"Then you also are of this opinion?"

"Most assuredly, senora."

"But report says that Donna Maria is greatly attached to the King. Do you think she will suffer Don Pedro to thus desert her?"—"She is a woman—she is weak, and will succumb like the Lady Blanche; only the death of the one was a murder, whilst that of the other will be an expiation."

"An expiation! Then according to you, Donna Maria has something to expiate?"

"Not according to me, senora, but according to all the world."

"Then it is your opinion that Maria Padilla will not meet with the same pity as Blanche of Bourbon?"

"Assuredly not; although when they are both dead, it is probable that the mistress will have been as unfortunate as the Queen."

"Then you will pity her?"—"Yes; although I am the last person from whom she deserves it."

"And why so?" demanded the young woman, fixing her large dark eyes, dilated with astonishment, upon him.

"Because it was she, they say, who persuaded the King to murder Don Frederick, and Don Frederick was my friend."

"Can you be that Frank chevalier with whom Don Frederick had made an appointment?"

"Yes; and to whom the dog brought his master's head."

"Chevalier! Chevalier!" exclaimed the young woman, seizing Agenor's hand, "listen to what I say. On my soul's salvation!—by Maria Padilla's hopes of paradise!—I swear to you it was not she who gave the King this counsel, but Mothril."

"But she was aware that the murder was about to take place, and did not oppose it." The lady was silent. "This is enough to make God punish her," continued Agenor; "or, rather, she will be punished by Don Pedro himself. Who can say that the blood of Don Frederick, rising between them, is not the cause of his already loving her less?"

"You are perhaps right," said the unknown, in a deep voice; "but patience! patience!"

"You seem to hate Mothril, senora?"—"Mortally!"

"How has he wronged you?"—"He has wronged me as he has all Spain, by dividing the King from his people."

"Yet women seldom, for a merely political cause, evince the deep hatred to a man that you do to Mothril."

"Because I have personal reason to complain. For a month past he has hindered me from rejoining my husband."

"How is that?"

"He has set such a watch over Don Pedro, that neither message nor messenger can reach either him or those who serve him. Thus, I have dispatched two emissaries to my husband, neither of whom have returned, so that I am ignorant whether I can enter Soria, and if you——"

"Oh, I shall gain admittance, for I come as an ambassador." The young woman shook her head ironically.

"You will only gain admittance if he pleases," said she, in a voice half stifled by some violent secret emotion.

Agenor stretched out his hand and displayed the ring given him by Henry de Transtamare. "Here is my talisman," said he. It was an emerald ring, with two interlaced E's on either side of the stone.

"Yes," said the unknown "by the aid of that you may perhaps succeed in making your way through the guards."

"If I succeed in doing so, you shall do the same; for you belong to my suite, and shall be respected."

"You promise, then, that if you gain admittance to Soria, I shall enter with you?"

"I swear it on my honour as a chevalier."

"Well, and in exchange for this oath, I conjure you to tell me what would at this moment give you the greatest pleasure?"

"Alas! what I most desire is out of your power to accord me."—"Never mind; tell me."

"To behold and be able to speak to Aïssa."

"If I enter Soria, you shall both see and speak to her."

"Oh, thanks! I shall indeed be grateful to you."

"Who can say that I shall not be the one most deeply obliged?"

"But you have given me new life."

"And you will have restored me to more than life," said the young woman, with a singular smile. Whilst exchanging these vows, and ratifying their treaty of alliance, they reached the village where they intended to halt. The fair unknown, therefore, sprang lightly from Agenor's horse, and, as this companionship of Christians and Bohemians might have had a somewhat strange appearance, it was agreed that they should rejoin each other next day on the road at about a league from the village.

CHAPTER XXXV.

THE PAGE.

NEXT day, the chevalier, in spite of his early rising, found the Bohemians already breakfasting beside a fountain at the prescribed distance from the village. They proceeded to make the same arrangements as on the preceding evening, and resumed their journey in the same order. At last they came within sight of Soria. It was only a second-class town, but in these warlike times, even towns of little importance were surrounded with walls.

"Senora," said Agenor, "here is Soria; if the Moor keeps such a watch as you imagine, it is not probable that he limits his visits to the gates and battlements; he must also reconnoitre the plain; therefore, I advise you to at once take all needful precautions."

"I was thinking the same," said the young woman, looking round her, as though to examine the locality; "and if you and your squire will walk slowly onwards, my precautions

will be taken in less than half an hour." Agenor obeyed.
The young woman dismounted, and led her nurse into the
thick underwood, whilst the two men continued their way.

"Come, come, sir squire! Do not keep turning your head
thus—imitate your master's discretion," said the nurse to
Muscaron, who resembled the damned souls of Dante, whose
dislocated heads looked back whilst their bodies moved forwards. But notwithstanding this injunction, Muscaron could
not prevail upon himself to turn his eyes in any other direction, so strongly was his curiosity aroused by the disappearance of the two females in a clump of horse-chestnut and
yew trees.

"Decidedly, master," observed he, when he was convinced
that his eyes could not penetrate the thick screen of foliage
which concealed the two women—"Decidedly, I am afraid that
instead of their being great ladies, as we at first supposed, our
companions will prove nothing but gipsies." Unfortunately
for Muscaron, this was no longer his master's opinion.

"You are a babbler, and presume on my indulgence," returned Agenor. "Be silent!" Muscaron obeyed.

After riding on so slowly that they had scarcely gone half
a quarter of a league, they heard a sharp and prolonged cry; it
was the nurse calling to them. They turned their horses' heads,
and beheld a young man advancing towards them, attired in
the Spanish fashion, and wearing a small mantle flung across
his left shoulder. He made signs with his hat for them to
wait for him, and in a few minutes he came up to them.

"I am here, senor," said he, addressing Agenor, who, to his
great surprise, recognised his travelling companion. Her raven
hair was concealed beneath a light peruque, her shoulders,
widened by the mantle, seemed those of a robust youth; her
mien was bold, and her complexion itself seemed to have assumed a deeper tint since the change in the colour of her hair.

"You see that my precautions are taken," said the seeming
youth. "And I should imagine that your page could gain
admittance with you into the town without any difficulty."
And he sprang up behind Muscaron with the lightness and
agility he had before displayed.

"But your nurse?" said Agenor.

"She will remain in the neighbouring village with my two
attendants, and there await my summons."

"Then all is well; let us enter the town."

Agenor, preceded by Muscaron and his new page, then directed his course towards the principal gate of Soria, which they perceived at the end of a long avenue of old trees. But they had scarcely proceeded half way down this avenue, before they found themselves surrounded by a band of Moorish soldiers, sent against them by the sentinels on the ramparts, who had observed their approach. They questioned Agenor as to his business. He had no sooner declared that it was to have an interview with Don Pedro, than they closed round him and conducted him to the governor of the gate, a creature of Mothril's.

" I am sent," said Agenor, on being again interrogated, "by the Constable Bertrand Duguesclin, to demand a conference with your prince."

At the sound of this name, which all Spain had learnt to respect, the officer appeared uneasy.

" And who are your companions ?" asked he.

" My squire and my page, as you see."

" Good; remain here, and I will report your demand to the Lord Mothril."—"Do as you will," returned Agenor; " but I warn you that I will speak neither to Mothril nor to any one except to the King, Don Pedro; therefore beware of carrying this investigation, which begins to be insulting, too far."

The officer bowed. " You are a knight," said he, " and therefore aware that the commands of my chief officer are not to be disputed, and that whatever he has prescribed, I must execute." Then turning to those around him, " Let his Highness the Prince Minister be informed that an envoy from the Constable Bertrand Duguesclin demands an audience with the King."

Agenor glanced towards his page, and remarked that he was looking both pale and uneasy. Muscaron, more accustomed to such adventures, did not quake at such a trifle.

" Comrade," said he, "this is how your precautions will succeed; you will be recognised in spite of your disguise, and we shall be hanged as your accomplices. But what does that matter if it suits my master ?"

The unknown smiled; she had already regained her presence of mind, which proved that she, no less than Muscaron, was not altogether a stranger to danger. She therefore seated herself at a little distance from Agenor, and appeared perfectly indifferent to what was passing around her. The travellers, after having been conducted through several apartments, thronged with guards and soldiers, now found themselves in a guard room built in the centre of the tower, and approached by a single door. On this door all eyes were now fixed, in momentary expectation of Mothril's entrance. Agenor continued to converse with the officer, whilst Muscaron chatted with several Spaniards, who made inquiries of him concerning the constable, and their various friends and acquaintances in the service of Don Henry de Transtamare. The young page was also surrounded by the pages of the governor, who led him hither and thither, and treated him like an insignificant boy. Mauleon was the only real object of watchfulness, although his courteous behaviour had completely re assured the officer; besides, what could a single man do against two hundred? The Spanish officer offered the French one fruits and wine; in order to procure these refreshments, the governor's attendants had to pass through the crowd of guards.

"My master is accustomed to take nothing from any hand but mine," said the disguised page. And he followed the pages into the outer apartments.

At this moment the sentinel gave the signal to present arms, and the cry of "Mothril! Mothril!" echoed through the guard-room. Every one arose from his seat. Agenor felt a shudder pass through his veins; he lowered his visor, and through its bars cast his eyes around him in search of the young page to re-assure him, but he was no longer to be seen.

"What has become of our travelling companion?" asked he of Muscaron, who with the greatest coolness replied in French,

"Messire, she thanks you much for the service you have rendered her in gaining her admittance to Soria. She charges me to tell you she is deeply grateful, and that you shall soon be convinced of it."

"What do you say?" said Agenor, in surprise.

"What she charged me to say, when she took her departure."

"Her departure?"

"*Ma joi!* yes," returned Muscaron. "She is gone. No eel ever glided more nimbly through the meshes of the net, than she did through the ranks of guards posted around. I saw in the distance the white plume of her cap disappear in the shade; and as I have not seen her since, I presume she has escaped."

"God be praised!" ejaculated his master; "but be silent."

In fact, the neighbouring apartment now echoed with the footsteps of a great number of cavaliers, and Mothril hastily entered.

"What is it?" inquired he, casting a keen and penetrating glance around him.

"This knight," said the officer, "the envoy of Messire Bertrand Duguesclin, Constable of France, demands an interview with his Majesty Don Pedro." Mothril approached Agenor, who stood with lowered visor, like a statue of iron.

"Behold," said Agenor, drawing off his gauntlet, and displaying the emerald ring given him by Don Henry as a token.

"What is this?" asked the Moor.—"An emerald ring once belonging to Donna Eleanora, the prince's mother."

Mothril bowed. "Then what are your wishes?"

"Those I will tell to the King."

"You desire an interview with his Majesty?"

"I insist upon it."—"Sir knight, you take a high tone."

"I speak in the name of my royal master, Don Henry de Transtamare."

"Then you must wait awhile in this fortress."

"I will wait; but I warn you not for long."

Mothril smiled ironically. "Be it so, sir knight; wait then." And he left the guard-room after saluting Agenor, whose eyes flashed lightning through the bars of his helmet.

"Keep good guard," whispered Mothril to the officer. "These are important prisoners, and I make you answerable for them."

"What shall I do with them, my lord?"

"I will tell you to-morrow. Meanwhile, do not let them hold communication with any one—do you hear?" The officer bowed.

"Decidedly we shall be hanged, and this stone-box will serve as our coffin," observed Muscaron, with the greatest coolness.

"What a glorious opportunity I had of strangling that miscreant!" said Agenor. "Oh, if I had only not been an ambassador!"—"One of the inconveniences of grandeur!" said Muscaron, philosophically.

CHAPTER XXXVI.

THE SPRIG OF ORANGE BLOSSOM.

AGENOR and his squire both passed a very bad night in their temporary prison : the officer, in obedience to Mothril's commands, had not again made his appearance. Mothril intended to pay them a second visit on the following morning; for summoned at the moment he was about to accompany Don Pedro to a bull-fight, he had now all the night before him to arrange his plans. Thus, if nothing occurred to change his mind, a second interrogation would decide the fate of the chevalier and his squire. It was still possible that the constable's envoy might be allowed to reach the King, but not before he had by some means or other learnt the object of his mission. The grand secret of political improvisatores consists in knowing beforehand the subject on which they will be called upon to improvise. On leaving the two prisoners, Mothril bent his steps towards the amphitheatre, where, as we have before said, the King was giving his court the spectacle of a bull-fight. This spectacle, which was usually given by day, on this occasion took place by night, which doubled its magnificence; three thousand torches of perfumed wax lighted the arena. Aïssa, seated on the right hand of the King, and surrounded by courtiers, who worshipped in her the newly-risen star in the horizon of royal favour, gazed without seeing, and listened without hearing. The King, gloomy and preoccupied, sat with his eyes fastened on her face, striving to read in it the confirmation of the hope unceasingly awakened by the changeless pallor of her pure brow, and the dreamy gaze of her half-veiled-eyes with their slumbering fires. Suddenly his brow darkened; for in contemplating the icy expression of the Moorish girl, he remembered the passionate mistress he had left at Seville—that Maria Padilla whom Mothril accused of being unfaithful to him, and changing with his fortunes, and who by her silence gave a colour to his suppositions; and he experienced a double suffering in the present coldness of Aïssa, and the recollection of the past love of Donna Maria. Thus, in thinking of this woman, his adoration for whom had been attributed to magic, a bitter sigh escaped from his breast, and like the breath of a storm, bowed the heads of his attentive courtiers. It was at this moment that Mothril entered the royal box, and understood at a glance the general state

R 2

of mind of its occupants. He observed the tempest raging in Don Pedro's breast; and guessing that it was caused by Aïssa's coldness, addressed a look full of hatred and menace to the young girl, who, although she well understood it, remained perfectly unmoved.

"Ah, you are there, Mothril," said the King. "You arrive at an unfortunate moment, for I am growing weary."

"I bring your Majesty news," said Mothril.—"Important ones?"

"Undoubtedly; should I disturb my King for trifles?"
The minister whispered to the King.

"It concerns an embassy sent you by the French."

"See, Mothril," interrupted the King, without seeming to have heard what the Moor said. "See how Aïssa dislikes our court. Truly, I think you would do well to send her back to her native Africa, which she seems to regret so deeply."

"Your Majesty is mistaken," returned Mothril. "Aïssa was born at Granada, and never having seen her native land cannot regret it."

"Has she then any other cause for regret?" demanded Don Pedro, turning pale.—"I believe not, sire."

"But then if she has nothing to regret, why does she behave thus; girls at sixteen talk and laugh, but she seems dead to everything."

"You know, sire, that nothing is so chaste, so reserved as an Eastern maiden, and I have already told you that, although born at Granada, Aïssa is of the blood of the Prophet. She bears upon her brow a rude crown—that of misfortune; therefore she cannot possess the careless smile, the empty gaiety of the women of Spain." Don Pedro bit his lips, and glanced at the unconscious Aïssa. "A day cannot change a woman's nature," continued the Moor, "and those who long preserve their dignity in like manner retain their affection. Donna Maria almost offered herself to you, and therefore has thus forgotten you." As Mothril pronounced these words, a sprig of orange blossom, flung from one of the upper galleries, fell on Don Pedro's knees with the directness of an arrow that reaches its mark. The courtiers exclaimed at this insolence, and some of them bent forward to ascertain from whence it came. Don Pedro picked up the sprig, and found a billet attached to it. Mothril made a movement as though to seize it, but Don Pedro stretched out his hand to prevent him.

"Stay," said he; "this billet is addressed to me, not to you." At sight of the writing he uttered a cry, and as he perused the first few lines, his countenance brightened.

Mothril anxiously watched the effects of this mysterious missive. All at once the King arose from his seat. The courtiers arose also, in readiness to attend him.

"Remain where you are," said Don Pedro. "The spectacle is not finished: I desire you to remain."

Mothril returned to the royal box, and mixed with the courtiers, who were lost in conjectures. He caused a search to be made on all sides for the bold perpetrator of the deed, but it was quite useless. A hundred women held bouquets of orange blossom in their hands; there was therefore nothing to betray from whence came the billet. On returning to the palace he questioned Aïssa, but she had seen nothing, remarked nothing. He tried to obtain access to Don Pedro, but the door of his apartment was closed against every one. The Moor passed a terrible night. For the first time an event of the highest importance had baffled his sagacity, and without being able to ground his dread on any positive circumstance, he felt a presentiment that his influence was about to encounter a rude shock. Sleep had not yet visited his eyes, when he received a summons from Don Pedro. He was introduced into the most retired apartments of the palace.

Don Pedro left his chamber, and advanced to meet his minister, first carefully closing the door behind him. The King was even paler than usual, but it was not chagrin that had given him this appearance of weariness; on the contrary, a smile of extreme satisfaction rested upon his lips, and there was an unusual softness and joyousness in the expression of his face. He seated himself, nodding in a friendly manner to the Moor, and yet Mothril fancied he perceived on his countenance an expression of firmness strangely at variance with his usual relations with him.

"Mothril," said the King, "you yesterday spoke to me concerning an ambassador sent to me by the French."

"Yes, sire," replied the Moor; "but as you made me no reply, I did not continue the subject."

"Besides which, you were not anxious to confess that you had ordered them to be imprisoned for the night in the tower of Porto-Basso."

Mothril started. "How did you know that, sire?" inquired he.

"I do know it, and that is sufficient. And why, since they announce themselves as ambassadors, have you placed them in confinement?"

"They call themselves so, it is true," said Mothril, who in a moment had regained his self-possession.

"And you say the contrary—is it not so?"

"Not exactly, sire, for in fact I am ignorant——"

"But if you were only doubtful, you should not have caused them to be arrested."—"Then your Majesty orders——"

"I order them to be immediately conducted to my presence." The Moor recoiled. "But it is impossible," he said.

"By the blood of our Lord! has anything happened to them?"

"No, my lord."—"Then hasten to repair your fault, for you have violated the rights of the people."

Mothril smiled: he knew the respect Don Pedro, in his hatred, had for these rights of the people, which he now invoked. "I will not permit my sovereign," said he, "to thus rashly expose himself to the danger that threatens him."

"Fear nothing for me!" retorted Don Pedro, stamping his foot; "rather fear for yourself."—"I have nothing to fear, having nothing to reproach myself with, sire," said the Moor.

"Nothing to reproach yourself with, Mothril! Reflect a little."

"What means your Majesty?"

"It means that you have a no less dislike to ambassadors coming in an eastern direction than to those coming in a western one." Mothril began to feel uneasy; little by little these interrogations were assuming a threatening aspect, but as he did not know as yet from what side to expect the attack, he waited in silence. The King continued, "Is this the first time you have arrested messengers sent to me, Mothril?"

"The first time, sire!" repeated Mothril, staking all on one throw: "there have been perhaps a hundred, not one of whom I have allowed to pass." The King arose from his seat, in a furious rage. "If," continued the Moor, "in keeping from the palace of my King the assassins hired by Henry de Transtamare and Bertrand Duguesclin, I have sacrificed a few innocent persons among so many guilty ones, my head is here to answer for the faults of my heart."

The King recovered himself, and again seating himself, said, "It is well, Mothril: by reason of the excuse you have made, I pardon you; but do not let it happen again. Let every messenger—whether he comes from Burgos or Seville—have access to me. As to these Frenchmen, I know them to be really ambassadors, and consequently I choose them to be treated as such. Let them be immediately released from the tower, and conducted, with all the honours due to their rank, to the best house in the city. To-morrow I will grant them a solemn audience in the grand saloon of the palace. Go." Mothril bowed his head and quitted the apartment, overwhelmed with surprise and mortification.

CHAPTER XXXVII.

THE AUDIENCE.

MEANWHILE, Agenor and his faithful squire were each, in their own fashion, lamenting their hard fate ; and Muscaron was already examining the stone walls to see if there were no means of scaling them, when Mothril appeared upon the threshold, followed by an escort of officers, whom he left at the door. Notwithstanding the suddenness of his entrance, Agenor had time to lower the visor of his helmet.

"Frank!" said Mothril, "answer me truly, if for once you can speak without falsehood."

"You judge of others by yourself, Mothril," retorted Agenor, who although not wishing to aggravate his position by giving way to anger, could not brook being insulted by the man whom of all others in the world he most hated.

"What mean you, dog!" vociferated Mothril.

Agenor seated himself, and shrugged his shoulders. "Have you only come here in order to talk this folly, Mothril?" said he.

"No ; I have important questions to put to you."

"Put them, then."

"First confess the means you have taken to correspond with the King."—"With what King?" demanded Agenor.

"I acknowledge but one King, envoy of the rebels, and that one my master."

"Don Pedro !—you ask me how I was enabled to correspond with Don Pedro ?"

"Yes."—"I do not understand you."

"Do you deny having demanded an audience with the King?"

"No; since it was to yourself I made the demand."

"Yes; but it was not I who communicated your demand to the King, and yet——"

"And yet?" repeated Agenor.—"He was aware of your arrival."

"Ah!" ejaculated Agenor, in amazement.

"Then you will confess nothing?" said Mothril.

"What would you have me confess?"—"First of all, by what means you corresponded with the King."

Agenor a second time shrugged his shoulders.

"Ask our guards," said he.

"Do not flatter yourself, Christian, that you will obtain anything from the King without having first gained my consent."

"Ah!" said Agenor, "then I shall see the King."

"Hypocrite!" exclaimed Mothril, furiously.

"Well," continued the chevalier, "since I am to have an audience with the King, we shall see, Mothril, whether my words will have as little weight as you imagine."

"Confess what you have done to make the King aware of your arrival—tell me the conditions on which you are come to offer him peace, and you shall have all my support."

"What need is there of my purchasing a support, which your very anger proves I can do without?" said Agenor, laughing.

"At least let me see your face," said Mothril, rendered uneasy by both the voice and the laugh of the strange knight.

"You will see it when I am in the presence of the King; before him, I shall speak with both face and heart revealed."
—All at once, Mothril struck his forehead with his clenched hand, and glanced round the chamber.

"You had a page," said he.—"Yes."

"What has become of him?"

"Search for him—make what inquiries you please, it is your right."—"Therefore, I ask you."

"Hear me; you have a right to question your officers, your soldiers, or your slaves, but not me!"

Mothril turned to his attendants.

"There was a page with this Frank," said he. "Find out what has become of him." There was a moment's silence whilst the search was being made, during which Mothril paced to and fro before the door, like a sentinel on his rounds, or rather, like a hyena in its den, and Agenor remained seated mute and motionless as a statue of iron, with Muscaron by his side, silently devouring the Moor with his eyes. The answer was, that the page had disappeared on the preceding evening, and had not since been seen.

"Is this true?" demanded the Moor of Agenor.

"Dame!" responded the chevalier, "they are men of your faith who say so; do infidels also lie?"

"But why has he fled?" Agenor understood it all.

"Doubtless to inform the King of his master's arrest."

"No one gains access to the King whilst Mothril watches over him!" said the Moor. Then, suddenly striking his brow, he exclaimed, "Ah! the orange blossom! the billet!"

"The Moor is decidedly going mad," observed Muscaron.

But Mothril almost immediately recovered himself; what he had just discovered was doubtless less terrible than what he had at first dreaded.

"Well," said he, "be it so; I congratulate you on your page's address. The audience you desire shall be granted you."

"And when?"—"To-morrow," said the Moor.

"God be praised," ejaculated Muscaron.

"But," continued the Moor, addressing Agenor, "beware lest your interview with the King has not the happy results you expect."—"I expect nothing," replied Agenor. "I fulfil my mission, and that is all."

"Let me give you one counsel," said Mothril, his voice assuming an almost affectionate tone.

"Thanks," replied the chevalier, "I wish to receive nothing from you."—"And why not?"

"Because I receive nothing from an enemy." And in his turn the young man pronounced these words in a tone of such intense hatred that the Moor shuddered.

"Good," said he. "Adieu, Frank."—"Adieu, Infidel!" said Agenor.

The Moor quitted the tower; in a word, he had learnt all he wished to know. The King had been informed, but by a little formidable voice. It was not as he had at first feared. Two hours after this interview an imposing guard came to escort Agenor, with the greatest marks of respect, to a house situated on the Plaza del Soria. Here vast apartments, as sumptuously furnished as possible, were prepared to receive the ambassador. Muscaron made a tour of the different rooms, inspecting the carpets, the furniture, the hangings, and every moment repeating—"We are decidedly better off

here than in the tower " Whilst Muscaron was thus employed, the chief governor of the palace entered, and inquired
whether it was the chevalier's pleasure to make any change
in his attire before appearing before the King."

"None," said Agenor; "I have my sword, my helmet, and
my cuirass; it is the dress of a soldier, and I am only a soldier
sent hither by his captain."

The governor left him, giving orders for the trumpet to be
sounded. An instant afterwards, they led up to the door a
superb horse, magnificently caparisoned.

"I do not require any horse but my own," said Agenor.
"It was taken from me, and all I wish is to have it restored."
Ten minutes afterwards, his own horse was brought him. An
immense crowd lined the road leading to the palace of Don
Pedro; but the young man vainly sought to discover among
the groups of women filling the balconies the face of his travelling companion, and he soon desisted from the attempt.
All the nobility remaining faithful to Don Pedro formed a
body of cavalry ranged in the inner court of the palace; and
their gold and silver coats of mail and glittering arms formed
a spectacle dazzling to behold.

Agenor had no sooner alighted from his horse, than he
found himself somewhat embarrassed. Events had succeeded
each other with so much rapidity, that he had not had time
to think of his mission, persuaded as he was that it would
never be accomplished. His tongue seemed glued to the roof
of his mouth—he had not a single connected idea—all his
thoughts were vague and undecided, and jostled together in
his brain, like the clouds on a foggy autumn day. His
entrance into the hall of audience resembled that of a blind
man suddenly restored to sight in the midst of a burst of sunshine, which envelops everything around him in a haze of
gold, and purple, and waving plumes. All at once, a shrill
voice which he recognised as having heard one night in the
gardens at Bordeaux, and one day in Caverley's tent, sounded
in his ears.

"Sir knight," it said, "you wished to speak to the King;
you are in his presence."

These words enabled the chevalier to fix his eyes on the
point from whence they proceeded, and he beheld Don Pedro.
On his right hand sat a veiled female, and on his left stood
Mothril. Mothril was deadly pale; he had just recognised

in the unknown knight Aïssa's lover. This inspection was as rapid as thought.

"Monseigneur," said Agenor, "I did not imagine for a single instant that I was arrested by your highness' orders."

Don Pedro bit his lip. "Knight," said he, "you are French, and therefore, perhaps, ignorant that, in addressing the King of Spain, it is usual to style him Sire, or your Majesty."

"I was in the wrong," said Agenor, bowing, "for you are King at Soira."

"Yes, King at Soira," returned Don Pedro, "whilst he who has usurped the title is not so anywhere."

"Sire," said Agenor, "happily these are not the subjects I have to discuss with you. I am come on the part of Henry de Transtamare, your brother, to propose a good and loyal peace, of which your people stand in great need, and which would also be congenial to your feelings as brothers."

"Sir knight," said Don Pedro, "if you are come to discuss this point with me, tell me why you now come to propose what eight days ago you refused?"

Agenor bowed. "Sire, said he, "I am not the judge between your royal highnesses, I only report the words with which I was charged—I am but a road from Burgos to Soria, extending from the heart of one brother to that of another."

"Then you do not know why peace is now offered me," returned Don Pedro; "well, I will tell you." Whilst waiting for the King to continue his speech, a profound silence reigned through the court. Agenor profited by the moment to cast his eyes on both the veiled female and the Moor. The former sat silent and motionless as a statue, whilst the latter was as pale and haggard as if in one night he had endured the sufferings of a lifetime. "You offer me peace in my brother's name," resumed the King, "because he wishes me to refuse it, and knows beforehand that I shall reject the conditions he names."

"Sire," interrupted Agenor, "your Majesty is as yet ignorant of what they are."—"I know that you have come to offer me the half of Spain, to demand hostages, and among others, my minister Mothril and his family."

Mothril from pale became livid, his burning eye sought to read to the bottom of Don Pedro's heart, to assure himself that he would persist in this refusal. Agenor started, for he

had not mentioned these conditions to any one except the
Bohemian, to whom he had said a few words on the subject.

"Your Majesty is indeed well informed," said he; "although
I cannot tell how or by whom." At this moment, the female
seated beside the King lifted her veil, and by a natural and
careless movement flung it back over her shoulders. Agenor
could not repress a cry of alarm; for in this female seated on
Don Pedro's right hand he recognised his fellow-traveller.
The blood rushed to his face; he now understood from whence
the King had obtained the information that had spared him
the trouble of stating the conditions of the proposed truce.

"Sir knight," said the King, "learn from my own lips, and
repeat it to those who sent you hither, that whatever may
be the conditions they propose to me, there is one which I
will never cease to resist—that of sharing my kingdom. It
belongs to me alone, and I choose to be at liberty to dispose
of it according to my own good pleasure."

"Then your Majesty chooses war?"

"I do not choose, I submit to it," replied Don Pedro.

"This is your Majesty's unchangeable decision?"—"Yes."

Agenor slowly drew off his steel gauntlet and cast it at the
King's feet. "In the name of Henry de Transtamare, King
of Castile," said he, "I proclaim war against you."

The King arose from his seat, amidst loud murmurs and
clashing of weapons. "You have faithfully fulfilled your
mission, sir knight," said he; "it remains for us to do our
duty as a King. We offer you four-and-twenty hours' hospitality in our city, and if it is agreeable to you, our palace
shall be your residence and our table yours."

Agenor silently saluted the King; and, on raising his head,
glanced at the veiled lady seated by his side. She returned
the glance, smiling gently; he even fancied that she raised her
finger to her lips, as if to say, "Patience! hope still."

CHAPTER XXXVIII.
THE RENDEZVOUS.

NOTWITHSTANDING this sort of tacit promise, on which Agenor
besides did not place much value, he quitted the audience-
chamber in a state of mind easily to be imagined. The only
thing bearing the semblance of probability was that this disguised Bohemian, with whom he had journeyed so familiarly,

was none other than the celebrated Maria Padilla. It was neither Don Pedro's resolution, nor the foreknowledge he had obtained of the object of his mission, that gave him uneasiness, but Agenor remembered having also confided to the Bohemian his dearest and most cherished secret—his love for Aïssa. The jealousy of this terrible woman once aroused, who could tell where the frenzy, which had already sacrificed so many innocent heads, would stop.   These gloomy thoughts arising together in Agenor's mind, prevented his remarking the withering looks of Mothril and the Moorish nobles, whom the proposition made in the name of Henry de Transtamare had wounded at once in their pride and their dearest interests. Brave and quick-tempered as he was, the chevalier would otherwise have scarcely preserved under their provocations the cool imperturbability necessary to an ambassador At the moment when he would have perhaps remarked and replied to them, another event occurred to distract his attention. Scarcely had he quitted the palace, and made his way through the crowd of guards surrounding it, than a woman, muffled in a long veil touched him on the arm, beckoning to him mysteriously to follow her.   Agenor hesitated for a moment ; he knew with how many snares Don Pedro and his vindictive mistress encompassed their enemies—what fertility of means they developed when vengeance was their object ; but thinking to himself that he had long struggled against fate, that it would be happy for him if his career were to finish one way or another, and that if destiny had fixed this hour to be his last, it would be welcome ; he followed the old woman, who made her way through the vast concourse of people, and doubtless certain of not being recognised deeply veiled as she was, bent her steps towards the house which had been assigned to the chevalier, and where Muscaron awaited him on the threshold. They had no sooner entered, than Agenor conducted the old woman to one of the most retired apartments; Muscaron, who saw something fresh was about to happen, bringing up the rear. The old woman lifted her veil, and they both recognised the nurse of the Bohemian.   After all that had taken place at the palace, this apparition did not in the least surprise Agenor ; but Muscaron, in his ignorance, uttered a cry of astonishment.

"My lord," said the old woman, "Donna Maria Padilla wishes to speak with you, and consequently begs that you

will repair this evening to the palace. The King purposes
reviewing the newly arrived troops; during that time Donna
Maria will be alone—may she depend on your visiting
her!"

"But," said Agenor, who could not feign towards Donna
Maria feelings that he was far from possessing, "why does
Donna Maria wish to see me?"

"Then do you consider it a great misfortune, sir knight,
to be invited by such a woman as Donna Maria to a private
interview?" asked the nurse, with a sly smile.

"No," said Agenor; "but I confess I prefer a rendezvous
given in the open air, in a spot where there is no want of
space, to which a man may go with his horse and his lance."

"And I with my crossbow," added Muscaron.

The old woman smiled at these tokens of distrust. "I see,"
said she, "that I must deliver the whole of my message;" and
she drew from her pocket a little pouch containing a letter.

Muscaron, on whom, in all such cases, the post of reader
devolved, seized the paper and read:—

"This, sir knight, is a pledge of safety from your travelling
companion. Seek me at the time and place my nurse will tell
you, that we may talk of Aïssa."

At these words Agenor started; the name of Aïssa seemed
a solemn assurance of safety, and he immediately declared himself ready to follow the nurse whithersoever she would.

"In that case," said she, "nothing can be more simple, and
I will await you in the castle chapel. This chapel is public
to the officers of our lord the King; but at eight o'clock they
close the gates, therefore you must be there at half-past seven,
and conceal yourself behind the altar."

"Behind the altar!" said Agenor, shaking his head, with
all his northern prejudices strong within him. "I do not
like a rendezvous given behind the altar."

"Oh, don't be alarmed!" said the old woman, naïvely; "God
is not offended in Spain by these little profanations, which
are the custom here. Besides, you will not have long to wait
there, for behind this altar is a door communicating with his
Majesty's apartments, by which he and the members of his
household can gain admittance to the chapel. This I will
open for you, and you will take your departure unobserved
by the secret way."

"Yes, without any one being the wiser," remarked Muscaron, in French. Hum, hum, Sire Agenor, this sounds terribly cut-throat! what do you say to it?"

"Never fear," replied the chevalier, in the same language. "We have this woman's letter—although only signed with her baptismal name—as a guarantee. If anything befalls me, you will return with it to the constable and Don Henry de Transtamare, explain to them my love, my misfortunes, and the ruse that has been practised to draw me into the snare; and, if I know them both, they will take such vengeance on the traitors as shall make Spain tremble."

"Very well," remonstrated Muscaron; "but, meanwhile, you will none the less be murdered."

"True, Muscaron; but if it is really to speak of Aïssa that Donna Maria requires my presence?"

"Master, you are in love—that is to say, you are mad, and a madman always thinks himself in the right, no matter how extravagant his ideas may seem to others. Pardon me, master, but it is the truth. Still, I yield the point; go." And honest Muscaron sighed deeply as he concluded this peroration. "But why," he suddenly resumed, "why should not I go with you?"

"Because there is an answer to deliver to the King of Castile, Don Henry de Transtamare," replied the chevalier; "and if I were dead, you alone could relate the results of my mission." And Agenor related clearly and succinctly Don Pedro's reply.

"But at least," persisted Muscaron, who would not consider himself beaten, "I may keep watch outside the palace."

"For what purpose?"

"Body of St. James! to defend you!" exclaimed the squire. "To defend you with my cross-bow, which would lay low half a dozen of these yellow-faced villains, whilst you could cut down another half dozen with your sword. That would make at least a dozen infidels."

"My dear Muscaron," said Agenor, "on the contrary, do me the favour not to show yourself. If I am slain, the walls of the Alcazar alone will know it. But, listen," he continued, with the confidence of an upright heart; "Donna Maria cannot bear me any personal malice; I never recollect insulting her; nay, I have even rendered her some service."

"Yes; but the Moor Mothril, you have insulted him sufficiently, have you not, both here and elsewhere? If I am not mistaken, he is governor of the palace, and to give you an idea of his disposition in your favour, would have willingly caused you to be arrested at the gates of the city and thrown into a dungeon. It is not the female favourite you have to fear, but the male one."

Agenor was somewhat superstitious. He turned towards the old woman, saying, "If she smiles, I will go." The old woman smiled. "Return to Donna Maria," said he to the nurse, "and tell her the thing is agreed upon; at seven o'clock I will be at the chapel."

"Good! and I will await you there with the key of the door," said the nurse. "Adieu, Senor Agenor; adieu, gracious squire."

Muscaron wagged his head, the old woman disappeared.

"Now," said Agenor, turning to Muscaron, "no letters for the constable, for you might be stopped and have them taken from you. You will tell him that war is declared, and that he must commence hostilities. You have our money, and can make use of it in journeying as quickly as possible."

"But you, master? For, after all, we must take into consideration that you may not be killed."

"I have need of nothing; if I am betrayed, I shall offer up the sacrifice of a life of fatigue and disappointment of which I am heartily weary. If, on the contrary, Donna Maria protects me, she will enable me to procure horses and guides. Set out then, Muscaron, this very moment; their eyes are fixed on me, not you; they will know I remain, and that is all they require. Go, your horse is good and your courage great!"

This project, adventurous as it appeared, was nevertheless in their present situation a wise one, and therefore Muscaron, more from conviction than courtesy to his master, ceased to dispute the point. A quarter of an hour afterwards Muscaron set out, and quitted the city without difficulty, whilst Agenor at the appointed time repaired to the chapel where the old woman awaited him. She beckoned to him to quicken his pace, and hastily opening the little door, drew him in after her. After passing through a long range of corridors and galleries, Agenor found himself in a low dimly-lighted apartment opening on to a terrace filled with flowers. Here he beheld a female, seated beneath a sort of canopy, attended by a slave, whom she dismissed on the chevalier's entrance.

The old woman also discreetly disappeared after introducing the chevalier.

"Thanks for your punctuality," said Donna Maria, addressing Mauleon, "I knew you were both generous and brave. I wished to offer you my thanks, even after having apparently been guilty of perfidy towards you." Agenor was silent. It was to speak of Aïssa he had been summoned, and had obeyed. "Draw nearer," continued Donna Maria, "I am so fondly attached to Don Pedro, that it was my duty to consider his interests even in injuring yours; but my love is my excuse, and you who also love ought to understand me." Maria approached the object of the interview; nevertheless Agenor contented himself with a silent bow. "Now that my affairs are disposed of, sir knight," continued Maria, "let us speak of yours."

"Of which of them, senora?"

"Of those in which you are most deeply interested."

Agenor at the sight of this frank smile, this gracious gesture, this cordial address, felt himself disarmed.

"Come, seat yourself here," continued the enchantress, pointing to a place beside her. The chevalier did as he was ordered. "You believed me your enemy," resumed Maria Padilla, "but I am nothing of the kind, and to prove it I am ready to render you services at least equal to those I received at your hands." Agenor gazed at her in astonishment. Maria went on: "Were you not my protector during our journey, and unintentionally a good counsellor?"

"Most unintentionally so," replied Agenor; "for I was completely ignorant to whom I was speaking."—"Yet, thanks to your information, I was none the less able to serve the King," said Maria, smiling; "therefore cease to deny having been useful to me."

"Well, then, I will confess it, senora; but as to yourself—"

"You do not believe me capable of serving you. Oh, chevalier, you doubt my gratitude!"

"You have perhaps the desire, senora; that I do not dispute."

"I have both the will and the power. Suppose, for instance, you were detained at Soria?" Agenor started. "I am able to facilitate your departure from the town."

"Ah, senora!" said Agenor, "by so doing you would serve Don Pedro's interests as much as mine; for you would prevent the King being taxed with cowardice and treachery."

"I admit it," replied the young woman, "if you were a simple ambassador coming here on a merely political mission, which could excite hatred and mistrust in no breast but the King's; but think well, have you no other enemy—an altogether personal one—at Soria?" Agenor grew visibly troubled. "Cannot you understand," continued the lady, "that if such were the case, this enemy without consulting the King, without thinking of anything but his own private vengeance, would, in order to revenge himself, lay snares for you, of all participation in which the King would be entirely innocent; and this it would be easy to prove to your compatriots in case there were ever need of an explanation; for remember, chevalier, you are here as much to watch over your own private interests as those of Don Henry de Transtamare." Agenor could not repress a sigh. "Ah, I thought you would understand me," said Maria. "Well, if I ward off from you the danger that menaces you in this meeting?"

"You would preserve my life, senora, and many would esteem that an invaluable boon; but for myself I scarcely know whether I should be properly grateful for your generosity."

"And why not?"—"Because I do not care for life."

"Not care for life?"—"No," replied Agenor, shaking his head.

"Because you have some great grief—is it not so?"

"Yes, senora."—"And if I know what it is?"

"You!"—"And can show you its cause!"

"You! You can tell me! You can show me!"

Maria Padilla rose, and walking towards the silken hangings veiling the terrace, flung them aside, saying, "Look!"

He now perceived a lower terrace, separated from the first by clumps of orange-trees, pomegranates, and rose laurels. Here, surrounded by flowers and bathed in the beams of the setting sun, hung a purple hammock in which a young girl was swinging herself.

"Well?" said Donna Maria.

"Aïssa," exclaimed Agenor, clasping his hands in an ecstasy.

"Mothril's daughter, I believe," said Donna Maria.

"Oh, senora!" exclaimed the young man eagerly, scanning the space separating him from Aïssa. "You are right; there is the happiness of my life!"

"So near, and yet so distant," returned Donna Maria, smiling.

"Are you mocking me, senora?" said Agenor, uneasily.

"God forbid, sir knight! I only say that Donna Aïssa is at this moment the very emblem of happiness. How often it appears as though we had only to extend the hand in order to grasp it, and yet some invisible, but insurmountable obstacle intervenes."

"Alas! I know it. She is watched—guarded."

"She is imprisoned, sir knight—imprisoned by good gates and strong locks."

"If I could only attract her attention!" exclaimed Agenor; "only see and be seen by her."

"Would that then be so great a pleasure to you?"

"Supreme!"

"Well, then, I will procure it for you. Donna Aïssa has not yet observed you; she shall do so even if it only increases her unhappiness; for it is but a poor consolation to lovers to stretch out their arms to each other, and confide their kisses to the air. Do better than this, sir knight."

"Oh, what must I do, senora? Command, or rather counsel me!"

"You see this door," said Donna Maria, showing him an outlet from the terrace itself. "This key—the largest of these three hung together on a ring—belongs to it. A long passage, similar to the one you traversed in coming hither, will conduct you to the neighbouring garden, whose trees appear on a level with the terrace occupied by Donna Aïssa. Ah! I see you begin to comprehend."

"Yes, yes, senora," responded Mauleon, literally devouring the words as they fell from Donna Maria's lips.

"The entrance to this garden is closed by an iron gate," she continued, "the key of which hangs beside the first. Once there, you can approach still nearer Donna Aïssa, by making your way to the foot of the terrace where she is now swinging; only the sides of it are perpendicular, and it is impossible to scale them. But you can at least call your mistress, and speak to her."

"Thanks! thanks!" cried Mauleon.

"Good," said Donna Maria, "you are already better satisfied; nevertheless, there is danger in conversing thus, for you may be overheard. I warn you of this, although Mothril is absent; he has accompanied the King to a review of the troops newly arrived from Africa, and will not return till ten

s 2

o'clock, or at earliest half-past nine—and it is now eight."—
"An hour and a half! Oh, senora, quick! Give me the
key I beseech you."

"Oh, there is plenty of time. Let the last rays of the
setting sun, now reddening the horizon, die away—it will only
be a minute or two. Meanwhile," added she, smiling, "shall
I tell you?"—"Speak, senora!"

"Unfortunately, I cannot separate this third key from the
two others, and it being one given by Mothril himself to Don
Pedro, I had much difficulty in procuring it."

"To Don Pedro!" said Agenor, with a shudder.

"Yes," resumed Maria; "and fancy, this key opens the
door conducting to a most convenient staircase ending in the
terrace, where Aïssa is, doubtless, at this moment dreaming
of you." Agenor uttered a cry of wild delight. "So that
this door once closed upon you," continued Donna Maria,
"you will be at liberty to converse for an hour and a half
with Mothril's daughter without fear of interruption. Besides,
if any one comes, it can only be through the house, and you
have your retreat secured on this side."

Agenor fell on his knees, and covered his protectress's
hand with kisses. "Senora," said he, "ask for my life at any
moment it could prove useful to you, and it shall be yours."

"Thanks, sir knight, but rather preserve it for your mistress. The sun is now set—in a few moments it will be dark
night—you have but an hour. Go, and do not compromise
me with Mothril." Agenor rushed down the steps of the
terrace, and disappeared. "Sir Frank," cried Maria, as he
hastened away, "in an hour your horse will stand in readiness at the door of the chapel; but do not let Mothril suspect anything, or we are both lost."

"In an hour, I swear to you," answered the already distant voice of the chevalier.

CHAPTER XXXIX.

THE INTERVIEW.

It was indeed Aïssa, who, pensive and alone, reclined on the
terrace of the palace adjoining her own and her father's
apartments; and who, dreamy and indolent, like a true child
of the East, was inhaling the evening breeze, and watching

the last rays of the setting sun. When these had faded away, her gaze wandered over the magnificent gardens of the Alcazar, seeking beyond the walls—beyond the trees—what she had vainly sought in the horizon; for this long-lived remembrance taking no account of time or space, which men call love, is an eternal hope. She was dreaming of the greener and more diversified landscapes of France, of the garden at Bordeaux, whose protecting shade had sheltered her during the happiest moments of her life; and at the same instant, her thoughts reverted to the garden at Seville, where Agenor so unexpectedly appeared before her. But her reverie was suddenly interrupted by the sound of a rapid footstep echoing on the stone staircase. She fancied it was Mothril already returned, and coming, as he sometimes did, to surprise her in the midst of her sweetest dreams; as if within the spirit of this man existed a penetration, a sagacity, which, like an infernal torch, illumined everything about him, leaving only his own deep and all-powerful mind shrouded in mystery and darkness. Nevertheless, these footsteps could not be Mothril's, for they proceeded from a direction altogether opposite to that in which he usually came. Then, with a shudder, she thought of the King, whose attentions, since the arrival of Donna Maria, she had ceased to dread, and had almost forgotten. The staircase, too, from whence the sounds proceeded, was the one constructed by Mothril to afford a secret mode of entrance to his sovereign. She hastened then to rouse herself from her soft reverie, and prepare to face the enemy. If it were Mothril, she could cow him by her indomitable will—if Don Pedro, she had her poniard. With affected indifference, she turned her back upon the door, in momentary expectation of hearing the harsh accents in harmony with the threatening footsteps that had already made her shudder. All at once she felt herself clasped in two mailclad arms; she uttered a cry of anger and disgust, but it was stifled by two eager lips pressed to her own; and she recognised Agenor kneeling on the marble pavement at her feet. She with difficulty repressed the cry of joy that was ready to burst from her lips.

"You, Agenor!" she murmured. "You in Don Pedro's palace! You restored to my fond heart. Oh! the days of absence are too long—God has two measures for time—for the moments when I behold you, and which pass swift as a

shadow, and the days when you are absent, and which **are**
like centuries !"

"Oh, we have met again, and you are still mine !" cried
Agenor. "What matters to me Mothril's hatred or the King's
love. I can now die happy !"

"*Die !*" repeated Aïssa, with tearful eyes and quivering
lips ; "die ! oh, no, my well-beloved, you shall not die. I
saved you at Bordeaux, and I will save you here also. As
to the King, think you that in this heart, filled with your
image and beating only for you, there is room for even the
shadow of another love."

"Oh, God forbid," said Agenor, "that I should for a
moment fancy that my Aïssa could forget me; but where
persuasion fails, violence sometimes succeeds. Have you not
heard the story of Leonora de Ximenes, to whom the King's
brutality has left no resource but a convent ?"

"Leonora de Ximenes is not Aïssa. It will never be with
the one as it has been with the other."

"I well know you would defend yourself, but in so doing,
you might meet with your death."

"And would you not rather have me dead, Agenor, than
belong to another ?"

"Oh ! yes, yes," cried the young man, straining her to his
breast with a feeling of love almost amounting to terror.
"Die, if it must be so—but be mine, and mine only !" For
some time a silence like death prevailed : the lovers' hearts
were both too full to speak. Agenor was the first to break
it, by girding on his sword, whose steel scabbard rang upon
the marble pavement.

"What are you doing ?" cried Aïssa, seizing his arm.

"You said, my beloved, that time has two measures—
the moments for happiness, the ages for despair. I must
depart."

"But you will take me with you—is it not so ? We shall
depart together." The young man disengaged himself from
her clinging arms.

"Impossible !" said he.—"How impossible ?"

"Yes; I am come hither under the sacred title of ambassador. It is that protects me: I dare not violate it."

"But I will not quit you!" cried Aïssa.

"Aïssa," replied the young man, "I came hither in the
names of the good constable and Don Henry de Transtamare,

who have confided to me—the one the honour of France, and the other the interests of the throne of Castile. What would they say when they found that, instead of fulfilling this double mission, I was only occupied with my own love ?"

"And who could tell them so ? What is there to prevent your concealing me from all eyes ?"—"I must return to Burgos, and it is three days' journey from Soria."

"I am strong, and accustomed to rapid marches."

"You are right, for the marches of the Arab horsemen are infinitely more rapid than our own. In an hour's time Mothril would discover your flight: he would pursue us, and I cannot enter Burgos as a fugitive."—"Oh, my God! my God! are we again doomed to be separated ?"

"I swear to you that this time, at least, our separation shall be a brief one. Let me discharge my mission, return to Don Henry's camp, resign the office with which he has invested me, and again become Agenor, the French chevalier who loves and lives but for you; and then I swear to you, Aïssa, that under no matter what disguise, even if it be that of an infidel, I will return to you, and bear you away."

"No, no," persisted Aïssa.

"But think of our protectress, Aïssa — the generous woman who guided me to you, that poor Maria Padilla, on whom Mothril would revenge himself; and you know in what fashion he revenges himself on his enemies."

"Then at least let me rejoin you," said the Moorish maiden, turning pale, as she felt a superior power—that of reason—separating her from her lover. "I have two mules, so fleet that they would outstrip the swiftest horse. Point out to me some spot where I may either wait for or rejoin you, and rest assured I will be there."

"Aïssa, it is impossible."

The young girl fell on her knees at Agenor's feet, supplicating—beseeching him. At that moment the sad and plaintive notes of a guzla sounded above their heads, imitating the summons of an anxious friend. They both started.

"Whence comes that noise ?" said Aïssa.

"I guess," replied Agenor. And he raised his eyes towards Maria Padilla's terrace. The night was dark, yet by the faint light of the stars the young people could distinguish a white form leaning on the parapet, and turned towards them. They might perhaps have doubted whether it was a phantom or a woman they thus beheld, but at that moment the same sonorous chord again sounded in the same direction.

"She calls me," said Agenor.   "Do you hear, Aïssa?"

"Come, come," said Maria, in a low voice, which sounded as if descending from heaven.

"Do you hear, Aïssa?" said Agenor again.

"Oh, I hear, I see nothing!" faltered the young girl.

At that moment, the trumpets which usually announced the King's return to the palace, were heard to sound.

"Allah!" exclaimed Aïssa, whom this sound at once changed into a weak and trembling woman.   "They come—fly, my Agenor, fly!"—"One more adieu!" said Agenor.

"Perhaps the last!" murmured the young girl; and returning his embrace, she hurried him down the steps of the terrace.   His footsteps had scarcely ceased to echo, when those of Mothril were heard in the corridor, and the door leading to Maria Padilla's apartments was scarcely closed ere that of Aïssa opened.

CHAPTER XL.

PREPARATIONS FOR BATTLE.

THREE days after the events we have just related, Agenor rejoined Muscaron, and rendered an account of their journey to Henry de Transtamare.   No one could doubt the dangers Agenor had encountered in the accomplishment of his mission ; thus the constable praised and thanked him, and directed him to take his place among his bravest Bretons, under the command of Sylvester de Budes.   On all sides were preparations for war.   The Prince of Wales had joined Don Pedro, bringing with him a fine army to add to his African troops.   The English adventurers, on their side, decidedly rallied round Don Pedro, promising themselves to exchange a few hard knocks with their deadly enemies the Bretons and Gascons.   We need not say the wildest projects fermented in the brain of our old friend Hugh Caverley.

Henry de Transtamare was not behindhand in these warlike preparations.   He had been joined by his two brothers, Tello and Sancho—had appointed them to posts of command—and was now marching by short stages to meet his brother Don Pedro.   Agenor, in a measure left to himself, turned over in his own mind all the means possible or impossible by which to reach Aïssa, and bear her away, so as not to be obliged to await the chances of the approaching battle. For this purpose he had, thanks to Bertrand's liberality, purchased two Arab horses, which Muscaron every day accustomed to take long journeys, and endure both hunger and thirst. At last they learnt that the Prince of Wales had passed through the defile, and encamped with the army he had brought with him from Guyenne, near the village of Vittoria, at a little distance from Navaretto. He had with him 30,000 horse, and 40,000 foot soldiers—a force about equal to that of Don Pedro.

Henry de Transtamare on his side had 60,000 foot and 40,000 horse. Bertrand, encamped in the rear with his Bretons, let the Spaniards indulge in their rhodomontades, and on all sides celebrate the victory they had not yet gained; but he nevertheless had spies who day after day brought him intelligence of the movements that took place in Don Pedro's army—nay, even in that of Don Henry. As to Caverley, he was acquainted with all his projects, almost as soon as the prolific brain of the adventurer conceived them. He consequently knew that the worthy captain—allured by the royal capture he had already made—had offered the Prince of Wales to terminate the war at a single blow. Nothing could be more simple than the plan he proposed to adopt; it was that of the bird of prey, which, hovering so high in the air as to be invisible to its intended victim, suddenly descends at the very moment it was least expected, and at one swoop bears it away.

Sir Hugh Caverley, accompanied by John Chandos, the Duke of Lancaster, and a portion of the English vanguard, were to make a sudden descent upon Don Henry's quarters, and carry off both himself and his court; thus at once making twenty prisoners, each of whose ransoms would make the fortune of five or six adventurers. The Prince of Wales had accepted this offer; he had everything to gain and nothing to lose by the proposed plan. Unfortunately, Messire Bertrand Duguesclin, as we before said, employed spies, who brought him intelligence of all that took place in the hostile army; more unfortunately still, he had an old grudge against the English in general, and above all against Caverley in particular. He therefore charged his spies not to sleep for a single moment, or if they did, at least to do so with one eye open; and he was

consequently informed of the captain of the adventurers
slightest movement.   An hour before the worthy captain
quitted the Prince of Wales' camp, the constable placed
himself at the head of six thousand Breton and Spanish horse,
and sent Agenor and Le Bègue de Vilaine by a road opposite to the one pursued by himself, to post themselves with
the troops under their command in a wood bordering each
side of a mountain defile.   The two troops were, therefore,
placed parallel to each other, so that when the English had
once passed through the defile, it would be closed behind
them.   Meanwhile, Henry de Transtamare forewarned of what
was about to take place, had all his men under arms.   Caverley would thus find himself hemmed in between two bodies
of enemies.   Horses and men took their stations at nightfall, each cavalier lay flat upon the ground, holding his horse
by the bridle.   Towards ten o'clock Caverley and all his company entered the defile; the English marching in so much
security, that they did not even examine the surrounding
wood, a precaution which the darkness would besides have
rendered it very difficult, if not impossible to take.   Behind
the English, the Spaniards and Bretons, issuing from their
places of concealment on either side of the road, joined like
the broken links of a chain united by a skilful workman.
Towards midnight a great tumult was heard; it was Caverley
making his attack on Don Henry's quarters, where he was
received with cries of "Don Henry and Castile!"   Then
Bertrand, with Agenor on his right hand, and Le Bègue de
Vilaine on his left, galloped forward with his troops, shouting
their war-cry—" Duguesclin!"   At the same moment great
fires burst into a blaze on either side, lighting up the scene
and displaying Caverley and his five or six thousand adventurers taken between two armies.   Caverley was not the man
to seek a glorious but useless death; and as by yielding he
ran the risk of being hanged, he set spurs to his horse and
managed to make his escape.   All his baggage, a considerable
sum in gold, and a casket of jewels and precious stones, the
produce of three years' rapine, fell into the hands of Agenor
de Mauleon.   Whilst the dead were being despoiled, and the
prisoners fettered, Muscaron reckoned their value, and found
he was now in the service of one of the richest chevaliers in
Christendom.   This change (and it was certainly a great one)
had taken place in less than an hour.   The adventurers had

been cut to pieces—two or three hundred alone had with difficulty escaped. This success inspired the Spaniards with so much boldness, that Don Tello, the younger brother of Don Henry de Transtamare, urged his horse forward and wished to proceed at once, and without further preparation, against the enemy.

"One moment, my lord," said Bertrand; "I presume you do not intend marching alone against the enemy, and being ignominiously made prisoner?"

"The whole army will march with me, I suppose," returned Don Tello.—"Not so, my lord," said Bertrand; "not so."

"Let the Bretons remain behind if they will," exclaimed the prince, hotly; "for my part, I shall advance with the Spaniards."

"To do what?"—"To defeat the English."

"Pardon!" said Bertrand. "The English have been beaten by the Bretons, but they will never be so by the Spaniards."

"What!" exclaimed Don Tello, impetuously, and advancing towards the constable. "And why not?"

"Because," returned Bertrand, unmoved by his anger, "the Bretons are better soldiers than the English; but the English are better soldiers than the Spaniards."

An angry flush mounted to the young prince's brow.

"It is a strange thing," said he, "that here in Spain our master should be a Frenchman; but we will soon see whether Don Tello will obey instead of commanding. Here, my men, follow me."

"My eighteen thousand Bretons will not stir an inch until I give the word of command," said Bertrand. "As to the Spaniards, I am only their master so long as your sovereign and mine commands them to obey me."

"How prudent these Frenchmen are!" exclaimed Don Tello, in exasperation. "How coolly they meet, not only danger, but insult! I congratulate you upon it, my lord constable."

"Yes, monseigneur," replied Bertrand, "my blood is cool whilst I restrain myself, but warm when I am aroused." And ready to burst with rage, he clenched his mailed hands tightly together.

"Nay, you are wondrously cool I tell you," persisted the prince; "but that is because you are growing old, and with age comes fear."

"Fear!" interrupted Agenor, spurring his horse up to Don Tello. "He who once says the constable is afraid shall not say so a second time."—"Silence, friend!" said the constable. "Patience, and leave fools to their folly."

"Respect the blood royal!" cried Don Tello. "Do you hear me?"

"Preserve your own self-respect, if you wish others to respect you," said a voice that made the young man start; for it was his elder brother's, who had been by some means or other informed of the altercation. "And above all, do not insult our heroic ally."

"Thanks, sire," said Bertrand, "you are generous in thus sparing me the always unpleasant task of chastising the insolent. But it is not you, Don Tello, to whom I allude; for you already feel how much you have been in the wrong."

"In the wrong for having said we were about to give battle to the enemy. Is it not true, sire?"

"Give battle to the enemy, and at this moment, too!" exclaimed Duguesclin. "But it is impossible!"

"No, my dear constable," said Henry. "The thing is so little impossible, that by day-break the battle will have begun."

"My lord, we shall be defeated."

"And why so?"—"Our position is bad."

"There is no such thing as a bad position," exclaimed Don Tello. "It all depends whether we are brave men, or cowards!"

"Sir constable," said the King, "my nobles demand this battle. They have beheld the advances of the Prince of Wales, and feel that we have the appearance of shunning the encounter."

"Besides," sneered Don Tello, "the constable is at liberty to watch our proceedings, and repose whilst we fight."

"Monseigneur," replied Duguesclin, "I shall do as much as the Spaniards, and more, too, I hope; for bear this in mind—in two hours' time you commence this attack, do you not?"—"Yes."

"Well, then, in four hours' time you will be flying across this plain before the Prince of Wales, whilst I and my Bretons shall remain firm, without either foot soldier or cavalier having retreated so much as an inch. Wait, and you will see."

"Come, sir constable," said Henry, "be moderate!"

"I state the truth, sire. You still persist in giving the enemy battle?"

"Yes, constable, I persist, for I feel I ought to do so."

"Then be it so!" and turning to his Bretons, he said, "My children, prepare for battle. Sire," he continued, "before night-fall, all these brave fellows, as well as myself, will be either slain or taken prisoners; but your will shall be done. Only remember that whilst I lose life or liberty, you will lose a throne."

The King let his head fall on his breast; turning to his followers, he said, "The good constable is hard upon us this morning, my lords; nevertheless, make your preparations for battle."

"Then it is true we are all going to be killed to-day?" observed Muscaron, loud enough to be overheard by the constable.—"Mon Dieu! yes, my worthy squire," returned he, with a smile. "It is an undoubted fact."

"It is annoying," said Muscaron, slapping his well-filled pockets, "to be killed just as we were going to enjoy life!"

CHAPTER XLI.

THE BATTLE.

AN hour after this mournful soliloquy of the worthy squire, as Duguesclin called him, the sun rose over the plains of Navaretto as brightly and as peacefully as if it were not about to shine on one of the most celebrated battles ever known in the annals of the world. By sunrise, the plain was occupied by Don Henry's army, disposed in three bodies. The left wing, composed of twenty-five thousand men, was commanded by Don Tello and his brother Sancho. Duguesclin commanded the main body, consisting of six thousand foot, and nearly twenty-eight thousand horse. Don Henry himself held the position on the right, with twenty-one thousand horse and thirty thousand foot.

It was the 3rd of April, 1368, and the preceding day had been overpowering from heat and dust. King Henry, mounted on a splendid Spanish mule, rode from one to the other of his squadrons, praising some, encouraging others, and above all, representing to them the terrible fate they would risk in falling into the hands of the cruel Don Pedro. As to the constable, who sat cool and resolute at his post, he hastened to him and embraced him, saying, "This arm is about to win me a crown ; why is it not the crown of the universe, that I might offer it to you, my brave ally, for none other is worthy of you!"

In moments of danger, kings are always profuse in promises like these ; it is true that the danger in passing by, bears them away with it as the whirlwind does the dust. Henry then fell on his knees, and, bareheaded, performed his devotions, in which he was imitated by all his army. At this moment the rays of the sun were reflected on the English lances, as they appeared above the brow of the mountain, and slowly descended its side. Among the banners, Agenor recognised Caverley's, rearing itself even more proudly and boldly than at the moment of the night attack. Lancaster and Chandos, who, like our captain, had escaped on the night of the defeat, shared the command with him, feeling the more resolute from having a terrible revenge to take. All three took up a position facing Duguesclin. The Prince of Wales and Don Pedro placed themselves opposite Don Tello and Don Sancho ; whilst the Captal de Buch, Jean Grailly, confronted Don Henry de Transtamare.

The Black Prince, touched at the sight of so many thousand men preparing to spill each others' blood, shed tears, and instead of haranguing his army, besought God to grant him not the victory, but that right which is the device of the English crown. Then the trumpets sounded—the earth trembled beneath the horses' feet, and a sound like the meeting of two opposing thunder clouds, was heard in the air. The two main bodies of troops, composed of resolute, and above all, experienced men, had, however, only advanced one step forward. The air was first darkened by a flight of arrows, and then the knights rushed upon each other, and silently fought hand-to-hand—a terrible and exciting spectacle for those not yet engaged in the strife. The Black Prince fought among his men like a common soldier ; at the head of his troop, he charged at full gallop the wing of the army commanded by Don Tello. This was the first set battle in which this young prince had ever been an actor, and he found himself suddenly confronted with men, who, with the exception of the Bretons, passed for the best soldiers in the world. His courage failed him, and he gave way. On seeing this, his cavalry turned their horses' heads, and in an instant, the whole left wing of the army had taken to flight under the influence of one of those panics by which even the bravest are sometimes carried away. In passing by the Bretons, Don Tello redoubled his speed and turned away his head. As to Don Sancho, encountering the contemptuous look of the constable, he, beneath its powerful influence, paused in his flight, turned back, and was taken prisoner. Don Pedro, who, with the Prince of Wales, was in pursuit of the fugitives, eager to profit by this first success, and seeing the left wing completely routed, turned immediately towards his brother Henry, who was struggling bravely against the Captal de Buch ; but attacked in the flank by seven thousand fresh troops, flushed with success, he yielded tŏ the shock. Amid the sounds of steel clashing against steel, the neighing of horses, and the shouts of the combatants, Don Pedro's voice was heard rising above it all, and crying, "No quarter to the rebels! no quarter!" He was himself fighting with a gilded battle-axe ; but the gild· ing, from the blade to the handle, was lost beneath the blood in which it was steeped. Meanwhile the body of reserved troops were routed and put to flight ; Duguesclin and his Bretons alone remained, and as they promised, had not receded a step ; but formed into an impenetrable mass, appeared like a rock of iron, around which the victorious battalions would soon coil themselves like long and greedy serpents.

Duguesclin cast a rapid glance over the plain—he saw that the battle was lost. Thirty thousand soldiers were flying in all directions, and where, an hour before, stood friends, nothing was now to be seen but the foe. He knew there was now nothing to be done but die in doing as much injury as possible to the enemy. He cast his eyes to the left, and perceived a ruined wall, the former rampart of some demolished town. Two bands of English lay between them and this shelter, which, once gained, would oblige all attack to be confined to their front. He gave an order in his full and sonorous voice—the two companies were trampled under foot, and the Bretons found themselves supported by the wall. Here Bertrand re-formed his ranks, and took breath for a moment. Le Bègue de Vilaine and the Maréchal d'Andreghem did the same. The constable profited by this momentary respite to raise the visor of his casque, and wipe his heated and dusty visage, as he gazed around him, and coolly counted the number of men remaining tc him.

"The King!" he demanded.   "The King!   Where is he? Is he slain, or fled?"

"No, messire," said Agenor.   "He has neither fallen nor taken to flight.   He is yonder, retreating towards us."

Don Henry, covered with blood, partly his own, and partly his enemies', and the crown on his helmet broken by the blow of a battle-axe, was bravely fighting his way back to rejoin the constable ; and harassed—breathless—retreating, without flying—and still keeping his horse's head turned to the enemy, slowly drew near the little body of Bretons, bringing on his faithful allies a crowd of English, who, like ravens, coveted this rich prey.   Bertrand ordered a hundred of his men to go to the assistance of the prince, and free him from his assailants.   These hundred men threw themselves upon ten thousand—opened a passage, and formed a living belt around the prince, in the midst of which he could regain his breath.   But no sooner did he feel himself at liberty, than Don Henry changed horses with a squire, flung aside his helmet, dinted with blows, snatched another from his page's hands, convinced himself that his blade was firm in the hilt, and strong as another Antæus, who, to renew his strength, needed but to touch his mother earth, "Friends," cried he, "you have made me a king, see if I am worthy of being one!"   And he again plunged into the melée. Four times they beheld him raise his sword, and at each blow fell a foe.

"To the King! to the King!" cried the constable.   "Let us save the King!"   And it was indeed time, for the English had closed round Don Henry as the sea closes on the swimmer.   He was on the point of being made prisoner, when the constable reached his side.   Bertrand seized him by the arm, and whilst several Bretons flung themselves between him and the enemy, he said, "Enough of courage like this, sire ; more would be folly.   The battle is lost ; fly, it is for us to die here in covering your retreat."   The King refused. Bertrand made a sign : four Bretons seized Henry de Transtamare.   "Now," cried the constable.   "Our Lady of Guesclin! forward! forward!"   And lowering his lance, he awaited the charge of thirty thousand cavaliers, which seemed as though it would overthrow the very wall against which the little troop leaned for support.

The armed masses came thundering on—nothing was visible, amid the clouds of dust, but a forest of lowered lances, when suddenly, at the risk of being borne down by the advancing squadron, a knight in black armour, with a black helmet surmounted by a crown of the same colour, and having in his hand a field-marshal's baton, rushed between the two opposing foes. "Stay!" he exclaimed, raising his arm. "The first that advances is a dead man."

At the sound of this powerful voice, the eager horsemen suddenly drew rein, thereby flinging many of the horses back upon their haunches. And the prince standing alone in the empty space, gazed with the sadness for which he was remarkable, and which shed a halo round his name, on the intrepid little band of Bretons, so lately on the point of disappearing before the number of their assailants.

"Valiant knight," said he; "you and your brave followers must not perish thus. Look! a god could not resist us." Then advancing towards Duguesclin, he saluted him, saying, "Good constable, I am the Prince of Wales, and I wish you to live, for your death would leave too great a void in the ranks of the brave. I entreat you to give me your sword."

Duguesclin was a man capable of appreciating true generosity, and that of the prince touched him. "It is a loyal gentleman who speaks thus," said he. "I understand English spoken in that fashion." And he lowered his sword. At a signal from the prince, the English slowly advanced with lowered lances. The constable took his sword by the blade, and was about to present it to the prince, when all at once, Don Pedro, covered with blood, and with his armour broken in a dozen places, rode up to them on his reeking horse. He had quitted the pursuit of the fugitives, and returned to those who still resisted.

"What!" he exclaimed, rushing upon the constable, "you allow these fellows to live! We shall never be masters whilst they exist. No quarter to the rebels! Death! death!"

"Ah," said Duguesclin, "this is a brute beast, and he shall die like one!" And as the prince flung himself upon him, he raised his sword by the blade, and let its iron hilt descend with such force on Don Pedro's head that he swayed in his saddle beneath a blow that would have felled an ox, and sunk back on his horse's crupper stunned and half lifeless.

T

Duguesclin again lifted his terrible flail, but whilst on his side rushing forward to attack the prince, he left behind him a vacant space, which was instantly filled by two English soldiers. As he raised his arm, they seized him, the one by the helmet and the other round the body ; the former pulling him backwards, whilst the latter endeavoured to lift him from his saddle.

"Sir constable," they exclaimed together, "surrender, or die!"

Bertrand raised his head, and powerful as a wild bull, he tore the soldier who had seized him by the helmet, from his stirrups, whilst thrusting the point of his sword through the neckpiece of the one who had seized him round the body, he pierced his throat, and stifled the menace in his own blood. But a hundred others gathered round him, eager to strike a blow against this giant.

"Stay!" exclaimed the Black Prince, in a voice of thunder. "Let us see who will be so bold as to lay a finger upon him." At these words even the most furious of his assailants retreated, and Duguesclin again found himself at liberty.

"Enough, my prince," said he. "I owe you my sword twice over. You are the most generous conqueror in the world." And he offered his sword to the prince. Agenor did the same.

"Are you mad!" said Bertrand to him. "You are mounted on a fresh horse. Fly! hasten to France, and inform the good King Charles that I am taken prisoner; and if he will do nothing for me, go to my brother Oliver!"

"But, monseigneur," objected Agenor,—

"They will pay no attention to you—go, I command you!"

"Quick, quick!" said Muscaron, who desired nothing better than to gain the open country; "let us profit by our present insignificance; when we return, we shall be of more importance." In fact, whilst the English were disputing for the possession of Le Bègue de Vilaine, the maréchal, and the great captains, Agenor stole from among them, followed by Muscaron; and both setting spurs to their horses escaped beneath a shower of arrows, with which, when too late, they were saluted by Mothril and Caverley.

CHAPTER XLII.

AFTER THE BATTLE.

THE number of prisoners made this day was considerable. The victors having drawn lots for them, Duguesclin fell to the Prince of Wales, and was by him consigned to the guardianship of the Captal de Buch. Jean de Grailly approached Bertrand, and taking him courteously by the hand, drew off his gauntlet, whilst his squires began to divest him of his various pieces of armour. Bertrand quietly submitted, for no violence was shown him. He continued to count and recount his friends, sighing each time there was one missing in his mental roll-call.

"Brave constable," said Grailly, "behold the inconstancy of fortune; you made me prisoner at Cocherel, and now you are mine."

"Nay," retorted Bertrand; "you mistake, my lord; I took you prisoner at Cocherel, as you say, but here, at Navaretto, you are only my jailor."

Jean de Grailly coloured, but so great was the respect shown in those days to misfortune, that he refrained from making any reply. Duguesclin seated himself on a bank, and beckoned to Le Bègue de Vilaine, d'Andreghem, and the rest to join him, for the Prince of Wales had caused the trumpets to sound as a signal for the troops to reassemble.

"They are going to offer up thanks," said the constable, "for his highness is both a brave and pious prince. Let us also pray."

"What, thank God for having saved you for this?" said Le Bègue de Vilaine.

"To ask him for revenge," said Duguesclin.

In fact, the Prince of Wales, after thanking God on his knees for this great victory, called Don Pedro, who, without having bent the knee for even a single moment, stood wrapped in gloomy contemplation.

"You behold yourself victorious," said the Black Prince; "nevertheless, you have lost a great battle."

"How?" demanded Don Pedro.

"A king is vanquished who only recovers his crown by shedding the blood of his subjects."

"Of rebels!" exclaimed Don Pedro.

"Well; has not God punished them for their rebellion? Tremble, sire, lest he punish you likewise for deserting those whom he has confided to your charge."

T 2

"My lord," said Don Pedro, turning pale with shame and anger, "I owe you my crown, but, prithee, do not be more merciless than the Almighty. Spare me, and accept my thanks."

And he bent his knee. Prince Edward raised him. "Offer your thanks to God," said he; "you owe me nothing." And turning his back upon him, the prince entered his tent to take some refreshment.

"Soldiers," exclaimed Don Pedro, at last giving the reins to his savage desires, "strip the dead, the day's booty is yours!" And mounting a fresh horse, he rode across the battle-field, examining the heaps of slain, and directing his course toward the bank of the river—the spot where Don Henry de Transtamare had encountered the Captal de Buch. Here he dismounted, and sticking a long sharp dagger in his belt, with his feet slipping in the pools of blood, silently commenced his search.—"You are certain you saw him fall?" he said at last to Grailly.

"I am sure of it," replied the captal; "his horse fell under him, struck by a battle-axe thrown by my squire with the skill for which he is unequalled."

"But his rider?"—"He disappeared beneath a cloud of arrows. I saw his armour covered with blood, and a moun-tain of dead bodies fall upon and bury him."

"Good, good!" exclaimed Don Pedro, with ferocious joy. "Let us continue our search. Ah, yonder is a golden circlet!" And with the agility of a tiger he sprang upon the heap of corpses, and dragged from amongst them the body of the knight wearing the golden circlet. With trembling hand and dilated eye, he raised the visor of the helmet. "His squire!" he exclaimed; "only his squire!"

"But this is the prince's armour," said Grailly. "See, there is the coronet upon the casque."

"Tricked—deceived! The traitor must have given his armour to his squire, the better to enable him to fly. But I had foreseen this; I caused the whole plain to be sur-rounded—he could not cross the river—and see! my faithful Moors are bringing me fresh prisoners—he must be among them!"

"Continue your search among the bodies of the dead," said Grailly to his soldiers; "and five hundred piastres to who-ever finds him living."

"And a thousand ducats to whoever finds him dead," said Don Pedro. "We will go and meet the prisoners Mothril is bringing us." Don Pedro remounted his horse, and followed by a numerous train of cavaliers eager to see what would follow, spurred towards the limits of the plain, where a cordon of white-robed Moors were driving before them a herd of fugitives whom they had gathered together afar off.

"I think I can perceive him!" roared Don Pedro, galloping towards them. He uttered these words as he passed the Breton prisoners. Duguesclin overheard them, and he cast his piercing eyes over the plain.

"Good God!" he exclaimed; "what a misfortune!"

These words seemed to Don Pedro a confirmation of his hopes. To better enjoy his good fortune, he determined on overwhelming the constable by the sight of it, and thus strike his two most powerful foes, the one through the other.

"Let us remain here," said he. "Go, seneschal, and order Mothril to bring his prisoners hither before these Breton lords, the faithful friends and allies of the vanquished usurper! the champions of a cause with which they had no business to interfere, and which they did not know how to render victorious."

To these sarcasms, this vindictive rage unworthy of a man, the Breton hero made no reply—nay, did not even appear to have heard them. He remained seated, and conversing indifferently with the Maréchal d'Andreghem.

Don Pedro dismounted, and leaning upon a long battle-axe, fidgeted with the hilt of his dagger, and stamped his foot with as much impatience as if he could thus hasten the arrival of Mothril and his prisoners. As soon as they were within earshot, he exclaimed, "Well, my brave Saracen, my valiant white falcon, what quarry do you bring me?"

"A good one, my King," replied Mothril. "Behold these colours!" And, in fact, he carried rolled round his arm a fragment of cloth of gold broidered with the arms of Henry de Transtamare.

"It is he, then!" exclaimed Don Pedro, transported with joy. "It is he, then!" And, with a threatening gesture, he pointed to a knight in full armour, with a crown round his helmet, but without either sword or lance, and bound in the coils of a silken cord, from the two ends of which depended a large leaden ball.

"He was making his escape," said Mothril, "but I sent after him twenty horses of the desert. My captain of the archers overtook him, and received a mortal wound; but one of the others entangled him in the coils of his lasso; he fell, and his horse with him, and we captured him, banner in hand. Unfortunately, one of his friends escaped, whilst he turned and confronted us alone.

"Off with his crown," cried Don Pedro, brandishing his axe.

An archer advanced, and severing the fastenings of the neck-piece, brutally struck off the crowned helmet. A cry of rage and affright escaped from the King's lips, whilst a shout of intense joy rose from the little band of Bretons.

"Agenor de Mauleon!" they vociferated. "Noël! Noël!"

"The ambassador! malediction!" muttered Don Pedro.

"The Frank!" faltered Mothril, half speechless with rage.

"Myself," said Agenor, saluting Bertrand and his friends by a look.—"Ourselves," chimed in Muscaron, who, though somewhat paler than his wont, was still dealing kicks right and left to the Moors.

"Then he has escaped?" said Don Pedro.

"Good heavens! yes, sire," replied Agenor; "I exchanged helmets with his Majesty behind a bush, and gave him my fresh horse."

"You shall die!" yelled Don Pedro, blinded with rage.

"What!" exclaimed Bertrand, placing himself at one bound between the King and Agenor, "lay your hand on him!— kill an unarmed prisoner! But, oh, you are coward enough even for that."

"Then, miserable adventurer, it is you who shall die!" cried Don Pedro, trembling and foaming at the mouth with rage. And he rushed with upraised dagger upon the constable, who clenched his fist as though preparing to fell a bull. But a hand was laid upon Don Pedro's shoulder, like that of Minerva, which, according to Homer, seized Achilles by the hair.

"Stay!" exclaimed the voice of the Prince of Wales. "Would you dishonour yourself, King of Castile? Stay, I command you, and cast aside that dagger." His nervous arm nailed Don Pedro to the spot where he stood; the murderous steel fell from the assassin's hands.

"At least sell him to me!" vociferated the furious prince. "I will pay for him his weight in gold"—"Beware! you insult me. Know, that were Duguesclin yours, I would pay for him his weight in precious stones. But he is *mine*, and remember it well—back!"

"King," muttered Duguesclin, scarcely able to restrain himself, "wicked and murderous King, who slays even his prisoners, wo shall meet again!"

"I trust so," retorted Don Pedro.

"Conduct the Constable of France immediately to my tent," said the Black Prince.

"Yet a moment, my honoured prince; the King will bo left alone with the Comte de Mauleon, and will murder him." —"Oh, I do not deny it," returned Don Pedro with a ferocious smile. "But I believe that this prisoner at least belongs to me."

Duguesclin shuddered; he looked beseechingly at the Prince of Wales. "Sire," said the prince, addressing Don Pedro, "to-day not a single prisoner should be put to death."

"To-day? Be it so with all my heart," said Don Pedro, exchanging a meaning glance with Mothril.

"It has witnessed too glorious a victory," continued the prince. " Is it not so?"—"Certainly, my lord."

"And you will do something to oblige me?" Don Pedro bowed his head. "I ask you to give me this young man," said the prince. A profound silence followed these words, to which Don Pedro, pale with rage, did not immediately reply.

"Oh, my lord," said he at last, "you make me feel you are the master. To lose my vengeance!"

"Then, if I am master," said the prince, indignantly, "I command this knight's bonds to be unloosed, and his horse and arms restored to him."

"Noël! Noël! to the good Prince of Wales!" shouted the Bretons.

"At least a ransom," suggested Mothril, to gain time.

The prince cast a side glance on the Moor. "How much?" asked he. The Moor was silent. The prince detached a diamond cross from his breast and offered it to him. "Take it, infidel," said he. Mothril bowed his head, and murmured in a low tone the name of the prophet. "You are free, sir knight," said the prince, addressing Agenor. "Return to France, and announce that the Prince of Wales, content with having had the honour of gaining by force of arms possession of the most redoubtable chevalier in the world will, at the end of the campaign, send him back free and without ransom."

"As an alms to the beggars of France," sneered Don Pedro.

Bertrand overheard him. "My prince," said he, "your friends make me ashamed of your generosity. I belong to a King who will pay my ransom a dozen times over, if I chance to be so often taken prisoner, and that, too, if I were each time estimated at the price of a king."

"Then fix your own ransom," said the prince, courteously.

Bertrand reflected a moment.

"Prince," said he, "I am worth seventy thousand gold florins."

"God be praised," ejaculated Don Pedro. "He will be lost through his own pride. Charles V. has not one-half the sum in his treasury."

"It may possibly be so," said Bertrand; "but since the Chevalier de Mauleon returns to France, he will ride through Brittany with his squire, and in every village, on every highway they come to they will cry, 'Bertrand Duguesclin is prisoner in the hands of the English. Spin, women of Brittany, spin! for he looks to you for his ransom.'"

"With God's assistance I will do so!" exclaimed Mauleon.

"And you will bring back the sum before I shall have had time to grow weary of my captivity, were that possible, were it even to endure for a lifetime, in the society of so noble and generous a prince." The prince held out his hand to Bertrand. "Chevalier," said he, addressing Mauleon, who now joyfully grasped his sword again, "you have conducted yourself like a loyal soldier. By saving Don Henry de Transtamare you have deprived our victory of its greatest value, but I bear you no malice for having left open a path to lead to future encounters. Take this golden chain, and the cross that yonder infidel refused." He remarked Don Pedro speak aside to Mothril, and receive in reply a smile of doubtful signification.

"Let no one stir!" he exclaimed, "I will punish with death the first one who crosses the boundary of my camp, whether he be prince or king! Chandos," he added, "you are a brave knight; you will conduct the Sire de Mauleon as far as the first town, and furnish him with the requisite safe-conduct."

Mothril, again defeated by this clear-sighted and persevering interpretation of his hideous plots, cast a glance of disappointment at his master. Don Pedro had fallen from the height of his triumphant joy; he could no longer revenge himself. Agenor bent his knee to the Prince of Wales, and kissed Duguesclin's hand, who taking him in his arms whispered, "Tell the King that our devourers have glutted themselves; they need a little rest, and then if he sends me my ransom I will lead them where I promised. Tell my wife to sell even our last estate, for I shall have many Bretons to ransom."

Agenor, deeply touched, mounted a fleet horse, bade a last adieu to his comrades, and set out. Muscaron followed, grumbling to himself, "Who would ever have imagined that I should like an Englishman any better than a Moor?"

CHAPTER XLIII.

THE TREATY OF ALLIANCE.

AT the same time that the victory declared itself in Don Pedro's favour, Duguesclin fell into the hands of the enemy, and Mauleon, following the constable's advice, fled from the battle-field to which he was so soon to be brought back in the helmet and mantle of Don Henry, a courier was directing his course towards the village of Cuello. There, two women, at a hundred paces from each other, the one in a litter, surrounded by Arabs, the other on a superb Andalusian mule, with a train of Castilian cavaliers, awaited in all the anguish of alternate hope and fear tidings of the events of the day. Donna Maria dreaded lest the loss of the battle should complete Don Pedro's ruin, and that he should be taken prisoner. Aïssa only desired some event to take place that would bring back her lover to her side. It mattered little to her whether Don Pedro fell, or Don Henry was victorious, provided he reappeared, whether following th bier of the one or the triumphal car of the other.

Maria, however, was more than uneasy, she was jealous. She knew that Mothril victorious would have nothing else to do but minister to the pleasures of the King; she had guessed his designs, and Aïssa in her simplicity had confirmed her instinctive suspicions. Thus, although the young girl was, as usual, shut up in her litter, and guarded by twenty trusty slaves, Maria kept her in sight.

The Moor, unwilling to expose his precious treasure to the chances of the battle, and the brutality of the English allies, had left the litter at the village of Cuello, which consisted of

a cluster of miserable hovels at about two leagues' distance
from Navaretto. He had given his slaves strict orders to
await him there, and to open the carefully closed litter to no
one but himself. But in case of his falling in the combat, or
not returning, he had given other instructions, which we shall
presently learn. Thus Aïssa awaited the issue of the battle
at the village of Cuello. As to Maria, Don Pedro had left
her well guarded at Burgos, where he expected her to await
the tidings of his fate. She had a large sum in gold and
jewels, and he had faith enough in her devoted love to know
that in case of reverses she would be even more fondly
attached to him than in prosperity. But Maria could not
suffer that torment of women of inferior minds, jealousy.
Her principle was that it was better to bear a misfortune
than to be ignorant of a treason. She knew Don Pedro's
weakness, and Cuello was at too short a distance from Navaretto. She, therefore, accompanied by six squires, and twenty
men-at-arms, rather humble friends than servants, took up
her quarters at the foot of a little hill, behind which rose the
hamlet of Cuello. Standing on the summit of this hill, she
beheld the advance of the two battalions; she could have
witnessed the combat, but so much was at stake that her
heart failed her. It was here she encountered Aïssa. She
had sent a trusty messenger to the scene of action, and
awaited his return at a short distance from her rival, around
whose litter her attendants sat crouching on the grass. The
messenger arrived, and announced the gain of the battle.
Being not only a man-at-arms, but one of the chamberlains
of the palace, he knew the principal knights of the hostile
army by sight. He had seen Mauleon at the solemn audience
granted him at Soria; besides, Maria had particularly pointed
him out. He therefore announced that Henry de Transtamare was vanquished, Duguesclin taken prisoner, and that
Mauleon had made his escape. These tidings, whilst crown-
ing all Maria Padilla's proud and ambitious hopes, awoke a
host of jealous fears in her heart. To behold Don Pedro
victorious, and reseated on this throne, was the dream of
both her love and her ambition; but the thought of Don
Pedro happy, envied, and exposed to the temptations of
Mothril, was the spectre that haunted it, the shadow of this
anxious and devoted affection.

Maria formed her plan with all her characteristic boldness.

She ordered her men-at-arms to follow her, and descended the hill, conversing with her messenger.

"You say the Comte de Mauleon has fled?" said she.

"Yes, senora, like a lion beneath a cloud of arrows." He spoke of Agenor's first flight; for he had quitted the field of battle, when our hero was brought back disguised in Don Henry's armour.

"And whither think you he will direct his flight?"

"To France; as the bird escaped from the fowler's net flies towards its nest."

"It is so," thought she; then she continued aloud, "Sir knight, how many days' journey is it from here to France?"

"Twelve, senora, for a lady like yourself."

"But for a person dreading pursuit; the Comte de Mauleon, for instance?"

"Oh, senora, in three days he might defy his deadliest enemies. Besides, they did not pursue this young man, they only thought of the constable."

"But Mothril, what has become of him?"

"He has received orders to surround the plain with a cordon of troops, so as to prevent the escape of the fugitives, especially Henry de Transtamare, if he is still living."

"Then he will no longer trouble himself about Mauleon," thought Maria. "Follow me, sir knight." She approached Aïssa's litter, but as she drew near the guardian Moors started from the grass on which they had been negligently reclining.

"Who commands here?" demanded she. "I do, senora," replied the leader, who was easily distinguished by the purple hue of his turban, and the scarf round his waist.

"I wish to speak to the young maiden concealed in this litter."

"Impossible, senora," replied the Moor, laconically.

"You do not know me, perhaps?"

"Oh, yes! well," replied the Moor, with a half smile; "you are Maria Padilla."

"Then you ought to know I have the right to command."

"The people of his Majesty Don Pedro," retorted the Moor, gravely; "but not those of the Saracen Mothril."

Donna Maria beheld with uneasiness this commencement of resistance. "Have you orders to the contrary?" she inquired in a gentle tone.

"I have, senora."—"At least tell me what they are."

"I should refuse to repeat them to any one but yourself, senora. If the battle is lost, or the Lord Mothril does not immediately return, I am to retire with my troop, and on no account resign Donna Aïssa to any one but himself."

"The battle is won," said Maria.

"Then Mothril will soon be here."—"But should he be dead?"

"Then," said the Moor, "I am to conduct Donna Aïssa to his Majesty Don Pedro ; for the least the King can do is to be guardian to the daughter of the man who has sacrificed his life for him." Maria shuddered.

"But he lives—he will soon be with you, and meanwhile, I have a few words to say to Donna Aïssa. Do you hear me, senor?"

"Senora," said the Moor, hastily, as he drew nearer the litter, "do not force the senora to speak to you, for in that case I have a terrible order to execute."

"And what is that?"

"To slay her with my own hand, if, in opposition to his will, any communication with a stranger takes place."

Donna Maria started back in affright, for she knew the savage and intractable manners of this race, and their blind obedience to a superior power. She returned to her escort, who stood awaiting her, lance in hand, like so many statues.

"I must gain access to this litter," said she. "But it is well defended, and the Moorish chief threatens to slay the female who is behind those curtains, if any one approaches her."

The knight she had employed as her messenger was a Christian, and consequently full of imagination and gallantry. He possessed the mind that invents, and the courage and strength that executes.

"Senora," said he, "this yellow-faced rascal, to whom I owe a grudge for having alarmed you, does not reflect that if I were to pin him to the pole of his litter, he would be unable to molest the lady it encloses."

"What! kill a man for obeying his orders? See what good watch he keeps ; he has made his companions resume their arms."

These words were pronounced in pure Castilian.

The Moors regarded them with looks of astonishment, for although understanding the Arabic spoken by Donna Maria, and the threatening gestures of the knights accompanying her, they were evidently ignorant of the Spanish language.

"See, senora! if we do not retire, these bloodthirsty dogs will commence the attack," continued the knight, who had a strong desire to wield his lance under the eyes of this fair and noble lady.

"Stay!" said Maria, "stay! You think they do not understand Castilian?"—"Speak to them in it, senora, and try?"

"I have an idea," said Donna Maria; "Donna Aïssa," continued she, in Spanish, speaking in a loud tone, and turning towards the knight as though addressing him, "you can doubtless understand me? If so, shake the curtains of your litter." At these words the brocade curtains of the litter were agitated several times. The Moors did not notice it, absorbed as they were in watching their movements.

"You see, not a single one has turned round," said the knight.

"It is, perhaps, a ruse," returned Maria. "Let us await a little longer." And she continued, as before, to address Aïssa.

"Only one side of the litter is guarded; the Moors having all assembled to watch us, leaves you so far at liberty. If the litter is closed, cut the curtains with your knife, glide from it, and take refuge behind the large tree you will see at a couple of hundred paces' distance. Obey me promptly; for I am come to enable you to rejoin, you know whom."

Maria Padilla, still preserving the semblance of indifference, had scarcely pronounced these words, before she perceived a slight oscillation of the litter. Her escort feigned to make a hostile movement towards the Moors, who on their side, began to advance, bending their bows, and loosing their maces. The Castilians, however, had no sooner beheld the fair Aïssa fly like a dove across the space between her litter and the sheltering tree, than Donna Maria said to the Moors, "Well, be it as you say; fear nothing, but keep your treasure, we will not touch it. Only draw on one side, and let us pass."

The chief, whose brow instantly cleared, obeyed, and Donna Maria's escort passed swiftly by them, and placed itself between Aïssa and those who but an instant before were her guardians. When Aïssa beheld this protecting barrier of twenty armed men ranged before her, she understood it all. She threw herself into Donna Maria's arms, kissing her hands in a transport of gratitude. The Moorish

chief, on beholding the empty litter, understood the trick
that had been played him, and uttered a cry of rage. For a
moment, he thought of rushing headlong on the armed troop ;
but terrified at engaging in so unequal a combat, he preferred
throwing himself upon a horse, and setting off at full speed
for the scene of action.

"There is no time to be lost," said Donna Maria to the
Spanish knight. "My lord, my eternal gratitude will be
yours, if you will carry off this maiden, and conduct her by
the route taken by the Comte de Mauleon."

"Senora," returned the knight. "Mothril is the favourite
of our King—this lady is his daughter, and consequently belonging to him, therefore, I should be robbing him of his child."

"You will obey me, sir knight ?"

"Senora, I would give my life for you, if it were necessary ;
but should the King discover that I have quitted my post
beside you, what excuse can I make—and my fault will be
the greater for having disobeyed my King."

"You are right, my lord, and it shall never be said that
the life and honour of a brave knight like yourself were placed
in peril by a woman's caprice. Point out the way, and
Donna Aissa shall accompany me on horseback until we
reach the route taken by the Comte de Mauleon, and then,
—well, then we will leave her, and you shall escort me back."
But such was not Donna Maria's design, she only sought to
gain time by thus quieting her companion's scruples. With
her, to will a thing was to accomplish it, and she trusted to
her usual good fortune.

After mounting Aïssa on a white mule of rare vigour and
beauty, the little party set off at full gallop, and skirting the
plain, on the left of the field of battle, directed their course
towards the route to France. Not a word was spoken—
their only thought was to double the speed of their panting
horses. Two leagues were already accomplished, when on
turning a corner of the road, Maria beheld a knight advancing towards her at full gallop. She recognised his plume
and sword-belt.

"Don Ayalos !" she exclaimed, accosting the prudent
stranger, who was already making a detour to avoid a ren-
contre with them, "is it you ?"

"Yes, noble lady," returned the Castilian, recognising the
King's mistress.

"What news?" asked Maria, reining up her steed.

"Strange ones. It was believed that Henry de Transtamare was captured, but, on raising the visor of the prisoner who wore the prince's helmet, he proved to be no other than the Chevalier de Mauleon, the French ambassador, who, after having fled, allowed himself to be retaken to save his master."

Aïssa uttered a cry. "He is taken!" she ejaculated.

"Yes, he is taken; and when I left them, the King, transported with anger, was threatening him with his vengeance."

Aïssa raised her eyes to heaven in despair.

"He would kill him?" said she. "Impossible!"

"He was very near killing the constable."

"But he shall not die!" exclaimed the young girl, urging her mule towards the field of battle.

"Aïssa! Aïssa!" remonstrated Donna Maria, "you will ruin us both!"—"He shall not die!" repeated the young girl, frantically, continuing her course.

Donna Maria, breathless with anxiety and uncertain how to act, was endeavouring to collect her senses, when they suddenly heard the trampling of a troop of horsemen approaching at full speed.

"We are lost!" said the knight, rising in his stirrups. "It is a detachment of Moors, sweeping along more swiftly than the wind, and preceded by their chief." In fact, before Aïssa had proceeded many paces, this furious cavalcade bore down upon them, and surrounded the little group, not excepting Donna Maria herself, who, despite all her resolution, remained pale and half fainting near the knight, in whose intrepidity she had not been deceived.

Mothril, mounted on his Arab horse, advanced from among his men, and seizing the bridle of Aïssa's mule, inquired, in a voice half choked with rage, where she was going.

"I am seeking Don Agenor, whom you wish to destroy," returned she.

Mothril now perceived Donna Maria. "Ah, in company with Donna Maria!" he exclaimed, grinding his teeth; "I guess it all."

The expression of his countenance became so terrible, that the knight put his lance in its rest. "Twenty against a hundred and twenty," thought he; "we are lost!"

CHAPTER XLIV.

THE TRUCE.

But a combat was not what Mothril desired. He turned leisurely towards the plain, cast a last glance over the battle-field, and, addressing Donna Maria, said, " I fancied, senora, that, our lord the King had appointed you a place of retreat. Can it be possible that he has changed his mind, and you are obeying fresh orders ?"

"Orders !" retorted the proud Castilian. " You forget, Saracen, that you are addressing one who is accustomed to give, not to receive them."

Mothril bowed his head. " But, senora," he resumed, " if you are able to act as you please, you cannot suppose that you possess the power of disposing of Donna Aïssa at your pleasure. Donna Aïssa is my daughter." Aïssa was about to reply by some furious exclamation, but Maria interrupted her.

"Senor Mothril," said she, " God forbid that I should sow dissension in your family! Those who wish to be themselves respected must respect others. I found Donna Aïssa alone, and in tears; she was dying with anxiety, and I brought her with me."

Aïssa could no longer contain herself. " Agenor !" she cried. " What have you done with my knight, Don Agenor de Mauleon ?"

"Ah !" said Mothril, " was it not about this senor my daughter was so anxious ?" And a gloomy smile passed across his face. Maria was silent. " Was it not to the arms of this senor you were charitably conducting my weeping daughter ? Speak, senora !"

"Yes," interrupted Aïssa. " And I persist in going to seek him. Oh, your frowns do not terrify me, my father. I will find Agenor de Mauleon. Conduct me to him."

"An infidel !"—" Yes, an infidel; for this infidel——"

Maria interrupted her. " Here is the King," she exclaimed; " he is coming towards us."

The Moor made a sign to his slaves, and Aïssa was immediately surrounded, and separated from Maria Padilla.

"You have murdered him !" she shrieked. " Then I will die, too !" She drew from its gilded sheath a small poniard sharp as the viper's tongue, which gleamed like a flash of lightning in the rays of the sun. Mothril rushed towards her. All his fury had disappeared: his ferocity had given place to the most grievous anxiety.

"No," cried he, "no! He lives! he lives!"

"Who will assure me of it?" said the Moorish girl, fixing her fiery glance interrogatively on the Moor.

"Ask the King himself. Will you believe him?"

"Good. Question him, and let him reply."

Don Pedro had now joined them. Maria Padilla threw herself into his arms.

"My lord," said Mothril, whose senses seemed forsaking him, "is it true that this Frank—this Mauleon—is dead?"

"No, by Heaven!" said the King, in a gloomy voice. "I could not even strike this traitor—this demon! No; the miscreant has escaped—sent back to France by the Prince of Wales. He has departed, free, happy, and mocking us, like the swallow escaped from the talons of the vulture."

"Escaped!" repeated Aïssa, "escaped! Can it be really true?" And she cast a questioning glance around her.

But Maria Padilla, who meanwhile had received positive information of what had taken place, and learnt all the particulars of Mauleon's release, made a sign to the young girl to apprise her that she might be at ease, for her lover was safe and sound. The Moorish girl was instantly appeased; she allowed Mothril to lead her away, following him with bowed-down head, too absorbed in the thought that Agenor was saved, and the sweet hope of again beholding him, to observe the eager looks cast upon her by Don Pedro. But these looks did not pass unremarked by Maria Padilla: she divined their meaning, but she also read in the countenance of the Moorish maiden the profound disgust Don Pedro's brutal speech had awakened in her mind.

"No matter," said she to herself; "Aïssa shall not remain at the court; she shall quit it, and I will reunite her to Mauleon. It must be so! Mothril will oppose it with all his power; but it has come to this—either Mothril or I must succumb in the struggle." And as she formed this resolution, she overheard the King whisper to Mothril, with a sigh, "She is indeed very lovely. I have never seen her looking so gloriously beautiful as to-day." Mothril smiled.

"Yes," muttered Maria, pale with jealousy; "here is all the subject of strife."

The re-entry of Don Pedro into Burgos was attended with all the splendour that a decisive victory gives to legitimate power. The rebels, having nothing more to hope for, submitted, and the enthusiasm of their recantation was as powerful as the Prince of Wales' exhortations in changing Don Pedro's ordinary cruelty into benevolence. He therefore contented himself with hanging a dozen of the bourgeois, causing a hundred of the chief mutineers to be shot by his soldiers, and levying heavy taxes and confiscations for the benefit of his treasury on the richest towns in Spain. Then, as he was weary of these bloody struggles, and fortune seemed to smile upon him, he made Burgos a royal residence, where *fêtes* and tournaments followed each other in quick succession ; honours and rewards were distributed, and war, and almost hatred, were forgotten. Nevertheless, Mothril did not relax his watchfulness; but instead of, like a prudent minister, guarding against the probable revival of the war, he lulled the King into a feeling of profound security.

Don Pedro had already dismissed the discontented English troops, whom a few strongholds still remaining in their possession indemnified both poorly and dangerously for the enormous expenses of the war. The sum due to the Prince of Wales was frightful. Don Pedro, feeling that it would be perilous to levy fresh taxes at the moment of his restoration, demanded time for payment. But the English prince knew the character of his ally, and refused to wait. Don Pedro, therefore, even in his apparent prosperity, was surrounded by the germs of such misfortunes that the most unlucky prince would have preferred his own situation to that of the King of Castile. But this was the moment waited for, perhaps foreseen by Mothril. Without affecting to be troubled by them, he smiled at the pretensions of the English, suggesting to Don Pedro that 100,000 Saracens were well worth 10,000 English ; would cost less, would open a path for Spain towards African domination, and that a double crown would be the result of this policy. At the same time he hinted that the only means of solidly uniting the two crowns upon one head was by an alliance; that a daughter of one of the ancient Arab princes, of the venerated blood of the Caliphs, seated beside him on the throne of Castile, would in the space of a year unite to it not only Africa, but all the countries of the East. And this daughter of the Caliphs was, as we know, Aïssa. Besides, the way seemed to grow smoother for the Moor; he appeared on the very verge of realizing his dreams. Mauleon was no longer an obstacle to his wishes, for he had quitted Spain. Besides, was he really one? Who was this Mauleon? A chevalier—a frank, loyal, and credulous dreamer. Could this be an antagonist for the gloomy and artful Mothril to dread? The only serious obstacle, therefore, seemed Aïssa herself. But the strongest resistance must at last yield to superior force. It was only necessary to prove to the young girl that Mauleon was unfaithful to her. This was an easy task, for his Arabs were equal adepts in discovering the truth, or giving the colour of it to a lie. But Mothril's brow darkened, as he remembered one impediment, even graver than the last; this haughty and beautiful woman already exercising, through the force of habit and the domination of pleasure, an all-powerful sway over the mind of Don Pedro.

Maria Padilla was no sooner aware of Mothril's plans than she laboured to counteract them with a skill worthy in every point of her rare and exquisite nature. She anticipated Don Pedro's lightest desire; she captivated his attention, and extinguished to the last spark the flame that another had kindled in his breast. Docile when alone with Don Pedro, imperious before the world, she contrived to keep up a secret intelligence with Aïssa, whom she had made her friend. By ceaselessly speaking of Mauleon, she prevented her thoughts from dwelling on Don Pedro; besides, the ardent and faithful young girl needed no reminding of a love which she felt could only end with her life.

Mothril had hitherto remained in ignorance of these mysterious interviews; his mistrust slumbered, for he beheld but one of the three threads of intrigue—the one he himself held. Aïssa had not appeared again at court; she silently awaited the fulfilment of the promise made her by Maria Padilla, to give her certain tidings of her absent lover. In fact, Maria Padilla had dispatched a messenger to France, charged with the task of finding out the Chevalier de Mauleon, apprising him of the state of affairs, and bringing from him some token of remembrance for the poor Moorish maiden languishing in the expectation of a speedy reunion. This messenger, a wary mountaineer, was one on whom she could depend, he being no other than the son of that old nurse with whom Mauleon had found her disguised as a Bohemian. This, then,

was the state of affairs in both France and Spain; and thus
two opposing interests only waited until by a brief period of
repose they had regained their full strength, to again clash
together. But for the present we must return to Agenor de
Mauleon, who, had it not been for the tenacious love which
attracted him to Spain, would have wended his way towards
France as lightly and joyously, rejoicing in his freedom, as
the swallow to which Don Pedro compared him.

CHAPTER XLV.

THE JOURNEY.

AGENOR comprehended all the difficulty of his position. The
liberty bestowed on him by the Prince of Wales was a privilege of which many persons might begrudge him the con-
tinuance. He therefore urged forward his horse at its fullest
speed, thanks to the exhortations of Muscaron, who shaking
his ears in the joy of still possessing them, made use of all his
eloquence to paint the dangers of pursuit, and the charms of
returning to one's own country. But honest Muscaron
wasted his time; for Agenor was not listening to him, his
thoughts were with Aïssa. Nevertheless, at this epoch the
sense of duty was so strong, that Mauleon, whose heart was
filled with indignation at being obliged to quit his mistress,
and throbbed with joy at the idea of secretly returning to her—
Mauleon, we say, bravely continued his journey at the risk of
losing for ever his Moorish lady love, in order to accomplish
the mission with which the constable had charged him. He
at last arrived at his destination, and hastened to throw himself at the feet of good King Charles, who was peacefully
nailing up his peach-trees in his beautiful garden at the Hôtel
St. Paul.

"Why, how is this? And what tidings do you come to announce to me, Sire de Mauleon?" said the King, on whom
nature had bestowed the faculty of never forgetting a face he
had once beheld.

"Sire," replied Agenor, bending his knee before him, "I
am the bearer of sad tidings. Your army has been defeated
in Spain."—"God's will be done!" ejaculated the prince,
turning pale. "But the army will rally again?"

"There is no longer an army, sire."—"God is merciful!"
said the King, in a lower tone. "How fares the constable?"

"Sire, the constable is a prisoner in the hands of the English."

The King gave a stifled sigh, but made no remark, and his brow almost immediately recovered its serenity.

"Relate to me the particulars of this battle," said he, a moment afterwards; "where did it take place?"

"At Navaretto, sire."—"I am listening."

Agenor related the whole of their disasters, the destruction of the army, the capture of the constable, and how he had been almost miraculously saved by the Black Prince.

"I must redeem Bertrand," said Charles V., "if they will accept a ransom for him."

"Sire, the ransom is already agreed on."

"At how much?"—"Seventy thousand gold florins."

"And who fixed this ransom?" exclaimed the King, starting at the magnitude of the sum.

"The constable himself."

"The constable! He appears to me to have been very generous."

"You think he has estimated his worth too highly, sire?"

"If he were estimated at his true worth," said the King, "not all the treasures in Christendom could purchase his freedom." But even whilst rendering this justice to Bertrand, the King fell into a gloomy reverie, the subject of which Agenor could not misunderstand.

"Sire," said he, "do not make yourself uneasy about the constable's ransom. He has dispatched me to his wife, Madame Tiphaine Raguenel, who has in her possession one hundred thousand crowns belonging to him, and will give them to redeem her husband."

"Ah, worthy chevalier!" said the King, recovering his cheerfulness. "He is then as good a treasurer as he is a warrior—I could not have believed it—a hundred thousand crowns! why, he is richer than myself. Let him, then, lend me these seventy thousand florins; I will soon repay them. But are you certain he still possesses them? Suppose they no longer exist?"

"How could that be, sire?"

"Because Madame Tiphaine Raguenel is extremely jealous of her husband's renown, and lives down there in a style at once charitable and magnificent."

"Then, sire, in case she has expended this money, the constable has given me another commission."

" And what is that ?"

" To ride through Brittany, crying, 'The constable is taken prisoner by the English ; pay his ransom, men of Brittany, and you, women of Brittany, spin !' "

" And," said the King, quickly, " you shall take with you one of my banners, and three of my men-at-arms, and let the cry resound throughout France. But," added Charles V., "only do this at the last extremity. If it be possible, let us ourselves repair the disasters of Navaretto."

" Impossible, sire ! You will doubtless soon see the fugi-tive prince Henry de Transtamare ; the English will trumpet their victory on all sides, and the poor Bretons, returning to their country wounded and in poverty, will relate their lamentable history to all they meet."

" It is too true. Go, then, Mauleon ; and if you again see the constable——" — " I shall see him, sire."

" Tell him from me, that nothing is lost so long as he is restored to me."

" Sire, I have still a few words to deliver from him. 'Tell the King,' he whispered, 'that our project is working well ; that numbers of the French rats have been killed by the heat of Spain before they could get accustomed to the climate.' "

" Brave Bertrand ! then he could jest even at that cruel moment."—" Always invincible, sire ; as undaunted in defeat as great in victory."

Agenor then took leave of the King, who presented him with three hundred livres, a magnificent gift, by the aid of which he furnished himself with two good war-horses, each of which cost him fifty livres. He gave ten livres to Muscaron, who wonderingly placed them in his leathern belt, and has-tened to renew his attire in the Rue de la Draperie. Agenor also purchased in the Rue de la Heaumerie one of the newly-invented helmets, closing with a spring, which he presented to his worthy squire, whose head had hitherto been an easy mark for the blows of the Saracens. They both set out on their journey in excellent spirits. On arriving at the fron-tiers of Brittany, Agenor requested permission of John de Montfort, the reigning prince, to enter his dominions, in order to visit Madame Tiphaine Raguenel and raise the money required for the constable's ransom. Muscaron's commission was a delicate one ; but the Earl of Montfort—son of the old Earl of Montfort, who with the Duke of Lancaster had made war against France, and who bore an ancient grudge against Bertrand, the principal cause of the siege of Dinan being raised—no sooner heard of the constable's misfortune, than he forgot all former enmity.

"If I will permit it!" he exclaimed; "on the contrary, I request it. Let all necessary contributions be raised in my dominions, for I wish to see him, not only at liberty, but my friend. My estates are honoured by having been the place of his birth." After having spoken thus, the earl received Agenor with the greatest distinction, loaded him with presents worthy of a royal ambassador, and, having honoured him with an escort, caused him to be conducted to the dwelling of Madame Tiphaine Raguenel, who resided on her family estates at La Roche Derrien.

CHAPTER XLVI.

MADAME TIPHAINE RAGUENEL.

TIPHAINE RAGUENEL, daughter of Robert Raguenel, Lord of La Bellière, a viscount and man of the highest birth, was one of those accomplished women to whom heroes but seldom have the good fortune to be united. In her youth, she had been surnamed by the Bretons Tiphaine the Fairy. She was learned in medicine and astrology, and it was she who, before Bertrand's two most celebrated battles, had foretold that he would prove victorious, to the great wonderment of the anxious Bretons. It was she who, when Bertrand grew weary of service and wished to retire to his estates, persuaded him by her counsels and predictions to resume the glorious life in which he won fortune and imperishable fame. Thus Tiphaine Raguenel exercised over her husband and throughout the surrounding country, an influence equal to that of a great queen. She was of high birth, and had been beautiful. Her cultivated mind gave her the advantage over many men, and to these fine qualities was added a disinterestedness almost rivalling that of her husband. When she heard of the arrival of a messenger from Bertrand, she went out to meet him, attended by her ladies and pages. Anxiety was depicted on her countenance. She had involuntarily assumed mourning attire, which, in the present state of things (for they were yet ignorant of the disasters at Navaretto), had inspired the domestics and serfs of La Roche Derrien with superstitious terror.

Tiphaine advanced to meet Mauleon, and received him on the drawbridge. The young chevalier had forgotten his gaiety, and assumed the grave demeanour befitting a messenger of evil augury. He first bowed, and then fell on one knee before her, even more impressed by the imposing appearance of the noble lady than the gravity of the tidings he brought her.

"Speak, sir chevalier," said Tiphaine, "I know you bring me bad news of my husband. Speak!" A deep silence reigned around, and the most intense anxiety was depicted on the manly Breton visages. They nevertheless remarked that the chevalier had no crape attached to either his sword or his banner, as was customary in cases of death.

Agenor collected his thoughts, and commenced the sad recital, to which Madame Tiphaine listened without manifesting the slightest astonishment. Only the cloud that rested on her noble brow grew darker.

"Well," said she, while the Bretons around her gave vent to their consternation by uttering exclamations of distress, and muttering their prayers, "you come from my husband, sir chevalier?"—"Yes, lady," replied Mauleon.

"And thus a prisoner in Castile, he has had his ransom fixed?"

"He fixed it himself, lady."—"At what sum?"

"At seventy thousand gold florins."

"Nor is it an exorbitant one for so great a captain. But where does he expect to procure this sum?"

"From you, lady."—"From me!"

"Yes; have you not the one hundred thousand gold crowns your husband gained in his last expedition, and deposited with the monks of Mont St. Michael?"—"True, sir messenger, the sum was one hundred thousand crowns, but it is gone."

"Gone!" involuntarily repeated Mauleon, remembering the King's words—"gone!"

"Spent as it should be, I believe," continued the lady. "I withdrew this sum from the hands of the monks to equip a hundred and twenty soldiers, to assist twelve knights of our province, and provide for nine orphan children, and as nothing remained of it to marry the two daughters of one of our friends, I have pledged my plate and jewels. The house no longer contains anything but the strictest necessaries; nevertheless, impoverished as we are, I trust I have acted according to the wishes of Messire Bertrand, and that he would approve of, and thank me for it, if he were but here."

The words, "If he were but here," fell so tenderly from those noble lips that they brought tears into every eye.

"Then," said Mauleon, "it only remains for the constable to thank you as you deserve, and wait for succour from God."

"And from his friends!" exclaimed several voices in their enthusiasm.

"And since I have the honour to be the faithful servant of Messire Duguesclin, I will at once commence the task he imposed upon me, foreseeing, as he did, all that has happened. I have the King's trumpeter, and a banner with the arms of France; with these I shall scour the country, announcing the news of the constable's capture. Those who wish to behold him safe, and at liberty, will rise and purchase his freedom."

"I would do so myself," said Tiphaine Raguenel, "but it will be better for you to do it, provided we can obtain the permission of the Duke of Brittany."

"That permission, noble lady, is already granted."

"Then, dear friends," continued Tiphaine Raguenel, casting an assured glance on the still increasing crowd, "you hear this; those who wish to testify their interest in the name of Duguesclin will do it by treating his messenger as a friend."

"And first of all," exclaimed a horseman who had just joined the group, "I, Robert Comte de Laval, will give forty thousand livres towards the ransom of my friend Bertrand. The money is following me; my pages are bringing it."

"May the nobles of Brittany imitate you, generous friend, according to their means, and the constable will be free to-night," said Tiphaine, greatly touched by this liberality.

"Come, sir chevalier," said the Comte de Laval, "I offer you my hospitality. You shall commence your collection to-day, and *ma foi!* it shall be a handsome one. Let us leave the Lady Tiphaine to her sorrow."

Mauleon raised the noble lady's hand respectfully to his lips, and followed the count amidst the blessings of a vast concourse of people drawn together by the news. The collection had already commenced in village after village. The humble dwelling of the labourer gave the price of a day's toil; the château the price of two bullocks, or a hundred livres; the bourgeois, no less generous or national, retrenched a dish on his table, a furbelow on his wife's petticoat. In eight days Agenor had collected one hundred and sixty thousand livres at Rennes; and this vein of gold exhausted, he proceeded to try others. It is, moreover, a fact that, according to the legend, the women of Brittany plied their spinning-wheels more industriously to obtain Bertrand's liberty, than they had ever before done to support their sons or clothe their husbands.

CHAPTER XLVII.

THE MESSENGER.

EIGHT days had elapsed since Mauleon took up his quarters with the Comte de Laval, when one evening, as he was returning home with a bag of gold, duly registered by the ducal scribe and the agent of Madame Tiphaine Raguenel, he remarked, on entering a ravine bordered on either side by hedges, two men of strange aspect, and occupying a singular position.

"Who are these fellows?" he inquired of Muscaron.

"Upon my soul one would fancy they were Castilians," replied the squire, gazing at a horseman followed by a page, both mounted on small Andalusian horses, with long manes, and who with helmet on head, and shield on breast, were drawn up against one of the hedges as though to dispute their passage.

"In fact they are accoutred in the Spanish fashion, and those long thin rapiers are Castilian."

"Does not the sight of them awaken a certain sensation, master?" demanded Muscaron.—"Yes, certes; but I fancy this horseman is going to accost me."

"Or to take your bag of gold, messire; fortunately I have my cross-bow."—"Leave your cross-bow alone; see, they have neither of them touched their weapons."

"Senor," began the stranger in Spanish.

"Are you speaking to me?" said Agenor in the same language.

"Yes."—"What do you require of me?"

"Have the kindness to direct me to the Château de Laval," said the horseman, with the politeness that distinguished not only the man of rank, but even the humblest Castilian.

"I am going there, senor," replied Agenor, "and will act

as your guide ; but I warn you that the master of the château is absent : he set out this morning on an excursion in the neighbourhood."

"Then there is no one at the château!" exclaimed the stranger, with evident disappointment. "What, still to search!" he muttered to himself.

"Nay, I did not say there was no one at the château, senor."

"You, perhaps, mistrust me, senor?" said the stranger, raising his visor, which, like Agenor, he had hitherto kept lowered—a prudent custom adopted by all travellers, who in these times of doubt and danger were in continual fear of attack or treachery. But the Castilian had scarcely disclosed his face before Muscaron ejaculated, "O Heaven!"

"What is it?" asked Agenor, in surprise. The stranger looked at him in seeming astonishment at this exclamation.

"Gildaz!" whispered Muscaron in his master's ear.

"And who is Gildaz?" asked Agenor in the same tone.

"The man whom we met on our journey in company with Donna Maria—the son of the good old Bohemian who came to summon you to that rendezvous in the chapel."

"Gracious Heaven!" exclaimed Agenor, filled with uneasiness. "What can have brought him here?"

"He is come in pursuit of us, perhaps."

"We must be prudent!"—"Oh, you know, Sir Agenor, there is no occasion to remind me of that."

During this colloquy, the Castilian examined the two interlocutors, and drew back, as if afraid.

"Bah! what have we, here in the middle of France, to fear from Spain?" said Agenor, after a moment's reflection.—"Then they are merely the bearers of some tidings," said Muscaron. —"Oh, it is at that I shudder! I fear events more than men. No matter ; let us question them."

"On the contrary, master, let us be prudent ; they may be emissaries of Mothril."—" But you remember having seen this man in the employ of Maria Padilla."

"And did we not find Mothril with Don Frederick?"

"True."—"Then let us be upon our guard," said Muscaron, bringing the cross-bow slung from his shoulder-belt within reach of his hand.

The Castilian remarked the action.

"Of what are you afraid?" demanded he. "Have we been guilty of any discourtesy, or is it the sight of my face that has displeased you?"—"No," said Agenor, hesitating. "But what is your business at the château of the Sire de Laval?"

"I will willingly tell you, senor. I have occasion to see the chevalier who is at present his guest." Muscaron cast a glance at his master through the bars of his helmet.

"A chevalier! and his name is?"

"Oh, senor, do not, in exchange for the service you render me, require me to be guilty of an indiscretion. I would rather await the chance of meeting with some less curious traveller."

"True, senor, true. I will not question you further."

"I conceived a great hope on hearing you reply to me in my native language."

"What hope?"—"That of the speedy success of my mission."

"To this chevalier?"—"Yes, senor."

"But what harm would it do to mention his name, since I shall know it when we reach the château?"

"Then, senor, I shall be beneath the roof of a lord who will not suffer me to be maltreated." A happy idea occurred to Muscaron, who was always brave when danger threatened his master. He resolutely lifted his visor, and approached the Castilian. "Vala me Dios!" exclaimed the stranger.

"Well, Gildaz, good day to you!" said Muscaron.

"You are the very man I am in search of!" cried the Castilian.

"Behold me, then," returned Muscaron, drawing his heavy cutlass.

"Is this lord your master?"—"What lord and what master?"

"Is this chevalier Don Agenor de Mauleon?"

"I am he," interrupted Agenor. "Come, let me know my fate. I am in haste to know whether it is good or evil."

Gildaz regarded the chevalier with a lingering mistrust.

"But if you are deceiving me?" said he.

Agenor made an impatient gesture.

"Nay, listen. A prudent messenger ought to be on his guard."

"You recognise my squire, foolish fellow!"

"Yes; but I do not know his master."

"What, you doubt me, scoundrel!" cried Muscaron, furiously.

"I doubt all the world when the right performance of my duty is in question."—"Beware, yellow face, lest I correct you! My knife is sharp."

"Eh!" said the Castilian. "And so is my rapier. You are unreasonable; would my mission be the better discharged by the death of either you or myself? Let us, if you please, proceed gently towards the Château de Laval; there let some one, without being warned beforehand, point out to me the Sire de Mauleon, and I will immediately execute my mistress's orders."

Agenor started at this last word.

"Good squire," cried he, "you are right, and we were wrong. You come to me from Donna Maria, perhaps?"

"You will know directly, if you are really Don Agenor de Mauleon," said the obstinate Castilian.

"Come, then!" exclaimed the young man, in a fever of impatience; "yonder are the turrets of the castle. Quick, you shall soon have every satisfactory proof, good squire. Set spurs to your horse, Muscaron!"

"Then, prithee let me go first," said Gildaz.

"As you will, only go quickly."

And the four cavaliers urged forward their steeds.

CHAPTER XLVIII.

THE TWO MESSAGES.

AGENOR had scarcely entered the château before the Castilian squire, whom not a word or gesture had escaped, overheard the major domo of the household say, "Welcome home, Sire de Mauleon."

These words, added to the reproachful look cast on him from time to time by Muscaron, were enough for him.

"Can I speak a few words in private to you?" said he, accosting Agenor.—"Will this court, planted with trees, suit you?" said the chevalier.

"Perfectly, senor."—"You know," continued Mauleon, "that I have no secrets from Muscaron, who is rather my friend than my servant. As to your companion——"

"My lord, you perceive he is a young Moor, whom I found, nearly two months ago, on the road leading from Burgos to Soria. He was dying of hunger, and had been beaten till the blood flowed by Mothril and his people, who had threatened his life because the poor youth had shown some inclination for the Christian religion. I found him lying pale and bleeding. I brought him to my mother, whom your lordship," he added, smiling, "may perhaps remember. She fed and tended him, and ever since he has been like a faithful

dog. Thus, when two weeks ago, my illustrious mistress,
Donna Maria——" (here the squire lowered his voice.)

"Donna Maria!" murmured Mauleon.

"Herself, senor. When my illustrious mistress, Donna
Maria, summoned me to her presence, and confided to me an
important and dangerous mission, 'Gildaz,' said she, 'mount
your horse, and repair to France. Put plenty of gold in your
valise, and take a good sword with you. Seek along the
route to Paris a gentleman [and my mistress described you,
senor] who is certainly on his way to the court of Charles
the Wise. Take with you a faithful companion, for I warn
you the mission is a perilous one.' I immediately thought
of Hafiz, and said to him, 'Hafiz, mount your steed, and take
your poniard with you.' 'Good, master,' replied he; 'only
give me time to visit the mosque.' For with us, you know,
senor, there are churches for the Christians and mosques for
the infidels, as if God had two dwellings. I allowed the boy
to visit his mosque, whilst I myself prepared his horse with
my own, and hung at his saddle-bow the long poniard that
you behold yonder fastened by a silken string; and when,
half an hour afterwards, he returned, we set out. Donna
Maria has sent you this letter." Gildaz raised his cuirass,
opened his doublet, and said to his companion, "Your poniard,
Hafiz."

Hafiz, with his bistre-coloured face, white eyeballs, and
impassible stiffness of mien, had throughout Gildaz' recital
preserved the silence and immobility of a statue. Whilst the
good squire was enumerating his good qualities—his fidelity
and discretion—he gave no signs of pleasure; but when he
mentioned his half-hour's absence to visit the mosque, a sort
of redness, like a pale and lurid fire, mounted to his swarthy
cheek, and his eyes flashed with either remorse or uneasiness.
When Gildaz demanded his poniard he slowly extended his
hand, drew the weapon from its sheath, and presented it to
him. Gildaz unripped the lining of his doublet, and took
from it a letter wrapped up in silk.

Mauleon called Muscaron to his aid, who, tearing off the
silken envelope, commenced reading the contents of the
epistle to his master, whilst Gildaz and Hafiz remained at a
respectful distance.

"Senor Don Agenor," wrote Maria Padilla, "I am strictly
watched and darkly threatened, but the person you wot of is

even more so than myself. I have a deep regard for you, but that person loves you still better than I do. We think, now you are in the land of France, it would be agreeable to you to possess what you are now regretting the loss of; therefore, in a month after the date of this letter, hold yourself in readiness near the frontier of Rianzares. The precise date of your arrival there I shall learn from the faithful messenger I send you. Wait there silently and patiently. One evening you will behold approaching, not the litter that you know of, but a swift mule, which will bring you the object of your desires. Then, senor, fly. Renounce the profession of arms, or at least never again set foot in Spain. Swear this on your faith as a Christian knight. Then, rich in the dowry your wife will bring you, and happy in her love and beauty, guard vigilantly your treasure, and sometimes bless Donna Maria Padilla, the unhappy woman of whom this letter is the last adieu."

Mauleon was at the same time touched and transported with joy. He snatched the letter from Muscaron's hands, and pressed it ardently to his lips. Not a single detail of this scene escaped Hafiz; but he neither spoke nor moved.

"Tell Donna Maria——" said Mauleon.

"Hush! senor," interrupted Gildaz. "This name, aloud!"

"You are right," said Agenor in a lower tone. "Tell Donna Maria, then, that in a fortnight——"

"No, senor," returned Gildaz: "my mistress's secrets do not concern me. I am her courier, not her confidant."

"You are a model of fidelity and noble devotion, Gildaz, and poor as I am, you shall receive from me a handful of florins."

"No, my lord, nothing: my mistress has rewarded me sufficiently."

"Then your page—your faithful Moor."

Hafiz opened his great eyes at the sight of the gold, and every limb quivered with eagerness.

"I forbid you to receive anything, Hafiz," said Gildaz.

An almost imperceptible movement revealed to the quick-sighted Muscaron the furious constraint exercised over himself by the Moor. "The Moors are in general avaricious," remarked he to Gildaz, "and this one is more so than a Moor and a Jew put together. Besides, he cast a villanous glance at his comrade Gildaz."

"Bah! all the Moors are ugly, Muscaron; and the devil alone can equal their grimaces," replied Gildaz, smiling, as he returned the poniard to Hafiz, who clutched it almost convulsively.

Muscaron, at a signal from his master, prepared to write an answer to Donna Maria. The Sieur de Laval's secretary was at that moment passing through the court. Muscaron stopped him, borrowed a strip of parchment and a pen, and wrote as follows:—

"Noble lady, you overwhelm me with happiness. In a month's time—that is to say, on the seventh day of next month—I shall be at Rianzares, ready to receive the dear object you will send me. I shall not renounce the profession of arms, for I wish to become a great warrior, in honour of my well-beloved lady; but I swear to you, by our Lord, that Spain shall never again behold me unless you summon me thither, or some misfortune prevents Aïssa from reaching me, in which case I would brave hell itself to recover her. Adieu, noble lady; pray for me.—Agenor de Mauleon."

Meanwhile, Hafiz watched every movement of Gildaz more like a tiger than a faithful dog, and remarked him secure Donna Maria's letter beneath his cuirass. He observed where he placed it, and then appeared indifferent to what followed, as if he had now seen all he cared to see.

"And now, good squire," said Agenor, "what are your plans?"

"I shall depart again on my indefatigable horse, senor. I ought to be with my mistress in twelve days' time—such are her commands—so I must be diligent. It is true the distance is not great, and they tell me there is a shorter route by Poitiers."

"True; adieu, good Gildaz! adieu, Hafiz! But, good heavens! it must not be said that if you decline the recompence of a master, you also refuse the gift of a friend;" and so saying, he unclasped his gold chain, which was worth a hundred livres, and flung it round Gildaz' neck. Hafiz' dark face was lighted up by an infernal smile. Gildaz wonderingly set out on his journey. Hafiz rode behind him, as if fascinated by the brilliancy of the gold links hanging over his master's shoulders.

CHAPTER XLIX.

THE RETURN.

MAULEON immediately commenced his preparations. He felt nothing but joy. There was now the almost certainty of an indissoluble union with his mistress—security in his love. Rich, beautiful, and loving, Aïssa appeared to him the realization of one of those dreams which God sends to mortals during the hours of darkness, to show them that there is something beyond this terrestrial existence. Muscaron shared his master's enthusiasm. To dwell in a grand château in some rich province, to command valets and serfs, rear cattle, dress horses, and arrange hunting parties; such were the sweet visions that in a crowd assailed the active imagination of the worthy squire. Mauleon had already resolved on giving up his profession for a year, and devoting that time to Aïssa; for he owed to her, no less than himself, a few months of calm happiness to repay them for so many hours of sadness. He awaited with impatience the return of the Sire de Laval. The count had, in his turn, collected large sums towards the constable's ransom from many of the Breton nobles. The secretaries of the King and the Duke of Brittany discovered, on comparing their accounts, that the half of the seventy thousand florins was already found. This was enough for Mauleon; he trusted that the King of France would furnish the rest, and knew enough of the Prince of Wales to be certain that, on the arrival of even half the ransom, he would immediately liberate the constable, unless policy demanded his longer detention, in spite of the payment of a portion of the sum. But to satisfy his scrupulous conscience, Mauleon travelled over the rest of Brittany with the royal standard, making an appeal to the inhabitants. Every time he passed through a town, he caused himself to be preceded by the mournful cry, "The good constable is a prisoner in the hands of the English! people of Brittany, will you let him remain captive?" By this means he gained another six thousand florins, which he gave into the hands of Madame Tiphaine Raguenel. But another scruple presented itself to his mind Although he was now at liberty to set out and meet his mistress, his functions of ambassador were not yet all discharged. Agenor, who had promised Maria Padilla never to return to Spain, must, nevertheless, convey to the constable the fruits of his labours in

x

Brittany—the precious money for whose arrival the captive was doubtless sighing.

Agenor was therefore placed between two duties, and long hesitated between them. An oath, and this he had taken to Donna Maria, was a sacred thing, but his affection and respect for the constable appeared to him to be equally so. He confided his perplexity to Muscaron.

"Nothing can be more simple," returned the ingenious squire. "Ask of the Lady Tiphaine a dozen armed vassals to escort the money. The Sire de Laval will give you four lances; and the King of France, provided it costs him nothing, will grant you a dozen more soldiers; with this troop, which you will command as far as the frontier, the money will be perfectly safe. When you arrive at Rianzares, write to the Prince of Wales, who will send you a safe-conduct. By this means the money will safely reach the constable."

"But how to account for my absence?"

"The pretext of a vow."—"A lie?"

"Nay, sire, it is not a lie. You have sworn it to Maria Padilla. Besides, were it even so, happiness is well worth a slight sin."—"Muscaron!"

"Ah, monsieur! don't assume so much piety; you are going to espouse a Saracen, and that appears to me a mortal sin!"—"True!" sighed Mauleon.

"Besides, it would be very hard if the lord constable required both you and the money. But trust me, I know men, and whilst the florins glitter they will forget the collector of them. On the constable's return to France he can see you if he wishes, for I suppose you do not intend burying yourself alive."

As usual, Mauleon yielded; besides, Muscaron was perfectly right. The Sire de Laval furnished him with men-at-arms. The Lady Tiphaine Raguenel armed twenty vassals; the Seneschal of Maine sent a dozen soldiers in the King's name; and being joined by one of Duguesclin's younger brothers, Agenor set out for the frontier, using all possible means to arrive at the place of appointment, at least two or three days before the time agreed upon with Donna Maria. Mauleon directed his march so skilfully, that on the fourth of the month they arrived at Rianzares, a small town which has long ceased to exist, but which then enjoyed some renown from being a sort of connecting link between France and Spain.

CHAPTER L.

RIANZARES.

AGENOR made choice of a dwelling situated on the slope of a hill, from whence he could easily distinguish the white and tortuous path winding between two perpendicular walls of rock. Muscaron had composed, in his best style, one epistle to the constable and another to the Prince of Wales, to apprise them of the gold florins; and a man-at-arms, attended by a Breton squire, one of the vassals of Lady Tiphaine, had been sent with them to Burgos, where it was said the prince was to be found at this moment, owing to the rumours of renewed warfare, which had recently spread throughout the country. By the help of the perfect knowledge he possessed of the localities, Mauleon every day reckoned the probable marches of Gildaz and Hafiz. According to these calculations, the two messengers must have crossed the frontiers at least a fortnight before. During this fortnight they would have had time to return to Donna Maria, who would then be able to prepare for Aïssa's flight. A good mule can travel twenty leagues in one day; six days would therefore be enough for the Moorish girl to reach Rianzares. Mauleon cautiously inquired whether the squire Gildaz had passed that way; for it was by no means impossible that the two travellers had availed themselves of this defile at Rianzares—an easy, safe, and well-known route. But the mountaineers replied, that at the time mentioned by Mauleon, they had only seen a single Moorish horseman, who was both young and ferocious-looking.

"A Moor—and young!"—"Twenty at most," replied the countrymen.

"Was he clad in red?"

"Yes, senor, with a Saracen morion on his head."

"Armed?"—"With a long poniard hanging from his saddle-bow by a silken chain."

"And you say he passed alone through Rianzares?"

"Absolutely alone."—"What did he say?"

"He asked in broken Spanish, which he pronounced badly and rapidly, if the path over the rocks was safe for horses, and whether the little river at the foot of the mountain was fordable? On our replying in the affirmative, he set spurs to his swift black horse, and disappeared."

"Alone," said Mauleon; "that is strange."

"Hum!" chimed in Muscaron; "that is singular."

"Gildaz must have crossed the frontier at some other spot, to avoid exciting suspicion. What do you think of it, Muscaron?"

"I think, messire, that Hafiz had a very ugly face."

"Besides," said Mauleon, thoughtfully, "how can we be certain that it was really Hafiz who passed through Rianzares?"

"It is better to think it was not."

"And then," added Mauleon, "I have observed, that the man who has almost arrived at the goal of his happiness, mistrusts, and beholds an obstacle in everything."

"Ah, master! happiness is indeed almost within your grasp; and if I am not mistaken, it is to-day we may expect Donna Aïssa. It would be as well if we kept good guard near the river during the whole night."

"Yes; for I do not wish our comrades to witness her arrival. I fear the effects of this flight on their narrow minds. For a Christian to be enamoured of a Moor would be enough to daunt the most intrepid courage; they would attribute all the misfortunes that have befallen us to a chastisement from God. But in spite of myself this solitary Moor dressed in red, with his poniard at his saddle-bow, this strange resemblance to Hafiz, haunts me."

"In a few hours, or at the most days, we shall know what to think of it," replied the philosopher. "Until then, monsieur, since we have no cause for sorrow, let us be joyful."

But the first day, the seventh of the month, passed away, and still nothing appeared on the road besides dealers in wool, wounded soldiers, or fugitives from Navaretto, who were regaining their native country, after passing through a thousand privations and dangers. Agenor learnt from these poor fellows, that war had again broken out in several places; that Don Pedro's tyranny, added to that of Mothril, weighed so heavily upon Castile, that the emissaries of the pretender, vanquished at Navaretto, found no difficulty in exciting the inhabitants against this abuse of power. These fugitives assured him, that they had already beheld many bodies of troops organized in the hope of the speedy return of Henry de Transtamare. They added that a good number of their comrades had seen letters from the prince, in which he promised soon to arrive with an army levied in France. These rumours of war inflamed Agenor's martial spirit; and since Aïssa had not arrived, it was beyond the power of love to calm in him

that fever aroused in young soldiers by the clashing of arms.
Muscaron began to despair. He knitted his brows more frequently than usual, and bitterly reverted to Hafiz, to whom,
as to some malignant demon, he obstinately attributed Aïssa's
delay. As to Mauleon, like a body seeking its lost soul, he
wandered incessantly along the road, with every bush, stone,
and shadow of which his eyes were familiar, and his ear could
distinguish the tread of a mule at two miles' distance. But
Aïssa came not, nor was anything to be seen approaching from
the direction of Spain. On the contrary, there arrived from
France, at intervals, as regular as if managed by clock-work,
troops of armed men, who took up their position in the neighbourhood, and seemed to await a signal to enter simul-
taneously. On the arrival of every fresh body of troops, the
leaders of the different bands parleyed together, exchanging
a countersign which appeared perfectly satisfactory, since men
of all countries and denominations traded and dwelt together,
with evidently a good understanding subsisting between them.

Mauleon, one day wishing to know at greater length the
reason of these arrivals of men and horses, learnt that they
were only awaiting the coming of their leader with fresh reinforcements to pour into Spain.

" And the name of this leader?" inquired he.

" We are ignorant of it; he will tell us it himself."

" Then every one will enter Spain but me!" exclaimed
Mauleon, in despair. " Oh, my oath! my oath!"

" Eh, messire?" said Muscaron. " Disappointment has
turned your brain. If Donna Aïssa does not arive, the oath
is no longer binding. She has not done so, therefore let us
push forward."

" It is not yet time, Muscaron; I have still hope."

" I should like to have half an hour's conversation with that
black-faced Hafiz," grumbled Muscaron. " Only to look him
well in the face."

" Pshaw! what could Hafiz do against the all-powerful will
of Donna Maria? It is she you must accuse, Muscaron, or
rather my ill luck."

Eight days passed away, and still no one arrived from
Spain. Agenor was almost mad with impatience, and Muscaron with fury. At the end of these eight days, five thousand armed men were assembled at the frontier. Waggons
laden with provisions (some said with money), were escorted

by this imposing force. The Comte de Laval's soldiers and
Lady Tiphaine Raguenel's Bretons impatiently awaited the
return of their messenger to know whether the Prince of
Wales consented to liberate the constable. The messenger at
last returned, and Agenor eagerly hastened to the river-side
to meet him. The soldier had seen the constable, been feasted
by the Prince of Wales, and received a magnificent present
from the princess, who had besides graciously deigned to say
that she hoped to see the brave Chevalier de Mauleon, and to
recompense his devotion. The messenger added that the
prince had accepted the thirty-six thousand florins, and that
the princess, seeing him hesitate for a moment, had said to
him, "Sire, I wish the good constable to receive his freedom
from me, who admire him as much as his compatriots. We
inhabitants of Great Britain are partly Bretons; I will therefore pay thirty thousand florins towards the ransom of
Messire Duguesclin." The consequence was, that the constable would be liberated, if he were not already so, even before
the arrival of the money.

These tidings filled the Bretons escorting the ransom with
delight, and as that is more catching than sorrow, the troops
assembled at Rianzares, on hearing the success of the embassy,
shouted with joy until they shook the very mountains.

"Let us enter Spain, and bring back our constable," cried
the Bretons.

"It must be so, master," said Muscaron in a low voice to
Agenor. "No Aïssa, no oath! We are losing time; let us
march forward, messire." And Mauleon, yielding to his
burning anxiety, consented. The little troop, followed by
the good wishes and benedictions of all, passed through the
defile nine days after the time fixed by Maria Padilla for the
arrival of Aïssa.

"We shall, perhaps, meet her on the road," said Muscaron,
to confirm his master in his decision. Meanwhile, by preceding them at the court of Don Pedro, we may, perhaps, be able
to disclose to our readers the cause of this ill-omened delay.

CHAPTER LI.

GILDAZ.

DONNA MARIA remained in her terrace apartments, counting
the days and hours; for she dreaded, or rather foresaw some

misfortune, both to herself and Aïssa, from the persevering quietude of the Moor. Mothril was not the man to slumber thus; never before had he so dissimulated his thirst for vengeance, that for fifteen days nothing had betrayed it to his enemies. His ostensible occupations were giving fêtes to the King—causing gold to flow into Don Pedro's coffers, and preparing to introduce into Spain the Saracen auxiliaries, as the first step towards uniting the two promised crowns on his master's brow. He neglected Aïssa, whom he only saw for a moment each evening, and then almost always accompanied by Don Pedro, who sent her the rarest and most magnificent presents. Aïssa, warned both by her love for Mauleon and her friendship for Donna Maria, accepted them only to cast them aside in disdain, and continued to treat the Prince with her usual coldness, without suspecting that she was thus increasing his passion, seeking for approbation of her conduct in Donna Maria's approving glance whenever she chanced to meet her. Donna Maria's glance also said to her, " Hope! our plan is ripening; my messenger will soon return and bring you love and liberty."

The day so ardently desired by Donna Maria at last dawned. It was one of those brilliant summer mornings beheld only beneath a southern sky; the dew trembled on every leaf of the flowers on Aïssa's terrace, when Donna Maria beheld the old woman of whom we have before spoken enter her chamber.

"Senora!" said she, with a deep sigh, "senora!"

"Well, what is the matter?"—" Senora, Hafiz is here."

"Hafiz!—who is he?"—"The companion of Gildaz, senora."

" What! Hafiz, and not Gildaz?"

" Yes, senora, Hafiz, and not Gildaz."

"Good God! Admit him; do you know anything else?"

" No, senora; Hafiz would tell me nothing, and I weep, for his silence is more ominous than any other's gloomy words."

"Nay, take comfort," said Donna Maria, shuddering. "No doubt there is some little delay—a mere trifle, that is all."— "Then why did not Hafiz also delay?"

"On the contrary, it is this return of Hafiz that re-assures me. Knowing that I should be uneasy, Gildaz would not keep him with him, he sends him forward, therefore the news are good."

The nurse was not easy to console; besides, there was little probability in these hasty conclusions of her mistress. Hafiz entered. He was, as usual, calm and humble. His eyes expressed respect, like those of a cat or tiger, which, dilating at the sight of those who fear them, contract and half close when they encounter a glance of anger or superior will.

"What, alone?" said Maria Padilla.

"Yes, senora, alone," returned Hafiz, timidly.

"And Gildaz?"—"Gildaz, mistress," said the Moor, glancing around him, "Gildaz is dead!"

"Dead!" ejaculated Donna Maria, clasping her hands in anguish. "Dead! poor youth; is it possible?"

"He was attacked by fever on the road, senora."

"He, so robust!"—"Robust, indeed; but God's will is stronger than that of man," said the Moor, sententiously.

"A fever! Oh, why was not I informed of it?"

"Senora," replied Hafiz, "in travelling through a defile in Gascony, we were attacked by mountaineers, whom the sight of gold had attracted."

"The sight of gold! what imprudence!"

"The French senor was so overjoyed, that he gave us gold. Gildaz, thinking himself alone with me among these mountains, took it into his head to recount our treasure, when he was suddenly struck by an arrow, and we beheld several armed men approaching us. Gildaz was brave; we defended ourselves——"—"My God!"

"Until we were overcome by numbers; for Gildaz was wounded—his blood flowed."—"Poor Gildaz!—and you?"

"I was also wounded." And, turning up his wide sleeve, he displayed his naked arm, gashed by a poniard. "They took our gold from us, and left us."—"And what then?"

"After that, mistress, Gildaz was attacked by a fever, and feeling himself at the point of death——"

"Did he tell you nothing?" interrupted Maria.

"Yes, mistress. When his eyes grew heavy, he said to me, ' Go! you can escape. Be as faithful as I have been ; hasten to our mistress, and deliver into her hands the trust confided to me by the French chevalier.' It is here, senora." Hafiz drew from his bosom a silken wrapper, pierced with poniard strokes, and soiled with blood.

Donna Maria shuddered with horror as she took it and examined it. "This letter has been opened," said she.

"Opened!" exclaimed the Saracen, with a look of astonishment.

" Yes, the seal is broken."

" I did not know it," said Hafiz.

' You have yourself opened it?"

" I, mistress! I do not know how to read."

" Then some one has."

" No, mistress! examine it again. You see this opening close to the seal—a mountaineer's arrow has pierced through both wax and parchment."

"True, true," said Donna Maria, doubtingly.

" And the torn part is stained with Gildaz' blood!"

" True; poor Gildaz !" and the young woman, casting a last glance on the Moor, found his boyish countenance so perfectly calm, stupid, and devoid of expression, that she could no longer entertain any suspicion of him.

" Finish your recital, Hafiz."

" Gildaz had no sooner given me the letter, mistress, than he expired ; then I set out as he desired me, and although faint and weary, never stopped until I found you, and delivered my message."

"Oh, you shall be amply rewarded, boy," said Donna Maria, moved even to tears.   " You shall not quit me, and if you are faithful—if you are intelligent——"   A momentary flash lighted up the eyes of the Moor, but it died away immediately.

Maria then read the letter, with the contents of which our readers are already acquainted, and yielding to the natural impetuosity of her nature, exclaimed to herself, " Now, now, let us to work !"   She gave the Moor a handful of gold, saying to him, " Rest yourself, good Hafiz; but hold yourself in readiness, for in a few days I shall have need of you."

The youth took his departure, radiant with joy ; but as he crossed the threshold, the sobs of the poor nurse fell upon his ear—she had just learned the fatal news.

CHAPTER LII.

HAFIZ' MISSION, AND HOW HE FULFILLED IT.

ON the evening of the day preceding that on which Hafiz brought Donna Maria the letter from France, a shepherd presented himself at the gates of the city, and asked to speak with the Lord Mothril.   Mothril, who was performing his devotions in the mosque, quitted them to follow this singular messenger, whose appearance did not seem to denote a very

high or powerful ambassador.   The Moor had scarcely left
the city before he saw a little Andalusian horse browsing on
the neighbouring heath, and perceived, crouched among the
bushes, the Saracen Hafiz, watching with his great eyes all
who emerged from the town.   The goatherd, rewarded by
Mothril, hastened gaily to rejoin his lean goats on the hill-
side; and Mothril, forgetting his rank, seated himself beside
the dark youth.

"Allah be with you, Hafiz!   You are then returned?"

"Yes, my lord."

"And you have left your companion far enough off for him
to have no suspicions?"

"Very far off, my lord; and he will assuredly suspect
nothing."

Mothril knew his messenger. "You have the letter?" said he.

"Yes, my lord."—"How did you gain possession of it?"

"If I had demanded it of Gildaz, he would have refused me.
If I had attempted to take it from him by force, he would
have beaten, perhaps killed me—for he was stronger than I."

"Then you have used artifice?"

"I waited until we had arrived in the heart of the mountains forming the frontier of France and Spain.   The horses
were very weary. Gildaz let them rest, and himself fell asleep
on the moss at the foot of a large rock. I chose this moment;
I crawled up to Gildaz, and struck him in the breast with my
poniard; he stretched out his arms with a dull cry, and his
hands were covered with blood. But I knew he was not dead,
and that with his left arm he might be able to draw his cutlass
and strike me; I therefore pierced him to the heart, and he
immediately expired. The letter was in his doublet. I drew
it out, and mounting my swift horse, journeyed the whole
night in the direction of the wind. The corpse and the other
horse, I left to the wolves and ravens. I crossed the frontier
and continued my route without interruption.   Here is the
letter I promised you."

Mothril took the letter, the seal of which was unbroken, although Hafiz's poniard, in reaching Gildaz' heart, had pierced
it through and through.   With an arrow taken from the
quiver of a sentinel, he severed the silken string, and eagerly
perused the contents.

"Good," said he; "we will all be at this rendezvous;" and
he fell into a reverie.   Hafiz stood waiting.

"What shall I do, master?"

"Take this letter, remount your horse, and at daybreak knock at Donna Maria's door. Inform her that the mountaineers have attacked Gildaz, wounded him with arrows and poniards; and that in dying, he gave you this packet. That is all."—"Good, master."

"Go, wander about the whole night, that your garments may be soaked with dew, and your horse covered with sweat, as if you had just arrived; then await my orders, and for eight days do not approach my house."

"The Prophet is pleased with me?"—"Yes, Hafiz."

"Thanks, master."

This is how the letter became unsealed, and such the nature of the storm gathering over the head of Donna Maria.

Next morning, Mothril arrayed himself magnificently, and sought Don Pedro's presence. He found the King seated in a large velvet fauteuil, playing mechanically with the ears of a young wolf, which he took great delight in taming. Donna Maria, looking pale and irritated, was seated in a similar one on his left hand. She was evidently greatly annoyed; for, notwithstanding her close vicinity, the Prince, doubtless occupied with other thoughts, had not addressed a single word to her since she had been in his presence. Donna Maria, proud, like all her countrywomen, grew impatient under this neglect. She also was silent; but as she had no tame wolf to toy with, she occupied herself in heaping up in her heart doubt upon doubt, and project upon project. Mothril's entrance gave her an excuse for sweeping hastily and passionately from the room.

"Are you going, senora?" said Don Pedro, uneasy, in spite of himself, at this angry sortie, which he had provoked by his indolent reception of his proud companion.

"Yes," she replied, "I am going. I do not wish to encroach upon your kindness, which you are doubtless reserving for the Saracen Mothril."

Mothril overheard her, but without evincing any signs of irritation. Had Donna Maria been less furious, she would have been aware that the Moor's calmness arose from the secret assurance of some speedy triumph. But anger never calculates—it is in itself a sufficient satisfaction. It is really a passion, and to be glutted with it is to some natures an intense pleasure.

"Sire," said Mothril, feigning profound sadness, "I perceive that my King is not happy."

"No," replied Don Pedro, with a sigh.

" We have plenty of gold—Cordova has contributed."

" So much the better," said the King, carelessly.

" Seville arms twelve thousand men," continued the Moor.
" We have gained two provinces."

" Ah !" said the King, in the same tone.

" If the usurper returns to Spain, I reckon on being able,
in eight days from the present time, to blockade him in some
castle, or take him prisoner."

The name of usurper had hitherto never failed to raise a
violent storm in the King's heart; but this time Don Pedro
contented himself with saying calmly, " Let him come. You
have both gold and soldiers ; we will take him prisoner, try,
and behead him."   Mothril drew near the King.

" Yet my King is very unhappy," said he.

" And why, friend ?"

" Because gold no longer pleases you—power disgusts you.
Because vengeance has no longer charms for you; and, lastly,
you have not even a glance for Donna Maria."

" Doubtless, I no longer love her, Mothril, and through this
void in my heart nothing now appears to me desirable."

" Is not this seeming void in your heart, my King, caused
by its being filled with other desires."—" I know it."

" Then you love ?"—" Yes, in truth, I love."

" Aïssa, the daughter of a powerful monarch.   Ah ! sire, I
both pity and envy you, for you may be either very happy
or greatly to be pitied."

" Very true, Mothril.   I am greatly to be pitied."

" You mean she does not love you?"

" Yes; she loves me not."

" My lord, do you imagine that this blood—pure as that
of a goddess—is agitated by the passions to which another
woman would yield ?   Aïssa is not fitted for the harem of a
voluptuary : she is a queen, and will smile only from a throne.
There are certain flowers, my liege, which blossom only on
the mountain's summit."

" A throne !   I espouse Aïssa !   Mothril, what would the
Christians say?"

" Who can say, my liege, that Donna Aïssa, loving you,
and accepting you for her husband, would not resign her
religion to you as well as her heart ?"

A sigh of almost pleasure burst from the King's lips.

" She would love me !"

"Yes, sire, she would love you."—"No, Mothril."

"Then, my liege, give yourself up to despondency; for since you despair so soon, you do not deserve to be happy."

"But Aïssa shuns me."—"I imagined the Christians better readers of a woman's heart. How could the haughty Aïssa appear to love a monarch at whose side is always to be found a woman the rival of all those who love Don Pedro?"

"Aïssa would be jealous?"—The Moor smiled.

"With us, sire, the turtle dove is jealous of its mate."

"Ah, Mothril, I love Aïssa."—"Then espouse her, sire."

"And Donna Maria?"

"The man who caused his wife to be put to death because she displeased his favourite, hesitate to dismiss one whom he has ceased to love, in order to gain five millions of subjects and a love more precious than all the dominions of the earth!"

"You are right; but it would kill Donna Maria."

The Moor again smiled. "She dearly loves you, then.?"

"Loves me! Can you doubt it?"—"Yes, my liege."

Don Pedro turned pale.

"He loves her still," thought Mothril. "His jealousy must not be awakened, or he will prefer her to all others." "I doubt it, my lord," he continued, aloud—"not because she has been unfaithful (that I do not believe), but because, although knowing herself less beloved, she persists in remaining near you."

"I should call that love, Mothril."

"I, my lord, call such a feeling ambition."

"Then you would drive Maria away?"—"Yes, to obtain Aïssa."

"Then," exclaimed Don Pedro, "I will break with Donna Maria; but I will bestow on her a million of crowns, and in whatever country she fixes her residence, there shall not be a princess more rich and honoured than herself."

"Be it so. That will be the conduct of a generous prince; but this country must not be Spain, for Aïssa would not feel secure unless the sea separated your ancient love from the new"

"Then we will place the sea between them, Mothril'

"Good, my liege."

"But I am the King, and therefore cannot accept conditions from any one. But this bargain—somewhat like a bargain between Jews—cannot be completed without some concession on your part."

" And what is that, my liege ?"

" Donna Aïssa must be placed in my hands as a hostage."

" Nothing but that, sire," said Mothril, ironically.

" Fool !" exclaimed the infuriated King. " Know you not that, if you trifle with me, I can tear her from you ? Dare but to roll your angry eyes, and I will have you seized, and hanged where all the Christian knights may behold your distorted carcase when they come to do homage to my new favourite !"

" Your anger is terrible, my lord," said Mothril, humbly. " And he is indeed unwise who does not bow the knee before you."—" Then you will place Aïssa in my hands."

" If you command it, sire. But if you have not followed my advice—if you are not rid of Donna Maria, Aïssa will never be yours, for Donna Maria will kill her."

It was the King's turn to shudder and reflect.

" What do you wish, then ?" said he.

" Wait eight days, sire. Nay, do not interrupt me. Aïssa shall then be conducted to one of your royal residences, without any one being aware of either her flight or her destination. Meanwhile, Donna Maria's suspicions will be lulled to sleep : she will awake to find herself defeated, and the favourite exchanged for a queen. She will never pardon this infidelity, and will herself free you from her presence."

" Yes, for she has a proud spirit. In eight days, then."

" At the last hour of daylight Aïssa will leave the city, escorted by a Moor. I will myself be her conductor."

" Go then, Mothril."

" Until then, sire, beware of rousing Donna Maria's suspicions."

" Fear not. I have hidden my sorrow. Do you think I cannot conceal my joy ?"

" Then publicly announce, my lord, that you intend setting out for one of your country houses."

" I will do so, Mothril."

CHAPTER LIII.

TREACHERY.

SINCE the return of Hafiz Donna Maria had renewed her intercourse with Aïssa. " Dear Aïssa," said she, "your departure draws near. In eight days' time you will be far from here, and close to him you love. I do not think you will regret leaving this country."

"Oh, no, no! It is life to me to breathe the same air as he breathes."

"Then you will be re-united. Hafiz is a prudent and faithful youth, and full of intelligence. He is well acquainted with the route. Besides, you will not fear him as you would a man, and will therefore journey with greater confidence in his company. He is your countryman, so you will both be able to converse together in your own language. This coffer contains all your jewels. Remember that in France a very rich noble does not possess the half of what you will bear to your lover. Besides, my good offices will attend the young man if he goes with you to the end of the world. Once in France, you will have nothing more to fear. I meditate a grand reform here. The King must be induced to drive from Spain the Moors, those enemies of our religion, and who serve as a pretext for the envious to tarnish the glory of Don Pedro. You absent, I shall have no hesitation in at once setting to work."

"On what day shall I see Mauleon?" demanded Aïssa, who had heard nothing but her lover's name.

"You may be in his arms five days after your departure from this city."

"My journey, senora, will be accomplished in half the time it would take the fleetest horseman."

It was after this conversation that Donna Maria summoned Hafiz, and demanded whether he would accompany the sister of Gildaz back to France. "A poor girl who is inconsolable for her brother's death," she added, "and who wishes to give his remains Christian burial."

"Willingly!" replied Hafiz. "Fix the day of departure, mistress."

"To-morrow you shall mount a swift mule that I will give you; the sister of Gildaz shall have another; and the third shall carry my nurse, her mother, and some effects relating to the ceremony she wishes to perform."

"Good, senora. To-morrow I will set out; and at what hour?"—"At night, after the gates are closed and the lights extinguished."

Hafiz had no sooner received this order than he trans-mitted it to Mothril. The Moor hastened to Don Pedro.

"My lord," said he, "this is the seventh day. You may now set out for your summer palace."

"I was expecting you," said the King.

"Set out then, my King; it is time."

"All the preparations are made," returned Don Pedro, "and I shall depart the more willingly, since the Prince of Wales sends a herald-at-arms to-morrow to ask for money."

"And the treasury will be emptied to-day, sire, for we must have the sum destined to assuage Donna Maria's wrath in readiness."—"Very good; that is enough."

Don Pedro gave orders for departure. He affected to invite several of the ladies of his court to join this excursion, but made no mention of Donna Maria. Mothril watched the effect of this insult on the haughty Spaniard, but she made no complaint. She passed the day with her women, playing on the lute and listening to the songs of her birds. Evening came. The court had retired, and Donna Maria declaring herself dying of ennui, ordered a mule to be got ready for her. At a signal from Aïssa, who was alone—Mothril having accompanied the King—Donna Maria descended the steps of the terrace, and enveloping herself in a large mantle, such as is worn by duennas, mounted her mule. Thus equipped, she herself went to seek Aïssa by the secret passage, and, as she expected, there found Hafiz, who had been nearly an hour in the saddle, peering into the darkness with his piercing eyes. Donna Maria displayed her pass to the guards, and gave them the countersign. The gates were opened. A quarter of an hour later the mules were rapidly traversing the plain. Hafiz rode first. Donna Maria remarked that instead of proceeding by the straight road he bore to the left.

"I dare not speak to him lest he should recognise my voice," said she, in a low tone to her companion; "but he will not know you, so ask him why he has taken a different road."

Aïssa put the question in Arabic, and Hafiz replied with surprise, "Because the route to the left is the shortest, senora."

"Good," said Aïssa; "but above all things take care not to lose your way."

"Oh, no!" replied the Saracen; "I know where I am going."

"Do not be uneasy," said Donna Maria, "he is faithful; besides, I am with you, and my only motive for thus accompanying you is that I may set you free in case of your being stopped in the neighbourhood. By morning you will have accomplished fifteen leagues, and then there will be no more danger of your meeting with bands of soldiers. Mothril keeps watch, but in a radius circumscribed by his own indolence and his master's indifference. Then I shall leave you to continue your journey, and retracing my steps, shall knock at the gates of the King's palace. I know Don Pedro, he is bewailing my absence, and will receive me with open arms."

"Then this château is near here?" said Aïssa.

"It is seven leagues from the city we have just quitted, but far on the left. It is situated on a mountain which we should behold yonder, against the horizon, if the moon were but risen." All at once the moon, as if obeying Donna Maria's voice, came from behind the clouds whose edges she had hitherto been silvering. Her soft and gentle lustre pouring down upon the woods and plain, the travellers suddenly found themselves bathed in a flood of light. Hafiz turned to his companions, and gazed around him. The road had given place to a vast plain bounded by high mountains, on which rose the bluish outline of the château.

"The château!" exclaimed Donna Maria. "We have lost our way!" Hafiz started, for he fancied he recognised this voice.

"You have lost your way?" said Aïssa. "Answer!"

"Alas!" returned Hafiz, simply; "can it be possible?"

He had scarcely finished speaking, when from the depths of a ravine, bordered with green oaks and olive-trees, darted four horsemen, whose spirited horses dashed down the steep with smoking nostrils and streaming manes.

"What does this mean?" said Maria, gloomily. "Can we be discovered?" And without another word she drew her mantle closer round her.

Hafiz began to utter piercing cries, as if overcome with fear, but one of the horsemen tied a handkerchief over his mouth, and seizing the bridle of his mule, led it away. Two others pricked the mules upon which the women were mounted with the point of their lances, so that they set off at a furious pace towards the château. Aïssa would have cried out, and attempted to defend herself.

"Be silent," said Donna Maria to her. "With me, you have nothing to fear from Don Pedro; with you, I have nothing to fear from Mothril. Be silent!" The four horse-

Y

men drove their captives before them, as though they were a
flock of sheep returning to the fold. "It appeared as though
we were expected," observed Donna Maria, "for the gates
are open without the horn being sounded." And, in fact, the
four horses and the three mules noisily entered the courtyard
of the château. One window was lighted up, and at this stood
a man who uttered a cry of joy on beholding their arrival.

"It is Don Pedro, and he was expecting us," murmured
Donna Maria, who recognised the King's voice. "What can
this signify?" The horsemen commanded the women to dis-
mount, and conducted them into the hall of the château.
Donna Maria supported the trembling Aïssa.

Don Pedro entered, leaning on Mothril, whose eyes sparkled
with joy. "Dear Aïssa," said he, eagerly advancing towards
the young girl, who, trembling with indignation, and with
flashing eye and quivering lip, seemed to demand from her
companion the reason of this treachery. "Dear Aïssa, pardon
me for having thus terrified you and this good woman.
Permit me to bid you welcome."

"And will you not welcome me also?" said Donna Maria,
throwing back the hood of her mantle. Don Pedro uttered
a loud cry, and recoiled with affright. Mothril, pale and
trembling, felt ready to sink into the earth beneath the crushing look of his enemy. "Come," continued Donna Maria,
"since you are our host, Don Pedro, let us be shown into an
apartment."

Don Pedro with faltering steps and downcast looks retreated into the gallery. Mothril also retreated, but fury had
already usurped the place of fear in his breast. The two
women clung closely to each other, and waited in silence. A
moment afterwards they heard the gates close. The major-
domo bowing to the ground, appeared to request Donna
Maria to ascend to her apartment.

"Do not leave me!" exclaimed Aïssa.

"I tell you, girl, there is nothing to fear! See, I have
discovered myself, and a single look was enough to daunt
these wild beasts. Come, follow me, I tell you; I will watch
over you."

"And you? Oh, do not you fear for yourself!"—"I?"
said Maria, with a disdainful smile. "Who then would dare
to molest me? It is not for me to know fear in this château."

CHAPTER LIV.

THE PATIO OF THE SUMMER PALACE.

THE apartment to which Donna Maria was conducted, was one well known to her. She had occupied it in the days of her dominion—her prosperity. Then all the court knew the way to these galleries supported by pillars of carved and gilded wood, of which a patio or garden of orange-trees surrounding a marble basin formed the centre. Then nothing was to be seen in these sumptuously illuminated galleries, but pages and valets in rich liveries, eager to offer their services. In the patio beneath, Moorish minstrels—whose strains so softly, so sweetly sad, seemed as they mounted from the lips of the singer, or the fingers of the musician, like rich perfumes ascending to heaven—were concealed under the thick branches of the flowering shrubs. Now all was silence. The gallery, separated from the rest of the palace, seemed dark and desolate, the heavy foliage of the trees looked gloomy and sombre, and the crystal water fell in the marble basin with a sound like the murmurs of an angry sea. At the extremity of one of the long sides of this parallelogram, a little door carved in ogives gave entrance to the gallery occupied by the King. This passage was long and narrow, like a stone canal. Formerly it had been hung, by Don Pedro's orders, with precious stuffs, and the pavement strewn with flowers; but during the long interval that had elapsed since his last sojourn here, the hangings had become faded and torn, and the dry and withered flowers crackled beneath the feet. All love's embellishments wither away when love itself is dead. It is like the passionate lianas, which flourishing when they twine luxuriantly around the tree they love, fall to the ground dry and withered when they no longer draw sap and life from its supporting trunk.

Donna Maria was scarcely installed in her apartment before she demanded her attendants.

"Senora," replied the major-domo, "his Majesty is only come to attend a hunting party, not to remain here, and has therefore not brought with him his usual retinue."

"Nevertheless, surely the King's hospitality will not permit his guests to lack necessaries."—"Senora, I am at your command, and all that you require——"

"Then bring us refreshments and writing materials."

The major-domo bowed and left them.   Night was fallen;
the stars sparkled in the sky, in the furthest depths of the
patio, beneath Donna Maria's casement, the plaintive cry of
an owl drowned the warbling of the nightingale. Aïssa in
the midst of this obscurity, overwhelmed by this untoward
event, terrified at the silent fury of her companion, stood
trembling at the further end of the apartment.   From thence,
she beheld Donna Maria pacing to and fro, like some pale
shadow, her hand upon her chin, and her eye gazing on va-
cancy, yet sparkling with projects.   She dared not accost her,
for fear of arousing this anger, or disturbing this grief.   The
major-domo presently appeared with waxen tapers, which he
placed upon the table.   A slave followed him, bearing on a
rich salver, two chased silver cups, dried fruits, and a large
flask of Xeres wine.

"The senora is served," said the major-domo.

"I see neither the ink nor the parchment I asked for,"
said Donna Maria.

"Senora, we have searched for some," returned the major-
domo with embarrassment.   "But the chancellor is not here,
and all the parchment is in the royal coffers."

Donna Maria knitted her brow.   "Good, I understand,"
said she; "thanks, now leave me."   The major-domo quitted
the room.   "I am devoured by thirst," said Donna Maria.
"Dear Aïssa, will you give me something to quench it."
Aïssa hastened to fill one of the cups with wine and offered it
her companion, who drank greedily.   "Have they not given
us any water?" asked she.   "This wine increases my thirst,
instead of quenching it."

Aïssa looked about her, and perceived a flower-painted
earthen jar, such as is used in the East to keep water cool and
fresh even in the sunshine.   She poured out a cup of pure
water, into which Donna Maria emptied the wine remaining
in her own.   But her mind had already ceased to occupy
itself with the wants of her body, and her thoughts returned
to their accustomed channels.

"What am I doing here?" said she.   "Why be thus losing
time when I ought to accuse the traitor of his treachery, and
endeavour to win him back again."   She turned abruptly to
Aïssa, who was anxiously watching her movements.   "Come,
young girl—you, in whose pure eyes one might fancy themselves able to read your soul—answer a woman, the most

unfortunate of her sex.   Have you pride ?   Did you ever envy
the splendour of my prosperity ? Have you for adviser during
the gloomy hours of the night a bad angel who lures your
feet from the path of love towards that of ambition.   Oh,
answer me! Remember that on the words you are about to
pronounce hangs my destiny. Answer me, then, as you would
answer God.   Were you acquainted with this intended ab-
duction—did you expect—did you hope for it?"

"Senora," replied Aïssa, in a tone at once sad and sweet,
"can you who have seen me fly so eagerly to my lover's arms,
ask whether I hoped to be clasped in those of another ?"

"You are right," said Donna Maria, impatiently ; "but
your reply, although perhaps expressing all the candour of
your soul, still appears to me a subterfuge. It may be because
my heart is not so pure as your own, and that all earthly
passions unite to darken and overwhelm it.   Therefore I
reiterate my question. Are you ambitious, and could you
console yourself for the loss of your lover by the hope of a
great fortune—a throne ?"

"Senora," replied Aïssa, shuddering, "I am possessed of
no eloquence, and I cannot tell whether I shall succeed in
convincing your grief ; but by the living God, whether he be
your God or mine, I swear to you, that in case Don Pedro
held me in his power, and endeavoured to force his love upon
me—I swear to you, I say, that I have a poniard with which
to pierce myself to the heart, or a ring like yours from which
to imbibe a mortal poison."

"A ring like mine !" exclaimed Donna Maria, recoiling
quickly, and hiding her hand beneath her mantle ; "you know !"

"I know from the whispers of every one in the palace,
that devoted to Don Pedro, and trembling lest, after the loss
of some battle, you should fall into the hands of his enemies,
you are in the habit of carrying in this ring a subtle poison
to set you free at will. For the rest, it is also a custom with
the people of my race. I should not be either less brave or
less faithful to Agenor, than you would be to Don Pedro.
Rather than he should lose his beloved, I would die !"

Donna Maria pressed Aïssa's hands, and even kissed her
brow with a sort of wild tenderness.   "You are a generous
child," said she, "and your words dictate my own duty, if I
had not something even more sacred than my love to protect
in this world.   Yes, I ought to die, having lost my future

and my glory; but who will watch over this ingrate, this coward, whom I even yet love? Who will save him from a shameful death, and a yet more shameful ruin? He has not a friend—he has millions of deadly enemies. You neither love him, nor will yield to his blandishments; this is all I wish, since all I feared was the contrary. Now, my line of conduct is ready traced. Before daybreak to-morrow there shall be a change in Spain with which the whole universe shall ring."

"Senora," said Aïssa, "beware lest your courageous mind carry you too far. Remember, I am alone in the world, and have neither hope nor happiness except in and through you."

"I have thought of all that; misfortune has purified my heart; having now no ordinary love, I am no longer selfish. Listen, Aïssa, my resolution is taken—I am going to seek Don Pedro. Search in the gold-inlaid coffer, which ought to be in the next chamber, there you will find a key: it is the key of the secret door opeinng into Don Pedro's apartments." Aïssa hastened to find the key, and brought it to Donna Maria, who took it from her.

"Must I remain alone in this gloomy place, senora?" asked the young girl.

"I have a safe retreat for you. Here some one might perhaps gain admittance to you; but at the lower end of the chamber from whence you have just brought this key, there is another door, opening into a chamber enclosed by walls and without other means of access. I will lock you up there; you will have nothing to fear."

"Alone? Oh, no! I should be afraid!"—"Child! but you cannot accompany me. It is only from the King you have anything to fear, and he will be with me."

"True, senora," said Aïssa. "Well, then, I resign myself to you. I will await your return, not in yonder dark and distant chamber, but here on the cushions on which you have just been reposing—here, where everything will recall to me your protecting presence."

"But you must take some repose."

"I do not need it, senora."

"As you will, Aïssa. Pass the moments of my absence in supplicating your God to cause me to triumph; since then, to-morrow, in broad daylight, and free from all apprehension, you will be able to take the road to Rianzares. To-morrow, on quitting me, you will be able to say, 'I am going to my husband, and no earthly power will be able to take me from him.'"

"Thanks, senora—thanks!" murmured Aïssa, bathing the hands of her generous friend in tears of joy. "Oh, yes! I will pray, and God will hear me."

At the moment these two young women were exchanging this tender adieu, a human head might have been seen forcing its way through the foliage in the lower part of the patio, until it was on a level with the gallery, where it remained buried in the darkest shade. The head thus confounded with the heavy masses of the surrounding foliage remained motionless. Donna Maria quitted the young girl, and lightly took her way towards the secret door. The head, without moving, followed her with its great white eyeballs, and beheld her enter the mysterious corridor. The sound of a door creaking on its rusty hinges was then heard at the extremity of the corridor, and the head immediately disappeared amidst the foliage, like that of a serpent making a hasty descent. It was the Saracen Hafiz, who thus glided down the polished trunk of a citron-tree. At its foot he found a dark figure awaiting him.

"What, Hafiz! already deserted your post?" said this personage.—"Yes, master; for there is nothing more to be seen in the apartment. Donna Maria has just left it."

"Where has she gone?"—"She went to the end of the gallery on the right, and there she disappeared.'

"Disappeared! Oh, by the sacred name of the Prophet, she has passed through the secret door, and gone to speak with the King. We are lost!"—"You know that I am at your command, Senor Mothril," said Hafiz, growing pale.

"Good; follow me to the royal apartments. All are asleep at this hour; there are neither guards nor courtiers about. Mount to the King's window, and listen, as you did yonder."—"There is an even simpler means, senor, by which you could listen for yourself."

"What?—Great Allah! Speak quickly."

"Follow me, then. I will climb up one of the columns of the patio until I reach a window, through this I will introduce myself, and glide on tiptoe through the door at the back, which I will open for you. By this means you will be enabled to easily overhear Don Pedro and Maria Padilla's conversation."

"You are right, Hafiz; the Prophet has inspired you. I will do as you say. Show me the way."

CHAPTER LV.

EXPLANATIONS.

DONNA MARIA did not deceive herself—the danger was extreme. Wearied by long possession, spoilt by success, and corrupted by adversity, which purifies good though erring natures, Don Pedro craved evil stimulants instead of good counsels. His whole soul required changing; and nothing would have been impossible with love; but this, it was greatly to be feared, Don Pedro no longer felt for Donna Maria. She therefore proceeded blindly along the dark path which was so well lighted for her enemy Mothril. Doubtless, had she encountered the Moor by the way, and grasped a poniard in her hand, she would have struck him to the heart without mercy; for she was sensible that the accursed influence that had darkened her life during the last year was now beginning to have dominion over her. These thoughts were passing through Maria's mind as she opened the secret door, and found herself in the King's apartments. Don Pedro, nervous and irresolute, was wandering like a ghost up and down the gallery. Donna Maria's silence, her calm anger, inspired him with more lively apprehensions than the most violent ebullition of rage would have done.

"She comes," he was saying, "to brave me even in the midst of my court—to show me that I am not master; and really I am not, since the arrival of a woman overthrows all my projects and destroys all my prospects of pleasure. This is a yoke that I must break, and, if I am not strong enough to do it alone, I will seek assistance." He was saying these words when Maria, who had glided over the polished china tiles, seized him by the arm, saying, "And who will assist you, sire ?"—"Donna Maria !" exclaimed the King, as though he had beheld a spectre.

"Yes, Donna Maria, come to ask you, her King, in what the counsels—the yoke, if you will—of a noble Spanish lady—of a woman who loves you, is more dishonouring or more heavy than the yoke imposed on you by Mothril, on a Christian

King, by a Moor ?"—Don Pedro clenched his hands with rage. "There is no occasion for either impatience or anger," said Donna Maria. "This is neither the hour nor the place for it. You are in your own apartments, and, believe me, I have not intruded on you to dictate terms. Thus master, as you are, why suffer yourself to be irritated, sire ? The lion does not quarrel with the ant."

Don Pedro was not accustomed to hear these humble protestations from Maria's lips. He paused in amazement. "Then what are your wishes, senora ?" said he.

"Very trifling ones, sire. It appears you love another woman ; it is your right, and I do not pretend to examine whether you use it ill or well. I am not your wife, and were I so, I should remember that, for my sake, you inflicted pain and grief on your former ones."

"Do you reproach me for it ?" said Don Pedro, fiercely, gladly seeking a pretext to grow angry.

Donna Maria bore his gaze without shrinking. "I am not God, to reproach kings with their crimes," said she. "I am but a woman, living to-day, dead to-morrow—an atom, a breath, a nothing. But I have a voice, and I will use it in telling you what you will only hear from my lips. You love, Don Pedro, and each time that has happened a cloud has passed before your eyes, veiling the whole universe from you. But you turn away your head. To what are you listening ? What attracts your attention ?"

"I fancied that I heard a footstep in the next chamber," said Don Pedro.—"No, 'tis impossible !"

"Why impossible ? Everything is possible here."

"Prithee look, sire, whether any one is listening."

"No ; there is no door to this chamber, and I have not a single attendant near me. It must have been the evening breeze lifting the hangings, and flapping them against the casement."

"I was saying," resumed Maria, "that since you no longer loved me, I was resolved to leave you." Don Pedro made an involuntary gesture. "I rejoice that my resolution gives you pleasure," said Maria, coldly. "I will leave you, then, and you shall never more hear of me. From this moment, sire, Donna Maria Padilla is no longer your mistress, but a humble servant, who is about to show you your true position. You have gained a battle, but it will be said that

others gained it for you; in such a case, your ally must be
your master, and this you will sooner or later prove. The
Prince of Wales already demands the considerable sums that
are due to him. This money it is out of your power to pay.
His twelve thousand lances, which have hitherto fought for
you, will now turn against you. Your brother has found
help in France; and the constable, the beloved of all who
bear a French name, will return hither thirsting for revenge.
Here are two armies to fight; with what will you oppose
them? An army of Saracens! O Christian King, you
have but one means of re-entering into the confederation of
Princes of the Church, and you deprive yourself of it.
You would draw upon yourself besides temporal arms the
anger of the Pope, and excommunication! Reflect; the
Spaniards are religious; they would abandon you. Already
the neighbourhood of the Moors terrifies and disgusts them.
Nor is this all: the man who urges you on to your destruction would not think it completed by mere misery and
disgrace; that is to say, in exile and defeat; he wishes
to entrap you into an infamous alliance—to make you a
renegade. God knows, I do not hate Aïssa; I love and
protect her, and would defend her like a sister, for I know the
purity of her heart and life. Aïssa, were she the daughter of a
Saracen King—which she is not, and I will prove it—would
not be more fitting for your Queen than myself, the daughter
of ancient knights of Castile, the noble descendant of twenty
ancestors equal to Christian Kings. But have I ever asked
you to raise me to the throne? and yet, certes, I might
have done so, for, Don Pedro, you loved me once!" Don
Pedro sighed. "Nor is this all. Mothril talks to you of
Aïssa's love. What am I saying?—he promises it you,
perhaps?" Don Pedro gazed at her uneasily—yet, with
vivid interest, as if ready to seize upon her words before they
were even uttered. "He promises that she will love you.
Is it not so?"

"How could that be, senora?"

"It might well be, sire; and you merit more than love.
There are certain persons in your kingdom, and these
Aïssa's equals, who feel for you more than adoration." Don
Pedro's face brightened. Donna Maria knew how to make
every chord of his heart vibrate beneath her skilful touch.
"But, in short," she continued, "Donna Aïssa would

never love you, for her affections are already bestowed upon another."

"Is this true?" exclaimed Don Pedro, furiously, "or is it only a calumny?"

"So little of a calumny, sire, that were you this very moment to question Aïssa—and that without her having held any communication with me—she would tell you word for word what I have just told you."

"Speak, senora, speak! by so doing you will indeed render me a service. Aïssa loves some one—who is it?"

"A French knight, called Agenor de Mauleon."

"The ambassador who was sent to me at Soria; and is Mothril aware of this?"—"He is aware of it."

"You assert this?"—"I swear it."

"And her heart is won in such a manner, that to promise me her love was on Mothril's part an impudent falsehood, an odious treachery!"

"Yes; an impious falsehood, an odious treachery."

"You can prove this, senora?"

"At any moment you command me to do so, sire."

"Repeat what you said, that I may convince myself that I heard aright."

With all his haughtiness, Donna Maria ruled the King; she did so through both his jealousy and his pride.—"'By the living God!' was Aïssa's declaration just now, and the words still ring in my ears—'I swear that in case Don Pedro ever holds me in his power, and attempts to force his love upon me, I have here a poniard with which to pierce myself to the heart, and a ring like yours containing a mortal poison.' And she pointed to this ring upon my finger, sire."

"This ring," repeated Don Pedro, in alarm. "What is this ring, then, senora?"

"It contains a subtle poison, sire; I have worn it during the last two years, to secure my freedom of body and soul, in case, among the reverses of the fortune I have so faithfully followed, I may some day meet with one that will deliver me into the hands of your enemies."

Don Pedro felt a remorseful pang at the sight of this simple and touching heroism.—"You have a noble heart, Maria," said he, "and I never loved a woman as I did you. But such reverses of fortune are far distant. You need not think of death."

"As he did love me," thought Maria, turning pale, and with difficulty refraining from betraying her emotion. " He no longer says, as he does."

"And this was Aïssa's own idea ?" resumed Don Pedro, after a pause.—" Entirely so, sire."

" This is idolatry for her French knight."

"It is a love equal to what I once bore you," replied Donna Maria.

"That you once bore me !" repeated Don Pedro, weaker than his companion, and betraying his wound at the first pang.—" Yes, sire."

Dod Pedro knitted his brow.—" Can I question Aïssa ?"

" Whenever you please, sire."

"Will she speak before Mothril ?"—" Yes, sire, before Mothril ?"

" She will relate all the details of her attachment ?"

" All, sire."

" Mothril ! Mothril ! every punishment would be too feeble, every torture too mild to inflict on you in expiation of this cowardly attempt ! Bring Aïssa hither, I entreat you, senora."

"I go, my lord ; but reflect ; I have betrayed this secret to serve the interests of my King. Will it not be better to trust in my word ? Cannot you believe me without exposing Aïssa ?"

" Ah, you hesitate ! you are deceiving me !"

" I do not hesitate, sire ; I only wish to awaken a little confidence in your Majesty's breast. The truth of what I assert will be proved in a few days, without exposure of any kind."

" It shall be proved immediately, and I summon you to produce your proofs, under pain of your accusations not being believed."

" My lord, I obey you," said Maria, greatly agitated.—" I shall impatiently await your return, Maria."—" My lord, you shall be obeyed."—"If you have spoken the truth, Donna Maria, to-morrow Spain shall not contain a single Moor who is not either a fugitive or proscribed."

" Then to-morrow, my lord, you will be a great King, and I, a poor fugitive and forsaken woman, shall be able to return thanks to God for the greatest happiness he has yet afforded me in this world—the certainty of your prosperity."

"Senora, you turn pale—you totter—shall I summon assistance?"

"Call no one, sire! No; I will return to my apartment, where refreshments are served. I left a cup of wine upon the table. I burn with thirst, and that once quenched, I shall be quite restored. Do not think of me, I entreat you. But I swear," exclaimed Maria, suddenly interrupting herself, and hurrying towards the neighbouring chamber, "I swear that some one is here! This time I am not mistaken, I heard a man's footstep."—Don Pedro seized a taper, Maria took another, and they both hastily entered the apartment. It was deserted—nothing announced that it had been lately tenanted, only the curtain beside the outer door, of which Hafiz had spoken, slightly shook.—"No one," said Maria, in surprise; "yet I distinctly heard what I said."

"I told you before it was impossible. Oh, Mothril, Mothril! what vengeance I will take on you for this treachery! You will return, then, senora?"

"Only give me time to apprise Aïssa, and return with her by the secret passage."—Saying this, Donna Maria took leave of the King, who, in his feverish impatience, almost confounded his gratitude for the present service with the remembrance of past love. In fact, Donna Maria was a beautiful and passionate woman, whom it was difficult to forget after having once seen. Proud and imperious, she imposed respect whilst she won love. More than once this despot King had trembled before her anger, and oftener still his worn-out heart had throbbed wildly in the expectation of her coming. Thus, when she quitted him after these explanations, he felt inclined to hurry after her, and say, "What matters Aïssa? you are all that I love."—But Donna Maria had closed the iron door, and the only sounds that met the King's ears were the rustling of her silken robe, and the crackling of the withered leaves as she trampled them under foot.

CHAPTER LVI.

MARIA'S RING AND AÏSSA'S DAGGER.

MOTHRIL'S foot had barely touched the ground, when Donna Maria fancied she heard a footstep; for before approaching the tapestry so as to overhear what was being plotted against

him, he had removed his sandals. The revelation of Aïssa's
secret had filled him with fear and horror. That Donna
Maria hated him he did not doubt; that she would endeavour to ruin him by aspersing his motives, and revealing
his ambition, the Moor was certain; but what he could not
support was the idea of Don Pedro becoming indifferent to
Aïssa. Aïssa, betrothed to Mauleon, would be for Don
Pedro an object without charm or value; and no longer to
hold Don Pedro by his love for Aïssa, was like dropping the
restraining rein of a furious horse. In a few moments the
whole of this scaffolding, raised with so much care, would
come tumbling down. Aïssa, sure of being protected, would
return with Donna Maria, and reveal to Don Pedro the secret
of her love. Then Donna Maria would regain her ascendancy, and Aïssa lose hers, whilst he himself, disgraced, confounded, driven away, and scouted as a miserable deceiver,
would tread with his compatriots the dreary path to exile,
admitting that he was not cast into a bloody grave by this
tempest of royal fury. These were the prospects that unfolded
themselves before the eyes of the Moor whilst Donna Maria
was speaking; and her words fell one by one on his ear
like drops of molten lead on a bleeding wound. Breathless,
bewildered—now cold as marble, now with the blood cours-
ing through his veins like boiling lava—Mothril asked himself, with his hand on his faithful poniard, why he should
not with one blow destroy both the speaker and the listener,
and thus save, not only his life, but his cause. Had another
guardian angel instead of Maria stood beside Don Pedro, he
would not have failed to warn him that he ran a terrible
risk. All at once the Moor's face brightened; the icy sweat
no longer stood upon his brow. Two words that fell from
Maria's lips had opened to him at the same moment the way
of safety through the path of crime. He calmly allowed
her to finish her recital; she might now tell all her thoughts
to Don Pedro; and it was not until the close of the conversation, when he had no longer anything to fear, that he
quitted his hiding-place. And the tapestry trembled behind
him, as Don Pedro and Donna Maria had observed. Mothril,
once more outside, paused for the space of two seconds, and
said to himself,—

"It will take her three times as long to return to her
apartment by the secret corridor as I shall be in reaching it

by the patio. Hafiz!" he continued, aloud, striking the young tiger, who stood awaiting his orders, on the shoulder, "hasten to the passage from the gallery. Stop Donna Maria when she appears—ask her pardon, as though you were struck with repentance. Accuse *me*, if you will—avow, reveal—do what you please; only detain her from entering the gallery for five minutes."

"Good, master," returned Hafiz; and crawling like a lizard up the carved pillar of the patio, he entered the passage whence the approaching footsteps of Donna Maria were already heard.

Meanwhile, Mothril made a tour of the garden, ascended the flight of steps leading to the gallery, and entered Donna Maria's apartment. In one hand he grasped his poniard, in the other a small golden flaçon, which he had just taken from amongst the folds of his ample vest. The waxen taper was guttering in its socket, and Aïssa, with closed eyes, lay softly slumbering on her cushions. From her half-opened lips a beloved name issued with her fragrant breath.

"First for Aïssa," said the Moor, with a gloomy look. "Once dead, she will be unable to confirm what Donna Maria has asserted. Yet to strike my child, my sleeping child! She for whom—if I do not too easily take alarm—Allah, perhaps, reserves a crown. Let me wait; she shall be the last to die. I will still preserve a ray of hope."

He approached the table, and taking up the silver cup still half filled with the draught prepared by Donna Maria herself, emptied the whole contents of the flaçon into it. "Maria," he muttered, softly, with a frightful smile, "forgive me if this poison is not equal to what you carry in your ring; but we poor Moors are mere barbarians. If my beverage displeases you, I will offer you my poniard." He had scarcely finished his talk before the supplicating tones of Hafiz, mingled with the more animated ones of Donna Maria, reached his ear from the secret corridor.

"For pity's sake!" the boyish monster was saying, "pardon my youth. I was ignorant of what my master made me do."

"I will see another time," returned Maria. "Now leave me. I shall know how to make inquiries, and gather from the testimonies concerning you the truth you are concealing from me."

Mothril hastened to conceal himself behind the tapestry

that curtained a window. Placed here, he could see and
hear all that passed, and rush upon Donna Maria if she
attempted to quit the chamber.

Hafiz, on being thus dismissed by her, proceeded slowly
down the long gallery. Maria then entered her chamber
and contemplated the sleeping Aïssa with indefinable emotion
"I have betrayed the secret of your love," said she—"clouded
your dove-like beauty; but the wrong I have done you, poor
child, shall be soon repaired. You are sleeping beneath my
protection. Sleep on! I leave you to your sweet dreams
still a moment longer." She advanced a step towards Aïssa;
Mothril grasped his poniard. But Donna Maria's movement brought her near the table where stood the silver cup
of ruby wine, inviting her parched lips. She took it up,
and drank a deep draught. She had scarcely swallowed the
last mouthful before the icy clasp of death seized upon her
heart. She staggered—her eyes became fixed—she pressed
her two hands on her breast; and divining from this intoler-
able suffering some fresh misfortune—perhaps some new
treachery—she gazed wildly around her, as if to question the
two mute witnesses of her agony—solitude and slumber.
Her breast burned like raging fire; the blood rushed to her
face—it seemed as though her heart had mounted into her
throat. She opened her lips, and endeavour to utter a cry.
Swift as lightning Mothril prevented her doing so, by placing
his hand over her mouth. In vain she struggled in his arms,
in vain she tore his fingers with her teeth. Mothril, whilst
retaining her in his hold, extinguished the taper, and Maria
was at the same moment wrapped in darkness and in death.
Her feet convulsively beat the floor for a few seconds, and
aroused her sleeping companion. Aïssa started from the
couch, and in endeavouring to make her way through the
darkness, stumbled over Maria's body. She fell into Mothril's
arms, who, seizing both her hands, flung her beside Maria,
at the same time gashing her shoulder with his poniard.
Deluged with blood, Aïssa fainted. Mothril then dragged
the ring containing the poison from Maria's finger, emptied
its contents into the silver cup, and replaced it on his victim's hand. Then staining the poniard the Moorish girl
was in the habit of carrying in her girdle with blood, he
placed it beside Maria, so that it appeared as if it had just
fallen from her grasp. This horrible scene occupied less

timo than it would have taken an Indian serpent to suffocate
in his coils two gazelles which he had watched sporting in
the sun on the grassy expanse of a savannah.   All that was
now necessary for its completion was for Mothril to place
himself beyond the reach of suspicion.   Nothing could be
more easy.   He re-entered the neighbouring patio, as if he
had returned from some journey of inspection.   He inquired
of the attendants whether the King had retired, and learnt
in reply that they had just beheld him impatiently pacing
to and fro the gallery.   Mothril asked for his cushions, desired one of the attendants to read him certain verses in the
Koran, and then appeared to sink into profound slumber.

Hafiz, although unable to communicate with his master,
had instinctively known what to do.   He had mixed with
Don Pedro's guards, preserving his usual gravity of demeanour.   Half an hour thus passed.   The most profound
silence reigned through the palace.   All at once a loud cry
was heard proceeding from the depths of the royal gallery,
and the King's voice shouted, " Help! help!"   Every one
rushed towards the gallery ; the guards grasping their naked
swords, the attendants armed with the first weapon that came
to hand.   Mothril, rubbing his eyes and stretching himself
as if still heavy with sleep, inquired what was the matter ?

" The King ! the King !" replied the eager crowd.

Mothril arose and followed them.   He saw Hafiz advancing in the same direction, also rubbing his eyes and looking
scared and astonished.   They then beheld Don Pedro, standing with a flambeau in his hand, on the threshold of Donna
Maria's apartment.   He was ghastly pale, and uttering loud
cries and imprecations, which he redoubled as from time to
time he turned towards the chamber.   Mothril pressed
through the mute and trembling crowd that surrounded the
half-frantic Prince.   A dozen flambeaus cast their blood-red
light over the gallery.

" See ! see !" cried Don Pedro.   " Dead, both of them !"

" Dead !" repeated Mothril ; " who are dead, my liege ?"

" Behold, shameless Saracen," exclaimed the King, whose
hair stood on end.

Mothril took a torch from the hands of a soldier, and,
slowly entering the chamber, recoiled, or seemed to do so at
the sight of the two corpses and the blood-stained pavement.
—" Donna Maria! Donna Aïssa !" he exclaimed.   " Great

z

Allah !"—The crowd repeated, with a shudder, " Donna Maria—Donna Aïssa, dead !"

Mothril flung himself on his knees and regarded the two victims with mournful earnestness. " My lord," said he to Don Pedro, who had buried his face in his two hands, " there has been murder committed here. Deign to command every one to retire. '—The King made no reply : at a sign from Mothril every one slowly withdrew.—" My lord," repeated Mothril, in the same tone of affectionate persistence, " there has been a crime committed."

" Wretch," exclaimed Don Pedro, recovering himself. " Do I behold you here—you who have betrayed me !"

" My King must be suffering deeply since he thus ill-treats his best friends," said Mothril, with unaltered gentleness.

" Maria—Aïssa—dead !" exclaimed Don Pedro, wildly.

" My lord," said Mothril, " I do not complain."

" You miscreant—you complain, and of what ?"

" That I behold in Donna Maria's hand the weapon which has shed the illustrious blood of my ancient rulers—slain the daughter of my venerated master, the Grand Caliph."

" It is true," murmured Don Pedro. " The poniard is in Donna Maria's hand ; but she herself—she whose features wear so frightful an expression, whose eyes are still filled with menaces, whose lips are covered with foam, who has killed her ?"

" How can I tell, sire ? I was asleep, and entered the chamber after you." And the Saracen, after having silently contemplated the livid visage of Maria, shook his head ; only he carefully examined the half-emptied cup.—" Poison !" muttered he.

The King bent over the corpse in gloomy terror, and seized its stiffened hand.

" Ah !" he exclaimed, " the ring is empty."

" The ring," repeated Mothril, feigning surprise. " What ring ?"

" Yes," continued the King, " the ring containing the mortal poison. Then Maria has destroyed herself. Maria, whose return I was awaiting—Maria, who might have still hoped that my love ——"

" Nay, my lord, I fancy you deceive yourself. Donna Maria was jealous, and knew that your heart had long been o cupied by another woman. Reflect, sire, that she must have been overwhelmed with shame and mortification, and her pride received a mortal wound in finding Aïssa thus summoned to your presence. The first burst of anger over, she would prefer death to desertion ; besides, she has not died without her revenge, and to a Spaniard revenge is dearer than life."

The tone of frank confidence in which this perfidious speech was uttered, imposed on Don Pedro for a moment ; but all at once carried away by his grief and resentment, he seized the Moor by the throat, exclaiming, " You lie, Mothril! You are mocking me : you ascribe Donna Maria's death to my desertion ; then you either are, or feign to be, ignorant that I preferred my noble love to all the world !"

" My lord, you did not say so the other day when you accused Donna Maria of wearying you."

" Do not remind me of that in the presence of this corpse, accursed Moor."

" My lord, I would fetter my tongue, I would resign my life rather than displease you; but I must act the part of a faithful friend in alleviating your grief."

" Aïssa—Maria !" repeated Don Pedro, in despair. " Oh, that my kingdom could repurchase an hour of your lives."— " Allah's will be done," said the Moor, mournfully. " Although he has taken from me the joy of my old age, the flower of my life, the pearl of innocence that enriched my dwelling."

" Miscreant !" exclaimed Don Pedro, in whom these words, purposely hazarded, reawakened his selfishness and consequently his fury, " you still vaunt Aïssa's candour and innocence—you who know her degrading love for the French adventurer."

" I !" vociferated the Moor, in a stifled voice, and with a burst of wrath none the less terrible for being feigned ; " who has dared to say this ?"—" One whom your hate can no longer harm—one whose lips falsehood never stained—the woman death has torn from me."

" Donna Maria !" said the Moor, contemptuously ; " she had an object in saying so. She might well seek to calumniate the girl her vengeance has now slain."—Don Pedro remained wrapped in silent reflection on this bold and logical accusation.—" If Donna Aissa were not stabbed with a

z 2

poniard it would perhaps be said that she had attempted to assassinate Donna Maria."

This last speech overstepped the bounds of audacity; Don Pedro took advantage of it.—"And why not?" said he. "Donna Maria revealed to me your daughter's secret. May not she have revenged herself upon her for this revelation?"

"You observe," said Mothril, "that Donna Maria's ring is empty—who can have emptied it besides herself? King, you are indeed blinded, since, by the death of these two women you cannot see that Donna Maria deceived you."

"But how? She went to bring me the proof of her words —to bring Aïssa to confirm them."

"Did she come?"—"She is dead."

"Because her coming was to prove what was false."

Don Pedro again bowed his head in bewilderment at this terrible mystery.—"The truth!" he murmured, "who will tell me the truth?"—"I will, sire."

"You!" exclaimed the King, with redoubled hatred; "you, the monster who persecuted Donna Maria, who wished me to abandon her, and have been the cause of her death. Well! you shall quit my kingdom and depart into exile—that is the only favour I will show you!"

"Hush, sire! a miracle!" replied Mothril, without noticing this outburst of Don Pedro's. "Donna Aïssa's heart throbs beneath my hand; she lives! she lives!"

"She lives!" exclaimed Don Pedro. "You are sure of it?"

"I feel the pulsation of her heart."

"The wound is perhaps not mortal—a doctor!"

"No Christian leech," said Mothril, with grave authority, "shall lay his hand upon a noble maiden of my race. Aïssa may not be saved, but if she is, it shall be by me alone."— "Save her, Mothril! save her, that she may be able to tell."

Mothril cast a meaning look at the King.

"That she may tell how both of us have been calumniated, my lord," said he.

Don Pedro, who was kneeling beside the two corpses, gazed first on the livid face of Maria, convulsed and distorted by a hideous death, and then on the calm sweet countenance of the lifeless Aïssa.—"Donna Maria was in fact very jealous," said he to himself; "and I remember she never tried to defend Blanche of Bourbon, whom I put to death to please her."—He rose from his knees, no longer wishing to think of anything but the young Aïssa.—"Save her, Mothril!" said he to the Saracen.

"Fear not, sire; it is my will that she lives; and she *shall* live."

Don Pedro withdrew, struck with a sort of superstitious terror. He fancied that Donna Maria's spectre rose from the ground and followed him down the gallery.—"As soon as the young girl is able to speak, either apprise me of it or bring her to me. I will then question her."

Such were his last words as he returned to his apartments with a heart void of regret, love, or hope.

Mothril ordered the doors to be closed. He then made Hafiz gather certain herbs, the juice of which he expressed and applied to Aïssa's wound—a wound which his skilful poniard had inflicted with all the dexterity of a surgeon's knife. After being made by Mothril to inhale several powerful essences, Aïssa came to herself. She was still weak, but memory revived with her returning strength, and her first act on regaining her senses was to utter a cry of affright.— She had caught sight of the inanimate body of Maria Padilla lying at her feet, the eyes glaring with anguish and despair.

CHAPTER LVII.

THE GOOD CONSTABLE'S PRISON.

MEANWHILE, Duguesclin had been conducted to Bordeaux, the residence of the Prince of Wales, where, although treated with the greatest kindness and respect, he found himself a close prisoner. The castle in which he was confined had both a governor and a jailor. A hundred men-at-arms composed the guard, and allowed no one access to the prisoner. Occasionally some of the most distinguished officers in the English army did themselves the honour of paying him a visit. John Chandos, the Sire d'Albret, and the principal nobles of Guyenne, obtained permission to frequently dine and sup with him; and Duguesclin, who was both a good host and a joyous companion, gladly received them, and in order to treat them well, borrowed money on his Breton estates. Little by little the constable lulled the doubts and fears of the garrison. He seemed to be happy in his prison, and expressed no wish for freedom. When the Prince of Wales visited him, and jestingly alluded to his ransom, he said, "Patience, monseigneur, it is being obtained." The prince then confided to him his annoyances; and Duguesclin, with his usual frankness, reproached him for having devoted his power and genius to the service of so bad a cause as that of Don Pedro. "How," said he, "could a prince of your merit lower himself by defending this robber, this assassin, this crowned renegade?"

"State reasons," replied the prince.—"And the wish to disturb France, was it not?" said the constable.

"Ah, Messire Bertrand! do not make me talk politics," returned the prince; and then they both laughed.

The Princess of Wales frequently sent Bertrand presents of little dainties or trifles wrought by her own hand, and this kindness made the prisoner's sojourn in the fortress more supportable. But he had no one near him to whom to confide his chagrins, and these were deep. He felt that time was passing away; and this army, levied with so much difficulty, was every day becoming more and more scattered, and more difficult to re-assemble when it would be needed. He had, almost under his eye, the spectacle of the twelve hundred officers and men taken prisoners with him at Navaretto—the nucleus of an invincible troop, which once free, would gather round it with ardour the scattered remains of that great power crushed by a single day of unexpected defeat. His thoughts often reverted to the King of France, doubtless, at this moment, greatly embarrassed. He beheld, from the depths of his gloomy prison, his dear and venerated master walking with bowed-down head in the trellised garden of St. Paul, sometimes lamenting, sometimes hoping, and murmuring, like Augustus, "Bertrand, give me back my legions." "And meanwhile," continued Duguesclin, in his silent soliloquy, "France is overrun by the reflux of the companies. Caverley and the Green Knight are, like locusts, devouring the remains of the poor harvest." Then his thoughts wandered to Spain, to Don Pedro's insolent abuse of power, and the obscure position of Henry, for ever cast from the throne so recently just within his grasp. And then the constable could not help blaming the cowardly indolence of this prince, who, instead of hotly pursuing his work— consecrating his life and fortune to the task of stirring up half the Christian world against the unfaithful Spaniards around Don Pedro—was probably leading an idle and do grading existence with some ignoble chatelain. When these thoughts crowded on the mind of the good constable, his prison became odious to him. He regarded the iron bars as Samson did the hinges of the gates of Gaza, and felt himself strong enough to carry away the walls on his shoulders. But prudence quickly counselled him to put a good face upon the matter; and as to his Breton loyalty he added a good deal of Norman craftiness—as he was at the same time brave and cunning—he never uttered so many shouts of laughter, never drank so roysteringly, as in the hour of weariness and despondency. Nevertheless, a superior authority caused the most rigorous surveillance to be exercised over the prisoner. Too proud to complain, the constable was ignorant to whom or to what he was indebted for this display of severity, which even went to the length of stopping all communication between him and France.

The English court regarded the capture of Duguesclin as one of the happiest results of the victory of Navaretto. In fact, the constable was the only obstacle that the English, commanded by such a hero as the Prince of Wales, could meet with in Spain.

King Edward, well advised, wished, little by little, to extend his power in this country ravaged by civil war. He foresaw that Don Pedro, through his alliance with the Moors, would sooner or later be dethroned—that Don Henry, vanquished and killed, there would remain no aspirants to the throne of Castile, which would then prove an easy prey to the victorious army of the Prince of Wales. But if Bertrand were free, it would make a great change in the face of affairs. He might return to Spain, regain the advantages lost at Navaretto, defeat the English and Don Pedro, place Henry de Transtamare finally on the throne, and thus put an end to a scheme of domination that for five years had occupied the attention of King Edward's council. Edward judged men less chivalrously than his son did. He imagined the constable might endeavour to make his escape, or if not, might be carried away; that even as a prisoner. chained and powerless within four walls, he might still give good counsel—a plan of invasion—a ray of hope to the vanquished party. Thus Edward had placed over Duguesclin two incorruptible guardians—the governor and the jailor, who were only to be relieved by the special directions of the

English court. Edward did not communicate to the emi-
nently noble and loyal Prince of Wales the secret designs of
his counsellors; he feared lest his magnanimous resistance
should place obstacles in his way. The fact was, the English
monarch was determined to on no account resign the prisoner
for any ransom whatever, and that he hoped by gaining time
to withdraw him eventually from the hands of the Black
Prince, and conduct him to London, where the Tower appeared to him a far safer place in which to deposit so illustrious a prisoner—so great a treasure—than the castle of
Bordeaux. Certes, if the prince had been warned of this
determination, he would have set Duguesclin at liberty before
receiving the official order for his detention. They were,
besides, waiting for matters to be well adjusted in Spain.
Don Pedro seated firmly on the throne, and France held
rigorously in check, to be able, by a sudden policy of state,
to recall, by an order from the privy council, the Prince of
Wales to London with his prisoner. For this favourable
moment the English monarch was waiting.

Duguesclin was in ignorance of the threatening storm.
He rested in perfect confidence on the power of his conqueror at Navaretto. The day so long desired by the illustrious prisoner at last broke through his prison bars. The
Sire de Laval arrived at Bordeaux with his ransom. It was
noon; the sunshine fell obliquely on the apartment of the
constable, who being at that moment alone, was sadly
watching the bright rays dance and flicker on the naked
wall. The trumpets sounded, the drums beat. Bertrand
comprehended that some illustrious visitor had just arrived.
The Prince of Wales entered his apartment bareheaded, with
a smile upon his lips.

"Well, sir constable," said he, as Bertrand bowed the
knee before him. "How do you like the sunshine? It is
indeed a fine morning."

"Truly, monseigneur," replied Duguesclin, "I love the
songs of the nightingales in my own country far better than
the squeaking of the mice in Bordeaux. But the will of God
must not be disputed by man."

"On the contrary, sir constable," said the prince, "God
sometimes proposes, and man disposes. Have you heard the
news from your country?"

"No, monseigneur," replied Bertrand, in a troubled voice.

"Then, sir constable, you will soon be free. The money has arrived." And so saying, the prince shook the hand of the stupified Bertrand, and smilingly left him. As he passed through the door he said to the officer charged with guarding the prisoner, "Sir governor, you will, if you please, allow the friend bringing his ransom free access to the constable." After saying this, the prince left the castle. The governor, gloomy and thoughtful, remained alone with the prisoner.

This unexpected arrival of Laval would frustrate all the plans of the English council; and Duguesclin would, in spite of all, be free. Without an express order from King Edward the governor dared not oppose the Prince of Wales' will, and this order had not arrived. Nevertheless, the governor was aware of the secret intentions of the English Government; he knew that the constable being set at liberty would prove a source of misfortune to his country, and chagrin to King Edward. He therefore resolved on attempting to accomplish by himself what the government had still left undone, so great had been Mauleon's expedition, so enthusiastic the eagerness of the Bretons to liberate their hero. The governor, therefore, instead of giving directions to the jailor, as the Prince of Wales had desired him, came himself to keep the constable company.

"Then you are free, sir constable," said he; "and it will be a real misfortune to us to lose you."

Duguesclin smiled.

"And why so?" said he in a jesting tone.

"It is so great an honour, sir constable, for a simple knight like me to have the guardianship of so celebrated a warrior as yourself."

"Good," returned the constable in his usual cheerful manner; "I am one of those persons who are always taken in battle. The Prince of Wales will infallibly make me prisoner again, and then you shall have the task of guarding me, for I swear you do it well." The governor sighed. "I have but one consolation remaining," said he.

"What is that?"—"I have all your companions—twelve hundred Bretons, prisoners like yourself, under my charge— I can talk to them about you."

Duguesclin felt all his joy abandon him at the thought of his friends remaining prisoners, whilst he, freed from captivity, was again beholding the sunshine of his native land.

"Your worthy comrades," continued the governor, "will lament your departure; but by my good offices I will lessen the weariness of their captivity as much as possible." Another sigh from Bertrand, who this time began silently to pace the paved floor of his chamber. "Oh what a glorious prerogative is that of genius and valour," continued the governor, "to cause a single man to be worth twelve hundred put together!"

"How is that?" asked Bertrand.

"I mean, sir constable, that the sum brought hither by the Comte de Laval to liberate you would be sufficient to pay the ransom of your twelve hundred companions."

"That is true," muttered the constable, more thoughtfully, more gloomily than ever.

"It is the first time," continued the Englishman, "that it has been visibly demonstrated to me that one man is worth a whole army. For in fact, sir constable, your twelve hundred Bretons are in themselves an army, and capable of undertaking a campaign alone. By St. George! if I were in your place, and rich as you are, I would only leave Bordeaux like an illustrious captain at the head of my twelve hundred soldiers."

"Here is a brave man," said Duguesclin, thoughtfully to himself; "he points out my duty to me. In fact, it is not right that a man made of flesh and blood like others, should cost his country as dear as twelve hundred brave and honest fellow-Christians." The governor watched with an attentive eye the success of his insinuations. "Then," said Bertrand all at once, "you think that seventy thousand florins would ransom the Bretons."

"I am certain of it, sir constable."

"And that on this sum being paid, the prince would set them at liberty?"—"Without haggling."—"Will you guarantee it?"—"On my honour, and my life!" said the governor, trembling with joy.

"It is well. Send, if you please, my friend and compatriot the Sire de Laval to me. Send my scribe also, with all that is requisite to draw up a schedule in proper form."

The governor lost to time; he was so overjoyed that he forgot his orders were to allow no one to have access to the prisoner except the English and the Navarrais, his natural enemies.

He transmitted Bertrand's orders to the astonished jailor, and himself hastened to apprise the Prince of Wales.

CHAPTER LVIII.

THE RANSOM.

BORDEAUX was in a state of tumult and agitation caused by the arrival of the Comte de Laval, with his four mules laden with gold, and fifty men-at-arms bearing the colours of France and Brittany. A considerable crowd had followed the imposing cortége, and on every visage was depicted either anxiety and disappointment when the face was English, or joy and triumph when it was either Gascon or French.

The Sire de Laval received in passing the congratulations of some, and the muttered imprecations of others. But his countenance was calm and unmoved; he rode at the head of his troop with one hand on the hilt of his dagger, the other on the rein of his powerful black horse; and with raised visor cleft the masses of the curious crowd without allowing any obstacle to either quicken or retard his progress. He arrived before the castle where Duguesclin was confined, and dismounting, gave his horse to his squire, and commanded the four muleteers to unpack the coffers containing the specie. They obeyed. Whilst they were unloading their mules one after another, and the curious crowd pressed closely around them, a knight, with a lowered visor, without either colours or device, approached the Sire de Laval, and said to him in pure French, " Messire, you are about to have the happiness of beholding the illustrious prisoner, and the still greater one of setting him at liberty, and bearing him away in the midst of your brave men-at-arms. I, one of the constable's best friends, shall perhaps not have an opportunity of speaking to him; will you, therefore, allow me to accompany you to his dungeon ?"

" Sir knight," said the Comte de Laval, " your voice falls pleasantly on my ear; you speak the language of my country, but I am not acquainted with you, and if any one demanded your name I should be forced to be guilty of falsehood."

" You can reply," said the unknown, " that I am the Chevalier de Mauleon."—"But you are not he," replied the comte, quickly. " For the Sire de Mauleon left us in order to reach Spain more speedily."

"I come from him, messire. Do not refuse my request.
I have one word to say to the constable—only one."—"Tell
it to me then, and I will faithfully transmit it to the constable."

"I can only say it to himself, and even then he would not
understand it without my showing him my face. I entreat
you, Sire de Laval, by the honour of the arms of France, of
which, I swear to you by God, I am one of the most zealous
defenders, not to refuse me !"

"I believe you, messire," said the comte ; adding, with a
feeling of wounded pride, "but knowing who I am, you place
little confidence in me !"

"When you know who I am myself, sir comte, you will
not say so. This is the third day I have passed at Bordeaux
vainly endeavouring to gain access to the constable, and
neither gold nor cunning has been successful."

"To me your conduct appeared suspicious," said the comte,
"and I will not for your sake burden my conscience with a
lie. Besides, what interest have you in visiting the constable when in ten minutes' time he will be at liberty ; in fact,
in ten minutes' time he will stand where you do now, and
you can then say to him this important word."

The stranger made an impatient gesture. "In the first
place," said he, "I am not of your opinion, nor do I look upon
the constable as free. Something tells me that his sortie
from prison will be attended with more disappointment than
you suppose. Besides, admitting that he will be free in ten
minutes, I should already be so far on my road. I should
avoid the delay of the ceremony of restoring him to liberty,
the visit to the prince, the thanks to the governor, the farewell feast. I entreat you take me with you ; I may be useful
to you." The stranger was at this moment interrupted by
the appearance of the jailor, who came to invite the Sire de
Laval to enter the constable's apartment. The comte took
leave of his petitioner, with an air of abrupt authority. The
stranger knight, whom he fancied shuddered beneath his
armour, retreated behind the men-at-arms, where leaning
against a pillar, he waited, as if still hoping, until the last
coffer had disappeared on its way to the dungeon. Whilst
the Sire de Laval was mounting the stairs, the Prince of
Wales, accompanied by the governor, and preceded by Chandos
and several other officers, was seen to pass along the open

gallery connecting the two wings of the castle. The conqueror of Navaretto was going to pay his last visit to Duguesclin, amidst the shouts of the populace and the flourishes of the French trumpets. The hero saluted them courteously, and as the door closed behind him, the crowd drew nearer the stairs, awaiting with noisy murmurs the sortie of the constable. At the expected sight of their great captain, for whom they would all have willingly given their lives, the hearts of the Breton men-at-arms beat violently. But half an hour passed away, and what only caused impatience in the spectators, became with the Bretons a subject of uneasiness. The stranger wrung his mailed hands together. At last Chandos appeared on the open gallery, speaking quickly to his officers, who seemed astonished and bewildered. Then when the gates of the castle reopened, instead of giving exit to the freed hero, no one appeared but the Sire de Laval, who, pale and downcast, and trembling with emotion, cast his eyes over the crowd. Several of the Breton officers hastened to him. "What has happened?" they anxiously inquired.

"Oh, a strange event! a great disaster!" replied the comte. "But where is the stranger—that prophet of misfortune?"— "I am here," said the strange knight, "I was awaiting you."

"Do you still wish to see the constable?"—"More than ever."

"Well, then, hasten, for in ten minutes it will be too late. Come, come! he is more than ever a prisoner!"—"We shall see," returned the unknown, lightly ascending the stairs behind the comte.

The jailor smilingly opened the dungeon door, and the assembled crowd began to comment on the event that had retarded the constable's release.

"So!" said the Breton leader to his men; "your hands upon the hilts of your swords, and attention!"

CHAPTER LIX.
PLOT AND COUNTERPLOT.

THE Englishman had not deceived himself; he knew his prisoner. The Sire de Laval had scarcely entered the apartment and flung himself into his friend's arms—the first moment of mutual joy was, in fact, scarcely past—before the constable, remarking the coffers of gold brought by the muleteers to the

landing outside his chamber—"My dear friend," said he,
"what a sum of money!"

"Never was a tribute more easily levied," returned Laval,
who, proud of his countryman, knew not how to do enough
to show his respect and friendship.

"My faithful Bretons!" said the constable. "And you,
too, my friend, have impoverished yourself!"

"You should have seen the pieces of gold pour into the
purses of the collectors," said the Sire de Laval, glad to annoy
the English governor, who had returned from visiting the
prince, and stood listening to the conversation, by this enthusiasm.

"Seventy thousand florins!" said the constable. "What
a sum!"

"A large sum when the question is, how to procure it; but
a small one when it is procured."

"My friend," interrupted Duguesclin, "you know that
twelve hundred of my countrymen are here prisoners like
myself?"—"Alas! yes, I know it."

"Well, I have found means to restore them to liberty. It
was my fault they were made captive, that fault I will now
repair."

"How will you do that?" inquired the Sire de Laval, in
astonishment.

"Have you been obliging enough, messire governor, to
summon your secretary?"

"He is at the door, sir constable," said the Englishman,
"and awaits your orders."

"Let him enter." The governor stamped three times with
his foot. The jailor admitted the scribe, who, no doubt, forewarned, proceeded to prepare his parchment, pen and ink.

"Write what I shall dictate to you, my friend," said the
constable.—"I am ready, my lord."

"Begin, then:—Know all whom it may concern, that we,
Bertrand Duguesclin, Constable of France and Castile, and
Comte of Soria, deeply repenting having, in a moment of in-
sensate pride, estimated our personal valour at the price of
twelve hundred good Christians and brave chevaliers, who,
certes, are worth more than ourselves——"

Here the good constable paused, without studying the
effect of his words on the surrounding visages. The scribe
wrote it faithfully down. "In order to repair this fault,

humbly entreating the pardon of God and our brethren, do herewith consecrate the sum of seventy thousand florins to the ransom of the twelve hundred prisoners made by his Highness the Prince of Wales at Navaretto, of mournful memory."

"What! mortgage your estates, sire constable!" exclaimed the Comte de Laval. "That would be an excess of generosity."—"No, my friend; my wealth is already dissipated, and I cannot reduce Madame Tiphaine to poverty; she has already suffered enough through me."

"Then what will you do?"

"The money you have brought me is really mine?"

"Most assuredly; but——"—"That is enough; if it is mine, I may dispose of it as I please. Write, master scribe—

"For this purpose I employ the seventy thousand florins brought me by the Sire de Laval."—"But, sire constable," exclaimed Laval, in affright, "you will remain prisoner!"

"And covered with immortal renown," interrupted the governor.—"But that is impossible," said Laval; "reflect upon it."

"You have written it?" said the constable.

"Yes, my lord."—"Then give it me to sign."

The constable took the pen, and rapidly inscribed his name. At this moment, the trumpets announced the arrival of the Prince of Wales. The governor had already seized upon the parchment. When the Sire de Laval perceived the English prince, he pressed forward, and bending the knee before him, "My lord," said he, "here is the money demanded for the ransom of the lord constable, do you accept it?"

"Right willingly, according to my word," said the prince.—"Then, monseigneur, this money is yours, take it," continued the comte.

"One moment!" said the governor; "your highness is not informed of what has just taken place. Will you deign to read this schedule?"

"To annul it!" exclaimed Laval.

"To cause it to be executed," said the constable.

The prince cast his eyes over the schedule, and was struck with admiration. "This is a noble act!" said he; "and I would willingly have been the doer of it myself."

"That would be useless, monseigneur; you are the victor," said the constable."—"Your highness will not detain the constable?" said the Comte de Laval.

"No, certes, if he chooses to depart," returned the prince.

"But I choose to remain, Laval. I ought to do so—ask these lords what they think about it." Chandos, D'Albret, and the rest, loudly expressed their admiration.

"Well," said the prince; "let the money be counted, and you, messieurs, order the Breton prisoners to be set at liberty."

It was then the English captains quitted the cell, and Laval, half mad with grief, recalled the gloomy augury of the unknown knight, and rushed from the castle to summon him to his aid. When he returned with him to the castle, an officer was already going over the list of prisoners; the coffers were already emptied of their contents, and the gold piled up in heaps.

"Tell the constable at once what you wish to communicate to him," whispered Laval in the stranger's ear, whilst the prince was chatting familiarly with Duguesclin. "And since you are possessed of so much natural and magical power, persuade him to take the ransom money for himself, instead of bestowing it on others." The unknown started; he stepped forward, and his golden spur rang upon the pavement.

"Who is this knight?" asked the govenor.

"My companion," returned Laval.—"Then let him raise his visor, and be welcome," said the prince.

"Monseigneur," said the unknown, in a voice which made Duguesclin start in his turn. "I have made a vow not to uncover my face; permit me to keep it."

"Be it so, sir knight; but you do not intend remaining unknown to the constable?"

"To him, as to every one else, monseigneur."

"In that case," interrupted the governor, "you will have to quit the castle, where I have orders to allow no one to enter but those known to me."—The knight bowed his head as though to signify his willingness to obey.

"The prisoners are free," said Chandos, returning.

"Adieu, Laval, adieu!" said the constable, with a heaviness of heart that did not escape the notice of his friend, for he seized Bertrand's hand, saying, "For the love of God, desist! there is yet time."

"No! on my life, no!" replied the constable.

"Do you, then, so begrudge him the renown he will win?" said the governor. "If not at liberty to-day, he may be so in a month's time. Money may be found, but opportunities like this of winning glory do not twice present themselves."

The prince seemed to applaud this speech; his captains imitated him. The unknown knight gravely approached the governor. "It is you who begrudge your master his glory, by urging him to act thus," said he, in a lofty voice.

"What are you saying?" exclaimed the governor, turning pale. "You insult me, sir knight! I envious of my prince's renown! You lie in your teeth!"

"Nay, do not cast down your gauntlet without first being aware whether it is worthy of my raising it. Messire, I speak truly; his Highness the Prince of Wales is injuring his renown by thus detaining the constable in this castle."

"You lie! you lie!" shouted angry voices, whilst swords clattered in their scabbards.

The prince, like the rest, resented this rude and unjust attack. "Who is this!" he exclaimed, "come hither to make me do his bidding? Is it by chance a king, who dares to speak thus to a king's son? The constable can pay his ransom, and depart—if he cannot pay it, he must remain, that is all; therefore why these angry complaints?"

The unknown knight remained unmoved. "My lord," he continued, "during the whole of my journey this is what I have heard said, that the constable's ransom was being taken him, but that the English feared him too much to set him at liberty."

"Good God!" muttered the prince. "They say that!"

"Everywhere, my lord."

"You see, they are mistaken, for the constable is at liberty to depart. Is it not so, constable?"

"It is, monseigneur," replied Bertrand, who, since hearing the voice of the unknown knight, had become strangely and inexplicably agitated.

"But," observed the governor, "since the constable has otherwise disposed of the money destined for his ransom, he will be obliged to await the arrival of a similar sum."

The prince remained for a moment buried in thought. "No," said he, at last. "I fix his ransom at a hundred livres!" A murmur of admiration ran through the assembly. Bertrand would have exclaimed against it, but the unknown knight placed himself between him and the prince.

"Thank God!" said he, holding him back. "France can

pay twice over for her constable. Duguesclin need not be obliged to any one. In this roll are draughts upon the Lombards, Agosti of Bordeaux, and among them, one for eighty thousand florins, payable at sight. Before two hours have elapsed, I will myself count down the requisite sum."

" And, I tell you," said the prince, angrily, "the constable either quits this castle on paying a hundred livres, or he does not leave it at all. If Messire Bertrand feels himself insulted by being my friend, let him say so. But I nevertheless remember, that he one day acknowledged me to be as good a knight as himself."

"Oh, monseigneur!" exclaimed the constable, throwing himself at the Prince of Wales' feet, "I accept your offer with so much gratitude that I will at once borrow the hundred livres from your captains."

Chandos and the other officers hastened to tender him their purses, from which he took the hundred livres, and brought them to the prince, who embraced him, saying, "You are free, Messire Bertrand! Let the gates be opened, and let no one say for the future that the Prince of Wales fears living man!" The dismayed governor gave the order; he had played his game so badly, that instead of losing a single prisoner, he had lost the whole army, and their captain to boot.

Whilst the prince was questioning both the Comte de Laval and his own officers as to the author of this piece of state policy, the unknown approached Duguesclin, and said to him, in a low-voice, "A false generosity was detaining you in prison —a false generosity has released you from it. You are now free; farewell, till we meet again, fourteen days hence, before Toledo." And bowing profoundly to the Prince of Wales, he disappeared, leaving Bertrand in a state of stupefaction.

An hour afterwards. the constable, free and gay, was passing through the town at the head of his Bretons, who rent the air with their acclamations. One person, however, did not join the crowd that followed Duguesclin. This was one of the Prince of Wales' officers—one of the leaders of the Free Companies, who bore the title of captains, and had a voice in the council, although their opinions went for nothing. It was, in a word, an old acquaintance, who having entered the constable's apartment with Chandos, had been struck with the voice of the unknown knight, and had never for a moment lost sight of him. Thus the knight had scarcely disappeared, before he assembled several of his men, made them mount their horses, and dispatched them to discover traces of the fugitive, whilst he himself, after making a few inquiries, took the route to Spain.

CHAPTER LX.
MUSCARON'S POLICY.

MEANWHILE Agenor, spurred on by the inextinguishable anxiety of a lover who has received no tidings of his mistress, hastened with the greatest possible speed towards Don Pedro's dominions. On his way—thanks to the reputation he had acquired by his expedition to France—he rallied round him the Bretons, who, after the ransom being gained, had come in search of, and to fight under, Duguesclin. He also met with a considerable number of Spanish knights bound for the place of rendezvous appointed by Don Henry, who, they said, was about to return to Spain, and enter into a treaty of alliance with the Prince of Wales, who was dissatisfied with Don Pedro. Every time he passed the night at either a town or a village of any importance, Agenor made inquiries concerning Hafiz, Gildaz, and Maria Padilla, asking whether any one had seen either a courier in search of a Frenchman or a young Moorish lady attended by two servants, and proceeding towards the French frontier; and each time an answer in the negative fell upon his ear, the young man struck his spurs more deeply into his horse's flanks. By dint of marching, Agenor gained ground; by dint of inquiries, he gained information. Twenty leagues still lay between him and the court at Burgos. He knew that a fresh army, devoted to their cause and eager for the fray, only awaited the signal to rally together, and oppose to the victor of Navaretto a hydra head more venomous, more dangerous than ever. Agenor asked Muscaron's opinion over and over again as to the prudence of concluding his negotiations with Maria Padilla before continuing his political ones. Muscaron confessed the goodness of the diplomacy, but he suggested that, in taking Don Pedro, Maria, Mothril, and Spain, they would also take Burgos, and with it Aïssa, if she still chanced to be there. This consoled Agenor, and he hastened onwards. Thus, little by little, the circle narrowed around Don Pedro, who,

A A 2

blinded by prosperity, was occupied, through the intrigues of
his favourites, with vain and futile trifles, whilst his crown
was in danger.

Muscaron, the most obstinate of men, especially since he
had felt himself rich, would not allow his master to run the
risk of being made prisoner by proceeding to Burgos in order
to confer with Donna Maria. On the contrary, he managed
to detain him among the Bretons and the partisans of Henry
de Transtamare, so that in a short time the young man found
himself at the head of a large body of troops, as much from
the relief felt from the success of his mission to France as by
his own assiduity. He welcomed all new comers, kept open
house, and corresponded not only with the constable, but with
his brother Oliver, who, at the head of five thousand Bretons,
was preparing to cross the frontier to join the constable, and
assist him in winning his first battle. Muscaron was becoming a tactician : he passed whole days in sketching plans
of battles and calculating the number of crowns Caverley
must have amassed since the last affair, so as, when they
should defeat him, to have the satisfaction of not having
miscalculated his wealth. It was in the midst of all these
warlike preparations, that important tidings reached Agenor.
In spite of all Muscaron's vigilance, an adroit emissary
announced to Agenor the departure of Don Pedro for his
summer palace, and the disappearance of Donna Maria and
Aïssa coincident with the King's journey. The same courier
also knew of Gildaz having died by the way, and of Hafiz
having returned to Donna Maria alone. In order to learn
all this, Agenor had only needed to give thirty crowns to a
countryman, who found out and conversed with Donna
Maria's nurse, the mother of poor Gildaz. Agenor no sooner
knew this than, in spite of Muscaron or his companions in
arms—in spite of everything, he flung himself on the best of
his horses, and spurred forward in the direction of the château
Don Pedro had chosen for his summer residence. Muscaro
grumbled and swore, but nevertheless followed his master.

CHAPTER LXI.

MOTHRIL'S SUCCESS.

IN Don Pedro's château, day, as it broke and lighted up
Donna Maria's apartment, only brought with it a fresh access

of grief and horror. Don Pedro had not retired to rest. Some of the attendants even asserted they had heard him weeping. Mothril had passed the night in a manner more advantageous to his interests—in arranging his plans so as to destroy even the smallest vestige of his crime. Alone with Aïssa, lavishing on her the tenderest cares with all the skill of the most expert physician, he had, from the commencement of the interview with her, moulded like pliant wax the still bewildered mind of the young girl. When Aïssa had cried out on beholding the body of Donna Maria, Mothril had pretended to be struck with involuntary horror, and had flung a mantle over the lifeless remains of the King's mistress. Then, as Aïssa gazed at him in affright, he murmured, " Poor child! render thanks to Allah for having saved you."

" Saved me!" repeated the young girl.

" Yes, dear child, from a frightful death."

" Who, then, stabbed me?"

" She whose hand still grasps your poniard."

" Donna Maria! she, so good, so generous—impossible !"

Mothril smiled compassionately. " The King's mistress good and generous to Aïssa, the object of the King's adoration! You do not believe it, my daughter ?"

" But," said Aïssa, " since she wished to send me away."

" To, as she said, restore you to this Frank chevalier—was it not so?" said the Moor, in the same calm and affectionate tone. Aïssa started up, pale with affright, at thus beholding her secret in the hands of the man most interested in frustrating her hopes. " Fear nothing," continued the Moor; " what Donna Maria was unable to effect on account of the King's love and jealousy, I will myself accomplish. You say you love him, Aïssa. Well, then, I will not only permit it— I will assist you; provided the daughter of my ancient kings is happy, I desire nothing more upon earth."

Aïssa, petrified at hearing Mothril speak thus, could not withdraw her eyes from his face. " He is deceiving me," thought she to herself; then remembering the body of Donna Maria—" Donna Maria is dead," she repeated, in bewilderment.—" And this, my beloved daughter, is the cause of her death. The King loves you passionately, and yesterday confessed it to Donna Maria, who returned hither maddened with rage and jealousy. Don Pedro proposed to unite himself to you by the ties of marriage, which had always been the object

of Donna Maria's ambition. Then she renounced life—
emptied her ring into yonder cup—and determined not to
leave you behind her, triumphant and a queen—to avenge
herself at the same time on Don Pedro and myself, who both
love you so much, though by different titles, she seized your
poniard and stabbed you."

"During my sleep, then," said Aïssa; "for I remember
nothing—a mist swam before my eyes—I heard something
like dull blows and stifled rattlings in the throat. I fancy
that I started from my cushions—that I felt cold hands grasp
mine—and immediately afterwards the gash of the icy steel."

"It was your enemy's last effort; she fell beside you—the
poison proved more powerful for her than the steel for you.
I found in you a spark of life—I fanned it, and had the joy
of saving you."

"Oh, Maria! Maria!" murmured the young girl. "You
were, notwithstanding, very good."

"You say that, my daughter, because she encouraged your
love for Agenor de Mauleon," said Mothril, endeavouring to
conceal his gloomy rage beneath an affectation of benevolence.
"Because she supplied him with the means of gaining access
to you at Soria."—"You know that?"

"I know everything. The King also knows it—Donna
Maria, before attempting to assassinate you, betrayed your
secret to Don Pedro."—"And the King?"

"The King is mad with love for you. It was he who in
the first instance corrupted Hafiz, and made him conduct you
to this château—whilst I remained in total ignorance of it—
and he now only awaits your convalescence to renew his
addresses."

"Then this time I will die," returned Aïssa; "for my hand
will not tremble, or the weapon glance aside, as it did with
Maria Padilla."—"You die!" exclaimed the Moor, falling on
his knees beside her. "You, my idol—my adored child—no;
you shall live, as I before said, happy, and blessing my name."

"I will not live without Agenor!"

"He is of a different religion, my daughter."

"I will embrace his faith."—"He hates me."

"He will pardon you when he finds you no longer interpose between him and his Aïssa. Besides, what does it matter to me? I love and I care for no other object in the world
but him I love."

"Not even him who has just saved your life—saved you for your lover?" said Mothril, humbly, and with an affected sadness that profoundly touched the young girl's heart. "You would sacrifice me, even when I am exposing myself to death for your sake."

"How is that?"—"It is assuredly so, Aïssa. You wish to fly to Don Agenor. I will assist you to do so."

"You!"—"Yes, Aïssa—I, Mothril."

"You are deceiving me!"—"But wherefore?"

"Prove to me your sincerity."—"That is easily done. You fear the King—well, then, I will prevent your beholding him. Will that satisfy you?"

"Not entirely."

"I understand you wish to again see this Frank."

"Above all things!"—"Wait until you are in a fit state to undertake the journey, and I will conduct you to him; I will place my life in his hands."

"But Maria was also conducting me to him."

"Certes, it was to her interest to get rid of you, and she would have preferred being spared an assassination. Before Allah's throne, on the day we appear before his tribunal, murder is a heavy burden." And as Mothril pronounced these terrible words, his pale visage assumed an expression such as we might fancy on the countenances of the damned, doomed to a torture without hope or intermission.

"Well, what will you do then?" demanded Aïssa.

"I will conceal you until you are cured; then, as I just told you, I will re-unite you to the Senor de Mauleon."— "That is all I ask; do that, and I shall regard you as my guardian angel. But the King?"

"Oh, if he were aware of our design, he would oppose it with all his strength. My death would be his best resource, as me dead, you Aïssa would be in his power."

"Or rather, I should be forced to die!"

"Would you rather die than live for the Frank?"

"No—oh! no. Speak, speak!"

"Listen, dear child; if by chance Don Pedro comes to visit you—speaks to you—questions you, concerning this Agenor de Mauleon, you must boldly maintain that Donna Maria lied in affirming that you were beloved by this Frank; and above all, that you returned his love. By acting thus, the King will no longer suspect your lover—he will cease to watch our actions, and leave us free and happy. You must also—and this, dear child, is of more consequence than anything—recall to your recollection, that Donna Maria spoke to you before stabbing you—that she urged you to avow your love to the King—that you refused to do so, and she stabbed you."

"I remember nothing!" exclaimed Aïssa, horror-struck, as every other pure and upright mind would have been at this exposure of the Moor's infernal tactics, "nor do I wish to remember anything. Neither will I deny my love for Agenor de Mauleon—this love is my light and my religion—my guiding star through life! Proud of being beloved by him, I am so far from wishing to conceal it, that I would proclaim it before all the kings of the earth. Do not depend upon me for these falsehoods. If Don Pedro questions me, I shall reply."

Mothril turned pale. This last—this feeble obstacle destroyed the results of a murder. The simple obstinacy of a child fettered the hands and feet of a strong man, who could have moved a world. He perceived he must not insist upon it further. He had nevertheless performed the task of Sysiphus; he had rolled the stone to the top of the mountain, only to behold it roll back again. Mothril had neither time nor fortune to recommence his labours. "My daughter," said he, "you shall act as you please; your happiness, as interpreted by your own heart, your own fancy, is my only law. Reply to the King as you will. I know that your avowal will cause me to lose my head, for I have involuntarily deceived my sovereign."

"Nevertheless I cannot tell a falsehood," returned Aïssa. "But why allow the King to have an opportunity of questioning me? It is easy to avoid him. Cannot you bear me to some lonely spot—in one word, conceal me? Is not my health, my wound, a sufficient pretext? My state itself aids you; but deny Agenor!—tell a falsehood!—no, never!"

Mothril vainly tried to dissemble the joy these words of Aïssa awakened in his soul. To depart with Aïssa; to avoid for a time Don Pedro's questions; to thus allow his anger, hatred, and regret, his remembrance of Maria Padilla to gradually grow weaker; to gain a month, it was to gain everything! This chance of safety Aïssa herself offered, and Mothril seized upon it eagerly.

"You wish us to quit this place, my daughter. Have you

any dislike to the Castle of Montiel, to which I have just been appointed governor?"

"My only dislike is to Don Pedro's presence. I will go where you please." Mothril kissed Aïssa's hands, and the hem of her garments, raised her gently in his arms, and bore her into the neighbouring chamber. He caused the body of Donna Maria to be removed; and summoning two Moorish women, on whose fidelity he could depend, he placed them beside the wounded girl, charging them on their lives not to exchange a word with her. Everything being thus arranged, he composed both his mind and his countenance, and went in quest of Don Pedro.

Don Pedro had just received several letters from the city, announcing that envoys from England and Brittany had made their appearance in the environs; that reports of approaching war were in circulation; that the Prince of Wales was surrounding the new capital with an iron belt, in order to force, by the pressure of an invincible army, his protégé of Navaretto to pay the expenses of the war, and turn his gratitude into coin. This news depressed, but did not dishearten, Don Pedro. He was sending for Mothril at the very moment he entered his chamber.

"Aïssa?" inquired Don Pedro, anxiously.

"My lord, her wound is both deep and dangerous; the victim will not be saved!"

"What! yet another misfortune!" exclaimed the King. "Oh, this is too much to bear! To lose Donna Maria, who so loved me—Aïssa, whom I love to madness; to have to recommence a bloody and implacable war—it is too much, Mothril, for the heart of one man to bear!" And Don Pedro showed his minister the letters sent by the Governor of Burgos, and the neighbouring cities.

"My lord," said Mothril, "you must forget love for the moment, and think only of war."

"The treasury is empty."—"A tax will refill it. Give your consent to the tax I proposed to you."

"It must be so. Can I see Aïssa?"

"Aïssa is like a flower hanging over an abyss; a single breath would cause her destruction."

"Has she spoken?"—"Yes, my lord."

"What did she say?"—"A few words which explained all. It appears that Donna Maria attempted to force her into an avowal which she thought would lower her in your Majesty's esteem. The courageous girl refused; the jealous Donna stabbed her!"

"Aïssa said this?"—"She will repeat it so soon as her strength is restored; but I tremble lest we should never again hear her voice in this world."

"My God!" ejaculated Don Pedro.—"One remedy alone can save her. A tradition of my country promises life to the wounded person who, by the rays of the new moon, applies a certain magical herb to his wound."

"This herb must be procured for her!" exclaimed the King, in a frenzy of superstition and love.

"It is not to be found in this province, sire; I have never seen it anywhere but at Montiel."

"At Montiel! Then send there, Mothril."

"I said, my lord, that the wound must be touched with this magic herb whilst it is still growing. Oh, it is a sovereign remedy! I would convey Aïssa to Montiel, but could she support the journey?"

Don Pedro replied, "She can be borne along as easily as the bird that poises itself upon its two wings. Let her go, Mothril; let her go. But you remain with me."

"But I alone, sire, can repeat the magic formula necessary during the operation."

"Then I shall be left all alone, Mothril."

"Not so, sire; when Aïssa is cured you can come to us at Montiel, and remain there."

"Yes, Mothril, yes; you are right! I will quit her no more; then I shall be happy! And Donna Maria's body, what has been done with it? I trust the greatest honours have been paid it!"

"I have heard it said, my lord," remarked Mothril, "that in your religion the body of a suicide is deprived of the rites of sepulture. The church must therefore be kept in ignorance of the cause of Donna Maria's death."

"All the world must be kept in ignorance of it, Mothril."

"But your attendants, sire?"

"I will announce to the court that Donna Maria is dead of a fever; and when I have said this, no one will dare to raise a dissentient voice."

"Blind fool!" thought Mothril.—"Then, Mothril," resumed Don Pedro, "you will set out at once with Aïssa?"

"This very day, my lord."—"I will superintend Donna Maria's obsequies; I will sign the edict, make an appeal to my army and my nobles. I will exorcise the storm!"

"And I," thought Mothril, "shall be safely sheltered from it."

CHAPTER LXII.

TOO LATE

LEAVING the officers, soldiers, and lovers of war to bewilder themselves with projects, plans, and stratagems, Agenor pursued the object he had in view, which was to find Aïssa, his dearest blessing. Love was beginning to gain the ascendancy over ambition—nay, even duty; since, in his impatience to enter Spain and obtain news of Aïssa, the young many as we have seen, had suffered the envoys of the King of France and Comte de Laval to proceed to Bordeaux, to pay the ransom the constable, in a moment of heroic pride, had himself fixed. Agenor and his faithful Muscaron journeyed rapidly towards the château to which Don Pedro had hoped to entice Aïssa. The young chevalier knew there was no time to be lost; he was too well acquainted with both Don Pedro and Mothril to amuse himself with hopes. "Who knows," thought he, "whether Maria Padilla herself has not, through weakness or fear, persuaded herself that an alliance with the Moor would be preferable to a rupture with Don Pedro, and whether—playing the part of an indulgent spouse—the favourite does not intend shutting her eyes to this caprice of her royal lover." These thoughts made Agenor's impetuous blood boil. He reasoned like a lover—that is to say, clothed all sorts of chimeras with the garb of probability. "When I have had but one hour's conversation with Maria Padilla!" he exclaimed, "I shall know all the present, and what to expect from the future!"

"But, messire, you will learn nothing, and you will finish by falling into the hands of this scoundrel of a Moor, who lies in wait for you as the spider does for the fly."

"You continually repeat the same thing, Muscaron; is a Saracen worth a Christian?"

"A Saracen, when he has any project in his head, is worth three Christians. You might just as well ask whether a woman is as good as a man, when every day we behold men governed and defeated by women; and do you know the reason why, master? Because, when a woman sets her mind upon an object, it is never out of her thoughts; whilst men generally act in a precisely different manner to what they resolve on."

" You conclude, then"—

" That Donna Maria has been prevented from sending you Donna Aïssa by some intrigue of the Saracen's."

" And what then?"—" That Mothril, who has known how to hinder Donna Maria from sending you your mistress, is lying in wait for you; that he will take you in a snare, as they do the larks among the green corn, and kill you, and then you will never obtain Aïssa."

Agenor only replied by an exclamation of rage, and spurred on his horse. He thus reached the château, whose appearance struck him with a sudden sadness. Palaces are eloquent; they speak a language intelligible to souls of a superior cast. By the light of the rising moon Agenor contemplated the edifice containing all his love—all his life. Even whilst he gazed upon it, the frightful assassination—the triumph of Mothril—was taking place within its mysterious walls. Harassed with so much fruitless exertion, Agenor, followed by Muscaron, at last wended his way towards a little village on the opposite side of the mountain. There, as we already know, dwelt several goat-herds; Agenor demanded a night's shelter from them, for which he liberally remunerated them. He succeeded in procuring a slip of parchment and some ink, and made Muscaron write a letter to Donna Maria, full of affectionate regrets and expressions of gratitude, but yet manifesting his doubt and uneasiness, expressed with all the delicacy of a French pen. Agenor, in order to insure the safe delivery of his missive, would willingly have entrusted it to Muscaron, but that worthy represented to his master that, being known to Mothril, he would run a far greater risk than a simple messenger taken from among the mountain shepherds. Agenor listened to reason, and sent the letter by a goat-herd. Then throwing himself on a sheepskin beside Muscaron, he endeavoured to sleep. But the slumbers of lovers are, like those of ambitious persons, madmen, and robbers, easily broken. Two hours after he had retired to rest, Agenor was standing on the brow of the hill, from whence the gates of the château, although at a great distance, were to be plainly distinguished, watching for the returi. of his messenger. This was the contents of his letter :—

"Noble lady, so generous, so devoted to the interests of two poor lovers, I have returned to Spain like a dog dragged back by its chain. I have heard no tidings of either you or Aïssa ; in mercy give me some. I am at the village of Niebra, where your reply will bring me either life or death. What has happened ?—what have I to hope or fear ?"

The messenger did not return. All at once the gates of the château opened, but it was not the goat-herd who appeared. A long file of soldiers, women, and courtiers coming, no one knew from whence, for the King had brought with him but few companions to this summer palace—in short, a long procession issued from them, following a litter containing a dead body. This was indicated by the mourning draperies with which it was hung. Agenor thought to himself this was a bad omen ; but as the thought passed through his mind, the gates were closed.

"This delay is very strange," he remarked to Muscaron, who shook his head in token of dissatisfaction.

"Go and make inquiries," added Mauleon ; and he seated himself on the side of a hillock among the dusty broom.

A quarter of an hour had scarcely elapsed before Muscaron returned, bringing with him a soldier, whom he seemed to have some difficulty in inducing to approach.

"I tell you," he was exclaiming, "that it is my master who will pay you, and that liberally."

"Pay for what ?" said Agenor.—"The news, my lord."

"What news ?"—"My lord, this soldier formed one of the escort conducting the corpse to Burgos."

"For God's sake ! what corpse ?"

"Ah, my dear master, you would not believe it from any one but me. The body now on its way to Burgos is that of Maria de Padilla."

Agenor uttered a cry of doubt and despair.

"It is true," said the soldier ; "and I must hasten to resume my place in the ranks of the escort."

"Woe ! woe !" exclaimed Agenor ; "but Mothril is at the château ?"

"Ah, my lord," returned the soldier, "Mothril has just set out for Montiel."—"He has gone with his litter ?"

"In which is the young girl, who is dying ?"—"Yes, senor."

" The young girl, Aïssa, dying! Ah, Muscaron, it has killed me!" sighed the unfortunate chevalier, falling to the earth as if really dead, greatly to the terror of the squire, who was little accustomed to see his master swoon.

"This is all I know about the matter, senor; and even this I learnt by chance. 'Twas I who, that night, raised the bodies of the young girl, stabbed with a poniard, and Donna Maria, who was poisoned."

"Oh, accursed night! oh, woe, woe!" exclaimed the half-maddened young man. "Here, my friend, take these ten florins, although you have just announced to me the bitterest misfortune of my life."

"Thanks, senor, and adieu," returned the soldier, hastening away at a rapid pace through the heath.

Muscaron shading his eyes with his hand, interrogated the horizon. "See, see! there, a long way off!" he exclaimed. "My dear lord, do you see those men—that litter crossing the plain? Do you see our enemy, the Saracen, on horseback in his white mantle?"

"Muscaron, Muscaron!" said the chevalier, rousing himself from his grief, " let us to horse—let us crush this miscreant; and if Aïssa must die, let me at least receive her last sigh."

Muscaron ventured to lay his hand on his master's shoulder. "My lord," said he, "we never reason justly on a too recent event. We are two, and they are twelve—we are weary, and they are fresh. Besides, we know they are bound for Montiel; we will rejoin them there. You see, my dear master, we must first of all get to the bottom of this story, which the soldier was unable to fully relate to you. It is necessary to know the reason of Donna Maria having died by poison, and Donna Aïssa being wounded by the stroke of a poniard."

"You are right, my faithful friend," said Agenor. "Do with me as you will."—"I will make you a happy and triumphant man, my master."

Agenor despondingly shook his head. Muscaron knew that the only cure for his malady lay in great excitement of both soul and body. He returned with his master to the camp, where the Bretons and the Spaniards faithful to Henry de Transtamare had already begun to conceal themselves less, and to more openly avow their plans, since the vague rumours had reached them of Duguesclin's liberation, and, above all, since they beheld their numbers daily increase.

CHAPTER LXIII.

THE PILGRIMS.

AT a few leagues' distance from Toledo, Agenor and his faithful Muscaron journeyed sadly along a sandy road, bordered by a wood of stunted pines, seeking a venta where they could repose their weary limbs, and cook a hare which Muscaron had shot on her form. All at once, they heard behind them the sound of rapid steps; it was the gallop of a fleet mule, bearing upon its sturdy back a pilgrim, whose head was covered with a broad-brimmed hat, and his face effectually concealed by a kind of veil attached to it. This pilgrim was spurring his mule and managing her like a man well versed in equestrian exercises. The animal, which was of the purest breed, flew rather than galloped, and was so quickly out of sight that they could not distinguish the traveller's voice, as he saluted them in passing with "Baya uste des con Dios," "God be with you." Ten minutes were scarcely elapsed, before Muscaron again heard a similar noise. He turned his head, and had scarcely time to draw his own and his master's horse on one side, before four horsemen came dashing along with the speed of lightning. The foremost of them wore a costume like that of the first pilgrim whom our travellers had just seen pass by. Only beneath this habit the prudent pilgrim concealed a suit of armour, the visor of which was drawn over his face, and, despite the darkness, this knightly visage presented a strange appearance peeping beneath the wide-brimmed hat of a palmer. The stranger immediately scented our travellers, as a bloodhound might have done; but Agenor had prudently lowered the visor of his helmet, and laid his hand upon the hilt of his sword. Muscaron also placed himself on the defensive.

"Senor," said a hollow voice, which seemed to issue from the bottom of a gulf, in bad Spanish; "have you not seen a companion of mine, a pilgrim like myself, mounted on a mule, swift as the wind?"

The sound of this voice disagreeably affected Agenor with a sort of confused remembrance, but his duty was to reply, and he did so courteously. "Senor pilgrim, or senor chevalier," replied he, also in Spanish, "the person of whom you speak passed by us nearly ten minutes ago, and he was indeed mounted on so swift a mule that few horses in the world could overtake her."

Muscaron fancied that Agenor's voice struck the pilgrim with surprise, for he came forward and said boldly, "This information is more valuable than you think, chevalier. It is, besides, given with so good a grace, that I should be charmed to make the acquaintance of the person who gives it me. I can tell from your foreign accent that we are both from the north, which is another reason for our becoming more intimate. Therefore, prithee, raise your visor, and let me have the honour of thanking you to your face."

"Uncover your own, then, sir pilgrim," replied Mauleon, whom this voice affected more and more disagreeably. The pilgrim hesitated, and ended by refusing in a manner that plainly showed how perfidious and interested his request had been. Without adding another word, he gave a signal to his companions, and followed at full gallop the route taken by the first pilgrim.

"Here is an impudent fellow!" observed Muscaron, when he was out of sight.—"And with a villanous voice, Muscaron, which it seems to me I have heard before in some evil moment or another."

"I think like you, my lord; and if our horses were not so fatigued, we should do well to hasten after these fellows. Something strange is about to take place."

"What does that matter to us, Muscaron?" said Mauleon, in the tone of a man who no longer takes an interest in anything. "We are going to Toledo, where our friends are to re-assemble. Toledo is near Montiel—that is all I either know or wish to know."

"At Toledo we shall receive news of the constable," said Muscaron.—"Probably also of Henry de Transtamare," said Agenor. "We shall receive orders, become machines—automatons—the only resource, the only consolation possible for those who, having lost their souls, no longer know what to do or what to say."

"There, there!" said Muscaron; "there is always time enough to despair. 'On the last day comes victory,' as a proverb of my country says."

"Or *death*. Is not that what you feared to add?"

"Well, my lord, one can but die once."

"Do you fancy I fear death?"—"Oh, my lord, you do not fear it enough: it is that grieves me."

Conversing thus, they reached the longed-for venta. It

was an isolated building, as are in Spain all these providential refuges for the weary traveller from the burning heat of the day and the cold of night—refuges as ardently desired and often as impossible to gain as the oasis of the desert, since, when quitting one, the traveller might perish of hunger, thirst, and fatigue, before he reached another. When Agenor and Muscaron had placed their horses in the stable, or rather when the worthy squire had performed this task alone, Agenor perceived in the low hall of the venta, seated before a bright fire and surrounded by groups of muleteers buried in profound slumbers, the two pilgrims, who, instead of conversing, were mutually turning their backs upon each other. " Ah ! I thought they were companions," observed Agenor, in surprise.

The pilgrim with the veil buried his face still more beneath its shade when the two travellers entered. As for the pilgrim with the visor, he seemed to watch with indescribable curiosity for the moment a corner of his pretended companion's veil should be lifted. This moment did not arrive. Mute, motionless, and evidently annoyed, the mysterious palmer, to avoid replying to his importunate questions and solicitations, ended by feigning a profound slumber. One by one the muleteers returned to the courtyard, and, wrapped in their cloaks, slumbered beside their mules. No one remained beside the fire but Mauleon, who had just finished supping with his squire, and the two pilgrims—the one still occupied in watching the pretended slumbers of the other. The one with the visor attempted to engage Agenor in conversation, by making several idle excuses for the manner in which he had quitted him on the road. He then inquired whether he did not soon intend retiring to his chamber, where he would doubtless sleep better than on the bench where he sat. Agenor, who still kept his visor down, was about to persist in remaining where he was, were it only to annoy the stranger, when it occurred to him that by so doing, he would learn nothing. It was evident to him that the other pilgrim was not asleep; something was therefore about to take place between these two men, who each desired to remain alone.

Agenor lived at a period and in a country where the indulgence of curiosity was often the means of saving the life of the curious person. He feigned, in his turn, to retire to the chamber pointed out to him by the host, but in reality he

B B

placed himself behind the door, which, although massive and
solid, was so badly joined, that through the chinks he could
plainly perceive the hearth. He was right, for a spectacle
well worthy of attention was reserved for him. The pilgrim
with the visor no sooner found himself alone with his apparently sleeping companion, than he arose from his seat, and
moved about the hall, as if to test the depths of his slumbers.
The sleeping pilgrim did not stir. The man with the visor
then approached on tip-toe, and stretched out his hand to lift
the veil concealing his features. But before he had touched
it the sleeper was upon his feet.

"What do you want?" demanded he, angrily; "and why
have you thus disturbed my slumbers?"

"Which, however, were not very deep, sir pilgrim with
the veil," said the other, in a tone of raillery.

"But which, nevertheless, ought to have been respected,
messire of the iron visage."—"You have doubtless some good
motive for wishing no one to be aware whether yours is flesh
or iron, sir pilgrim."

"My motive concerns no one; and if I wear a veil, it is
clear that I do not wish my face to be seen."

"Senor, I am very curious, and I am resolved to see your
face!" said the man with the visor, still in a tone of raillery.
The pilgrim immediately drew a long poniard from beneath
his robe.

"You shall first see this," said he.

The man with the visor thought for a moment, and then
hastened to shoot the heavy bolts of the door behind which
Agenor was watching and listening. At the same time he
opened a casement overlooking the road, and admitted four
men armed and cased in iron.

"You see," said he to the pilgrim, "resistance would be
useless—nay, even impossible, my lord. Therefore, in order
to spare a life which I believe to be very precious, deign to
reply to the following questions. The pilgrim, still grasping
his dagger, trembled with rage and uneasiness. "Are you,
or are you not, Don Henry de Transtamare?" The pilgrim
started.

"To a question like that, put in such a form and with such
preliminaries, I could not reply, if I am the person you
mention, without expecting death. I shall therefore sell my
life dearly, for I am really the prince whose name you have

pronounced." And with a majestic gesture, he uncovered his noble countenance.

"The prince!" exclaimed Mauleon from behind the door, which he endeavoured to force open.

"Himself!" cried the man with the visor, with savage joy. "I was sure of it; we have been long enough following him, comrades. It is some distance from Bordeaux. Oh, put up your dagger, my prince—I have no thoughts of killing you, but only of putting you up to ransom. Body of saints! I will be accommodating. Put up your dagger, put it up." Agenor, redoubled his blows upon the door, but the sturdy oak resisted all his efforts. "Stand beside yonder door, in readiness to secure that one, and leave me to persuade the prince," said the man with the visor to his armed companions.

"Brigand!" said Henry, contemptuously; "you wish to give me up to my brother."

"Yes; if he will pay me better than yourself."

"I was right in saying it would be better to perish here," exclaimed the prince. "Help! help!"

"Ah, my lord," said the bandit, "then you will oblige us to slay you. Your head will perhaps fetch less than your living and entire body; but we must be content with it, and we will carry your head to Don Pedro."

"We shall see that!" exclaimed Agenor, who, by almost superhuman efforts, had succeeded in forcing the door, and now fiercely attacked the brigand's four companions.

"The end of this will be that we shall be obliged to kill him at once!" said the man with the visor, drawing his sword to attack the prince. "My lord, you have there a very awkward friend: order him to remain quiet." But he had not ceased speaking before another pilgrim entered, whom, certes, they did not expect.

The new comer wore neither mask nor veil: he considered himself sufficiently disguised by his pilgrim's habit. His broad shoulders and enormous arms, his square and intelligent head, announced a vigorous and intrepid champion. He paused upon the threshold, and contemplated in astonishment, but without either fear or anger, this uproar in the hall of the hostelry.

"What, then, is fighting going on!" he exclaimed. "Hold, Christians! who are right and who are wrong?" And his deep and imperious voice rose above the tumult, as the voice

of the lion rises above the tempests in the gorges of Atlas.
The simple sound of this voice produced a singular effect on
the combatants.   The prince uttered an exclamation of surprise and joy; the man in the visor recoiled in affright, and
Muscaron cried out, " On my life, it is the constable !"

"Constable! constable!" exclaimed the prince; "here, they
wish to murder me !"—"You, my prince !" roared Duguesclin,
tearing off his pilgrim's robe to be more at liberty.   "And
pray, who wish to do that ?"

"Friends," said the brigand to his acolytes, "we must
either slay these two men, or die here ourselves.   We are
armed, they are not—the devil delivers them up to us.   Instead of a hundred thousand florins, double the sum now
awaits us—forward !"

The constable, with incomparable *sangfroid*, stretched forth
his hand, and seizing the speaker by the throat before he
had time to finish his speech, as easily as if he had been a
sheep, flung him rudely on the tiled floor at his feet.   Then
snatching away his sword, " Here am I, armed," said he.
" Three against three,—come on, my gentlemen of the road."

"We are lost !" muttered the bandit's companions, as they
fled through the still open casement.

Meanwhile Agenor had flung himself upon his knees beside
the fallen brigand, and unfastening his visor, exclaimed,—
" Caverley ! I guessed it !"

"It is a venomous reptile that must now be crushed," remarked the constable.—"I will undertake the task!" said
Muscaron, preparing to cut his throat with the knife he
carried in his belt.

" Mercy !" murmured the robber, " Mercy !   Do not abuse
your victory."—" Yes," said the prince, embracing Duguesclin
in a transport of joy.   " Yes, mercy.   We owe too deep a
debt of gratitude to God for having re-united us, to occupy
ourselves with this miserable wretch.   Let him live to be
hanged elsewhere."

Caverley, in the effusion of his gratitude, kissed the feet
of the generous prince.

"Then let him go," said Duguesclin.—"Go, bandit !"
muttered Muscaron, unwillingly opening the door.

Caverley did not need a second bidding; he ran so swiftly
that not even their horses would have been able to overtake
him in case the prince had changed his mind.   After having

indulged in a few mutual congratulations, the prince, the constable and Agenor, began to converse together on the subject of the approaching war.

"You see, sire," said the constable, "I was punctual to the appointment. I was on my way to Toledo, as you desired me at Bordeaux. Then you reckon upon Toledo."

"I have great hopes that Toledo will open her gates to me."

"But that is not certain," said the constable. "Since I have journeyed beneath this disguise—that is to say, during the last four days, I have learnt more than I should otherwise have done in two years. These Toledans lean to Don Pedro. There will be a siege to make."

"Dear constable! to how many dangers you have exposed yourself for me!"

"Dear sire, I had my word to keep. I promised that you should either reign in Castile, or I die. Besides, I have a revenge to take. Thus you had no sooner liberated me by your presence of mind at Bordeaux, than I hastened to King Charles, and within ten days regained the frontier. During the last eight, I have been following on your traces through Spain, since my brother Oliver and 'Le Bègue de Vilaine' had received information that you had passed through Burgos and were proceeding towards Toledo."

"That is true; I have passed through it. I expect to meet beneath the walls of Toledo all the officers of my army. I only assumed this disguise at Burgos."

"They assumed the same, monseigneur, and that gave me the idea. By this means the leaders went forward unnoticed, to prepare their soldiers' quarters. A pilgrim's habit is the fashion now-a-days—every one in Spain wished to make a pilgrimage—so much so, that this scoundrel Caverley has borrowed the dress as well as ourselves. But here we are, re-united. You will choose your quarters, and summon to you all the Spaniards of your party—I, the knights and soldiers of every land and nation. There is no time to be lost. Don Pedro is yet afloat—he has just lost his best adviser, Donna Maria, the only creature in the world who loved him. Let us profit by the stupor into which this has plunged him, and give him battle before he has time to recover himself."

"Donna Maria dead!" said Henry. "Are you certain of it?"

"I am sure of it," said Agenor, sadly. "For her corpse passed by me."—"And Don Pedro, what is he doing?"

"No one knows. He has caused the poor woman, his victim, to be interred at Burgos, and has since disappeared." —"Disappeared!—is it possible? But you say Donna Maria was his victim, constable: relate the story to me, for during the last eight days I have not dared to speak to a living soul."

"This is what my spies inform me has taken place. Don Pedro loved a Moorish girl, daughter to that accursed Mothril. Donna Maria suspected it—she even discovered that a secret understanding existed between them. Transported with rage, she took poison, after having first stabbed her rival to the heart."

"Oh, my lords!" exclaimed Agenor, "it is impossible! At so odious a crime, so black a treason, the very sun would have grown dark with horror!" Both the King and Duguesclin gazed in astonishment at the young man as he thus expressed himself; but they could extort from him no explanation of his vehemence. "Pardon me, monseigneur," said Agenor, humbly, "I have a young man's secret—a sweet and bitter secret, one half of which Donna Maria has carried with her to the grave, and the other half I will religiously keep."

"In love," said the constable; "poor boy!"

Agenor's only reply was, "I am at your command, sire, and ready to die in your service."

"I know," said Henry, "that you are a devoted friend—a loyal and indefatigable servant; therefore, depend upon my gratitude. But tell us; you know something touching these love affairs of Don Pedro?"

"I know everything, my liege, and if you command me to speak——"—"Where can Don Pedro be at this moment? —that is all we wish to know."

"Messeigneurs," said Agenor, "deign to grant me eight days, and I will tell you for a certainty."

"Eight days," repeated the King. "What do you think about it, constable?"

"I think, sire," replied the constable, "that these eight days are necessary for us to organize our army, and await reinforcements and money from France. We run absolutely no risk."

"And better still, my lord," added Mauleon; "if my project

succeeds, you will have in your power the true cause of the war, the veritable firebrand, Don Pedro, whom I will joyfully give up to you."

"He is right," said the King. "With the capture of one of us ends the war with Spain."

"Oh, not so, sire," exclaimed the constable. "I swear to you, that if you are ever made prisoner—which with God's help will never be—I will pursue the punishment of this miscreant Don Pedro, who slaughters his prisoners in cold blood and allies himself with infidels."

"I believe it, Bertrand," said the King; "but do not trouble yourself about me. If I am captured or killed, regain my body by a victory, and place it, inanimate as it is, upon the throne of Castile; provided that assassin—that traitor be lying at the foot of the throne, I shall declare myself happy and triumphant."

"Sire, it is said," replied the constable. "Now let us grant this young man his liberty."

"And a rendezvous before Toledo, which we shall invest?" said Mauleon.

"In eight days."—"In eight days."

Henry tenderly embraced the young man, who was quite overcome by such an honour.

"Let me do so," said the King. "I wish to show you that after having shared my evil fortunes, you will have a right to also share the good."

"And I," added the constable, "who in part owe to him the liberty I now enjoy, I promise to aid him with all my strength whenever he shall claim my assistance; for whatever purpose it may be, in whatever place, and against whatever person."

"Oh, my lords! my lords!" exclaimed Mauleon, "you overpower me with joy and pride. Two powerful princes to treat me thus! You open the gates of heaven to me!"

"And you are worthy of it, Mauleon," said the constable.— "No, my lord, no."

"Are you in want of money?"—"Oh no, my lord."

"The plan you meditate will put you to expense."

"My lord," said Mauleon, "do not you remember that I once gained possession of that brigand of a Caverley's strong box. It contained a king's fortune—it was too much and I lost it without regret. Since then I have received a hundred livres from the King of France—all the treasure I need, for it suffices for my wants."

"Oh, that was well said," murmured Muscaron from his corner, with tears in his eyes.

The King overheard him.

"That is your squire?" said he.

"A brave and faithful servant, who, after having more than once saved my life, now renders it supportable."

"He, too, shall be rewarded. Here, squire," continued the King, detaching from his robe one of the scallop shells embroidered on the stuff, "and the day on which you stand in need of anything—you or yours, in whatever generation it may be—this shell put into the hands of myself, or one of my descendants, will be worth a fortune to you. Go, good squire, go!"

Muscaron fell on his knees, his heart swelling, as though it would burst through his breast.

"Now, sire," said the constable, "let us profit by the darkness to reach the spot where your officers are awaiting you. We did wrong in letting Caverley go; he is capable of returning and falling upon us with triple forces, so as effectually to capture us—were it only to show his spirit."

"To horse, then," said the King. They resumed their arms, and confiding in their strength and courage, gained a wood where it would have been difficult to attack, and impossible to follow them.

Agenor then dismounted, and took leave of his two powerful protectors, who wished him success and a safe journey. Muscaron awaited his orders, to know towards which of the four cardinal points he was to turn the horses' heads.

"Where are we going?" asked he.

"To Montiel; my hatred tells me that sooner or later we shall there find Don Pedro."

"In fact," observed Muscaron, "jealousy is good for something, since it makes things visible which do not exist. Let us go to Montiel."

CHAPTER LXIV.

THE CAVERN OF MONTIEL.

By dint of hard travelling, Agenor in two days' time reached the end of his journey. Assisted by Muscaron, he arrived so stealthily at Montiel, that not a creature was aware of his presence there. Only through taking all these precautions, they had deprived themselves of the advantage of gaining information. Those who do not ask cannot learn. When Muscaron beheld Montiel seated like a granite giant upon a rocky pedestal—lifting its head towards heaven, whilst its feet seemed to bathe in the Tagus—when he had regarded by the bright moonlight the spiral turns of a path bristling with brambles and briars, the slope forming sharp angles, so that no traveller could see more than twenty paces before him whilst from the heights above the sentinels could behold every one making the ascent, he observed to his master—

" This is a true vulture's nest, my dear master, and if the dove is imprisoned here, we shall never be able to take her from it. In fact, Montiel is a place impregnable to all but famine, and two men cannot invest a fortress."

" What we require to know is this," said Agenor, "whether Mothril inhabits this retreat with Aïssa, Aïssa's position in the midst of our enemies, and, in one word, Don Pedro's conduct throughout the whole affair."

" All this we shall learn with patience," returned Muscaron, "only we have only four days to be patient in—remember that, my lord."

" I shall remain here until I have either seen Aïssa herself, or some one who can give me tidings of her."

"I fancy it will prove a wild-goose chase; besides, consider, master, whilst we are prowling about the castle, Mothril, Hafiz, or some one else, may let fly at us from above or below an arrow or a bolt that will pin us like frogs to the wall. The position is well chosen. See!"—" You are right."

" We must, therefore, make use of means more ingenious than mere ordinary ones. As to Donna Aïssa being here, I firmly believe it. I have even little doubt that she is confined here by Mothril himself. As to Don Pedro being here, I think we shall discover that by waiting a couple of days."— " And why?"

" Because the castle is small, and cannot contain a large garrison, therefore, is not well provisioned; and to obtain the fresh supplies necessary to entertain so great a King, they will be obliged to frequently quit it."

" But meanwhile where shall we find a shelter?"

" We have not far to go. I can see from here what will just suit us."—" Yonder cavern?"

" Is a fissure in the rock, from whence a spring takes its source. It is damp, but retired. No one goes near it, except to drink or fetch water. We shall be concealed in its recesses, and will seize upon the first who comes, and force him, either by menaces or promises, to speak."

" You are a brave and judicious companion, my Muscaron."

" Oh, trust me, Don Pedro has not many such advisers as I am. Do you agree to the cavern?"

" You forget two things; our food, with which the cavern cannot furnish us, and our horses, which cannot find shelter in it."

" True; one cannot think of everything at once. I have found the beginning, you find the end."

" We will kill our horses, and throw them into the Tagus which flows below."

" Yes; but what shall we do for provisions?"

" We will let the person, sent from the castle for provisions pass quietly by, and when he returns with them, attack him, and possess ourselves of them."

" Admirable!" said Muscaron; " only those in the castle, finding their purveyor does not return, will begin to suspect something."—" What does that signify, if we obtain the information we require."

It was decided that these two plans should be followed. But as Agenor was about to fell his horse with his mace his heart failed him.

" Poor beast!" said he, " who has served me so well!"

" And," added Muscaron, " who may serve you better still, in case you carry off Donna Aïssa from here."

" You speak prophetically; I will not kill my poor horse. Go, Muscaron, unsaddle him, and hide his harness and equipments in the grotto. The animal can wander about without being remarked, and more industrious than a man, will be able to provide for himself. The worst that can happen to either him or us is, that they may observe him, and take him to the castle. Besides, we shall be here all the same to defend him."—" Yes, messire."

Muscaron unharnessed the horse, and concealed his equipments in the depths of the little cave, whose floor was composed of a mass of damp clay, over which, Muscaron, to render it more healthy, spread a coating of sand, brought in his mantle from the brink of the Tagus, and dry heath. The remainder of the night was occupied by these labours. Daybreak found our two adventurers in the recesses of their solitary asylum. A singular phenomenon attracted their attention. By means of this spiral path, which mounted from the foot of the hill to the summit of the castle, they were able to distinguish the voice of those standing on the ramparts. The voice instead of simply mounting, was driven back, and echoed along this funnel until the sound burst forth like a torrent of water. The result was that Agenor from the depths of his cave was able to overhear the conversation of those three hundred feet above his head. The first fortification was situated above the fountain; so far every one had free passage, but the country was so desert, and in such a state of devastation, that few besides the inhabitants of the castle ever ventured to tread this maze. Agenor and Muscaron passed the first half of their day sadly enough. They drank water, for they were parched with thirst, but they were unable to satisfy their hunger. Towards the close of the day two Moors descended from the castle, leading an ass to carry the provisions they counted on obtaining at a neighbouring town a league's distance. At the same time four slaves came from the town bearing jars, which they proceeded to fill at the fountain. The Moors from the castle entered into conversation with the slaves, but in so barbarous a dialect that our two adventurers were unable to understand a word of what was said. The Moors accompanied the slaves back to the town, and returned two hours afterwards. Hunger is a bad counsellor. Muscaron wished to mercilessly slay the poor devils, fling their bodies into the Tagus, and then profit by their provisions.

"That would be a cowardly murder," said Mauleon, "and would injure our cause in the eyes of God. Another stratagem, Muscaron; see how dark the night is, and how narrow the path. The ass, laden with its panniers, will have great difficulty in passing along the pathway over the rocks. We have only to push against it, and it will roll to the foot of the hill. Then during the night we will pick up the scattered provisions."

"This is all very true, and like a good Christian, master; but I was too hungry to think of being merciful."

They did as Agenor said. The four hands of the two adventurers gave so rude a push to the small ass as it brushed against the rock that it lost its footing, and fell down the steep slope. The Moors uttered angry cries, and beat the poor animal to make it get up, but do what they would they could not replenish the empty panniers. They therefore returned, the one lamenting to the castle, the other to the town with the wounded ass. Our two hungry friends plunged boldly among the rocks and thickets, and picked up the bread, dried grapes, and leathern bottles of wine with which the ass had been laden. They had obtained at one stroke sufficient provisions to last for eight days. This copious repast restored them to strength and courage, and indeed they stood in need of it.

During the space of two whole days our vigilant sentinels neither saw nor heard anything, except the voice of Hafiz, as he paced to and fro the ramparts, deploring his servitude, Mothril giving his orders, and the soldiers going through their exercises. Nothing announced the King's presence at Montiel. Muscaron had the courage to emerge at night from his retreat, and make inquiries in the neighbouring town, but no one could give him the slightest information. Agenor did the same, but without receiving a single satisfactory reply. When we begin to despair, the time passes with redoubled quickness. The position of our two spies was a critical one. By day they dared not show themselves; at night they feared to quit their post, for fear some one should enter the castle in their absence, and that one be the King. But when two days and a half had passed, Agenor was the first to be discouraged. On the evening of the second day Mauleon returned from the neighbouring town, where he had emptied his purse without learning anything. He found Muscaron in the cavern plucking out his thin locks by handfuls in his despair. On questioning the honest fellow, he learnt from him that, wearied with remaining alone in the grotto, he had fallen asleep, and that during his slumber some horseman had ridden up to the castle without his perceiving him. He only heard the tramp of the horse or mule.

"Must we always be unfortunate!" exclaimed the squire.

"Do not distress yourself, this could not have been the King; the townfolks know him to be at Toledo. Besides, the King would not journey alone, and the noise made by his suite would have awakened you. No, it was not the King; he will not come to Montiel. Instead of wasting our time here, let us proceed straight to Toledo."

"You are right, master. All we should gain by remaining here would, perhaps, be, to hear Donna Aïssa's voice. It is a very sweet one, but, as we say in Bearn, ' The bird's song is not the bird itself.' "

"Let us at once put our plan into execution, Muscaron. Gather together our horses' harness; let us quit this place and proceed on our journey."

"I shall not be long about it, sir chevalier; you can scarcely believe how weary I am of this cave."

"Come, then," said Agenor. But at the moment he was about to rise from the ground, Muscaron checked him.

"Hush!" whispered he.—"What is it?"

"Be silent, master! I hear footsteps." And so great was his uneasiness that he presumed to pull his master back by the wrist.

Agenor returned to the cavern. They distinctly heard hurried footsteps on the path leading to the castle. The night was dark, and the two Franks were concealed in the depths of the cavern. Three men soon became visible; they were stealing along bent almost double, to prevent being seen from the fortress. They paused within a few paces of the spring. They wore the garb of peasants, but were all well armed with axes and knives.

"He has certainly gone this way," said one of them; "here are the prints of his horse's hoofs on the sand."—"Then we have missed him," said another, with a sigh. "The devil! how unfortunate we have been lately!"

"You hunt too large game," rejoined the first speaker.— "Lesby, you are a fool, and the captain will tell you the same."

"But——' "Silence! a large quarry once killed feeds the hunter for a fortnight; whilst a hare and ten larks make at most a sorry meal."

"Yes; but one snares the hare or the larks more easily than the stag or the wild boar."

"The fact is, he escaped us finely the other day; did he not, captain?" The one addressed as captain heaved a deep sigh; this was his only reply. "And, then," continued the obstinate Lesby, "why change every instant your track and your prey? Why not stick to one and take him?"

"Did you take the one you had followed from Bordeaux, at the venta, the other night?"

"Hem!" exclaimed Muscaron in his master's ear.

"Hush!" said Mauleon, listening with his ear to the ground. The man whom his companions had styled captain drew himself up and said, in an imperious voice,—"Be silent, both of you. Do not comment upon my orders. What have I promised you?"

"Ten thousand florins each."

"Provided you get them, what more do you require?"— "Nothing, captain, nothing."

"Don Henry is worth one hundred thousand florins to Don Pedro; Don Pedro is worth the same to Don Henry. I fancied I should be able to take the one, but I was mistaken; I was near, as you were witness, leaving my skin in the lion's den. Well, since the lion spared my life, I ought in gratitude to capture his enemy. I will capture him. I will not, it is true, give him up to Henry de Transtamare for nothing, but I will sell him to him; it is all one so long as he gets him in his power. In this way we shall both be content." His two companions replied by a growl of satisfaction.

"God forgive me!" whispered Muscaron in his master's ear, "if it is not that Caverley at our finger ends!"—"Silence!" said Mauleon.

Caverley (for it was really he) thus finished his profession of faith:—"Don Pedro has quitted Toledo; he is in this castle. He is very brave, and from prudence has journeyed alone, as a solitary traveller seldom attracts notice."

"No," said Lesby, "but he is taken prisoner."

"By our Lady!" said Caverley, "one cannot foresee everything. Now to conclude our plan. You, Lesby, rejoin Phillips who is holding the horses. The King will not remain in the castle later than to-morrow; for, as we know, he is expected at Toledo."—"And what then?"

"I and Becker will keep watch against he passes; but we must be on our guard against one thing."

"What is that?"—"That he has not given orders to his guards to precede him; we ought to manage our affairs on the spot. You, Lesby, are a good sportsman—find us some hiding-place among these rocks, where we may conceal ourselves."

"Captain, I hear the gurgling of water—it must be a spring.

Springs generally hollow out for themselves some bed in the rocks. We ought to find a grotto somewhere about here."

"We are lost! they are coming in here!" exclaimed Muscaron; but Agenor placed his hand over his mouth like a gag.

"See," cried Lesby, "the grotto is yonder."

"Very well," said Caverley. "Go, Lesby, and join Philips, and let the horses be ready by daybreak."

Lesby left them; Caverley and Becker remained alone.

"See what a thing it is to have wit!" said the bandit to his companion. "I am a sort of land pirate, and am the only man who understands the real state of affairs. Two men are disputing the possession of a throne; if one be removed, the war is finished. Thus, by acting as I do, I act the part of a Christian and a philosopher—I spare men's blood. I am a virtuous man, Becker! I am a virtuous man!" And the bandit indulged in a fit of stifled laughter.

"Come," said he, at length, "let us creep into the hole—now to watch for our game!

CHAPTER LXV.
CAVERLEY'S CAPTURE.

THE arrangement of the grotto was as follows:—First came the spring, whose crystal waters, falling from a rocky arch, had hollowed out a bed for itself in the flinty soil beneath. Further back was a winding grotto, approached by two natural steps. This cavern was dark during the day; at night only a fox could have discovered it. Caverley avoided the perpendicular waterfall, and mounted the two steps, feeling his way as he went into the inner cavern. Becker, more courageous, or more a friend to comfort, had already penetrated further into its recesses in search of shelter and warmth. Agenor and Muscaron felt, heard, and almost saw them. Becker ended by seating himself and inviting Caverley to follow his example, by saying to him, "Come, captain, there is room for us both."

Caverley suffered himself to be persuaded, and entered the cavern; but as he found some difficulty in finding his way, he repeated in an ill-humoured tone,—"Room for both! it is easy to say that!" and stretched out his hands to avoid striking himself against the rocky walls or sides of the cavern.

In doing this, he unfortunately encountered Muscaron's leg, and seizing hold of it, cried out,—"A dead body, Becker! a dead body!"

"No, pardieu!" exclaimed the valiant Muscaron, seizing him by the throat; "it is a living man, who is going to strangle you, my fine fellow!"

Caverley measured his length upon the ground unable to utter a word, whilst Muscaron held his wrists, and secured them with the bridle of one of the horses. Agenor had only to stretch out his hand to do the same to Becker, who was half dead with superstitious terror.

"Now, my dear captain," said Muscaron, "we are going to talk about ransom. Pay attention, for there is a good number of us; and the least movement, the slightest cry, would draw upon you an infinite number of poniard strokes in your body."

"I will neither move nor speak," murmured Caverley; "only spare me."

"We must first take all necessary precautions," continued Muscaron, despoiling Caverley piece by piece of his armour, both offensive and defensive, with the dexterity of an ape peeling a nut. This task being terminated, he proceeded to do the same to Becker. Their weapons being removed, Muscaron prepared to examine their pouches. His fingers alone displayed any delicacy in this operation; his conscience did not experience the least scruple. Two well-lined belts and bulky purses passed into Muscaron's possession.

"What, are you also a plunderer?" said Agenor.—"Messire, I am only depriving them of the means of doing evil."

The first moment of terror being over, Caverley asked permission to offer a few observations.

"You may do so," said Agenor, "provided you speak in a low voice."—"Who are you?" inquired the robber.

"Ah, my dear fellow, that is a question we shall not answer," replied Muscaron.

"You have overheard my conversation with my men?"

"Without losing a single word of it."

"The devil! Then you know my plans?"

"As well as yourself."—"Well, what do you mean to do with me and my companion?"

"That is simple enough: we are in Don Pedro's service, and shall deliver you up to him, at the same time relating all we know of your intentions with regard to him."

"That is not Christian," remonstrated Caverley, who turned
pale amid the darkness.   "Don Pedro is cruel: he will make
me suffer a thousand tortures.   Rather than that, strike me
at once to the heart."

"We do not murder in cold blood," said Mauleon.

"Yes; but Don Pedro will murder me."

A long silence on the part of his captors apprised
Caverley that he had convinced them, since they were unable
to make him any reply.   Agenor was reflecting.   Caverley's
unexpected appearance had revealed the presence of Don
Pedro at Montiel.   This man had been the hound whose
unerring scent had unearthed his master's quarry.   The
service thus rendered to Mauleon inclined him towards clemency.   Besides, his foe was unarmed, despoiled, and unable
to do any harm.   Caverley had employed this interval of
silence like the shrewd and cunning man that he was.   He
reflected that, from the commencement of the disagreeable
conversation he had just held with his unknown captors, two
voices only had spoken, and by feeling about him, he was
convinced that the grotto was small and narrow, and incapable of containing more than four men.   The numbers
were therefore equal, except in regard to weapons.   But to
regain these weapons he would require to use his hands, and
these hands were bound together.   The good fortune which
seems to attend scoundrels, and which is really only the
weakness of honest men, came to Caverley's aid.

"This Caverley," said Agenor to himself, "will be a great
annoyance to me.   Were he in my place, he would free
himself from embarrassment by stabbing me with his dagger,
and throwing my body into the Tagus.   These are means of
which I cannot avail myself.   He will hinder me when I
wish to quit this place, and that I shall do as soon as I have
received certain tidings of Don Pedro and Aïssa."   This
reflection was no sooner made, than Mauleon, who was expeditious in his movements, seized Caverley by the arm, and
began to unloose him, saying, as he did so, "Master Caverley,
you have, without knowing it, rendered me a service.   Yes,
Don Pedro would slay you, and I do not wish you to perish
by his hand whilst there are so many lofty gibbets existing
in both England and France."   At each word the imprudent
young man unfastened a knot.   "Therefore," continued
Mauleon, "I give you your liberty; profit by it to make

your escape, and endeavour to amend your courses." As he said this, he finished undoing the leathern strap.

Caverley's arms were no sooner freed, than he rushed upon Agenor, and endeavoured to wrest away his sword, exclaiming, "Give me back my purse as well as my liberty." He had already seized upon the steel, and was grasping the hilt in order to strike, when Mauleon dealt him a blow with his fist which sent him rolling into the pool of water at the foot of the steps to the grotto. Caverley, like a fish which, escaping from the fisher's basket, once more feels the ambient element that gives it life, inhaled the fresh air with delight, rushed out of the cavern, and took his way at the top of his speed towards the town.

"By St. James! master," said Muscaron, in a fury, "you have certainly done a wise deed. Let me run after him, and recapture him."

"And for what purpose, since I wish to give him the liberty of going where he pleases?" said Agenor.

"Folly! insane folly! The rascal will play us some trick —he will return; he will tell."

"Silence, fool!" said Agenor, nudging Muscaron's elbow, lest in his wrath he should betray anything before Becker. "If he returns we will give him up to Don Pedro, whom we will warn this very evening."—"That is a different thing," grumbled Muscaron, who understood the ruse.

"Come, friend, unloose the arms of this honest M. Becker, and tell him that so sure as the four illustrious chevaliers— Caverley, Lesby, Philips, and Becker—are found in this neighbourhood by to-morrow, they shall be all hanged to the battlements of Montiel; for in these parts justice is better organized than in France."

"Oh, I will not forget it, my lord," said Becker, intoxicated with joy and gratitude. He did not dream of endeavouring to arm himself against his benefactors: he kissed their hands, and disappeared with the swiftness of a bird.

"Oh, master!" sighed Muscaron, "what an adventure."

"Oh, sir squire, what lessons you have yet to learn!" said Agenor. "What! you did not see that this Caverley has unearthed Don Pedro for us; that not knowing who we are, he believes us to be the guardians of the King, and will consequently quit the country as soon as possible? In short, what would you have? You have gained both arms and money."

"Master, I was wrong."—"Very well."

"But let us watch, master; let us watch! That Caverley is as artful as the devil!"

"A hundred men could not force this grotto. We can take it in turns to sleep, and thus await news of my dear mistress, since Heaven has already given us tidings of Don Pedro."

"Master, I no longer despair of anything; and if any one were to tell me that Donna Aïssa intended paying you a visit in this adder's nest, I should believe it, and say, 'Thanks, good fellow, for your news.'" At this moment a faint noise in the distance, measured and in cadence, struck the practised ear of Muscaron. "Ma foi!" said he, "you are right. There is that Caverley galloping away. I swear I hear four horses. He has rejoined his men, and they are all flying from the gibbet, with which you threatened them—at least, if they are not returning hither. No; the noise becomes more distant; it dies away; a good journey to you. Au revoir, captain of the devil!"

"Why, Muscaron!" exclaimed Agenor, suddenly, "I have no longer my sword."

"That fellow has robbed you of it," returned Muscaron; "it is a pity to lose so good a blade."

"With my name engraven on the hilt. Ah, Muscaron, the brigand will recognise me!"

"But not before the evening, master, and by then, judging from appearances, he will be far distant. That cursed, Caverley, he must always be stealing something or other!"

The next morning at daybreak they heard two men engaged in eager conversation descend from the castle. It was Mothril himself accompanied by Don Pedro. This latter was leading his horse. At this sight Agenor's blood boiled. He was going to rush upon his foes, poniard them, and thus put an end to the struggle; but Muscaron stopped him.

"Are you mad, my lord?" said he. "Would you destroy Mothril without having won Aïssa? How can you tell that it is not the same as at Navaretto, and that her guardians have not received orders to slay her, in case of your either killing Mothril or making him prisoner?"

Agenor shuddered. "Oh, you really love me!" said he; "yes, you really love me."

"I should think so, pardieu! Do you think I should not

feel pleasure in killing this villanous Moor, who has done so
much evil. Yes; I will kill him, but at a fitting time and
opportunity."

They beheld the two objects of their legitimate hatred
pass within reach of them, indeed so close that their garments almost brushed against them, without daring to betray
themselves.

"Fortune is mocking us!" exclaimed Agenor.

"Do you complain, my lord," said Muscaron. "You who,
without Caverley, would have left here yesterday, left without knowing where Don Pedro was, or obtaining any
tidings of Aïssa. But, hush! let us listen to what they are
saying."

"Thanks," Don Pedro was saying to his minister; "I trust
she will be cured, and will then love me."

"Doubt it not, my lord, for Hafiz and I will gather, according to the prescribed rule, the herbs you know of. Then
she will love you, since there is no longer anything to displease her at your court. But let us speak on serious subjects. Convince yourself of the truth of these tidings. Ten
thousand of my compatriots ought by now to have disembarked at Lisbon, and mounted the Tagus as far as Toledo.
Go to Toledo where they love you, and encourage your
faithful defenders. The very day Henry enters Spain, we will
take both him and his army at a single blow, between the
town he is besieging and the troops of your Saracen allies,
at the head of which I will place myself when they shall
arrive in sight of Toledo."

"Mothril, you are a clever minister; whatever may happen,
you have always been devoted to my interests."

"Fancy the hideous face the Moor must be making in his
attempts to look gracious!" whispered Muscaron.

"One last counsel, sire, before I return to the castle," continued Mothril; "refuse all payment to the Prince of Wales,
until he has again joined your cause. These English are
perfidious."

"Yes; and besides the money is wanting."

"A reason the more for doing so. Adieu, sire; henceforth
you will be victorious and happy."

"Adieu, Mothril."—"Adieu, sire."

"The two adventurers had the additional trial of beholding Mothril with an infernal smile upon his lips, slowly

regain the castle, to which Agenor so ardently desired admittance.

"Let us mount after and seize him," exclaimed the young man. "Let us threaten him with death if he will not give up Aïssa, and he will resign her."

"Yes; and as we are redescending the mountain he will crush us beneath masses of rock. Our cause will then be greatly advanced. Patience, I say; God is good!"

"Well, then, since you refuse to have anything to do with Mothril, do not let us neglect the opportunity that offers itself with regard to Don Pedro. He has departed alone; we are two; let us capture him, slay him if he offers any resistance; and if he does not, take him to Don Henry de Transtamare to prove that we have found him."

"Excellent idea!" exclaimed Muscaron. "I adopt it; I follow you." They waited until Mothril had reached the platform of the castle, then they ventured to creep out of their hole. But when they gazed over the plain they beheld Don Pedro at the head of at least forty men-at-arms, tranquilly continuing his route towards Toledo. "Ah, pardieu! we were very stupid! Pardon, my lord, very credulous," said Muscaron; "Mothril would never have allowed the King to depart alone. The guards have come from yonder town."

"But apprised by whom?"—"By the Moors yesterday evening, or even by a signal from the castle."

"True. Let us now only think of, if possible, seeing Aïssa, and then returning to Don Henry."

CHAPTER LXVI.

HAFIZ.

During the whole of an entire day, the looked-for opportunity did not present itself. No one quitted the castle except the purveyors. A messenger also arrived, but the horn of the seneschal having signalled his approach, our adventurers did not judge it prudent to stop him. Towards evening, when all became silent, when the sounds mounting from the river to the mountain were softened and deadened, and the sky grew pale towards the horizon, our two friends overheard an angry conversation carried on by two well-known voices. Mothril and Hafiz were disputing together as they descended from the platform of the castle by the pathway leading to the gates.

"Master," Hafiz was saying, "you caused me to be kept in confinement whilst the King was here, and yet you had promised to present me to him. You also promised me a large sum of money. I grow weary of always being with this young girl, whom you make me guard. I wish to fight with my newly arrived countrymen, whose white-sailed boats are now mounting the Tagus; so pay me quickly, master, and let me go to the King."—"You wish to quit me, my són?" said Mothril. "Am I, then, a bad master?"

"No; but I do not wish to have any master at all."

"I may keep you with me, because I love you," said Mothril.

"I do not love you," retorted Hafiz. "You have forced me to commit wicked actions which people my slumber with frightful dreams and visions. I am too young to make up my mind to live thus. Pay me, and set me free, or I will go in quest of some one, and reveal all."—"You are right," said Mothril. "Return to the castle, and I will pay you at once."

Whilst descending the mountain, Mothril was before and Hafiz behind; in retracing their steps, the path was so narrow that Hafiz was then the foremost. The owl began to whoop in the crannies of the rock—the purple shadows began to assume a violet tint. Suddenly a frightful cry—a fearful oath rent the air, and a soft and bloody mass fell dull and heavy on the ground in front of the cavern. The night birds flew affrighted from their lairs, and the very insects were startled from their haunts. In a few moments a stream of blood mingled with and reddened the crystal water of the little cistern.

Agenor, pale and horror-struck, put his head out of his hiding-place, and Muscaron's livid face appeared beside it.

"Hafiz!" they both exclaimed, on recognising in the crushed and motionless form before them the companion of Gildaz.—"Poor boy!" murmured Muscaron, who had crept from his hold to render him help, if it were not too late.

Already the shadows of death were spreading over his bronzed face—his eyes, starting out of his head, were glazed and fixed —a heavy half blood-choked breath burst painfully from his crushed breast. He recognised both Muscaron and Agenor, and his countenance expressed superstitious terror. In fact, the miserable wretch fancied he beheld avenging spirits.

Muscaron raised his head, while Agenor fetched fresh water to bathe his brow and his bleeding wounds.

"The Franks! the Franks!" murmured Hafiz, drinking greedily. "Allah, pardon me!"—"Come with us, poor boy," said Agenor, "and we will cure you."

"No, I am killed—killed, like Gildaz," murmured the Moor. "Killed, as I deserved—murdered! Mothril flung me from the castle heights." The gesture of horror that escaped Mauleon was observed by the dying youth. "Christian," said he, "I hated you; but I no longer do so, for you can avenge me. Donna Aïssa has always loved you, and Donna Maria always protected your interests. It was Mothril who poisoned Donna Maria, and who profited by Donna Aïssa's swoon to stab her with his poniard. Tell this to the King, Don Pedro; tell it him quickly; but save Aïssa, if you love her, for in fourteen days' time, when Don Pedro returns to the castle, Mothril is to give her up to the King, drugged with some magic potion. I have wronged you; but I am now serving you; pardon, and avenge me! Allah!" He fell back exhausted, turned his eyes with a last and painful effort towards the castle, as though to curse it, and expired.

More than a quarter of an hour elapsed before our two friends could either collect their ideas or recover their coolness. This hideous death—these revelations—this threatening future, had struck them with unspeakable affright. Agenor was the first to recover himself.

"Fifteen days hence," said he, "we shall be at peace. Fifteen days hence, either Don Pedro, Mothril, or myself will be dead. Come, Muscaron, let us return to Henry's camp, and render him an account of the mission with which he charged me. But let us hasten—seek our horses on the plain."

Muscaron, his brain still whirling from the shock he had received, succeeded in finding the horses, which besides came running at the sound of his voice. He saddled them, loaded them, and springing lightly into his saddle, took the road to Toledo, along which his master had already preceded him. When they reached the plain, and the gloomy castle raised its dark profile against the bluish-grey background of the sky, "Mothril!" cried Agenor in a ringing voice, and shaking his fist at the casements of the castle, "Mothril, we shall meet again! Aïssa, my love, I shall soon behold you."

CHAPTER LXVII.

PREPARATIONS.

FIRE does not spread through a train of gunpowder more rapidly than did revolt through Don Pedro's dominions. Without fear of being invaded by the neighbouring kingdoms, the inhabitants of Castile had for the most part declared themselves in favour of Don Henry, so soon as a manifesto from him apprised them that he had returned, bringing with him a large army, and that this army was commanded by the Constable Bertrand Duguesclin. The roads were covered, in a few days, with soldiers of fortune, devoted citizens, monks of every order, and Bretons marching towards Toledo. But Toledo, faithful to Don Pedro, as Bertrand had foretold, closed her gates, armed her walls, and awaited the course of events. Henry lost no time. He invested the town, and commenced a regular siege. This state of hostility suited him marvellously well, since it gave time to his allies to collect round his banner. On the other hand, Don Pedro's forces were increasing. He sent courier upon courier to his ancient friends the Kings of Granada, Portugal, Arragon and Navarre. He entered into negotiations with the Prince of Wales, who, lying sick at Bordeaux, seemed to have lost somewhat of his energy in war and to be preparing himself by repose for the cruel death which snatched him, whilst still young, to a glorious immortality. The Saracens mentioned by Mothril had disembarked at Lisbon. They had taken a few days to recruit themselves, and then, by means of the boats with which the King of Portugal had furnished them, re-mounted the Tagus, preceded by three thousand horse, sent to Don Pedro by his Portuguese ally. Henry had with him the cities of Gallicia and Léon, and a heterogeneous army, of which five thousand Bretons, commanded by Oliver Duguesclin, formed the powerful nucleus. He was only waiting for certain tidings of Mauleon, when he returned with his squire to the camp, and recounted what he had seen. The King and Bertrand listened in profound silence.

"What!" said the constable at last, "Mothril has not gone with Don Pedro?"—"He is only waiting for the arrival of the Saracens, to place himself at their head."

"Before that takes place we can send a hundred men to

Montiel, and capture him. Agenor shall command the expedition, and as I suppose he has no great reason to love this Moor, he shall erect a tall gallows on the banks of the Tagus, and there hang this Saracen—this traitorous assassin!"

"My lord, my lord," said Agenor, "you were good enough to promise me your friendship—to promise me your help. Do not refuse me now. I entreat you to allow the Saracen Mothril to remain quiet and unsuspecting in his castle of Montiel."—"Why so? It is a nest that must be destroyed."

"Sir Constable, it is a haunt of which you will at some future time prove the utility. You know that when they wish to entrap the fox, they do not appear to remark his hiding-place, but carelessly pass it by; otherwise he leaves it, and does not return to it."—"What then, chevalier?"

"My lords, let Mothril and Don Pedro fancy that their presence is unsuspected at Montiel, and who knows that we shall not at last take them both in one net?"

"Agenor," said the King, "this is not your only reason?"

"No, sire; I have never told a lie—it is not my only reason. The true one is, that the castle contains a friend, whom Mothril would slaughter if he were too closely pressed."

"Say so, then!" exclaimed Bertrand, "and never fancy that we should hesitate to grant any request you might make us."

After this conversation, which relieved Mauleon's mind with respect to Aïssa, the leaders of the army vigorously pursued the siege of Toledo. The inhabitants defended themselves so well, that it was the scene of many feats of arms, and many of the illustrious besiegers were killed and wounded in the skirmishes and sorties. But these combats were only the prelude to a general action, as thunder and lightning are to a storm.

CHAPTER LXVIII.

TOLEDO FAMISHING.

DON PEDRO had commenced in Toledo—a strong city full of resources,—regulating his affairs with both his subjects and his allies. The Toledans, during this interminable course of civil wars, had leaned now to one party, now to the other; it was therefore necessary to strike a final blow, and bind them eternally to the cause of the victor of Navaretto. This was Don Pedro's best title. In fact, if the Toledans did not on this occasion support their prince (and he was as victorious in this battle as in the last), it would be all over with Toledo. Don Pedro would never pardon her desertion. The artful prince well knew that the population of a large city know no other impulses than those produced by hunger and avarice. Mothril repeated it to him every day. It was therefore only necessary to feed the Toledans, and to excite their hopes of rich spoils. But in these two things Don Pedro did not succeed. He made great promises for the future, but performed nothing in the present. When the Toledans perceived that provisions were wanting in the markets, and the granaries were empty, they began to murmur. A league of twenty wealthy shopkeepers, either devoted to the interests of the Comte de Transtamare or animated by merely a spirit of opposition, fomented the murmurs and the bad dispositions of the town. Don Pedro consulted Mothril.

"These people," returned the Moor, "will play you the evil trick of, while you sleep, opening the city gates to your competitor. Ten thousand men will enter, take you prisoner, and the war will be at an end."

"What, then, is to be done ?"—"A simple thing enough. They call you in Spain Don Pedro the Cruel."

"I know it; and I have only gained this title through a few somewhat energetic acts of justice."

"I am not discussing that point. But if you have once gained this name, you must not shrink from meriting it again. If it has been unjustly bestowed upon you, hasten to prove its justice by making a few examples, to teach the Toledans the force of your arm."

"Be it so," replied the King. "I will act so this very night." In fact, Don Pedro caused the discontented individuals before mentioned to be pointed out to him. He made himself acquainted with their dwellings and habits; then that same night, accompanied by a hundred soldiers, whom he commanded in person, he broke open the houses of each of the malcontents, and had them murdered. Their bodies were thrown into the Tagus. A little nocturnal disturbance, a good deal of blood carefully wiped up, this was all the Toledans learnt of the future administration of the city, and how the King intended to practise justice. They therefore no longer murmured, but commenced eating their horses for the first thing. The King congratulated them upon it.

"You do not require horses in the city," said he; "the journeys are not long, and as to the sorties on the assailants, well, we will make them on foot."

After their horses, the Toledans were obliged to eat their mules. This is a hard necessity in Spain. The mule is a national animal: they regard it almost as a compatriot. Certes, they sacrifice the horses in bull-fights, but they employ the mules to drag the bulls and horses killed by each other off the arena. The Toledans therefore ate their mules, sighing as they did so. This slaughter of their mules aroused the energies of the Toledans. They made a sortie in quest of provisions, but Le Bègue de Vilaine and Oliver de Mauny, who had not devoured their Breton horses, cruelly repulsed them, and obliged them to remain within the town. Don Pedro suggested that they should eat the fodder which the horses and mules, being dead, could no longer consume. This lasted for eight days, at the end of which time it was necessary for some other expedient to be resorted to. Their circumstances were certainly not prosperous.

The Prince of Wales, annoyed at not receiving the sums of money owing him by Don Pedro, had dispatched three deputies to Toledo, to present the account of the expenses of the war. Don Pedro consulted Mothril about this fresh embarrassment.

"The Christians," replied Mothril, "dearly love ceremonies, fasts, and public *fêtes*. Whilst we had bulls, I should have advised you to give them a brilliant bull-fight; but as there are no longer any, we must think of something equivalent."—"Speak! speak!"

"These deputies are come to ask you for money. All Toledo awaits your reply. If you refuse, it will be because your treasury is empty; and then no longer count upon the Toledans."—"But I cannot pay this sum—we have now no money."

"I, who manage the financial affairs of your kingdom, sire, know it well; therefore, instead of money, we must have wit. You must invite the deputies to repair in great pomp to the cathedral; there, in presence of all the people, who will be charmed to behold your royal robes, the gold and jewels of the sacerdotal ornaments, the rich armour, and the hundred and fifty horses remaining in the city, like specimens of curious animals of which the race is extinct—there you will say, 'My lord deputies, are you invested with full powers to treat with me?' 'Yes,' they will reply; 'we represent our gracious lord, his Royal Highness the Prince of Wales.' 'Well, then,' you will say, 'his Royal Highness demands the sum of money which it was agreed I should pay him?' 'Yes,' they will answer. Then, my prince, you must say, 'I do not deny this debt; only it was agreed between his Royal Highness and myself that, in return for the sum demanded, I should have the protection, the alliance, and the co-operation of the English.' "

"But I have had it," said Don Pedro.

"Yes; but you will have it no longer, and run the risk of having just the contrary. Thus we must above all things obtain their neutrality; since if, besides Henry de Transtamare's army, and the Bretons commanded by the constable, you have to encounter the Prince of Wales and his twenty thousand English, you are lost, my prince, and the English will pay themselves by despoiling you."

"They will refuse, Mothril, as I cannot pay them."

"If they meant to do so it would have already been done. But the Christians have too much self-esteem to confess that they have been deceived. The Prince of Wales would sooner lose all you owe him, and pass for having been paid, than be paid without the world knowing it. Let me finish: the deputies will summon you to pay them; you will reply, 'I am menaced on all sides with the hostility of the Prince of Wales. Were such the case, I would sooner lose the whole of my kingdom than suffer the shadow of an alliance to subsist between myself and so disloyal a prince. Therefore, swear to me, that for two months from the present time, the Prince of Wales will keep—not the promise he made to aid me—but his former one of preserving a strict neutrality; and in two months' time I swear to you by the Holy Bible, which you behold here, that you shall be paid; I have the money in readiness.' The deputies will pay for the privilege of returning quickly to their own country. Then your people will be relieved, joyful, sure of having no more fresh enemies, and after having eaten their horses and mules, they will devour all the rats and lizards in Toledo, which on account of the neighbourhood of the rocks are numerous enough.

"But in two months, Mothril?"

"You will not any the more pay then, it is true; but you will have either gained or lost the battle that is about to take place. In two months' time you will have no reason, either as victor or vanquished, to pay your debts; because, as victor, you will have even more credit than you require, and, as vanquished, you would be worse than bankrupt."

"But my oath upon the Scriptures?"

"You have often talked of turning Mahometan; this will be the time for it, my prince. Devoted to Mahomet, you will no longer have anything to do with other prophets."

"Execrable Pagan!" murmured Don Pedro. "What counsels!"

"I do not deny it; but your faithful Christians give you none at all, therefore mine are worth something."

Don Pedro, after deep reflection, put Mothril's plan into execution. The ceremony was imposing, the Toledans forgot their hunger at the sight of the splendours of the court and the paraphernalia of warlike pomp. Don Pedro displayed so much magnanimity, made so fine a discourse, and took such solemn oaths, that the deputies having sworn neutrality, appeared even better satisfied than if he had paid them at once. "After all," said Don Pedro to himself, "what does it matter to me? Things will last my time." He was more fortunate than he anticipated; for, thanks to Mothril's foresight, a large reinforcement of Africans arrived by the Tagus, and forced the enemies' lines to revictual Toledo; so that Don Pedro, on reckoning his forces, found himself commanding an army of eighty thousand men—Jews, Saracens, Portuguese, and Castilians. He had kept himself apart during all these preparations, devoting extreme care to his person and leaving nothing to chance that could by any means cause him to lose the result of the grand stroke he meditated.

Don Henry, on the contrary, like a King assured of his throne, was already organizing a government. He wished the day following the action which would obtain him the crown, to witness this royalty as solid and sound as that already consecrated by a long peace. Meanwhile, Agenor kept his eye on Montiel, and knew by means of well-paid spies, that Mothril, having established a cordon of troops between the castle and Toledo, went nearly every day, mounted on an Arab barb swift as the wind, to visit Aïssa, now entirely recovered from the effects of her wound. He had tried every

means in his power to either gain entrance to the castle, or
to apprise Aïssa of his presence, but all his attempts had
been hitherto unsuccessful.   Muscaron's anxiety had thrown
him into a fever.   Agenor at last saw no hopes of success,
except in a speedy and general combat, which would enable
him to slay Don Pedro with his own hand, and take Mothril
alive; so that he might obtain Aïssa free and living as a
ransom for this odious life.   This sweet thought, this constant
dream, wearied the young man's brain by its ardent assiduity.
He had conceived a deep disgust for everything that was not
active and decisive war; and as he was one of the council of
chiefs, his opinion was always to give up the siege, and force
Don Pedro to a pitched battle.   He met with serious opposition in the council, since Henry's army did not amount to
more than twenty thousand men, and many of the officers
considered it would be folly to risk the chances of a battle
under present circumstances.   But Agenor represented to
them that if Don Henry, since the publication of his manifesto, had at his disposal only twenty thousand men, and if
he did not make his name known by some brilliant exploit,
his forces would diminish instead of augmenting, whilst
every day the Tagus brought Don Pedro reinforcements of
Saracens and Portuguese.

"The cities are undecided," said he; "they waver between
the two banners; observe the address with which Don Pedro
reduces you to inaction, which is above all a proof of our
want of power.   Abandon Toledo, which you cannot take.
Remember that if you are victorious, the town will be forced
to yield, whilst at the present moment nothing presses it;
on the contrary, Mothril's plan is being carried into effect.
You will soon be enclosed between walls of stone, and walls
of steel—the Tagus behind you bordered by eighty thousand
foes.   Then you will only be able to fight and die.   To-day
you may attack and conquer."

It is true self-interest was at the bottom of this speech, but
what good counsel is not more or less interested?   The constable was too clear sighted, and had had too much experience
in war not to support Mauleon.   There only remained the
King's indecision to vanquish; for he felt all the risk he ran
in hazarding a stroke of fortune without having first taken
precautions to insure its success.   But what man fails to do
God's will brings to pass.

CHAPTER LXIX.

THE BATTLE OF MONTIEL.

DON PEDRO was as eager as Agenor to obtain possession of what, after his crown, he most desired on earth to call his own. Every evening when, his affairs of state being over, he could make his way through the throng of devoted soldiers, and hastening to Montiel, contemplate the fair Aïssa, pale and sad as she was, for a quarter of an hour, he was happy. Mothril, however, rarely granted him this happiness. The Moor's project was ripe, his well-spread net had taken its prey; it now only remained to keep it; for an ensnared monarch is like a lion caught in a net, never less securely held than when apparently captured. Mothril was urged by Don Pedro to let him espouse Aïssa, and place her on the throne.

"No," had been the Moor's reply. "It is not on the eve of a battle that a King celebrates his nuptials; it is not when so many brave men are shedding their blood for him that he should think of love. No; wait until the victory is gained, then everything shall be permitted you." He thus restrained the eager King; but his designs were so transparent, that, had not Don Pedro been either blinded or intoxicated with this new passion, he must have seen through them.

Mothril wished to make Aïssa Queen of Castile, because he was well aware this union of a Christian with a Mahometan would outrage all Christendom—that the whole world would then abandon Don Pedro, and that the so often vanquished Saracens were in readiness to reconquer Spain, and install themselves there for ever. Then Mothril, who stood so high in the estimation of his countrymen—Mothril, who, during the last ten years, had guided them step by step towards this promised land, until their rapid progress was remarked by all except this mad or drunken monarch—Mothril would become King of Spain. But as, in bestowing Aïssa, in managing a return of adversity to Don Pedro, it was, nevertheless, necessary to act slowly and surely, Mothril waited for a decisive victory to destroy the most dangerous enemies the Moors would encounter in Spain. It was necessary for the Moors to gain, in Don Pedro's name, some great battle, so as to slay Henry de Transtamare, Bertrand Duguesclin, and all the Bretons—in short, to show all Christendom that Spain was

a country easy to enter, but only to furnish graves for its in-
vaders. It was also necessary that the greatest obstacle to
Mothril's project, Agenor de Mauleon, should be killed; so
that his young mistress, first buoyed up by promises and as-
surances of a speedy re-union, then discouraged by his unexpected death on the field of battle, should allow herself, in
her despair, to be made subservient to Mothril's ends, which
she no longer suspected or distrusted. The Moor redoubled
his tenderness—his care; he even went so far as to accuse
Hafiz of having been in league with Donna Maria to deceive
or to betray Agenor. Hafiz was dead, and could no longer
either defend or justify himself. He procured for Aïssa either
true or forged tidings of her lover.

"He thinks of you," he said; "he loves you. He remains
with his master, the constable, and never misses an opportunity of communicating with the messengers I dispatch to
obtain tidings of him."

Aïssa, reassured by these words, waited patiently; she even
found a certain charm in this separation, which thus showed
her how anxiously Mauleon sought to be re-united to her.
Her days were passed in the most retired apartments of the
castle. There, alone with her women, she indolently and
dreamily contemplated the country from a casement overhanging the abyss formed by the perpendicular rock of
Montiel. When Don Pedro came to visit her, she treated him
with that cold and measured courtesy which, with women incapable of dissimulation, is the supremest effort of hypocrisy—
coldness so unintelligible that presumptuous men are apt to
mistake it for the timidity of dawning love. The King had
never before encountered resistance. The proudest of women
—Maria Padilla—had loved and preferred him to every one.
Why, then, should he doubt Aïssa's affection, above all, since
Maria's death and Mothril's calumnies had persuaded him that
the young girl's heart was pure from all thoughts of love?
Mothril kept a strict watch over the King in each of his
visits. Every word that fell from the Prince's lips had
for him its value, and he would not suffer Aïssa to make a
single reply—his excuse being, that her invalid state rendered silence imperatively necessary. Besides this, he experienced constant anxiety lest Don Pedro should corrupt some
of the inhabitants of the castle. Mothril, sovereign master

at Montiel, had thus taken every precaution. The best of all was to convince Aïssa that he approved of her love for Agenor, and of this the young girl was now persuaded. The result was, that on the day Mothril was obliged to quit Montiel to take command of the African troops newly arrived for the battle, he had only two cautions to give, one to his lieutenant and one to Aïssa herself. This lieutenant was the same who, before the battle of Navaretto, had so badly guarded Aïssa's litter, and who now burned to have his revenge. He was more soldier than servant. Incapable of stooping to the servility of Hafiz, he only understood the obedience due to a chief and the respect due to the commands of religion.

"I am going to join the battle," said Mothril to Aïssa. "I have entered into a compact with the Sire de Mauleon that we mutually spare each other in the combat. If his party prove victorious, he will come and fetch you from this castle, whose gates I will open to him; and you will fly with him— with me, if you love me as a father. If vanquished, he is to come to me—I will lead him to you, and he will owe to me, at the same time, his life and his mistress. Will you not dearly love me, Aïssa, for so much devotion to you? You understand that if his Majesty Don Pedro heard a single word—formed the slightest suspicion of this plan—my head would roll at his feet before an hour had elapsed, and you would be for ever lost to the man you love."

Aïssa uttered a thousand protestations of gratitude, and hailed this day of blood and mourning as the dawn of her liberty—her happiness. When he had thus prepared the young girl, he gave his instructions to his lieutenant.

"Hassan," said he to him, "the Prophet is about to decide the fate and fortunes of Don Pedro; we are about to give our enemies battle. If we are defeated—or even if we are victorious, and I do not return hither the evening after the battle—whether I may be dead, wounded, or a prisoner— open the door of Donna Aïssa's chamber (here is the key of it), poniard her and her two women, and fling the bodies from the heights of the rock into the ravine beneath; since it is not right that good Mussulmans should be exposed to the insults of a Christian, whether he be called Don Pedro or Henry de Transtamare. Keep better watch than at Nava-

D D

retto; there vigilance was at fault; then I pardoned you—
I spared your life; this time the Prophet will punish you.
Swear, therefore, to execute my orders."

"I swear it," returned Hassan, coldly; "and when the three
women are dead, I will poniard myself with them, so that my
spirit will keep guard over theirs."

"Thanks," said Mothril, throwing his gold chain over his
neck; "you are a faithful servant; and if we are victorious,
you shall have the command of this castle. Let Donna Aïssa
be kept in ignorance, until the last moment, of the fate that
is in store for her. She is a woman—she is weak—she need
not suffer death twice over. As to the victory," he added
hastily, "I do not believe that we can fail to gain it; therefore, my orders are an almost unnecessary precaution." After
having thus spoken, Mothril took his weapons, his fleetest
horse, and leaving the command of Montiel in Hassan's
hands, he set off during the night, followed by ten men-at-
arms, to rejoin Don Pedro, who impatiently awaited him.
Mothril reckoned upon gaining the victory, nor did he do so
without cause. These were the chances in his favour:—Fresh
troops every moment arriving; all the gold of Africa poured
into Spain by the power of a dark and immutable will bent
upon conquest—a design often deferred, but never abandoned;
whilst the European knights joining in the struggle, some from
cupidity, some from religious motives, fought coldly enough,
and were easily discouraged by a reverse of fortune. If ever
an event burst forth in the midst of well-laid schemes, it was
the battle to which history has given the poetic name of the
Battle of Montiel.

Don Pedro impatiently collected all his troops between
Montiel and Toledo. His army covered a space of two leagues,
stretching, cavalry and infantry, like the rungs of a ladder,
until it reached the mountains. He had besides a splendid
ordnance. There was no more hesitation for Don Henry. To
sustain the attack like a man constrained to fight would be
degrading to a competitor for the crown, who, on his arrival
in Castile, had adopted as his device "Rester roi ou mort."
He therefore hastened to find the constable, and said to
him, "Once more, Sire Bertrand, I place in your hands the
fate of my kingdom. You shall be the commander of my
army. You may be more fortunate than at Navaretto,
although you cannot be braver or more skilful than you were

there. But we Christians know that what God will not permit at one time He will at another."

"Then I am to command, sire?" said the constable, quickly.

"Like a king; I am but your first or your last lieutenant, sire constable," returned the King.

"And you will say to me, as King Charles V., my wise and glorious master, said to me at Paris, when he bestowed on me the sword of constable."

"What did he say to you, brave Bertrand?"

"He said to me, sire, 'Discipline is badly observed in my armies, which are often lost through the want of justice and submission. There are some princes who blush to obey a simple chevalier; but a battle has never been gained without all agreeing to follow the will of one. Therefore, Bertrand, I give you the command, and every disobedient head, be it even that of my own brother, shall either fall or be humbled, if it will not submit.'" These words, uttered before all the council, recalled to their minds the misfortunes at Navaretto, where the imprudence of Don Tello and Don Sancho, the King's brothers, had caused the ruin of a great army. The princes were both present, and the colour mounted into their cheeks on hearing Duguesclin's words.

"Sire constable," said the King, "I have said that the command of the army is yours, therefore you are master. Whoever refuses to obey your wishes or your orders, I will myself strike with the battle-axe I hold in my hand, whether he be my ally, my relation, or my brother. Those who love me, ought to wish me to be victorious, and I shall only be so by all obeying the wisest captain in Christendom."

"Be it so," replied Duguesclin. "Then I accept the command; to-morrow we will give them battle."

The constable passed the whole of the night in listening to the report of his couriers and his spies. The former informed him of the devastations committed on the country, which for the last month these eighty thousand men had ravaged like a cloud of locusts; and the latter brought him intelligence that fresh bands of Saracens had disembarked at Cadiz.

"It is time this were ended," said the constable to the King, "otherwise your kingdom will be eaten up by these fellows before it comes into your possession."

Agenor, at once joyful and anxious, like every one on the eve of a long-desired event which is to decide some important question—Agenor endeavoured by displaying an unheard-of activity to drown his uneasiness. He was continually on horseback, bearing orders, re-assembling and grouping the different companies, reconnoitring the ground, and assigning to each troop its position on the morrow. Duguesclin divided his army into five parts—four thousand five hundred horse, commanded by Oliver Duguesclin and Le Bègue de Vilaine, formed the vanguard. The French and Spanish nobility, to the number of six thousand, formed the body of the army, and was commanded by Don Henry de Transtamare. The Arragonese and other allies formed the rear-guard. A reserve of four hundred horse, commanded by Oliver de Mauny, were placed so as, if necessary, to cover a retreat. As to the constable, he placed himself at the head of the three thousand Bretons, commanded by young De Mauny, Carlonnet la Houssaie, and Agenor. This troop, well mounted and composed of men of invincible courage, appeared like a powerful arm ready to put forth its strength whenever the eye of the constable should judge it necessary in order to gain the day. Bertrand aroused his soldiers at daybreak, and each one marched leisurely to his post in such a manner that before dawn the army was ranged in battle array, without either fatigue or noise. He did not make a long harangue. —" Only remember," said he, " that you have each four foes to kill ; but that you are each worth ten of your adversaries. This mass of Moors, Jews and Portuguese cannot resist the soldiers of France and Spain. Strike without mercy—strike all who are not Christians. I have never caused blood to be unnecessarily shed ; to-day necessity compels me to shed it. There are no ties between the Moors and the Spaniards— they mutually detest each other—interest alone unites them ; but as soon as the Moors find themselves sacrificed to the Spaniards—as soon as they behold you in the *mêlée,* sparing the Christian in order to slay the infidel, terror and distrust will spread through their ranks, and the first feeling of despair over, they will quickly turn their thoughts towards safety. Slay, then, without mercy."

This speech produced the usual effect ; an extraordinary enthusiasm circulated through their ranks. But Don Pedro was also at work ; they beheld him manœuvring his undisciplined but immense African battalions, whose armour and sumptuous vestments glittered in the sun.

When Duguesclin beheld from the summit of the hill he had selected as his post of observation, this innumerable multitude, he began to fear that the small number of his soldiers would inspire his adversaries with too great confidence. He therefore thinned his rear ranks to place his men closer together in the front ones, in such a manner as to make them both appear equal. He also placed a group of standards so as just to appear above the brow of the hill, that the Saracens might fancy them surrounded with soldiers.

Don Pedro beheld all this; his genius seemed to increase in proportion to the danger. He made an eloquent speech to his faithful Spaniards and brilliant promises to the Saracens; but brilliant as they were, they did not equal the hopes already conceived by his allies themselves, as to the booty they hoped to obtain. The trumpets sounded on Don Pedro's side, and were echoed by those of Duguesclin. Then the earth trembled as though two worlds were about to rush against each other. The effects of Duguesclin's recommendation was immediately apparent. The Bretons, by refusing to make Moorish prisoners, and slaying all, whilst they spared the Spaniards and other Christians, awakened a deep distrust in the midst of the infidels, which ran through their ranks like a shudder, and quenched their ardour. They immediately fancied an understanding subsisted between the Christians on both sides, and that whether Henry was victor or vanquished, the Moors would be the only victims. In fact, their first battalions had been attacked by Duguesclin's brother and Le Bègue de Vilaine; these intrepid Bretons had made so great a massacre amongst them, that their chiefs and even the Prince of Bennémarina himself having been slain, the Moors took fright and fled, the whole of their main body having been cut to pieces. The second still remained, and advanced valiantly enough to the encounter. Duguesclin gave the word to his three thousand Bretons, and himself at the head of them, charged the infidels so rudely that half of them turned their horses' heads and fled. Then commenced a second massacre; chiefs, nobles, soldiers—all were slain—not a single one escaped. Duguesclin had returned to his post, and was wiping his heated visage, when he saw Don Henry also returning from the pursuit, and, according to order, preparing like himself to resume his place in the ranks.

"Welcome, monseigneur!" said Bertrand. "So far all has

gone well. We have only lost about a thousand men, whilst twenty-five thousand Saracens bite the dust; you see how we have scattered them—all goes on well."

"If it only continue," murmured Henry.

"At least we will do our best to make it," said the constable. "See how Mauleon is rushing on the third body of Saracens commanded by Mothril. The Moor has perceived him and has given orders for him to be surrounded—some of the horsemen have already commenced doing so. They will kill him. Sound a retreat, trumpeters!" The trumpets sounded. Agenor heard and obeyed the summons as though he were merely accomplishing some feat of horsemanship, and returned to his post under a shower of arrows, which only clattered on his good armour.

"Now," said the constable, "my vanguard will attack the Spaniards. They are good soldiers, monseigneur, and we shall not gain a cheap victory over them. We must here divide into three bodies and attack them on three sides. The King," he continued, "will take the left, Oliver the right, I myself shall wait." Our readers will perceive that he touched neither his reserved troops nor his light cavalry. The Spaniards received the shock like men resolved to conquer or die. Henry, in attacking the body of troops commanded by Don Pedro, encountered the resistance of both skilful valour and hatred. The two Kings recognised each other at a distance, and exchanged menacing gestures without being able to meet. Between them was a crowd of men and clashing weapons; then this crowd fell away, and the earth was flooded with blood. Henry's strength suddenly began to fail him; Don Pedro had the advantage—he fought not only like a soldier, but like a lion. One of his squires had been already killed; he had twice changed his horse, but had not received a single wound, and his arm brandished with unslackened vigour and precision the battle-axe which with each blow struck down a man. Henry found himself attacked by not only Mothril's Moors, but Mothril himself, who, if Don Pedro were a lion, was certainly a tiger. The French nobles were terribly mown down by the yataghans and scimitars of these infidels, their ranks began to thin, and some of the arrows reached the King's breast. Already one Moor, bolder than the rest, had touched him with his lance.

"It is time!" exclaimed Duguesclin. "Forward, my

friends! Our Lady of Guesclin to the victory!" The three thousand Bretons rushed forward with a terrible noise, and forming an angle penetrated like a steel wedge into the heart of Don Pedro's twenty thousand men.

Agenor had at last obtained the long-desired permission to encounter and capture Mothril. In a quarter of an hour the Spaniards were broken up—destroyed. The Moorish cavalry could not stand against the shock of these men-at-arms and the blows of their terrible maces. Mothril attempted to fly, but his retreat was cut off by the troops of Le Bègue de Vilaine led on by Agenor. Agenor was already deeming himself master of his enemy's life and liberty, when the Moor, accompanied by at most three hundred men, burst through the Breton ranks, and losing in the struggle two hundred and fifty horsemen, effected his escape; and in doing so struck off, with a blow of his scimitar, the head of Agenor's horse, which was following closely on his traces. Agenor rolled in the dust. Muscaron let fly an arrow which missed its aim, and Mothril, like a flying wolf, disappeared behind the heaps of corpses in the direction of Montiel.

Don Pedro now saw that all was lost. He felt, so to speak, the hot breath of his deadliest enemy upon his face. But the golden circlet had been broken from his helmet, and his standard-bearer slain, and what made the shame of the prince saved the man. Don Pedro was no longer to be recognised; an indiscriminate carnage was taking place around him. It was at this moment that an English knight, with black armour and carefully closed visor, took his horse by the bridle and hurried it from the field of battle. Four hundred cavaliers, concealed by this prudent friend behind a hillock, was the fugitive King's sole escort. It was all that remained to Don Pedro of the eighty thousand men who were living for him at the beginning of the day. As the plain was covered in all directions with fugitives, Bertrand could not distinguish the King's little troop from the other scattered bands. It was not even known whether Don Pedro was living or dead. The constable therefore sent at hazard the reserved troops and the fifteen hundred horse of Oliver de Mauny after the fugitives; but Don Pedro—thanks to the excellence of his horses—was too far in advance. They did not think of following him besides, no one recognised him; he was for every one only an ordinary fugitive. But Agenor, who knew the road to

Montiel, and the interest Don Pedro had in seeking refuge
there—Agenor kept watch on this side. He had seen Mothril
fly in that direction; he guessed who the English knight was
who had assisted Don Pedro. He beheld a body of cavaliers
escorting a single horseman, who, thanks to the fleetness of
his magnificent steed, was far in advance of them. He recognised the King by his broken helmet, his golden spurs
stained with blood, and the eagerness with which he gazed
at the distant towers of Montiel. Agenor cast his eyes around
him to see whether there was no body of troops that could
assist him in following this precious fugitive and cutting off
the retreat of his four hundred horsemen. He could only see
the band of Le Bègue de Vilaine, who were resting their
panting horses for a few moments before taking part in the
general pursuit. Bertrand was at a distance pursuing the
fugitives and completing the victory.

"Messire!" cried Agenor to Le Bègue de Vilaine; "come
quickly to my aid if you wish to secure Don Pedro, for it is
he who is flying yonder towards the castle."

"Are you sure of it?" exclaimed Le Bègue.

"As of my life, messire!" rejoined Agenor. "I recognise
the leader of the band of horsemen—it is Caverley. Without
doubt he is escorting the King so carefully in order to take
him at his ease and sell him—it is his trade."

"Yes," said Le Bègue; "but we must not let an English
adventurer perform this feat, whilst we have here so many
brave French lances." Then turning to his men, he said, "To
horse, all! and let ten men hasten to apprise the constable
that we are going towards Montiel in quest of the vanquished
King."

The Bretons set out with so much eagerness that they overtook the escort. The English leader immediately divided his
troop into two bands—one following the individual they supposed to be the King, the other barring the progress of the
Bretons.

"Charge! charge!" cried Agenor. "They only wish to
gain time to enable the King to reach Montiel." Unfortunately for the Bretons, they were at the entrance of a
mountain gorge, where they could only fight six abreast.

"They are escaping us—we shall lose them!" cried Agenor.
"Courage, Bretons, courage!"

"Yes, we shall escape you, devilish Bearnais!" roared the

English knight, heading the escort. "Besides, if you wish to take us, come on." He spoke thus confidently because Agenor, carried away by his jealous eagerness, had outstripped all his companions, and stood almost alone before the two hundred English lances.

The intrepid young man did not pause before this terrible danger; he only struck his spurs more deeply into the flanks of his reeking horse. Caverley was brave, and his natural ferocity urged him to a combat, in which he knew he must infallibly be victorious. Placed as he was in the midst of his men, he seated himself more firmly in his stirrups, and awaited Mauleon. Then the curious spectacle presented itself of a single knight rushing headlong on the points of two hundred lances.

"Oh, the cowardly Englishmen!" vociferated Le Bègue. "Oh, coward, coward! Stay, Mauleon, this is too chivalrous!"

Caverley was covered with confusion. After all, he was a knight, and owed a few blows of a lance to the honour of his nation and his golden spurs. He quitted the ranks, and placed himself in battle array. "It is not here, as in the cavern of Montiel," he exclaimed to Mauleon, who came thundering on.

"I have already your sword; and before long, I shall have your whole suit of armour."

"Then first take my lance," retorted the young man, aiming so furious a blow at him, that Caverley was borne from his saddle, and fell to the earth together with his horse.

"Hurrah!" shouted the Bretons, wild with joy, and rapidly drawing near the combatants, which the English perceiving, they turned their horses' heads, and endeavoured to overtake their companions, who were already flying across the plain, leaving the King to be carried by his fleet horse to Montiel.

Caverley attempted to rise, but his ribs were broken; his horse in its endeavours to free itself gave him a violent kick on the breast, and he again fell to the earth, deluged in black blood. "The devil!" he muttered, faintly, "it is all over with me—I shall never stop any one again—I am dying!" and he sank back. At the same moment the Breton cavalry came up, and the eleven hundred iron-shod horses passed like a whirlwind over the crushed and mangled body of the famous King taker. But this delay had saved Don Pedro. In vain Le Bègue, by his heroic efforts, inspired his Bretons with triple spirit. The Bretons dashed furiously along at the risk of killing their horses, but they only came within sight of Don Pedro at the moment he was passing safely through the first barrier of the castle, and the gate closed behind him, leaving him to thank Heaven for his escape. Mothril had arrived a quarter of an hour before him. Le Bègue, in his despair, tore out his hair by handfuls.

"Patience, messire," said Agenor, "let us lose no time in investing this place. What we have not accomplished to-day, we will to-morrow."

Le Bègue followed this advice; he dispersed all his horsemen around the castle, and night fell as the last point of issue was closed to any who attempted to quit Montiel. Duguesclin also arrived with three thousand men, and learnt from Agenor the important news. "It is unfortunate," said he, "for the place is impregnable."

"We shall see, my lord," replied Mauleon; "at least, if we cannot gain entrance, no one can gain exit."

————

CHAPTER LXX.

AÏSSA.

THE constable was not credulous. He had as high an opinion of Don Pedro's talents, as he had a low one of his character. After he had made the tour of Montiel, and convinced himself by reconnoitring the place, that with a good and trusty guard it was possible to prevent even a mouse from issuing from the castle, he said to Agenor, "No, Sire de Mauleon, we are not so fortunate as you would have us believe. No; the King, Don Pedro, is not at Montiel, for he knows too well that we should blockade and reduce it by famine.

"I protest to you, my lord," said Mauleon, "that Mothril is in Montiel, and Don Pedro with him."

"I will believe it when I see him," said the constable. "What garrison has the castle?"

"Nearly three hundred men, my lord."

"These three hundred men, if they only think fit to roll down stones upon our heads, could slay five thousand of us, without our being able to reach them with a single arrow. To-morrow Don Henry will be here; he is occupied in summoning Toledo to surrender. As soon as he arrives, we will deliberate whether it will be better to take our departure, or waste a month here for nothing."

Agenor attempted to reply, but the constable was as obstinate as a Breton, and would not listen to any answer, or rather would not allow himself to be persuaded. Next day, Don Henry arrived, flushed with victory. He brought with him his army intoxicated with success; and when his counsel had deliberated on the question, whether Don Pedro was or was not at Montiel—

"I think with the constable," said the King, "that Don Pedro is too cunning to have knowingly shut himself up in a place from whence there is no issue. We must, therefore, leave a small body of troops to harass Montiel, and force it to surrender, so that it may be unable to pride itself on our not being able to take it; but for ourselves, we will proceed elsewhere, for please God, we have other tasks to perform, and Don Pedro is not here."

Agenor was present at the discussion. "My lord," said he, "I am both very young and very inexperienced to raise my voice among all these valiant captains; but my conviction is such, that nothing can shake it. I recognised Caverley following the King, and Caverley has been killed. I saw Don Pedro enter Montiel; I knew his broken helmet, his shattered shield, his golden spurs stained with blood."

"And why might not Caverley himself be mistaken? I changed armour at Navaretto with a faithful chevalier, and why may not Don Pedro have done the same?" said Don Henry. His last reply gained the general assent; Agenor again found himself defeated. "I hope you are persuaded?" said the King to him.

"No, sire," he replied, humbly; "but I can say nothing against your Majesty's arguments."—"You must be convinced, Sire de Mauleon—you must be convinced."

"I will try to be so," said the young man, with a sadness which he could not conceal. It was, in fact, a cruel position for a lover.

Don Pedro, exasperated by his defeat, and having now no reason for caution, was shut up with Aïssa; and with the prospect of a speedy death before him, was it likely that this faithless prince would risk the chance of the young girl he loved, and whom he might obtain by violence, falling into the power of another. Besides, was not Mothril there—that

inventor of odious stratagems—capable of anything that
would advance his sanguinary and greedy policy a step. This
was what rendered Agenor half mad with grief and rage.
He understood that by longer guarding his secret, he exposed
himself to allowing Don Henry, the constable, and the army
to depart; that then Don Pedro, greatly superior in mind
and talent to the already disgusted officers, who would be
left before Montiel, would succeed in making his escape.   He
suddenly took his resolution, and demanded a private interview with the King

"My lord," said he, "this is why Don Pedro, in spite of
appearances, has taken refuge at Montiel.   It is my secret,
but it is my duty to disclose it for your interests.   Don Pedro
is passionately enamoured of Aïssa—Mothril's daughter.   He
wishes to espouse her.   It was on this account he suffered
Mothril to murder Donna Maria Padilla—as to please Maria
he caused Madame Blanche of Bourbon to be put to death."

"Well," said the King; "then Aïssa is at Montiel?"

"She is there," said Agenor.

"Another thing, my friend, of which you are no more sure
than of the former one."—"I am sure of it, my lord, because
a lover always instinctively knows the spot containing his
cherished mistress."

"You love Aïssa—a Moorish girl!"

"Like Don Pedro, I love her passionately, my lord; but
there is this difference—for my sake, Aïssa would become a
Christian, whilst she would sooner destroy herself than become
Don Pedro's prey."

This avowal plunged Don Henry into deep perplexity.
"This is one reason," he muttered.   "But tell me how you
know that Aïssa is at Montiel."   Agenor related word for
word the murder of Hafiz and his account of Aïssa's wound.

"Tell me—have you formed any project?" asked the
King.

"I have, sire; and if your Majesty will lend me your
assistance, I will in eight days' time deliver Don Pedro into
your hands as surely as I before gave you certain tidings of
him."   The King summoned the constable, to whom Agenor
repeated what he had said.

"I do not any the more believe that so cunning, so heart-
less a prince, would suffer himself to be taken through his
love for a woman," replied the constable; "but the Sire de

Mauleon has my promise to aid him whenever he requires it, and I will perform it."

"Then have the place invested," said Agenor. "Let a moat be made round it, and with the earth dug out of it raise an embankment, behind which let not common soldiers, but vigilant officers, be concealed. I and my squire will conceal ourselves in a spot of which we know, and from whence we can overhear all the sounds from the castle. Don Pedro, if he behold a strong besieging army, will begin to be suspicious, and suspicion is the safety of so skilful and dangerous a man. Let your army set out for Toledo; only leave behind your earthen rampart two thousand men, a force amply sufficient to invest the castle and resist a sortie. When Don Pedro believes that you keep careless guard, he will endeavour to leave the castle—I give you warning of it." Agenor had scarcely finished unfolding his plan, and succeeded in gaining the King's attention, when an envoy from the governor of Montiel to the constable was announced.

"Let him be brought here," said Bertrand, "and then he can explain his business."

It was a Spanish officer named Rodrigo de Sanatrias; he announced to the constable that the garrison of Montiel beheld with uneasiness this display of troops, that the three hundred men shut up in the castle were unwilling for a protracted struggle, as hope had deserted them since the departure and defeat of Don Pedro. At these words both the King and the constable looked at Agenor, as much as to say, "Do you hear ?—he is not there."

"Then you will surrender ?" said the constable.

"Yes, messire, like brave men; but after having waited a certain time, since Don Pedro, on his return, must not accuse us of having betrayed his cause without striking a single blow."—"It is said that the King is still with you," said Don Henry.

The Spaniard laughed. "The King is far enough away," said he. "What should he do here, where men surrounded, as you have surrounded us, have nothing to do but either surrender or die of hunger ?" The King and Bertrand again glanced at Agenor.

"Then what are your real demands ?" questioned Duguesclin. "State your conditions formally."

"A ten days' truce," replied the officer, "to give Don

Pedro time to come to our aid; after that, we will surrender."
—"Listen," said the King.   "You positively assure me that
Don Pedro is not in the place?"

"Positively, monseigneur.   Without that being the case,
we should not ask to quit the place, as you will then see us
all, and would consequently recognise the King.   If we have
deceived you, you can punish us; and if you take the King,
you will doubtless show him little mercy?"   This last
sentence was a question to which the constable made no
reply, whilst Don Henry with difficulty concealed the bloodthirsty expression that glared from his eyes at the idea of
Don Pedro's capture.

"We grant you the truce," said the constable, "on condition that no one leaves the castle."

"But our provisions, my lord?" objected the officer.

"You shall be supplied with them; we will visit you, but
you shall not leave the castle."

"Then it is not an ordinary truce," muttered the officer.

"Why do you wish to leave the castle?   To escape when,
after ten days, we grant you your lives?"

"I have nothing more to say," replied the officer.   "I
accept the terms.   Have I your word, messire?"

"May I give it, my liege?" demanded Bertrand of the
King.—"Give it, constable."

"Then I grant you," said Duguesclin, "a ten days' truce,
and the lives of the garrison."—"Of all, my lord?"

"Of course," exclaimed Mauleon.   "Why should there be
any restrictions, when you have yourself declared that Don
Pedro is not with you?"   These words escaped from the
young man's lips in spite of the respect he owed to his leaders;
and he congratulated himself on having uttered them, for a
visible pallor passed like a cloud over the features of Don
Rodrigo Sanatrias.   He bowed and retired.

"Are you at last convinced, obstinate youth—poor lover?"
said the King, after he was gone.

"Yes, sire—convinced that Don Pedro is at Montiel, and
that you will have him in your power before a week is over."

"Oh, this is really obstinacy!" exclaimed the King.

"And yet he is not a Breton," said Bertrand, laughing.

"Monseigneur, Don Pedro is playing the same game as
ourselves.   Sure of not being able to escape by force, he essays
stratagem.   You are persuaded, as he wishes, that he is else-

where—you grant a truce, and keep negligent guard. Well, he will outwit you, and escape; but I trust we shall be there. The very circumstances that have convinced you of his not being at Montiel have only proved to me that he is there."

Agenor quitted the King's tent with an eagerness easy to conceive. "Muscaron," said he, "find out the highest tent in the camp, and fasten my banner to it, so as to be plainly seen from the castle. Aïssa will see and recognise it, and knowing me to be near her, will not lose her courage. My foes, seeing my pennon on the embankment, will fancy I am there, not suspecting that we are again going to creep into the grotto of the spring. Come, my brave Muscaron, come. This last effort, and the goal is reached!" Muscaron obeyed, and Mauleon's banner floated proudly above the rest.

CHAPTER LXXI.

THE RUSE OF THE VANQUISHED.

DON HENRY, accompanied by the constable, led the army from before Montiel. Only two thousand Bretons and Le Bègue de Vilaine remained surrounding the earthen embankment. Love had inspired Mauleon, every one of his observations had hit upon the truth. In fact, he had spoken as though he had overheard all that had passed in the castle. On his arrival after the battle, Don Pedro, breathless, suffocated, foaming with rage, flung himself upon a carpet in Mothril's chamber, and remained there motionless, mute, and unapproachable, making superhuman efforts to bury in the depths of his heart the fury and despair boiling within him. All his friends dead, his fine army destroyed, so many hopes of vengeance and of glory annihilated in the space of time it takes the sun to make the tour of the horizon. Nothing now remained but flight, and exile, and misery, fruitless and shameful conflicts, an inglorious death upon an inglorious field of battle. No more friends! This prince, who had never loved a single creature, experienced the most cruel grief in doubting the affection of others. Kings for the most part confound the respect which is their due with the affection they ought to inspire. Possessing the one, they excuse the other. Don Pedro beheld Mothril enter the chamber covered with blood. His armour was pierced in a thousand places, and through each hole welled blood which was not that of his enemies. The Moor was livid, and his eyes expressed gloomy resolution. It was no longer the submissive and cringing Saracen, but the proud harsh man addressing an equal.

"King Don Pedro," said he, "you are then vanquished." Don Pedro raised his head, and read in the cold eyes of the Moor the transformation that had taken place in his character.

"Yes," replied he, "irremediably so."

"You despair," said the Moor ; "then your God is not worth ours. I who am also vanquished, and wounded as well, do not despair. I have prayed, and am strengthened."

Don Pedro bowed his head resignedly. "True," said he, "I had forgotten God !"—"Unhappy King ! you are not yet aware of the greatest of your misfortunes. With the crown you will lose your life."

Don Pedro started, and cast a terrible look at Mothril. "You are going to assassinate me ?" said he.

"I—I your friend ! You are mad, Don Pedro. You have enemies enough without me ; and if I desired your death, I have no need to steep my hands in your blood. Rise, and look with me over the plain." In fact, the lances and cuirasses with which the plain was thronged, glittering in the setting sun, formed by degrees a fiery circle round Montiel, which imperceptibly narrowed. "Surrounded ! we are lost ! Do you see it well, Don Pedro ?" said Mothril. "For this castle, impregnable if well provisioned, can neither feed you nor the garrison. You have been seen ; you are surrounded ; you are lost !"

Don Pedro did not immediately reply. " I have been seen ; who has seen me ?" said he at last.

"Do you imagine that the banner of Le Bègue de Vilaine halts before Montiel in order to take the useless fortress ? and see, yonder is the pennon of the constable. Does he want Montiel ? No, it is you they want. You they are in search of."

"They shall not take me alive !" said Don Pedro.

Mothril in his turn was silent. Don Pedro resumed in an ironical tone, "The faithful friend ! the man full of hope, who has not even enough to say to his King, ' Live and hope.'"

"I am considering how to effect your escape from here," said Mothril.—"You would banish me !"

"I wish to save my own life. I do not wish to be forced

to destroy Donna Aïssa, for fear she should fall into the hands of the Christians." At Aïssa's name the blood mounted to Don Pedro's brow.

"It was through her," he muttered, "that I fell into this snare. Had it not been for my desire to see her again I should have hastened on to Toledo. Toledo can defend herself; I should not perish there of hunger. The Toledans love me, and would give their lives for me. Beneath the walls of Toledo I could have, for the last time, given them battle, and found there a glorious death; or who knows? perhaps, caused that of my enemy Henry de Transtamare. A woman has led me to my ruin."

"I would have rather seen you at Toledo," rejoined the Moor, coldly, "for I should then have arranged your affairs and my own."

"Instead of now being unwilling to do anything for me!" exclaimed Don Pedro, whose fury began to find vent. "Well, miserable slave, I may perhaps end my days here, but I will still punish you for your crimes and disloyalty. Aïssa, whom you have used as a lure, shall be mine!"

"You deceive yourself," said the Moor, calmly. "Aïssa will not be yours. Do you forget that I command here three hundred men? Do you forget that you cannot quit this chamber without my permission; that if you stir from your seat, I will lay you dead at my feet, and fling your body to the constable's soldiers, who will receive my present with transports of joy?"

"Traitor!" murmured Don Pedro.

"Blind fool!" exclaimed Mothril, "rather say a saviour. You can escape, and with liberty regain fortune, crown, and renown. Fly, then, without loss of time, and do not further irritate God by your debaucheries and exactions, nor insult your sole remaining friend."

"A friend! who speaks to me thus?"

"Would you rather that he flattered you, and gave you up to your enemies?"

"I submit; what do you wish to do?"

"I am going to send a herald to these Bretons who are watching you. They believe you to be here; let us deceive them. If we see them give up all hopes of making so rich a capture, let us profit by it, and arrange your escape on the first opportunity their negligence affords you. Have you here

E E

any devoted and intelligent man whom you could send to them?"—"I have Rodrigo Sanatrias, a captain who owes everything to me."

"That is no reason for his being faithful. Does he still expect anything from you?"

Don Pedro smiled bitterly. "True," said he, "our only friends are those who still hope to receive benefits from us. Well, I will make him hope so."

"Then let him come to us immediately."

While the King was summoning Sanatrias, Mothril placed several Moors on guard at the entrance of Aïssa's chamber. Don Pedro passed a part of the night in discussing with the Spaniards the means of obtaining a conference with the enemy. Rodrigo was as ingenious as he was faithful; besides he at once saw that the King's safety was the safety of them all, and that to gain possession of the person of the vanquished King, the victors would sacrifice ten thousand men, demolish the castle, and cause all to perish by hunger and the sword, but what they would attain their object. At day-break, Don Pedro beheld with despair the banner of Henry de Transtamare. For a King thus to change his route and a constable his plans, was sufficient proof that they felt certain of taking in Montiel something more valuable than its garrison. Don Pedro immediately dispatched Rodrigo Sanatrias, who performed his mission with the skill and success we have already seen. He brought back tidings to the castle that filled all the prisoners with joy. Don Pedro demanded without ceasing details of the scene, and drew favourable imferences from all he heard. The departure of the troops of the King and constable completed the proofs of the wisdom and efficacy of the Moor's counsel.

"At present," said Mothril, "we have only to contend with an ordinary enemy. Let a dark night come and we are saved."

Don Pedro could not contain himself with joy; he became affectionate and communicative to Mothril. "Listen," he said to him, "I see I wronged you; you merit a better fate than that of being the minister of a vanquished king. I will espouse Aïssa, and ally myself to you by the strongest ties. God has abandoned me. I will forsake God. I will become a worshipper of Mahomet, since it is he who has saved me by your voice. The Saracens have ceen me in the field.

They know whether I am a good captain and brave soldier. I will assist them in re-conquering Spain, and if they judge me worthy of commanding them, I will seat upon the throne of Castile a Mahometan king, to shame the Christianity which occupies itself with intestine broils instead of seriously devoting itself to the cause of religion."

Mothril listened with gloomy distrust to these promises, dictated by fear and momentary enthusiasm. "First make your escape," said he, "then we shall see."

"I wish you," said Don Pedro, "to have a more solemn pledge of the fulfilment of my promises than my simple word. Summon Aïssa hither; I will plight her my troth—you shall put down my promises in writing, and I will sign the document. We will form an alliance together instead of an agreement." In entering into this engagement, Don Pedro had regained all his art—all his former strength. He felt that by holding out to Mothril the hope of a future, he prevented him from entirely abandoning his cause, and that without that hope Mothril was capable of giving him up to his enemies.

Mothril, on his side, had had the same idea; but he saw a glimpse of hope in saving Don Pedro—that is to say, in reviving a war of which he would reap all the fruits; whilst Don Pedro dead or taken prisoner, the Saracens would no longer have a pretext for carrying on a ruinous war against their hitherto invincible enemies. Mothril well knew that Don Pedro was a good soldier, and that knowing the resources of the Moors, he could by reconciling himself with the Christians, work them incalculable evil. Besides, Mothril was linked to him by both crime and ambition—mysterious and powerful ties of which it is impossible to tell either the strength or the duration. He therefore listened favourably to Don Pedro, and replied, "I accept your offers with gratitude, my King, and will place you in a position to realize them. You wish to see Aïssa—you shall do so, only do not agitate her by too passionate avowals. Remember she is scarcely yet recovered from a painful illness."

"I will remember everything," said Don Pedro.

Mothril went in quest of Aïssa, who was beginning to grow uneasy at not receiving any tidings of Mauleon. The clashing of arms, the hurried steps of men and soldiers, announced to her the imminence of the danger; but what she dreaded more than all was the arrival of Don Pedro, and of this she was still ignorant. Mothril, who had made her so many promises was still obliged to persist in his falsehoods. He dreaded lest she should reveal to Don Pedro the scene that had taken place at Donna Maria's death; yet he could not refuse to grant the King this interview. He had hitherto avoided all explanation; but now the King would question, and Aïssa reply. " Aïssa," said he to the young girl, "I am come to announce to you that Don Pedro is defeated, and has taken refuge in this castle." Aïssa turned pale. He wishes to have an interview with you; do not refuse him, for he is master here. Besides, he leaves here this evening, and it is as well to remain on good terms with him."

Aïssa was apparently convinced by the Moor's words; but the throbbing of her heart foretold that some fresh misfortune awaited her. " I will grant no interview to the King," said she, "until I have seen the Sire de Mauleon, whom you promised to bring here, whether victor or vanquished."

" But Don Pedro is waiting!"

" What does that matter to me?"

" But I tell you he commands here."—" I have means of freeing myself from his yoke, you know that well. What did you promise me!"

" I will keep my promises, Aïssa; but aid me."

" I will aid no one in deception."—" Very well, then cause me to lose my head—I am ready to die."

This menace had always its effect upon Aïssa. Accustomed to the expeditious manner in which Arab justice was administered, she knew that a gesture from the master was sufficient to cause a head to fall; she could therefore be easily made to believe that Mothril was deeply compromised.

" What has the King to say to me?" she asked. " And where is this interview to take place?"

" In my presence."—" That is not enough; I choose to have witnesses to our conversation."

" I promise that it shall be so."—" I will be sure of it."

" How?"—" This chamber opens upon the platform of the castle. Place a guard of men there, my litter shall be carried thither attended by my women, and I will there listen to what the King has to say."

" It shall be as you desire, Donna Aïssa."

" Now, what has Don Pedro to say to me?"

" He wishes to offer you his hand."

Aïssa made a violent gesture of refusal.

" I know it well," said Mothril; " but let him do it—remember he departs to-night."

" But I will not make him any reply."

" On the contrary, Aïssa, you will reply with courtesy. You see these armed men, Spaniards and Bretons, surrounding the castle? These men, if they find Don Pedro is amongst us, will take it by storm, and put us to death. Therefore, to insure our safety, let the King go."—" But the Sire de Mauleon?"

" He could not save us if Don Pedro were here."

Aissa interrupted him. " You lie!" said she. " You cannot even flatter me with the hope of being reunited to him. Does he live—where is he—what is he doing?" At this moment, Muscaron by his master's orders, raised the banner—so well-known to Aïssa—in the air. The young girl perceived the beloved signal; she clasped her hands in ecstasy, exclaiming, " He sees me—he hears me! Pardon me, Mothril, I suspected you wrongfully. Go, then, and inform the King that I will follow you."

Mothril cast his eyes upon the plain, saw and recognised the banner; and turning pale, faltered, " I go." Then he burst out furiously, " Accursed Christian ! then you still pursue me, but I will escape you."

CHAPTER LXXII.

EVASION.

DON PEDRO received Aïssa on the platform, in the midst of the witnesses she had requested. His love was not expressed in a very emphatic manner, for its ardour was considerably cooled by the preoccupation of his approaching flight. Aïssa had, therefore, nothing to reproach Mothril with on that account; besides, during the whole of the conference, she did not remove her eyes from Mauleon's welcome banner, which waved resplendently in the sun, at the further end of the embankment. Aïssa beheld an armed man standing beneath this banner, whom she mistook for her lover. This Agenor had calculated upon. Having thus found means of reassuring Aïssa—even whilst revealing to her his presence—and Mothril by banishing from his mind all suspicions of secret designs,

Don Pedro had decided that three of his most devoted
friends should hold themselves in readiness to go at night
and reconnoitre the entrenchments. There was really one
spot more carelessly guarded than the rest—namely, the side
of the rock descending perpendicularly on the ravine. Many
advised the King to descend into this ravine, by means of a
rope attached to Aïssa's window; but even if he succeeded in
reaching the ground, he would have no horse to bear him
rapidly away. It was therefore resolved that the entrenchments should be reconnoitred and a way forced—by scat-
tering or slaying the sentinels—through which the King,
mounted on a swift horse, could make his escape. But the
bright sunshine promised a clear night, which would be un-
favourable to the execution of the project. All at once, as
if fortune was determined to favour Don Pedro's every wish,
a west wind raised whirlwinds of the burning sand of the
plain, and long streamers of copper-coloured clouds appeared
on the verge of the horizon, like the vanguard of some terrible army. The sun had scarcely set behind the towers of
Toledo, when dark heavy clouds mantled the sky. Towards
nine o'clock in the evening, a blinding rain began to fall.

Agenor and Muscaron had proceeded immediately after
sunset to their hiding-place near the spring, where they sat
waiting side by side. The picked troops of Le Bègue de
Vilaine had hollowed out for themselves a shelter in the sun-
baked earth of the embankment, so that around Montiel,
there was an uninterrupted cordon of these concealed men.
According to the orders of Agenor—who since the constable's
departure had taken the initiative in everything—the sentinels were seen standing at regular distances, guarding, or
seeming to guard, the line of circumvallation. The rain had
obliged the sentinels to muffle themselves in their cloaks—
some of them were lying upon them. At ten o'clock, Agenor
and Muscaron heard the sound of men's footsteps upon the
rock. They listened more intently, and presently discerned
three of Don Pedro's officers, who, rather crawling than walking, were exploring the entrenchments at the place already
agreed upon. The sentinels had been purposely removed
from this spot. There only remained the officer concealed
beneath the embankment. Don Pedro's spies perceived that
the spot was left unguarded. They joyfully communicated
the discovery to each other, and Agenor overheard them ex-

changing congratulations, as they re-ascended the steep path. One of them remarked, "It is slippery, and the horses will scarcely be able to keep their feet in making the descent."

"Yes; but they will go better on the plain," rejoined another.

These words filled Agenor's heart with joy; he dispatched Muscaron to the entrenchments to inform the nearest Breton officer that some fresh event was about to take place. The officer communicated the tidings to his neighbour, who did the same, and so on until the intelligence given by Agenor had gone round Montiel. Half-an-hour had scarcely elapsed when Agenor heard a horse's hoof strike upon the platform. The noise drew nearer, and the sound of other horses' feet was perceptible—but to Agenor and Muscaron alone. In fact, the King had directed the horses' feet to be wrapped round with tow, so as to deaden the sound of their hoofs. The King came last, a little dry cough, which he could not repress, betraying his presence. He walked with great difficulty, holding up his horse, which kept slipping in the rapid descent, by the bridle. As each of the fugitives paused before the grotto, Agenor and Muscaron recognised them. When it came to Don Pedro's turn they distinctly saw his pale and anxious face. Arrived at the entrenchments, the two foremost fugitives mounted their horses, and leaped over the parapet; but they had scarcely gone ten steps, before they fell into a pitfall ready prepared for them, where twenty soldiers gagged and carried them noiselessly away. Don Pedro, suspecting nothing, in his turn leaped on his horse, and in a moment was seized by Agenor, who encircled him with his strong arms, whilst Muscaron bound a belt over his mouth. This done, Muscaron pricked the horse with his dagger, and it bounded over the embankment, and galloped off, its hoofs ringing on the rocky road. Don Pedro struggled with all the strength of despair.

"Take care," muttered Agenor in his ear; "I shall be obliged to kill you if you make a noise."

Don Pedro succeeded in gasping out, "I am the King; treat me in a knightly manner."

"I am well aware that you are the King," said Agenor. "I was waiting for you here. On the word of a chevalier, you shall not be ill-treated." He took the King on his robust shoulders, and thus traversed the line of entrench-

ments, in the midst of the officers, whose hearts bounded
with joy. "Silence, silence, messieurs!" said Agenor. "No
noise, no cries. I have attended to the constable's affairs;
now, do not make me spoil my own." He bore his prisoner
into the tent of Le Bègue de Vilaine, who flung himself on
his neck, and warmly embraced him.

"Quick! quick!" exclaimed this leader; "couriers for the
King, who is before Toledo; couriers for the constable, who
keeps to the open country, to tell him that the war is
finished!"

CHAPTER LXXIII.

DIFFICULTY.

WHILST the whole of the Breton camp passed the night in
the intoxication of success, horsemen mounted on the fleetest
steeds in the troop went to carry the intelligence to Don
Henry and the constable. Agenor had remained during the
night with the prisoner, who, buried in moody silence, alike
refused all consolation and all alleviation of his situation.
They could not allow a king to remain bound; they therefore
unloosed his bonds, after having made him give his "parole"
not to escape.

"But," observed Le Bègue to his officers, "we know the
value of Don Pedro's word; therefore double the guard, and
let the tent be surrounded in such a manner that he cannot
even dream of making his escape."

They found the constable about three leagues from Montiel,
driving the remnants of the army, defeated on the preceding
evening, before him like flocks of sheep, and by the capture
of prisoners with rich ransoms, completing this important
day's victory; for the Toledans had refused to open their
gates to even their defeated allies, so greatly did they fear a
deceit common to those barbarous times, when cunning often
took the place of strength.

The constable had no sooner learnt the news, than he exclaimed, "This Mauleon had more wit than we had!" And
he spurred his horse towards Montiel with a joy difficult to
describe.

Dawn was silvering the crests of the mountains, when the
constable arrived, and embraced Mauleon, who modestly
received his congratulations on this triumph. "Thanks,

messire," said he, "for your clearsightedness and courageous perseverance. Where is the prisoner?" he added.

"In Le Bègue de Vilaine's tent," replied Mauleon. "But he is either sleeping or feigning to do so."

"I do not wish to see him," said Bertrand. "The first person who has an interview with Don Pedro must be Don Henry, his conqueror and his master. Is he well guarded? Some evil spirits need only utter a good prayer to the devil to be delivered."

"There are thirty chevaliers around the tent, messire," replied Agenor. "It is impossible for him to escape unless some agent of Satan carries him away, like the Prophet Habacuc, by the hair of his head."—"Then we should see him go, and I would send him in the air a bolt that would make him arrive in hell before the Angel of Darkness!" said Muscaron.

"Let a camp bed be spread for me in front of the tent," commanded the constable. "I, like the rest, will guard the prisoner, and present him to Don Henry." The constable's orders were obeyed, and his couch, a board covered with heath, placed at the very door of the tent. "By the bye," said Bertrand; "he is almost a felon, and capable of destroying himself. Have his weapons been taken from him?"

"We have not dared to do so, my lord. His is a sacred head: he has been proclaimed King before God's own altar."

"True; besides, we have from the first received orders from Don Henry to treat him with all respect."

"You see, my lord," said Agenor, "how grossly this Spaniard lied when he assured you that Don Pedro was not at Montiel."—"Therefore," said Le Bègue de Vilaine, coolly, "we will hang him and all the garrison. By this lie, he has freed the constable from his promise."

"My lord," rejoined Agenor, quickly, "these poor soldiers have been guilty of nothing but obeying the orders of their leader. Besides, if they surrender, it will be committing murder; and if they do not, you will be unable to take them."

"We shall reduce them by famine," said the constable.

The idea of seeing Aïssa perish by famine carried Mauleon beyond the limits of his natural discretion. "Oh, my lord," he exclaimed, "you will not be guilty of cruelty."

"We will punish disloyalty and falsehood," said the constable. "Besides, should we not congratulate ourselves on a falsehood which will give us an opportunity of punishing the Saracen Mothril. I am going to send a messenger to this miscreant to inform him that Don Pedro is taken; and consequently was at Montiel—that he has deceived me, and in order to give an example to all felons, the garrison will be put to death if they surrender, and condemned to perish by hunger if they do not."

"And Donna Aïssa?" said Mauleon, pale with uneasiness.

"It is well understood that we will spare the women," replied Duguesclin, "since cursed be the warrior who does not spare old men, women, and children."

"But Mothril will not spare Aïssa; that would be leaving her, after his death, to another. You do not know Mothril—he will kill her. But you promised to grant me a boon, messire. I ask of you Aïssa's life.

"And I grant it you, my friend—but how will you save her?"

"I entreat you to send no other messenger to Mothril than myself, leave me at liberty to say what I please, and I will answer for the prompt submission of the Moor and the garrison. But for pity's sake, the life of the unfortunate soldiers—they have done nothing."

"I see that I must yield. You have done me such good service that I can refuse nothing. The King, on his side, owes you as much as myself, for you have taken Don Pedro, without whom our victory would be incomplete. I may therefore, in his name as well as my own, grant you what you desire. Aïssa is yours—both officers and men of the garrison shall have their lives spared, but Mothril shall be hanged."—"My lord!"—

"Nay, do not ask that of me again, for you will not obtain it. I should offend God if I spared this wretch."—"Monseigneur, the first thing he will demand will be whether his life is to be spared. What can I reply?"

"What you please, Sire de Mauleon."

"But you would have done so according to the articles of the truce made with Rodrigo Sanatrias?"

"Him!—never. I said the garrison. Mothril is a Saracen, I do not reckon him among the defenders of the castle; besides, I have to render an account to God, I tell you. So long as you have Donna Aïssa, nothing else concerns you. Let me do as I please."

"Once more, monseigneur, let me supplicate you. This Mothril is a wretch—his chastisement would please God—he is disarmed—he can no longer do harm!"

"You might as well talk to a statue, Sire de Mauleon," replied the constable, "so be good enough to leave me to my repose. As to the message you bear to the garrison, I leave you at full liberty to say what you please—go !"

This admitted of no reply. Agenor well knew that Duguesclin, when once engaged in a project, was inflexible, and never to be turned aside from it. He also knew that Mothril, on learning that Don Pedro had fallen into the power of the Bretons, would no longer adopt mild measures, since he was well aware that his life would not be spared. In fact, Mothril was one of those men who know how to bear the weight of the hatred they inspire, and submit to the consequences. Implacable to others, he resigned himself in his turn to receive no mercy. On the other hand, he would never consent to resign Aïssa. Agenor's position was most difficult.

"If I tell a falsehood," thought he, " I shall dishonour myself. If I promise Mothril his life, and not keep my word, I shall become unworthy of woman's love and man's esteem." He was still plunged in this cruel perplexity, when the trumpets announced King Henry's arrival before the tent. It was already broad daylight, and they could see from the camp the ramparts of the castle, where Mothril and Rodrigo were walking together engaged in deep conversation.

"What the constable would not grant you, King Henry will," said Muscaron to his master, whose sadness he remarked. "Ask, and you will obtain it. What does it matter whose lips say yes, so long as you have a positive yes, which you can without falsehood report to Mothril."

"Let us try," said Agenor. And he hastened to throw himself on his knees beside the stirrup of Henry, whom a squire was assisting to alight from his horse.

"Good news, seemingly ?" said the King.

"Yes, my liege."—"I wish to reward you, Mauleon ; ask from me what you will—even a province."

"I ask you, sire, for Mothril's life ?"—"That is worth more than a province, but I grant it you."

"Set out quickly, master," whispered Muscaron, "for yonder comes the constable, and if he overhears this it will be too late.'

Agenor kissed the King's hand, who alighted from his horse, exclaiming—

"Good day, dear constable! So the traitor is ours?"

"Yes, monseigneur," said Bertrand, who feigned not to have remarked Agenor's conversation with the King.

The young man sped away as if he were carrying off some treasure. As an accredited messenger he had the right of taking with him two trumpeters. He chose them, made them precede him, and, followed by the inseparable Muscaron, mounted the path leading to the outer gates of the castle.

CHAPTER LXXIV.

LOVE'S DIPLOMACY.

THE gates were opened without delay, and as they advanced they were able to judge of the difficulty of the approach. Sometims the path was not more than a foot in width, and everywhere the rock descended perpendicularly into the ravine. The Bretons, little accustomed to mountains, felt their heads grow dizzy.

"Love makes us sadly imprudent, master," said Muscaron; "but God watches over all."

"Do you forget that our persons are inviolable?"

"Eh, messire! what would restrain this accursed Moor, and is there anything on this earth he would regard as inviolable?" Agenor imposed silence on his squire, continued to ascend the mountain, and reached the platform, where Mothril, having recognised him as he approached, awaited him.

"The Frank!" he muttered. "What signifies his presence at the castle?" The trumpets sounded. Mothril made signs that he was listening.

"I come," said Agenor, "on the part of the constable, to tell you thus:—'I made a truce with my enemies on condition that no one quitted the château; on this condition I granted them their lives. To-day I have changed my mind, for you have broken your word.—'"

"In what?" asked Mothril, turning pale.

"This very night," continued Agenor, "three horsemen passed the entrenchments in spite of our sentinels."

"Well," said Mothril, restraining himself by a violent effort, "they must suffer death since they have perjured

themselves."---" That would be easy if we had taken them,"
said Agenor, " but they have escaped."

" How was it you did not stop them ?" exclaimed Mothril,
unable, after having experienced such lively inquietude,
to conceal his joy.—" Because our guards, confiding in
your word, kept less vigilant watch than usual ; as according to the reasoning of the Senor Rodrigo beside you, no one
had any inducement to take to flight, all lives being spared."

" You conclude to do this ?" said the Moor.

" Somewhat changing the conditions of the truce."

" Ah, I suspected so !" said Mothril, bitterly. " The clemency of the Christian is fragile as a glass ; in drinking from
it we must be careful not to shatter it.   You are come to
inform us, then, that several soldiers—were they soldiers ?—
having escaped from Montiel, you will be forced to put us all
to death."—" But first of all, Saracen," said Agenor, stung
by this supposition, " you ought to know who these fugitives
were."

" How can I tell ?"—" Count your garrison."

" I do not command it."—" You do not form part of the
garrison !" retorted Agenor, quickly ; " then you are not in-
cluded in the truce."

" You are very cunning for a young man."

" I have learnt to be distrustful through associating with
the Saracens ; but answer."—" I am in fact their chief," said
Mothril, who feared to lose the chances of a capitulation,
were such a thing possible.

" You see I had reason to be cunning, since you were telling me falsehoods. But that is not the question. You
confess that the conditions have been violated."

" You say so, Christian."—" And you ought to believe
me," said Mauleon. " But here are the commands of
our leader, the constable. This place must be surrendered
this very day, or the blockade will be rigorously commenced."

" Is that all ?" inquired Mothril.—" That is all."

" You will starve us ?"—" Yes."

" And if we choose to die ?"—" You are at liberty to
do so."

Mothril regarded Agenor in a strange manner, which the
latter perfectly comprehended.

" All ?" said he, dwelling on the word.—" All," replied

Mauleon ; "but if you perish it will be by your own choice for, believe me, Don Pedro will not rescue you."

"You think so ?"—"I am sure of it."

"Why so ?"—"Because we have an army to oppose him, he has no longer one, and before he has collected one you will be dead with hunger."

"You reason justly, Christian."—"Therefore save your life, whilst it is in your power to do so."

"Ah, you offer us our lives !"

"On the faith of the King, who has just arrived."

"Who has just arrived !" repeated Mothril, uneasily, "but I do not see him."—"Behold his tent, or rather that of Le Bègue de Vilaine."

"Yes, yes ; you are sure that he will grant us our lives ?"

"I will guarantee it."

"And to me also ?"—"To you, Mothril, I have the King's word."

"We shall be allowed to retire where we please ?"

"Where you please."

"With attendants, baggage, and treasure ?"

"Yes, Saracen."—"That is very fine !"

"You do not believe me ? You are mad ! Why should we entreat you to yield to us to-day, when we are certain of having you either dead or living by remaining here a month ?"

"Oh, you may fear the coming of Don Pedro."

"I assure you that we do not fear him."

"Christian, I must have time for reflection."

"If, in two hours' time, you do not surrender !" exclaimed the impatient young man, "look upon yourself as dead. The iron belt will not open again."

"Two hours ! That is no great stretch of generosity," said Mothril, anxiously interrogating the horizon, as if a saviour was about to appear at the bottom of the plain.

"Then this is all your reply ?" said Agenor.

"In two hours !" faltered Mothril.

"Oh, messire, he will surrender; you have persuaded him !" whispered Muscaron in his master's ear.

Mothril suddenly fixed his gaze on the Breton camp, with an anxiety he no longer sought to disguise. "Look !" he muttered, pointing out to Rodrigo Le Bègue de Vilaine's tent.

The Spaniard leaned over the parapet in order to have a better view.

"To judge from appearances," said Mothril, "it seems as though the Christians were tearing one another in pieces. See how they are rushing towards the tent." In fact a crowd of officers and men were hurrying towards the tent with signs of the most lively anxiety. The tent swayed to and fro, as though shaken by some violent struggle taking place within it.

Agenor beheld the constable rush towards it with angry gestures. "Something strange and terrible is taking place in the tent where Don Pedro' is confined," said he. "Let us go, Muscaron."

The Moor's attention was distracted by this incomprehensible tumult, and that of Rodrigo was even more so; Agenor profited by this forgetfulness to descend the difficult steep with his Bretons. When about half way down, they heard a horrible cry mounting from the plain towards heaven. It was time they reached the barriers; the last gate had scarcely closed behind them when Mothril cried out in a voice of thunder, "Allah, Allah! the traitor has deceived me. Don Pedro is taken! Seize the Frank, and let him serve as an hostage; to the gates—close them!—close them!" But Agenor had gained the entrenchments; he was in safety, and could even behold the terrible spectacle the Moor had witnessed from the height of the platform.

"God be thanked!" exclaimed Agenor, trembling with rage, and raising his arm towards heaven, "in another moment we should have been taken and lost; but what I see in yonder tent would have excused Mothril taking the most bloody revenge!"

CHAPTER LXXV.

LE BÈGUE DE VILAINE'S TENT.

DON HENRY, after having quitted Agenor, and granting him Mothril's pardon, wiped his flushed face, as he said to the constable, "My friend, my heart throbs wildly. I am about to witness the humiliation of the man I mortally hate; it is a joy mingled with bitterness, and at this moment I cannot comprehend the mixture."

"That proves, sire," said the constable, "that your Majesty's heart is great and noble, for it would otherwise contain nothing but triumphant joy."

"It is strange," added the King, "that I enter this tent with such reluctance, and, as I said before, such oppression at my heart. How is he?"

"Sire, he is seated on a bench, with his head buried in his hands; he seems greatly cast down."

Henry de Transtamare made a sign with his hand, and every one withdrew. "Constable," said he, in a low tone, "one last piece of advice, I entreat you. I wish to spare his life, but must I banish him, or imprison him in some fortress?"

"Do not ask me to advise you, sire," returned the constable, "for I cannot do so. You are wiser than I am, and about to stand face to face with a brother; God will inspire you."

"Your words have decided me, constable—thanks."

The King raised the flap of canvas closing the entrance of the tent, and entered. Don Pedro had not quitted the posture described by Duguesclin to the King, only his despair was no longer mute; he betrayed it, now by desponding exclamations, now by furious ones. One would have pronounced it the beginning of madness. At the sound of Henry's footsteps, he raised his head. No sooner did he recognise his majestic countenance, and the golden crest in the form of a lion, than he gave way to his fury.

"You are come!" he vociferated. "You have dared to come!" Henry made no reply. "I vainly sought you in the *melée*," continued Don Pedro, gradually lashing himself into fury; "but you have only the courage to insult a vanquished foe; and at this very moment you hide your face lest I should see its pallor!" Henry slowly unfastened the clasps of his helmet, and laid it upon the table. His face was indeed pale, but his eyes preserved a sweet and serene expression. This calmness exasperated Don Pedro. He arose from his seat. "Yes," said he, "I recognise my father's bastard, the self-styled King of Castile, forgetting that whilst I live Castile can know no other King."

Henry endeavoured to hear with patience these galling taunts of his enemy; but an angry flush mounted to his brow, and drops of cold sweat rolled down his face. "Take care!" said he, in a trembling voice. "Remember that you are here in my power. I have not insulted you, and you are dishonouring your birth by expressions unworthy of us both."

"Bastard!" cried Don Pedro; "bastard! bastard!"

"Wretch! then you wish to arouse my fury?"

"Oh, I am quite easy on that score," retorted Don Pedro. approaching him with flashing eyes and livid lips; "you will not let your anger go further than is necessary for the preservation of your safety—you are afraid——"—"You lie!" vociferated Don Henry, exasperated beyond measure.

Don Pedro, in reply, seized Don Henry by the throat, while Don Henry grasped Don Pedro in both his arms. "Ah!" said the vanquished prince, "we only needed this encounter, and you shall see it shall prove a decisive one." They wrestled so furiously together that they shook the whole tent; the canvas swung to and fro; and at the noise the constable, Le Bègue de Vilaine, and several officers, came running to the spot. They were obliged, in order to force an entrance into the tent, to rip up the canvas with their swords. The two foes, locked together—interlaced like two serpents—were clinging to the hangings with their spurred feet. When the interior of the tent, and the murderous struggle taking place in it, were disclosed, the constable uttered a loud cry. A thousand soldiers immediately rushed in the direction of the tent. It was then that Mothril from the height of the platform, and Agenor from the foot of the embankment, caught sight of this spectacle. The two adversaries continued to wrestle, rolling over each other, and, every time they had an arm at liberty, seeking to seize a weapon. Don Pedro was the most fortunate; he succeeded in getting Henry de Transtamare under him, and holding him down with his knee, he drew a small dagger from his belt, with which he prepared to strike him. But the danger he was in gave Henry fresh strength—he flung off his brother and raised himself on his side. They lay side by side, breathing into each other's faces the devouring fire of their powerless hate.

"There must be an end to this!" exclaimed Don Pedro, seeing that no one dared to separate them—so much the majesty of royalty and the horrors of their situation awed the spectators. "To-day there may no longer be a King of Castile, but there shall no longer be a usurper. I shall have avenged myself, although I have ceased to reign. They will kill me, but I shall have drunk your blood!" And, with unexpected strength, he flung himself upon his brother, who was exhausted by the struggle, seized him by the throat, and

F F

raised his hand with the intention of burying the dagger in his breast.

Duguesclin then perceiving that he was searching for the opening between the coat of mail and the cuirass, in which to deal his blow, seized Don Pedro's foot in his strong grasp, and made him lose his equilibrium. In his turn, he fell under Henry. " I neither make nor unmake kings," said the constable, in a gloomy voice; "I aid my sovereign lord."

Henry, on being able to breathe again, had recovered his strength and drawn his sword. There was a lightning flash, and the bright steel was buried in Don Pedro's breast. A stream of blood, stifling the terrible cry that broke from Don Pedro's lips, spouted into the victor's face; the wounded man's hand relaxed his hold, his eyes became fixed, his head fell back and struck heavily on the ground.

" Oh, what have you done ?" exclaimed Agenor, who, rushing into the tent, beheld, with bristling hair, the corpse swimming in its own blood, and the kneeling conqueror, his weapon in his right hand, whilst with his left he was endeavouring to support himself.

A fearful silence reigned throughout the assembly. The kingly murderer let fall his reddened blade. They then beheld a stream of blood gush from the corpse, and slowly trickle down the rocky slope. Every one recoiled before this blood, which smoked as though still seething with anger and hatred.

Don Henry no sooner rose to his feet, than he retreated to a distant corner of the tent, and there seating himself, buried his face in his hands. He could not support either the light of day or the gaze of the spectators. The constable—equally gloomy, but more energetic—quietly rose and dismissed the witnesses of this terrible scene. "Certes," he observed, "it would have been better to shed this blood in the fray with your sword or your battle-axe. But God orders all things, and the deed is done. Come, sire, take courage !"

" "His death was his own choice," murmured the King ; "I was going to pardon him. See that his remains are not too long exposed to the public gaze—that honourable burial"——

" Sire, banish all such thoughts from your mind. Leave us to do our duty."

The King retreated behind a crowd of silent and horrified soldiers, and sought refuge in another tent. Duguesclin summoned one of his Bretons. " Cut off his head," said he, pointing to Don Pedro's corpse. " And you, Le Bègue de Vilaine, dispatch it to Toledo. It is the custom of this country, where, at the very least, the usurpers of the names of the dead have no longer any right to come and trouble the reign and the repose of the living." He had scarcely finished speaking, when a Spaniard from the fortress came to announce, on the part of the governor, that the garrison would lay down their arms at eight o'clock that evening, according to the conditions imposed by the constable's envoy.

CHAPTER LXXVI.
THE MOOR'S RESOLUTION.

THE whole of this brief but terrible scene had been beheld from the castle of Montiel, thanks to the curtains of the tent being cast aside, and the agitation of the principal actors.

We have seen that during the interview between Agenor and Mothril, the latter, whilst listening to the propositions of the former, frequently turned his gaze towards the plain, where something seemed to attract his attention. Agenor had endeavoured to make him believe that the Bretons were in ignorance of the names of the last night's fugitives. He had also made him believe that they had not been taken.

These tidings re-assured Mothril as to Don Pedro's fate, for the obscurity of the night had prevented those in the castle from remarking the results of the attempted escape, and the Bretons had taken care to observe the most profound silence whilst making the capture. Mothril had, therefore, every reason to believe Don Pedro safe. Thus he began by disdaining Mauleon's propositions'; but, on looking towards the plain, he beheld three horses wandering among the heath, and distinctly recognised—he whose sight was so sure—Don Pedro's white horse, the noble animal that had borne his master from the field of battle, and should have carried him like a flash of lightning beyond the reach of his enemies.

The Bretons in their enthusiasm had seized the riders and forgotten the horses, which, finding themselves at liberty, and terrified by the precipitation of the aggressors, had fled beyond the entrenchments, and taken to the open country. They had wandered about, browsing and sporting with each other, all the rest of the night; but at daybreak, instinct, or perhaps fidelity, had made them return to the neighbourhood of the castle, from whence Mothril perceived them. They had not retraced the circuitous path by which they had left it, therefore the ravine was still between them and the fortress—a ravine deep and precipitous, which effectually stayed their progress. Hidden by the piles of rocks, they from time to time raised their heads to gaze at the castle, and then continued to browse on the mosses and resinous madronios they found in the crevices of the rock, and whose berry resembles the strawberry in both colour and perfume.

When Mothril caught sight of these animals he turned pale, and began to conceive doubts of Agenor's veracity. It was then he began to discuss the conditions and bargain for his own life being spared. Then all at once the scene in the tent presented itself before him in all its horrors. He recognised the golden lion, the badge of Henry de Transtamare —the bright hair of Don Pedro—his violent and energetic gestures ; he recognised his voice when the last cry—the death cry, burst shrill and despairing from his pierced breast. Then it was he sought to detain Agenor, to make a hostage of him, or to tear him limb from limb. Then beholding the assassination of Don Pedro, and knowing neither the cause nor the results of the quarrel, he whispered to himself that he was indeed lost—he the instigator of the murdered King. From that moment he comprehended the whole of Agenor's tactics. That he promised him his life in order to let him be massacred at the sortie from Montiel, and to thus gain possession of Aïssa.

"I may possibly die," said the Moor to himself ; "nevertheless, I will endeavour to save my life ; but, accursed Christian, Aïssa shall never be yours except dead, like myself." He agreed with Rodrigo to conceal Don Pedro's death, which they alone had witnessed, and to assemble the officers of the garrison. All were of opinion that it would be better to surrender. Mothril vainly endeavoured to persuade these men that death was preferable to trusting to the mercy of the victors.

Rodrigo himself combated his design. "They may, perhaps, bear malice towards Don Pedro," said he ; "but we, whom they spared in the affray—we who are Spaniards, like Don Henry, why should they massacre us, when our safety is guaranteed by the constable's word? We are neither Saracens nor Moors—and we invoke the same God as our conquerors."

Mothril plainly saw that with the resignation of his comrades all would be finished. He bowed his head on his breast, and fenced himself round with a terrible and immutable resolution. Rodrigo announced that the garrison were ready to surrender immediately. Mothril contrived that the capitulation should not take place until towards the evening. For the last time they yielded to his desire. It was then the messenger came to Duguesclin, and proposed eight o'clock in the evening for the surrender of the place. Mothril shut himself up in the governor's apartments to, as he said to Rodrigo, pass his time in prayer.

"At the appointed hour," said he—"that is to say, at night, you will make the garrison quit the castle,—first the men, then the under officers, then the officers themselves. I will come last with Donna Aïssa."

Mothril was no sooner alone than he proceeded to open the door to Aïssa's apartments. "You see, my child," said he, "all has succeeded as we hoped. Don Pedro is not only gone from here—he is dead!"

"Dead!" repeated the young girl with an expression of horror in which still lingered the remains of doubt.—"Here!" said the Moor, phlegmatically, "come and see for yourself."

"Ah!" murmured Aïssa, hesitating between terror and a desire to know the truth.

"Do not hesitate thus, Aïssa; I wish you to see how the Christians, whom you love so much, treat their vanquished and captive foes." He drew the young girl from her chamber to the platform, and showed her the tent of Le Bègue de Vilaine, in which still lay the corpse. As Aïssa, pale and mute, contemplated this frightful spectacle, a man knelt beside the body, and with one blow of a Breton axe, severed the head from the body. Aïssa gave a loud shriek, and fell half fainting into Mothril's arms. The Moor carried her into her chamber, laid her upon her couch, and, kneeling at its foot, "Child," said he, "you have seen it; you know the same fate awaits me. The Christians have offered to capitulate and grant me my life; but they promised the same to Don Pedro. See how they have kept their word. You are young and inexperienced; but your heart is pure, your mind upright. Advise me, I entreat you!"

'I advise you!"—" You are acquainted with a Christian."

"And a Christian," interrupted Aïssa, "who will never break his word; but will save you, for he loves me."—" You think so?" said Mothril, gloomily shaking his head.

"I am sure of it," added the young girl, with all the enthusiasm of love.—" Child," said Mothril, "what authority has he among his companions? He is only a simple chevalier, and has above him captains, generals, a constable, a king! That *he* would pardon me, I agree; but the others are implacable—they will kill us!"

"Kill *me!*" repeated the young girl, with a momentary burst of egotism, which she could not repress, and which allowed the Moor to read to the bottom of her heart to see the depth of the peril and the necessity of a prompt resolution.

"No," said he; "you are a beautiful young maiden. These captains, these generals, this constable, and King, will pardon you, in hopes of obtaining a smile from your lips. Oh! the French and the Spaniards are gay gallants," he added, with a hollow laugh. "But I—I am only a dangerous foe to them: they will sacrifice me."

"I tell you that Agenor is there—that he will protect me with his life!"

"And if he were dead, what would become of you?"

"I have death for a refuge!"

"Oh, I contemplate death with less resignation than you, Aïssa, for I am nearer it."

"I swear to you that I will save you."

"You swear to me by what?"—" By my life. Besides, I repeat to you, you are mistaken as to the influence possessed by Agenor. The King loves him—he has been a faithful servant to the constable. They confided an important mission to him—you remember—at Soria."

"Yes; and it appears you also recollect it, Aïssa," retorted the Moor, with a glance full of jealousy.

Aïssa blushed, but resumed, " My chevalier will therefore save us both; if necessary, I will make this a condition——"

"Listen, child !" interrupted the Moor, irritated at beholding this loving obstinacy embarrass him at every step of the path along which he was longing to rush. "Agenor is so little able to rescue us, that he was here himself a short time ago."

"He was here!" exclaimed Aïssa—"here! and you did

not tell me."—" To open all eyes to your love ! You forget your dignity, young girl. He came, I say, to find means of saving you from the outrages of the Christians. At this price he promised to defend me."

"Outrages!—to me! to me about to embrace Christianity."

Mothril uttered a cry of rage, which imperious necessity immediately made him repress. " How shall I act ?" said he. " Advise me, for time presses. This evening the place is given up to the Christians; this evening I shall die, and you will become a portion of the infidel's booty."

" But what, then, did Agenor say?"

" He made a terrible proposition, which only proves the imminence of the danger."—" He suggested a means of safety —a means of escape. Speak !"

"Look out of this window. You will see that on this side the rock of Montiel is perpendicular—impracticable, and descends to the bottom of the ravine in such a manner that surveillance there would be superfluous, since birds that fly and adders that crawl could alone ascend or descend these heights. Besides, since the cessation of their watch for Don Pedro, the French have totally abandoned the spot."

Aïssa gazed fearfully into the gulf, already darkened by the shadows of approaching night. " Well," said she.

" Well, the Frank advised me to fasten a rope to the iron bars of this grating, and to lower it into the ravine, as we wished to do for Don Pedro, and should have done had it not been necessary for him to find a horse below. He advised me to fasten myself with you in my arms to this cord, to lower myself into this ravine whilst the Christian army were engaged in relieving the garrison, which will defile unarmed about eight o'clock this evening.

Aïssa listened with flashing eyes and quivering lips, and a second time gazed down upon the yawning abyss " He advised this?" said she.

"When you have descended," continued the Moor, " you will find me awaiting you. I will furnish you with the means of flight."—"What! he will abandon us! he will leave me alone with you !"

Mothril turned pale. "Not so," said he. " Do you see those three horses browsing yonder on the opposite side of the ravine?"—" Yes, yes, I see them."

" The Frank has already kept half his promise. He has

sent his horses to await us. Count them, Aïssa: there are three of them. How many of us, then, are to fly?"

"Oh, yes, yes!" she exclaimed. "You, I, and Agenor! Oh, Mothril! to fly with him I would descend into a gulf of flames! We will go."

"You will not be afraid?"—"When he awaits me!"

"Then be prepared, the moment you hear the drums announce the departure of the garrison."

"The rope?"—"Is here; it would support a weight triple that of ours; and as to its length, I have measured it by lowering a leaden ball at the end of a thread. You will be strong and courageous, Aïssa?"

"As if I were going to my nuptial *fête* with my chevalier!" replied the young girl, joyfully.

CHAPTER LXXVII.

THE HEAD AND THE HAND.

NIGHT descended upon Montiel—night cold and gloomy, enveloping in a misty shroud all forms and colours. At the appointed time the trumpets gave the signal, and a procession bearing torches, descended the steep and rocky path leading from the principal gate of the castle. The soldiers and officers one by one appeared, and making their submission, were kindly received by the constable and the other Christian leaders, who, standing beside the embankment, overlooked the sortie of the men and baggage. All at once an idea occurred to Muscaron. He approached his master, and whispered in his ear, "This accursed Moor has treasures; he is capable of flinging them down some precipice to prevent our profiting by them. I will go and make a tour of the place; for I see as clearly at night as a cat, and take no great pleasure in watching these bands of Spanish prisoners defile."

"Go," said Agenor; "there is one, my most precious treasure, which Mothril will not fling down a precipice. For that I am keeping watch at this gate, and upon that I shall seize the moment it appears."—"Eh, eh!" said Muscaron, with an air of gloomy doubt, as he scrambled through the heath in the moat, and disappeared.

The soldiers continued to defile, then came the horsemen. It took some time for two hundred horsemen to descend, one by one, such a path as that leading to Montiel. Mauleon's heart was devoured by impatience, a fatal presentiment darted like a sharp arrow through his brain. "Fool that I am!" thought he. "Mothril has my word; he knows that the least misfortune happening to the young girl will expose him to the most terrible torments. Then Aïssa, who must have seen my banner, must have taken her precautions. She will soon make her appearance—I shall behold her—I was mad!"

All at once he felt Muscaron's hand upon his shoulder. "Master," said he, softly, "come quickly!"

"What is the matter? How agitated you are!"

"Master, come, in Heaven's name! What I predicted has come to pass. The Moor is removing things through a window."—"What does that matter to me?"

"I am afraid it matters a great deal to you; the objects that are descending from it have all the appearance of living beings."

"We must give the alarm!"

"Beware of doing so. The Moor—if it be he—will defend himself, he will slay some one; the soldiers are brutal, and not in love, they will spare nothing. Let us conduct our affairs ourselves."

"You are mad, Muscaron! For the sake of a few miserable coffers you would make me lose the first glance of Aïssa."

"Then I will go alone!" said Muscaron, impatiently; "if I am killed it will be your fault." Agenor made no reply. He quietly, and without attracting attention, left the group of captains, and gained the embankment. "Quick, quick!" cried the squire; "let us strive to arrive there in time." Agenor redoubled his speed, but nothing could be more tedious than having thus to make their way through the lianas briars and small shrubs. "Do you see?" said Muscaron, pointing out to his master a white form which glided down the dark wall to the bottom of the ravine. Agenor uttered a cry.

"Is that you, Agenor?" asked a sweet voice.

"Well, master! what do you say to this?" said Muscaron.

"Let us hasten to the brink of the ravine and surprise them!" cried Mauleon.

"Agenor!" repeated the voice of Aïssa, whom Mothril vainly attempted to silence by energetic exhortations made in an under-tone.

"Let us throw ourselves down on the edge of the ravine; do not let us speak, or in any way show ourselves."

"But they will make their escape that way."

"Oh, we shall always be able to capture the young girl, more especially as she asks for nothing better than to fall into our hands. I tell you, my dear master, let us lie down here."

Mothril was listening as a tiger listens at the mouth of his den before carrying off his prey, and hearing nothing more, he regained his courage, and ascended with an agile step the steep bank of the ravine. With one hand he held and supported Aïssa—with the other he grasped the trees and bushes. He gained the summit, and paused to take breath.

Then Agenor sprang up, exclaiming, "Aïssa! Aïssa!"

"I was sure it was he!" said the young girl.

"The chevalier!" roared Mothril, furiously.

"But Agenor is there!—let us go that way?" remonstrated Aïssa, endeavouring to disengage herself from Mothril's arms and hasten to her lover.

Mothril's only reply was to clasp her more closely and drag her towards the spot where he had beheld Don Pedro's horse. Agenor hurried after them, but stumbled at every step; the Moor outstripped him, and drew near the horses.

"This way! this way!" Aïssa continued to cry. "Come, Mauleon, come!"—"If you breathe another word, you are dead!" hissed Mothril in her ear. "Do you wish every one to be attracted hither by your foolish cries? Do you wish to prevent your lover from ever rejoining us?" Aïssa was silent. Mothril found the horse, seized it by the mane, sprang into the saddle, and placing the young girl before him, set off at full gallop. It was the horse of one of the officers captured with Don Pedro.

Mauleon heard the tramp of the steed, and uttered a shout of anger. "He is escaping! he is escaping! Aïssa, Aïssa, answer!"

"I am here! I am here!" cried Aïssa; but her voice was lost in the thick folds of the veil which Mothril, at the risk of stifling her, held over her mouth.

Agenor rushed madly and despairingly after them, but fell on his knees, breathless and exhausted. "Oh, God is not just!" he muttered.

"Master, master! here is a horse," cried Muscaron. "Courage!—Come, I have hold of him!"

Agenor sprang up joyfully. With renewed strength, he placed his foot in the stirrup, which Muscaron held, and followed swift as lightning upon Mothril's traces. His steed proved to be that marvellous courser, with flame-coloured spots, which had not its equal in Andalusia; so that, as it were, devouring space, Agenor drew near to Mothril, and cried out to Aïssa, "Courage! I am here!"

Mothril ploughed his horse's flanks with his poniard till it snorted with pain.

"Give her up to me, and I will not harm you," said Agenor to the Moor. "By the living God, I will let you escape!" The Moor replied by a disdainful laugh. "Aïssa! Aïssa! slip from his arms."

The young girl was uttering half-stifled groans of despair, beneath the vigorous hand pressed upon her mouth. At last Mothril felt the fiery breath of Don Pedro's horse upon his back. Agenor was able to seize his mistress' robe, and drag her toward him.

"Resign her to me, Saracen," said he, "or I will kill you!"

"Loose her, Christian, or you are dead!"

Agenor tightened his grasp on the white woollen robe, and raised his sword; but Mothril with an oblique blow of his poniard severed Agenor's left hand at the wrist. This hand remained clinging to the stuff, and Agenor uttered so piercing a cry that Muscaron heard it afar off, and bellowed with rage. Mothril now fancied he should be able to make his escape, but it was no longer Agenor who pursued him, but the horse excited by the chase. Besides rage had redoubled the young man's strength; his sword was again raised, and if Mothril had not made his horse spring on one side, it would have been all over with him.

"Yield her up to me, Saracen!" said Agenor, in a fainter tone; "you see I shall kill you. Yield her up to me, I love her!"

"And I also love her!" retorted Mothril, again spurring his horse forward.

A voice, that of Muscaron, pierced through the darkness. The honest squire had found the third horse; he had scrambled through bushes and over stones, and come to his master's aid. "I am here; courage, master!" said he.

Mothril turned round, feeling himself lost.

"You wish to have this maiden?" said he.

" Yes, and I will have her !"—"Well, then, take her !"

Agenor's name, followed by a stifled moan, escaped from the veil, and some heavy body wrapped in the long floating folds of the white scarf rolled under the feet of Agenor's horse. Mauleon sprang from the saddle to seize what Mothril had abandoned to him ; he flung himself on his knees to embrace the veiled form of his mistress, but no sooner had it met his gaze than he fell senseless to the earth. When dawn cast her lurid light upon this horrible scene, the chevalier might have been seen pale as a spectre, pressing his lips to the cold blue ones of the severed head flung him by the Moor. At a few paces' distance, Muscaron sat weeping. The faithful servant had found means during his master's long swoon to stanch his wounds ; he had saved his life in spite of himself. Further off lay Mothril, his brain pierced by the sure and death-dealing arrow of the worthy squire, and still clasping in his arms the mutilated corpse of Aïssa. Even in death a triumphant smile rested on his lips.

Two horses wandered hither and thither among the grass.

THE END.